Darkness fell over Blair like a smothering blanket.

This blackout hadn't been caused by a power failure. The impending danger had caught up with her. Outlined against the walls, she saw a shadow. He was here with her…

Watching. Waiting.

"Who's there?" she whispered. "Who are you?" Her trembling voice echoed off the tiles, bouncing back at her in desperate mockery of her fear.

She heard the sound of shuffling feet. Where was he? How close? Blair looked up and saw a crouching form, hunched over.

He didn't even look human.

"What do you want?" Blair asked.

One word. A guttural growl.

"You."

Rocky Mountain Mystery

CASSIE MILES

SILHOUETTE®

INTRIGUE™

Thank you, Patience and Denise, for believing
in this series. And, as always, to Rick.

*First published in Great Britain 2006
Silhouette Books, Eton House, 18-24 Paradise Road,
Richmond, Surrey TW9 1SR*

© Kay Bergstrom 2005

ISBN 0 373 22820 1

46-0606

*Printed and bound in Spain
by Litografia Rosés S.A., Barcelona*

CASSIE MILES

lives in Denver in a high-rise, not unlike the apartment described in this book. She also shares the heroine's fondness for luxurious chocolate. This is a story close to her heart, and she wouldn't mind at all if a dashing hero joined her on the balcony to count the stars.

When she's not writing, Cassie is a movie buff who regularly attends the annual Denver Film Festival where she can overdose on three or four movies a day and ponder the true meaning of Scandinavian subtitled films.

CAST OF CHARACTERS

David Crawford—Haunted by the murder of his sister, he became an investigative journalist, focusing on serial killers.

Dr Blair Weston—Injuries from a devastating car accident caused her to retire from her position as a medical examiner in the coroner's office.

Eddy Adderly—Convicted of the Fisherman serial murders and on death row, he is dying from liver cancer.

Jake Zitti—A newspaper photographer and ladies' man, he was driving the car when Blair was injured.

Ted Hurtado—A newspaper columnist who received the threat notes from the Fisherman.

Adam Briggs—Head of Colorado Crime Consultants.

Molly Griffith—Secretary at Colorado Crime Consultants.

Colorado Crime Consultants (CCC)—A nonprofit organisation of private citizens with special skills who are called upon to help solve crimes in the past, present and future.

Chapter One

David Crawford had been on airplanes since noon—seven hours ago—with nothing to eat but a bag of peanuts. He was tired and hungry. Worse than that, the person who picked him up at the airport was a guy instead of a warm, welcoming, beautiful woman. Even worse, the May weather was rainy, and David couldn't see the rugged outline of the Rocky Mountains west of town.

But he wasn't complaining. He settled back in the passenger seat of his friend's sporty Miata and allowed a wave of nostalgia to wash over him. Home again. Here in Denver, he went to high school, kissed his first girlfriend, bought his first car, got his first job. It was here, in a well-groomed cemetery, that his sister was buried.

The Miata swerved in the rain on the airport road, dodging around an SUV, and David braced his arm against the dashboard. "Slow down, Jake."

"Don't want to be late for my date tonight."

"You've already got a new woman lined up?"

"Already?" Jake scoffed. "It's been ten days since what's-her-face kicked me out."

Jake Zitti, a news photographer for *The Denver Post,* never wasted time regretting relationships gone bad. Each time he was thrown, he dusted himself off and got right back on the horse, so to speak. "I don't know how you do it," David said.

"Nothing hard about dating, pal. You ought to give it a try."

"I date," David said. "I'm more selective than you are." A fruit fly was more selective than Jake.

"You'd do well playing the field. The ladies like your type. You're practically one of the Baldwin brothers with your blue eyes and black hair, which looks to me like it's getting a little gray around the edges."

"At least I've got hair." David stared pointedly at his friend's clean-shaved skull. "This new woman of yours. Is it serious?"

"Why do you care?" Jake asked.

"I want to know when you're moving your sorry butt out of my guest bedroom."

"You love it when I'm staying at your town house," Jake said. "I'm a fun guy."

David cringed as the Miata plunged forward, throwing up a backwash that splashed as high as the windows. "Yeah, real fun."

"So, David, how long are you in town this time?"

"It depends."

David's job took him all over the country. As an investigative crime reporter, he flew to wherever the breaking news was. It wasn't a career path he'd consciously planned.

Five years ago, when he was a sports reporter at *The Denver Post,* the closest he got to criminal activity was reporting on scandals with the local high school football team. Those were the good old days. Lots of skiing. Beer drinking. Hanging out with friends like Jake. Then David's world turned upside down.

His kid sister, Danielle, became the fourth victim of

a serial killer who drowned his victims and left their bodies near water with their feet tied together like a mermaid's tail. He was nicknamed the Fisherman, and he killed twice more after Danielle.

David hadn't coped well with the tragedy. Even after the Fisherman was apprehended and convicted, David couldn't assuage the pain of losing his sister. Instead of following the sports news, he wrote impassioned editorials and columns on victims' rights and the court system. He was obsessed.

When another serial killer struck in Nevada, he took a leave of absence from his job at *The Post* and went there. His interviews with witnesses, suspects and cops resulted in a series of articles which he sold to a national magazine. They liked his work and paid his way to the next crime scene in Florida. His reporting on serial killers, mass murderers and unsolved crimes turned into a regular feature, and he developed a reputation, even appearing on television news shows as an expert.

His reporting was respected. He was well paid and highly visible. But not satisfied. Racing from one brutal crime scene to the next, he never found the answers that would ease his own uncompromising grief and rage. How could such violence happen? Why? And why to Danielle?

To Jake he said, "Actually, I'm planning to stay in Denver for a while."

"Yeah? Is this a story I ought to know about?"

"Old news. The Fisherman."

Jake frowned. "Why rake up the past?"

"Because he's dying." The convicted murderer of David's sister had liver cancer. He was dying in prison where he waited for the process of appeals on his death sentence. "And I need to know the truth. What if it wasn't him?"

"He confessed," Jake said. "His DNA was found on the last victim."

"But not on my sister."

"You're wasting your time. The cops are never going to reopen that investigation."

"I'm not going through the police." A week ago David had contacted Colorado Crime Consultants, a nonprofit network of private citizens who used their skills to investigate crime. CCC's experts included entomologists, doctors, lawyers, chemists and psychologists who volunteered their time to find the truth. They'd agreed to look into the Fisherman serial murders.

Jake's cell phone played the opening notes to "You've Lost that Loving Feeling," and he answered. As he engaged in a loud, one-sided conversation, the Miata careered wildly along I-70, and David couldn't help remembering that Jake already had one near-death driving accident.

David snapped, "Watch the road."

"The road's not going anywhere." The Miata swooped toward the exit ramp. "That call was from the city desk. I need to make a stop to take some photos. Do you mind?"

"Hell, yes. I'm starving."

"Too bad. There is a crime scene at City Park and we happen to be five minutes away." If anyone else had been driving, they'd have been fifteen minutes away. "It's a woman. Her body's near the lake."

Found near water. Like the victims of the Fisherman. David's hunger pangs tightened into a hard knot in his gut.

Inside City Park, the Miata squealed to a stop. Jake

leaped from the car and grabbed his camera equipment from the trunk.

Stepping out into the fading drizzle, David turned up his collar. A sense of foreboding weighted his stride through the wet grass. Though he'd been to dozens of crime scenes, he'd never gotten accustomed to the horror. In every victim, he saw his sister.

Halogen police lights illuminated the area near the lake, turning dusk into harsh daylight. Yellow crime-scene tape draped over leafy shrubs. The hum of tense conversation mingled with static from police radios.

David slipped around the edge of the police cordon where uniforms and other forensic investigators converged on the body. He caught a glimpse of her delicate white feet, tied with cord at the ankles.

Impotent rage crashed against his forehead with the impact of a jackhammer. This couldn't be happening again. His muscles clenched. *Please, God, not again.*

SWIMMING LAPS was a form of therapeutic exercise for Blair Weston. In the accident, she'd shattered her wrist. Her right leg had been broken in four places, including a compound fracture of the right tibia and fibula. For a long time, the only place she'd been able to move without pain was in the pool.

Now, five years later, she was mostly recuperated, but she still swam a hundred laps a day in the seventy-five-foot-long pool in the garden level of her high-rise condo building. The pale-turquoise water—a color that someone once told Blair matched her greenish-blue eyes— felt like a cool liquid caress, gently embracing her body as she stroked back and forth. An excellent morning workout. The exertion got her blood circulating and her heart pumping. Not unlike sex.

What a pleasant idea! Sex! Blair could hardly remember the last time she'd been to bed with a man. Was five years ago long enough to recertify her as a virgin at age thirty-four? Rather a depressing thought.

At the deep end, she rolled under the water and pushed away from the edge, gliding half the length of the pool underwater. Silence surrounded her. Through her goggles, she gazed at the flowing pattern of light and shadow in soothing ripples. When she broke the surface and caught a breath, she heard her name being called.

"Hey, Blair!"

Her first instinct was to dive, to ignore the intrusion. She preferred to keep swimming in lithe contemplation. But she paddled to the shallow end and looked up at the two men who awaited her. One was Adam Briggs, the head of Colorado Crime Consultants. Good! Adam was probably bringing her a project—something more to occupy her mind than contemplation of her status as a reborn virgin.

Before the accident, Dr. Blair Weston had been a medical examiner in the Denver Coroner's Office. She still wasn't able to go back to full-time work—didn't have the stamina to stand for a long time without moving. Also, her head injuries caused uncontrollable dizzy spells. And her wrist, though healed, was still too shaky for detail work. Doing part-time consultation on medical forensics for CCC was all she could handle in spite of an ever-increasing need to bring in more income than she received from insurance disability.

When she glanced toward the other man, she felt a pleasant spark of recognition. She peeled off her goggles and grinned. "David."

The last time she'd seen David Crawford was over a year ago when they'd bumped into each other in the grocery store. They'd exchanged phone numbers. He'd never called, and she'd assumed there was nothing more to talk about.

He squatted at the edge of the pool. "How're you doing, Blair?"

"I'm fine." If he really cared, he would have telephoned her the last time they met. Therefore she assumed David was here for another reason. "What can I do for you?"

"You look great," he said.

Pushing away from the edge of the pool, she ducked her head under the water so her bangs would plaster over her forehead, covering the scar near her hairline. She assumed that David would revise his opinion of how "great" she looked if he could see the Frankenstein scars on her right leg.

"You're the one who's looking good," she said. He'd aged well. The hint of silver in his thick, black hair added a touch of mature elegance. Though he was smiling, his grin was incomplete—lifting only on the left side in a way that made his face seem asymmetrical and interesting. She wondered if he had ever truly smiled after the death of his sister. "I saw you on TV. Some program about serial murders in Texas."

Her voice echoed in the tiled pool room, giving this meeting a surreal, dreamlike quality—as if she were imagining these two men at the edge of the pool.

Adam didn't stoop to talk to her. Though he'd left the military years ago, he maintained a rigid posture. He said, "Blair, I have a project for you."

"Go ahead."

"It's about the Fisherman."

She bobbed under the water again. *I don't want to hear this!* Five years ago, before her life came undone, the Fisherman serial murders had been her case. She'd autopsied all six of the victims. "I really don't think I want to—"

"Get out of the damn pool," Adam said. "We can't have a sensible conversation while you're splashing around like a dolphin."

She looked away from Adam, turning her attention toward David. If she left the sheltering waters, he'd see her poor, battered leg. He'd notice her clumsy stride; he was a reporter and noticed everything.

"Blair." Adam repeated her name as if she should snap to attention. "This consultation has important ramifications."

"Like what?"

"There was a murder last night in City Park. Some of the particulars resemble the Fisherman crimes."

She shuddered. Though she'd heard a news flash on the radio, she had no idea about the connection. "But it can't be the Fisherman. He's in jail."

"Maybe not," David said. "What if the wrong guy was convicted?"

"No way." She couldn't accept that possibility; it was too scary. During the earlier investigation, there had been threats aimed directly at her. The Fisherman knew who she was, knew her preferences and habits. "Eddy Adderly was convicted. After he was put in jail, there were no more murders."

"Until now," David said.

"That doesn't fit any kind of psychological profile. Serial killers don't take five years off before striking again."

"Out of the pool," Adam ordered. He held her towel. "Come on, Blair."

"What's the big rush?"

"I've arranged for you to observe the autopsy on this victim. This afternoon at 1530."

"What time is that in civilian terms?"

Adam rolled his eyes. "Three-thirty this afternoon. At the Coroner's Office."

An autopsy? At her old office? A bevy of emotions charged through her brain: excitement at once again being part of a complex forensic investigation; satisfaction at the idea that she might be able to help; fear of plunging back into the fray.

"Let's go," Adam snapped.

Here came another emotion. She felt intensely self-conscious about climbing out of the pool. *Don't be silly!* She wasn't a giddy teenager who fretted about her body image. Blair was a grown woman, an adult. It shouldn't matter to her what David thought.

Her thigh muscles flexed, and she stood up in the shallow water. A veil of droplets slid off her electric-blue, one-piece swimsuit with the French-cut legs that always seemed too high. She strode through the water and hoisted herself onto the concrete ledge.

Her first instinct was to grab the towel from Adam and cover the grotesque scarring on her leg, but she forced herself to follow her regular routine. She rubbed the moisture from her short brown hair, draped the towel over her shoulders and stood, revealing all five feet, eight inches of her body. Her angular shoulders. Her jutting hipbones. Her minimal breasts. And her right leg that was seven-eighths of an inch shorter than the left.

She felt David's gaze upon her and avoided looking back at him, embarrassed by what she might read in his expression. Walking slowly to minimize her limp, she went to a hook at poolside where she grabbed her full-length terry cloth robe and wrapped it around her, tying the sash tightly at her waist. Her feet slipped into a pair of rubber thongs with a bright yellow daisy at the juncture of her first and second toes.

"Your answer?" Adam asked. "Will you attend the autopsy?"

"What's my role in this?" Though her pulse raced, she kept her voice level and businesslike. "Why has CCC been called in? We usually don't get involved in ongoing crime investigations."

"Because of me," David said. "About a week ago I asked CCC to take another look at my sister's murder."

"Why?" she asked.

"Eddy Adderly is dying, and it made me think. I want to know—without a shadow of doubt—that the right man was arrested and convicted, that the Fisherman will never harm another woman."

She could hear the frustration in his voice. When she finally looked at David, she saw a troubled man who wanted the truth and didn't care what she looked like. He didn't think of her in terms of her appearance. And why not?

Her ping-pong shift in emotions was rather annoying. Only a moment ago she wanted to hide from David. Now, contrarily, she wanted him to notice her. Why shouldn't David Crawford be interested in her as a woman?

"Listen, Blair, I don't have any right to ask for your help. You don't owe me anything. But I know—"

"How's Jake?" Her tone was brittle.

"He's fine," David said warily.

"Still playing the field?"

"With a vengeance."

She'd met David through his friend, Jake Zitti, whom she'd been dating at the time of the Fisherman murders.

Jake was driving the car at the time of the accident. Jake the Snake dumped her before she was out of the hospital.

David was a whole different story. He'd made a dozen hospital visits, bringing flowers and magazines she couldn't read because she was out of her mind on pain medication and didn't care what she looked like. Other issues loomed larger. Would she ever walk again? Would she regain the use of her arm? David had been kind and encouraging. In some ways, she thought, he'd treated her with the tenderness and attention he was unable to lavish upon his murdered sister.

The memory of Danielle Crawford returned Blair's attention to the Fisherman. Should she observe the autopsy? She turned to Adam. "I need to think about whether I want to be involved in this consultation. I'll call you back at one o'clock. That would be, um, 1300 hours."

"I know you'll make the right decision." Adam gave a brisk nod. "Call me on the cell."

He pivoted and went out the door. She was left alone with David.

"Mind if I stick around?" he asked.

"You won't influence my decision one way or the other," she warned.

"Not even a little?"

"I don't like looking backward. The Fisherman serial murders got real personal." She shrugged off the remembered fear. "It's a time in my life that I'd rather forget."

"I understand."

She rather doubted that. His response to those tragedies had been the extreme opposite of hers. Instead of trying to forget, David had obsessed over his sister's murder. He'd plunged deeper and deeper into the horrifying world of serial killers and snipers and mass murderers. He'd travelled all around the country, searching for...what? "Why do you do it?" she asked. "Why do you keep digging into these crimes?"

He glanced at the pool. "Why do you swim?"

"A typical reporter." She grinned. "Answering one question with another."

"It's my nature," he said.

"You know, David, even though you're a hotshot TV consultant, you still dress like a beat reporter."

"How's that?"

"You're not quite put together. Khaki trousers with a belt that doesn't match your loafers. Wrinkled blue shirt with the sleeves rolled up. Loosely knotted necktie. I bet you're still wearing the same brown tweed sports jacket you had five years ago."

"It's in the car," he said. "And you didn't answer my question about swimming. Why do you do it?"

"Because it's good for me."

"But it's not necessary physical therapy."

"Not anymore," she said.

"You're pretty much recovered from your injuries," he said. "Tell me, Dr. Blair Weston, why haven't you gone back to work as a medical examiner?"

She held up her wrist, displaying the pale scars from two operations. "My hand is still too shaky."

"For working on dead people?"

"For your information, there's a certain degree of precision required in an autopsy."

"Let me see that wrist."

He caught hold of her forearm and pushed up the sleeve of her robe. With his thumb, he traced the line of scars along the tender flesh at the inside of her forearm.

Though his hands were warmer than hers, his light caress sent shivers through her body.

She lifted her gaze to meet his and found herself fully engaged in a study of his intense, compelling eyes. A darker rim circled multifacets of blue, nearly as splintered and complicated as the man himself. As she stared at him, the tiled pool room and the rippling expanse of turquoise water faded into a soft, pleasant blur.

"I think there's another reason you haven't gone back to work," he said gently. "I don't know the label. Trauma. Fear. Sorrow. All of the above."

"Maybe." Blair had tried psychological therapy and quit when she didn't make measureable headway.

"Were you ever able to recall what happened in the accident?"

She shook her head. She remembered driving with Jake. The windows on the car were down, and there was a breeze. Riding in a car with Jake behind the steering wheel was always a harrowing experience. Too fast. He always drove too fast. "I don't remember the crash. My mind is a blank until I woke up in the hospital. I assume I was in shock."

"Me, too," he said. "After Danielle was killed, I went into emotional shock. The way I coped was writing about it. So there's the answer to your question. I keep writing, keep digging into serial killings because I need to make sense of it. For my sister. And for myself."

He might have undertaken an impossible task. "Do serial killings ever make sense?"

"Not in a rational way."

She couldn't quite believe that they were standing here, holding hands and talking about heinous crimes. "I should get going. Adam needs my decision in less than two hours."

"I'd like to see you again," David said. "Can I take you to lunch sometime?"

"How about now? Come upstairs with me, and I'll make you a terrific tuna salad sandwich."

"You're on."

Side by side, they left the swimming pool, crossed the lobby and boarded the elevator. Though Blair suspected that David was coming upstairs to convince her to investigate the Fisherman, his attention pleased her. He'd asked her to lunch. He wanted to spend time with her.

At her condo on the fifth floor, she unlocked the door. "Make yourself at home. I'll just run into the bedroom and get changed."

"Do you have to change?" David followed her into the living room. "I like the blue bathing suit. It shows off your curves."

Her curves? Apparently, David had noticed more about her than her damaged leg. "Were you ogling me?"

"I'm a reporter. A trained observer."

"And what have you observed?"

"Curves. Nice curves."

His blue-eyed gaze rested warmly upon her. His masculine appreciation was unmistakable.

Blair didn't know what to think of this attention from David Crawford, whom she'd always placed in the category of friend rather than boyfriend. Of course, she'd considered the possibility of dating him. With his black hair and blue eyes, he was handsome. And he was funny. And kind. Could there be something more between them than friendship?

"Come on, Blair." His eyebrows lifted, teasing. "Let me see that bathing suit again."

"If you want curves, take a drive down the Pikes Peak."

"Are you scared to give me another glimpse?"

He was definitely flirting with her. It had been ages since she'd played this kind of game with a man. "Scared of you? No way."

"Then do it."

"Open my robe?"

"Or forever be branded a coward," he said.

"I'm no chicken." She untied the terry cloth sash. She literally put her best leg forward as she slowly parted the material and offered him a view.

"Very nice." The corner of his mouth curved in a half-grin, and he reached toward her. His hands slipped inside her robe and rested on either side of her rib cage. "You're perfectly proportioned."

"Nobody's perfect."

"Lady, you're close."

She ought to object to his overture. Blair wasn't the kind of woman who tumbled easily. She had more self-control in her little finger than most people had in their whole body. But, instead of pulling away, she leaned toward him.

She wanted to be held—wanted her electric-blue swimsuit to leave a damp impression on his rumpled shirt and khaki trousers. And she offered no objection when his lips touched hers. The pressure of his mouth was firm but tentative. This wasn't a passionate kiss but more of an exploration, a testing of boundaries.

Then his hands encircled her torso, and he pulled her closer, crushing her against him.

His kiss became more demanding. His tongue forced her lips to part.

A sudden, pleasant heat shimmered through her body

like a mirage. Her boundaries crumbled as she swooned against him. It had been so long. She'd missed this tenderness, this passion, this intimacy. She wanted to let go of all inhibitions and tear away their clothes.

But that would be crazy. Foolish. She would never risk her heart again. Awkwardly she separated from him, taking a clumsy step backward, ending their delicious embrace. "How did that happen?"

"I could show you again," he offered.

"I think not." When she turned away from him, a secret smile of pure delight played across her lips. "Now, I'm going to change clothes."

"I like black lingerie," David said.

"Dream on."

"I will."

As he watched her leave the room, David exhaled the breath he'd been holding. He felt like a very lucky man. Three times lucky.

Once lucky because when he contacted CCC, the first name Adam mentioned was his old friend, Blair.

Twice lucky because Blair was glad to see him.

Lucky times three, because she kissed him back. He'd felt her body yearning toward him, and he could tell that she was as hot as he was. Maybe even hotter.

He strolled across the carpet and sank into a recliner chair. Why hadn't he kissed her sooner? Years sooner?

Leaning back in the chair, he checked out her condo. The recliner where he sat was the only comfortable piece of furniture. The rest of the room was exercise equipment: a treadmill, a stationary bicycle and a mat for floor exercises. There was a small table with two chairs in the dining area—not a space that was large enough for entertaining. The blinds were drawn.

David recognized the no-frills decor. This was a

purely functional space for a single person. In that way it reminded him of his own town house, which was nicely furnished but unused except for the desk and the bed.

In just a few minutes she returned to the living room. She wore jeans and a purple jersey shirt with a white collar. Her gait was different. He assumed that her black shoes were fitted with lifts that made walking easier. She'd blown dry her short brown hair in a cute tousled style that made him want to run his fingers through it.

"I have a question," she said. "About the woman who was killed yesterday, what was her profession?"

David knew exactly where she was going. The Fisherman chose his victims carefully. Though he was subtle, there was evidence that he stalked these women before he abducted and killed them. His six victims came from three workplaces: hospital, newspaper and law enforcement. "She was a cop."

Blair cringed. "I assume she wasn't on duty."

"She was retired," he said. "A former homicide detective. She quit the force last year to stay home with her family."

"Oh, no. She had kids?"

"Two boys. They're both grown and in college. The victim spent most of her time taking care of her aging parents." There was one more piece of information he needed to tell her. "This latest victim was one of the investigators on the Fisherman murders five years ago."

"Her name?"

"Pamela Comforti."

Blair gasped. "I knew her."

David was beginning to regret his request that Blair get involved in the investigation. She'd been through enough. She didn't need to be dragged back into this tragedy. "I'm sorry."

She glanced at her wristwatch. "There's not much time before I need to call Adam. What do you think I should do?"

"I'm torn," he said honestly.

"Why?"

"Of course I want your input. You were the medical examiner in charge of the prior murders. You're smart. You know how to interpret the data. And you know the Fisherman's modus operandi."

However, as she'd mentioned before, the prior investigation had become personal. At the time, Blair had been assigned a bodyguard. "Why did the police consider you a target?"

"Godiva chocolate." She went toward the kitchen. "Come in here with me while I make sandwiches."

He followed her to the small galley kitchen. Though David knew most of the details on the Fisherman murders, her reference wasn't familiar. "What about Godiva chocolate?"

"It was a detail that the police kept secret," she said as she went to the fridge and took out the makings for sandwiches.

"Are you going to tell me?" he asked.

She turned and faced him. Her green eyes, surrounded by thick black lashes, shone bright. "Because I did the autopsy on the first victim, the Fisherman serial murders became my case."

He nodded. Standard procedure for the Coroner's Office was to maintain consistency on related murders. "Go on."

"My autopsy results on the contents of the stomach

and upper GI showed that every victim, after the first one, had eaten chocolate a few hours before her death.''

"So?"

"Specifically, it was Godiva chocolate."

David still didn't get it. "What does this have to do with you?"

She pointed to a gold foil box on the kitchen counter. "I've always had a passion for Godiva chocolate. Some of the forensics people even called me Lady Godiva. The police deduced that the Fisherman was feeding his victims my favorite chocolate before he killed them."

"As a sick threat to you."

"Very sick," she said.

David's jaw tightened. "Call Adam right now. Tell him to forget about the autopsy. I don't want this psycho coming after you again."

"Neither do I." Pensively she frowned. "But it's not my choice. It's up to the Fisherman. He makes the decision about who's next."

Chapter Two

Blair opened the gold box of Godiva and popped a mini-truffle into her mouth. The rich chocolate melted comfortingly on her tongue. Of course she worried about the Fisherman and the scheduled autopsy and an investigation that might turn deadly. She'd be crazy not to be nervous. However, a different concern was uppermost in her mind. David.

As she made sandwiches at the kitchen counter, he stood near enough that she could feel the warmth of his body. She could smell him—a clean scent like soap and fresh laundry.

"Blair." The way he spoke her name sounded like an endearment. "I don't want you to do anything that might be dangerous."

Like kissing you? While she'd been changing clothes, the fact that they'd kissed had absorbed into her consciousness. There was an obvious sexual buzz between them, but she didn't understand why or where it might be going. Was she ready for a real relationship? Would she be satisfied with less?

"Blair, are you—"

"Fine, I'm fine." She flapped her hand, brushing away his concern. "There's nothing dangerous about my life, David. The way I figure, my odds of being attacked by a serial killer are about a hundred thousand to one.'' Which was roughly equivalent to the odds of a single thirty-four-year-old woman who seldom left her house finding a meaningful relationship with a man. ''Wildly unlikely.''

''Wrong,'' he said. ''The Fisherman isn't a random killer. His targets are—''

''I know. Women who work in medicine, law enforcement or the media. None of which applies to me. In case you haven't noticed, I don't work anywhere.'' Without turning around to look at him, she groped for the door to the refrigerator. ''What do you want to drink?''

''Any kind of soda pop that's not diet.''

Her teensy kitchen wasn't big enough for two people, but he continued to hover as if lurking within a three-foot radius would somehow protect her from a psychotic murderer. She grabbed two cans of pop from the fridge and circled to face him. ''Excuse me, David. It's a bit crowded in here.''

''I should hire a bodyguard for you.''

''What?''

He dropped his hands to her shoulders and stared intently at her. ''Let me do this. I'll hire somebody who won't get in the way. Not a guy. A woman bodyguard. A really big woman who knows martial arts.''

''You want to hire Xena the Warrior Princess to look after me?''

''If that's what it takes,'' he said.

This time, when she looked up into his well-meaning eyes, she didn't have the urge to kiss him. It was the opposite: she wanted to punch that lantern jaw. Who did he think he was? What gave him the right to come in here and disrupt her life?

He said, "You need protection."

"What I need is space."

She pressed the icy aluminum cans in her hands against his chest, and he recoiled.

"Damn, Blair. That's cold."

"Be glad the pop cans aren't open. I might have dumped the contents on your pointed head." She glared. "I don't need a bodyguard."

"How can you be so sure?"

"The Fisherman is in jail." She nodded toward the other room. "We're ready to eat. Go sit at the table."

He left the kitchen but didn't sit. "I'm not letting go of this, Blair. Yesterday's victim was involved with the prior investigation. Just like you."

"Enough." She slammed the pop cans down on the table. "As of this moment, I'm officially declaring a moratorium on discussion of the Fisherman."

"You can't ignore this," he said.

"Accept my conditions or leave."

He pulled out a chair and sat.

Silently she counted to five, allowing her emotions to settle. "We're going to have a nice lunch. Just a couple of old friends, renewing our acquaintance."

She glanced at her small, round dining table that was old enough to qualify as antique but not polished. She should have covered the scratched-up veneer with a tablecloth or thrown together a centerpiece—something to make their lunch more cosy. But her tablecloths were stuck away in a linen drawer. What could she do to make this lunch more civilized?

"Wine?" she asked.

"No."

"Music," she said, turning on the radio, set to the classical station. "Rossini."

"Oh, yeah. Nothing like a good rotini."

"That's a pasta, David."

"Whatever."

She opened her vertical blinds. Daylight from the floor-to-ceiling windows splashed into her condo. On the fifth floor, she was just above the leafy green treetops. Her windows faced west, and it would've been a spectacular panorama if other high-rise buildings hadn't been in the way. As it was, she could only see slices of the Rockies.

Busily, she set lunch on the table. Tuna salad sandwiches and blue corn chips. Her fiesta-ware plates looked…festive, but the paper napkins were terminally tacky. At the very least, she ought to have decent glasses for the soda pop. Returning to the kitchen, she climbed onto the counter to reach the top cabinet shelf where she kept her crystal. The goblets were dusty.

"Blair? What are you doing in there?"

"Nothing." She climbed down and grabbed two plain water glasses that she filled with ice and brought to the table. "Should I light a candle or something?"

"Not on my account," David said.

But she wanted their lunch to be pleasant—free from thoughts about serial killers, free from the tragedies of the past. She wanted to pretend that David was here because he found her attractive and interesting. This casual lunch was the closest to a date she'd had in months. Pathetic! "I've got to get out more."

"Likewise." He took a bite of his sandwich. "I keep telling myself that I need a hobby, like golf."

"An old man's game," she said as she sat.

"Not since Tiger Woods."

David's expression seemed wary as he peered across the table and chewed. She sensed that he was waiting for the right moment to launch into more talk of the Fisherman, his personal obsession. Not just yet, old pal. She was determined to engage in polite conversation, and the topic was golf. "I used to caddy for my father," she said. "I think he uses a cart now."

"Where are your parents living now?"

"Near Tucson. Yours?"

"They're still here in Denver."

She asked if he'd read any good books or seen any movies. And he asked what she put in her tuna salad. Gosh, they were boring! If their small talk got any more amiably bland, they'd both fall asleep. "Okay," she said. "Tell me about your travels."

He raised an eyebrow. "Which bizarre crime scene would you like to hear about?"

Actually, she was rather interested in neurological damage in the Texas hammer murders, but she didn't want to start down a slippery slope that might lead to the Fisherman. "You were in Texas. Tell me about the wide-open spaces."

He wrenched the knot loose on his necktie. "How long are we going to dance around the issue, Blair?"

She tossed her napkin on the plate, symbolically throwing in the towel. "All right. The Fisherman. Talk."

David laced his fingers together and cracked his knuckles like a concert pianist preparing to play Rachmaninoff. "Everybody assumes that the right man was convicted because the killing stopped when he was arrested. Like you said, it's not typical for a serial killer to take a break. But not unheard of. For example, the Green River murders in Washington. That guy killed more than forty women in two years. Then he stopped."

"He was recently apprehended," she said. "Was there an explanation for why he stopped?"

"He might have continued killing in a different location. The cops are trying to link him to various other unsolved crimes."

"What are some other explanations for a time lapse?"

"The killer moves. Or dies. Sometimes, they get arrested. Then, when they're released, they start up again."

Another possibility occurred to her. "Maybe yesterday's murder wasn't committed by the Fisherman. It might be a copycat crime."

"We'll find out soon enough," he said. "Part of the Fisherman's thrill was a power trip. He liked outsmarting the cops. Remember? He used to send notes to a columnist at *The Post.*"

"Ted Hurtado." He was another friend of Jake's. "Wonder whatever happened to him."

"I'll look him up," David said. "Ted's a good place to start."

She was a bit confused about the logistics. David had contacted Adam at CCC, but it sounded like he had plans of his own. "Are you going to investigate? You personally?"

"That's what I've been doing for the past five years. Looking into crime and analyzing."

"What part does CCC play?"

"Adam said he would compile the old case files and court records. If I came up with questions, he would have volunteer experts who can help." He gave her a lopsided smile. "You were the first name he mentioned. He said you were the best at reviewing forensic medical evidence."

For a moment, she had a glimmer of déjà vu, remembering when she was a medical examiner working with the other forensics experts and detectives. She liked being part of that team, tracking down clues and putting together the pieces of a puzzle.

Her part in crime-solving wasn't often a source of pulse-pounding excitement. Rather, her work involved meticulous study, attention to detail, science and reasoning. But when she was able to contribute to an arrest, she experienced a deep satisfaction.

Should she attend the autopsy? Was there any way her presence would help unravel the past or solve the present crime?

David asked, "How did you get involved with Adam?"

One day he showed up on her doorstep without prelude or introduction. In direct, no-frills terms, he told her of his mission: reviewing old cases, offering expert evaluation when called upon by the police or looking into suspicious events. When Blair agreed to act as a consultant, CCC paid her expenses and, sometimes, offered a small stipend. But she didn't do this work for the money. Her disability insurance payments and savings were sufficient to live on.

"Adam came to me, and I couldn't say no." She believed in his goal to help the surviving family and friends find closure. "I have skills. They were going to waste."

"Have you thought about other work options?" David asked. "Like teaching?"

"I've considered teaching forensic medicine."

But she wasn't ready to settle for less, to take a diminished position. When the accident forced her to leave the Coroner's Office, she was at the top of her game. All the cops wanted to work with her. Her opinions were sought after.

She didn't want to return to the field as a pathetic loser—a has-been who never really was. It felt as if she'd failed. The thought of limping back to the Coroner's Office this afternoon seemed like an exercise in humiliation. "I think I'm going to take a pass on the autopsy this afternoon."

David nodded. "There's another issue I want to talk to you about. I'd like to see you again."

She couldn't imagine why. They obviously had nothing in common but a weird interest in violent crime. She and David were both damaged people, struggling to overcome the disasters in the past. If she was smart, she wouldn't see him again. Why sign up for a voyage on the *Titanic* when you know it's going to run into an iceberg?

"Tomorrow's Friday," he said. "May I take you out to dinner?"

"Yes." The word popped out of her mouth. "What should I wear?"

"Something skimpy." He stood and pulled his wallet from his trouser pocket. He placed his business card on the table. "Call if you need anything. Otherwise, I'll see you at seven tomorrow night."

She accompanied him to the door. "One question, David. When I saw you a year ago in the grocery store, why didn't you call?"

"Timing." He had a ready excuse. "I was on my way out of town. When I came back, it seemed like too long. Why didn't you call me?"

"Because I'm old-fashioned. I believe in letting the man make the first move."

"Yeah, right." David doubted that she had one nonassertive, old-fashioned bone in her entire delectable body.

"There were other reasons," she said, "that you didn't call me."

"Right." When he saw her a year ago, David had pitched backward in time. She reminded him of the investigation, the Fisherman. "I wasn't ready."

"For what?"

"Memories. Keeping the past where it belongs."

"The past isn't all bad," she said.

"Not entirely." He remembered taking care of her after the accident, nursing her. There was something very satisfying about being needed. "We've been through a lot, haven't we?"

She nodded. "And we both survived."

He looked down into her turquoise eyes. "It's time to write a new chapter in our story—one that includes a lot of kissing."

"You sound awfully romantic for a true crime reporter."

"Tomorrow," he said as he closed the door behind himself and went down the hall to the elevator.

Her condo building had fairly decent security, but David didn't think it was enough if Blair was really in danger. No surveillance cameras on the floors. And there wasn't a doorman. Earlier today, he and Adam had gained access to the swimming pool by buzzing the resident manager and asking where they could find Blair.

Until he knew what was happening with the investigation, he wanted to make sure she was safe. Since she wouldn't let him hire a bodyguard, he'd take on that duty for himself.

At his Cherry Creek town house, David parked in front and ran up the concrete steps. He unlocked the door and charged inside, full of purpose. His gun, if he remembered correctly, was in a shoe box on the top shelf of the downstairs linen closet. He glanced past the sunken living room to the kitchen counter where Jake stood, eating pizza in the midst of scattered newspapers.

"Hey, bud," Jake called out. "What's up?"

"Shouldn't you be at work?"

"In about an hour. There's a press conference on last night's murder."

At the linen closet, David pushed aside the stacked sheets on the top shelf. He found the box, opened it and took out his black Glock automatic. The heft of the weapon felt good in his hand. He held the gun straight out and sighted down the barrel.

"What the hell?" Jake stood at the end of the hall. "What's going on?"

"I need protection."

"Is somebody coming after you?"

"Not me," David said. "Blair."

"Blair Weston?" Jake stumbled back a step. He looked like somebody had punched him hard in the gut, knocking all the hot air out of him. "Damn."

At least, David thought, his friend had the belated decency to realize he'd behaved badly toward Blair. After nearly killing her in the car accident, Jake had ended their relationship.

"She looks great," David said. "Her hair's short. Real cute. It makes her eyes look huge."

"What happened to her was a damned shame," Jake said. "Poor kid."

Disgusted, David turned away. He couldn't stand to look at this supposed fun guy—love-'em-and-leave-'em Jake Zitti. "Don't waste your pity on Blair. She's completely recovered."

"After the accident..." Jake's voice faltered. "I couldn't stand to see her all beat up like that. It wasn't really my fault. Some jerk cut me off. Hit-and-run. They disappeared.''

"Face it, Jake. You had an accident because you drive like a madman.''

And Blair had paid the price. Reaching into the shoe box where he'd kept his gun, David took out his permit to carry a weapon. He tossed aside the box and went into his first-floor office. In the bottom desk drawer, he had several clips of bullets filed among the computer discs.

He snapped in a clip and swiveled around in his desk chair to face Jake. "Now all I need is the shoulder holster.''

"Tell me again why you're packing heat.''

"I'm investigating," David said cryptically. "Which reminds me. Is Ted Hurtado still working at *The Post?*''

"Teddy's back. He took off for a while to write a book or something. But I saw him the other day." Jake glanced at the gun. "I can help you out with the holster. I've got one that should work. You just clip it onto your belt.''

David raised a skeptical eyebrow. "You carry a gun?''

"Not all the time. But there was this girl that I dated. Great-looking woman. Long red hair all the way to her butt. Anyway, she was…''

"Married?''

"Right," Jake said. "I broke it off. But her husband was the jealous type and I thought he was going to kill me.''

David shook his head. "Jackass.''

AFTER BLAIR MADE THE CALL to Adam, telling him that she wouldn't be at the autopsy, she began second-guessing herself. Should she go? If the murder yesterday was connected to the Fisherman case, she might be able to help. On the other hand, if David was right and she was targeted as a victim, she'd be smart to lie low.

Uncertain, she paced through her condo. The two-bedroom space had never felt so confining. When she stood outside on the balcony and peered at her glimpse of the mountains, she felt trapped as a baby bird in a nest, afraid to fly. *Grow up, Blair! You can't spend the rest of your life hiding out.* She needed to get out, even if it was only to go to the bookstore or grab an espresso.

She grabbed her car keys and backpack. While recovering from her many operations, a lot of her time was spent on crutches, which meant she needed both hands free. She'd gotten into the habit of using a backpack or fanny pack instead of a purse.

Heading out the door and down the hall to the elevator felt like a victory march. She didn't know exactly where she was headed, didn't have a plan. But at least she wasn't cowering.

Inside the elevator, Blair hit the button for the basement level where her car was parked. As soon as she opened the door to her Camry, she was met with a sickening stench. What was that smell?

On the passenger side, staining the upholstery, was a dead, gaping trout. Blood and guts spilled across the seat.

A cold dead fish. From the Fisherman.

Chapter Three

With a gasp, Blair yanked herself out of the car. Her gaze flitted to the far corners of the underground garage. "Anybody here?"

Her voice echoed back at her, and she could hear the sound of her own fear. Her panic. He could be anywhere. Hiding inside the stairwell. Ducked behind another parked car.

In spite of the stink, she climbed behind the steering wheel of her Camry and locked the doors. The inside of her head whirled like a centrifuge. She was about to black out. An overwhelming vortex dragged her down into darkness. She was falling, unable to catch herself.

She blinked, forcing herself to see. Through the windshield, the concrete wall wavered as her vision faded. The light and shadow blurred.

Fighting dizziness, she turned the key in the ignition. Her fingers shook. She had to get away from here. Slowly she backed from her slot, turned and drove up the ramp onto the street where May sunlight splashed in a burst of ironic cheerfulness.

Breathing hard, she drove to the corner, turned right, drove two more blocks and parked. The sense of vertigo began to ebb, leaving her trembling and confused. She stared out at the street. Quite literally, she didn't know which way to turn.

It wouldn't do any good to return to the condo, run upstairs and lock her door. He knew where she lived.

Call the cops? Eventually, she'd turn over the dead fish for forensic analysis. There might be prints or fibers. But right now she wasn't ready to face a police interrogation.

Escape? She could move in with a friend. Go to Tucson and stay with her parents. But what if he followed? She couldn't be responsible for bringing danger to someone else's doorstep.

Blair knew what she must do.

The dead fish in the passenger seat took precedence over her prudent, don't-get-involved attitude. Like it or not, she was a part of this inquiry. She needed to be at the autopsy.

And she wanted David at her side.

After a stop at a convenience store, where she bought a newspaper and used it to wrap the fish, which she stashed in the trunk, she got back into the driver's seat and rolled down all the windows hoping to blow away the stench. Ventilation didn't help. The disgusting odor clung to her, sinking deep into her pores, reminding her of the danger. He'd been close enough to put the dead fish in her car. And he could come even closer.

Checking the address on the business card David had given her, she aimed toward the Cherry Creek area. Though David lived only fifteen minutes away from her high-rise—close enough that they both went to the same grocery store—his town house was obviously in a higher tax bracket. The row of six two-story units, set back from the street, were expensively charming with molded stucco curves swooping around large windows. Each unit had its own attached garage. To afford a place like this, David must be doing very well for himself.

Walking up the sidewalk to his door, Blair hesitated. How could David help her? He wasn't a cop. What did she expect from him?

Comfort, she decided. Earlier today, when he'd held her and kissed her, she experienced a blissful relief. For that one moment in his arms, she forgot about her failures, her scars and her disappointments. She felt nearly happy, and she needed that feeling again—something to erase the stinking miasma of threat and danger.

Jabbing with her index finger, she pressed the buzzer.

The door opened. Jake Zitti! Though his thinning hair was now shaved bald, Blair knew him. There he was. The man who had destroyed her life. She saw confusion in his dark eyes, a nervous quiver at the corner of his mouth.

As she stared at him, she felt…nothing. She was detached—as if she'd surgically removed this cancerous man from her life. Jake the Snake was nothing to her, less than zero.

"Where's David?" she asked.

"Hey, Blair. It's great to see you."

Not bothering with a polite response, she pushed past him into the town house. "David?"

He appeared in the foyer, carrying a gun.

She pointed at the automatic pistol. "What are you doing?"

"Cleaning my weapon."

From behind her back, she heard Jake snicker as he said, "Polishing his rod."

What a jerk!

Jake continued, "Checking his clip."

Ignoring him, Blair said to David, "I've decided to

observe the autopsy. Come with me. I'd like you to drive."

"Let's go."

He came toward her with the Glock automatic still in his hand. Though Blair was concerned about the fishy threat from the Fisherman, she didn't want to drag David into the role of protector. "When was the last time you fired that thing?"

"Years ago."

At the Coroner's Office there were dozens of armed police. She ought to be safe. "Leave the gun."

"Right." He handed the pistol to Jake. "Put this away. Someplace safe."

As they whisked out the door, Jake called after them. "Have fun. See you. Bye."

"Jackass," David muttered under his breath.

"Does he live with you?"

"Temporarily. He moved in about a week and a half ago after his latest girlfriend kicked him out." David flinched as if trying to shake off the sticky tentacles of an unpleasant parasite. "I'm sorry you had to run into him like this."

"Doesn't bother me," she said. "I always wondered what would happen when I saw him again. Now I know."

"You've forgiven him?"

"Not really," she said. "But hating takes too much effort."

At the curb, David held open the passenger door to a bronze Acura and she climbed inside. She fastened her seat belt and gritted her teeth. Ever since the accident, she was uncomfortable riding in cars when other people were driving. This time, she had no choice; the stink made her own vehicle unbearable.

David started up the car. "Why did you change your mind about the autopsy?"

"Why did you have a gun in your hand?"

He gave her one of his poignant half grins. "I'm the reporter. I'm the one who's supposed to answer a question with a question."

Blair knotted her fingers together on her lap and kept her eye trained on the road, alert to any potential hazard as he pulled away from the curb. "You first."

"The gun is for self-defense. I don't know how dangerous this investigation might get, and I want to be prepared."

"The Fisherman never attacks men."

"Not yet." He turned west on Eighth Avenue, merging with acceptable expertise. "You changed your mind. It sounds like you're certain that we're dealing with the original Fisherman."

"Maybe."

"Less than an hour ago, you told me he was in jail and the current murder might be the work of a copycat. What happened, Blair?"

A gutted trout in the passenger seat of her car didn't seem so scary now that she was with David. And she didn't want to admit that she'd been terrified by a fish, driven to the brink of passing out.

She pointed to a minivan that edged too close on the passenger side. "Watch out for this guy."

David slowed to let the minivan pull ahead on the three-lane street approaching central Denver. "Why did you change your mind?"

"Gosh, you're persistent." She fidgeted. "Let's just say that I didn't have anything better to do this afternoon."

"Did you tell Adam you'd be at the autopsy?"

"I guess I ought to do that." She pointed to the next corner. "I think there's a pay phone at that gas station."

"Don't you have a cell?"

The modern dependence on mobile communication was unnecessary in her case, she hardly left her condo. "Anybody who needs to reach me can leave a message on my home phone."

David reached into his jacket pocket and pulled out a ridiculously tiny phone.

"Pull over," she snapped. "No driving while you're on the phone."

"Right. Okay. You're kind of a back-seat driver, Blair."

"Kind of."

He eased to the curb and put the car in Park while he called Adam. And she concentrated on breathing slowly, calming herself. She certainly didn't want her former colleagues at the Coroner's Office to see her behaving like a crazy woman. The only thing she had left was her previous reputation.

David ended the call. "Adam says he's glad that you've decided to participate. And he wants us to stop by his office in Golden when we're done."

She nodded.

David held the tiny phone toward her. "I want you to take this. To use in case of an emergency."

She pushed it back toward him. "Don't need it."

"Give me a break, Blair. You won't let me hire Xena as a bodyguard, won't let me carry my Glock. At least, take the damn phone. You might have to call 911."

"Fine." Though she didn't like being contradicted, it was nice to have someone fussing over her.

As they neared the Coroner's Office, where the autopsy would take place, she gave a series of directions, leading to the most convenient parking lot.

David pulled into a slot and turned to her. "Would it be better if I dropped you off near the door?"

"Why?"

"I know you can swim like a dolphin, but I wasn't sure how you are with walking."

"Not a problem," she said defensively. "My right leg is seven-eighths of an inch shorter than the left, but I have a corrective lift. I'm fine with walking. In the right shoes, I can even jog."

"I didn't mean to insult you, but I remember what it was like right after the accident." His voice was gentle, without a trace of condescension. "All the pins you had in your leg. All the operations. For a while the surgeons weren't sure you were going to be okay."

"Guess I showed them."

His gaze melted over her like warm honey. "I'm proud of you, Blair."

Basking in his approval, her heart lifted. The day seemed more golden and bright. "I could get accustomed to these compliments."

"I'm not lying," he said. "You amaze me."

Her cheeks warmed. "Now you're feeding me a line."

"Don't get me confused with Jake. He's the slick one, the pick-up artist. I'm the dork who sits in the corner, not drinking so he can be the designated driver."

"The caretaker."

She remembered, too. David had always taken responsibility, made sure everybody else was all right. He was kind enough to open his home to an annoying jerk like Jake. He wanted to hire a bodyguard for her. Though his motivation was partially due to a generous nature, she suspected a darker rationale. He took care of others *because he hadn't been able to save his sister.*

Losing Danielle was the defining moment in his life. And that worried her. She wasn't sure if David could ever heal from that terrible wound.

ENTERING THE CORONER'S OFFICE where he had come five years ago to identify his sister's body, David realized how much he needed to know the truth about her murder. Throughout the trial of Eddy Adderly and all the way through the sentencing, he had doubts. The evidence was inconclusive. Alibis didn't match. There was a lack of tangible proof for every murder except the last one.

But he accepted the verdict. For the past five years he tried to convince himself that justice had been done. But now he didn't believe it. The Fisherman had struck again.

"Excuse me." A tall, thin man stepped up beside them while they were signing in and getting their visitor badges. "Aren't you David Crawford?"

"That's right." David looked directly into the man's round, black glasses. "And you are?"

"Justin Hunter." His smile was shy and somehow furtive. His handshake was the same. "I'm a fan of your work."

Though some of the magazines that printed David's articles ran a small photo, he wasn't often recognized. "Do you work here, Justin?"

"I sell medical supplies."

As Justin continued to stare with a weird intensity, David moved away from him. "Nice meeting you."

He fell into step beside Blair. As she proceeded down the hall, he felt as if he was escorting royalty. Everybody who had known Dr. Blair Weston before the accident greeted her enthusiastically. New employees approached her with deference. She had a sterling reputation as a medical examiner. Almost legendary.

The head M.E., a husky man with a ruddy complexion, enveloped her in a bear hug. "Good to see you, Dr. Weston."

"Back at you, Dr. Reinholdt." Blair's radiant smile was wonderful to behold. "You look hale and hearty."

"A little too hearty," Reinholdt said, patting his ample belly. "The wife has me on tofu and salad."

"A wise woman," Blair said.

"Of course you'd take her side," he said. "You women always stick together."

Blair winked. "Because we're always right."

Unnoticed, David observed the interactions of the small but boisterous crew of pathologists. These were people who performed all manner of chemical analysis, ranging from DNA tests to toxicology. They were scientists—smart, well-trained people with high IQs. Also quirky. David noticed a definite nerd gene in their collective personality.

At the door to the autopsy suite, he encountered a more familiar face—a detective from Denver PD, Homicide Division. His name was John Weathers, and he'd been part of the team investigating the original series of Fisherman killings.

David had never been impressed with Weathers's abilities. He was a bland, by-the-book cop with beige hair and a brown suit, average height, average weight. He had no imagination when it came to tracking down a killer who was unfortunately near genius in his crimes.

Willing to let bygones be bygones, David stuck out his hand. "Detective Weathers. I was sorry to hear about

Pamela Comforti. My condolence on the loss of your co-worker.''

"You're David Crawford, right?" As he shook hands, a realization dawned and his brown eyes narrowed. "The reporter."

"That's right."

"Get out," Weathers said. "I don't want the press in here."

"I'm not covering this case as a journalist," David said. "It's personal."

"I don't want you here."

That was too damned bad. David straightened his shoulders. "I'm not leaving."

It probably would've been smarter to talk his way around the detective's objections, but David wasn't inclined to be reasonable. At issue was his sister's murder. If the cops had screwed up five years ago and arrested the wrong man...

Weathers beckoned to a uniformed cop who stood farther down the corridor near the metal detectors at the exit. "Escort this man from the building."

Blair joined them. "Is there a problem?"

"Dr. Weston," Weathers acknowledged her. "I appreciate your willingness to help out on this case."

"I'm sure you do," she said, "especially since I'm not on the clock as a county employee."

The uniform approached with a rolling gait. His meaty fist rested on the gun clipped to his utility belt.

David braced himself. His adrenaline level surged; he was prepared to take on both the uniform and Weathers. Again, not the smartest plan.

Blair touched his arm. "Please come with me, David. They're ready to get started."

"Sorry, ma'am," Weathers said. "This man is press. He's not allowed to—"

"Then I'm leaving," Blair said.

Dr. Reinholdt stepped up behind her. His brow furrowed as he glared at Weathers. "What's going on? Detective, I need Dr. Weston's opinion."

Blair added, "And I won't stay without David."

"Right," the detective snapped. He turned to David, "If I see one word about this autopsy in print, you'll be sorry."

Suppressing the urge to gloat, David gave a quick nod and followed Blair into the autopsy suite where the body of the deceased, covered by a sheet, lay on a wide metal gurney under bright lights.

As Blair slipped into a gown and put on a pair of latex gloves, she whispered, "What was that all about?"

"Not important."

David had attended part of one autopsy and had seen the aftermath of another—enough to know he didn't want to stand too close. Edging back, he leaned against a stainless steel counter and folded his arms across his chest to keep from accidentally touching something he should avoid.

From the opposite side of the room, he saw Detective Weathers's eyes watching him as though David were a dangerous felon. Some cops, like Weathers, had a problem: they got so wrapped up in their own authority that they forgot the real crime and the real criminals. Determining who was in charge was a whole lot less important than the dead woman on the autopsy table.

Dr. Reinholdt removed the sheet. "We've already completed the external examination and taken photos. There are a few details I'd like to point out."

Blair and three others—M.E.s and forensic pathologists—leaned forward to study the body.

Reinholdt said, "The ligature contusions at the wrists
and ankles indicate that she was tied up and struggled
against her bonds."

"Nylon rope?" Blair asked.

"Yes."

"Cause of death?"

"Drowning."

From where he stood, David saw a length of marbled
white thigh, slightly bluish. He could also see her head.
In profile, her nose seemed prominent. Her cheek sank
in. Her hair was a limp tangle of auburn.

"David," Blair called to him. "Come closer."

Though he was fine where he was, he didn't want to
appear squeamish. David put on his reporter's face. It
was his job to observe and make deductions; he could
handle this. Stepping forward, he looked where she was
pointing.

"See here," she said, "on the abdomen. There's an
oddly shaped circle of pinprick scars. Postmortem injuries?"

"Yes," Dr. Reinholdt said. "Those puncture wounds
were made after death."

With a gloved finger, Blair probed the flesh. "It's a
jagged tear. Not a pin." She looked up at Reinholdt. "A
fish hook."

"Good call, Dr. Weston." He glanced toward one of
the forensic pathologists. "I told you she was sharp."

Blair lifted the right hand to study the pattern of
bruises on the forearms. "Her hands were tied in front
of her. She lifted her arms to cover her face. Or to lash
out."

"She put up a fight," Dr. Reinholdt said. "But we

found no tissue under the fingernails. Matter of fact, we've found very little. No semen. No DNA. No fingerprints.''

"A clean kill," said the pathologist. "Very clean. After death, the body was washed thoroughly with a strong lye-based soap."

Blair peeked over her shoulder at David. "Except for the circle of wounds on the abdomen, this murder is consistent with the Fisherman."

"I see." He saw too much. His view of the inert body on the cold metal table churned up a serious revulsion in his gut. He might have puked right here, embarrassing himself badly, if he hadn't also felt a hard burning rage. It was wrong for this innocent victim to be lying here. The man who killed her and terrorized her before death deserved to be caught, tried and brought to justice. He deserved to be confined for all eternity in his own private hell.

David stepped back when he saw Reinholdt take a scalpel from a tray of instruments.

Though the temperature in the autopsy room was cool, a sweat broke across David's forehead. He adjusted the knot on his necktie. His throat tightened; it was hard to swallow.

Reinholdt made a Y-shaped incision from the shoulders to the middle of the chest, then straight down. The dark red blood had congealed. The heart was no longer pumping. The flesh was opened to reveal the internal organs.

It wasn't necessary for David to stay in the room. He didn't know enough about anatomy to notice any unusual clues, and he wasn't particularly interested in learning. He could leave right now and wait for Blair to tell him the important details.

Struggling to swallow, he glanced across the room at Detective Weathers and the uniformed cop who stood beside him. Neither of them were looking directly at the body. The uniformed officer's complexion had paled and his jaw flexed tight. *If they can take it, so can I.* David forced himself to watch as Reinholdt removed an organ and placed it on the kind of hanging scale found in grocery stores.

The autopsy team worked quickly and efficiently, keeping up a running commentary that was recorded by an overhead microphone for later transcription. After removing and weighing various organs, they took tissue samples.

Blair stepped back beside him for a moment. "Any questions?"

"What do they do with those pieces?"

"We preserve the body fluids and tissues for microscopic and toxicological testing."

"Wasn't she drowned?"

"Beyond cause of death, the body can reveal a lot of clues."

When she looked directly at him, David worked hard at being cool. He'd already wiped the sweat off his forehead, but his mouth was cottony, and his lips stuck together.

She cocked her head and asked, "Are you okay?"

"You bet." He nodded slowly so his head wouldn't get dizzy and fall right off his shoulders onto the tiled floor.

She patted his arm and turned back to the autopsy table. The inside of the body wasn't tidy like those neat overlapping transparencies in biology class that showed the layers of sinew and muscle, then different-colored organs, then a white skeleton. This work was messy, and there was a pungent smell that defied description.

David had to look at something else. He concentrated on the back of Blair's head. Her soft brown hair made a pleasant distraction. She leaned forward to get a better view, and he could see part of her profile—high cheekbones and sharply defined chin. Her hands were clasped behind her back, and her fingers twitched as though she was itching to take a more active part.

"I'm particularly curious about the stomach contents," she said.

"When we have the analysis, I'll call," Reinholdt promised. To the pathologist, he said, "Be careful with the liquid from the lungs. We want to know where that water came from."

Time passed, and the process became a little less unsettling. David had grown accustomed to the odor. He found that if he stared at one body part at a time, he could forget that this was a whole person who once had a life.

Across the room, he saw Weathers and the uniformed cop leaving. Hah! He'd beaten them. He'd toughed it out. David felt like a forensic pathology ace. *Go ahead and toss me that spleen, I can handle it!*

Blair glanced over her shoulder at him, and David flashed an "okay" sign. He was cool.

Reinholdt had the scalpel again. He made an incision at the hairline. David instinctively turned away. He heard the whine of a Stryker saw, then the grinding noise as the blade hit the solid bone of the skull.

This part of the autopsy was why Weathers and his companion had left. They knew what was coming. David, in his naiveté, thought the worst was over.

Though he didn't want to wimp out and disappoint

Blair, there was no way he'd turn around and take a peek. His imagination told him plenty.

"David?" Blair was standing beside him.

He whipped around to face her. Her hands, in the latex gloves, were bloody. He concentrated on her green eyes. "Hi."

"I think you were correct," she said in a low voice. "This murder was the work of the Fisherman."

If he hadn't been afraid of losing his lunch, he would have grinned. Through clenched teeth, he said, "Stomach contents."

"We'll know after analysis."

Behind her left shoulder, Reinholdt was doing something at the victim's head. David raised one hand to his eyes, shielding his vision.

Blair glanced at the big clock on the wall over the door. "We should try to get over to Adam's office before six. Are you ready to leave?"

"Way ahead of you."

Chapter Four

The office for Colorado Crime Consultants was west of Denver in Golden, a small town nestled against the foothills. Blair hadn't done much talking on the drive. Her mind was preoccupied, focused on the autopsy she'd just witnessed. Her reading of the medical findings told her this "clean kill" was performed by the same perp who'd committed the earlier crimes. Yet there were differences—most obviously, the fish hook scars on the abdomen.

The Fisherman was taunting them, sending a message. But why? And what was he trying to say? The answers weren't evident in forensic analysis. Pursuing this investigation might require old-fashioned police work—interviewing witnesses and suspects.

Speaking of old-fashioned forensic police work, she had confided in Dr. Reinholdt before they left the Coroner's Office, telling him about the stinky fish in the trunk of her car. He had taken her car keys and would notify the forensic investigators though neither of them expected to find fingerprints on a trout.

David found a parking space just off the main street with its quaint, Old West atmosphere, and they strolled down a covered sidewalk toward the opposite corner. "We're like a couple of tourists," he said.

"But we're not here to shop." She paused to peer in the storefront window of a candle shop. The smell of scented wax wafted through the open door. "I wonder if we can get access to the forensics gathered by the Denver PD and CID on the current investigation."

"Doubtful," David said. "Detective Weathers doesn't seem inclined to share with me."

"Well, of course not," she said. "You're from the press. Even worse than that, you're an investigative reporter. Speaking on behalf of everyone in forensics and the cops, *your* people can be a major distraction."

"*My* people? You make it sound like we're a tribe of hyenas."

"An apt analogy."

"You think I'm a dog?"

She peeked up at him and grinned. He looked much better now than during the autopsy. The color had returned to his face, and his gaze was steady. "If you were a dog," she asked, "what breed would you be?"

"Something macho. Maybe an Irish wolfhound."

"Macho?" she teased. "Like you were in the autopsy suite?"

"Hey, it took guts to hang in there." He linked his arm with hers and started along the sidewalk again. "*Guts* probably isn't the best word to describe watching an autopsy. Fortitude. I showed fortitude. I should get a Boy Scout badge for fortitude."

"Didn't you find the process interesting?"

"In a word…no!"

"At least you're honest."

"And I should get another badge for that." He turned

right at the corner and started up the block. "How about you, Blair? What kind of dog would you be?"

"Not a poodle," she said quickly. Nothing fluffy or cute. "A dog that likes swimming. Maybe a Labrador retriever."

"Most of the Labs I've known have been a little wild. Is that you? Wild and exuberant?"

She hadn't been crazy and out of control in years, certainly not after her accident. And before that? Her career left very little time for fun and games. She'd gone directly from college to med school, then an internship and field research. "Maybe I'm not wild, but the potential for exuberance is there."

"That's something I'd like to see." His voice slipped into a lower register. "The wanton, uncontrolled, passionate side of Dr. Blair Weston."

His intimate tone suggested passion in the bedroom. And, when she confronted his sexy blue eyes, similar thoughts popped inside her head. All too easily, she imagined discarded clothing at the foot of the bed. She and David, meshed together on the sheets. Their legs entwined. Their arms grasping and clawing at each other. Their lungs screaming with unfettered lust. *Oh, my.*

She pushed open the gate in the white picket fence surrounding a gingerbread Victorian house that had been converted to office space. The sidewalk was flagstone, lined by a border of yellow dahlias and pansies. On the veranda, David opened the door to the charming yellow house with white trim. Inside was a foyer with hardwood floors, an imitation Persian rug and several potted ferns. Colorado Crime Consultants was the first door to the right.

Behind the antique front desk sat Molly Griffith. If she'd been a dog, Blair guessed Molly would have the looks of an Afghan hound with her long neck and swoop of straight, blond hair, but her personality was pure terrier—quick, smart and tenacious.

After she greeted them, Molly held up her wristwatch and announced, "One minute until six o'clock. End of the day."

Blair asked, "Do you have a quitting time or does Adam make you stay all night?"

"I'm flexible." She bent down, opened her bottom desk drawer and removed a bottle of Jack Daniels. "Sometimes I don't come in until noon. Sometimes I leave at two. Time is unimportant to me. Not like Adam. He's predictable as a metronome."

She poured three fingers of Jack Daniels into a plain glass tumbler. "In precisely ten seconds, he'll open the door to his office and come out here for his evening drink."

"Why?" Blair asked. "Something to do with the Marines?"

Molly shrugged. "It's just Adam."

The wooden door to an inner office opened, and Adam Briggs stepped through. His right hand was outstretched. He grasped the tumbler and took a sip.

"Told you," Molly said. "This is the most predictable man on the planet."

With a hint of a smile, he said, "Structure leads to productivity."

"Or terminal boredom."

As he swirled the amber liquid in his glass, Adam regarded her with an expression of fond indulgence. These two had worked together since the inception of Crime Consultants. He was the brains, and she was the heart. They made a good team.

Adam asked his office manager, "Do you have the information for Blair and David?"

"I picked up the last bit this afternoon," Molly said. "From Gary O'Hara. For an FBI guy he's kinda cute. Is he married?"

"Not your type," Adam said.

"He's got a pulse. That's about all I require these days." Molly nudged Blair. "I'm not getting any younger."

"Gary O'Hara," David repeated the name. "He was the FBI Special Agent assigned to the Fisherman investigation five years ago. I thought he'd left Denver."

"He was reassigned to Langley," Adam said. "He's been back here since the first of the year."

"What kind of information did you get from him?"

"Copies of his personal notes on the prior murders." Adam took another taste of his drink. "We won't get data on the current investigation, but the past is a closed case. Therefore, it's relatively accessible."

Molly stepped out from behind her desk and led the way toward another closed door at the rear of their office. "I put everything back here in the conference room. O'Hara's notes. Partial transcript from the trial. Newspaper clippings. Interviews. Web site information."

"Impressive," David said. "You're thorough."

"I'm just the collection point," she said. "We have a couple of researchers who work for us on a volunteer basis, including a former court reporter who knows how to navigate that system. Shh, don't tell anybody about her."

Blair and David stepped into a conference room. Above wainscoting, the walls were painted a deep red. Framed maps hung from the walls. At the end of the polished table sat a large cardboard box with a lid.

Molly stood at the doorway. "Would either of you like something to drink?"

"I'll have what Adam's having," David said.

"Water for me," Blair said.

"I'll get it." Molly turned toward the outer office and glanced impatiently toward her boss. "Come on, Adam. We're waiting."

He sauntered up beside her. "Don't rush me."

Molly planted her fists on her hips and tossed her head, flipping a wing of blond hair out of her eyes. "Any particular reason you're dragging your feet?"

"As you know, Molly—" he tasted Jack again "—I only have one drink a day and…"

"You like to savor," she finished his sentence. "It's the slow burn and the aftertaste."

"Exactly." He drained the liquid from the tumbler and handed the glass to her. As he seated himself at the head of the table, he turned to Blair. "Tell me about the autopsy."

"Manner of death—homicide," she said. "Cause of death was drowning. No evidence of sexual assault. Contusions on wrists and ankles indicated that hands and feet had been bound."

She explained the postmortem marking on the stomach and concluded, "We'll know more after analysis on the water from the lungs and the stomach contents."

"What do you expect?" Adam asked.

"If this is the Fisherman or a copycat who is conversant with the particulars of the prior murders, the drowning will have been in a bathtub. The stomach contents will reveal Godiva chocolate."

"Is there a significance to the candy?"

"Me," Blair said. "After I was assigned to the first

murder, every victim was fed that particular brand of chocolate. It's my favorite.''

"Mine, too," Molly said. "Are you sure that's significant?"

"My nickname at the Coroner's Office was Lady Godiva," she said. "And it wasn't because of riding naked on horseback."

"There's a direct threat to you?" Adam exchanged a worried look with David. "I didn't know."

"Neither did I," David said. "If I'd been aware that Blair might be a target, I never would have wanted her to be involved."

Molly placed their beverages on the table and Blair drank deeply of the cold bottled water. Now might be the time to mention the threat from this afternoon—the gutted trout in her car. But she was reluctant to take that step. She didn't want the investigation to be about her vulnerability.

"Are you in danger?" Adam asked.

"I'm not sure." She turned to David. "You've reported on a lot of these cases. How do people know when they're really and truly in danger?"

"Some don't," he said, "until the ax falls."

"Why not?"

"Lack of imagination," he said.

That certainly wasn't her problem. It only took a lowering of his voice for her to leap into a full-blown fantasy of lovemaking. "I don't suffer from that lack. Much of my work as an M.E. is based on an ability to imagine what might have happened."

"Sometimes," he said, "people hide their fear by building emotional walls of defense, telling themselves over and over that nothing bad will happen to them, until they believe it's the truth. No matter what the facts."

"De-nial," Molly said. "It's not just a river in Egypt. If you're in danger, Blair, we have bodyguards that we can contact."

"Not yet," she said. "I promise to be careful."

"I'll make sure you do," David said.

"Whoa there, cowboy." Adam leaned back in his chair and squinted at him. "What makes you think you're qualified as a bodyguard? Do you have training in hand-to-hand combat?"

"No training." Though David was in decent physical condition, he knew little about karate, kung fu or any other technique that might be used to fight off a crazed serial killer. David's weapon was his pen...more accurately, the word-processing program on his laptop computer. "I have a gun."

"Which you probably haven't fired in years."

"Correct."

"How do you intend to protect Blair?" Adam demanded.

"By keeping her out of harm's way."

"The Fisherman has never attacked anyone who was accompanied," Blair said. "He's not likely to take sudden, precipitous action. This is a guy who leaves no forensic clues behind. He's careful."

"And dangerous," Adam said.

"I know." David swallowed his drink in two quick gulps that set his throat ablaze. He didn't need a reminder that the Fisherman was lethal; the bastard had murdered his sister.

He nodded toward the box on the table. "I'd like to take this information with me tonight."

"Why?"

"To determine which leads we should be following. I'll need to interview some of the witnesses." He was anxious to get his hands on the detailed files. "It's been five years. People might remember things differently."

"None of this can be for publication," Adam warned. "I won't compromise any of my sources."

"Don't worry." This was one crime he had no intention of writing about.

EVENING CAME QUICKLY in Denver. As soon as the setting sun disappeared behind the Rockies, the blazing skies faded and darkness unfurled across the Queen City of the Plains. By the time they returned to the center of the city and Blair's condo building, David had his headlights on. He parked in front.

"Until we know otherwise, we'll assume that you're in danger, Blair. That means I'm staying with you."

"All night?"

Her voice sounded husky, and he hoped she was coming on to him. "I can stay the night."

"Not necessary. But if you bring that box upstairs, we can go through the information together."

She flung her car door open.

"Wait!"

"What's wrong?" she asked.

He scanned the streets with a watchful eye. This area was condo city with lots of high-rise buildings. He spotted a couple of people on the sidewalk. Were they dangerous? Or just out for a walk? "Wait until I can walk you to the door."

"Oh, please," she scoffed. "Do you really think I'm going to be attacked here? On this well-lit street? In front of witnesses?"

How should he know? David had never before tried to think like a bodyguard. Lifting the cardboard box from the back seat, he followed her toward the entry to her building. He wished he had his gun with him.

A man stepped from the shadows. He wore a black suit—not the expected garb of a serial killer, but there was menace in his stillness.

Was this an attack? David knew he should respond with lightning reflexes. He dropped the cardboard box in front of himself. Should he jump on top? Dodge around the side? Maybe he ought to just trip over the damn thing and get the probable humiliation over with.

He confronted the shadowy figure. "Who are you?"

FBI Agent Gary O'Hara stepped into the light. Though he was solidly built, he moved silently as a wraith. "Good evening, David. Dr. Weston."

"Agent O'Hara," David said. "Good to see you."

"Wish I could say the same." His voice was low as a clandestine whisper. "You've only been in town a day, David. And you've already got the local cops in an uproar."

"I had a little showdown with Weathers. No big deal."

"I've been specifically instructed not to consult with you on the current murder investigation," O'Hara said. "However, nobody mentioned the prior murders."

"We have the data you gave to Adam Briggs." David pointed to the box. "Is there something else you wanted to tell us?"

"Denver PD is taking the position that they arrested and convicted the right man five years ago. However, the murder of Pamela Comforti is assumed to be connected to the Fisherman. The police want to believe this killer is a copycat."

"What do you believe?" David asked.

"I think it's him. The Fisherman."

David's blood stirred. They were on the right track. "How do we find him?"

"Start with the past," O'Hara said. "Dig into the old crimes, the leads that weren't followed. Concentrate on suspects who've been out of Denver for a significant portion of the last five years."

David asked, "Can we use you to check into VICAP and the National Crime Information Center?"

"Go through Adam," O'Hara advised. He held out a business card. "If you come up with valid evidence, contact me."

"Thanks."

When O'Hara focused on Blair, his dark eyes lingered. He reached out and grasped her hand. "Always a pleasure, Dr. Weston."

"Same here."

O'Hara pivoted. In just a few strides, he went around the corner of the building and disappeared.

Blair wasted no time hustling inside the front vestibule where she unlocked the inner door. A shudder rippled across her shoulders. "O'Hara's a little spooky."

"Molly thinks he's cute," David said.

"Not really," Blair said. "She's just teasing Adam. Anybody can see that those two are in love."

"They are?"

"Not in the conventional sense." She held the door for David. "I mean, they're not sleeping together. But there's a bond between them...like an old married couple."

"A married couple who doesn't have sex?"

"Don't bother puzzling it out," Blair said as she boarded the elevator. "Men don't understand relationships."

"And you do?"

"Better than you. I've spent plenty of time talking to my friends about their significant others. I've read the magazine articles and looked up the horoscopes to see what sign matched my own. Even if I never was a girly-girl."

He suspected she was a tomboy, the kind of kid who dissected her Barbie dolls to see what made them work. "Tell me how reading a magazine makes you a relationship expert."

"I can see the signs." She exited the elevator and trooped down the hall to her condo. "Maybe it's female intuition."

He set down the box while she opened the door to her condo. His intention was to enter the condo ahead of her and to search, making sure there was no threat. "Let me go first."

"Why?"

"Because that's what a real bodyguard would do."

She pushed open the door and stepped back. "While you're bodyguarding, what should I do? Do I leave the door open or closed?"

It didn't seem smart to leave her standing in the hall. There could be a psycho lurking in the stairway. "Come inside and close the door."

When he glanced at her, he saw the flicker of a smirk playing on her lips. And he felt damned silly. He wasn't a former Marine like Adam, wasn't a federal agent like O'Hara who could materialize out of the shadows and disappear just as fast. David was just an average guy, flying blind and trying to do the right thing.

When she closed the door, they were both standing in the narrow hall that led into her condo. He went first into the living room, dining area and kitchen. Down the hall and into the bathroom, he peered behind the shower curtain. He checked in the cabinet beneath the sink.

"What do you expect to find under there?" Blair teased. "A midget psycho?"

"You're not making this easier," he grumbled.

"Because it's a waste of time."

"Not when you consider the facts," he said. "Two of the victims were abducted from their homes. They were women who lived alone, like you."

In her second bedroom which she used as an office, he opened the door to the closet. This room was filled with clutter, books, a desk and computer. But there were no good hiding places.

He entered her bedroom. Unlike the rest of her functional living space, this room was pretty and feminine. He could easily imagine the woman who lived in here reading girlish magazines and thinking about the perfect relationship. On the bedside table was a single white orchid in a bud vase. The furniture was dark wood, and the covers on her four-poster bed were white with a sprinkle of tiny pink and yellow daisies. After looking in the attached bathroom, he returned to the bedroom. It smelled great, like cinnamon and honeysuckle.

"Is it safe?" Blair asked from the doorway.

When he saw her standing there, so close to her bed, his thoughts proceeded down a risky path. He wondered if he could manufacture a valid precaution that might include lying down on the bed, possibly removing some of her clothing.

"David?" Her gaze was cool and sardonic. "Are you done in here?"

"I should look under the bed." He bent down and did so. "And the closet."

Her walk-in closet was impeccably organized. He

reached out, and lightly touched her silky blouses and dresses. The fabric caressed his fingers. "These are pretty."

Behind him she said, "I never wear dresses anymore. You know, because of my leg."

Dozens of shoe boxes were stacked in a corner, reaching from floor to ceiling. He gestured to them. "Do you wear all those?"

"Not for the past five years." She pivoted abruptly and walked away, leaving him in the closet.

David winced, feeling like an ass for being so insensitive. If he'd concentrated for two seconds, he would have realized that she didn't wear the fancy shoes anymore. She needed a seven-eighths-inch lift.

But it was hard for him to remember that Blair was handicapped, especially after watching her at the autopsy where she was obviously smart and competent and respected by her peers. Yeah, sure, there were scars on her leg, but she didn't seem limited in any way.

He came out into the living room and found her curled up in the one decent chair, nibbling at a Godiva chocolate. She was irritated. He could almost see the miniature storm cloud above her head.

"Okay, Blair. There's one more hiding place I need to check, and you need to help me."

"I'm really tired."

"One more thing." He caught hold of both her hands and pulled her to her feet. "The balcony."

"Fine. Take a look."

"Come with me," he said. "If there's a wall-crawling psycho out there, I'm pretty sure I'll need your help to subdue him."

"For goodness sake, David!" She tried to wrench

free, but he held on tight, dragging her along with him to the sliding glass doors. "Just open the blinds."

"Not sufficient," he said. "We can't see in the corners."

They stepped outside onto the fifth-floor balcony. Beyond the rooftops, the lights of downtown Denver shimmered like diamonds in vertical trays. The gold dome of the state capitol gleamed against a dark purple background of sky and sheltering mountains. Spreading lights of the city and suburbs glimmered into a faraway perspective, consumed by the velvet prairie night.

Of all the places David had traveled, he loved Denver the most. Definitely a city. But there was also a sense of natural isolation, a home for the rugged individual. He leaned his elbows on the balcony railing and inhaled a breath of springtime air. "Nice."

"I like the view." Standing beside him, Blair exhaled a sigh. "If we were up higher, we'd see more of the mountains. But I prefer being at this level, even with the treetops."

For a long moment they stood, secluded by the night, lulled by the sounds of the city stretched out below them. He placed his hand atop hers. "It's good to spend time with you again."

"Even though I'm a smart aleck?"

"I like your sass."

"My what?"

He grinned. "Doesn't seem like we've ever been apart."

"But we were never really together, David. We didn't date. We weren't a couple."

He gazed down into her moonlit face, a perfect oval dominated by turquoise eyes. "I would've made a move on you the first minute I saw you. Except for Jake."

"Jake the Snake," she said automatically. "But you're not remembering correctly. Five years ago, when we met, you'd just lost your sister. You were a raw nerve ending."

"I've healed." He stroked his fingers through her soft brown hair. "All better now."

"Are you?"

"Kiss me, Blair."

Chapter Five

The scent of cinnamon and honey—Blair's perfume—
enveloped David as he pulled her close. He'd asked for
a kiss but wasn't willing to wait while she considered
the alternatives and came up with excuses from ladies'
magazines. He had to kiss her now, right now, while
they stood on her balcony with the twinkling city lights
as a backdrop.

His mouth slanted across hers, tasting gently, savoring
the smooth texture of her lips. Her fragrance swirled
around him, arousing him to the erotic possibilities of
Blair—who would never call herself a girly-girl, but was
all woman.

She responded to him. Her supple arms wrapped
around his shoulders, and she held on tight. Their bodies
tensed. In five seconds' time, they'd gone from zero
miles per hour to 120. He needed to slow down before
they crashed. His grasp lightened. He left her gasping
lips and kissed her cheek, her earlobe, the sharp edge of
her jawline. His hands outlined the shape of her body,
the slender indentation of her waist and the sexy flare of
her hips. Each caress fed his rising passion.

Her fingers kneaded his back, and he hoped those
skilled hands, medically trained, would teach him the

special secrets of her anatomy. She shuddered as he cupped her breast. The pliant weight and hard nipple, a taut little bud of passion, drove him crazy.

David hadn't expected to make love to Blair today, but her touch felt so right. Her body was made for him. On some level, he had always wanted her.

When she started to pull away, he wouldn't let her go. He kissed her again, not wanting her to speak. He didn't want to hear that they were moving too fast.

Playfully she pushed against his chest. "No, David."

"Yes, Blair."

He silenced her with another kiss. Her lips parted. Her tongue engaged with his.

Then again, she tore herself away, panting. "No."

Though he had to respect her stated refusal, he knew she was hot. And he was on fire, up to his neck in boiling lava. "I don't want to stop."

"A relationship between us…" Turning away from him, she stood at the railing, staring toward the glistening downtown skyscrapers and the mountains beyond. "You and me? David, it just won't work."

"You're wrong, Dr. Weston."

He came up behind her, and she leaned her back against his chest. As his arm encircled her, she moaned softly. "Please, David. No."

He rubbed his cheek against the top of her head. Her soft brown hair tickled his nose. "Give me a chance."

"It's not going to happen."

With an effort, she shoved away from him. Why was she was fighting the natural urge that drew them together? Her eyes shone with a strange desperation. She almost looked scared. Well, damn. He didn't want her to be frightened of him.

David took a step backward, giving her space. "I'd never do anything to hurt you. You understand that."

Her chin lifted. "We can't get involved. You and me, we're both damaged people. A couple of victims, clinging to each other."

"Victims?"

"Caught in the past." She pivoted and whipped through the glass door into her condo. "We don't have a future."

He was much too aroused to chase after her. His body was set on high, ready for steamy, hot passion. Not logic! The hell with rational thinking! Seeking calm, he stared into the night heavens. Slowly he counted the pinpricks of cool distant stars. His breathing settled into a more normal pattern, but his mind was still agitated.

He wanted to make love to her, and he didn't believe her diagnosis. Why wouldn't a relationship between them work? David didn't consider himself a victim.

When he stepped inside her condo, he left the sliding glass door open a crack to allow the night breezes inside. Blair stood across the room with one hand resting on the handlebars of her stationary exercise bike. Her posture was rigid.

She held up her hand, forestalling any comment from him. "I need to say this, David. It's not fair to either of us if I don't thoroughly explain my position."

"Go ahead."

"I can't look at you without thinking of who I was before the accident. When we first met, I had a career, doing significant work," she said. "I was a whole person with my life ahead of me."

"You're still a whole person," he said. "And anytime you want to go back to work at the Coroner's Office, they'll take you. They love you there. They respect you."

"My job was important, but there was something more—something I took for granted before I lost it." She raised one hand to cover her mouth, then lowered it. "I was pretty."

He stared, uncomprehending. "But you're beautiful."

"Stop," she snapped. "It's not the same. Before the accident, I was in my prime, wearing miniskirts and flimsy, fancy sandals." Her hand curled into a fist which she tapped against her injured leg. "My sandal-wearing days are over."

"Damn it, Blair. If this is about shoes—"

"Don't joke. You can't dismiss what happened to me. Or to you. We can't pretend it didn't happen." As she paced across the room toward the table, her limp was evident. "We're rooted in the past, anchored by our separate pain."

"What if I told you how attractive you are right now? Right at this moment." He wasn't lying. "What if I told you that your eyes are the most intriguing shade of green I've ever seen? Your smile is a miracle. You're soft and strong at the same time. Your body is slender, hot and sexy."

"I'd say you were the one in denial." She sighed. "Face it, David. You didn't come here because of my allegedly hot bod. The only reason we're together right now is to review a murder. You and me, we're still stuck in the past."

He had to acknowledge a grain of truth in what she said. "I'm attracted to you, Blair. And I admire you. You're a survivor. You recovered from your injuries."

"Did I? I still can't go back to work because I have these unexplainable dizzy spells. The docs can't find a neurological explanation for my weakness.'' Her lower lip trembled. ''It's in my head. I can't accept who I am.''

''I can.''

''Liar!'' She shook away the unshed tears. ''And look at you! You say you're not a victim, but your whole life is devoted to the study of crime, trying to make sense of your sister's death. There isn't room in your heart for anything else.''

A stab of realization cut through him. Though he'd made peace with his past on a rational level, his heart still ached. He couldn't deny the pain. Or the effect.

David hadn't been able to sustain any kind of relationship after his sister's murder. Sure, he pretended that he was being selective in dating, but that was a lie. He held back, still mourning Danielle. And when he thought of her, he was enraged, consumed by a driving need that could only be about revenge, a relentless poison.

Until he knew without doubt that the real killer was on death row, David would be incapable of giving himself completely.

''You might be right,'' he said.

''Of course I am.''

''This investigation may be more important to me than I thought.''

She sank into the chair beside her dining room table. ''I know. I could see all the signs.''

''What signs?''

She braced her elbow on the table and rested her forehead against the heel of her hand, avoiding his gaze. ''While I was working in the Coroner's Office, I saw the next of kin who came to identify their loved ones. I saw the investigators who became obsessed with the crimes and criminals.''

''I've seen them, too.'' Much of his investigative

work involved interviews with those who were left behind—suspects, killers and victims. "They're all different."

"All damaged. Whether they're crying or screaming or yelling, there's a common need. An emptiness that must be filled before they can, once again, participate in life."

Blair's telephone rang. She rose from her chair and went into the kitchen to answer, leaving him alone with a mountain of self-doubt.

He knew that Danielle's murder was an important turning point. But had it crippled him emotionally? Had he spent the past five years in limbo, unable to feel anything? He was familiar with the psychology of survivor's guilt and post-traumatic stress disorder, but he hadn't applied those terms to himself. Until this moment it hadn't seemed necessary.

David wasn't altogether sure he wanted to let go of his rage. That intensity drove his work. Maybe it was time for his impossible quest to end.

Blair returned from the kitchen. "That was Dr. Reinholdt. Some of the sample analysis from the autopsy is complete. It was tap water in the victim's lungs, probably from a bathtub."

"Like the Fisherman," he said. "What about the stomach contents?"

"Chocolate. Godiva chocolate." She frowned. "If this is a copycat, he's precise."

"Which means you're in danger," he said. "He stalked you before. He's stalking you now."

"Maybe," she said quietly.

This was a definite call to action. He could almost hear the trumpets blare. The sooner he got this investigation under way, the sooner it would be solved. Then he could have a life. "I need to get started with that box of information. Can I use your office?"

"Let me tidy up the clutter."

She walked past him with her eyes downcast and her shoulders sagging. She looked exhausted, but David knew better than to approach her. Blair had her own battles to fight, and she'd made it clear that she didn't want his help.

While Blair scooped her personal stuff—bills and letters and documents into the drawers, he centered the box on her desktop and opened it.

The information from CCC was neatly arranged in file folders with identifying tabs indicating forensic reports, Agent O'Hara's notes, newspaper clippings and court transcripts. Molly had done an excellent job in pulling this together. Additionally, she'd set up individual files for each victim which she labelled Mermaid 1 through Mermaid 6. David's sister was the fourth mermaid killed by the Fisherman.

Blair peered over his shoulder. "Give me the forensic evidence file."

Since there was only one desk chair in the room, she perched on the edge of the desk to peruse the file.

David looked down at the remaining data. Danielle's file was the place he had to start. He opened the flap of the manila folder. His sister's heart-shaped face stared up at him from a formal eight-by-ten photograph taken after she'd graduated from college. The camera caught a sparkle in her eyes that matched the diamond pendant she often wore. Tiny gems outlined the shape of a *D*. Danielle and David were the Crawford children, and their mother was Diana. They called themselves the Three Ds. *Oh, Danielle...* She should have had a long life, children of her own. She should not have been murdered.

His stomach lurched. Bile rose in his throat. His rage and horror remained unquenched, even after all these years and the supposed conviction of her murderer.

"Look at this," Blair said.

She held up the arrest photograph of Eddy Adderly. The convicted killer's name was as bland as his appearance and personality. With his thinning blond hair and squinting myopic eyes, Eddy Adderly never looked smart enough to elude the police. But David had learned from his subsequent investigations that the face of evil is often nondescript. A stone-cold killer might be the guy next door, somebody you pass on the street without a second glance.

"He's an ugly little vermin," she said.

Preoccupied by the files, David nodded.

"Hungry?"

"I guess so."

"I'm thinking we should order pizza."

"No anchovies."

She left the office, and he flipped the photo of his sister facedown. Quickly he skimmed the autopsy report, crime-scene report and investigative notes from the police, including Detective Weathers. There were no surprises, and the information was scanty as David knew it would be. None of the evidence indicated his sister had a personal connection with the killer.

He opened up the file for the first mermaid. Because the cops had no pattern when she was killed, there was a lot more focus on the family and friends of this woman. She'd been a nurse, like Danielle, and was engaged to an anesthesiologist, Kevin MacKay. From the looks of these reports, he'd been considered a suspect.

On the outer side of the folder, David made a note to talk with Kevin MacKay. As he proceeded through the files, his list of people to interview grew. He had nearly twenty when Blair appeared in the doorway.

"Pizza's here," she announced.

He'd forgotten his hunger, his lust and virtually everything else. Concentrating on his work, David had fallen into an all-consuming state of research. Pieces of data ricocheted inside his head as he pushed away from the desk and followed her to the tiny table in the dining area where a large pizza box awaited.

"Wait a minute," he said. "How did this pizza get here?"

"Not a mystery. The delivery guy buzzed at the front door. I ran downstairs and—"

"Hey! I'm supposed to be your bodyguard," he said. "You could have been killed."

She arched an eyebrow. "While picking up a pizza?"

He didn't appreciate her attitude. "The whole idea of protecting you is for you to stay here, safely locked inside."

"Whatever." She opened the pizza box and pushed a paper plate toward him. "Something to drink?"

"Beer?"

"Sorry," she said. "I have cranberry juice and soda pop. Oh, and I think there's vodka somewhere."

"Just water."

At his town house there was beer. And a comfortable space in his office. And his computer. While investigating other crimes, he'd come up with a system of spreadsheets to outline suspect profiles.

If Jake hadn't been living there, David would have suggested that she move in with him for a while. Clearly, that was impossible. Blair didn't need to be reminded of her past by having Jake around. And David knew there would be no chance of further kissing with her ex-boyfriend in the next room.

He bit into a slice of hot, cheesy pizza.

"So," she said. "Are you finding anything interesting?"

"I've got a list of people to interview."

"I want to come with you," she said.

David always worked alone. He found that his subjects were more willing to talk to one person. Plus, he was sharper when he concentrated his entire attention on each interview. Having Blair with him would be a distraction. "Why?"

"The Godiva chocolate for one thing. There's a direct threat to me, and I need to confront it."

"What else?" He sensed that she was holding back. "And what's the other thing?"

"A dead fish," she said. "When I went down to the parking lot this afternoon, I found a gutted trout in my car. That's why I changed my mind about attending the autopsy and—"

"Did you tell the police?"

"I told Dr. Reinholdt. The CSI team is going over my car. I don't really expect they'll find any trace evidence."

He stuffed more pizza into his mouth to keep from exploding. Unsure of whether he was more ticked off at her for concealing evidence from him or more enraged about this obvious threat from the killer, he chewed furiously.

"Leaving a big fat clue, like the trout, wasn't typical of the Fisherman," she said. "I know he selected his victims and stalked them."

"Right," David said.

"But did he threaten them before he abducted them?"

"I'll check the files."

"It just seems weird, leaving the fish in my car."

David swallowed a blob of pizza grease too fast. It stuck in his throat. In more ways than one, he was choking. "What are you saying?"

"Maybe this killer really is a copycat."

"Doubtful," he said. "Serial killers have specific reasons for their actions. There's something about the details of the execution that satisfies them. And the Fisherman is very precise. It's not likely that somebody else has the same fantasy."

"The copycat's thrill could be simply that," she said. "Copying the first guy. Outsmarting the cops and making them look foolish."

It was possible. Typically, serial killers got a kick out of the power they had over law enforcement. They liked to sit back and watch while everybody ran around trying to find them.

"Frankly, Blair, I'm more concerned about your safety than the psychological profile. Aren't there security cameras in your parking area?"

"Only one, and it isn't aimed at my car." She frowned. "I should've handled this differently. I should have reported the dead fish right away. Keeping a crime scene pristine and untampered with is vital to a thorough forensic investigation."

He nodded.

"I didn't want to admit that I was scared," she said. "Maybe you're right. Maybe I really do need a bodyguard."

Hallelujah! She was beginning to catch on. "Let me hire a pro."

"I'd rather stick with you."

Though he wasn't trained for the job, David was motivated. He'd fight to the death to protect this woman. "Okay, fine."

"Therefore," she said with a self-satisfied grin, "I should stay with you all the time, even when you're interviewing suspects and witnesses."

He opened his mouth, then closed it as he finished off his slice of pizza and reached for another. Her plan sucked. Though being with her 24-7 sounded like he'd just won the lottery, he wasn't supposed to touch her or even think about a relationship. Plus, she'd be a major distraction during his interviewing process.

"I'm right," she said. "Aren't I?"

"Don't gloat."

"We'll work together very well. I'm sure of it."

David felt like a moron in a chess game with a Mensa genius. Outplayed. Manipulated. "I'm going back to your office."

"I'll stay out here and go over the forensics," she said. "When you've reviewed everything, maybe you could give me an update."

"Sure."

In her office, he sank into the chair behind her desk. Surrounded by reports and evidence of six brutal murders, he could only think of the crafty, clever woman in the other room. Blair wasn't his idea of a victim. She'd played him like a concert pianist and had gotten what she wanted. Being around her was a constant challenge.

But he liked the idea of matching wits. Sooner or later he'd come out on top…in more ways than one.

With renewed energy, he dug into the files. Concentration consumed him. He stared for several seconds at a name. Justin Hunter. That was the guy at the Coroner's

Office, the medical supplies salesman who claimed to be a fan of David's writing.

For a while Agent O'Hara focused his suspicions on Justin Hunter, who ran a Web site devoted to serial killers. It couldn't be coincidence that Hunter happened to be at the Coroner's Office at the time of the autopsy.

There were other names. Family members and associates. David's list of interview potentials was growing. When he finally looked at his wristwatch, four hours had passed. It was nearly midnight—time for him to go home, take a shower and catch a few hours of sleep before tomorrow morning. But he didn't want to leave Blair unprotected.

He stood and stretched and yawned.

There was no place for him to sleep in her condo. She didn't even own a sofa. Her bed? Not a chance, not if he wasn't supposed to touch her.

He went to the front room to pose this problem to Blair and found her curled up in the recliner chair in front of the television, sound asleep under a crocheted blanket. On the table beside her chair were three crumpled paper cups that he knew had held Godiva chocolate.

Her face, in repose, had a sweetness that was absent when she was alert. Her bangs fell haphazardly across her smooth forehead. Her lashes made dark crescents above her pink cheeks.

Though he hated to wake her, he knew she'd be more comfortable in her bed. He leaned close and whispered, "Blair."

Not even a twitch. Apparently, she was a sound sleeper.

"Come on, Blair."

Gently he removed the blanket. She'd changed into a long, pink, jersey nightgown that subtly outlined her slender curves. On her feet were fuzzy slippers. And she still wasn't moving.

"Time for bed," David said. He slipped one arm beneath her knees and the other under her shoulders. When he lifted her into his arms, her head drooped. Still asleep, she nuzzled warmly against his chest as he carried her from the chair down the hall and into her bedroom.

Gently he stretched her out on the queen-size bed and pulled down the covers. She rolled onto the sheets and grabbed the pillow without opening her eyes.

He stood beside her bed, smiling down at her. Blair would hate being described as adorable, but that word came readily to his mind. She was sweet and cuddly as a kitten.

Reaching down he took off her slippers. Her injured ankle was crisscrossed with pale, puckered scars where pins and rods had been implanted. Farther up her leg were more marks from her surgeries. David bent down and kissed the places she'd been hurt, wishing he could erase her pain.

"You're beautiful," he whispered as he pulled the covers up over her shoulders.

Chapter Six

Blair wakened slowly. Her body rose gently from the pleasant lethargy of sleep, floating upward toward the surface. It was morning. Rolling to her side, she glanced at the bedside clock. After nine o'clock? Amazing! She was usually up with the dawn, completely alert.

But yesterday had been packed with activity. It was a three-ring circus with more thrills, chills and excitement than she usually encountered in a month. The Fisherman's threats were less than amusing. But her moments with David? His kisses? A lazy grin spread across her face.

She shouldn't be thinking about him that way. Time to make coffee.

In the front room, she stopped in her tracks and stared. David had fallen asleep in the recliner chair. The sleeves of his shirt were rolled up, and his muscular forearms clenched across his chest. His shoulders hunched. His head drooped at an uncomfortable angle. Ouch! He was going to be stiff. She knew the morning-after ache of sleeping in that chair because she often drifted off while watching late-night television.

As far as she could remember, that was what had happened last night. She'd been staring at the tube, hoping to distract herself. She'd closed her eyes, just for a minute, to rest them. Had she gone to sleep? Apparently not. Somehow, she must have staggered down the hall to the bedroom, leaving David to fend for himself.

Talk about a terrible hostess! Guiltily she reached out and tapped his shoulder. "David, do you want to get up?"

He growled like a bear coming out of hibernation. Even before he opened his eyes, his hand rubbed at the base of his neck, and he winced. "What time is it?"

"Not too late," she said brightly. "A little after nine."

He wrenched himself out of the chair. His eyes were bloodshot. The rugged stubble on his chin made him look disheveled. His khaki trousers and cotton shirt from yesterday were so wrinkled that they looked like the sagging skin of a shar-pei puppy.

He cleared his throat. "We've gotta get moving."

"Why?"

"I have an appointment at ten-thirty with Ted Hurtado."

"The reporter who got all those letters from the Fisherman?"

"Right," he said. "I set it up yesterday."

"That still gives us an hour," she said. "Enough time for me to shower and swim."

"Afraid not, Blair. I need to go back to my place for a change of clothes. And you're coming with me."

Though she'd been insistent yesterday about taking part in all his interviews, they didn't have to be joined at the hip. If she didn't do her regular swimming, she'd be cranky all day. "Why don't you go home and change, then come back and pick me up?"

"We stay together." He crammed his feet into his loafers. "I'm taking this bodyguard stuff seriously."

"Okay, fine. I'll be ready in five minutes," she said. "But we're stopping at a Starbucks on the way."

"Five minutes," he snarled.

"Not exactly Mr. Congeniality in the morning," she mumbled as she hustled down the hall. From her years as an intern working double shifts, Blair knew how to throw herself together in a flash. Her short hair required only a bit of tousling. Face washed. Teeth brushed.

In just over five minutes, she was dressed in black slacks, a red silk shirt and a gray blazer. She strode out of the bedroom. "Ta-da!"

David grabbed the box of information from CCC. "Nice work, partner. You look good."

She couldn't honestly say the same for him. She reached up to pat his stubbled cheek. "How's your neck?"

"I'll live," he said.

They were off and running.

HIS TOWN HOUSE was pleasantly empty of Jake, and Blair had a chance to check out the surroundings while David was in the shower. She wandered around, sipping her Starbucks latte.

From the outside, his home qualified as upscale with its flowing modernistic design, and the interior reinforced that impression. The floor plan for the living room, dining room and kitchen was open space under a swooping cathedral ceiling.

Blair started in the kitchen, hoping she might find food. The appliances behind a black marble countertop were state-of-the-art, but the refrigerator held only a half loaf of bread, a six-pack of beer and catsup. Could she make toast? She eyed the bread suspiciously. Not quite sprouting mold, but the half loaf had probably seen better days.

She moved on.

In the sunken living room, the decor featured a lot of leather and heavy masculine furniture that seemed to suit David's taste. But there were also designer touches that made her think he'd hired a professional to furnish his home. Instead of family photos, there was geometric artwork on the walls. Directional lights focused on interesting sculptures and a few artistic silk flower arrangements.

When he emerged from the bedroom down the hall, buttoning the front of his blue cotton shirt, she pointed to a dramatic display of orange and white lilies. "I had no idea that you were a flower kind of guy."

He stared at the arrangement as if seeing it for the first time. "Orange lilies. In the language of flowers, they stand for hatred. White lilies are for purity."

She raised an eyebrow. "What's the message? I hate purity?"

"I didn't choose the flowers. I hired a decorator, and she did the whole thing. Furniture doesn't much interest me, and I'm on the road a lot."

"So why did you decide to spruce the place up?"

"I started dating somebody," he said. "It seemed like the right time to buy a sofa."

In spite of Blair's stated refusal to have a relationship, the mention of another woman caused a ping of jealousy in the pit of her stomach. She didn't want to hear about other girlfriends. Instead, she returned to the display of orange and white lilies. "Hatred and purity?"

"That's right," he said. He slowly twisted his head from side to side. "My neck's killing me."

"One more question," she said. "Why do you know the meanings of flowers? It's a kind of Victorian, maiden-aunt thing."

"Forget it." He continued to rub his neck.

"Come on, David. I'm sure there's an interesting story involved."

His blue eyes focused sharply upon her, and Blair had the sense she'd probed too deeply. What kind of dark secret could possibly be connected with a silk flower arrangement?

"There was a serial killer case in Montana," he said. "Four victims. The killer always left behind a bouquet. Black roses, symbolizing death. Gardenias for a secret love. And lilies. He used lilies, too. The sick bastard."

David strode across the room to the side table where the vase of artistically arranged silk lilies stood. Gripping the bouquet by the stem, he lifted the flowers and crushed them, heads down, into a trash can.

His abrupt action startled her. "What are you doing?"

"Erasing a reminder."

As he went into the kitchen, she saw only a glimpse of his profile. His taut jaw and the deepening of lines at the corners of his eyes were enough to show his tension.

"The flower killer was caught," David said tersely. "Unlike the Fisherman, he was sloppy. There was enough DNA evidence and fibers to convict on all four murders."

Unlike the Fisherman. Every part of his life—his entire livelihood—related back to that case. She had to do something to relax him before he exploded. "You need a massage."

"We don't have time."

"May I remind you that I'm a doctor? I can fix that ache in your neck in under ten minutes. Come over here,'' she ordered, pointing to one of the chairs by the dining room table. "Take off your shirt and sit."

He strode toward her, tearing open the buttons he'd fastened only a moment ago. He draped his blue shirt over a chair back and turned to face her. "Okay, Doctor, do your stuff."

She smiled. His chest was firm, lightly muscled with a sprinkle of black hair that arrowed down to the waistband of his trousers. Very nice, Blair thought. "Sit backward on this chair," she said. "The chair back is a good height. Rest your arms on the top and your chin on your hands."

As she arranged him on the chair, she especially enjoyed the dorsal view. His spine was perfectly straight. With each small movement of his arms, the muscles from shoulders to blades to rib cage flexed and extended in subtle, enticing ripples. Very nice, indeed.

She couldn't help remembering how his arms enfolded her last night on the balcony. And she'd pushed him away? Obviously, Blair had been out of her mind. A sane woman would have dragged him into the bedroom and had her way with him.

"Relax, David."

Her fingertips worked at the knotted muscles at the base of his neck. She lightly massaged, then went deeper, releasing the knots of tension.

He groaned. "Oh, yeah. This is good."

She turned his head from one side to the other, worked her way out to his shoulders and returned to his nape. He smelled like soap, fresh and—to her mind—sexy.

"Is this medical?" he asked.

Not really. Blair wasn't a chiropractor. But she knew that the first step to a cure was having the patient believe.

"Of course it's medical. I'm loosening the intersecting flexors."

"Whatever you're doing, keep at it."

She kneaded her way down his spine and up again. As David relaxed, she grew more tense. Excited, really. Touching his naked flesh couldn't help but arouse her sensual imagination.

She needed a distraction. "Last night, going through the information, did you figure anything out?"

"The trial transcripts were interesting," he said. "It didn't seem to me like there was enough hard evidence to convict Eddy Adderly."

Her review of the forensic data led to the same conclusion. "Go on."

"On the other hand, his confession was full and detailed. With information he couldn't have known unless he was the killer."

"You're tightening up again," she said. "Relax."

"Right."

She could have massaged him for hours, enjoying the pleasure of touch. And she wanted his hands on her body, returning the favor. Blair exhaled a sigh. "What's your conclusion? Is Eddy Adderly the Fisherman?"

"I don't know." David's head lolled to one side. "But I mean to find out. That's why I contacted CCC. I need to know, once and for all, who killed my sister."

"When you have your answer, what happens?"

"Revenge," he said darkly.

The edge in his voice worried her. There was no easy cure for his wound. His pain went deeper than muscle, deeper than bone. He'd been stabbed through the heart with grief. Still bleeding after five years, he was more crippled than she would ever be.

She lightly stroked his shoulders with her fingernails. "Done."

He sat up straight, stretched and yawned. "Nice job, Doctor. I feel human again."

She took a few steps away from him and clasped her hands behind her back. Her fingers tingled, and she felt flushed all over.

He slipped into his shirt. "Unless you want beer for breakfast, we'll have to grab fast food on the way to Ted Hurtado's house."

She picked up her blazer and headed toward the door. "Coffee is enough for me until lunch."

Outside, on another gorgeous spring day, she climbed into the passenger seat of his car and fastened her seat belt, still uncomfortable with someone else behind the wheel. Not that she had a choice. Forensics had impounded her car.

They crossed the city on Speer Boulevard to north Denver, entering an older, genteel area with aging residences on spacious lots. David parked outside a sprawling house of dark-brown brick. Trapped in the shadows of two towering spruce trees, the house was enveloped in permanent gloom. There were signs of neglect: a broken sidewalk, weeds among the iris, chipped paint above the wide porch.

"Doesn't seem right for Ted Hurtado," David said. "I never knew him well, but his columns were always hip and witty. This house looks like Dracula might keep a coffin in the basement."

Blair remembered Ted as a neat, well-dressed man with thick brown hair combed back from his forehead. Not bad looking. He'd made a play for her while she was dating Jake. "Didn't he take some time off from the newspaper to write a novel?"

"That explains it," David said as he opened his car door. "Novelists are weird."

On the porch, a coating of dust covered wicker furniture and matching urns of dead flowers and weeds. David pressed the bell.

The door opened immediately, as if the person inside had been waiting for them. She was petite, dressed in skintight leopard-patterned pants and a deep-purple blouse that showed a lot of cleavage.

"I'm Doris." She smiled through thick scarlet lipstick. "Teddy's mother. Please come in. We'll have tea."

"Thank you, ma'am." David introduced them both. As a reporter, he'd trained himself not to form hard-and-fast opinions based on first impressions. Though Doris Hurtado, Ted's mother, had a platinum-blond hairdo taller than she was, though she wore wacky clothing, it didn't mean the woman was color-blind or crazy. However, as he and Blair followed the bustling little lady into her house, David couldn't help wondering if her offer of tea included a drop of gin.

To the left of the marble-tiled foyer was a formal parlor. Unlike the shabby exterior of the two-story brick house, this room was impeccable with fancy, claw-footed Victorian furniture, ornate picture frames and shelves full of weird little keepsakes all dusted and shiny. Above the fireplace mantel was a huge portrait of an angry-looking man in a black suit.

"Nice place you've got here," David said. "Who's the gentleman in this picture?"

"That's Daddy." With mincing steps, Doris bounced up to the picture and blew him a kiss. When she tilted her head to behold the portrait, her towering curls were strangely immobile. "Daddy passed away seven years ago but is never forgotten. Not for a minute."

When she turned back toward them, her squinty raisin eyes were damp, and she dabbed away the moisture with the sleeve of her purple shirt. "Teddy told me that you'd be visiting, David. But I didn't know you'd be bringing your girlfriend."

Blair said, "I'm not his girlfriend. We're colleagues."

"Do you work at the newspaper?" Doris asked.

"I'm a medical examiner," Blair said. "A coroner."

"A doctor." Doris beamed. Tiny wrinkles crackled across her face. It was impossible for David to guess this woman's age. She could have been a hard-living fifty-five or a well-preserved seventy-five.

Doris chirped, "Remind me, Doctor, to tell you about a pain I have in my tummy, right above my boom-boom. But first, we'll have tea."

As she set out toward the kitchen, David followed. He was curious to see the rest of her domain. "Allow me to help, Mrs. Hurtado."

"Call me Doris. All my boyfriends do."

They passed through a formal dining room, also immaculate, into a disaster area of a kitchen. Clutter and gunk covered the countertops. Cupboard doors hung open. The sink was full of dishes. But the chaos didn't seem to bother Doris at the least. She gestured toward a cookie sheet encrusted with scorched blobs. "My muffins," she said, "didn't quite turn out."

"We already ate," David said quickly.

As she placed a chipped enamel teapot on the stove to boil, Doris picked through the mess in the sink. Filmy water lapped around the sloppily stacked dishes. It looked like a breeding pond for mosquitoes. "Let me see," Doris said, "I'll need to find cups."

"Please don't trouble yourself," said Blair who had followed them. "We'll just chat with you until Ted shows up."

"That wouldn't be proper." Doris continued to hover at the sink, poking at glasses with one long fingernail. "I always offer refreshments to my visitors."

Unless David missed his guess, most visitors—those who survived—were smart enough to decline the offer. "We're fine, Doris. Let's go back in the other room."

When she lifted out a cup, coated with unnamed globules, David took action. He grasped her arm. "Step away from the sink."

"Well, well." She beamed up at him. "Aren't you the he-man!"

"We're going back to the parlor."

As he escorted her, Doris rubbed herself against his arm. Was this loony little woman flirting? Her tiny eyes beamed up at him. "I've seen you on the television, David. You're very cute."

"Thanks, ma'am."

In the parlor he tried to seat her in a chair, but she insisted on sitting beside him on the sofa. When he moved to the far edge, she stuck with him. She was so close that he could smell her cloying perfume.

"Tell me about Ted," David said. "He's been writing a book."

"My Teddy is a genius. He should be on television, too."

The front door swung open, and Teddy the Genius came inside. He had his mother's squinty little eyes which he rolled when he saw Doris plastered up against David.

"Here's my darling boy!" Doris said as she sprang to her feet and ran to her son. She tugged on his sleeve until he lowered his face so she could kiss his cheek, leaving a smear of lipstick.

"Sorry," Ted said to David. "I was running late."

"Teddy." His mother still clung to his arm. "David was making a pass at me."

He glanced apologetically toward David and Blair, then gazed down to his mother and said, "That's what happens when you're the prettiest lady in Denver."

"You're silly!" she said.

"Mom, you'll have to excuse us," Ted said. "We have some work to take care of."

After a few more compliments to his fawning mother, he extracted them from the tidy parlor. They went across the foyer into an office with a sliding wood door. Ted closed it and pointed to a couple of modern chairs.

His office, like the parlor and dining room, was sleek and functional. He sat behind the desk. "Mom can be a little over the top, but she means well."

"Do you live here?" Blair asked.

"Every time I move out, Doris has a crisis." He shrugged. "It's not so bad. There's a guest apartment over the garage where I can grab some privacy."

"This is a big place," she said. "It seems like a lot for your mother to take care of."

"I have a cleaning service twice a week."

It was hard for David to believe that the disaster in the kitchen had accumulated in just a few days. "So, Ted. I understand you took some time away from the paper to write a book."

"A thriller. The manuscript is with an agent and we're optimistic about finding a publisher. In the meantime, I went back to *The Post*. It's been about six months." He glanced at his wristwatch. "What can I do for you, David?"

"I'm working with Colorado Crime Consultants, look-ing into the Fisherman murders."

"The current thing?"

"I'm leaving that to the cops," David said carefully. After FBI Agent Gary O'Hara's warning, he didn't want anybody to think he was going to mess up the ongoing investigation. "I'm more concerned with the past."

"Why?"

"Eddy Adderly is dying in prison. Before he goes, I want to be sure he's the man who killed my sister."

Ted frowned. "You shouldn't get involved, David. You're too close to the crime."

"It's been five years," David said. Not that he had to justify his decisions to anybody.

"My advice? Let somebody else do the investigat-ing."

"As it so happens," David said coolly, "I'm the best person I know for conducting true crime interviews. That's my job."

"And we all know you've been real successful." Ted didn't bother to disguise the bitterness in his voice. "Jake always tells us about your accomplishments. Ohh, did you see David on television? Aah, David got quoted in *Vanity Fair*. But those investigations are different. You're not personally connected to those crimes."

David reined in his temper. "Thanks for your concern. Do you mind answering a couple of questions?"

Ted paced to a file cabinet, pulled it open and took out a folder. "These are copies of all the notes the Fish-erman sent to me. There were ten in all."

David had already reviewed copies of the notes that had been printed in the newspaper. Most were taunts along the line of "You'll never catch me." Or threats, stating when the next victim would appear.

"I'm more interested in your impressions," David said. "Did you ever get the idea that he knew his victims? Maybe that he stalked them before he attacked?"

Ted plucked one sheet from the file and read it aloud, "Cops are stupid. I'm not. Next mermaid comes on Friday. Do you see? You are dumb." Ted looked up at them. "The first letter of the first word in each sentence spells out CINDY, and that was the next victim."

"So he knew," Blair said. "He already had selected her."

"And we were all too stupid to understand his little code," Ted said. "Not until after the murder."

"Were there other clues like that?"

Ted shook his head. "Far as I can tell, it was the only time he gave a name in code."

"There were references to food," David said. "Like 'she's sweet as pecan pie.'"

"I think those were meant for me." Ted straightened his shoulders, preening a bit. "I was writing restaurant reviews at the time, and the Fisherman must have read them."

His rationale answered a question that had been bothering David. Why Ted? Why not an investigative reporter with a front-page byline? "You think he selected you because he was a foodie?"

"The cops thought so," Ted said. "They staked out the restaurants I reviewed."

From outside the office, David heard Ted's mother shuffling around. It sounded as if the front door opened and closed.

Blair must have heard it, too, because she said, "Maybe I should go check on Doris."

"She's fine," Ted said.

"About the current murder," David said. "Do you think it's him, the same guy as before?"

"No way. Eddy Adderly is the Fisherman, and he's in jail."

There was a hammering on the office door. In a high-pitched voice, Doris squealed, "Teddy, come quick. Oh, dear. Teddy, hurry."

He stalked to the sliding door and opened it. "What's wrong, Mother?"

"The mail!" She held up a plain white envelope, addressed to Ted. "I didn't mean to open it, but I just did. And this was inside."

Her hand trembled as she waved the sheet of lined notebook paper toward them.

Ted took the paper and read. "I'm fishing again. I want more mermaids and you can't stop me. The next one comes on Friday."

Chapter Seven

With one hand, Ted patted the quivering shoulders of his mother who had plastered herself against his chest. With the other, he held out the threatening note so David could study it.

"Don't touch," Ted warned. "There might be fingerprints."

David leaned close to scrutinize the scribbled words. Like the other notes from the Fisherman, it was written in pencil with blockish letters. Though it would take a handwriting expert to determine if this note was written by the same person who penned the other threats, it looked similar. "Same guy? What do you think, Ted?"

"At first glance it's the same."

"Not quite." Blair—who was much more conversant with forensics than either of them—held a copy of a previous note beside the new one for comparison. "The new one has more capital letters. Look at the word *mermaid.* Both the *A* and *I* are written small but are uppercase."

"A code," David suggested.

"Or a purposeful misdirection," she said.

"It's different in other ways," Ted said. "Very brief and to the point. And there's no mention of food."

''It's not so sneering,'' David said. The other notes made derogatory comments about cops and the media. He repeated the catchphrase from several other notes. '''You can't catch me.' That was a more challenging tone.''

''More direct,'' Ted said.

''I can't believe you two,'' Blair said. ''You're critiquing a threat note from a psycho.''

Doris sobbed loudly against her son's chest. ''Oh, Teddy. What will we do? He's going to kill us.''

Blair stepped in, gently touching the older woman's shoulder. ''Come with me and sit down, Doris. This has been a terrible shock for you.''

She tightened her grasp on her son. ''That's right. A terrible shock.''

''Come with me,'' Blair repeated. ''I'm a doctor, remember?''

When Doris transferred her grip to Blair, who carefully escorted her to the other room, David breathed a little easier. How the hell did Ted put up with this woman? Doris Hurtado took the concept of *clingy* to a whole new level. ''Weren't the other notes sent to you at the newspaper?''

''That's right. Addressed to me personally and marked Private.''

So this was another deviation from the original pattern of the Fisherman. Though it seemed like a small change, David didn't downplay the significance. Serial killers generally followed the same ritual down to the last detail. ''Why would he do it different this time?''

Ted rubbed at his shirtfront, which was smeared with his mother's lipstick. ''Look at this mess! It's a Hugo Boss shirt. Probably ruined.''

''Maybe this killer is a copycat, after all.''

"That would be my analysis." Ted looked up from his shirt, clearly irritated. "If you ask me, the whole thing is a pain in the rear."

"That's an interesting take on the brutal murders of several women," David said coldly. Ted wasn't exactly the King of Empathy.

"Don't moralize with me," Ted snapped. "This isn't my beat."

"It could be." David was a little surprised that Ted hadn't already cashed in on his unique position as the recipient of the Fisherman's threat notes.

"You're right," Ted murmured. "I could do a couple of TV interviews. I should call my agent."

David read the note again, memorizing it. The next killing would take place on Friday. Only four days from now. If he was following the pattern of the original Fisherman, the next victim would work for the news media or would be a medical person. *Like Blair.*

Doris wailed from the other room, and Ted exhaled a long-suffering sigh. "You have to leave, David. I need to take care of my mother and call the cops."

"And your agent?"

"I could follow in your footsteps," he said. "You seem to have turned serial killers into a full-time profession."

Wallowing in violent crime hadn't been David's original intention. He'd wanted to use his investigative reporting to heal himself and others. Now, his profession disgusted him. It might be time to get out. "Thanks for your time, Ted."

Staring straight into David's eyes, Ted's attitude was confrontational. "Like I said before, it's a bad idea for you to dig into these crimes."

"And I told you that—"

"Stop!" Ted held up his hand, palm out. "Leave the investigating to the professionals at CCC."

"Actually, they're not pro. They're citizen experts. Like you and me."

"Whatever. You ought to back off. You'll only get hurt."

If David had been pursuing these killings as an investigative reporter, he would have made more of an effort to leave Ted Hurtado on a positive note. But this was his own private hunt, and he could be honest. "I don't need your advice, Ted."

"Because you're so smart?"

"Because you know nothing about me. Or my life."

With a quick pivot, Ted turned his back and went into the other room where Blair sat on the sofa beside his mother, patting her hand and listening as Doris rattled on about her physical ailments and how this terrible shock would probably kill her.

David stood with the front door half-open, waiting while Blair extricated herself. Quickly as possible, she joined him. On the porch, she shuddered from head to toe. "That is one weird family."

"Agreed."

"People like Doris are one of the reasons I became an M.E. for the Coroner's Office. Dead people don't talk back."

Side by side they walked down the sidewalk to the car. "What's next?" she asked.

"I need to make some phone calls," he said. "Do you still have my cell?"

She unzipped a pocket on her backpack, but before she turned over the phone, she said, "No cell phone while you're driving."

"Here's an idea," he said. "You drive. I'll sit in the passenger seat and make my phone calls."

The approving smile that lit her face told him that he should have figured out this solution a long time ago. If Blair was behind the wheel, he wouldn't have to listen to her constant back-seat driver commentary, telling him to watch out for the other cars, for bumps in the road, for lane changes.

"I'd be delighted," she said.

Behind the wheel of the Acura, Blair made adjustments to the seat and the mirrors. Carefully she eased the car onto the residential street. "Where to?"

"St. Ignatius Hospital," he said.

For a little while she tried to listen to David's end of phone conversations, but her mind drifted as she drove back toward the center of town. Coming from the west, the skyline was a reverse image of her usual view. Sunlight sparkled in brash reflections off the skyscraper windows. The skies above were blue and clear.

Though she'd grown up in Indiana, she considered Denver to be her home. The city was large enough to have urban advantages, but there was still a small, cow town feeling within the various neighborhoods. The fabric of the city was stitched together like a quilt with each scrap representing a diverse locale with its own architecture and population—like Ted's house in an older section where brick two-stories stood side by side, looking out at a quiet street where few children played. Ted Hurtado seemed out-of-place in that dark brick home. He was a sophisticated guy who belonged in a classy downtown loft where he could walk to performances at the Denver Center for the Performing Arts. Why had he stayed with his mother?

More important, why had the Fisherman chosen to

send his threat notes to Ted? Could it possibly be—as he suggested—because he wrote a restaurant column?

She had a sense that Ted knew more information about the Fisherman but didn't want to share with David. On the other hand, he seemed to like her. If Blair could schedule some time alone with him, he might be more forthcoming.

Not that she was thrilled by the process of interviewing witnesses and suspects. It was too inaccurate. If you showed five witnesses the exact same scene, they'd come up with five different stories. People lied. Or they avoided the truth. Or they simply didn't see what needed to be seen.

She much preferred the exactitude of science. Just the facts, ma'am.

David completed his calls and clicked the cell phone closed. "Here's what we're going to do. I just talked to Jake, and he's clearing his stuff out of my town house. You'll stay with me."

She thought for half a second and said, "No."

"I need to be in my office, using my own computer to make notes on these interviews and—"

"I wanted to ask about that," she said. "You didn't jot down any notes while you were talking to Ted. How do you remember what was said?"

"If the interview gets complicated or if I need accurate quotes, I use a tape recorder. Otherwise, I remember," he said. "And don't change the subject. Why can't you move into my place?"

"You don't have a swimming pool." Seemed obvious to her. "Swimming every day is important to me. It keeps me in balance."

"No problem. I'll make sure we get back to your

place every day for a swim. But you're going to stay
with me. It's safer.''

She had to agree that moving in with David seemed
like a good protection strategy. In the past, the Fisherman only targeted women who lived alone. Still, she
didn't want to pick up and move. It was a huge disrup-
tion. Her condo was comfortable; her daily routine was
settled. She might not have the most wildly ecstatic
lifestyle, but she wasn't miserable. Only a little bit
lonely. Okay, so she was occasionally very lonely. Desperately isolated.

What was the real reason she didn't want to move? It
was an admission that she was in danger—an acceptance
of the possibility that the Fisherman might target her
next. Friday, four days from now, was the deadline.

''Okay, David. I'll move in with you. The change will
do me good.''

''I promise to get food,'' he said.

''And coffee,'' she said. ''And—''

''Chocolate,'' he said. ''I know.''

She found a parking space down the street from St.
Ignatius Hospital. ''What are we doing here?''

''I'm hoping we can hook up with Dr. Kevin MacKay.
He's an anesthesiologist. His fiancée was the first victim.''

''Is Kevin MacKay a suspect?''

''The cops seemed to think so. At the time of the first
murder, they really worked him over. Then the second
body showed up, and this turned into a serial killer investigation.''

''Do we have an appointment with him?''

''I just talked to him. He said he'd try to meet us in
the cafeteria within the hour.''

She groaned. ''Hospital food for lunch.''

IN THE HOSPITAL'S beige cafeteria, Blair assembled a palatable lunch: a bag of chips, bottled water and a turkey sandwich. The secret to decent eating in any kind of institutional setting was to avoid foods that required expert preparation—like the goopy bowl of chili on David's tray.

He opened his skinny briefcase on the Formica tabletop and pulled out a photograph. "This is an old picture of Dr. MacKay. See if you can spot him in here."

With his red hair, snub nose and pale-blue eyes, he looked like an all-American guy with no secrets and no nefarious agenda. She scanned the cafeteria. The people in street clothes—patients, their friends and family—shared an attitude of resigned anticipation as they poked at their food, waiting for medical results. The hospital staff was far more varied in their poses. They were on the job. Some weary. Some happy. Some tense. None of them were Kevin MacKay. "I don't see him."

David was already halfway through his chili. "This isn't half-bad. I might have to go back for seconds."

"Two bowls of chili? You must have a cast-iron stomach."

"As long as it's food, I'm okay."

She wondered if, while she was staying at his home, they'd cook meals together. The idea of sharing domestic duties made her smile. The last time she'd lived with another person was in med school when she'd rented a bedroom in a large old house with three other roommates. She remembered big dinners of salad and spaghetti. It might be fun to try out her more experienced culinary skills on David.

"Hello, Blair."

The tenor voice came from over her left shoulder. She turned and looked up at the redheaded man from the photograph. Dr. Kevin MacKay. He seemed to know her. "Hi," she said tentatively.

"You don't remember me," he said as he set his tray on the table beside her. "We interned at the same time. That was at Rose Hospital."

"But you're an anesthesiologist." Logically their paths wouldn't cross. "I was never on a surgical rotation."

"We didn't work together, but I noticed you." His smile seemed forced. "You looked real cute in your purple scrubs."

"Right. Baggy scrubs are so adorable."

His laugh was cold. "I even asked you out on a date. You turned me down."

"I didn't date much." This was turning uncomfortable. "We were so busy as interns."

"Sure," he said. "That was the same excuse you used back then."

She still couldn't place him. Had they really interned at the same time? He looked to be in his late forties, at least ten years older than she was. "What have you been up to, Kevin?"

"This and that." He carefully unwrapped the cellophane on his cafeteria sandwich. "I just got back from Peru. For the past four years, I've been working with International Medical Relief. Which means I've been all over the world. Africa, Asia and South America."

"So you've been away from Denver for quite a while."

"I like the travel."

As David introduced himself and explained his investigation, Blair's thoughts turned inward. If Kevin MacKay could be considered a suspect, if he might be the Fisherman, his travel patterns would explain the gap of five years between the earlier murders and the killing of Pamela Comforti.

The perfect escape for a serial killer was to move from place to place so the authorities wouldn't recognize a pattern. Even more brilliant would be moving from country to country. A killing in Peru would never be connected to the murders in Denver.

The thought sickened her. It was grotesque to imagine someone from International Medical Aid as a serial killer. Their job was to provide relief to a desperate population, not to harm them. The revulsion must have shown in her expression because Kevin said, "Something wrong, Blair?"

Had he targeted her? Was he looking at her as his next victim? "I'm fine."

David said, "I hate to rake up the past, Kevin. But sometimes we have a different perspective when we look back."

"What do you want to know?"

"I'm interested in the time right before the murder of your fiancée. Did you notice anything unusual?"

"Like what?"

"A change in her regular routine?"

"Hard to tell," he said. "She had a bee in her bonnet about setting a date for our wedding. Kept pressuring me about it. Every time I saw her, she was carrying one of those bride magazines."

"Was that behavior different?"

As Kevin considered the question, he arranged the food on his tray and started eating in a clockwise progression, taking a bite of sandwich, a sip of milk, then a bite of apple. Very precise.

The way he dressed was equally obsessive. Under his starched white medical jacket, his scrubs were ironed.

The four pens in his pocket were identical. He wore a large wristwatch with several dials and functions. Blair suspected it was an alarm clock wristwatch—one of those annoying devices for people who were oh, so important.

She really wasn't being fair to Kevin. Attention to detail was a positive trait for an anesthesiologist. And for a serial killer?

"As I look back," Kevin said, "I'd say Marion was more excitable than usual. You know, giggly. She mentioned three or four times that she wanted to move in with me."

"You weren't living together?"

"Of course not." He frowned. "Not before marriage."

"You were a priest," Blair said. "I remember now. When you started interning, you'd just left the priesthood."

"Because I believed I could do more good in a medical profession," he said.

"That's why you've been working for International Medical Aid. To do good."

"That wasn't my first plan. I expected to get married, settle down and have kids. After Marion was killed, that changed."

"Did you find someone else? Are you married now?"

"Not yet. But I'm still looking."

With this new evidence, Blair absolutely had to revise her opinion of Kevin. He was a former priest *and* a volunteer for medical aid. It didn't sound like the résumé for a serial killer.

"Back to Marion," David said. "Did you ever have the impression that she was being stalked?"

"Not really. She didn't get weird notes or phone calls."

"Anything more subtle? Somebody asking her out even though she was engaged?"

"Well, that happened all the time." He sipped his milk. "Marion was a very beautiful woman."

"Looking back," David said, "was it possible that she wanted to move in with you because she felt threatened?"

"I don't think so." He nibbled his apple. "Marion enjoyed the attention of men. All men. She encouraged them, tossing her hair and swinging her pelvis when she walked. And all that giggling. She had an aura. Very sexy. I wasn't surprised she attracted a serial killer."

Blair couldn't believe his words. "Surely you don't blame her for what happened?"

"I don't condemn her. She couldn't help the way she was. Women don't realize what they do to men. Like Eve in the Garden. The temptation of the flesh."

Before she could tromp all over his idiotic opinion, David said, "Do you think Marion knew the killer?"

"Certainly," he said. "She allowed him to get close enough to take her captive. When her body was found at Sloan's Lake, she was wearing tight leather pants I disapproved of. If she'd done as I said—"

"Wear Amish clothes?" Blair snapped. "Or never leave the house?"

"There's something to be said for modesty." Kevin tasted his sandwich, his milk, his apple.

Outraged, she pushed away from the table. "I'll wait for you in the hall, David."

"Sorry," Kevin said. "I didn't mean to offend you. I'm being honest."

Honestly offensive. She was appalled by his suggestion that female victims deserved to be attacked or murdered because of their clothing. Tight leather pants didn't justify an assault. Blair had never believed the "she's asking for it" theory.

Walking as quickly as possible, she left the cafeteria and stepped into the hallway. Even the faintly antiseptic smell of the hospital was a relief after listening to Kevin's rancid opinions.

Blair leaned her back against the wall and folded her arms below her breasts. Impotent anger surged through her. Right now, she seriously needed a swim—something refreshing to wash away this disgusting, slimy sensation.

But she knew the swim would have to wait.

They spent the rest of the day talking to other people connected to the first murder, Marion's murder. According to her sister and other friends, Marion had been an average woman in her mid-twenties. A nurse. She liked dressing up and considered herself lucky to be engaged to Kevin. None of these people suspected Kevin of anything more than being opinionated.

It was after dark when the returned to Blair's condo so she could gather up the necessary clothes and toiletries for a stay at David's place. Before she went anywhere, she intended to take a swim.

She emerged from her bedroom wearing her robe over her bathing suit. Her apartment keys were in her robe pocket. "I'm going down to the pool."

He pried himself out of the recliner. "I'll come with you."

"That's not necessary," she said, rolling her eyes. Though she enjoyed David's company, they'd been joined at the hip all day. "Take a break."

"What kind of bodyguard would I be if I let you—"

"A sensible one." Placing her hands on his chest, she pushed him back toward the recliner. "I swim every day and nothing ever happens to me. Besides, the Fisherman set his deadline for Friday. Four days from now. I'll be fine."

He glanced longingly toward the television. "I'd like to catch the evening news and see if there's been progress on Pamela Comforti's murder."

She picked up the remote and clicked on the news broadcast. "I'll be back in half an hour."

With a sigh, David sank into the chair.

Before he could change his mind, she whipped down the hall, out the door and ran to the elevator. She liked David, but she needed a break from the incessant talking. All the spoken words crammed inside her head and rattled around in a jumbled mess. Too much—it was definitely too much human contact for someone like Blair who usually spent her days in relative quiet.

The tiled pool room was empty. As usual. She always found it hard to believe that with more than a hundred people living in her building, the pool was so often deserted.

She hung her robe on a wall hook, put on her goggles and stepped to the edge. Her neat dive into the cool blue water instantly revived her senses. A delicious shiver rippled through her.

With vigorous strokes, she swam two laps, then rolled onto her back and set a more leisurely pace. The gentle exercise relaxed her body and eased her mind. Tension flowed from her. Swimming was such a clean sport. No sweating. No straining. Only a smooth ripple.

And then the overhead lights in the pool room went out. Darkness fell over her like a smothering blanket.

Chapter Eight

Confused by the sudden darkness, Blair splashed in a circle, treading water, staying afloat. Unable to get her bearings, she tore off her goggles. A faint illumination spilled from two high windows that were shuttered for privacy. It was just enough light to reflect off the water. The waves shimmered around her like a hundred sharp knives pointed straight at her heart.

This blackout hadn't been caused by a power failure. The impending danger had caught up with her.

There was only one door out of the pool room, and she peered toward it. Beside the door was the light switch. "Who's there?" she whispered.

Outlined against the tile walls, she saw a shadow, a solid presence. He was here with her. Watching. Waiting.

"Who are you?" Her trembling voice echoed off the tiles, bouncing back at her in desperate mockery of her fear. Screaming for help was useless. No one lived on this level. No one would hear.

The shadow moved, furtively gliding along the wall, circling the edge of the room. Where was he?

She couldn't tell, couldn't see anything. Her only

landmarks were the tiny slashes of light from the windows. Could he see her?

She swam toward the shallow end of the pool. Before she grasped the edge, she decided this was a bad idea. Once she got out of the water, she was exposed. If she stayed in the center of the pool, surrounded by water, he couldn't reach her.

She pushed away from the side and paddled halfway back to the deep end. At least, that's where she thought she was. In the dark, her familiar surroundings became alien territory. She straightened her body in the water and bobbed below the surface. The deepest part of the pool was eight feet. She wasn't there yet.

When she broke the surface, she heard the sound of shuffling feet against the concrete. Where was he? How close?

If he dove into the water after her, she could pinpoint his location and flee from him. She was a fast swimmer. But where was he? Where would the attack come from?

Concentrating hard, she stared at the tiled walls all the way around the room. There seemed to be no one. No shadow. Nothing.

Then she looked up. On the diving board above her head, she saw a crouching form. Hunched over, he didn't even look human.

Instinctively she took a breath and dove as deep as she could. Absolute silence engulfed her. A dark void. It was the most horrible emptiness she'd ever experienced. Totally alone, she was in limbo, a prelude to hell but safer here than on the top where he could find her. The engulfing waters would cushion and protect her. How long could she stay down? Forever? It would be better to die here than to be caught by the Fisherman.

But Blair wasn't ready to die. Not here or anywhere

else. Fear expanded inside her lungs. She pressed her lips together, holding back the terrified gasps that could drown her.

She had to come up for air.

As soon as her head was out of the water, she heard a splash. It seemed to be only inches away from her. Then another. He was slapping at the water, hitting at her with something long and dangerous. One of the poles used for cleaning the pool.

She ducked again and stroked furiously toward the shallow end. When she stood, the beam of a flashlight blinded her. He was directly in front of her.

The light went out. Again, she felt the splash from that pole.

Diving back and kicking with all her strength, she raced to the opposite end of the pool. Clinging to the side, she gulped down air. Though she knew the darkness had lasted for only a few minutes, it felt like hours.

The flashlight beam caught her, and she squinted. She couldn't make out his features, couldn't even tell if he was tall or short.

"What do you want?" she asked.

"You." One word. A gutteral growl, distorted by the tile acoustics.

How could she fight him? Terror clawed at her throat. She couldn't breathe. Her arms and legs felt limp and helpless. She was broken again. Like a marionette off its strings.

The flashlight went out. He was moving again, coming after her, slashing the surface of the water with the long pole.

She had to move, to swim, to escape. Her hours of exercise in the pool should be good for something.

Not knowing where he was, she swam from one side

to the other and back in a crazy pattern so he wouldn't guess where she was headed next.

Back and forth at the deep end, she hoped to lure him there. Back and forth. Stroking for her life, her arms churned the water. And when she felt certain that he had taken a position at that end of the pool, she changed direction and sprinted toward the shallows where she would climb out and race for the door. It couldn't be locked from this side. That would be her escape. Not much of a plan, but it was all she had.

As Blair pulled herself out of the pool, she saw him, faintly outlined by the light from the window. He stood directly in front of her. A shadow come to life. Before she knew what was happening, she felt a glancing blow on the side of her head.

Falling back, she was in the water again. Half-conscious, she tried to struggle, but her arms were too weak. And she was dizzy, near blacking out forever.

All she could manage was to float on her back toward the center of the pool. Soon, she knew, the air would leave her lungs. The dead weight of her body would pull her under, and she would drown. Her struggles and pain had been for nothing. In the end she was helpless as a fish in a bucket. A mermaid.

The overhead lights flashed on.

The sudden flare blinded her. She looked up, directly into the light—circular and bright. Like in an operating room. Or in the Coroner's Office. What was going on? What other horror did he have planned for her?

She stood. Her bare feet planted solidly on the bottom of the pool. The water was high as her breasts.

Her gaze searched. She turned in a circle.

No one else was in the room.

IN FRONT OF the television set, David talked back to the screen. "You're an idiot, Weathers."

In a prerecorded interview, Detective Weathers stood behind a half dozen microphones and answered questions from the media. "This is not the Fisherman," he said firmly. "The man who terrorized our city five years ago has been convicted and is in prison."

David scoffed. "That's what you want us to believe."

An off-screen reporter asked, "What about the note? Do you expect more killings?"

Weathers drew back from the microphones. Though he was obviously trying to appear calm and controlled, David saw the nervousness in the detective's manner. His lips thinned. His eyes squinted under the unforgiving glare of the television lights. Weathers said, "We can't predict what will happen next. However, we urge citizens to use extra caution."

"Which citizens?" A reporter asked, "Who does the Fisherman attack?"

"As I said before, this is not the Fisherman. It's a copycat crime. Probably an isolated incident."

Though Weathers clung steadfastly to that line, David didn't buy it. The cops were protecting themselves and the court system. The didn't want to admit they'd convicted the wrong man.

The TV news story shifted to Ted Hurtado who must have reached his agent. Unlike Weathers, Ted carried himself well. Poised as a movie celebrity, he was dapper, cool and ultrasuave in a charcoal suit jacket and dark-maroon shirt. His mother would be pleased to see her boy making such a good appearance on the tube.

Far more glib in his comments, Ted looked into the camera and said, "The note I received was similar to the earlier messages from the Fisherman but not exactly the same. Some of the letters were uppercase instead of lower.''

David muttered, ''Which you didn't notice until Blair pointed it out.''

''Five years ago,'' Ted continued, ''the Fisherman attacked women from three areas—law enforcement, the media and hospitals. Single women.''

''Which I reminded you about,'' David said.

He glanced away from the television as Blair unlocked the door to her condo. She was breathing hard, dragging herself down the hallway. There was blood on the side of her face.

David bolted from the chair and ran to her. ''What happened?''

She sagged into his arms. ''He attacked me. In the pool.''

He scooped her up in his arms and carried her toward the bedroom.

''Not the bed.'' She moaned. ''I'm bleeding.''

''You need to lie down. I'll call an ambulance.''

''Don't want to bleed on the bedspread,'' she said. ''Take me to the bathroom.''

Though he disagreed, now was not the time to argue with her. He carried her to the bathroom.

''Put me down,'' she ordered.

She stared into the mirror above the sink. Her fingers probed the edges of her head wound, pulling her hair aside so she could see clearly. Though there was a lot of blood, she'd only been scratched, not cut.

''It's nothing,'' she said. ''A superficial abrasion at the temple. I don't need stitches.''

''I'm calling 911.''

''No,'' she said firmly. ''I'm a doctor, and I know when I need medical attention.''

Equally firm, he took her by the shoulders and turned her toward him. David wasn't sure what symptoms to look for. She was cold. Her complexion was pale, but her eyes were clear and focused. "Be honest with me, and I'll trust your opinion. How do you feel?"

"I don't have a concussion," she said. "And I'm not in shock. Physically I'm not in bad shape."

"Emotionally?"

A shiver racked her body. She looked fragile and vulnerable. Her lips trembled. "Scared."

Gently David wrapped his arms around her and pulled her close. This was his fault. He should never have allowed her to swim alone. He'd failed as a bodyguard, and Blair was paying the price for his negligence.

She sighed against his chest. "He could have killed me, David."

"You're okay now." He would protect her. She came first. Her safety was more important than finding the Fisherman or tracking down old clues.

"But he didn't. He let me live." She tilted her head back to look up at him. "Why?"

Because, sometimes, we get a second chance. Life wasn't always a disaster, even if it felt that way. Every once in a while, there was reason to hope. David wouldn't let this chance slip through his fingers. He'd do everything in his power to make sure Blair was safe from harm.

"Why?" she repeated. "I mean, is this my fate? To be pushed to the edge and survive? Sometimes I think it would be easier to throw in the towel. To give up and die."

"Don't ever say that."

"I've lost so much." She shuddered. "My career. My

confidence. My looks. I know that's shallow, but it still hurts.''

"You can get it back," he said. "All of it."

"Look what happened to me." Angry tears glistened in her eyes. "For the first time since the accident, I went back to the Coroner's Office. And I liked it. I liked the attention. I was out in the world, investigating with you. I was excited about…being useful again."

"That doesn't have to stop." He kissed her forehead.

"But now I'm scared." She leaned against him. "I'm so tired of fighting."

He could feel the fear in her body and the bone-deep exhaustion that came from struggle in one impossible battle after another. But he knew she was strong. She'd conquered injuries that would have left a less-determined person in a wheelchair. "You're a survivor, Blair. You'll make it."

"Right." She slipped out of his embrace and sat on the edge of the tub. Her head drooped forward. "Tell me to stop feeling sorry for myself, David."

He knelt on the floor in front of her and took her hands. Her fingers were ice cold. "I can't tell you how to feel."

"I had a long time after the operations to lie around and whine. It's a waste of time."

"Whatever you say."

She lifted her head and gazed up at him. "I need to take a hot shower and dress this wound."

"I'm calling the police."

"Talk to Weathers," she said. "Forensics might find something near the swimming pool. And you also might call—"

"I'll handle it," David said. He stood and backed out

of the bathroom. "Take your shower. If you need anything, I'll be right here."

He closed the bathroom door. The focus of his investigation had completely changed. His search for the Fisherman was no longer a vague quest toward closure. It was about Blair, about keeping her safe. He couldn't stand to lose her.

WITH THREE PHONE CALLS David turned her isolated little condo into a bona fide madhouse. Detective Weathers brought a full forensics team with him, including photographers and crime-scene investigators. Most of them were down by the pool, but several stayed up here. Two guys were out on the balcony smoking.

Weathers and two other plainclothes cops were in the bedroom talking to Blair. There was a knock on the door, and David answered. It felt like the five hundredth time.

It was Special Agent Gary O'Hara. He didn't mince words. "You're an incompetent jerk, David."

"Nice to see you, too."

"How did you let her get into a dangerous situation?"

David could have offered a half dozen excuses, starting with Blair was headstrong and ending with a reminder that David was not, after all, a professional bodyguard. But they all sounded like the words of an incompetent jerk. "It won't happen again."

"Damn right, it won't." O'Hara's lantern jaw clenched. "She needs to be under twenty-four-hour-a-day surveillance."

"I'm convinced," David said. "Now talk to Blair."

"Where is she?"

"In the bedroom with Weathers."

As O'Hara strode past him, he muttered, "You did one thing right. Calling me."

"Yes, sir." Though Agent O'Hara was probably only a few years older than David, he was the kind of guy who inspired respect.

"Give me a quick run-through of what happened."

"She was swimming laps and the lights went out. Sounds scary as hell to me. She couldn't see the guy. He had a flashlight. And he kept poking at her in the water with one of those long poles they use for cleaning. He hit her once, then turned on the lights and left."

"Was she unconscious in the water?"

"A little stunned," David said. "She didn't think he meant to kill her."

O'Hara's eyebrows raised. "This is different from the Fisherman. He stalked his earlier victims, but he didn't physically attack until he snatched them."

"I know." The variation in routine pointed, once again, to the possibility of a copycat, inspired by the earlier serial murders and preparing to build his own legend. "If it is a different guy, how does he fit the profile?"

"Much the same," O'Hara said. "Murder excites him. He hates women. But this is more complicated than a sex crime. He craves the notoriety, the power. When he succeeds in a kill, he makes law enforcement look foolish, and that turns him on."

"Which is why he sends the notes."

O'Hara nodded. "These aren't those pleading psycho notes. 'Stop me before I kill again.' Oh no, not for this guy. He's a lot smarter than that, and he's gloating."

The most significant interview David had today was with Kevin MacKay. He was definitely smart and liked to feel superior. As for hating women? Kevin's disparaging remarks about his murdered fiancée's leather pants seemed like proof of a hostile, misogynist attitude. David had to wonder if their talk with Kevin at noon had spurred him to attack Blair tonight.

There was more knocking at the door, and David answered.

Jake Zitti stepped inside. His mouth was already flapping. "One photo of Blair. That's all I want. Just one candid to run with tomorrow's story."

"No press," Agent O'Hara barked.

"You heard the man," David said.

"But this is different," Jake pleaded. "Come on, David. We're buds. I used to date Blair."

And he nearly destroyed her life with his careless driving. Jake had no claim on Blair's sympathies.

A quiet anger built inside David. There were limits to friendship, and Jake had crossed that boundary too many times. "Is your stuff out of my house?"

"I got it all cleared out. Just like you said." He tried a grin. "You owe me, man."

He didn't owe Jake squat. David had bailed this jackass out of trouble more times than he liked to count, and Jake had taken advantage of his caretaking nature. No more. David didn't have to save the entire world. Just Blair. "Get out."

"And you call yourself a newspaper man? Sounds to me like you're on their side, the cop side."

"We didn't choose up sides. This isn't a game." David shoved him toward the door. "This is real life."

"You're protecting her."

"Damn right."

As Jake was leaving, grumbling to himself, Adam Briggs stepped through the door. "Thanks for calling me, David. How can I help?"

David led the way into the crowded front room. One of the cops was using Blair's treadmill. Two others were on their cell phones, pacing. It was chaos. "How about a lion tamer's whip and chair?"

"Active investigations are messy," Adam said. "Is Blair all right?"

"She wasn't seriously injured. Refused any kind of medical treatment. Dressed the wound herself."

David introduced Adam to Agent O'Hara. The two men shook hands and immediately fell into conversation. There was a definite similarity between those two. Both in excellent physical condition, they shared a rigid bearing. And they carried their own aura of intensity. David couldn't imagine either of them being scared or hurt. If they were in pain, they wouldn't flinch.

For a long time David had tried to be impervious to the ache of his own grief. He'd buried himself in work and had written stories about other people's tragedy. For him, it hadn't been a successful coping strategy. Deferred sorrow never went away.

Blair emerged from the bedroom with Detective Weathers and his two plainclothes cronies. She went directly to David. Under her breath she said, "Get me out of here."

"My place?"

"Yes." She clutched his hand tightly.

With Weathers in the room, there were too many bosses: O'Hara, Adam and the police detective. They were all ready to give orders, and nobody had a clear plan.

For a moment David thought he and Blair might be able to slip away unnoticed. She had to be exhausted, and he wanted to tuck her into a nice warm bed and let her sleep.

Then the attention turned toward them. O'Hara said, "I'm assigning you a bodyguard, Blair."

"Thanks for the offer," she said. "But I don't want somebody hovering over my shoulder."

"Not your choice," Weathers said, backing up Special Agent O'Hara. "This killer is stalking you. If we watch you, we might be able to catch him."

"I agree," she said crisply. "Put me under surveillance. But I don't want a bodyguard. David will be with me."

As they all stared at him, David straightened his shoulders. He wasn't the most macho guy in the room, not trained to tackle thugs or to gun them down. He'd never fired a gun at another human being. But he wasn't a wimp, and he had more motivation than anyone else. He cared about Blair's safety.

He straightened his shoulders and stared back at them, answering their unspoken questions with his own determination. No way in hell was he going to back down. Blair needed him, and he was equal to the challenge. "I'll take care of her."

Weathers frowned and glanced away. O'Hara nodded his approval. It was Adam who spoke. "You have a carry permit for a gun, don't you?"

"I do."

"Use it."

David nodded. Nobody was going to hurt Blair while he was around. She was his number one priority. She'd be safe with him.

Chapter Nine

After a police escort to David's town house and a thorough search of the premises by armed experts, she and David were alone. Finally.

Blair flung herself onto the sofa and watched as David reset the burglar alarm by coding numbers into a keypad in the foyer.

"Now we're safe," he said. "I just changed the deactivation code so nobody else has it. If anybody breaks a window or opens a door, this alarm goes off like an air raid siren."

"You usually don't use the alarm, do you?"

"Not when I'm in town." He stepped down into the sunken living room to join her on the fawn leather sofa. "Tired?"

"You bet."

"Well, we're in luck," he said. "My cleaning lady came today so the guest bedroom is all made up. And she also purchased some basic groceries. So we won't starve to death."

"She sounds like a jewel."

"The bachelor's best friend," he said. "Are you ready to crash into bed?"

"I'm not really sleepy." She was still stirred up,

cruising on an adrenaline rush. In the past two hours she'd gone through a terrifying attack and a grueling period of interrogation with all kinds of law-enforcement people getting right up in her face—asking questions, making demands. Weathers had been relentless in trying to get a description from her.

Though she told the detectives over and over that it was dark in the swimming pool, and she couldn't see, they insisted that she must have noticed something. "After all that questioning, I felt like making something up. I would have said anything to get those guys off my case."

"A lot of witnesses do." He leaned back on the sofa and casually draped his arm around her shoulder. "I usually do my interviews a couple of days after the police have talked to the witnesses. Many of them admit they aren't sure what they saw. But they remember other details."

"And you use those details when you're writing your story."

"That's the real story to me," he said. "How random violence changes people's lives."

She remembered reading one of his stories about a sniper who shot four people. Through the eyes of a witness, he described an approaching thunderstorm and the way the blood on the pavement was diluted by raindrops. Though he never directly mentioned sorrow at the senseless loss of life, she'd felt it. "I like the way you write."

"Thanks."

She glanced up at his profile. A handsome man. With his black hair and blue eyes, there was no denying his attractiveness. But men like David often got overlooked. He was steady and casual. Not a "bad boy." Nor was he the toughest guy on the block.

O'Hara, Adam and even Weathers were more macho. They swaggered and postured and vied for the position of top dog. And while those other men locked horns, it was David who quietly took control. Like tonight. From the moment he carried her into the bathroom to his showdown with Weathers and O'Hara when he backed her insistence not to have a bodyguard, he was supportive, steadfast and solid. Without making a scene, he hadn't allowed anybody to push her around.

Maybe he wasn't the type who won medals or led his troops into battle. But he was brave and strong in his own way. In her eyes, he was a hero.

She rested her head against his shoulder. "You were fantastic tonight."

"You're joking. I should have gone with you to the pool. You wouldn't have been attacked if—"

"Don't start second-guessing," she said. "I've played that game too many times. Looking back and saying, 'What if I'd done this or that.' It's a waste of time. The past never changes."

He lightly stroked her shoulder. "So, what do we do next?"

"About what?"

"The investigation," he said. "The Fisherman."

She hadn't really considered the next step. Tonight, she'd been so scared she almost wished she was dead. The idea of pushing forward, diving deeper into their investigation seemed reckless. "There's an army of cops and FBI agents on the case. Plus they have access to the most up-to-date forensic equipment."

"True." His voice sounded resigned.

"But I don't want to quit." Now that she'd had a chance to recover her wits, she was angry. She wanted that monster caught and locked away where he would never hurt another woman. "We should keep at it. Keep doing what we're doing."

He gave her a squeeze. "I hoped you'd say that."

"So, what's the game plan?"

"A couple more interviews. I have an appointment tomorrow with Justin Hunter. A real weird little guy. He works as a medical supplies salesman, but he also runs an Internet site on serial killers."

"Charming," she said. "What else should we do?"

"If I was writing an article about this case, I'd sit down and organize the information we gathered in today's interviews. Cross-referencing with other known data."

"Sounds mathematical," she said.

"In a way it is. I make spreadsheets. For example, timing. Assuming the guy who attacked you is the Fisherman, there's a five-year gap we have to explain. So I feed in all the names and figure out who was out of Denver at the time."

"Kevin MacKay." She strongly disliked the former priest who was so quick to disparage his murdered fiancée. "He was working for International Medical Aid. Out of Denver. Out of the country."

"But he doesn't exactly fit the profile. Remember, part of the reason this guy kills is for power, to show he's smarter than the cops." David snuggled her more closely against him. "Not very smart to start off your string of murders with your own girlfriend."

"Where are you getting the details for these profiles?"

"Mostly from O'Hara's notes." He dropped a casual kiss on her forehead. "FBI notes on profiling."

All this incidental touching was beginning to have a sensual effect on her, but Blair wanted to ignore the tickle of desire that centered a few inches below her stomach. She shifted position to get more comfortable, nestling in the crook of his arm. "David, what would you have done if I wanted to back off on the investigating?"

"I'd back off," he said.

"Just like that? You'd forget about your quest to find your sister's real murderer?"

"I'd put it off for another day," he said. "You're my number one priority, Blair. All that's important is keeping you safe."

She met his gaze and felt herself being drawn magnetically toward him.

Logically she ought to resist this impulse. Though the attack in the swimming pool made her feel vulnerable and she needed the reassurance of human contact, it wasn't right to lead him on. She and David shouldn't embark on a relationship while they were caught in this sticky web of hurt, regret and fear. She was pretty sure they didn't love each other.

Yet she continued to gaze up at him. The line of his cheekbone intrigued her. And the shape of his lips, his very sexy lips. One little kiss wouldn't hurt.

She closed her eyelids and arched her neck, waiting for him to respond.

It took only a brief moment. His lips touched hers lightly—the merest caress, a gentle wakening.

Then he kissed her with firm pressure, making his desire known to her. A warmth spun through her body, erasing her tension and focusing her sensations on just one thing. Passion.

He held her face in his hands and tasted her mouth with a fervent strength. Her breath quickened. She wanted more. Tonight she wanted to sleep in his bed.

But only a moment ago she'd told herself that sex with David was a mistake. She clasped his hands and lowered them. "David, I don't think—"

"That's good. Don't think."

Her heart fluttered. "We can't have a relationship."

"Too late. We're already friends."

"You know what I mean." The words of refusal came out of her mouth, but her body yearned toward him.

"You want to make love," he said, stating the obvious. "And so do I. Where's the problem?"

"I'm not interested in casual sex." Although, at the moment, it sounded like a lot of fun. "We need to wait until we understand what sort of relationship is possible."

"Okay, when will that happen?"

"After our investigation is over."

He groaned. His head fell back against the sofa. "That could take weeks."

Any decision they made right now would be precipitous, driven by the intensity of the situation. "If you still want me after the Fisherman is apprehended, then we can consider a real relationship."

"You know what this reminds me of? When you're a kid and you have to eat all your vegetables, even the brussel sprouts, before you get the dessert."

"I like brussel sprouts."

"What would happen," he said, "if we had the dessert first?"

Make love before any relationship basis was established? "Not a good plan."

"You love your chocolate." He tasted her lips again. "This could be sweet as Godiva truffles."

Her resistance was fading fast. She allowed him to kiss her again.

"Creamy filling," he whispered. "Coconut centers."

She sighed and kissed him back. "Strawberries dipped in melted milk chocolate."

This was a fine seduction—semilogical and potentially fattening. She felt the barriers of her self-control lowering with a blissful whoosh.

Still kissing him, she stroked his chest. Beneath his cotton shirt, she felt the nubs of his hard, flat nipples. She needed to touch him, to claim the warmth of his flesh. Her fingers unbuttoned his shirt, and she tore the fabric apart.

Rising on her knees beside him, she massaged his firm, muscular chest. The rough texture of his black hair excited her, and she leaned down to nuzzle her cheek against it.

When her hand slipped lower, he gasped. The sound aroused her even more. "Oh, David. I'm so ready for dessert."

"Yes," he said. "Oh, yes."

He slipped her shirt up and over her head. In seconds he'd unfastened her bra and discarded the flimsy bit of lace. His gaze devoured her. Then his hands. Then his lips. He nibbled a line from her throat to her belly button.

She was wildly aroused. Her body was singing, screaming in a trembling soprano about to hit high C. But when he touched the waistband of her jeans and popped open the button, she grasped his hands again.

"Not here." Though he'd already seen the scars on her leg, this was different. He might be distracted by her disfigurement when she wanted his admiration. Making love, she wished to feel beautiful.

"Where?" he asked.

In the bedroom there would be sheets and blankets to

cover herself with. They could turn out the lights. "Bed."

"Excellent plan."

Shirtless, they rose from the sofa and went up the staircase to his bedroom. The fact that she was half-naked amused Blair. "This is so unlike me."

"That's where you're wrong," he murmured. "To the rest of the world, you might be Dr. Blair Weston, ace medical examiner. But I knew from the minute I saw you swimming in your electric-blue suit that you had a wild, passionate nature."

"You knew that?"

"I'm a good judge of people." He turned on the over-head light in the bedroom.

"Too much glare," she said.

"But I want to see you."

"Too bad." She threw back the covers and sat on the sheets. "Turn it off. Close the door."

"Whatever you say."

As soon as the darkness closed around her, Blair knew she'd made a mistake. Her eyelids fluttered. In her mind she was back in the swimming pool, flailing at an invisible threat. Panic rose in her chest.

Instinctively, she leaped to the center of the king-size bed.

"Blair? What's going on?"

This was crazy. Worse than her dizzy spells. In her mind she felt the cool liquid lapping around her in rippling motion. The splintered reflection off the water. Like knives. Her hands flew to cover her mouth, but she couldn't hold back a wrenching sob.

David turned on a dim bedside lamp. "What's wrong?"

She wanted to explain, but she couldn't speak. And

when he reached for her, she scooted away. Frantically she pulled up the bedspread to cover her nakedness.

"It's okay." David took a step back from the bed. "Nobody's going to hurt you."

Waves of terror washed over her. She crumpled on the bed in a fetal position, still feeling the waves and the terror. She couldn't fight it. Her willpower was gone. The pent-up emotions of the past five years exploded, and she wept.

She felt David's hand, gentle and reassuring on her naked back. This wasn't fair to him. "I'm sorry," she choked out.

"It's okay." He arranged the blankets to cover her. "Let it out, Blair."

Torrents of pain and regret spilled over the shattered wall of her self-control. As she sobbed, her body relaxed. She was under the covers, still crying. Her face burrowed in the pillow. Would these damned tears never stop?

THE NEXT MORNING, David was still kicking himself. He never should have pushed her, should've known that Blair was vulnerable and needed rest instead of…what he'd been offering.

As he stood in the kitchen, waiting for his coffee to brew, he made a solemn vow to keep his sex drive under wraps, so to speak. No touching. No long, lust-filled stares. And definitely no kisses.

It wouldn't be easy. For the next several days she'd be living here. They'd be in constant contact.

He grabbed his coffee mug and went into the bathroom for a cold shower.

When he emerged, he looked in on Blair who was sleeping soundly in his bed with the small lamp on the table still lit. Even asleep, she didn't look completely relaxed. Her tousled brown hair plastered damply to her forehead. Her arm crooked at an uncomfortable angle, and she restlessly changed positions as if caught in a nightmare.

Quietly he closed the bedroom door.

In his office David booted up his computer and entered the information from yesterday's interviews. A few important details came to the surface.

In regard to stalking, none of the earlier victims reported such incidents to the police. But they seemed nervous to their friends and family. One had been drinking heavily. Another wrote in her diary that she felt as if someone was watching her.

Also, when David asked specifically about possible missing items, the sister of mermaid number three mentioned a missing bracelet. Number two had lost a pair of opal earrings. Apparently, in some cases, the Fisherman was taking souvenirs from his victims.

Though David tried to think of something his sister had lost, he came up blank. And it wouldn't help to ask his parents. Shortly after his sister's murder, they'd enlisted people from their church to clean out her apartment, donating all of her clothing and jewelry to charity.

It was their way of coping, and he didn't blame them. Everybody handled grief differently. If it had been up to him, David would have been more likely to build a shrine to Danielle.

He returned his attention to his computer. Kevin MacKay was the only person who'd come across as suspicious, but it was hard to fit him into the role of a serial killer. The guy was a former priest, and he worked for International Medical Aid.

The next best suspect was Justin Hunter, whom David

had scheduled for a lunch meeting today. Hunter wasn't personally connected with any of the victims. He came to the attention of the police when they checked his serial killer Web site where he displayed a detailed knowledge of the Fisherman.

Also, Hunter's job put him in contact with hospitals where two of the victims worked. He'd even been hanging around at the Coroner's Office where he'd introduced himself to David.

Online, David checked out Hunter's handiwork at a Web site that should have been called www.psycho.com. It was an encyclopedia of serial murders, ranging from Jack the Ripper to the Boston Strangler to the Fisherman. Quite a nasty little hobby.

When David saw his own name referenced, he cringed. He didn't like being part of this ghoulish network, this fascination with the horror show of serial murder. And yet, there he was.

With a shudder David went back to his charts, trying to make sense of the incomprehensible. He cross-referenced several factors: timing and alibi; childhood abuse; prior criminal activity; medical history.

It was after ten o'clock when Blair appeared in the doorway to his office. She was all showered, clean and dressed. The only evidence of last night's breakdown was a slight puffiness around her eyes. The swelling from her head wound was hidden behind her bangs.

"How are you feeling?" he asked.

"I'm fine." Her smile was determinedly cheerful. "Really, I'm okay."

"Do you want to talk about it?"

"No big deal." She shrugged. "I guess I'm not the kind of woman who can eat dessert first."

Though she was clearly on edge, he didn't push. If

Blair wanted to tamp down her fears and get on with her life, that might be the best way for her to handle the attack. "Okay, then. No dessert this morning. Let's start with coffee."

"And breakfast. I'm starving."

As he followed her to the kitchen, a difficult question began to form in his mind. He'd promised to take her along on his interviews. But she was fragile. He sure as hell didn't want to trigger another meltdown.

She peeked inside the fridge. "Blueberries!"

David continued to ponder. It would be easy to arrange for police protection while he was out.

"Yogurt!" she said. "And eggs. And lunch meat."

And what if Justin Hunter actually was the Fisherman? What if he was the man who attacked Blair last night? She might recognize him. There might be some detail in his voice or the way he moved that would identify him.

David couldn't be responsible for putting her in that kind of danger.

"Your cleaning lady is brilliant," Blair said. "She got all the right food. So, what do you want for breakfast?"

"A bite of cereal with blueberries," he said. "I have a lunch appointment in about an hour."

"Remind me again. Who are we meeting?"

Leaning an elbow on the marble countertop, he watched her, trying to gauge her reaction. "It might be better if I go alone."

"Don't be silly," she said. "I'm coming."

"My appointment is with Justin Hunter. He's somebody who should be taken seriously as a suspect."

"So?" After opening and closing a few cabinet doors, she found bowls.

"Hunter might be the Fisherman."

As she placed the bowls on the countertop, she hesitated. For an instant her resolute enthusiasm was disrupted. "What are you saying?"

"I can arrange police protection for you. There's no need for you to face this guy."

"Maybe there is."

"Why?"

"If I recognize him, this could all be over."

She opened the box of granola cereal and shook a portion into each bowl. As she took the milk from the refrigerator, Blair felt a trembling in her hands.

Last night, when the dam burst, she thought she'd washed away all her anxieties with her tears. She wanted to believe she'd had a final catharsis. But apparently there was more. Fear was endless.

Her fingers clenched into fists. "Just when I thought it was safe to go back in the water, here comes *Jaws* again."

"Then it's settled," David said. "I'll meet Hunter for lunch. And you stay here."

But she was tired of hiding from real life. For the past five years, she'd secluded herself in her apartment, afraid to face a world where she wasn't in control. Though she'd told herself that she couldn't go back to work because of physical injuries, the truth was that she'd been afraid. Afraid of not being the best, the prettiest, the most competent. "I have to go with you. I need to stay involved."

"Why?"

This was hard to explain. "I can't spend my whole life hiding from my fears."

His expression was unreadable, and she didn't blame him for not wanting to take her along. She hadn't exactly been a paragon of stability. "Please, David. I need this."

He rubbed his hand across his chin, considering. "I won't put you in danger."

"We'll be safe," she said. "You're carrying your gun, right?"

"I intend to."

"And we're not going to meet anybody in a dark alleyway."

"No way," he said.

"And I'm not completely helpless." She pointed to her foot. "These are the first custom-made shoes I bought after the accident. I was really nervous about reinjuring myself by bumping my foot and ankle." She pulled up her trouser leg to show him the lace-up, high-top boot. "Not only is there a seven-eighths lift, but the heel and toe are reinforced with steel. Kicking somebody with this boot is like hitting them with a hammer."

"Remind me not to take you dancing," David said.

"I can dance." She twirled in a circle. "But I can also kick butt."

"Okay, Blair." His mouth hitched in a half smile. "Don't eat much breakfast. We're leaving for lunch in about an hour."

Blair grinned. She'd gotten what she wanted. But was that really so clever? A wise man once warned: be careful what you ask for, you just might get it. She might have bought a one-way ticket to danger.

Chapter Ten

For this interview, Blair dressed as if she were going into battle. In addition to her bionic, steel-toed boots, she'd strapped an innocent-looking fanny pack at the front of her black jeans. Inside the pack, she carried a small can of pepper spray and the cell phone in case she needed to call for emergency assistance.

She sauntered into David's office. She waited for him to finish his phone call, her hands poised above her fanny pack like a gunslinger.

When he looked up, she said, "Check out these accessories."

In a quick draw, she whipped open the Velcro strip, grabbed her thin canister of pepper spray and aimed it at his nose. "Gotcha!"

Her other hand held the cell phone. "Then I dial 911. Pretty nifty, huh?"

"Fearsome." David was armed with a more lethal weapon. Under his sports jacket, he carried his Glock automatic pistol in a shoulder holster. "That phone call was from Hunter. Instead of lunch, he wants to meet at Cheesman Park for a walk."

"That's close to where I live." The proximity worried her. If Justin Hunter was the Fisherman, he'd already made two appearances at her condo building: planting the dead fish in her car; and at the swimming pool. "Why there?"

"He said he missed his morning exercise, and this was more convenient."

"Changing locale is kind of a power trip," she said. "He's letting us know that he calls the shots."

"Or maybe it means nothing more nefarious than convenience," David said. "Let's go."

THEY PARKED near the Eleventh Avenue entrance to the park where a wiry man with black-framed glasses stood waiting in the shadow of a conifer. When he smiled a shy greeting, Blair wondered if perhaps she'd gone over the top with her weaponry. Justin Hunter looked more like a grown-up Harry Potter than a depraved serial killer.

He stared at David with undisguised admiration. "We meet again, Mr. Crawford. Again, I have to say that your work means a lot to me."

"Please, call me David. And why?"

"Most crime reporters don't spend enough time with the details. They spew out the facts that the cops feed to them. Your stories give a real sense of, I don't know, the ambiance."

The ambiance of murder? Blair slightly revised her opinion. Hunter's fascination with these crimes was more than a little creepy. She studied him. Could he have been the person who attacked her at the swimming pool? Though she had the impression that her stalker had more bulk, it might have been this man.

When David introduced her, Hunter's dark eyes sparkled behind his glasses. He grasped her hand firmly between both of his and gushed, "I'm so honored, Dr. Weston."

"Really?" Blair couldn't wait to reclaim her hand, possibly to wash her fingers with disinfectant soap.

"When you were an M.E., your reports were always well considered and detailed." Hunter beamed at her. "Almost inspired."

She didn't often encounter autopsy fans and wasn't sure how to take the compliment.

"I studied you," Hunter continued.

Blair pulled her hand from his grasp. His intensity disconcerted her. "You studied me?"

Instead of responding, he checked his wristwatch. "I only have half an hour. We should start. Once around the park."

Walking three abreast with David in the middle, they followed a dirt path that led around the edge of the grassy inner-city park. Blair was well aware that they were only five blocks from her building. She often walked this very route. It was almost a mile in length.

She peered around David toward Hunter. "You said you'd studied me."

"Oh, yes." He rattled off a list of schools she'd attended and the titles of her three articles published in medical journals. "If I'd known you were coming to this meeting, I would have brought a box of Godiva chocolate."

Her heart thumped hard inside her rib cage. "How did you know I like Godiva chocolate?"

"I studied the Fisherman," he said. "I mean, it's one of the more compelling serial murders in Denver's history, and I'm right here where I can get firsthand information and—"

"How did you know about the Godiva?" Blair demanded.

"The autopsy reports indicated the presence of Godiva chocolate in the gastric contents, and I knew it must mean something. So I asked around." He peeked over at her. His eyes widened in pseudo-innocence. "You love those chocolates. Their presence was a threat to you, Dr. Weston."

"Who told you?"

He placed his forefinger across his lips. "I have my sources."

She wanted to smack that smug little smile off his face. How dare he dig into her life without permission! "Don't ever do that again."

"What?"

"Invade my privacy."

"I'm sorry, Dr. Weston. May I call you Blair?"

"No," she snapped.

David broke in. "Tell us about your Web site, Hunter."

"It's been real busy, especially with this new Fisherman-type crime. I've had e-mails from as far away as Oslo."

"Psychos," she muttered under her breath.

David placed a restraining hand on her arm, but she wasn't calmed. Her stomach was churning. At the very least, Justin Hunter was an annoying snoop. At worst, he was the Fisherman himself.

Either way, he was obsessed with these horrible crimes. He continued to chat as they strolled past the entrance to the Botanical Gardens and the white marble portico. Why should Hunter's interest in the Fisherman be anathema to her? Since she and David were doing much the same thing, digging into the crimes, she had no right to be disgusted.

But their focus was different. She and David sought justice for the victims. Hunter's fascination focused more on the killer, identifying with him, glorifying him.

As they rounded the southern edge of the park, passing several dog walkers and joggers, David continued to ask questions as if he were seeking out new information on the Fisherman. He didn't treat Hunter like a suspect.

"You're an expert," David said. "Do you think the murder of Pamela Comforti was committed by a copycat?"

"No way," Hunter said. "It's the same guy who killed the six other mermaids. The Fisherman."

"But the note to Ted Hurtado wasn't written exactly the same."

"A clever ploy," Hunter said. "You can't really disguise your natural handwriting, you know. So the Fisherman didn't even try. He wrote a couple of the letters different. To create doubt. To throw the police off the track."

"What about the five-year gap between prior crimes and this one?"

"Unusual, but not unheard of." He glibly cited several examples of other serial murderers. Hunter obviously relished this topic. "But I have another theory about the time gap."

"Don't keep us waiting," David said.

"The man who was convicted, Edward Adderly, is dying in prison. When he goes, his secrets go with him. I believe the Fisherman started killing again to keep his legend alive."

Blair glanced at David. His own motivation for re-opening an investigation was also based on the impending death of Eddy Adderly.

"You think Adderly is innocent," David said. "But his psychological profile fits the typical criteria for a serial killer. Abused as a child. A history of petty crimes. And he's the right age, turning thirty-three."

"Big hairy deal," Hunter said. "I'm thirty-one."

"And how was your childhood?"

"A little rocky," he admitted. Ironically, they had just come in sight of the playground where several children played on swings and slides. "My parents divorced. But Mom was great. Really pretty, you know. She had a lot of boyfriends."

Blair knew where David was headed with these questions. The typical behavior for serial killer during childhood included three aberrant aspects: fire starting, bed wetting and cruelty to animals.

"Divorce is tough on kids," David said. "I saw on your Web site that you had counseling when you were young."

"Lucky for me." There was a note of sarcasm in his voice. "Let's get back to Adderly. It's my theory that he's a sexual deviant and probably belongs in jail."

"But you don't think he's a killer?"

"He lacks the intelligence to pull off the Fisherman killings. I mean, these were really elegant crimes."

In spite of her revulsion, Blair found herself becoming interested. *Elegant* was an odd word to use in describing heinous murders. But in her autopsies she remembered being impressed with the killer's thoroughly clean kills, leaving not a trace of evidence. "Why do you say elegant?"

"Clean and smart. Everybody danced to the Fisherman's tune," Hunter said. "For example, he targeted his victims, and they weren't easy women to catch. Two of them were cops, not counting Pamela Comforti. And he somehow convinced these women to come with him. That takes smarts."

"It doesn't take a genius to sneak up and shove a chloroform-soaked rag in the victim's mouth." Blair recalled her autopsies. "All of the victims were sedated."

"But you can't tell when. Did he sedate them to grab them? Or later when he had them tied up?" Hunter answered his own question. "Doesn't matter. My point is that he somehow got close enough to administer a sedative."

"You're suggesting that the victims initially went along of their own free will." Blair wasn't really surprised by his analysis. Though her autopsies showed that the victims struggled, the pattern of their injuries indicated that their wrists and ankles were bound with nylon ropes at the time.

Hunter glanced around David to give her a sly smile. "The Fisherman was clever enough to appear nonthreatening until his mermaids were safely in his grasp."

Nonthreatening? That word was a perfect description of Justin Hunter with his glasses and lean, boyish frame. "How do you think the Fisherman got his victims to trust him?"

"Something simple," he said. "Like offering assistance if their car wouldn't start. Or asking them to assist him in some way. Ted Bundy wore a fake cast on his leg and asked women to help him carry packages to his car."

"Another possibility," David said, "is that he might have dressed like someone in authority. A uniformed cop. Or a doctor."

"Or," Hunter added. "Maybe he was someone they all knew and trusted."

"Nope," David said, "I've cross-referenced all the acquaintances of the victims. There's no commonality."

Hunter shrugged. "Whatever he did, he managed to get close."

Blair thought of last night's attack at her swimming pool. If the Fisherman had meant to take her captive, all he needed to do was wear a bathing suit and get into the water with her. She didn't know everyone in her condo building and wouldn't have suspected another swimmer.

Last night he hadn't meant for her to be a victim. Grabbing her at the pool would've been foolish. There was too much likelihood that he'd be observed. Lots of people went in and out of her building. Lots of witnesses.

But why had he attacked her? To scare her? If that was his plan, it worked. And yet she was bothered by the discrepancy with the past. Blatant stalking didn't fit his routine. Never before had he shown such bravado. It was a different profile.

Maybe the person who attacked her was a copycat, after all. Maybe someone like Justin Hunter who was thrilled by these crimes and wanted to take risks, barely escaping the police investigative net.

While he talked to David, she studied him in glances. Was he muscular enough to commit these crimes? In every murder, including the most recent one, the Fisherman had carried his victims some distance to leave them by water.

In her mind, the act of arranging the bodies was a haunting image. According to crime-scene investigators, he'd worn plastic gloves to avoid leaving prints, and his clothing had been equally impervious, probably a plastic rain slicker with a hood and rubber boots that left obscure footprints. It was all too easy for Blair to imagine that frightening, hooded figure carrying the body of a dead woman.

A quiver of tension flicked across her shoulders. The hairs on the nape of her neck bristled. He could be anyone, could be here in the park, could be watching her at this very moment.

Or the Fisherman might be Justin Hunter.

She tuned back in to David's interview. He was talking about the DNA evidence linking Eddy Adderly to the sixth murder.

"Easy to explain," Hunter said. "Let's assume that Edward Adderly is a deviant. He found the dead body and violated her. Which also explains why witnesses saw him near the scene."

"After he was arrested," David said, "the killing stopped."

Hunter frowned. "Yeah, I don't understand that part. Until then the Fisherman was playing a cat-and-mouse game with the cops. I don't know why he'd quit."

The cell phone in Blair's fanny pack buzzed, and she jumped. She wasn't accustomed to the electronic summons, and she fumbled before pulling the phone from her pack. "Hello?"

"It's Adam. Let me talk to David."

She held out the phone to him. For a moment they stopped walking. David stepped aside to take the call, leaving her in direct line with Hunter's bespeckled gaze.

"Dr. Weston," he said, "may I ask you a personal question?"

"Okay." But she might not answer.

"Why didn't you go back to work? I mean, you're great at your job. Why did you quit?"

She gave him the stock answer she used with everyone else. "I'm not ready. I have headaches. Not enough stamina to work full-time."

"But you could work part-time."

None of your business. "Why should my work schedule concern you?"

He leaned toward her. His voice lowered to a conspiratorial level. "Have you ever thought, Dr. Weston, that it might be all about you. The killings."

The shivers that had been marching up and down her spine coalesced into a frigid tension. "What do you mean?"

"Your car accident was about the same time as the police arrested Adderly. Maybe the Fisherman didn't quit because of the arrest. Maybe he quit because he wanted to match wits with you."

"That's ridiculous," she said.

"With you out of the picture, it wasn't as much fun for him."

"But I was never a threat to the Fisherman. My job as an M.E. didn't involve active investigation. I just did the autopsies."

"Think about it, Dr. Weston."

His mouth twitched in a sneer, and he removed his glasses to wipe them with a hanky. His dark, almost black eyes were burning in a weird, freakish contrast to his smooth baby face. It was obvious that he wanted to scare her.

But she wouldn't give him the satisfaction. Blair forced a laugh. "You've got a vivid imagination, Hunter. I'll bet you were a lonely little boy. Maybe a bed wetter."

"And a fire starter," he said. His voice seemed deeper, more menacing. "We didn't have pets, but I used to catch grasshoppers and pull their legs off. So, you see, I fit the profile.''

"Of a serial killer?''

"That's what you really wanted to know," he said. "You and David didn't arrange to meet me because you wanted my opinions or expertise. Oh no, not that. You don't respect my research. You suspect me.''

His gaze lifted, and she realized he was staring across the park at the top of her fourteen-story condo building. The threat was subtle. Or was it?

She cleared her throat loudly, hoping to attract David's attention. She wanted him off the phone and watching this transformation. "Is there a reason we should suspect you, Hunter?''

"That's for me to know and you to find out.''

He stuck his glasses back onto the bridge of his nose. The psycho moment had passed. He was, once again, a meek and mild salesman of medical equipment with an odd hobby.

Unaware of the strangeness that had transpired, David ended his phone call and returned to where they were standing. "Adam has someone he wants us to talk with. I guess we should hurry.''

She was more than ready to get away from Hunter, wanted to sprint the last hundred yards to the Eleventh Street exit. While David politely thanked Hunter for his time, she stalked toward the car and ducked into the driver's seat.

In a moment David joined her. "What's your problem, Blair?''

"While you were on the phone, Hunter turned into a drooling, mad-dog lunatic.''

He raised a skeptical eyebrow. "Drooling?''

"Maybe not frothing at the mouth," she said, "but I

swear he was different. Like Dr. Jeckyll and Mr. Hyde. Even his voice sounded different.''

''And what did he say?''

''The *real* reason the Fisherman stopped killing was because of my car accident. Like the whole thing was about me? Hah! Like I'm the center of the universe? Hunter said the Fisherman wanted to match wits with me.''

''And you took that comment as a threat?''

''Of course I did.''

''I hate to say this. I've considered a scenario similar to Hunter's. But it's not all about you.''

''Who is it about?''

''I'll talk while you drive,'' he said. ''Back to the town house. Adam called to tell me that Weathers and O'Hara would meet us there in half an hour to discuss evidence they found at the swimming pool.''

Warily he watched as she turned the key in the ignition. Blair had become the designated driver, and that was fine with him. Using her car was out of the question since the forensics team still hadn't returned her vehicle.

Noticing tension at the corners of her eyes, he asked, ''Are you okay?''

''Fine,'' she muttered. ''Do you think they're done with my car?''

''I wouldn't count on it,'' he said. ''The crime-scene investigators will want to go over it with a fine-tooth comb.''

She exhaled a sigh. ''Of course they'll search for prints, fibers and hairs. A waste of time. The Fisherman won't slip up on something so basic.''

He was inclined to agree with her, but procedure was procedure. ''Maybe they'll get lucky.''

"Okay, David. Tell me why Hunter's sick theory makes sense."

"Several unrelated events occurred at the time Eddy Adderly was arrested. You and Jake had the accident, taking you both out of the investigation."

"Jake? He wasn't involved."

"He's part of the media," David said. "He did a lot of photos around the crime scenes."

Though she was upset, she drove with her usual extreme caution. "What else happened at the same time?"

"O'Hara was transferred to another FBI office. It was a promotion for his good work on the Fisherman case. So he was removed from the area. It was election time, and a new district attorney came into office. A couple of cops retired. Anyway, it wasn't the same team."

"Why would that affect the Fisherman?"

"In his mind he was playing a game with all of you. Outsmarting you. He felt like he had a personal relationship with each and every person who was trying to catch him. When the team fell apart, the game wasn't as much fun."

"That's what Hunter said. It wasn't fun for him anymore."

The equation between serial murder and fun was a difficult connection for David to make. No sane person would think that way. But the Fisherman had always been on a power trip, proving his cleverness. "It's all a game to him."

"And he uses dead women as pawns."

David nodded. It disturbed him that Hunter had taken the few minutes while he'd had his back turned to frighten Blair with his theory. She wasn't safe. This was another example.

No matter how hard he tried to protect her, constant

threats bombarded them. And the clock was ticking. The Fisherman had promised another body in only three days.

When they pulled into the driveway in front of his town house, there was another car parked on the street. David had spotted someone behind the wheel, waiting.

"Stay here," he said to Blair. "Lock the doors."

As he left the car, his hand went to the Glock automatic in his shoulder holster. This wasn't his thing, but he was fully prepared to draw and shoot.

At the end of the driveway, David saw Kevin MacKay climb out from behind the wheel. His red hair spiked like the top of a flame as he charged toward David. "You son of a bitch," he said.

Apparently, swearing wasn't a problem for the ex-priest. "Nice to see you, too."

"I had a visit from the police today," he said. "Something about a swimming pool. And did I have an alibi for last night?"

"Did you?" David asked.

"Not that it's any of your damned business, but I was home alone."

No alibi. David tried to imagine this guy sneaking into Blair's condo and terrorizing her. It wasn't a huge stretch of the imagination. "Doesn't look good for you, Kevin."

"Damn you." He paced back and forth on the sidewalk. "I agreed to talk to you because I felt sorry for your loss. I wanted to help. And you pay me back by siccing the cops on me?"

"You know how investigations work," David said. "The cops are doing their job. They have to talk to everybody Blair came into contact with."

"This was her idea," he snarled. "I could tell she

was ticked off at me yesterday. To think I wanted to go out with that bitch."

"Hold it right there." David stepped in front of him. They were less than a foot apart. "Don't ever call her that again. Don't even think it."

Kevin huffed like a steam engine. "The cops came to the hospital. It was humiliating."

David didn't like Kevin MacKay, didn't like his attitude toward women, didn't completely believe in his innocence. "Stop whining."

"You can't talk to me like that."

For a man who'd spent several years working for International Medical Aid and helping disadvantaged people, Kevin was short on compassion and long on ego.

"This isn't about your inconvenience," David said. "Seven women, including your fiancée and my sister, have been murdered. Every lead has to be investigated."

"How can you suggest I have anything to do with those deaths?" His lips pulled back from his teeth in a snarl. "I ought to punch you right in the nose."

"Take your best shot."

David was usually good at talking his way out of any situation. Right now he'd welcome a fight. Any kind of action was better than wallowing around in unanswered questions and mucked-up clues.

Kevin stepped back and cocked his right arm. What a jerk! He telegraphed the punch more obviously than Western Union. When he swung, David sidestepped easily and fired a hard right to Kevin's midsection.

Immediately David retreated. He wasn't a brawler, and this particular fight could get nasty fast. While carrying a gun, he had no business throwing punches and allowing tempers to run high. "I'm sorry, Kevin."

The red-haired man doubled over, clutching his belly. He staggered to the curb and leaned against the hood of his car.

Before it had even started, this fight was over.

Chapter Eleven

David hadn't meant to hit him that hard.

Hacking and wheezing, Kevin MacKay braced himself against his car. His face was pale, and he looked as if he was going to puke. "I ought to sue you for this."

Not good. And David had the uneasy feeling that his problems were about to get much worse.

For starters, he'd punched one of his prime suspects. Was it possible to be a serial killer and a wuss? Either way, Kevin wasn't somebody David wanted to alienate.

And here came more potential trouble. Jake Zitti's sporty little Miata squealed to a stop on the other side of the street.

As if Jake's gadfly presence wasn't enough, law enforcement in the person of Detective Weathers and Special Agent O'Hara were on their way.

All these guys charging together was a formula for chaos, like throwing reactive elements into a beaker and shaking until it exploded. David glanced back at his driveway where Blair was following his instructions to stay inside the car with the doors locked. Good! At least she'd be safe.

Jake got out of his car and paused to assess the situation. Apparently, he figured that the fight had already happened. Then, and only then, Jake swaggered across the street. "Do you need some help here, David?"

"Everything's fine. No problem." *Go away!*

Ted Hurtado emerged from the passenger side of Jake's Miata. He didn't bother pretending that he would have joined in the fisticuffs. His crazy mother had probably taught him, early on, that good boys don't get in street fights. Ted ran a comb through his thick brown hair, repairing the damage done by riding with the top down. As he sauntered across the street, he looked down his nose, acting even more superior and aloof now that he'd been on television.

With a lurch and a groan, Kevin managed to stand upright. He glared at all of them. "So now it's three against one," he said bitterly. "This is typical of what I'd expect from you, David."

"Nobody wants to hurt you," David assured him. "But it might be best if you—"

"That's right." Blair joined the group. She homed in on Kevin like a robin to a worm. "If I were you, I wouldn't worry about them."

"Why not?" Kevin asked.

"Because I had the car window cracked, and I heard what you said about me. If there's anybody you need to be scared about, it's me, the big, bad b—"

"Enough," David said. "Kevin, it's time for you to go. Jake and Ted, what do you want?"

"I left a couple of CDs in the dining room," Jake said. "I wanted to pick them up. And, as long as I'm here, maybe I could get a photo of Blair to go along with the Fisherman stories."

"I don't think so," she said.

"Come on, Blair. We ran an old photo with today's story, and you look different now."

She glared at him. "Different how?"

Jake twitched his shoulders in a nervous shrug. "For one thing, your hair's shorter."

"Right, and so is my leg." Shoulders back and head high, she marched up the sidewalk toward the front door.

David wanted to run after her, offering assurance that she was beautiful and Jake was a jackass, but he couldn't leave these guys untended on the street.

He kept an eye on Kevin, who got behind the wheel of his car and drove away. Then he turned to the other two. "It's not a good time, guys."

"Give me a break," Jake said. "I'll be in and out before you know it."

From the porch Blair shouted, "From what I've heard, that's his standard technique with the ladies."

"Really not a good time," David repeated. "The cops are on their way over here to talk to Blair, and they won't want to see a reporter and a photographer."

"Wait a minute," Ted said. "You're a reporter. Why will they talk to you?"

"I'm off the record," David said.

"I can be off the record, too." He straightened his necktie. "I have a right to be here. I'm the one getting the Fisherman threat notes in the mail. Delivered to my house, damn it. You saw what that did to my mother."

David sympathized. Doris Hurtado was already loopy. It wouldn't take much to send her twirling off like a cyclone to Oz. "It's not up to me, Ted."

"David!" Blair called out from the porch. The door behind her was open; she must have used his house keys that were on the same key ring as the car keys. "How do I turn off the alarm?"

"Shit." David raced toward the front door.

The burglar alarm screamed louder than ten thousand

Bronco fanatics after a touchdown. David's eardrums throbbed as he flew past Blair into the town house and punched numbers into the keypad to turn off the alarm.

But it kept on wailing. He'd changed the deactivation code and forgotten the new one. *Think, you idiot.* He tried his birthday. The alarm seemed to get even more shrill. The first digits of his social security number? No effect.

He banged his head against the wall, trying to jog his memory. *Focus, damn it!* Why hadn't he gone with an obvious code? Maybe he had. He punched the keypad numbers in sequence starting with three.

Silence fell with a thud. When David looked up, they were all standing there. Jake, Ted and Blair. Even better, they'd been joined by Special Agent O'Hara and Detective Weathers—both of whom had drawn their guns and were doing the two-fisted aiming routine, fully prepared to assassinate his sofa.

Are we having fun yet?

David raced to the kitchen. Using the phone on the counter—a direct line from the house was necessary— he called the security company, who informed him that their men and the cops were already on the way and he would be assessed a fee for accidentally tripping his own alarm. "I suppose it's too late," David said, "to call off the—"

From outside he heard the police sirens.

"Never mind." He hung up the phone.

A battalion of cops and security men burst through the front door. More weapons in hand. A couple of David's neighbors joined the crowd. Disturbingly, they were also armed. There was enough firepower in his living room to launch a preemptive strike on neighboring Boulder.

"False alarm," David said as he walked toward them. "Everything's okay."

He definitely needed to bring calm to this situation. Then, behind his back, he heard somebody in the kitchen. David pivoted and stared at Jake, who was opening his refrigerator. What made Jake think he had the right?

"Hey," Jake called out. "Anybody want a beer?"

That was it! The last straw. David's self-control snapped. "Out! All of you, get the hell out!"

They gaped, slack-jawed.

David was tempted to draw his own pistol. He settled for pointing with a cocked forefinger. "You, you and you. Security guys. Go. You're not needed. And the rest of you? Figure it out for yourselves."

A couple of the gun barrels pointed in his direction. This was too much!

He strode across the room, grabbed Blair's hand and dragged her up the stairs to his bedroom. He slammed the door behind them and turned to her.

The hint of a grin teased the corners of her mouth. "Are you okay?" she asked.

"I'm just dandy. There's a herd of nutcakes and cops in my living room. I'm making zero headway in solving anything. Zero, Blair. Oh, yeah, I almost forgot. There's a psycho serial killer closing in."

Her hand covered her mouth. Her shoulders quaked with suppressed laughter.

"Not funny," he said.

"I love it." A light chuckle escaped her lips. "You're usually calm and controlled, the guy who takes care of everybody else. And you yelled. You walked away and left all those people in your living room."

She was right. His usual behavior was to be the peacemaker, the stand-up guy, the nice guy. He could always be counted on to do the right thing. Why the hell had he punched Kevin MacKay? "What's going on with me?"

Blair came closer, reached up and straightened the lapels on his jacket. Teasing, she said, "Tsk. Tsk. Not very responsible, David."

"Nor is this." He pulled her into his arms and planted a firm kiss on her warm, smiling lips. She gasped in surprise, and he allowed her just enough time to catch her breath before he kissed her again. It felt so good to hold her, to press her supple body against his. Oh, yeah. This kiss was the smartest thing he'd done all day.

He looked down into her shining green eyes and whispered, "I'm going to take you away from here. Away from all this craziness."

"What about our investigation?"

The threads of an idea knitted together in his mind. "I have a plan."

There was a sharp rap on the door, and Ted Hurtado stepped inside. He stared coldly at their embrace. "Isn't this sweet."

"Bite me," David said.

"But I'm sincere," Ted said with a heartfelt sneer. "The lovely but injured former M.E. and the aggrieved brother of a victim. You have so much in common."

"A word of advice," Blair said coldly. "Stick to your restaurant reviews. You don't have the heart to be Dear Abby."

"Ouch!" he said. "I never knew you could be so sarcastic, Blair."

"Is there some reason you came barging in here without knocking?"

"Detective Weathers wants to see you both in the

living room." He turned on his heel and walked away, leaving the door open.

"That was strange," David said. He'd known Ted for years and had worked with him. It was the same with Blair. They'd had a lot of shared experiences. But when Ted saw them together, he identified them with their roles in the Fisherman case. Maybe Teddy Boy was more involved in this investigation than he liked to admit.

"Let's go," Blair said.

"But I want them all gone," he said.

"We don't always get what we wish for."

They went down the hall and sat together on the living room sofa where they'd almost made love last night. David adjusted the shoulder holster under his jacket. Though it was probably safe to shed his gun, being armed in this group seemed prudent.

Detective Weathers perched at the edge of his chair, ready to flee at a moment's notice. He was probably a good cop, but he always looked uncomfortable, as if his underwear was too tight.

In contrast, Special Agent O'Hara radiated his usual coolness and authority.

Ted sat in an armchair with his legs crossed and the crease in his trousers razor-sharp. Apparently, he'd convinced Weathers and O'Hara to let him stay.

Blair spoke first. "How's my car?"

"Too damn clean," Weathers said. "Our guys found no decent forensic evidence."

Not a surprise. The Fisherman never left clues.

Weathers exhaled a ragged sigh. "Listen up, people. Everything we say here is off the record. Is that clear?" His glance flicked from David to Ted to Jake who stood behind the kitchen counter, sipping Coors from the can.

David nodded.

"This wasn't my idea," Weathers continued. "I think you all know how I feel about the press."

That they were sleazier than snail slime. David was amazed that the detective would even tolerate their presence, much less take them into his confidence.

"This is my plan," O'Hara said. He stood, immediately dominating the room with his mature presence. "I decided it would be useful to talk to you people since you all have a connection to the prior crimes. I want fresh input on the Fisherman."

"You want us to speculate?" Ted asked.

"That's right."

David suspected a ruse. The FBI didn't consult with former witnesses for theories. "I thought the official line was that the murder of Pamela Comforti was a copycat crime."

"Right," O'Hara said briskly. "That ties this case to the prior serial killings. And, according to the note sent to Mr. Hurtado, we have only three more days to figure it out before he kills again."

"Or two," Blair said. "In one of the prior cases, the Fisherman held his victim for at least a day before drowning her."

"Theories." O'Hara snapped his fingers. "Let's start with you, Mr. Hurtado."

Ted tilted back his head and frowned thoughtfully. He posed himself like a pundit on a television news show. "The first thing that comes to mind is a prison connection. Possibly, someone who was in jail with Eddy Adderly decided to take up where he left off."

"Why?" O'Hara asked.

"The fame of being a serial killer. The copycat might have learned details from Eddy." Ted warmed to his own theory. "If he pulls this off, he can also claim responsibility for the other murders."

"You think he wants to get caught?"

"Ultimately, yes." Ted gestured gracefully. "Don't all serial killers?"

O'Hara turned to Jake. "Any thoughts?"

"I dunno." Jake took another swig of his Coors. "The Fisherman was nuts. The copycat must be crazy, too. Maybe you should check with local shrinks."

"Oh, please." Ted rolled his eyes. "Information from psychiatrists is privileged."

"Not if their client plans to hurt somebody," Jake said. "I know that much."

"But I doubt a murderer would tell the details of his plot," Ted said. "If this guy is anything like the Fisherman, he's clever."

"Very true." O'Hara sat on the arm of the sofa nearest Ted. "And why do you think he's fixated on Blair?"

"That's obvious. The Fisherman probably meant to kill her before. Then she had the accident, and it wasn't viable to grab her. She's unfinished business."

David felt Blair stiffen beside him. She said, "But he didn't kill me. Last night he could have drowned me in the swimming pool. But he didn't."

O'Hara leaned toward Ted. "Why do you think he did that?"

"Beats me."

"David?" O'Hara turned to him. "Got any theories?"

The encouraging light in his eyes and the modulation of his voice reminded David of his own interview techniques: let the subject keep talking. Never contradict. Make him think he's important, that his opinion counts. Hope that he spills something incriminating.

Now David understood what was happening. O'Hara wasn't really looking for theories; he was subtly interrogating them. Were they suspects? He and Ted and Jake? He phrased his suspicion in a theory. "If this is a copycat, he could be someone intimately familiar with the details of the earlier crimes. Like somebody who was a reporter at the time."

O'Hara locked gazes with him. "Continue."

"It might even be a cop," David said.

Weathers glanced up sharply. "Not a cop."

But he could be. The Fisherman could be Kevin MacKay or Justin Hunter. Or any of the men in this room. David didn't have any answers.

He knew only one thing for sure. He needed to get Blair out of harm's way as soon as possible.

HOURS LATER, with everyone gone and the town house calmed down, Blair cleaned up the dinner dishes. She had missed her daily swim, but it was her choice to forgo the exercise. She wasn't quite brave enough to go back in the water. Nor did she want to add any more weight to David's load.

He seemed to have recovered his usual equilibrium, but it was hard to tell for sure. He'd spent most of his time on the telephone, hunched over his desk. He was arranging something but wouldn't tell her his plans. "Not until I'm sure I can pull this off."

"Does this plan include getting out of town?"

He'd smiled. "Definitely."

She liked the idea. A vacation sounded fantastic. It had been too long since she'd gone away, except for the occasional visit to her parents in Tucson. Maybe they'd take a lovely trip to Maui? Blair frowned to herself. She wasn't up for tanning and preferred to keep her scars covered. How about Maine? She and David could take long walks on windswept beaches.

Her fantasies of a getaway caused a slight twinge of regret. It didn't seem right to abandon their investigation. On the other hand, she wasn't opposed to a strategic retreat. If she wasn't within range of the Fisherman, she wouldn't be a victim.

But someone else would die. Another innocent woman.

Though it didn't seem as though she and David were making progress, they had to keep trying. They couldn't turn their backs and walk away.

David came into the kitchen with the mobile phone. "You didn't have to clean up," he said. "I'd have helped."

"Or called your brilliant cleaning lady." She tossed down the dishrag. "You can finish up."

He held out the phone toward her. "This call's for you."

How odd. Nobody knew she was staying here, except for her parents who she warned in case they called her condo and found her gone. "Hello?"

"It's Reinholdt."

Dr. Reinholdt from the medical examiner's office? "It's after eight o'clock. Working late?"

"We're under a lot of pressure here, investigating the Fisherman killing."

"You mean the copycat?" she asked.

"That's our problem," he said. "Everybody wants a definitive answer. Was Pamela Comforti killed by the same person who committed the other murders?"

She didn't envy his dilemma. Technically, a medical examiner wasn't supposed to make those sorts of judgments. Their job was to provide the facts and let the detectives sort out the conclusions. "There was one major difference," she said. "That odd-shaped circle on the abdomen."

"Right," he said. "And there's her age. Pamela Comforti was at least ten years older than any of the other victims."

An important variation. Serial killers generally fixated on the same general type of victim. "However," she said, "from what I could see, she was in excellent physical condition. Her hair was red, not gray."

"You see my problem," Reinholdt muttered. "I can't say that this was the same guy. Or somebody else."

"Did you have a specific question for me?"

"Right," he said. "The other vics were gagged. This one had tape over her mouth."

"Actually, there was one other with duct tape. I'm sure I noted it at the time of the autopsy."

"Let me check."

Through the phone, she heard him shuffling papers. The sound brought back memories of Dr. Reinholdt's big, cluttered desktop with files spilling in all directions. Behind him in the medical examiner's office was a wall of bookcases, also messy, and plastic models of the human heart and brain. In the corner hung a life-size plastic skeleton that the staff decorated for seasonal occasions. "How's Mister Bones?"

"Since it's almost summer, he's wearing sunglasses and baggy shorts."

Blair grinned as she strolled away from the kitchen to the living room. "Mister Bones always was fashionable."

"Not really. The shorts are neon pink and green. I wish I could convince you to come back here and help us monitor his style."

"Me, too."

"Anytime you say the word, Blair. We've got a place for you."

A pleasant warmth spread through her. It was nice to be wanted. "Thanks."

"Aha, here it is," he said. "Residue of masking tape on the third victim. Damnation! I thought I might have another clue."

"Is there anything else I can do to help?" she asked.

"I'd love to have you come down here and review our autopsy. You might pick up something we missed."

"I doubt that," she said. Reinholdt and his staff were thorough and capable. "But I promise to stop by more often."

"Listen, Blair." His tone held a chiding note. "I heard about the attack on you. And I also heard that you refuse to have a police bodyguard."

"Don't worry. I'm fine. In fact, I'm thinking about leaving town for a few days."

"Excellent plan! You take off and forget all about this stuff."

They said their good-nights, and she disconnected the call. She didn't want to leave the investigation. She thought of Reinholdt working late in his office and O'Hara with his far-fetched scheme of speculating on the crime and Weathers struggling with the police evidence. She belonged in that world.

As David joined her in the living room, she said, "About this trip—"

"It's all set up. We leave tomorrow morning."

Blair wasn't sure she liked the way he'd taken charge without consulting her. If he'd purchased plane tickets to Maui, he might have to cancel. "I don't want to quit. We should keep investigating."

"We will be," he said. "We're driving south to Cañon City, home of the maximum security penitentiary. I've arranged for us to talk to Eddy Adderly."

The Fisherman himself.

Chapter Twelve

Perfect! Blair fell back on the sofa and laughed out loud. A vacation with David didn't mean an idyllic trip to Maui or the Bahamas or even the windswept shores of Maine. In a stroke of genius, he'd managed to combine the need to get out of town with continuing their investigation. "David, you're fantastic."

"So, you'll go?"

"Wouldn't miss it for the world."

"I'm glad you're pleased." He eyed her curiously. "Most women don't burst into laughter when faced with the prospect of visiting a maximum security prison to meet a serial killer."

"You should know by now that I'm…" She puzzled for a moment, trying to come up with exactly the right word. "I guess I could say that I'm unique."

"I've noticed," he said dryly.

Her uniqueness wasn't exactly a plus. When she was growing up, her mother often disapproved of her behavior. "Mom always wanted me to fit in, to be more ladylike. She'd say, 'Blair, dear, quiet down.' 'Blair, dear, nobody likes a pushy girl. A pushy girl will never be prom queen.'"

Instead of joining her on the sofa, David sat in the

chair beside her, keeping a buffer between them. His long legs stretched out in front of him. "Were you?"

"Was I what?"

"Prom queen?"

"Definitely not. But I did have a date with the captain of the lacrosse team. I wore a strapless red dress and a white orchid corsage."

"Pushy girl makes good," he said. "That must have made your mom happy."

"Not really."

With a sigh she leaned back against the sofa pillows. Blair knew she got away with her smart-aleck attitude because she was also fairly attractive. It seemed cocky to say so, but facts were facts. Her features were proportionally well balanced, and her anatomy was sound. Simple as that. It wasn't a gift she asked for and had never fully appreciated until after her accident when she was in a wheelchair with Frankenstein pins in her leg or hobbling around on crutches with people staring at her for all the wrong reasons.

She missed being pretty. Maybe, in her heart of hearts, she yearned for the very things her mother had planned for her: a home with a white picket fence, children and a loving spouse.

"Tell me more," David said.

"Too boring. High school was something I got through, not especially remarkable. I didn't really come alive until med school and interning."

"Why?"

"The challenge. I like working hard."

"As a medical examiner," he said.

"An occupation that makes my mother want to scream. She'd say, 'Blair, dear, you could be a pediatrician.' 'Blair, dear, even a psychiatrist.'"

''But that's not you.''

''Afraid not.'' She was happiest when she was up to her elbows in an autopsy, searching for clues, finding the key that would unravel a crime. ''I've been thinking that I might try to go back to work.''

David's blue eyes shone with quiet approval. ''Good for you.''

''Obviously, they're shorthanded at the Coroner's Office if Dr. Reinholdt has to stay this late. I could probably help out.''

For the first time in ages, she had a positive feeling about returning to her profession in spite of all the reasons why she shouldn't—the lack of stamina, the shaky wrist, the headaches.

Could she dismiss those physical symptoms? They hadn't suddenly disappeared. She held up her right hand and studied it. Rotating the wrist from side to side, she felt a strain. Her fingers weren't shaking but they would. If she thought about any of her pains, they would return. ''I might be making a mistake.''

''You can do whatever you put your mind to,'' he said. ''I've always known that about you.''

She appreciated his sentiment but couldn't quite accept it. ''How have you always known?''

''Remember, Blair, I was with you after the accident. I saw the surgeries you went through. I saw you at physical therapy, sweating up one T-shirt after another.''

''Thank you for that lovely image.''

''Lovely to me,'' he said. ''You didn't quit.''

''But I wasn't one hundred percent. And I never will be.'' And for five long years she'd refused to face that fact. She'd cut back on her lifestyle and managed to scrape by on disability insurance and her dwindling savings. She hid out in her condo with the shades drawn, pretending that daily swims and workouts on her exercise bike were enough of a life for her. "Maybe seventy percent is enough."

"You're more than enough." A half smile lifted the corner of his mouth. "You're plenty woman to handle anything."

His calm support touched her. Within his strong lean body was a core of strength and sincerity that stirred her blood. He made her believe she could do anything.

"Determination," he said. "That's what makes you unique."

A gush of affection flooded through her. She wanted to bolt from the couch, throw herself on top of him and kiss him so hard that his teeth rattled. The only thing holding her back was the memory of last night's panic attack. It wasn't fair to David if she started something she couldn't finish. Maybe tomorrow.

She cleared her throat. "When we go to Cañon City, let's get one room instead of two."

"I'll make the reservations."

When he stood and headed toward his office, she wanted to grab him and hold on. But making love tonight would be…too soon. She couldn't stand it if they finally got into bed together and it wasn't perfect. Better to go slow. Better to wait.

DAVID BOOKED THEM a suite in a Cañon City motel with two important features: a two-person whirlpool tub in the room and a huge swimming pool in the center courtyard.

While he was checking in, Blair disappeared.

He found her in the courtyard, standing near the edge of the pool and staring down into the cool, turquoise waters.

Carrying both their overnight bags and his laptop, he came up beside her.

"I want to swim," she said.

"I suggest you put on your bathing suit first."

"Do we have time?" she asked. "Is there anything else we need to do today?"

"Our meeting with Eddy Adderly isn't until tomorrow afternoon. Today, we relax."

She took her bag from his hand. "First, we swim."

He led the way to the elevator and down the hall to their room. Since David's regular occupation meant he was on the road more often than not, he was an expert when it came to motel rooms. This corner suite on the second floor was better than he expected for a small town. The bedroom was separate from a decent-size living area with a stocked refrigerator, table and chairs, and a desk with a hook-up for his computer. Opposite the cabinet that held the television was a huge, oblong Jacuzzi whirlpool tub, beige with gold faucets. A little tacky, but not bad.

Blair was less judgmental. "I love this! We can bubble around in our own private hot tub while we're watching the tube."

Bubbling around together sounded good to him. "Should we start with the Jacuzzi?"

"Swimming first."

Water sports had never been his favorite thing. Though he'd always been athletic, he gravitated toward skiing and team sports, many of which he covered when he worked at *The Post* as a sports reporter. Of course, he knew how to swim. He just wasn't fond of it. He hated being cold.

Without unpacking the rest of his clothes, he slipped into his trunks. As soon as the air-conditioning hit his arms and legs, he was chilly. He shivered. The only good thing about swimming was that he'd get to see Blair in that sexy blue swimsuit.

Unfortunately, when she came out of the bathroom, she already had her long terry cloth robe cinched tightly at her waist. Her eyes sparkled like emeralds, but her smile seemed forced.

"I'm a little nervous," she said. "Getting attacked in the pool was traumatic. I'm not sure how I'll feel about getting into the water again."

This small flash of vulnerability was endearing. "We'll take it slow," he promised.

"No way." She tossed her head, and her short brown hair ruffled. "One of the best things about swimming is the rush when you dive in, and the water swirls around you."

"The cold water," he said. David preferred wading, allowing his body to gradually accustom itself to the temperature. "I've never been the kind of person who plunged in."

"We'll see about that."

He grabbed one of the motel robes from the bathroom and followed her down the carpeted hallway to center courtyard. The vaulted ceiling rose four stories above the pool area, which was separated by a half wall of planters and shiny, green foliage. There were only three other people in the pool, two kids splashing around in the shallow end and another man doing laps.

Blair paused at the deep end. Her voice was a whisper. "I was so scared when the lights went out. The water made me feel disoriented. I couldn't tell where he was."

He grasped her hand and squeezed. "It'll never happen again."

"I'm glad you're with me, David."

She tilted her head up. Her luminous eyes searched his face for encouragement that he was glad to give. At that moment he would have done anything for her. "I'm glad, too."

"Dive in with me."

He winced. "Without even sticking my toe in the water?"

"Please, David." She slipped the robe off her shoulders. "If I'm scared, you'll be right beside me."

He nodded, wishing she'd asked for something less difficult. Like fighting off twenty thugs. Or battling a killer anaconda.

"We dive on three," she said. "One. Two..." Her robe was off, arms arched above her head. "Three."

Her entry into the water was smooth and splashless. He threw his robe toward hers and belly flopped. Cold! Very cold! His entire body screamed with shock. Freezing water blasted his face, his chest, his entire body. He clawed to the surface with a gasp.

She bobbed a few feet away from him. "It's nice. Not that chilly."

"Ice water," he sputtered.

"I'm so glad we're doing this. I love swimming. It's so sensual."

"If you're a polar bear."

While he frantically trod water, she rolled to her back. Her arm lifted in a graceful stroke. God, she was beautiful. She looked like a magical water sprite.

He lumbered along beside her, taking choppy grabs at the water and kicking hard. His ability to float was less than zero. Every part of his body conspired to sink, which meant he had to work twice as hard to swim. Probably a good thing. The exertion would warm him up.

After two laps he decided he might survive.

After four laps, he was bored. Swimming back and forth didn't hold his interest. In other repetitive exercise, like jogging, you at least had a change of scenery.

At the deep end, she caught hold of the side. She lifted both arms above her head like a dancer about to perform a twirl. With a smile, she slipped below the rippling turquoise waters. When she returned to the surface, liquid sluiced from her shoulders, dripping like diamonds. With her hair slicked back, he could appreciate the natural beauty of her features. Delicately arched eyebrows. High cheekbones. "Come down with me, David. Keep your eyes open."

He caught a big gulp of air and allowed himself to sink to the bottom. The quiet enveloped him. This was a different world—a place he didn't like a whole lot. But Blair did. Suspended in water, she was incredible. She flipped in a somersault, and he watched, mesmerized until his lungs reminded him that he needed to breathe.

He pushed off the bottom and surfaced. Clinging to the side, he caught his breath.

"I love the water," she said. "It's the only place I feel completely free. No limp to hold me back."

"Not feeling any residual fear from the attack?"

"Nope. But I wouldn't be real happy if the lights went out." A tiny frown creased her forehead. "I think it was the darkness that terrified me."

Judging from her panicked reaction in his bedroom, David had to agree. "We'll always keep a light on," he promised.

He swam a bit more, lagging behind as she churned up the waves, lap after lap. Her obvious pleasure gave him a nice feeling of warmth. A little warmth. Not enough to stay in the water.

"I'm getting out," he told her. "You keep swimming as long as you want."

Outside the pool, he wrapped himself in the terry cloth robe, trying to ward off the chill. It felt as though the temperature was near freezing. But he couldn't go back to the room and warm up, leaving her alone and unguarded. He'd already made that mistake once.

Though Cañon City was a three-hour drive from Denver, beyond the typical attack range of the Fisherman, he intended to keep a careful eye on Blair. Until this madman was caught, she was still in danger.

David strolled over to the bar in a thatched-roof tiki hut with potted palm trees that seemed out-of-place in the Colorado high plains. Showing his room key, he ordered scotch, straight up, then returned to the pool where Blair continued to swim.

Drink in hand, he sat in a lounge chair. The scotch warmed his throat, made him feel nearly human. His heartbeat returned to normal. Watching Blair, he slipped into reporter mode, mentally recording the atmosphere for this story. His story. And Blair's.

There were a lot of ironies here.

Her affinity for water made Blair a mermaid, like the victims of the Fisherman.

Also, her approach to the pool delineated the difference between them. Blair plunged in, embracing the experience. And he held back, clinging to bodily warmth the way he clung to the past.

Obviously, if he wanted his life to move forward, he needed to change, to take the plunge.

Her head popped up at the edge of the pool near him. "Would you grab my robe for me?"

He brought the full-length terry cloth robe to the aluminum ladder leading up from the deep end. When she climbed out, he wrapped the robe around her, leaning close enough to plant a light kiss at the juncture of her jaw and throat.

"That's nice," she murmured as she leaned back against him.

"It's just a start."

She tilted her head back to kiss his neck. "I think I know what's at the finish line."

Hand in hand they returned to their nice, warm room, the nest they would share for the next few days. It was three o'clock in the afternoon, twenty-four hours from when they were scheduled to meet with Eddy Adderly at the prison.

David glanced over at the Jacuzzi, then he looked at Blair. "More water?"

"Let's dry off for a while. Is there anything we ought to prepare before talking to Eddy Adderly?"

"Probably." Though he didn't really have investigating on his mind, there were a few necessary preparations. "We'll only have twenty-five minutes with him. So we need to know exactly what to talk about."

"I'll get changed," she said. "And we can start."

In the bathroom, she peeled off her bathing suit and jumped into the shower to rinse off the chlorine. Her swim had energized her; she felt as if she could take on the world.

When she returned to the front room, David had plugged in his laptop computer. The menu listed several different options. "Here's the part you need to study. The autopsies."

"What am I looking for?"

"Think of three questions, things that might determine if Eddy Adderly really committed the murders."

She nodded. "Like, what did you use to gag the victims?"

"Right."

David's robe hung open, offering a view of his bare chest. The black hair made neat whorls that narrowed down his torso. When she lifted her gaze to his face, it was obvious that he'd caught her peeking. His gaze was hot, inviting her to touch, to kiss and more. But not yet. She wanted the moment to be perfect.

A bit nonplussed, she said, "And what will you be asking him about?"

"Contacts," he said. "People he knew. People who knew him."

"Do you think he'll tell us the truth?"

"We can hope."

As David went to take his turn in the shower, she sat at the desk and clicked through the information stored in his computer. Apparently, he'd scanned the documents, because they were complete with photographs. Very useful for refreshing her memory of the autopsies.

When she came to mermaid number four, David's sister, she found no crime-scene photographs. Instead, there was a posed picture of a lovely blond woman with a perfect smile. Her eyes were blue like David's, and there was a resemblance in the jawline. She wore a diamond necklace that spelled the letter *D* for Danielle.

It was so impossibly cruel to think that this young woman, whose life was full of promise, had been murdered. Was she only a pawn in the Fisherman's game?

When she heard David coming out of the bathroom, she clicked forward to another file.

"How's it going?" he asked.

"I thought of a couple of questions." She turned around in the desk chair. "None of the autopsies showed indications of rape or torture, but the ligatures on the wrists and ankles indicated that they were kept alive, possibly tied up for several hours. What was he doing with them?"

"In his confession," David said, "Eddy said they were sedated and gagged."

"But he took their gags off long enough for them to have water and food. Like the Godiva chocolate. I think he was talking to them."

David reached over to the computer and clicked to another file. "This is a theory from an FBI profiler."

She scrolled down the page. In professional language, the profiler explored motivations. These murders weren't sex crimes. The precision of the perpetrator suggested compulsive behavior. His obsession was control and power. The victims were tied up and helpless, fulfilling a fantasy of dominance. But they weren't mistreated. The perpetrator took pleasure in telling his story, emphasizing how he had outsmarted everyone. He lacked empathy for his victims, saw them as a means to an end.

The profiler said they should look for a white male in his late twenties or thirties. A loner. Probably not successful. Someone with mother issues.

"Someone who hates women," she said. "Sounds like Kevin MacKay to me."

David nodded. "Don't forget Justin Hunter. A boring job. Definitely a loner."

"The other big forensic question," she said, "is how did he manage such clean kills? Until the last victim, we didn't find a hair or a shred of fabric. No skin under the fingernails."

"Eddy Adderly described the outfit he wore," David said. "Gloves and boots. A hooded slicker."

The image revolted her. "I have a ton of questions. Do you think he'll tell us the truth?"

"We'll find out tomorrow," he said. "By the way, the instructions for prison visits are very explicit for what clothing is acceptable. No dangly earrings or jewelry. And nothing slinky."

"So, the backless black satin negligee is out."

David's eyes opened wide. "Black satin?"

"I'm joking."

"I guess that was too much to hope for."

But she wouldn't disappoint him tonight. Blair had already decided that their lovemaking would be perfect. She had a plan.

After they reviewed the files, they hit the town for dinner. She bought several candles at a gift shop, and he bought a bottle of wine.

When they returned to the room, it was seven o'clock. "Time for the Jacuzzi," she said.

David was more than ready. He had his shirt unbuttoned in two seconds.

"Wait," she said. "I want to set the mood. You take these two candles into the bedroom, light them and wait in there until I tell you to come out."

With David out of the room, she went to work, filling the Jacuzzi with steamy hot water and turning on the jets. A shiver of anticipation went through her. When David first came into her condo for lunch, she'd been unprepared for entertaining. Now she took her time to make the moment exactly right.

On the in-room sound system, she found a station that played slick, sultry jazz. Next she uncorked the wine and found two glasses. Unfortunately, they weren't stemmed wineglasses, but she didn't want to wait for room service to bring the proper crystal.

After placing six candles around the hot tub and lighting them, she turned off the lights. A little too dark, and the candles might go out. She turned on a lamp. Too bright. She didn't want to ruin the mood by having him see the scars on her leg clearly. She dragged the standing lamp behind the curtain, allowing just enough light to reflect on the wall.

Then she stepped back to survey her handiwork.

Very sexy! Though Blair would never be the perfect homemaker her mother had wanted her to be, she'd done a good job on this. The mood was pure seduction. Exactly what she wanted.

Slipping out of her clothes, she got into the Jacuzzi. "Okay, David. I'm ready."

With the water jets churning around her, she waited.

When David came into the room, he barely noticed her elaborate preparations. His gaze focused on her.

"Do you like it?" she asked.

"Better than Disneyland." He stepped out of his shoes and pulled off his socks. "I feel like I ought to do a striptease or something."

"Go right ahead."

Moving in time to the jazz beat, he flashed open his unbuttoned shirt on one side, then the other. Then he tore it off. He laced his hands behind his head and wiggled his hips.

She clapped. "More, more. Take it off."

He unfastened his belt, turned around and swung his butt from side to side. "How about it? Am I the next Gypsy Rose Lee?"

"Don't quit your day job."

He took off his trousers and underwear in one quick sweep. As she beheld his naked body, the laughter faded from her lips. He was incredible. Exactly the way she wanted a man to look. His body was firm and strong but not overly muscular.

With his striptease over, he walked to the whirlpool with a confident strut, and she knew that the silliness was over. Tonight he would make love to her in a way she'd never forget.

Chapter Thirteen

David lowered himself slowly into the hot, churning water. Bubbling jets massaged his lower back and spine. Yet he wasn't relaxed. The anticipation of making love to Blair was too intense.

The light from six candles flickered on her face, her throat, her shoulders. Below the water's surface, he saw the outline of her firm, high breasts.

She held a glass of Merlot toward him. "Sorry about the water glass," she said. "No stem. I didn't think to bring—"

"It's perfect," he said. Everything about this setting was exactly right.

He reached out and tipped his glass toward hers. She leaned toward him. Her arm curved gracefully as she clinked her glass against his.

The wine tasted sweet, and he licked his lips. This moment had been worth waiting for. He inhaled a deep breath, catching a hint of exotic fragrance from the scented candles. From the radio, he heard the low throb of a jazz clarinet. "A treat for the senses," he said. "Taste, smell, sound, sight. Every sense but one."

"Touch," she whispered.

She glided the short distance across the tub toward

him. Her pale skin glowed in the candlelight. She was golden.

Her hand caressed his cheek, compelling him to look directly into her enchanting green eyes. Her fingernails trailed down his neck to his chest, feathering across his skin.

The heated tub suffused him with languorous passion. Slowly he pulled her body against his. She rose from the churning water and slid up to his neck and down again, soft and sultry as a warm ocean tide.

"You take my breath away," he said.

"That's okay," she said, returning to her side of the tub. "I'm a doctor. I know CPR."

He took another drink of the wine, set his glass on the ledge and went toward her. Kneeling in front of her, the water didn't quite reach his chest. "One more sip, Blair."

After another taste of her wine, her expression was half tease and half challenge. "Then what?"

He removed the glass from her hand. "Then I kiss you."

Their slick, wet bodies molded together as the jets eddied around them in a fantastic whirlpool. His mouth claimed hers. Every nerve in his body was on fire. Every muscle pulsed. This was a rush.

She pushed against him, and he fell back in the water, dragging her with him, still joined by a kiss. His head bobbed under, and he came up laughing as he released her. "I'd like swimming better if all the pools were this warm."

"They have hot springs at Glenwood."

"We'll go there." He wanted to take her everywhere, to share the world with her.

She picked up her glass again. "More wine?"

"Don't need it. You intoxicate me."

He kissed her again and again. They splashed around in the water until it began to cool. He stood in the tub. "It's time for bed."

"We'll get the sheets wet."

"Not if we dry off first."

As he stepped out of the tub and offered his hand to help her out, Blair hesitated. She loved the sensual buoyancy of the Jacuzzi. Underwater she was flawless. Once she emerged, her feet would be flat on the ground. Her scars would be visible.

Still she climbed out. The promise of going to bed with him was enough to encourage her. Quickly she grabbed a towel. "I'll dry you."

Lightly she patted the drops of water from his lean, muscular body. His shoulders seemed so very broad. The pattern of black hair on his chest fascinated her as did his smooth torso. The heat from the bath gave color to his skin, otherwise he would have reminded her of a perfect marble statue.

"My turn," he growled.

"No," she said, not wanting close inspection of her body.

"Come on, Blair. We don't want to get the sheets wet."

"I said no." Her tone was firm, almost harsh.

"What's wrong?"

Damn it! She didn't want to ruin this perfect mood with her insecurities. Trying to put him off, she said, "Nothing's wrong."

His direct gaze demanded the truth. "Tell me."

Her lips pinched together, but she had to speak, had to answer him. "I don't want you to look at my leg."

He gently stroked her damp hair back from her forehead. "I've already seen the scars. When Adam and I came to the pool in your condo and you got out of—"

"This is different." How could she explain the turmoil she felt inside? She gazed up at him with tortured eyes. "I want everything to be perfect."

"It is," he said.

"Not anymore, David." Why couldn't he understand? "I want to be the way I was before."

"So do I." He draped a towel over her shoulders. "I want to sleep without seeing my sister's face, to wake up without remembering how she died. But it's not going to happen. We are who we are. With all our flaws. With all our past."

He dabbed the moisture from her face and lifted the towel to rub her damp hair. "I wouldn't change a thing about you, Blair. Not one damn thing."

"But I would," she said.

He grabbed another towel and lightly dried her breasts, ending his gentle massage with a tiny kiss on each nipple that sent a shiver through her body.

When he smiled at her, she stared. Something was different in his expression. His eyes? The lift of his chin? No, it was the most obvious feature. His smile.

This wasn't one of his tight half grins. He smiled fully without holding back. It was a smile of truth, and she knew she could trust him with her body, with her heart, with her very soul.

His hands circled her waist. "Hold still so I can finish drying you off."

He rubbed her tummy and leaned down to kiss her belly button. His lips tickled, and she wriggled.

"Nice," he said. "I like that."

"No more tickling."

Towel in hand, he cupped her buttocks and pressed

her against his thick, hard arousal. Renewed excitement whirled through her.

He crouched before her. She looked down at his shining black hair as he stroked both of her legs and caressed her feet. Before rising, he rested his forehead against the thigh of her scarred leg and kissed her knee.

Then he stood before her. His gaze was calm. His smile held true. And she could see that he had not been disgusted. He accepted her. Exactly the way she was.

"Now," he said. "I want you in my bed."

"Gladly."

The separate bedroom was softly lit by two more candles. David threw back the covers and eased her down onto the cool white sheets. As she stretched out, Blair experienced a freedom she hadn't felt in years. Acceptance seemed like such a simple thing to do; she couldn't imagine why she'd resisted.

In bed, the pace of his lovemaking accelerated. His touch bespoke an urgency. And she responded.

Their passion exploded in frantic caresses and hungry kisses. Too many to count. More sensations than there were stars in the velvet night sky.

When he finally entered her with a hard thrust, she shattered into a million sparkling pieces. Fulfilled. Happy. Excited and yet at peace.

AT TWO O'CLOCK in the afternoon following the best night of her life, Blair couldn't believe she was about to enter a maximum security prison to visit a serial killer. Talk about a return to harsh reality!

She stared at her reflection in the bathroom mirror. It was the same face she saw every other morning of her life, but today she looked different. A little softer, maybe younger. She sighed. If it was possible to become a reborn virgin after five years of no sex, she'd certainly lost that status last night. Three times. Then again this morning.

"Blair!" David tapped on the bathroom door. "We need to get moving."

"I thought the appointment wasn't until three o'clock."

"There might be complications. I want to get there early."

"Complications?"

"You never know with the prison system," he said. "To make this appointment with a death row inmate, I had to get clearance from Eddy Adderly's lawyer, a judge and the warden. Not to mention an okay from Eddy himself."

She pulled a short-sleeved cotton sweater over her head and opened the door. "I'm ready."

He studied her for a moment. In spite of the warm appreciation in his eyes, he shook his head. "No way can you go into a prison dressed like that. You look too sexy."

"Sexy is in the eye of the beholder." She went up on tiptoe to kiss his cheek. "Don't worry. I'll cover my wildly erotic slacks and a sweater with a blazer."

"Great." He turned away and paced toward the Jacuzzi. Then to the kitchen. Back again.

His tension was palpable, and she couldn't blame him for being nervous. If Eddy Adderly really was the Fisherman, David was about to come face-to-face with the man who'd brutally murdered his sister. Maintaining journalistic distance might be hard for him.

"For what it's worth," she said, "I don't think Eddy is the Fisherman."

"I agree." He continued to pace, talking too fast. "I

think Justin Hunter had it right. Eddy saw the Fisherman arrange the body of mermaid number six. He waited until the killer left, then he took a closer look at the dead woman. He touched her. He kissed her, leaving his saliva in her mouth and dropping a couple of hairs that you tested for DNA. When he took off, a witness spotted him."

"That would be my guess," she said.

"But how did he know the details of the other crimes? Why did the killing stop after he was arrested?" He came to an abrupt halt. His hands rested on the tabletop. "Why the hell did he confess?"

"You and I both know that a lot of confessions are false," she reminded him. "They come from fear. Or from a sick need to be recognized, even for something as horrifying as serial killing."

"I sat through the whole trial," he said. "Eddy's lawyers never claimed he was innocent. Only insane."

She placed her hand atop his, wishing she could ease his frustration, knowing that the only cure would be when the real Fisherman was apprehended. She reached into her backpack and took out the car keys. "You drive."

"Really?"

She nodded. If she intended to truly accept herself, she needed to give up her phobia about having someone else behind the wheel.

Hesitating, he looked down at the car keys in his hand. "Are you going to give me a hard time about every traffic hazard, real and potential?"

"Not a bit. I trust you."

"Thanks."

When he looked into her calm, beautiful face, David felt a little less edgy. Her faith in him might be the boost he needed for this interview. From past experience, he knew that jailhouse visits were never fun. This one might be worse than all the others combined.

Outside the motel, the sun shone brightly in an azure sky rimmed with puffy white clouds. Cañon City was a pleasant little town backed up against Sleeping Ute Mountain and bordered by the Royal Gorge, a tourist attraction that featured the highest suspension bridge in the world.

"Is it just me?" Blair asked. "Or is this a particularly gorgeous day?"

"Both," he said.

"Why do you suppose all these prisons sprouted up around here?"

"Politics. Fremont County housed the earliest territorial prisons in the 1860s. They bidded for the others and won. Plus this area is naturally isolated but not far from larger cities like Colorado Springs and Pueblo. In this area, there are nine state prisons and four federal penitentiaries including Supermax."

"Super maximum security?"

"Right. It's been home for a lot of criminal celebrities, like the Unabomber, Tim McVeigh and John Gotti. If we'd been trying for an interview there, it would have taken weeks to get clearance."

It was a surprisingly short drive from the bustling little town to the prison complex situated on several acres surrounded by chain-link fences topped with barbed wire, then enclosed by solid walls and guard towers.

At each checkpoint David's tension increased. By the time they were escorted into the penitentiary building—a structure with all the architectural charm of a giant shoe box—his heart hammered so loudly that he was sure other people could hear it.

"I hate jails," Blair said. "How many prisoners are here?"

"Over seven hundred in maximum security."

"And on death row?"

"A handful."

"All this hate and violence bottled up in one place." Her voice trembled. "It's scary."

David wasn't afraid but apprehensive. Uncertain of his own reaction. He might be speaking to the man who murdered his sister, a man he despised. "Digging out the truth is never easy."

"And if he lies?"

"We'll find something," he said with a show of confidence. His palms were sweaty, and he wiped them on his trousers before he grasped Blair's hand and squeezed.

She didn't seem to need much reassurance. As they proceeded through the system, her attitude was calm and friendly. It was much the way she behaved in the Coroner's Office—efficient, cooperative and in control. She chatted with the guards in khaki shirts who walked them through a scanner and relieved them of all personal items—keys, cell phone, David's wallet and Blair's backpack.

David held up his small tape recorder. "I checked with the warden. He said this would be okay."

"Sure," the guard said. "Now, here are the rules. You'll be shown into a small room. Both of you sit on one side of the table. There will be no physical contact between you and the inmate. You'll be observed on a video monitor. An officer will be present."

They were patted down and escorted through a narrow hallway into a plain, windowless room, not much larger than the cells where the prisoners were housed. David took a seat at the Formica-topped table.

Almost immediately the door opened and Eddy Adderly entered. His face was gaunt and sallow. The cancer had taken a toll. His wrists were cuffed to his belt. His ankles were shackled.

The first words out of his mouth were, "You've got to get me out of here. I belong in the infirmary."

David's tension vanished, quick as the snap of his fingers. His professional manner took over. "If you cooperate with us, we'll see what we can do."

Eddy slouched in the chair on the opposite side of the table. "You're nobody. You can't do nothing."

"Trust me, Eddy. We're all you've got." He turned on the tape recorder. "There's been another Fisherman-style killing."

"I heard."

David posed the number one question on his list. "You never killed those other women, did you? It was somebody else. And he's acting again."

"It was me." Eddy's flat eyes were dark holes in his skeletal face. "I'm the famous Fisherman."

"A criminal genius," David said, playing along. "There's a computer Web site with all the details. Ever heard of it?"

"Yeah, the guy who runs it sends me fan mail."

"What's his name?" David asked.

"Hunter, Justin Hunter. He says if I send him written notes, he can auction them off."

His scrawny shoulders straightened. He was proud of his notoriety.

"What kind of notes?" David was interested in this connection between Hunter and Eddy Adderly. "Notes like the ones you sent to the newspaper?"

He nodded, seeming to lose interest. His gaze wandered toward Blair. "Who are you?"

"Dr. Blair Weston," she said.

"You're pretty." He gave a rheumy cackle. "Why don't you take off that jacket and give a dying man something to look at."

Instant rage exploded in David's gut. His need to protect her was instinctive and strong. With an effort he suppressed his anger. They only had twenty-five minutes. Every second counted. "About those notes, Eddy. Why did you send them to Ted Hurtado?"

"Because he's got the same name as me. We're both Edward. Eddy and Teddy. I seen him on television yesterday. What a loser!"

"Sounds like you know him," David said.

"He interviewed me. Like you're doing now." He grinned at Blair. His face was a death mask. "I got you figured out. You're the chick who does autopsies."

"That's right," she said.

Blair glanced toward David, silently asking if she should interrupt his questions. He nodded.

Clearing her throat, she said, "You used a sedative on your victims—"

"My mermaids," he said.

He disgusted her. The physical wasting of his body didn't bother her. She'd seen much worse. It was his utter depravity that turned her stomach.

For the first time in a career that included some truly grotesque autopsies, she felt like throwing up. "Where did you get the sedatives, Eddy?"

"Around."

"Who gave them to you?" she asked.

"I got them on the street."

She doubted that very much. In one case, he'd used

a hypodermic to administer a sedative. "Okay, I have a different question. How did you feed your victims?"

"Through the mouth." He cackled again. "Took off the gag and put food in their mouth."

"Why?"

"They were hungry," he said.

"But you intended to kill them. Why would you care if they were hungry?"

"You're trying to trick me." He lurched toward her, rattling his chains. "It won't work. I'm the Fisherman. Me. That's what it's going to say on my gravestone."

The prison guard at the door stepped forward, placing a restraining hand on Eddy's shoulder. The guard said, "You have ten more minutes."

Blair had other questions about how he kept the crimes so clean, how he'd washed the victims and what he'd worn. But there was no point in asking. She was certain that this pathetic creature, Eddy Adderly, had not killed those women.

David said, "Did you have any help? Maybe there was somebody who helped you carry the bodies."

"Nobody. It was me. Alone."

"The cops found newspaper clippings about the murders in your apartment. Did you talk to anybody about what you'd done?"

"I heard plenty," he said.

"Where?" David asked.

Blair noticed the vacant quality in Eddy's expression. He must be on pain medication.

"Where?" David repeated. "Did you hear people talking about the Fisherman on the street? In a bar?"

"That's right." He leaned against the back of his chair. "The Red Rover. A bar where cops go. I used to sit and listen to them trying to figure out what the Fisherman was doing. What I was going to do next.''

Blair almost gasped out loud. The Red Rover must be where Eddy had gotten his inside information on the cases. ''Why wasn't this bar mentioned in the police reports?''

''They're stupid,'' he said.

The omission of this information was more than stupid. It was tantamount to a cover-up.

''Any cop in particular?'' David asked. ''Maybe one of the Feds.''

''Cops are cops.'' He glowered at the prison guard. ''Pigs.''

''Give me a name,'' David said. ''Who did you hear talking in the bar?''

''You're crazy. I never been in a bar.''

Blair wanted to shake the truth out of him. ''You're dying, Eddy. Tell us. Before you die, tell us what really happened.''

His thick tongue protruded. He licked his dry lips. ''You can be my next mermaid, Doc. I can make you famous.''

''Godiva chocolate,'' she said.

''Huh?'' His eyes darted, searching for the answer she wanted to hear. Then, he bobbed his head. ''That's right. I fed my mermaids chocolate.''

''Why?''

''Get me out of here. Get me a bed in the infirmary. I'll tell you anything.''

''More lies,'' David said.

''You don't know nothing.''

The prison guard stepped forward. ''Time's up. Let's go, Eddy.''

His scrawny body wrenched upright. His chains rattled as he shuffled toward the door with shoulders slumped. A dying man. She didn't think he'd last another month.

"Eddy." David stood. "What part was true?"

"You figure it out." He turned his head and gave them a look of pure evil. "See you in hell."

Chapter Fourteen

Throughout the reverse process, as he and Blair left the maximum security prison and drove through the checkpoints at the perimeter, David kept his thoughts to himself. Unsure whether he was closer to the truth or deeply misled, he had much to consider.

Eddy Adderly had implicated the law-enforcement community. He'd overheard police conversations in the Red Rover bar that gave details of the Fisherman's crimes.

The fact that Eddy chose to hang out in a bar frequented by cops didn't surprise David. There were a lot of guys who hung around the edges of law enforcement like groupies with rock bands. These "cop groupies" fantasized about wearing a badge and gun, having that kind of authority. Or becoming a criminal who was even smarter than his heroes.

Unfortunately, this revelation didn't point to the real killer. What Eddy had gotten from his barroom eavesdropping was information. Confidential information. Likely, he used those details to confess to the famous Fisherman crimes and gain the notoriety that was even more important to him than life itself.

David found it more interesting that Eddy admitted

knowing Justin Hunter, who was a groupie of another sort. Or was he? Hunter was smart enough to be a leader instead of a follower. Behind those innocent-looking Harry Potter glasses, he had a kind of deviant cleverness. But was he a mastermind? Capable of manipulating Eddy and the investigators, capable of getting away with murder?

As soon as they passed the final gate outside the penitentiary complex, Blair said, "What if the Fisherman was a cop? He could have arranged for Eddy to overhear the details of the crime and then framed him."

"Too random," he said. "How could he frame Eddy?"

"By luring him to the scene of the last crime," she said.

"Then what? Convince Eddy to leave his DNA on the body? I don't think so. The Fisherman is into control. He wouldn't trust a pathetic loser like Eddy Adderly to keep his secrets."

"How can you be sure?" she asked.

"I can't." He pulled onto the shoulder of the road and set the parking brake. "Come here."

She eased across the space between the seats and into his waiting arms. Her warmth comforted him, reminded him that there were good things in the world as well as the danger, the secrets and lies. "I need a change," he said.

"From what?"

"Crime reporting. I'm sick of it. The criminals. The cops. The creeps like Justin Hunter. Suspects. It feels like, for the past five years, I've been wallowing in filth." His decision was clear. "This is my last crime story."

"Will you go back to sports reporting?"

He snuggled her closer against him, rested his cheek on the top of her head. Her short, silky hair smelled clean. "Oh, yeah, that sounds like heaven. A lazy afternoon at a baseball game with the sun shining on my face. The green grass in the field. The athletic precision of a battle between pitcher and batter. I love that stuff."

"Why did you quit doing it?"

"You know the answer." He'd been obsessed with crime, ferreting out the truth. "I had to make sense of my sister's murder."

"Ironic," she said. "You're ready to leave investigative procedures behind. I'm thinking about going back. We've both changed." She looked up at him. "I wonder why."

He dropped a light kiss on her forehead. "Mostly I want to change because of you, Blair. When I'm with you, the future seems like a good, decent place."

"I'm glad." She snuggled against his chest.

"All of a sudden I'm hearing birdsong, smelling the scent of piñon pine on the breeze. It used to be when I closed my eyes I'd see horror. Now my vision is you. Wet from the tub. Naked. Beautiful."

She exhaled a soft sigh. "Like Justin Hunter said, you're good at creating ambiance."

"You bet. Words are my business."

"And autopsies are mine."

Though their professions didn't seem to share much in common, he knew better. They both aimed for a similar goal. "You're a doctor, Blair. A healer."

"Really? I've never had one of my 'patients' wake up from an autopsy."

"But you provide a cure." She used her skill to find the answer to crime. To find the truth. "You heal the people left behind. People like me."

"Seems to me," she said, "that we both have bright lives ahead of us. We should get busy, get this investigation over with."

He nodded his agreement.

She continued, "And I still think we should take a closer look at the cops involved with the Fisherman case. At the very least, there was a cover-up. If Eddy overheard details of the crime at a bar, his confession should have been suspicious."

"You're forgetting something. After Eddy was arrested, the killing stopped." That was the most damning evidence against Eddy Adderly. Circumstantial or not, Eddy confessed and nobody else was murdered. Case closed. "The cops wanted him to be guilty."

"But he's not." She tilted her head back to stare at him with intent, searching eyes. "Eddy didn't buy those sedatives on the street, and he certainly didn't have the expertise to administer a hypodermic injection with the proper dosage."

An image of Kevin MacKay, the anesthesiologist, flashed across David's mind. Kevin would know all about proper methods of sedation.

Blair continued, "When we talked to him, Eddy didn't recognize me. He didn't even know who I was. The mention of Godiva chocolate confused him."

"Maybe he was lying. Trying to throw us off."

"He didn't fake that blank stare," she said. "Even though he's on pain meds, he wouldn't forget about the Godiva chocolate. It would have been really hard to convince those women to swallow the candy."

He brushed a wisp of hair off her smooth cheek. Her skin was so soft. She was so delicate and lovely. She deserved poetry, sonnets praising the curve of her chin and the tip of her nose. So how come they kept talking about murder?

David dragged his focus back to the topic. "Bottom line—you think a cop might be involved."

"Might be the killer," she said. "We've speculated about how the Fisherman got these women to come along with him. If he was a cop, they'd trust him."

"When we get back to the motel," he said, "I'll run some of the key law-enforcement personnel through my database to see if they fit the profile."

She gave him a quick peck on the cheek and scooted back to her seat. "Some of those cops built their careers on the successful arrest and conviction of Eddy Adderly."

David started up the car and headed toward town.

She continued, "Special Agent O'Hara was promoted. Weathers is now a lead detective, talking to the media."

"Eddy also mentioned that he'd talked to Ted Hurtado. Eddy and Teddy."

"And we should check him," she said. "And Jake, too."

"Jake Zitti?" His pal might be a jackass, but he didn't strike David as the type who'd be a serial killer. "Definitely not a loner. And he's got a different girlfriend every week. He loves women."

"Trust me," she said. "He's more misogynist than you think."

They were already approaching the little town, passing fast-food restaurants on the main drag. "Hungry?" David asked.

"No way. The prison made me nauseous. As did Eddy."

He knew exactly what she meant. Revulsion had turned his own stomach inside out.

"I think maybe you need a nice, long soak in the Jacuzzi bath," he suggested hopefully.

"You know how much I love water." She tossed her head, and the sunlight played in her hair. "But shouldn't we be getting back to Denver?"

"There's no rush." He intended to keep her out of Denver until the Fisherman's murderous deadline had passed. One more day.

BACK IN THE MOTEL ROOM Blair watched as David took a seat at the computer and worked his magic. His gaze was riveted to the screen of the laptop as his fingers raced across the keyboard. Frowning, he concentrated hard, and he looked as adorable as a kid figuring out a puzzle.

A basic instinct rose within her. Being close to him was too much enticement. She wanted to tease him, to ruffle the forelock of black hair that fell across his forehead.

More than that, she wanted to push aside the computer and make love to him on the desktop. Or in the tub. Or the bedroom. Wherever. Whenever. She wanted to feel his skillful hands caressing her body, to revel in the sensual pleasure of his kisses.

Pacing across the room and back again, she wished that she'd been smart enough to bring along a stash of Godiva. A chunk of milk chocolate would go a long way toward calming her down.

She peeked over his shoulder. "Tell me about this program of yours."

"After years of doing my investigative reporter thing, I developed these spreadsheets to keep the suspects straight."

He pulled up a screen. A vertical column listed the

initials of possible suspects. A horizontal column across the top showed numbers.

"What are the numbers?" she asked.

"They stand for physical evidence."

"Like what?"

"Lack of alibi for the time of the crimes. Physical size of the suspect. Access to sedative drugs. Acquaintance with victims. Did they leave Denver in the past five years? Criminal record."

There were probably twenty names on his list. Only two were marked in across the board: Kevin MacKay and Justin Hunter.

Blair stared at the screen. "I can see why you zeroed in on those two."

"Don't get too excited," he warned. "This isn't verified proof. And a lot of it is circumstantial. Like the issue of alibis. Because both Hunter and MacKay are unmarried and live solitary lives, they're less likely than married men to have alibis."

"I didn't know Hunter had been out of town during the past five years."

"Occasionally," he said. "He goes to conferences for his job as a medical supply salesman."

David typed his way through a couple of documents that featured his own special code, then went back to the spreadsheet. He pointed to a new set of initials at the top of the sheet. "This stands for Special Agent Gary O'Hara."

Across the board, there were a couple of *x*s and several zeros.

"What does that mean?" Blair asked.

"Zero stands for insufficient data. Basically, our only physical evidence on O'Hara is that he's physically capable of murder and carrying a corpse, has access to sedatives and was out of Denver for a significant portion of the past five years.''

''It doesn't seem like much,'' she said.

''To learn more, I need to ask more questions.''

Entering a new code, he changed the screens. The configuration was similar. ''This is the psychological profile. I compiled information from FBI profilers and cops.''

She nodded. ''What's the profile for the Fisherman?''

''Male. An introvert. Probably unmarried. A control freak. Obsessive-compulsive disorder. He feels power-less or unappreciated in his job. He was an only child or youngest son. Had a lack of male role models while growing up and an unhealthy relationship with his mother.'' He pointed to a horizontal row of pluses and minuses. ''A healthy relationship is a plus.''

''How did you find out all this stuff about your sus-pects?'' she asked.

''Some info came from police reports or interviews with friends. Mostly it was talking directly to the sus-pects. It's amazing what people will tell you if you care to listen.''

''Like Eddy telling us about the Red Rover,'' she said. ''But how do you know if they're telling the truth?''

''I don't.'' He shrugged. ''None of this information is scientific, Blair. I haven't given these people tests or technical profiles. Mostly, it's guesswork on my part.''

She pointed to the row of minuses and a few pluses that stood for Kevin MacKay's profile. ''Tell me how you came up with this interpretation for MacKay.''

He turned around in the chair to face her. ''He's an unmarried introvert who doesn't have a high opinion of women. On the plus side, he's a former priest who spent the past five years doing noble work in Third World countries.''

"You might not be a real profiler, but that sounds accurate to me. How about Justin Hunter?"

"Unmarried introvert in dead-end job. Likely abused as a child. He has a morbid fascination with serial killers." He paused. "Actually, that obsession might be a plus because he uses his Web site as an outlet for his craziness."

Unable to resist him any longer, she took David's hands and pulled him away from the computer. "How about Detective Weathers?"

"I think he's married."

"Divorced," she said. "With two kids."

"He likes to boss people around. That fits the profile. But he's uncomfortable in the spotlight. That's not like the Fisherman, who craves attention and recognition."

"What do we think about O'Hara?"

When she tugged on his hands again, he planted his feet firmly. "Where are we going?"

"I'm thinking a Jacuzzi might be nice." She flashed a flirty little grin that really wasn't her style. At least, it hadn't been her style before she and David made love. Boldly she added an eyelash flutter. "We should wash off the stink of the prison."

His response was immediate and predictable. "You convinced me."

Within moments they were in the Jacuzzi. The familiar waters churned. The jets massaged her body. And David came to her, as she'd known he would. Her lips had grown accustomed to his kisses. Her body fit against his as if they were meant to be together. She couldn't imagine any reason they would ever be apart.

AFTER WONDERFUL LOVEMAKING and a room-service dinner, they went back to the Jacuzzi. Languidly she murmured, "We didn't make much progress toward solving the case."

"Might be best to leave investigating to the police."

She eyed him curiously. Solving his sister's murder had been an obsession for five years. "Are you comfortable with giving up?"

"There's something more important, Blair. Your safety."

"Are you suggesting that we stay here until the police take someone into custody?"

"I wouldn't mind," he said. "We could drive down to New Mexico. Santa Fe is fantastic this time of year. We could check out the art galleries, go for long walks at sunset when the sky turns a hundred lingering shades of red and gold."

What a lovely picture he painted! She was tempted to throw this investigation out the window and glide along with him, following a purely sensual bliss. Yet she knew they couldn't quit their investigation. "We can't do it."

"Why not?"

"The cops pulled a cover-up when they indicted Eddy Adderly. It could happen again."

"And you'd still be in danger." His blue eyes darkened. There was a peculiar sadness in his expression. "I don't want you to spend the rest of your life looking over your shoulder. But I'm not sure that we can figure this out."

"We can't give up. You've invested too much of your life looking for the truth. Can you really turn your back and walk away?"

"I want to."

"Come on, David. We were making progress. Let's think about the potential suspects. What about O'Hara?"

"Not again." He rolled his eyes. "He really doesn't fit the profile."

"But he was out of town for five years. Then he returns to Denver, and the killing starts again. Coincidence?"

"I don't believe in coincidence," he said. "But I think O'Hara's return falls under the category of motivation. Remember? We talked about this with Hunter."

"Refresh my memory." She was too easily distracted by the vision of his broad shoulders and the pattern of hair on his chest.

"After Eddy Adderly was arrested, the team of investigators fell apart. Several people dispersed. Some left town. You were injured and out of action. Pamela Comforti retired. Even Ted Hurtado took off to work on his book."

David spread his hands wide, rippling the surface of the water. "Now you're all back on the case. That's why he killed again."

"You're probably right, but I don't like to think about this theory." A shiver flickered across the surface of her skin. In spite of the heated Jacuzzi, she felt cold inside. For five years the Fisherman had been watching her. "I don't like to think of him monitoring my progress."

His attention scared her, but hiding out was not an option. She needed to be right smack in the middle of the ongoing investigation. She needed for the Fisherman to be caught, gutted and filleted.

"Let me take this theory one step further," David said. "Though I'd like to think he's not targeting you as a victim, he killed Pamela Comforti. She was part of the earlier investigative team."

Her tension heightened. She slipped down in the tub so the water was all the way up to her chin. "Do you think, this time, he means to attack the investigators?"

"In his twisted mind that might be the ultimate challenge."

"Killing the people who are pursuing him." In a horrible way his theory made sense. "I feel like I have a bull's-eye painted on my forehead."

"That's why we have to be careful." He half rose from the water and grabbed the remote from the floor beside the tub. He pointed at the television and clicked. "It's almost ten o'clock. Let's check the news."

The Fisherman was the lead story. An anchorwoman with a serious face looked directly into the camera. "This just in. The Fisherman has struck again. The body of a woman was found approximately one hour ago at the Congress Park swimming pool…"

Blair felt relieved. It wasn't her name that the anchorwoman was about to report. She wasn't his latest victim. At the same time she experienced a pang of guilt. If David's theory was correct, someone else had died in her place.

Chapter Fifteen

In spite of his wonderful night with Blair—a night that had been filled with world-class sexual activity—David woke with a start. Eyes wide open and alert, he shot quick glances into the corners of the motel room. He looked toward the window where sunlight spilled around the edges of the curtain. Then to the open bedroom door.

His fingers clenched into fists, but there was nothing to fight. No visible threat.

Leaning back on the pillows, he gazed down at Blair, still asleep on her back. She looked so pretty, so peaceful and innocent. Her rose-petal lips were slightly parted as she breathed steadily. Her left arm was thrown artlessly above her head with her slender fingers slightly curved. He marveled at the delicate, pale skin of her inner arm.

Careful not to wake her, he crept from the bed, slipped into his boxers and went into the other room to order room-service breakfast and a newspaper.

Last night they'd decided to drive back to Denver today. Blair wanted to participate in the autopsy of the latest victim. And David had an agenda of his own. He wanted to talk to O'Hara about his theory on why the Fisherman had started killing again. And especially on the possibility that he might be targeting previous investigators.

Was it worth the risk to go back? He sat on the sofa and stared at the blank screen on his laptop computer. During the past five years he'd stayed in hundreds of motel rooms, digging through thousands of documents, crime-scene photos, court transcripts and transcribed notes from his interviews. He'd seen carnage. He'd looked into the fathomless eyes of stone-cold killers. None of it had really scared him. Until now.

After room service arrived and he'd poured himself a cup of black coffee, Blair emerged from the bedroom. Wearing only a thin pink nightshirt and no shoes, she walked with an off-kilter gait that he found adorable. "Good morning," she murmured as she leaned down to kiss his cheek. "What's up?"

The front-page story in *The Denver Post* was the Fisherman murder. David summarized, "The victim was the producer of a local TV news broadcast. She left the station at ten in the morning yesterday. Her body was found last night."

Blair squeezed her eyes closed. For a second he thought she was going to cry. Then her eyelids popped wide. Her lips thinned. "Never talk to me about murder before I've had my coffee."

He snapped the newspaper and folded it closed. What the hell was he supposed to say? "How was your night? Did you sleep well?"

She poured herself a cup of coffee. "I could do without the sarcasm."

"It's a mistake to go back to Denver." He pushed himself out of the chair and paced across the room. "I'm putting you in danger."

"What makes you think my safety is your responsibility?"

"Because I care about you."

She sat at the table and neatly crossed her right leg over the left. Her scars reminded him of her vulnerability, but her voice was firm and unshaken. "I can take care of myself, David."

He wasn't being overprotective. The danger was real. "Here's an interesting detail from the latest murder," he said. "This victim was thirty-eight. Pamela Comforti was forty-seven."

"Five years ago," she said, "his oldest victim was twenty-seven."

"He's going after older women," David said. "How old are you, Blair?"

"Thirty-four."

"You fit in either group. And, if he's following the same pattern as last time, he's killed one woman from law enforcement and one from the media. The next one will have a medical profession. Do you understand what I'm saying, Dr. Weston?"

"I get the point." She sipped her coffee. "But I won't give in to fear. I've been hiding for years. It's time for me to come out of my shell."

Of course, he was glad that she was giving up the life of a lap-swimming hermit. But did she have to take on the Fisherman? "I'll be watching you like a hawk, Blair. You go nowhere by yourself."

"Goody." She grinned. "Does that mean you'll be coming with me to another autopsy?"

His stomach plummeted. "I can handle it."

BY TEN O'CLOCK they were on the road, headed back to Denver. Blair fidgeted in the passenger seat. Though David was an excellent driver, she couldn't help the twinges of nervousness that came from having someone else behind the wheel.

She pressed her lips together to keep from nagging at him. They'd come close enough to conflict this morning. Wasn't that always the way? A couple of nights of great sex and then the relationship crumbled like a cookie.

It was small solace that she'd been right. When they first kissed and she said they shouldn't go any further, she knew they were both too damaged to have any kind of decent relationship. He was too protective, still carrying a load of survivor guilt about his sister's murder.

Still, when she peeked over at his strong profile, the sight of him made her smile. He'd been good for her. With David's unflagging encouragement and acceptance, she finally had the courage to think about a future that included working again in a profession she loved.

When he took a curve at eight miles per hour over the posted limit, she blurted out, "Slow down."

He eased off the gas pedal. "I think we're safe. The weather is perfect. This little two-lane road is relatively flat. And there's no traffic to speak of."

She gazed through the windshield at the rolling hills of buffalo grass, sprigged with the occasional stand of conifers. At roadside, there were springtime wildflowers. The landscape provided small comfort for the turmoil in her mind. "Oh, sure. What could possibly go wrong on a day like this?"

"Now who's being sarcastic?"

She rolled down her window to feel the breeze flowing down from the foot hills. "David, it's really okay if you don't come to the autopsy with me. You probably have some interviews you'll want to do."

"Not today," he said. "I talked to Adam this morning

and told him I needed some basic data for our new list of suspicious people.''

''Good idea.'' She remembered how thorough Molly had been in putting together their first crate of information. ''Who's on that list?''

''The Fisherman strikes in three areas—law, media and medicine. Even though Eddy only mentioned hanging out at a cop bar, I targeted former investigators in all three.''

''Medical?''

''It's impossible to consider all of the docs and nurses in Denver, but I suggested a couple of people from the Coroner's Office.''

She rolled her eyes. As if Dr. Reinholdt was a serial killer? ''What about media? Did you include Jake?''

''Both him and Ted Hurtado,'' he said. ''Actually, Ted might fit the profile of a serial killer.''

''The poor guy definitely has issues with his crazy mother.'' Doris Hurtado—with her platinum hair and leopard pants and the kitchen from hell—was the most clingy woman she'd seen in a long time.

''After being raised by Doris, I'm surprised Ted can even talk to women.''

''He's unmarried,'' David said. ''Loves attention and being in control. His classy wardrobe hints at compulsive behavior.''

''Or unusually good taste.'' But she didn't dismiss Ted as a suspect. It was easy to imagine him taking the care to remove every trace of evidence from his victims. ''Does he have access to drugs?''

''I wouldn't be surprised to find out that his mother requires the occasional sedative.''

''A nice shot of elephant tranquilizer,'' Blair said. ''Did you believe what Eddy said about choosing Ted to send the notes to? Because their names were the same.''

''Kind of a creepy link between them. Eddy and Teddy.''

Instead of taking the highway on the last leg of their trip from Colorado Springs to Denver, David had chosen a back route that added forty-five minutes to their drive time. But this ride was far more mellow. At times the two-lane road followed the twisty curves of a small creek. There were more trees in this area. Cottonwoods and aspen groves.

''This is pleasant,'' she said. ''Almost makes me forget where we're going.''

''We could keep driving. Straight through Denver and north to Wyoming.'' He exhaled a breath. ''But we won't. Not until we're sure the Fisherman is caught.''

Tentatively she asked, ''And then what happens? To you and me?''

''I'm not sure.'' His forehead crinkled as he considered her question. ''Did you ever go to the old roller coaster at Elitch Gardens?''

''Once,'' she said. ''It was rickety, made out of wood.''

''Remember how the roller-coaster car would climb, real slow to the top? It ratcheted up one click at a time. I feel like that's what we're doing. Gathering info, reasoning, building a case. Each fact takes us a bit higher. Click, click, click. Then, when we finally have the answer, we'll take a screaming dive, straight down. After that, life will even out.''

''We just have to wait,'' she said. ''No promises or assurances.''

It was hard to make a lifetime commitment when you didn't know if the only life you had left was a matter of days or hours.

She noticed David peering into the rearview mirror, and she turned. There was a big, black pickup truck coming up behind them, following too close. Though she'd sworn not to nag, she said, "Pull over and let him pass."

"I will as soon as there's space."

The shoulder was only a few feet wide, then down a slight embankment to the trees bordering the creek.

David sped up.

"What are you doing?" she asked.

"Giving him some room."

The speedometer showed they were going only fifty miles an hour, but it felt like 150 to Blair. The green branches of trees lashed past her window in a dizzying blur.

The road curved. She leaned against the passenger door. *Too fast. They were going too fast.* The road widened slightly. Beside them was a wide meadow bordered by a barbed wire fence.

The truck behind them honked.

"David, please." Every nerve in her body gnarled with tension. They were going to have an accident. "Stop the car."

"Can't. He'll run right over me."

The pickup pulled out to pass. His engine roared as he raced up beside them.

At the next curve a red station wagon appeared from nowhere. It was headed toward them. In the same lane as the pickup.

David stood on the brake as the pickup swerved in front of him.

She heard the sickening crunch of metal against metal as the rear of the pickup clipped the front fender of David's car. The nose of the Acura spun toward the field. They were on the narrow shoulder, churning up pebbles and dust. Out of control.

Blair screamed. *Oh, God, not again.* She couldn't stand for this to happen again.

She was aware of David fighting the skid. His airbag exploded, blocking his vision. She heard the screech of the tires. Her body jostled against the seat belt. Terror consumed her.

She squeezed her eyelids closed but didn't lose consciousness. She was too scared to pass out, afraid that she'd wake up in a hospital. Broken. Destroyed.

The car stopped.

They hadn't crashed.

Beside her she heard David cursing and struggling with the airbag. His hand grasped her shoulder.

"Blair, are you okay?"

She wanted to speak, but her mind was frozen in time. Her memory cleared. This was exactly what had happened before. When Jake was driving, the car that tried to pass wasn't a truck, but it had forced them off the road. Someone else had been responsible for the accident.

All along Jake had claimed that the accident wasn't his fault. He told her there was another car involved, but Blair couldn't remember and didn't believe him. She'd cursed him, thrown him out of her life, despised him. And he wasn't to blame.

"Blair!"

She opened her eyes. "I owe Jake an apology."

HER NEAR-MISS ACCIDENT with David wasn't exactly the same as the disaster five years ago when Jake had been driving. With David, the other two vehicles stuck around and exchanged insurance information. The Acura sustained serious body damage but was still driveable. And, most important, David had controlled the skid and managed to stay on the road.

But the choreography was very similar to what had happened in the first accident—*the accident that hadn't been Jake's fault.* Blair had wasted a lot of time and effort, hating him for no good reason.

When David finally returned to the car, she said, "Jake didn't dump me."

"Whatever." His eyebrows pulled down in an expression of deep concern. "Are you certain you're not injured?"

"I dumped him. Told him that I never wanted to see him again." She frowned. "It was pretty cruel."

"My God, Blair. Don't waste time feeling guilty about Jake. If I remember correctly, he recovered fast."

"He tried to tell me it wasn't his fault, but I wouldn't listen." She gazed directly into David's eyes. "I wouldn't let him help me. I pushed him away."

Was she making the same mistake with David? For much of her life she'd clung to a misguided sense of independence. The result was not freedom. But bone-deep loneliness.

David checked his wristwatch. "We can still make it back to Denver in time for the autopsy. What do you want to do?"

"I'll attend the autopsy." Too much of her life and livelihood had already been lost. "Then I'll decide." She looked up at David, linking her gaze with his, and she amended her statement. "We'll decide. You and me."

Right up at the top of her list was the need to apologize to Jake. It seemed important to wipe that slate clean.

GLOVED AND GOWNED in the autopsy room, Blair observed as Dr. Reinholdt opened the body cavity. The corpse was anorexically thin. Though her wrists and ankles showed the ligatures typical of being bound, there was little bruising. Possibly her captor had used too much sedative for a woman of such low body weight, and she'd been too weak to struggle. Unlike Pamela Comforti, there were no unusual markings on this victim's abdomen.

Reinholdt's dissection to free the large intestine was uncharacteristically sloppy, and Blair looked up in surprise. What was wrong with him? Above his surgeon's mask, dark circles ringed his eyes. His ruddy complexion was faded to an ashen hue. He was obviously exhausted, weighed down by heavy stress.

Someone else should be handling this important autopsy. Blair glanced toward the other doctors who were assisting. The man she knew from five years ago was a pathologist, not qualified as a medical examiner. The other was young—too junior to take over.

Though it was the height of presumption for her to interfere, Blair had to relieve Dr. Reinholdt of this burden. He'd never forgive himself if he overlooked a clue because he was too tired to do a proper job.

She cleared her throat. "Dr. Reinholdt, would you mind if I participated in the autopsy? It would mean a lot to me."

Quickly, he stepped back from the stainless steel autopsy table. "Be my guest, Blair."

As she glanced toward the other medical examiner, she saw him nod. She was doing the right thing.

Blair put on a mask and stepped up to the table. Was she ready for this? She hadn't done an autopsy since before her accident. Her gloved fingers grasped the razor-edged scalpel firmly. She focused on the body that lay before her. Basic anatomy. Intestines, bile duct, liver, stomach.

She took a deep breath. "I'll start with the lower gastrointestinal area."

"Yes, Doctor."

"You take the lungs."

"Right."

For a moment she paused. Her wrist trembled, and she was afraid. What if she messed up? What if she couldn't do this work?

Her gaze lifted. Though David had declined the opportunity to join her in the autopsy room, he was here. Standing in the corridor, he watched her through the glass window. His gaze met hers. He smiled and gave her a thumbs-up signal.

He believed in her, and she didn't want to let him down. What was more important, she had something to prove to herself.

WATCHING FROM THE HALLWAY, David worried that Blair was taking on too much. At the same time he was proud of her. If she hadn't been up to her elbows in somebody else's innards, he might have run into the autopsy room and kissed her.

He turned away from the window and saw a familiar figure leaning against the opposite wall. Justin Hunter pushed his glasses up on his nose, straightened the lapels on his sports jacket and sauntered toward David. "Nice to see you again."

It couldn't be a coincidence that he was here, lurking around outside the room where the Fisherman's latest victim was being autopsied. This was the second time he'd shown up for the Fisherman autopsies. In a way,

Hunter's appearance was like returning to the scene of the crime. "What are you doing here?"

"I sell medical supplies." Hunter gestured ingenuously. "This is a medical facility."

Even if Hunter was the Fisherman, David wasn't concerned about safety. Not for Blair or for himself. There were cops all over the Coroner's Office, including a uniformed officer posted outside the door to the autopsy room. "I thought this area was restricted."

"I had an appointment. Besides—" he flashed a twinkly smile "—nobody notices a guy like me. I come and go and do my job and nobody even remembers I was here."

"I doubt that," David said.

"And you'd be right. I make myself known."

His boast could have been directly transcribed from the psychological profile for serial killers' manual. Phony self-deprecation combined with a need to be acknowledged and in control.

Since it might be worrisome for Blair to see Hunter while she had her hands full, David started strolling with him toward the exit. "I saw a friend of yours. Eddy Adderly."

"In Cañon City?"

"That's right." David watched for a reaction. "He mentioned you."

Hunter's chin lifted. His expression was smug, as if he'd done something clever. "How about that! Edward Adderly knows who I am."

"He mentioned that you wanted to sell copies of his Fisherman notes. I don't think that's strictly legal. Eddy's not allowed to profit from his crimes."

"Who said anything about sharing the profit?" Hunter

chuckled. "And it's not like I'd declare the sale of criminal artifacts on my income tax."

"Do you sell other artifacts?"

He stopped walking, leaned toward David and waggled his index finger. "You're trying to trip me up, David. I'm not about to reveal all my secrets to you. You're a reporter, after all."

What secrets? "How are you going to get the acclaim you deserve if nobody knows what you're doing? You don't want to stay anonymous."

"Lots of people know about me," he protested. "That's what my Web site is about."

David pushed a bit harder. "You can tell me your secrets. I'd write about you. Make you famous."

Behind his glasses, his eyes went cold as he considered David's proposition. "Why don't I show you instead?"

"Show me what?" David remembered the souvenirs the Fisherman had taken from his crimes. Bits of jewelry from his victims that had never been recovered.

"Come with me now."

David hesitated. He couldn't leave Blair here alone, but he wanted to see what Hunter was hiding. This might be evidence, might be the key to finally proving a case. If Hunter was the Fisherman…

"I don't live far from here," Hunter said. "Maybe twenty minutes away. In the Washington Park area. By the lake."

His mention of living near water clinched David's decision. "You're on," he said. The autopsy ought to last for another hour. "Let me leave a note for Blair."

He took a pen from the inside of his jacket pocket and scribbled a note on the back of one of his business cards. Quickly he paced down the hall toward the autopsy room and gave it to the cop. "Please give this to Dr. Weston when she's done."

"Who?"

"The lady doctor doing the autopsy. Brown hair. Green eyes."

"The cute one."

"That's the one." David nodded. "Whatever you do, don't let her leave. She's an important witness. Protected. Do you understand?"

"Sure."

David hurried down the corridor toward Justin Hunter. Somewhere in the back of his mind, it occurred to him that it wasn't a very smart idea to go home alone with the man he suspected of being a serial murderer. But David was carrying his gun in his shoulder holster, and he was willing to take the risk. Maybe he was finally going to catch a break.

Chapter Sixteen

By the time Blair completed her portion of the autopsy, she was physically tired. The muscles in her leg were tense from standing so long in one position. Her wrist felt weak. But her heart was soaring. She'd done a good job.

In the hallway outside the autopsy suite, Dr. Reinholdt engulfed her in a huge bear hug. "Thanks, Blair. As soon as I stepped back from the table, I realized how stressed I was."

She ought to be thanking him. His willingness to step aside had given her the last nudge she needed to make her decision. "I want to come back. I want to work for you again. Full-time."

He held her at arm's length and regarded her with glowing paternal pride. "Name the date."

"Two days after the Fisherman is apprehended."

"Done," he said. "I don't need to tell you that my wife will be pleased. With you back here, I can relax, maybe even take a family vacation."

And David? Would he be pleased? Of course, he would be. He was consistently supportive—her best and most handsome cheerleader. She scanned the hallway.

Where had he gone? She couldn't wait to share her happy news with him.

A uniformed cop approached her. "Dr. Weston, your friend left you this note."

She took David's business card and read the scribble on the back: "Be back in a sec. Don't go anywhere alone."

"What's up?" Reinholdt asked.

"Apparently, David got called away." No big deal. "He'll be back."

"He seems like a good man."

"A very good man." Five years ago, when she'd been working with Reinholdt, he'd taken more interest in her dating pattern than her own mother. According to Dr. Reinholdt—who was no Dr. Phil—a doctor was only as good as his or her spouse. "I know you'd approve of him."

"Travels a lot, doesn't he?"

"David is thinking about changing his job focus, maybe going back to sports reporting."

"Excellent choice. You need someone who can be home for dinner more often than not, a shoulder to lean against, a friend. In our business, it's vital not to take your work home with you."

"As if I'd try to sneak out with a spare gall bladder?"

"You know what I mean, Blair."

"It's good advice for you, too. Tonight, promise me that you'll get a good night's sleep."

"Glad you're back on the team." He patted her shoulder. "I'll call with the forensic analysis results."

She waved goodbye and started toward the exit.

The cop who had given her David's card blocked her way. "I'm sorry, ma'am. But you're supposed to wait here."

But she was too excited to stand around and wait for David to return. She needed to move. If not to dance, at least to stretch her legs and breathe fresh air. She smiled up at the cop. ''I won't go far.''

''You're a protected witness.''

Right at the moment, there was nothing to protect her from. The Fisherman had already made his strike. She dodged around the cop. ''I'll be fine.''

Her words echoed ominously inside her head. The last time she'd refused protection was when the Fisherman attacked at the swimming pool in her apartment. But this was different. She wouldn't go far.

Outside the Coroner's Office, a brilliant sunset settled over Denver. Reflected glory streaked the spring skies with magenta and painted the underbellies of clouds with pure Rocky Mountain gold. A balmy breeze kissed her cheeks.

Nothing bad could happen on a day like this. She'd said it before with sarcasm, now she meant it. This was a wonderful, significant day.

She thought back to their near accident on the drive from Colorado Springs. Now might be a good time to call Jake. Reaching into her fanny pack, she took out the tiny cell phone and punched in the main number for the *Denver Post*. Their offices weren't far from here. Maybe she could stop by and talk to Jake personally. Though she didn't usually like to admit she'd been wrong, this was an apology she was looking forward to.

As she strolled on the sidewalk with a steady stream of traffic to her left, Blair felt safe enough. She wasn't being careless. Even if the Fisherman was after her, he was too careful to grab her in front of so many witnesses.

She reached Jake's extension. A woman answered and informed her, "He's not around."

No big surprise. "Do you know where he's staying?"

"I'm not supposed to tell."

That was typical of Jake. He probably had a dozen angry ex-girlfriends after him. "Don't worry," Blair said. "I'm his doctor."

"He's staying with a friend. Ted Hurtado."

Blair thanked her and disconnected the call. She was tickled to think of Jake, trapped in that dark brick house with Ted's nutsy mother. Doris would likely be plying him with burned cookies and asking his advice on fuschia nail polish.

With an impatient sigh, Blair realized that she'd walked as far as the lot where her little Toyota was parked. She looked to the car, then to the street, then to the skies. Where was David? He must have been detained. Surely he wouldn't expect her to wait all night.

Almost before she realized what she was doing, Blair had crossed the asphalt parking lot and slipped behind the steering wheel. She sat with the doors locked. Even after several days and a thorough investigation by the police forensics team, the faint odor of rotting fish lingered.

Now what? Continue to wait? She took out the cell phone and looked at the green screen. There were messages. From David? Though he'd told her how to retrieve them, she didn't remember. If he really needed to reach her, he'd call again.

In the meantime, she started up the car. She could whip over to north Denver, talk to Jake quickly and return to David's town house in half an hour. Shouldn't be a problem.

DAVID CHECKED HIS WRISTWATCH and strode toward the front door of the bungalow house that Justin Hunter shared with a roommate. "Time to go," David said.

"But you haven't seen everything." Hunter pouted like a child, pursing out his lower lip. "I have detailed information on sixteen serial killers, and we only looked at the Fisherman stuff."

And that was plenty. In addition to Hunter's own neatly archived account of the crimes, he had several scrapbooks. One was entirely devoted to Ted Hurtado's columns and the notes he'd received from the Fisherman. The front page of that scrapbook was autographed by Ted himself. Likewise with photographs taken by Jake Zitti, also autographed.

"Before you go," Hunter said. "I don't have all your articles compiled in a special scrapbook because you've written about so many different cases. But I'd like your autograph."

David didn't want to play a part in this gallery of horror. "No autograph."

"Aren't you proud of your work?"

"It's what I do." But there was a difference between researching serial killings and glamorizing them. He no longer wanted to be part of that world. "Crime reporting is what I used to do."

"Please." Hunter held out a plain piece of paper and a heavy silver pen, highly polished.

His ploy was transparent. "As soon as I leave, you're going to lift my fingerprints off the pen. Right?"

Hunter grinned sheepishly. These murders were a game to him, like playing cops and robbers.

"Let's go," David said. "I don't want to keep Blair waiting."

"Fine." Hunter snatched his car keys and walked toward the door. On a small table to the right of the doorway was a black-and-white photograph in a silver heart-shaped frame. He paused to straighten the picture, then to straighten it again. His motion had a compulsive rhythm, like a ritual, and David guessed that Justin always touched that photograph before he went out the door.

"Who's in the picture?" David asked.

"Mama. She was a wonderful woman. Died five years ago."

"At the time of the Fisherman killings?"

"It was about three months before the first victim." He pushed his glasses up on his nose. "This sounds a bit morbid. But I was almost glad when the murders started. It distracted me, you know."

Or was his mother's death a motivation for murder? Though Hunter's obsession with serial murder put him clearly in the category of crackpot, David was careful not to underestimate this skinny, unpresuming guy. He might be the Fisherman. If he'd been distraught at losing his mother, he might have acted out with murder. "We all handle grief differently."

"And you know all about grief, don't you?"

His tone was snotty, childish and angry. Under Hunter's bland exterior, hostility seethed. "What are you implying?"

"Your sister's death really messed you up," Hunter said. "You never got over it. Well, that's okay. I can understand. I still miss Mama. She died suddenly. A heart condition."

"Sorry." If Hunter had said that his mother was murdered, it would have made him the number one suspect on David's list. "Let's go."

"Mustn't be late for Blair." His voice was as sing-song as a playground taunt, but his eyes were cold and ageless. "You don't deserve her, you know."

"Probably not." David walked through the door.

Hunter followed. "She's a genius. Truly brilliant at what she does. Her autopsies are like poetry."

"You think she deserves someone who could appreciate her work?" David hurried down the sidewalk to Hunter's car. "Maybe someone like you?"

As he came around to the driver's side, he raised his eyebrows and sneered. "I'd make sure she was satisfied."

That was an odd way to put it. Was he talking about sex? David's jaw clenched. He'd better not be talking about sex. "Satisfied?"

"Whatever she wanted, I would give to her." He opened his car door. "If Dr. Blair Weston was my responsibility, I wouldn't leave her alone at the Coroner's Office. That's for sure."

He had a point. David felt uncomfortable about taking off and leaving her unprotected. He'd thought a conversation with Hunter might break his investigation open. Wrong again.

Ducking into the car, David fastened his seat belt and asked, "Can I borrow your cell phone again?"

Hunter held it toward him. "I hope you can reach her this time."

Was that a threat? Or was David's imagination working overtime? He punched in the numbers for his own cell phone. *Come on, Blair. Pick up.*

When he heard her voice, he exhaled a sigh of relief. "How are you doing?"

"Great," she said. "Hold on. Let me pull over so I don't crash my car."

She was driving? She'd left the Coroner's Office? Renewed tension tightened his gut. If she'd stayed in the Coroner's Office, she'd be protected by uniformed cops and a metal detector. On the street she was an easy target.

"I'm back," she said.

"Where are you? Why didn't you—"

"Big decision, David. I'm going back to work. Dr. Reinholdt already said I could have my job back."

"Good. Now where—"

"I'm so excited! Tonight we have to celebrate."

"Blair!" He almost shouted. "Where the hell are you?"

"I'll meet you back at the town house. I have one stop to make first. See you in a few."

"No stops," he said. He didn't want her driving all over town, alone and vulnerable. "Listen to me. I want—"

"I'm so grateful to you, David. I never would've gotten my confidence back without you. Bye."

She hung up. Just like that. Had she forgotten that there was a serial killer on her trail? David couldn't believe her indifferent attitude. Independence was one thing. This was insanity.

"Trouble?" Hunter asked.

David shook his head. Now was not the time to start confiding in a suspected serial killer. "I worry too much."

He gave Hunter the directions to his house and settled back in the passenger seat, staring straight ahead, counting the seconds, hoping nothing would go wrong. Over and over, he told himself that she'd be fine. She'd meet him at the town house, and everything would be all right. But somewhere in the back of his mind, David sensed that their investigation had gotten out of control. Events were taking on a momentum of their own, and he was powerless to stop them.

"Well," Hunter said. "Aren't you going to ask me the big question?"

"What question?"

"Who did it? Who is the Fisherman?"

If anybody ought to know, it would be Justin Hunter. He'd studied every aspect of these killings. "Okay," David said. "Who?"

"I wrote the name down on a piece of paper and mailed it to you. My return address is in the corner. You can wait until the police make an arrest and then open it."

"This isn't a magic show." David felt his temperature rising. "Women are dying, being killed by this monster. If you have evidence, you need to tell me. This isn't a game."

"That's where you're wrong." His pointed chin jutted out. "The Fisherman is a master gamesman."

"Do you have evidence? A witness?"

He scowled. "No."

"Is it you, Hunter? Are you the Fisherman?"

"No."

"Then I don't give a damn about your theories."

They rode the rest of the way in silence. David's anxiety level was off the chart. He wanted Blair safely in his arms. Nothing else mattered.

When Hunter pulled up to the curb, David didn't see her car. She wasn't yet here.

He leaped out and slammed the door. "Thanks for the ride."

Hunter drove off without another word. He was an enemy now, and David didn't care. He raced up the sidewalk to his front door, whipped it open and went directly to the keypad to disengage the alarm system.

The house was quiet and dark. Hadn't he turned on the light when he came in? It didn't matter. He reached out and flicked on the small lamp on the side table where his mail was stacked.

On top was a letter from an attorney. David ripped it open and glanced at the thick parchment with letterhead. Kevin MacKay was suing him for assault. Great!

He dug through the pile, looking for the letter from Hunter. Maybe the little creep really did have an insight.

He found it. The address and return address were printed in the same style that the Fisherman used on his notes. Nice touch, Hunter. *You psycho.*

David ripped open the envelope and read the name. ''This is nuts.''

From behind his left shoulder he heard a shuffling sound. In his peripheral vision he caught sight of movement. Nothing definite. More a stirring of air than an actual vision.

Then he felt the blow to the back of his skull. His head exploded. Darkness came fast. He was falling. Going unconscious. *Blair! He had to warn Blair.*

REHEARSING WHAT SHE WOULD SAY to Jake, Blair pressed the buzzer at the front door of the Hurtado house. Though no one appeared immediately, there was the sound of movement. Crazy Doris was in the house.

Blair counted to ten before buzzing again. She also knocked. The heavy door swung inward, framing little Doris Hurtado with her mountain of platinum curls. Her scarlet lipstick was smeared, and one of her false eyelashes hung by a thread.

Blair introduced herself. ''Remember me?''

"The doctor," Doris said delightedly. "Come in, come in."

Blair opened the screen door and stepped inside. The antique-looking parlor was immaculate, and she wondered where Doris spent her time during the day. Surely not in here. There would have been clutter.

Doris straightened her wig. "I haven't been feeling at all well, Doctor."

"I'm sorry to hear that," Blair said.

Her gaze went from the hair to the multicolored, paisley overblouse to the tight red leggings. At her throat, Doris wore a tasteful piece of jewelry. The necklace was so out of character that Blair took a closer look. The pendant was diamonds shaped like the letter *D*.

"My tummy," Doris complained, "is so upset that I can hardly eat. What do you suggest for that?"

Blair knew she'd seen that pendant before. Quickly she searched her memory. A photograph. She remembered the picture of a young woman, David's sister. She'd worn that necklace.

The realization hit like an earthquake. Before Blair's eyes was the first piece of tangible evidence in the Fisherman case. A diamond pendant worn by a dead woman. *D* for Danielle.

Keeping the tension from her voice, Blair said, "That's a beautiful piece of jewelry. Did your son give it to you?"

Doris pointed with her painted fingernails. "I'm sure it's not real diamonds, but it is nice."

"Where did you get it?"

"Oh, dear. Let see." She flounced into the parlor and stood before the huge portrait of her father, lost in thought.

"The necklace?" Blair prompted.

"It was a thank-you gift."

"From Ted?"

"Would you like a drink, dear?" Doris turned to face her again. She was enjoying this cat-and-mouse game. "I was just about to pour myself a jot."

Blair wanted to shake her, to force her to concentrate. "You know, Doris, that necklace might be worth something. If you'd like, I could have it appraised."

"What a wonderful idea!"

When she reached behind her neck and unfastened the chain, Blair was surprised that her ruse had worked so easily. Doris had to be one of the most trusting people on earth.

Holding the pendant, Blair felt her breath quicken. She was certain that this piece of jewelry was a souvenir of the Fisherman. The letter *D* was significant. *D* as in Doris. *D* as in Danielle. "Who did you say gave this to you?"

"It was one of Teddy's friends. I think his name begins with a *J*. But it's not Jonathan."

"Justin," Blair suggested. "Was it Justin Hunter?"

"No, but Justin's a very nice boy. One afternoon he came over with a scrapbook of Teddy's columns." Her eyes widened. "A real fan."

A crazy fan. And a murderer? Blair knew she had to get away from here as quickly as possible. She could feel the presence of the Fisherman emanating from that necklace. She wasn't safe. Not by a long shot.

"It was Jake," Doris said. "The photographer. Jake Zitti. He's staying here, you know. And he gave me this necklace."

It seemed impossible. Jake was the Fisherman.

Chapter Seventeen

Blair's mind whirled faster than a tornado. Could she believe crazy Doris Hurtado? The woman couldn't even keep her wig on straight. How could anything she said be trusted. But what reason would she have to lie?

The traffic light changed, and Blair pulled forward. Though she wanted to race back to David's house and tell him what she'd found, all these cars blocked her way, and she was—above all—a cautious driver.

To think she'd been on her way to apologize to Jake! Maybe she'd been wrong about her memory of what happened five years ago. Or, possibly, the unexpected accident had saved her life. When they went off the road and crashed, Jake's plans might have been interrupted. His original intention might have been to take her to his lair where he would have killed her Fisherman-style.

What lair? Jake was the most footloose person she knew. Occasionally, he had a place of his own, but he was usually in transit, moving from one relationship to another, from one apartment to another.

Was he clever enough to be the Fisherman? The answer, Blair knew, was yes. Though Jake seemed like a dim bulb, he had innate smarts and talent. And charm. He had a way of looking at a woman that made her think she was the only one in the world. It was easy for her to imagine how he'd convinced his victims to come along with him. He seemed funny and willing to please.

Was it all an act? It had to be! Blair had tucked Danielle's necklace into her fanny pack, and that necklace was proof. The letter *D*. She remembered the markings on Pamela Comforti's abdomen. A lopsided circle? It was a *D*. He had branded her with that letter.

But why? Was it a reference to Doris Hurtado? Pamela was the oldest victim, closest in age to Doris. But that didn't make sense. Jake had no special reason to hate Doris, to kill over and over again in her name.

After navigating an eternity of traffic, she finally reached David's town house. Through the settling dusk, she peered at the entryway. The lights were still off. He wasn't home yet.

Dusk had fallen. Streetlights were lit. The path to David's front door was obscured in dangerous shadow. The hairs on the back of her neck prickled. Someone could be watching her. Jake could be watching.

If only David were with her. He wasn't a trained bodyguard, no expert in kung fu. But he made her feel protected—sometimes overprotected. She'd never before had that sense—the feeling that he would sacrifice himself to take care of her.

Chased by invisible phantoms, Blair raced up the sidewalk, turned her key in the lock and darted inside to plug the code into the keypad.

The stillness of his town house settled around her. Something was wrong here. She could feel it.

The overhead light flashed on. She whirled around. It wasn't David who awaited her. "You!"

"I thought you'd never get here."

"How did you get inside?"

"Don't you remember, Blair? I was here when David was punching numbers into the keypad. I memorized the code to deactivate the alarm."

"But the door key?"

"I made a wax copy of your keys. All of your keys."

"When?"

"That lovely night when I turned out the lights and you were swimming in the dark. Your keys were in the pocket of your terry cloth robe."

Ted Hurtado preened. He wasn't dressed in his usual tailored suit. His clothing was slick black leather from head to toe, unlikely to leave fibers for a forensics team to investigate. His hair was covered by a cap. Thin black gloves encased his hands. He held a gun with the barrel aimed at her belly.

"You're the Fisherman," she said.

"Welcome to my world." His smile was predatory and cruel. "Before you do anything trite, like scream for help, you might want to turn around."

Slowly she looked down the hallway. David! He lay motionless on the floor. Blood matted the hair on the back of his head. Instinctively Blair went toward him.

Ted grasped her arm. "Don't touch him. He's still alive."

"What did you do to him?"

"A little tap on the head. And a mild sedative. He'll wake up in an hour or so."

She felt for David's pulse. It was strong. Thank God!

Ted yanked her away from him. "Right now I have no reason to harm David. I knocked him unconscious before he saw me. But I might change my mind if you don't cooperate."

"Damn you!" She clawed toward Ted's face, the only exposed skin. If Blair was to die, she wanted his skin under her fingernails. She wanted the autopsy to show his DNA.

He slapped her hand away with the barrel of the gun. "If you don't do exactly as I say, I'll kill David. A bullet to the brain. Not my style, but I'm capable of improvising."

The fight went out of her. The inside of her head clenched in a tight spasm, and she squeezed her eyes shut. She couldn't pass out. Not now.

When she opened her eyes, the room was distorted. Ted seemed twelve feet tall. The angles tilted, threatening to collapse upon her.

"Breathe," he ordered.

She gasped. If there was any time in her life that Blair needed her wits about her, it was now. Careful not to hyperventilate, she concentrated on regulating her intake of oxygen. She fought the desperate aching inside her skull.

"How…" she asked. "How did you get Jake to give your mother the necklace?"

"What? You were at my house?" His grasp on her arm tightened. "I wish I'd known. You could have saved me a lot of trouble."

"The necklace," she said. "The diamond *D*. Your mother said—"

"Doris is impossible." He released Blair's arm. His gun pointed down at David's head. "I assume you're talking about the *D* for Danielle necklace. No one gave that jewelry to Doris. Certainly not Jake."

"But she said he did."

"Doris has a lot of imaginary boyfriends. Since Jake has been staying at the house, he's her pick of the week." He sneered. "Stupid woman. She must have gone through my things and found the necklace."

The hatred in his voice was palpable. "You want her dead."

"Matricide? I think not. A bit too obvious."

"The marking on Pamela Comforti's abdomen. That was a *D* for Doris. Did you imagine you were killing her?"

"Again and again. But the stubborn old hag still won't die." He nudged David's body with his toe. There was no response. "Your boyfriend isn't much of a fighter. Went down like a sack of potatoes."

Anger rose from Blair's heart, pumping fresh blood through her veins and arteries. Anger gave her strength, cleared her mind. "Leave him alone."

"I warned him. Told him he had no business poking around in the past."

She needed to distract Ted, to pull him away from David. "What do you want from me?"

"Can't you guess? You're my next victim."

From her knowledge of the autopsies, she knew this was the time when he would drug her. Press a cloth saturated with chloroform to her nose. Or plunge a hypodermic into her thigh. She took a backward step. Her balance was unsteady, and she gripped the edge of the side table. Half-opened mail was scattered on the floor.

"Let's go," he said.

"I can't." She tried to buy time. "I'm too weak."

"Don't make me shoot you, Blair."

"Why not? I'm going to die, anyway."

"There are fates worse than death. You remember." His voice turned low and seductive, not at all nervous. He was enjoying this, reveling in the power he held over her. "You remember the pain of your injuries after the accident. The agonizing recovery process. Think of what it would be like if I fired a bullet into your kneecap."

He couldn't have chosen a better threat. Faced with severe injury, she almost preferred the ultimate release of death. "I'll do what you say."

"We'll return to my house. To be exact, the guest apartment behind my mother's hideous dwelling." He gestured with the gun. "Move along. You'll drive. I'll hold the gun."

She had no choice. Head down, she shuffled toward the door.

"Not that way," he snapped. "Through the kitchen. I parked in David's garage."

She should have known. He wouldn't be careless enough to leave his car on the street where a neighbor might notice and remember. Ted had thought of everything. In the garage she slipped behind the wheel of his car and adjusted the seat forward.

First, she'd get far enough away from David that Ted couldn't use him as a threat. Then what? "I'll bet the interior and trunk of this car are full of evidence. Fibers and DNA."

"You'd be wrong," he said. "I'm a very tidy person. After I'm done with you, I'll have the car supercleaned and detailed, inside and out. Twice."

She backed out onto the street. "This isn't your usual plan. Why haven't you sedated me?"

"Because this will be so much more instructive and you have a lot to learn."

"Like what?"

"No doubt, you're thinking that you could pull into traffic and cause an accident. But you won't. You can't. You wouldn't want to risk hurting someone else. And the thought of another accident terrifies you more than anything else."

He knew her weakness. Her greatest fear. She gripped the steering wheel with both hands.

"You'll never forget the crash," he said. "It destroyed your life, disfigured you. If I remember correctly, you were trapped behind the dashboard for almost an hour. The pain must have been incredible."

Her head was throbbing. She could hardly maintain her focus on the road. The taillights of the car in front of her glared like the fierce red eyes of a demon.

Her only chance for escape was to yank the steering wheel and swerve into the car beside her. *Do it!* She could, at least, end his reign of terror.

"By the way," he said. "An accident would be no guarantee that I'd be apprehended. And I promise that you'd be dead."

"How?"

"I'd snap your neck. The injury would be blamed on the accident."

She forced herself to keep driving, to stay within the speed limit, to avoid other cars. There was no escape. Helpless tears streamed down her cheeks. He'd thought of everything.

When they reached his mother's house, Ted directed her into the driveway that stretched toward the back of the house. As soon as she parked, he covered her nose and mouth with a chemical-smelling cloth. The fumes went straight to her brain. Sleep came quickly.

THROUGH A FOG David heard a hammering. Somebody was calling his name. He tried to open his eyelids, but they were too heavy.

Voices echoed in his brain. Someone talking to Blair. David had to get to her.

He dragged himself up. He was on hands and knees.

His body felt disconnected. And his head hurt like hellfire.

"David, open the door! David!"

Stumbling, he managed to disengage the alarm and open the door. Justin Hunter spilled inside. Behind his glasses, his eyes were huge. "Thank God you're alive," he said.

"Blair," David said. His mouth was dry. His tongue weighed at least a pound. "Where is she?"

"He's got her. The Fisherman."

David looked down at the piece of paper scattered amid the mail. The name Hunter had written was Gary O'Hara. Special agent for the FBI. "O'Hara?"

"No. It's Ted Hurtado. I saw him in the car with Blair. He had a gun."

"We need to call the cops," David said. It was a cogent thought. A good sign. He was coming around. "Call the police."

"What if I'm wrong? What if it's Agent O'Hara?"

David staggered toward the door. Whatever he'd been drugged with was going to wear off soon, and he'd be in a world of hurt. Didn't matter. All that was important was Blair. "We have to go to Ted Hurtado's house. You're driving."

Stumbling like a drunk on a bender, David charged into the dusk. The cool air should help to revive him. He was in the passenger seat of Hunter's car. "What were you doing here?"

Hunter started up the car. "I felt bad about the way we parted. You know, David, you really are one of my heroes."

David's attempt at laughter sounded like a garbled wheeze. "Don't try to be like me, kid."

He'd thrown away five years of his life, searching for

a truth that was right in front of his nose. Blair was his truth. His life. His love. If anything happened to her...

"This is all very illogical," Hunter said. "Ted Hurtado is—"

"He's the Fisherman," David said. "Give me your cell phone."

Going through information, David called Adam Briggs on the twenty-four-hour-a-day hotline for CCC. "It's David."

"You sound like hell. What's wrong?"

"He's got Blair."

And David would rescue her. Blair was the woman he loved, and he would not allow the Fisherman to steal his future.

WHEN BLAIR WAKENED, her hands were tied in front of her with a nylon rope. Still fully dressed, she was on the floor in a sterile white bathroom. White tiles on the floor and halfway up the walls. An old-fashioned, claw-foot bathtub. White sink. Her ankles were also tied.

"Oh, goodie," Ted said. "You're awake."

He hadn't bothered to gag her, which meant her screams would probably go unanswered. "Where am I?"

"An apartment on top of the garage behind my mother's house. It's the only place I can get away from her."

The place where you did your killing. Though the inside of her head throbbed, she felt surprisingly alert. Her adrenaline level must be so high that it counteracted the sedative.

He started running the water in the tub.

"Wait," she said. "Aren't you going to feed me? You

gave all the other women Godiva chocolate at least an hour before you drowned them.''

"But that was to teach a lesson to you, Blair. That was to show you that I outsmarted you and your forensic examiner buddies.'' He shrugged. ''Now there isn't much point.''

She didn't want to die. *Keep him talking.* ''The five years. Why did you quit for five years?''

"I quit after Eddy was arrested because his confession was just too perfect. I have no idea how the little sap learned all those details, but I made sure to visit him in jail. Interviews for my column. The kind of thing David does. And I filled in a few blanks for him.''

"But you stopped killing.''

"Did I?'' His eyes were as cold and dangerous as black ice. ''I took some time off to work on my book, and I traveled. It's a big country. There were other executions, other women who disappeared without a trace.''

"Why start the Fisherman killings again?''

"I'm not sure.'' He tilted his head back, considering. ''I started following Pamela Comforti. And you.''

She shuddered and pulled her hands tightly against her body, trying to protect herself. She realized that she was still wearing her fanny pack. The cell phone was inside. And the pepper spray.

"Eddy was in the news again,'' Ted said. ''He was dying. And there were recaps of the Fisherman legend. Maybe I thought I should give them something new to write about.''

"You went back to work at *The Post.*''

He frowned. ''A dead-end job. It's entirely possible that if my book had sold, I would have moved to New York, a nice town for a predator.''

She peeled back the Velcro on her fanny pack slowly. The sound of water running in the tub helped to cover the noise. "The police think you're a copycat."

"And I'll prove them wrong. In the next note to myself, I'll enclose one of my souvenirs from the earlier crimes. Perhaps the necklace from Danielle."

"What about your mother?" Blair slid her fingers inside her fanny pack. "She'd notice the necklace."

"She won't figure it out." He stood, towering over her. "Enough about me. I believe it's time for you to beg for your life."

Blair's fingers closed around the small canister of pepper spray. She held it with the nozzle pointed outward. "I have nothing more to say to you."

"Nothing?" His eyebrows raised. "Not even a curse? Not even something about your darling David?"

When he leaned down to pick her up, she raised her arms. A blast of pepper spray hit the side of his face. He shrieked and backed away from her. "What did you do?"

The bathroom door crashed open. It was David.

His attack on Ted wasn't pretty. He launched himself across the bathroom, shoving Ted into the sink. Still weakened from the drugs, he swung wildly.

But Ted was half-blinded. He reached for his weapon.

"Gun," Blair screamed. "David, he has a gun."

David grabbed Ted's wrist. His grasp was clumsy. With sheer force of strength David slammed him into the white tile wall. Holding Ted by the collar, he swung him around and threw him into the tub. It was full. Water splashed over the sides.

Blair could see what was coming next. David intended to drown the Fisherman.

"No," she shouted. "David, no. Don't kill him."

"He deserves to die."

With one arm, David pushed Ted's face under the water. His arms flailed, but he couldn't get a grip. And David looked down into the distorted face of evil, a predator, a serial murderer. He deserved to be in hell, drowned in the tub he'd used to kill.

But that wasn't David's job. He wasn't an executioner. He pulled Ted up, allowing him a gasp of air.

"Finally," David said, "I know the truth."

Adam Briggs and Justin Hunter came through the door. Adam was armed. He passed a set of handcuffs to Hunter. "Cuff him."

"Me?" Hunter's eyes were shining.

David patted his shoulder. "You're the real hero. If it weren't for you, we wouldn't have gotten here in time."

He went to Blair. Curled on the floor, her frightened gaze locked with his. He cradled her in his arms. "I'm never letting you out of my sight. Never again."

"But I'm safe now."

"The world is a dangerous place." He kissed her forehead. "I don't want you locked away from it. Life is nothing if we don't take chances."

She smiled unsteadily. "Would you untie me now?"

"Not until you give me a promise," he whispered. "Spend every night, forever, in my bed."

Simply, she said, "Yes."

When he held her against his chest, David finally felt a deep, profound sense of peace. She was all he ever wanted. For the rest of his life.

* * *

Don't miss Rocky Mountain Manhunt, out next month.

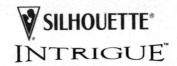

SILHOUETTE®
INTRIGUE™

ROCKY MOUNTAIN MANHUNT
by Cassie Miles

Colorado Crime Consultants

When Kate Carradine woke up with no memories of who or where she was, only one thing was clear: someone was trying to kill her—and she had to go into hiding. Then suddenly, a sexy stranger materialised, offering his protection. But would Liam MacKenzie accept her once she regained her memory, or would he long for the wild woman he'd rescued?

DENIM DETECTIVE by Adrianne Lee
Cowboy Cops

Sheriff Beau Shanahan's life fell apart when his mistrust led to his family's demise. And then his wife returned—with a killer on her trail and the belief that their baby was alive. Would his mistakes cost him the two people he loved the most…again?

OUT FOR JUSTICE by Susan Kearney
Shotgun Sallys

Kelly McGovern suspected the town was covering up her brother's murder, and the one man the townsfolk didn't trust was the only one she wanted watching her back. Between dodging bullets and town interrogations, could she convince dangerous rebel Wade Lansing their attraction needed some private investigation of its own?

THE SEDGWICK CURSE by Shawna Delacorte
Eclipse

Donovan Sedgwick's great-grandfather had loved a woman with an obsession that had left them both dead and their families cursed. Now, a century later, Taylor MacKenzie invaded Donovan's life, questioning the Sedgwick curse and looking too beautiful to resist. When a rash of murders began, it seemed the past was repeating itself. But, this time, were Taylor and Donovan destined to love…or destined to die?

On sale from 16th June 2006

www.silhouette.co.uk

SUSPICIOUS by Heather Graham

When police officer Jesse Crane returned to his Florida
home town, he was shocked to discover a rash of mysterious
killings. Lawyer Lorena Fortier, who was working
undercover at an alligator farm with mysteries of its own,
was the key he needed—and wanted—to solve the case. Her
beauty intrigued him, but mixing business with pleasure was
never a good idea—or so he thought.

ROMANCING THE RENEGADE
by Ingrid Weaver

Payback

Timid bookworm Lydia Smith had no idea she was the
daughter of a legendary gold thief, but sparks flew when
dashing FBI agent Derek Stone recruited her to find a lost
shipment of gold bullion. Together they uncovered her secret
past...and a chance for love worth treasuring.

ONE MAJOR DISTRACTION
by Linda Winstead Jones

When Flynn Benning and his team went undercover in
an all-girls school to crack a robbery and murder case,
he hardly expected to fall for school chef Tess Sanford.
Although Flynn was keen on keeping his relationships
casual, Tess was not a casual kind of woman. But once
Flynn finished his mission, this one major distraction was
sure to change his ways...

On sale from 16th June 2006

*Available at WHSmith, Tesco, ASDA, Borders, Eason,
Sainsbury's and most bookshops*

www.silhouette.co.uk

0606/18a

0606/18b

AKA GODDESS by Evelyn Vaughn

The Grail Keepers

Modern-day grail keeper Maggie Sanger was on a quest, charged with recovering the lost chalices of female power. But when her research was stolen and suspicion fell on her ex-lover, Maggie was challenged to uncover the truth about the legacy that she'd been born into—and the man she once loved.

EMBRACING DARKNESS by Margaret Carter

Until she met Max Tremayne, Linnet Carroll had led an ordinary existence. But Max claimed to be a 500-year-old vampire…and Linnet believed him. Now they needed to join together to hunt down the renegade vampire responsible for the deaths of Max's brother and Linnet's niece. Even if they succeeded, would this mismatched couple ever be able to have a life together?

WILD WOMAN by Lindsay McKenna

Bombshell: Sisters of the Ark

Pilot Jessica Merrill's risk-taking actions had earned her the nickname Wild Woman. Now she'd been charged with retrieving the powerful Native American totem from the madman who would use it to gain immortality. But Jessica's doubtful partner, Mace Phillips, was less enthusiastic about the mission. It was up to her to save the tribe—and show Mace that sometimes you had to take wild chances to get what you wanted…

On sale from 16th June 2006

Available at WHSmith, Tesco, ASDA, Borders, Eason, Sainsbury's and most bookshops

www.silhouette.co.uk

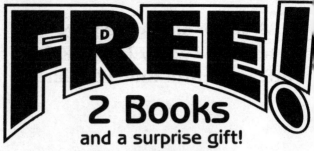

FREE!
2 Books
and a surprise gift!

We would like to take this opportunity to thank you for reading this
Silhouette® book by offering you the chance to take TWO more specially
selected titles from the Intrigue™ series absolutely FREE! We're also making
this offer to introduce you to the benefits of the Reader Service™—

- ★ **FREE home delivery**
- ★ **FREE gifts and competitions**
- ★ **FREE monthly Newsletter**
- ★ **Exclusive Reader Service offers**
- ★ **Books available before they're in the shops**

Accepting these FREE books and gift places you under no obligation to buy
you may cancel at any time, even after receiving your free shipment. Simply
complete your details below and return the entire page to the address below.
You don't even need a stamp!

YES! Please send me 2 free Intrigue books and a surprise gift. I understand
that unless you hear from me, I will receive 4 superb new titles every
month for just £3.10 each, postage and packing free. I am under no obligation
to purchase any books and may cancel my subscription at any time. The free
books and gift will be mine to keep in any case.

16ZE

Ms/Mrs/Miss/Mr ....Initials....................................
BLOCK CAPITALS PLEASE

Surname..

Address...

....Postcode ....

Send this whole page to:
UK: FREEPOST CN81, Croydon, CR9 3WZ

Sterling Seagrave grew up on the China-Burma border. For many years an investigative journalist in Asia, he is the author of *Yellow Rain*, *Soldiers of Fortune*, *The Marcos Dynasty*, *Dragon Lady*, the bestselling *The Soong Dynasty* and *Lords of the Rim*. He and his co-author Peggy Seagrave live in Europe.

International acclaim for *The Yamato Dynasty*:

'The Seagraves have discovered one of the biggest secrets of the 20th century'
Iris Chang, author of *The Rape of Nanking*

'[A] remarkable and disturbing book . . . A story of deception, corruption and political chicanery that would test a political thriller writer'
Martin Booth, author of *The Dragon Syndicates*

'[*The Yamato Dynasty*] unveils some of the most enduring secrets of the war in the Pacific . . . with a reality that is both shocking and absorbing for the reader' *Business Age*

'An incisive biography . . . contains all the elements of a political thriller: family squabbles, power struggles, duplicity and murder. It involves a huge pile of treasure – bullion worth billions stashed all over the world – and secret operations to retrieve it. And best of all, it's all true'
The South China Morning Post, Hong Kong

'I urge you to read this enthralling/gripping book'
Nouvel Observateur, Paris

'*The Yamato Dynasty* reveals a bewildering game of deception and long hidden war secrets . . . Finally the terrible truth is coming to the surface'
De Telegraff, Holland

'A provocative, thrilling and exciting book'
Der Tagesspiegel, Berlin

'A deeply disturbing chronicle of pervasive corruption and greed, of unspeakable violence visited upon people, values, and the truth' *Kirkus Reviews*

'Drawing on recently discovered sources, including imperial diaries, longtime Asian expert Sterling Seagrave (*The Soong Dynasty*) and his wife and collaborator, Peggy, connect, in this penetrating yet remorselessly bleak account, the personal histories of Japan's emperors, their wives and other members of the imperial family through five generations (from 1868 – the year of the Meiji Restoration – to the present) to Japan's political and economic culture. The authors contend that the imperial system, with all its isolation and mystification, was a veil behind which plutocrats and militarists have always exerted unobtrusive control over Japanese society. Even today, they argue, Japan is a "one-class dictatorship by a financial elite evolved from the clan lords of previous centuries" who "rule by manipulation, intimidation and corruption". The Seagraves extensively study the long reign of Emperor Hirohito assigning him and other members of the imperial family a measure of guilt for Japan's military aggression, wartime atrocities and looting of stupendous wealth from all corners of Asia. They criticize US officials, especially MacArthur, for orchestrating a postwar exorcism by which only a handful of Japanese war criminals were punished, while Hirohito and his family were restored to power without having to account for their wartime depredations . . . This book dramatically brings the imperial family – and those behind it – to life, offering readers an intriguing glimpse behind the long-maintained veil of secrecy' *Publishers Weekly*

Also by Sterling Seagrave

THE MARCOS DYNASTY
THE SOONG DYNASTY
YELLOW RAIN
SOLDIERS OF FORTUNE
LORDS OF THE RIM

With Peggy Seagrave

DRAGON LADY

THE
YAMATO
DYNASTY
THE SECRET HISTORY OF JAPAN'S IMPERIAL FAMILY

Sterling Seagrave

and

Peggy Seagrave

CORGI BOOKS

THE YAMATO DYNASTY
A CORGI BOOK : 0 552 14709 5

Originally published in Great Britain by Bantam Press,
a division of Transworld Publishers

PRINTING HISTORY
Bantam Press edition published 1999
Corgi edition published 2000

1 3 5 7 9 10 8 6 4 2

Set in 11/12pt Sabon by
Phoenix Typesetting, Ilkley, West Yorkshire.

Corgi Books are published by Transworld Publishers,
61–63 Uxbridge Road, London W5 5SA,
a division of The Random House Group Ltd,
in Australia by Random House Australia (Pty) Ltd,
20 Alfred Street, Milsons Point, Sydney, NSW 2061, Australia,
in New Zealand by Random House New Zealand Ltd,
18 Poland Road, Glenfield, Auckland 10, New Zealand
and in South Africa by Random House (Pty) Ltd,
Endulini, 5a Jubilee Road, Parktown 2193, South Africa.

Printed and bound in Great Britain by
Cox & Wyman Ltd, Reading, Berkshire.

To Elizabeth and John Murray

CONTENTS

LIST OF ILLUSTRATIONS

Second plate section

Shogun meets Emperor, Hirohito and MacArthur (*Popperfoto*)
General Bonner Fellers (*UPI/Corbis*)
Emperor Hirohito planting rice (*Hulton Getty*)
General Tojo (*Popperfoto*)
Premier Konoe (*Keystone/Sygma*)
President Herbert Hoover arrives in Japan (*UPI/Corbis*)
Joseph and Alice Grew (*UPI/Corbis*)
The financier Thomas Lamont (*UPI/Corbis*)
Kishi Nobusuke (*Associated Press*)
Prime Minister Hatoyama (*Popperfoto*)
Tanaka Kakuei (*Camera Press*)
Takeshita Noboru (*Associated Press*)
The imperial family of Emperor Hirohito, 1947 (*Hulton Getty*)
The imperial family in 1972 (*Hulton Getty*)
Crown Prince Akihito (*Hulton Getty*)
Akihito as a student (*Hulton Getty*)
Elizabeth Gray Vining (*UPI/Corbis*)
Emperor Hirohito meets the British royal family (*Hulton Getty*)
Emperor Akihito and Empress Michiko meet the British prime
    minister
    (*PA Photos*)
Crown Prince Naruhito with the Princess of Wales (*PA Photos*)
Emperor Hirohito and Mickey Mouse (*Popperfoto*)

CAST OF MAIN CHARACTERS

Japanese nomenclature is used throughout – family name first, personal name last.

Akihito, Emperor. Current emperor, 125th of the dynasty. Son of Hirohito and Empress Nagako.

Asaka Yasuhiko, Prince. Uncle of Emperor Hirohito, married one of the Meiji emperor's four daughters. Ordered Rape of Nanking, but never prosecuted.

Chichibu, Prince. Most dynamic son of Emperor Taisho and Empress Sadako. Brother of Emperor Hirohito, Prince Takamatsu and Prince Mikasa.

Fellers, General Bonner. MacArthur's aide, lifelong agent of Herbert Hoover. Suborned Japanese war crimes witnesses to exonerate Emperor Hirohito.

Grew, Joseph. Longtime US ambassador to Japan, pawn of Herbert Hoover. Aligned to ultra-right American and Japanese big money.

Haruko, Empress. Wife of Meiji emperor and adoptive mother of Meiji's son, Emperor Taisho. Japan's first popular, modern empress.

Higashikuni, Prince. Playboy uncle of Emperor Hirohito, married one of Meiji emperor's four daughters. Prime minister at the end of World War II.

Hirohito, Emperor. Controversial 124th emperor of the dynasty, son of Emperor Taisho and Empress Sadako. Reigned from 1926 to 1989.

Hoover, Herbert. Former US president. Worked secretly with Fellers, Grew and others to rescue Hirohito and make Japan an ally against communism.

Ito Hirobumi. Brilliant impresario, Japan's greatest man 1880–1910. Wrote Meiji constitution, created democratic image, but undercut by Yamagata.

Kido Takayoshi. 'The Pen'. Great hero of the Meiji Restoration. An idealist and romantic, he tried to humanize the emperor.

Kishi Nobusuke, Prime Minister. Canny manipulator, backed army–gangster alliance, dodged war guilt, helped create the postwar LDP bribery machine.

Kodama Yoshio. Underworld godfather, wartime admiral, war criminal. Looted conquered countries, financed the LDP, then hired by the CIA.

Konoe, Prince. Brilliant but erratic leader, tried repeatedly to stop the war, then alienated MacArthur's men. Was probably murdered to silence him.

Lamont, Thomas. Headed Morgan Bank, backed huge loans to Japan in 1920s and 1930s, setting stage for postwar alliance of US–Japanese big money.

MacArthur, General Douglas. US Pacific commander, headed occupation of Japan. Fired by President Truman in 1951 for insubordination in Korean War.

Michiko, Empress. Daughter of a wealthy businessman, wife of Emperor Akihito, mother of Crown Prince Naruhito, and a target of endless backbiting.

Mikasa, Prince. Scholar son of Emperor Taisho, youngest brother of Hirohito, the only imperial prince to speak out against Japanese war atrocities.

12

Mutsuhito, Emperor. Meiji emperor, 122nd of the dynasty, son of murdered Emperor Komei. Ito's drinking companion, no taste for power or majesty.

Nagako, Empress. Wife of Hirohito, mother of Akihito. Her marriage was engineered to free the imperial family from the clutches of General Yamagata.

Naruhito, Crown Prince. Son of Akihito, married attractive Owada Masako, but remained childless after six years. Not highly regarded by younger Japanese.

Okubo Toshimichi. 'The Despot'. A Meiji Restoration hero, with Saigo and Kido. A devious tyrant. Undercut his rivals, and was brutally murdered.

Sadako, Empress. Wife of Taisho, mother of Hirohito, perhaps a Christian. Invisible to the outside world, she exerted great influence for half a century.

Saigo Takamori. 'The Sword'. Military hero of the Meiji Restoration. Undercut by court intrigues and died magnificently leading a samurai uprising.

Takamatsu, Prince. Brother of Hirohito. Convinced by 1942 that Japan would lose the war, worked secretly for peace and pressed Hirohito to abdicate.

Takeda Tsuneyoshi, Prince. Cousin of Hirohito, grandson of Meiji. A financial wizard, oversaw the collection and hiding of Japan's war loot.

Tanaka Kakuei, Prime Minister. Scandal-ridden master of LDP money-politics. Found new ways to corrupt Japan's postwar bureaucracy.

Terasaki Hidenari. Western-educated diplomat and pacifist, tried to stop Pearl Harbor attack. Later served as key liaison between Hirohito and MacArthur.

Vining, Elizabeth Gray. American Quaker tutor to Crown Prince Akihito. Provided many intimate insights into life in the imperial palace.

Yamagata Aritomo. Japan's most powerful military man, 1880 to 1920, turned the country into a police state. Emperor Meiji was frightened of him.

Yoshihito, Emperor. The Taisho emperor, 123rd of the dynasty, son of Meiji by a court lady. Yamagata portrayed him as a drunken buffoon. It was not true.

THE DOOR TO HEAVEN

The Yamato Dynasty is the first collective biography of the Japanese imperial family, both men and women, covering five generations since the Meiji Restoration in the nineteenth century. When we asked a Japan scholar what he would like to see in our book, he said, 'Everything! It has never been done.' Well, maybe not everything.

Most books focus on Hirohito and whether he was responsible for the Pacific War, with only passing reference to his empress, his brothers and others. Ours is an effort to portray them all, their personalities, aspirations, disabilities, achievements, failures and fateful relationships, as monarchs of a very different nation that has risen, fallen and risen again to exceptional world power. It is the first biography to benefit from the recent discovery in a warehouse of the diaries of Hirohito's brother, Prince Takamatsu, totalling eight volumes in their first Japanese edition. And from the publication of a memoir by Princess Chichibu, wife of another brother who was regarded as an alternative emperor, and who led a secret life during World War II that we reveal for the first time. Fragments of Hirohito's diaries have also surfaced, but the Imperial Household has tried to suppress them. Wherever possible, we use Japanese sources and authorities.

15

Clustering this material produces interesting discoveries. Previously, historians neglected the princesses, so until now we have been unaware of a discreet network of Christians around the throne – centred on Hirohito's mother, Empress Sadako – and the pivotal role they played in rescuing the imperial family from prosecution for war crimes after World War II. This discovery leads to others.

Though no single book could be a complete and comprehensive history of Japan or of its imperial family, *The Yamato Dynasty* reflects what we found intriguing during the decades when six of our books were being published in Japan, and one evolved into a major kabuki theatre production. The name Yamato comes from a river valley near Kyoto where the imperial house was first established after moving up from Kyushu in prehistoric times. This epoch was called the Yamato Chotei. Japanese sometimes call themselves the Yamato people. Traditionally, they hold that a single dynasty has 'reigned unbroken since time immemorial' – tracing the family lineage back to the Yamato Chotei, before which there is only legend. So we have chosen to call them the Yamato dynasty. They are the world's longest-reigning dynasty. The dynasty may have reigned but it rarely ruled, so we devote equal attention to the strongmen in the shadows behind the throne, and promise a few disturbing surprises. The main entrance to the Kyoto palace is called the Door to Heaven – the first of many deceptions.

Sterling and Peggy Seagrave, 1999

ACKNOWLEDGEMENTS

We have been investigating the hidden face of Japan, and the role of Japan in East Asia, for forty years, so it would be impossible to acknowledge all the help we have received. Many of our Japanese sources sensibly prefer to remain anonymous. But for the biographical side of this volume, we are especially indebted to Jim Raper, Robert Curtis, Dr Joan Pengilly, Laurie Saurborn, Elizabeth Murray, Deborah Marquardt, Hamish Todd and Norman Haynes. But the way we have presented the material and the conclusions we have drawn are the responsibility of the authors alone.

Mariko Terasaki Miller was remarkably generous in helping us understand the role her father played as liaison between Emperor Hirohito and General MacArthur, spending a week with us in Europe. The late Nancy Gillespie of Washington, DC, helped with the personal papers of her father, General Bonner Fellers. Bruce Merkle of Vienna, Virginia, who was General Fellers's secretary and confidant, kindly provided insights, documents and tape recordings.

John Easterbrook unearthed many unpublished papers for us at the Hoover Library in California, while Jim Raper made groundbreaking discoveries at the

MacArthur Library in Norfolk, Virginia, and fitted many pieces together. Laurie Saurborn spent months combing through the Joseph Grew papers at Harvard.

Dr Joan Pengilly juggled a dozen archival projects at once in the US.

This is the fourth book Elizabeth Murray has helped us with, in England, and it is to her and her husband that this edition is dedicated. At the British Library Oriental and India Office Collections curator Hamish Todd kept the Japanese identities straight, and guided us through the genealogical maze. His computerized database on the genealogy of the imperial family is outstanding.

Sam Garchik helped with Japanese hospital ships and naval details.

Medical help on meningitis and brain lesions came from Dr David Alleva in San Diego, California, and from France's brilliant Dr Charles Fattal. Dr Lionel Gania helped us bridge the medical gap from French to English.

At French archives we wish to thank Luis Amigues, Directeur des Archives, Ministère des Affaires Étrangères; Colonel Pierre Jacob, Adjoint au Secrétaire Général, Le Saint Cyrienne; Jean-Pierre Defrance, Conservateur, Chef de la Mission des Archives Nationales, Ministère de l'Intérieur, Paris; Paule Rene-Bazin, Conservateur Général Chargée de la Section du XXe Siècle, Archives Nationales; and Colonel Andre Bach, Chef du Service Historique de l'Armée de Terre. Special thanks to Joel Legendre for many clarifications.

We are indebted to Thomas D. Hamm, archivist and Associate Professor of History at Earlham College, and to archivists at Hoover Presidential Library, MacArthur Library, the Harvard East Asian Institute, Sidwell Friends Alumni Office, the British Library, Imperial War Museum, the London Library, the London University

Library and the School of Oriental and African Studies.

In many ways our greatest debt is to our literary agent Marcy Posner at the William Morris Agency in New York, who supported this project vigorously from the outset. On that score thanks are due to Michelle Lapautre, Peter Fritz, Stephanie Cabot, Eugenie Furniss, Gerald Trageiser, Christiane Schmidt and Simon Thorogood, and to Ursula Mackenzie, our publisher, whose first-hand knowledge of East Asia has been crucial.

HOKKAIDO

Sea of Japan

HONSHU

● Nagano

Kanto Plain
Tokyo
Yokohama

Oki-Shoto ○

Kyoto
Osaka Nara
Tsushima
Hagi Hiroshima YAMATO ● Grand shrine
CHOSHU of Ise
Nabeshima Kochi
SHIKOKU
Nagasaki
SATSUMA *Pacific Ocean*
Kagoshima KYUSHU

J A P A N
Home Islands

KEY	
··············	The Japanese Empire in 1931
— — —	Farthest extent of Japanese expansion, 1942–1943
████	Post-surrender limits of the Japanese state, 1945

JAPAN AND
SURROUNDING COUNTRIES
*Showing extent of Japanese occupation
during the Second World War*

EMPRESS EISHO ~ **EMPEROR KOMEI** > LADY NAKAYAMA YOSHIKO
(1833 – 1897)   (1831 – 1867)   Official Concubine

LADY YANAGIWARA NARUKO < **MUTSUHITO** ~ EMPRESS HARUKO > LADY SONO SACHIKO
Official Concubine   **EMPEROR MEIJI**   (1850 – 1914)   Official Concubine
(1855 – 1943)   (1852 – 1912)   (1867 – 1947)

YOSHIHITO ~ EMPRESS SADAKO   Princess Masako ~ Prince Takeda
EMPEROR TAISHO | (1884 – 1951)   (1888 – 1940)   Tsunehisa
(1879 – 1926) | (1882 – 1919)

HIROHITO ~ EMPRESS   Prince Chichibu ~ Princess Chichibu   Prince Takamatsu ~ Princess Takamatsu
EMPEROR SHOWA | NAGAKO   (1902 – 1953)   (1909 – 1995)   (1905 – 1987)   (1911 –)
(1901 – 1989) | (1903 –)   no issue   no issue

AKIHITO ~ EMPRESS   Princess Shigeko ~ Prince Higashikuni   Princess   Princess Kazuko ~ Takatsukasa
EMPEROR HEISEI | MICHIKO   (1925 – 1961)   Motohiro   Sachiko   (1929 – 1989)   Toshimichi
(1933 –) | (1934 –)   issue   (1916 – 1969)   (1927 – 1928)   no issue   (1923 – 1966)

CROWN PRINCE ~ CROWN PRINCESS MASAKO   Prince Akishino ~ Princess Akishino   Princess Nori
NARUHITO | (1963 –)   (1966 –)   (1966 –)   (1969 –)
(1960 –) | no issue by 2000   single in 1999

Princess Mako   Princess Kako
(1991 –)   (1994 –)

Princess Fusako ∼ Prince Kitashirakawa
(1890 – 1974)   Naruhisa
issue   (1887 – 1923)

Princess Nobuko ∼ Prince Asaka
(1891 – 1933)   Yasuhiko
         (1887 – 1981)

Princess Toshiko ∼ Prince Higashikuni
(1896 – 1978)   Naruhiko
         (1887 – 1990)

Prince Mikasa ∼ Princess Mikasa
(1915 –)   (1923 –)
       issue

Prince Takeda
Tsuneyoshi
(1909 – 1992)

Prince Asaka
Takahito
(1912 – 1994)

Prince Higashikuni
Motohiro
(1916 – 1969)

Princess Atsuko ∼ Ikeda Takamasa
(1931 –)   (1926 –)
no issue

Prince Hitachi ∼ Princess Hitachi
(1935 –)   (1940 –)
       no issue

Princess Takako ∼ Shimazu Hisanaga
(1939 –)   (1934 –)
issue

THE   YAMATO   DYNASTY
The Japanese imperial family,
1831 to present day

PROLOGUE

EMPEROR MEETS SHOGUN

Just before 10 a.m. on 27 September 1945, a maroon
1930 Rolls-Royce with a canvas-covered top whispered
out through the Sakurada Gate of the imperial palace in
Tokyo and crossed the bridge over its broad moat,
followed by three black Daimlers. Japanese pedestrians
knew who it was, turned and bowed deeply. Maroon
was a colour reserved for the emperor's cars. Emperor
Hirohito was on his way to a fateful first meeting with
Japan's new shogun, General Douglas MacArthur.
Sitting on jump seats in the Rolls facing Hirohito – by
custom no subordinate could share the emperor's seat –
were his most senior adviser, Marquis Kido, and a
trusted English-language interpreter. In the Daimlers
were other members of Hirohito's inner council. The
emperor's personal physician accompanied him wherever he went, but on this occasion he had a particular
reason: Hirohito was suffering deep depression made
worse by jaundice. Since Japan's surrender the previous
month, the emperor had slept badly, and today in particular his hands trembled more than usual.

How different from four years earlier, when he had
shaken with rage. Then, in September 1941, three
months before Pearl Harbor, the emperor had been given

a detailed briefing on the High Command's plans for a surprise attack on the United States Navy base and a coordinated lightning conquest of Southeast Asia. Hirohito had asked the army chief of staff, General Sugiyama, how long it would take. Circumspectly, the general had replied that the conquest of Southeast Asia would take only three months. (It took precisely one week longer than that.) But he did not give an estimate for the subduing of America. Testily, Hirohito pointed out that when the war with China had begun in 1937, General Sugiyama had said it would be over in a month, yet it had dragged on for four years and was far from over in the autumn of 1941. Sugiyama protested that China was vast. This increased Hirohito's anger. 'If you call the Chinese hinterland vast, would you not describe the Pacific as even more immense?' The general squirmed with embarrassment, and sucked his breath in sharply. Hirohito was calmed only by repeated assurances that a diplomatic settlement with America would get first priority after Japan got the upper hand. In this, his ministers lied, for both the Imperial Army and Navy by then were committed to total war, with no serious intention of quitting while they were ahead. Only a major last-minute concession from America such as dropping its oil embargo of Japan could have altered events, and everyone knew this was unlikely. A formal declaration of war had been prepared long in advance, with the understanding that, 'due to a most unfortunate last-minute delay in the English translation', it would not be delivered in Washington until after the attack on Pearl Harbor had already begun.

The mood in all four cars was sombre. What could be seen of Tokyo made it worse. The Navy Ministry was nothing but rubble. Bomb craters and bombed-out cars

26

were everywhere. During the Pacific War, 1.5 million Japanese men died in combat. Some 8 million Japanese civilians were killed or wounded, and 2.5 million homes in Japan were destroyed or badly damaged. During the biggest of these B-29 raids on Japan, when 1,700 tons of incendiary bombs were dropped on Tokyo, 100,000 people were killed in a single day and 125,000 homes destroyed. Although the war was now over, it was estimated that 10 million Japanese might yet starve to death. The population of Tokyo had fallen from 6.75 million to about 3 million, many living in shanties among the ruins. Osaka and other cities were teeming with disabled veterans, homeless children, desperate women and vagrants. In Tokyo each day, trucks hauled piles of bodies to crematoriums. At night, the homeless crowded into subways to sleep. Others froze to death sleeping rough in Ueno Park. Many died of malnutrition, and tuberculosis was epidemic.

As the cars sped towards the US embassy compound, there was no military police escort to halt traffic. To put his visitor at a further disadvantage, MacArthur had deliberately avoided assigning an escort to the motorcade. When the traffic light at Toranomon intersection turned red, cross traffic made it necessary for the emperor's Rolls to come to a stop like all the other cars. Nobody in the Daimlers could remember that ever happening before.

MacArthur had been in Japan only a month. He had arrived at Atsugi Air Base from the Philippines at the end of August, two weeks after Japan's surrender. By then, only 6,000 American troops had arrived to take control of the Tokyo area, where there were still some 2 million fully armed Japanese soldiers. The emperor's radio appeal to all Japanese to lay down their arms had been effective. But there was no certainty that fighting would not flare up again. Bluff was all important. More so than anyone realized.

During those first weeks in Japan, MacArthur had been pressed repeatedly to summon the emperor to a private meeting, to resolve certain delicate matters, but MacArthur chose to wait. Conservative policy-makers in Washington, including former president Herbert Hoover, had come to the conclusion that it was crucial for America's future security interests in East Asia to get the behind-the-scenes cooperation of the imperial family, and of powerful financial leaders in Japan – but not to be seen in public as making any concessions to Hirohito, whose image in the West was as bad as that of General Tojo Hideki, Japan's wartime prime minister. Together, Tojo and Hirohito were widely seen as the driving forces behind the war. Hirohito's name came at or near the top of all lists of prospective war criminals who were to be tried by Allied military tribunals. Through intermediaries, MacArthur let it be known that the emperor must take the initiative, and ask for a meeting with him. Secret negotiations went on through MacArthur's military secretary and former chief of psychological warfare, Brigadier General Bonner Fellers, who had unusual private channels in Japan.

Persuaded by his own family and advisers that such a meeting would be critical to the preservation of the dynasty, Hirohito responded by arranging through Foreign Minister Yoshida to see MacArthur on 27 September. Because of the sensitive nature of the meeting, it would take place privately in the general's living quarters at the embassy, rather than at occupation headquarters in the old Dai Ichi Life building opposite the imperial palace.

Despite the unusual secrecy that still surrounds this meeting, both in America and Japan, the superficial details are well known. After passing the Okura Museum, the motorcade turned into the embassy gate and rolled up the drive to the ambassador's residence, where MacArthur was living with his wife and son. General Fellers, waiting with other US Army officers at the entrance portico, stepped out to meet the Rolls as it came to a halt. As Hirohito and Marquis Kido emerged, the Americans saw with some amusement that the emperor had abandoned his customary military uniform and was dressed in 1930s diplomatic attire, with a formal black tail-coat, wing-collar, striped cravat and striped trousers. He was carrying a silk top hat, which he now put squarely on his head, as coached by his chamberlains. At five feet three inches, Hirohito looked small and frail next to the Americans. His moustache and wire-rimmed glasses did nothing to disguise his fragility. He seemed bewildered and tense. General Fellers saluted, then, to put the emperor at ease, smiled warmly and reached out to shake his hand, saying, 'Welcome, sir!' Hirohito responded uncertainly by putting out his own hand, an uncharacteristic gesture that would have astonished most Japanese. Not even his most senior adviser, Marquis Kido, ever shook the emperor's hand. As Fellers guided the emperor into the building, Kido tried to stay with them but another American officer politely but firmly asked the marquis to step to one side. Only Hirohito's interpreter was allowed to follow. The rest of the emperor's entourage was herded with Kido into a conference room for their own discussions with Fellers and others.

While waiting for the motorcade to arrive, General MacArthur had been moving furniture nervously a few inches this way and that in the deeply carpeted reception room. In front of a fireplace, he put a side chair next to a big chesterfield where he planned to sit with the emperor. This side chair, MacArthur explained to his personal physician, Dr Roger Egeberg, was there in case the emperor brought along an interpreter, to give him time to think before answering questions. The emperor would not really need an interpreter, MacArthur explained, because as a young man he had gone to school in America and spoke good English. (This amazing remark, recorded at the time by Dr Egeberg, reveals how little MacArthur really knew about the emperor of Japan, his enemy for the past four years; he may have been thinking of Hirohito's younger brother, Prince Chichibu, who had studied in Britain and spoke elegant English.)

When word came that Hirohito had arrived, MacArthur stepped to the door to greet him, calling him 'Your Majesty' and giving him an unsmiling but business-like handshake. In contrast to the emperor's formal attire, the general had deliberately chosen to wear khaki 'suntans' with no hat, no ribbons or insignia of rank, and his collar open wide. A well-briefed US Army photographer was waiting and, as agreed in advance, took three official photos of the general and the emperor. Hirohito stood stiffly at attention, face frozen, arms rigid at his sides, while MacArthur towered over him, at ease, legs apart, arms akimbo and hands jauntily on his hips. This was one of MacArthur's favourite poses. He was a theatrical man who had staged dramatic publicity photographs throughout the war, repeatedly wading ashore at island after island while his favourite photographer took dozens of exposures to get the effect just right.

As they were shown to their seats before the fire,

Hirohito chose to sit alone in the side chair, so the general ended up on the chesterfield with the interpreter. This annoyed MacArthur and he badly wanted to smoke, so he leaned forward to offer the emperor an American cigarette. Although Hirohito did not smoke, he was so determined to be positive that he accepted anyway, his hand trembling as the general lit it. He smoked the entire cigarette, without inhaling, while MacArthur puffed at his corncob pipe, and this gave both men a chance to gather their thoughts. A Japanese servant brought coffee rather than the traditional pot of very hot green tea, but the emperor did not touch it. There was speculation later that he was warned to consume nothing for fear of poison, but it is more likely that he was simply too tense to pick up a cup.

MacArthur, who was then 65, opened the conversation by remarking that he had been received by Hirohito's father in 1906, at the close of the Russo-Japanese War. During the forty-minute conversation, the emperor's interpreter made selective notes. His job was to see that whatever the emperor said on the spur of the moment was put so skilfully in English that no nuance could be misconstrued, and conformed with policy decisions made at the palace before the meeting. One copy of his notes later went to the Ministry of Foreign Affairs, and another into the emperor's personal files. Although MacArthur and Hirohito had agreed that their talk would be kept absolutely secret, years later in his memoirs MacArthur quoted the emperor as saying: 'I bear sole responsibility for whatever happened, for whatever incidents occurred in conjunction with Japan's prosecution of the war. Furthermore, I bear direct and sole responsibility for every action taken in Japan's name by every commander, every soldier, and every politician.

As for my own life, whatever judgment you choose to make, it does not matter to me. I bear sole responsibility.' MacArthur grandly concluded that the emperor's willingness to assume responsibility for everything that had gone wrong made him unquestionably 'the first gentleman of Japan'. In December 1975, a Japanese magazine published what it said were the interpreter's notes. The two versions did not agree. The interpreter's notes made no mention of Hirohito offering to take 'sole responsibility'. The Japanese people would have liked very much for Hirohito to take some responsibility for the war, and were deeply disappointed when he did not. It is unlikely that a statement of such historic significance would be left out of the written record. Exactly what Hirohito said to MacArthur remains a mystery, unless we believe the general's memory. Given his confusion about Hirohito going to school in America, that is risky. But, as we will see, this was not the only time MacArthur (and others) put words in Hirohito's mouth.

Ten minutes after their meeting was supposed to end, MacArthur and the emperor came out with happy looks on their faces. The general was introduced to the emperor's aides and then escorted Hirohito to his car. On his way back to the palace, the emperor seemed relieved and talked much more than usual. He slept better as well. He was certain now that he could escape arrest or prosecution for war crimes.

What was it that put smiles on their faces so soon after a war without mercy, and the horrors of Hiroshima and Nagasaki?

Two people who eavesdropped on the meeting were the general's wife Jean and Dr Egeberg, who – with MacArthur's full knowledge – hid behind the red velvet drapes in the reception hall, but later claimed that they only overheard an occasional phrase.

We can eavesdrop in a different way. To read the bare details recounted so far is to see this great turning point with only one eye, in flat two dimensions. We can now open the other eye, for today we know what else was going on. It is a surprising and deeply disturbing story.

The general's chief concern that day, quite naturally, was to ensure his own public success as America's proconsul in Japan, which he hoped would lead to his being chosen by the Republican Party as its candidate for president in the 1948 elections. Becoming president of the United States had obsessed MacArthur since the early 1930s, and had shaped many of his actions.

Liberal Washington policy-makers, particularly New Deal Democrats, wanted to alter the postwar power structure of Japan permanently to make it more democratic. MacArthur was a reactionary conservative, not a liberal by any measure, yet he had to appear to be carrying out Washington's orders. He and his inner circle of advisers, including Herbert Hoover, concluded that his success in occupied Japan would depend upon manipulating Hirohito. The way he went about this would have to be kept absolutely secret because of the methods to be used and the trade-offs involved. He would have to frighten the emperor with the threat of being indicted, prosecuted and hanged (or shot), and then offer to protect him in exchange for his secret collusion. Using carrot and stick, and outright extortion, he would induce Hirohito to give them inside knowledge of Japan's financial cliques and other vital power relationships, so that key people could be put under pressure, deals could be made and Japan's postwar power structure

33

could be rearranged to suit MacArthur's conservative political and financial backers, rather than American liberals.

During those first weeks after the surrender, great effort already was being made to distance the emperor from direct responsibility, for Pearl Harbor in particular, shifting the blame entirely to General Tojo. This had been decided in secret talks between conservative American and Japanese envoys in Switzerland, long before the war ended. To rescue Hirohito, everyone would have to be persuaded that the emperor was 'a captive of Tojo and the militarists' who were 'exclusively responsible for the war'.

In keeping with this strategy, two days before seeing MacArthur, Hirohito said in written replies to questions from a *New York Times* correspondent that Tojo was responsible for the government's failure to communicate Japan's declaration of war to Washington prior to the Pearl Harbor attack. This was untrue; the delay was a ruse they had all agreed upon in September, long in advance of the attack.

At no time during the remaining forty-four years of his life did Hirohito ever publicly accept personal responsibility for the war, whether for starting it (which angered Americans) or for losing it (which angered Japanese). Marquis Kido became so distressed by Hirohito's refusal to accept responsibility that he privately advised the emperor to abdicate rather than disgrace his ancestors. Hirohito grieved over the tragedy that had befallen his country, but felt no responsibility whatever for the failure of his military commanders, who had assured him of victory repeatedly only to let him down. Although the ultimate decision to continue the war for two more years remained with Hirohito, he saw it as their failure, not his.

34

The rescue of Hirohito would have to be drawn out over several years. If he was exonerated too quickly, he could slip off the hook. Whenever he became obstinate, evasive or hesitant, MacArthur would frighten him with word of new demands for his prosecution, from Congress, from the Allies or – most dreaded of all – from the Kremlin. To be sure, this extortion would have to be carried out with great tact and subtlety. But MacArthur had long experience of being vague and oblique.

Indeed, as they left the embassy in the Rolls, Hirohito told Marquis Kido that MacArthur had said: 'I believe Your Majesty knows about the people and important men in the [Japanese] political world, so from now on, I would like to have your advice on various matters.'

In what follows, we will unfold new evidence of the massive fraud that ensued, who was involved, and how major witnesses including General Tojo himself were suborned by MacArthur's staff and forced to falsify their testimony and perjure themselves before the international war crimes tribunal. At least one general was hanged for a crime at which he was not even present, forced to take the fall to protect Hirohito's uncle Prince Asaka, the butcher of Nanking, who escaped punishment of any kind. But it did not stop there. Soon matters got completely out of hand.

Mistakenly, MacArthur and his inner circle thought it was enough to take the emperor himself hostage. They got it wrong. Real power in Japan remained in the shadows. He could squeeze the emperor like a lemon till his pips squeaked, but the real power-brokers felt no pain. They watched from the wings and from backstage, and figured out what MacArthur was really after. The secret exorcism of Hirohito involved a lot of horse trading, which was skilfully used by Japanese negotiators. Once they had participated with MacArthur and his aides in perjuring witnesses to rescue the emperor, they could pressure MacArthur repeatedly for the rescue of others. This led first to the exoneration of the whole imperial family, then to that of the entire financial and industrial elite of Japan (a group that had been the Allies' explicit target for purge and prosecution). All the big Japanese banks and *zaibatsu* financial cliques that had bankrolled the war were originally to be dissolved, but were let off. They were excused from paying war reparations on the argument that Japan was 'bankrupt'. While Germany paid some £30 billion in compensation and reparations over the years, Japan paid only £2 billion. Even today, Germany continues this programme of compensation and reparations, but Japan dug in its heels and said it was all settled in 1951. Instead of encouraging the democratization of Japan and the growth of alternative political parties, MacArthur thwarted opposition groups, clamped down on postwar labour unrest and jailed any and all demonstrators. Next came freedom for all the indicted war criminals locked up in Sugamo Prison, including underworld figures who had participated in the looting of billions of dollars in treasure from a dozen conquered countries. Finally, there was exoneration for all the 220,000 people who were initially blacklisted by America for their roles in the war. It may not have been MacArthur's original intention to let all these people off, but once the emperor's advisers realized what the general wanted, it was a simple matter to take advantage, patiently, step by step. Extortion can work both ways.

Most Japanese learned about the private meeting between the emperor and the general only when MacArthur insisted on publication of the photo in every major newspaper in Japan. This caused an uproar because it made the formally attired emperor look absurdly subordinate to the rudely casual American. Previously only carefully vetted photographers had been able to take pictures of the emperor, using a telephoto lens from a distance, showing only the upper part of his body and never showing him in relation to others. Many Japanese still believed that if they looked directly into the emperor's face they would be blinded. The photograph of Hirohito with MacArthur was a masterful political stroke, of a sort. But it backfired when MacArthur's efforts to manipulate Hirohito were turned to Japan's advantage.

When the transition government in Tokyo objected to the publication of the photo, MacArthur flexed his muscles by repealing all of Japan's restrictions on publishing. This was followed by a directive on civil liberties that effectively outlawed all of Japan's secret police and internal security organs. Prince Higashikuni, another uncle of the emperor, resigned his post as head of the transition government in protest. MacArthur did this to show what he *could* do when provoked. The last thing he wanted was to open the way for genuine civil liberties, which would invite political change in Japan. That would be entirely too radical. From his point of view, anyone who was not ultra-right was a communist.

We can only guess at what repercussions there might have been in Japan, America and Europe if the real nature of the secret meeting with Hirohito had become known to the general public.

It is a cliché that in Asia things are rarely what they seem. Nobody puts more effort into deception than the Japanese. So it is hardly surprising that MacArthur and his staff thought they were doing the manipulating while they were being manipulated. Their mistake arose from being fascinated by the similarities between Japan and the West, when they should have focused on the differences. The differences were dangerous. The similarities were disarming, reassuring and seductive. Take, for example, the Quaker network in Japan. It comes as a surprise that Quakers, despite their small number, are sprinkled throughout Japanese society, and have remarkable leverage.

Let us begin with General Bonner Fellers. He was not just the greeter in the embassy portico. Fellers was an unusual army officer with interesting connections. Through his family he had ties to a Japanese diplomat, Terasaki Hidenari, who was riding in one of the black Daimlers in Hirohito's motorcade on that day. Both Fellers and Terasaki were intelligence officers. 'Terry' Terasaki had held the senior post of first secretary at the Japanese Embassy in Washington at the time of Pearl Harbor. He and his American wife and daughter were interned, swapped for other diplomats, then spent the war years miserably in Japan. Now Terasaki had been transferred to the Imperial Household organization, which took care of all practical matters for the emperor and the imperial family. Essentially, his job was to act as Hirohito's personal liaison with General Fellers and General MacArthur.

Terry was perfect for the job. He loved America and knew it well. Bonner Fellers was a cousin of Terry's American wife, Gwen Harold, who came from a long line of Quakers. Bonner Fellers had attended a Quaker college in Indiana, where he became friends with Japanese Quaker exchange students. Two of these, Watanabe Yuri and Kawaii Michiko, became leading educators in Japan and had palace connections. In postwar Tokyo they were helping Fellers carry out his secret mission. In short, Fellers and Terasaki were part of a network of Quakers and near-Quakers that reached from Herbert Hoover at one end deep into the imperial palace at the other, to the personal entourage of Hirohito's mother, Dowager Empress Sadako, and other members of the imperial family. A number of Japanese men in the ruling hierarchy, who were themselves Buddhist or Shinto, had Christian wives. So the inner core of an aggressively warlike Buddhist–Shinto state, in the volatile 1920s, 1930s and 1940s, had a nucleus of Christians, many of them Quaker pacifists. They influenced England and America greatly between the wars. They did not have enough power to prevent the war, but they tried to stop it. Some of these palace officials used their links to Swiss, British and American Quakers to send secret peace feelers to London and Washington by way of Switzerland. After the war, they intervened in every way they could to save the imperial family from humiliation and prosecution as war criminals. While this may seem commendable in some respects, it had a dark side. The same network was used very cynically by Bonner Fellers and others to achieve MacArthur's personal objectives, and those of his conservative backers.

On the Allied side, this quasi-Christian network was a cat's cradle of powerful connections. One of its leaders was US Undersecretary of State Joseph Grew, the prewar US ambassador to Japan. Grew had longstanding ties to General Fellers and to former president Herbert Hoover. Grew's wife, Alice Perry Grew, was a descendant of Commodore Matthew Perry, who had opened Japan to Western commerce in the nineteenth century. As a child, Alice attended school in Tokyo, became fluent in Japanese and was intimate friends with aristocratic Japanese girls, one of whom grew up to become

Hirohito's mother. So Alice and Joseph Grew had unique access to aristocratic circles in Japan. One of Grew's cousins, Jane Norton Grew, was married to Jack Morgan, son of J. Pierpont Morgan, whose banking empire was known in Japan as 'the Morgan *zaibatsu*'. Morgan Bank made huge loans to Japan in the 1920s and 1930s, and helped many big American corporations like General Electric to make major investments there. So Grew, part of the extended Morgan family, also enjoyed a very cosy reception in the Japanese financial world. While he served as US ambassador to Japan in the 1930s, Grew associated with Japanese men and women who were reassuringly like the Boston Brahmins of his own childhood. With so many Quakers and other Christians among them, Grew felt he was dealing with the Asian equivalent of New England Puritans. The Japan he saw was neat and tidy, freshly scrubbed. The Japanese financial elite he met were so crisp, elegant and beautifully mannered that he failed to see – or chose not to see – the profound institutional corruption that was deeply embedded in the Japanese system (and remains embedded to this day).

At the centre of the Yamato dynasty during the first half of the twentieth century was Empress Sadako, Hirohito's mother. A tiny woman of great character, she was an invisible force in imperial affairs from the 1910s to her death in the early 1950s. In a matrilineal society like Japan, an emperor's mother had leverage that can never be overestimated. Although she was a Fujiwara, one of the top families that provided brides for emperors over many centuries, Sadako had been raised in the countryside by Japanese Quakers. She was said to read the Bible every day, and there are strong indications that she was a practising Christian, although the Imperial

Household kept this carefully obscure. For thirty years, the dowager empress surrounded herself with Japanese Quakers and other Christians, men and women, adding them to her retinue and discreetly arranging for them to be appointed to senior posts in the Imperial Household and in the government bureaucracy. That there were a surprising number of Christians like Sadako in the upper strata of society does not, however, alter the fact that they were first of all Japanese, with overriding loyalties to their own society.

This was largely a network of mothers, wives, sisters and daughters, unnoticed by Japanese men, committed to altruistic values and to pacifism at a time when Japan was becoming increasingly violent and militaristic. That this secret network was composed largely of women is not surprising. In ancient times Japan was often ruled by women.

Historically, the Yamato dynasty was founded in the first century AD by a 'witch' named Himiko, a priestess with unusual powers who had her court in the Yamato river valley near what is today Kyoto. Chinese court records from that period state clearly that Japan was ruled by women at the time. Himiko was thought to be descended from a line of priests and priestesses going back some six hundred years. Those earlier prehistoric roots of the dynasty were in the warm southern island of Kyushu. It was there, according to legend, that the sun goddess Amaterasu first created the imperial line that has led 'unbroken' down 2,500 years to Emperor Akihito and Crown Prince Naruhito.

The Yamato people ruled by Himiko were not the earliest known inhabitants of Japan. Those were the more primitive Ainu, whose origins are still unknown. The Yamato people were more recent arrivals.

Immigrants from China first brought wet rice culti-vation to the lowlands of Kyushu, then more warlike immigrants from Korea settled along the mountainous north shore. Over several centuries of conflict these two immigrant cultures mingled, and their most powerful clans sorted out a feudal pecking order. In search of better farm land they gradually migrated eastwards up the Inland Sea to the big fertile plain around what are now Kyoto and Osaka on the main island of Honshu, pushing back the Ainu and taking over their land. There, by the Yamato river, the dynasty coalesced in the first century around Himiko, the leader of the strongest clan.

Himiko was succeeded by a line of emperors who also served as high priests of Shinto – 'the way of the gods'. But women continued to have strong influence, some-times ruling alone, sometimes acting as regents for young emperors or as marital pawns in power struggles. This ended in the twelfth century when a military dictatorship was set up by the shoguns, or generalissimos, of rival samurai clans. The imperial family then went into a long eclipse.

The survival of the Yamato dynasty was often in jeop-ardy. The gravest challenges came from the emperor's own relatives, who found ways to gain control of the throne and turn the emperor into a puppet. For most of its history, as a consequence, Japan's imperial family has had more spiritual influence than temporal power. At times emperors even were reduced to selling noodles in the street. Many were packed off to Buddhist mon-asteries, others were exiled to remote islands, while several were simply murdered.

Powerless as they often were, emperors provided supernatural cover for the tyranny of invisible men behind the throne. No group portrait of Japan's imperial family can begin without quickly sketching these other faces in the background. From the time of Himiko to the Meiji Restoration in 1868, five families gained extraordinary power over the throne: the Soga, Fujiwara, Minamoto, Ashikaga and Tokugawa families. The Soga and Fujiwara were wealthy noble families who married their daughters to emperors and then ruled indirectly as regents for the offspring, generation after generation. They hired samurai mercenaries to protect their interests, and these mercenary armies gradually grew into powerful military establishments. The other three families – Minamoto, Ashikaga and Tokugawa – were samurai warrior clans who set themselves up as dictators starting in the twelfth century, and ruled Japan for the next 800 years, usually treating the imperial family with contempt or ignoring it entirely. Shoguns were subject to the same kind of manipulation. Typically, the first one or two shoguns in each epoch were shrewd, tough men who ruled by violence and treachery, but they were succeeded by weaklings who were manipulated by their own regents, wives and advisers.

The Soga family in the fifth century were the first in Japan to perfect the technique of using the emperor as a front man, deflecting attention from themselves so they could operate in complete secrecy. For three centuries the Soga fended off all rivals, then were toppled and exterminated by the Fujiwara. Although the style of the Fujiwara was different, they used the same Soga devices to stay in control. To hide their manipulation, corruption and murder, it was essential to preserve the imperial family as a cosmetic device. As Sons of Heaven, emperors could be seen as pure and sacred. Nobody dared to criticize an emperor because to do so would be a sacrilege, punishable by beheading. For the same reason, nobody dared to criticize the emperor's advisers. This allowed the men behind the throne to be as corrupt as they wanted, without fear of being challenged or overthrown. Danger usually came only from palace rivals, who tried to gain the upper hand by conspiracy, by bribery or poison, or by putting their own daughters in the imperial bedchamber.

The Fujiwara used every means available to destroy initiative on the part of each new emperor, so that a passive state of mind became inbred over the centuries. It was extraordinarily cunning to put the emperor in a position to enjoy all the benefits of authority with few of the responsibilities. To resist would require unusual moral courage. Few had it. Most emperors were awash in luxury, with hundreds of sexual companions, and all the food, drink and entertainment they could consume. Emperors continued to have tremendous inferential power, but they rarely sought to use it without clearing their actions in advance with whoever happened to be the current strongman.

For the better part of those eight centuries under the shoguns, most Japanese were unaware that emperors still existed, and only a small circle of court nobles continued to regard them as divine. When the shoguns were toppled in the Meiji Restoration of 1868, Japan's new strongmen gained control of the current Son of Heaven, a boy of 15, and announced that the whole country had 'submitted to rule by the divine emperor'. This was sheer bluff. Even today, there are huge credibility gaps in Japan. If there were a Japanese version of the fable *The Emperor's New Clothes,* the tailor would be executed for exposing the truth, the little child for speaking the truth and the peasantry for seeing the truth.

The Meiji Restoration of 1868 was not a revolution. Japan has yet to experience a true social revolution, although one may be about to begin. During the Meiji coup, real power simply was transferred from one ruthless backstage clique to another, and the boy emperor was moved from Kyoto to the shogun's palace in Tokyo. They made sure that the emperor appeared to rule, but he was only decoration. Just as with the Soga and Fujiwara, real power remains to this day in the hands of invisible men behind the throne, heading rival power cliques.

No other royal family is so guarded. Seclusion is imperative because the imperial family is – in a certain sense – held hostage by the cliques that actually rule Japan. Who controls and manipulates the emperor controls and manipulates the people. This isolation prevents rival forces from taking similar advantage.

The emperor has magical, supernatural influence as a divine icon – he is 'above the clouds'. Because he is a demigod, he cannot be criticized. By extension this applies to his advisers and his government, so they too are protected. For most of Japan's history, lese-majesty has been punished by beheading. Even constructive criticism was impossible. The sacred hid the profane.

From time to time, liberals or other 'deviants' have tried to separate the emperor from the strongmen, so that the government could be criticized without implying criticism of the emperor. But the Meiji strategists who designed the modern Japanese system anticipated this, and skilfully identified the emperor with every decision and every aspect of the regime. It was a Meiji Restoration, a Meiji government, the imperial will, an imperial decree, the imperial army, a decision of the throne, 'a dynasty unbroken since time immemorial'.

Because of this mystification, only Hirohito became well known outside Japan. Very little is known of his father and mother, his brothers and uncles, or any other members of the family. Now, thanks to the gradual accumulation of scholarship, plus the recent discovery and publication of family diaries, it is possible to fit many tiny pixels together into a collective portrait of all five generations – four emperors and a crown prince – in the modern period.

Even the Meiji emperor remains obscure, his real personality hidden by image-building. In public he was an operatic figure. In private he was completely different, an indolent and self-indulgent man who loved women, horses and flowers, and drinking the night away with his favourites. Keeping him under control was difficult. Because Meiji was so troublesome, his ministers decided to take a different approach with his children and grandchildren. Great effort was put into making them compliant, completely dependent upon their privy councillors and chamberlains. The Imperial Household staff grew to number more than ten thousand.

They failed in the raising of Meiji's son and heir, the Taisho emperor. Most historians write Taisho off as a misbegotten clown not deserving serious consideration. They say he was mentally unbalanced and a drunken womanizer. When Taisho is compared to his father, 'the great Meiji emperor', he is always found wanting. But these are false comparisons, because the father's image was as grossly inflated as the son's image is cruelly diminished. On closer study, Taisho turns out to be refreshingly different. The caricature of him as a lunatic libertine was largely the invention of General Yamagata, who turned Japan into a secret police state and launched it on its binge of militarism. Yamagata glorified the throne, while diminishing the emperor. By calculated leaks to the press, he destroyed the reputation of the young emperor, and was stopped only by the steadfast counter-attack of Empress Sadako and her allies. Moving behind the scenes, she was able to humiliate the old general in a contest over the choice of a bride for Crown Prince Hirohito. Yamagata was trying to plant his own female agent in the palace bedchamber. When he failed, the general went into terminal decline. But his ruthless, cold-blooded style poisoned Japan for the rest of the twentieth century.

By the 1920s, the imperial myth had become dogma. Thought police were at every level of society to inform on neighbours and family. It could cost your life to raise an eyebrow, and all critics of the regime were jailed or executed under harsh new laws. In this atmosphere of terror – Asian in style but reminiscent of Europe's Inquisition – the militarists emerged and were able to take control of Japan in partnership with big business and financial cliques.

Hirohito was raised to be different from his grand-father and his father. To avoid the indolence of Meiji and the audacity of Taisho, the Imperial Household oversupervised Hirohito, giving him a lifelong dependence on advisers and complicating the process of decision-making. This had tragic consequences in World War II when Hirohito waited interminably for Japan to regain the upper hand, so he could sue for peace from a position of advantage. His reign was the longest in Japan's history, and the most controversial.

Emperor Akihito's resistance to similar manipulation led him to marry outside the aristocracy, and to identify more with the Japanese people. Crown Prince Naruhito has continued this refreshing trend, bringing into the palace as his bride the most independent princess since Sadako.

They have their enemies. Japanese conservatives block and frustrate both Empress Michiko and Crown Princess Masako, to keep them from developing the leverage wielded by Hirohito's mother. Both women have been the target of vicious backbiting. While it may still be dangerous to criticize the emperor, it is open season on the empress and crown princess.

Recent scandals reveal that money – not Shinto – is the state religion of Japan. Because greed is so fundamental a religion, we will examine how it replaced politics as the main motive force behind the Meiji Restoration, and how greed steered the ship of state into secret alliances, war and disaster. In the 1920s, the promising Anglo-Japanese diplomatic alliance was replaced by a vast web of private financial alliances between America and Japan. On the advice of Morgan Bank's Thomas Lamont, America made huge private loans and investments. When the economic bubble burst – first in Japan and then on Wall Street in 1929 – it became apparent that much of this prosperity was built on unsecured sweetheart deals. In America, this resulted in major reforms of the banking and financial sectors, and radical social programmes to help the common man. None of this happened in Japan, where all energy and resources went into rescuing the financial elite from their own folly. Nothing was done to ease the desperation of the people, and hundreds of thousands of girls were sold into prostitution by families unable to feed themselves. Instead of reforming the system, Japan's power cliques arrested and executed critics and reformers. Today, seventy years later, the same financial corruption has brought Japan to its worst economic crisis yet.

During World War II, Japan's militarism became a heady mixture of glory and greed as the army and navy embarked upon a binge of conquest and looting, from which Tokyo could not extricate itself. We know a lot about the conquest, but amazingly little about the looting. In the Japanese holocaust, millions were killed and billions were stolen, but the loot vanished. One of the great mysteries of World War II is what happened to the billions of dollars' worth of treasure confiscated by the Japanese Army from a dozen conquered countries. The answer involves the imperial family, so it is an essential part of this biography.

Recognizing after the Battle of Midway in June 1942 that the war was going badly, a number of imperial princes devoted the rest of the war to hiding the loot ingeniously to give Japan a hedge against disaster. This systematic campaign of looting and hiding treasure, codenamed Golden Lily, was under the direct supervision of Hirohito's brother Prince Chichibu. Until now, he was assumed to have spent the war on medical leave from the army, recuperating from tuberculosis at a country estate beneath Mount Fuji, nursed by his wife. In fact, he travelled all over occupied China and Southeast Asia supervising the collection of plunder, using hospital ships to carry much of it to Manila for onward shipment to Japan. From early 1943 till mid-1945 he was in the Philippines overseeing the hiding of this loot in bunkers, in vaults beneath old Spanish churches and in vast underground tunnel complexes. Golden Lily stripped Asia of currency, gold, platinum, silver, gems, jewellery, art treasures and religious artefacts, including more than a dozen solid gold Buddhas, each weighing more than a ton. According to Japanese who participated, some $100 billion worth of gold and gems was hidden at more than two hundred sites in the Philippines when it became physically impossible to move the loot to Japan. We have corroborated accounts from eyewitnesses and participants, including Japanese, and members of Prince Chichibu's personal retinue.

Faced with Allied invasion of the Home Islands, and the total destruction of Japan's heritage, Emperor Hirohito was finally persuaded to opt for a quick surrender. This was a bitter pill, but it allowed Japan to survive the war with the bulk of its assets intact, including many billions of dollars of loot that would help put the nation back on its feet. Since the war, the gold hidden in a number of sites in the Philippines has been recovered by teams from Japan and other countries, and these recoveries have been verified. A Swiss court disclosed in 1997 that one of the solid gold Buddhas is now in a bank vault beneath Zürich's Kloten Airport, along with a large quantity of other gold bullion recovered by former Philippine president Ferdinand Marcos and held in Marcos family accounts. In 1997, a Japanese investigative team from Asahi Television was taken to an underground vault in Luzon where they filmed (and took core samples of) 1,800 gold bars worth $150 million – gold that was stolen from Sumatra, Cambodia and Burma. This gold had been melted down in occupied Malaya, recast and marked in accordance with the accounting procedures of Golden Lily, and then sent to Manila on fake Japanese hospital ships. Treasure looted from China was taken to Japan by way of Korea and hidden in underground vaults in the mountains near Nagano, the site of the 1998 Winter Olympics. Gold bullion aboard ships at the time of surrender in 1945 was sunk in Tokyo Bay and other points along the coast, and some of it has since been recovered.

Thanks to Prince Chichibu and Golden Lily, when the US occupation ended in 1952 'bankrupt' Japan was able to begin a 'miraculous' recovery, on its way to becoming the world's second-richest economy. War reparations were dodged, the imperial family evaded punishment, and Japan's financial elite resumed control as if the war had not occurred. Claims that Japan and its imperial family were left virtually penniless by the war would therefore appear to be completely false. War loot also provided a huge pool of black money used by postwar politicians to corrupt Japan's bureaucracy, bringing the country full circle again at the millennium to the verge of economic collapse.

Although there have been many investigations of Nazi war loot, there has never been a formal investigation of the looting of Asia by the Japanese, nor has Japan ever been forced to account for the plunder. The amounts involved dwarf the Nazi looting many times over. The truth about Japan's looting of Asia puts a completely different spin on history.

Emperor Akihito, who was only a child during the war, has begun the process of putting the imperial family in tune with the people of Japan rather than with the power elite. He has effectively cut the umbilical to heaven. But he and his family are still hostages to the myth contrived during the Meiji Restoration long ago. Today, instead of being manipulated by Meiji oligarchs, or Hirohito militarists, the imperial family is window-dressing for financial manipulators who milk Japan like a cash cow.

There is a glass ceiling separating 90 per cent of the population from the elite and their militant disciples. The long-suffering Japanese people have now discovered that even their meritocracy has been corrupted. There are signs that the long-awaited social revolution has begun. Ordinary people are voting with their money by not spending it. Rather than keeping it in Japanese banks, they are investing it abroad. Like a huge supertanker, however, the ship of state will take a long time to slow and turn around.

So this is a double-image, this family portrait, of those on the throne and significant others looming behind it. What was true under the Soga and Fujiwara remains true today – real power in Tokyo is in the hands of secretive financial cliques, bureaucratic factions, political king-makers and outlaws whose roles are little known and poorly understood. They remain hidden because they have learned that 'all trouble comes from the mouth' and 'when you cease being invisible, you take the first step towards defeat'.

The public role of the imperial family is like a kabuki troupe. Their highly stylized drama unfolds with magnificently costumed and masked players moving around a curious figure draped from head to toe in black. This dark figure, while clearly observed by everyone, is never acknowledged by actors or audience. By tradition he is totally invisible, and therefore does not exist. He is the stage manager, moving the scenery and furniture, altering the set as the drama goes on around him. He is called the *kuromaku*, the man behind the black veil, and he goes back long before kabuki to the ancient puppet theatre of Japan, where audiences could clearly see the puppetmaster and his assistants. Japan's imperial family is comprehensible only if we understand the part played by the *kuromaku*. Life at the top in Tokyo involves many veiled players. The emperor and his family are surrounded by them.

CHAPTER 1

REINVENTING THE EMPEROR

The future Meiji emperor was only eight months old in July 1853 when four large, black-hulled American Navy ships appeared off the entrance to what is now called Tokyo Bay. Two of the heavily gunned warships were steam-powered, spewing smoke and terrifying on-lookers. Commanding the squadron was Commodore Matthew Perry, carrying a letter to the Tokugawa shogun from the president of the United States asking Japan to establish commercial and diplomatic relations. For centuries, Japan had been closed to foreigners. Past shoguns had distrusted Western traders and regarded Christian missionaries as subversives who encouraged opposition to the military regime. All Westerners were expelled except a few merchants restricted to a man-made island in the port of Nagasaki. Contact with the outside world became illegal, and Western ships were turned away from Japanese harbours. Commodore Perry refused to be diverted, however, and demanded that the president's letter be accepted by an official representative of the shogun. After six days of tense confrontation, the Japanese complied and Perry delivered his letter, adding that he expected a positive answer the coming year, when he would return with a larger squadron. To drive his point home he steamed his black ships directly across the bay towards the shogun's capital. Expecting bombardment, people panicked. Savouring the moment, Perry turned and sailed away.

In his wake he left Japan in crisis, climaxing fifteen years later with the overthrow of the shogun, the restoration of an ancient monarchy after eight centuries in eclipse, and a teenage Meiji emperor on the throne. The Meiji Restoration was followed by other dramatic changes, and in only a few decades Japan was transformed into a world power, today the second biggest economic force on the planet. But in Japan things are rarely what they seem – powerful mythology hides what is really going on. After making a great public display of restoring the emperor to power, the new state obliged the emperor and the imperial family to resume their deep seclusion, hidden by a screen of ritual, protocol and mystification. As one of Meiji's grandsons exclaimed, they are like 'caged birds'. Japan might be liberated from centuries of feudal samurai dictatorship, and be thoroughly modern in most other respects, but the Sons of Heaven, and heaven's daughters, remain hostages of the past.

Keeping hostages for long periods is a venerable tradition in Asia. What better than to hold the gods themselves captive. This is not just a turn of phrase. For eight centuries Japan's emperors were kept hostage by military regimes, and defiant emperors were roughly treated. Plots to capture the emperor were central to the overthrow of the shogun in 1868. Once young Meiji was on the throne, he remained in effect a political prisoner to prevent any countercoup by rival forces. And for other important reasons.

On the surface Japan seems to be a passive society

devoted to loyalty and consensus. But underneath it is a power country. Treachery, so common throughout its history, made loyalty admired precisely because it is so rare and beautiful. Consensus is idealized, because everyone cheats or colludes behind the scenes. In such a corrupt situation, an icon of divine purity is handy to solve power struggles. As the Son of Heaven, directly descended from mythic gods, and as chief priest and embodiment of all supernatural qualities in the national religion, Shinto, the emperor provides that divine icon. In the past, Japanese strongmen who held the emperor hostage claimed that they derived their office from the throne (meaning from the gods). Anyone who challenged their rule was not only treasonous but blasphemous, deserving terrible punishment. Out of this grew a mythic tradition and a double standard that keep most Japanese submissive and silent even today.

Given the fact that they were gods, it is astonishing how badly the Yamato emperors have been treated over the centuries. While some lived in perfumed silks, others were betrayed, poisoned, dethroned, exiled or driven to suicide. Those who cooperated were surrounded by chamberlains and court ladies who often were snoops and spies for the real strongmen. Under those conditions, being a god was far more dangerous than being ordinary. As gods, emperors were magical, but in reality they were powerless because all real power was held by regents or shoguns. Nothing has changed today.

As a child, Meiji's future was highly uncertain. He was not the son of an empress, but of Emperor Komei's favourite concubine, Nakayama Yoshiko, daughter of a court noble. He was born on 3 November 1852, at his mother's childhood home, one of many noble mansions built around the edge of the imperial palace grounds in

Kyoto. As a precaution, the baby was given his first bath in the Well of Divine Help. They called him Sachi no Miya – Miya being one of three words for prince. In 1860, when he was eight years old, he was adopted by the empress as the formal heir, and given the name Mutsuhito Shinno (Prince Mutsuhito). Meiji was a formal reign title chosen later when he became emperor. (Because it is confusing to call one emperor by his reign title (Meiji) and another by his given name (Hirohito), we will use given names for our main characters where possible, reserving reign titles for certain purposes.)

Of Emperor Komei's six children – two boys and four girls – Mutsuhito was the only one to survive beyond the age of four. Infant mortality ran high in the nobility after centuries of inbreeding for strategic marriages and political liaisons. Because the aristocracy isolated itself from ordinary people, it developed little natural resistance to infections or endemic diseases like meningitis. Komei himself was one of fifteen children, but only three reached maturity.

In a highly competitive court, infanticide was also a danger, so during his first five years Prince Mutsuhito was separated from his parents and sheltered from intrigue at the home of his maternal grandfather, Lord Nakayama. Two wet nurses were with him around the clock as imperial infants were fed every two hours day and night. In 1854, when Mutsuhito was two years old, the Kyoto imperial palace burned down, so the emperor came to live for a while at the Nakayama mansion and grew fond of his son.

Physically delicate and rather effeminate, like a tender asparagus shoot, Mutsuhito was a headstrong child who would fly into tantrums, break his toys and hit his noble playmates, who were forbidden to retaliate. Little

Japanese boys are rarely disciplined. Mutsuhito's tantrums continued even as a grown man. To strengthen the toddler, Lord Nakayama gave him a wooden horse and a bamboo sword, and encouraged him to play samurai. From this the boy developed a love of horses and swords, not as weapons but as playthings and treasures. Strenuous exercise gave him a hearty appetite and a robust appearance, although he was never really robust. From Lord Nakayama's diary we know he hovered over his grandson, worrying about every bruise. At age five the crown prince was taken back to the rebuilt palace, to live in a new pavilion with white walls and a black tile roof overlooking a pond full of carp and gardens of evergreens, weeping plum and black-stemmed bamboo. There his father gave him lessons in poetry while scholars tutored him in a range of subjects. History and geography were his favourites. Many of his questions concerned the foreigners who were appearing in Japan in increasing numbers since the arrival of Perry's black ships. He saw them in the streets of Kyoto on those rare occasions when he was allowed out of the palace to see the changing autumn leaves or the spring clouds of cherry blossoms. These excursions were made in a black lacquered cart, a black box on wheels drawn by two carefully washed white bullocks. In the wagon, the crown prince was shielded from view by roll-down bamboo shades, through which he peered with great excitement.

In the palace, Mutsuhito was surrounded by nearly three hundred women. They controlled who saw him, what he could do and not do, what he wore, what he ate and when he went to bed. These ladies-in-waiting were chosen from families of nobles when they were young girls, and most spent their entire lives in the palace.

Parents were eager to volunteer their daughters because having a family member in the emperor's inner apartments gave them influence at court. All spoke an archaic form of Japanese called *gosho kotoba* or palace language, incomprehensible to most Japanese. A rigid pecking order gave great power to court ladies of higher rank. They could keep an emperor isolated, to the fury of his ministers. Among them over the centuries were individuals of extraordinary intellect and talent, such as Lady Murasaki in the eleventh century, who wrote a masterpiece, *The Tale of Genji*. But there were also many who were ignorant, or conspiratorial. It was their responsibility to serve or amuse the emperor and make certain he had plenty of heirs, if the empress failed to oblige. Mutsuhito's mother was a court lady fortunate enough to become an imperial concubine. These women had their own intelligence network reaching all corners of Japan, so it was often from them that the emperor had his first news of events outside Kyoto, or heard of conspiracies.

Meals were served by court ladies wearing cotton masks over their mouths for hygiene. When they knelt to perform obeisance, only the backs of their hands touched the mats, to avoid contamination. They could not put on their own socks, and when they sewed garments for the imperial family they could not moisten the thread with their own saliva. The crown prince ate with chopsticks, but his were one inch longer than those of anyone else except the emperor, who had nine-inch chopsticks. In Japan, the presentation of food was all important, so the eyes were better fed than the stomach. Sometimes Mutsuhito tried Western foods, but he rarely ate meat other than chicken.

Emperor Komei did not share his son's interest in

foreign things. He made no secret of his intense dislike of all foreigners. One of his poems goes, 'Perish my body neath the cold clear wave of some dark well, but let no foreign foot pollute the water with its presence here.' Still in his early twenties when Perry arrived, the emperor bitterly criticized the shogunate for not standing up to the West. This was not entirely true. For many years, probes by European trading nations had been blocked, some fired upon. Russian vessels were turned back, their crews imprisoned. In 1846, when two American sailing ships arrived under the command of Commodore James Biddle, they were intercepted and towed back to sea. Generally, however, foreign skippers were treated with courtesy, supplied with food and water, and only then urged to leave because of the exclusion law. When sail gave way to steam, Japan became important as a coaling station, as a bad-weather refuge for whalers and as a big potential market for products of the industrial revolution. America increasingly saw itself as a Pacific player, so Commodore Perry was ordered to open up Japan, by force if necessary.

Many Japanese were in favour of foreign trade, foreign ideas and foreign technology. With Japan closed, food was not imported even during famines. Opening Japan to the world, they argued, meant opening the world to Japan, with all that could mean in manufacturing technology, education, science and medicine, and the exploitation of natural resources elsewhere that the islands lacked. Others disagreed violently. Japan had multiple personalities: friendly, hostile, humane, brutal, enlightened, barbaric. Contrary moods swept over the islands like pods of rain squalls. For all those eager to open up, there were fanatics ready to behead them.

The shogun's samurai armies were not up to any

serious contest. China's quick defeat by Britain in the First Opium War in 1842 made it obvious that losing would bring humiliation, which Japan could not face with the same resignation as China. The best strategy was to avoid war by making a bargain. So on his return a few months later, Commodore Perry was given a favourable reply. Without asking for the consent of Emperor Komei (a good measure of his insignificance), the shogunate signed a treaty with America, followed later by similar treaties with Great Britain, Russia, Germany, Holland and France. The treaty-holders were exempted from Japanese law, and were allowed to export goods to Japan at favourable prices. After centuries of seclusion, the intrusion of foreigners was traumatic to many Japanese. The garish dress and behaviour of Westerners was offensive. One official mourned, 'For more than ten years our country was in a state of indescribable confusion.'

The weakness of the shogun's government had been apparent to some for a long time, but was made obvious to everyone by these lopsided new treaties. Once a powerful military dictatorship, the shogunate had been set up to benefit Japan's feudal military class, the samurai. Tyrannical shoguns became decadent in their private behaviour. In the first half of the nineteenth century, Japan suffered under the most degenerate shogun in history, Ienari, an 'exhausted voluptuary' who kept a harem of nine hundred women and fathered at least fifty-five children. His ministers were famously corrupt, procuring girls and boys for their master, arranging bribes and swindles through court ladies in the shogun's bedchambers. Corruption was becoming contagious in Japan. The reckless printing of unsupported

60

paper money fed a craze of pleasure-seeking in the cities, and brothels boomed.

The issue facing most Japanese in the middle of the nineteenth century was economic survival. Most of the shogun's samurai supporters had mismanaged their feudal estates. Some squandered assets on sumptuous living, or wasted their lives on conspiracy. Only the hardest-working remained strong, on great estates far from the capital, relatively independent of the central government. Even so, lords of the greatest domains were obliged by the shogun to maintain lavish households in the capital, which was ruinously expensive. Smaller fiefdoms also were deeply in debt. The growth of a money economy encouraged people to borrow ruinously, and wealth shifted from old gentry to money-lending upstarts. Merchants and bankers grew rich but lived in constant danger of being victimized by the predatory regime. Many were the horror stories, like the rich merchant who died in prison while his sons and business manager were crucified, and all their wealth confiscated.

This corruption came to an end in a great famine (1832–7). Like earlier famines, first the horses, dogs and cats were eaten, then great numbers of people starved. In villages of forty or fifty households not a single person survived, corpses went unburied, and there were the usual reports of cannibalism. Plague followed, with peasant uprisings and urban riots. In one province, when 50,000 starving farmers attacked the mansions of the local gentry, the shogun had 562 demonstrators crucified. In the cities, naked government spies lurked in the steaming waters of public bath houses, waiting to arrest any man or woman who revealed the slightest criticism of the government. When the degenerate

Ienari died in 1841, at 69, reformist ministers expelled a thousand women and men from the shogun's palace, and sumptuary laws were enacted to impose frugality on society as a whole. These measures were so drastic that the economy was strangled. The reforms came too late, as powerful secret alliances were already plotting the regime's downfall.

Enemies of the shogun differed about what to do. The most vigorous conspirators were samurai clans who had lost earlier power struggles. Among them the conservatives hoped to preserve the existing military government but with new men in charge. The more radical wanted to end the military regime and to 'modernize' Japan by bringing the emperor out of obscurity and making him the figurehead of a new style of government built around a coalition of stronger clans. As these radicals gained support, the concept of the emperor became more and more important as a rallying point. Disaffected lords and vassals took up the slogan *Sonno Joi* – 'revere the emperor, expel the barbarians'. Unexpectedly, Emperor Komei found himself stronger politically than any of his ancestors for generations. To embarrass the shogunate, firebrands murdered foreigners and burned their warehouses and legations. The outraged West demanded huge indemnities, crippling the shogun's treasury.

Chief among the conspirators were the great Choshu and Satsuma clans. Choshu looked north, towards Korea, Manchuria and Siberia. Satsuma looked south, towards Taiwan, south China, the Indies and Southeast Asia.

Second largest of Japan's domains, Satsuma, on the southern island of Kyushu, had its capital at the busy port of Kagoshima. A mountainous region with a rugged coast, Satsuma bred some of Japan's fiercest warriors and most ambitious entrepreneurs, an aggressive mixture of greed and patriotism. The clan was rich because it had long carried on an illicit trade with China and the West, despite Japan being officially closed. Some of this clandestine trade was done directly, some in league with Chinese pirates, and some by way of the Ryukyu Islands whose king paid tribute to the Satsuma lord. Cane sugar from the tropics was their biggest import. While the rest of Japan suffered economic decline, Satsuma's Lord Shimazu spent money lavishly, enlarged his army and improved his arsenal with the secret help of Westerners, most of them British traders or American adventurers based on the China coast. When Shimazu ran up debts so huge they could never be repaid, he simply defaulted. His creditors were powerless, for nobody challenged Satsuma lightly. The clan went on with life as usual, profits pouring in.

Just across the Strait of Shimonoseki from Kyushu, on the western end of the main island of Honshu, lay the rival domain of Choshu, with its capital at Hagi. Half the size of Satsuma, its rich farmland gave it equal wealth, and supported one of the largest samurai contingents in Japan. Choshu had been a staging base for the invasion of Korea in the sixteenth century, and its Lord Mori kept a secret slush-fund of wealth first accumulated during that campaign. Because Choshu controlled the Strait of Shimonoseki and access to the Inland Sea, it was able to tax coastal trade to the commercial hub at Osaka. During the recent hard times, Lord Mori had prospered by encouraging merchant guilds, providing cheap loans to farmers, local traders and lesser samurai. Unlike Satsuma, which profited from foreign trade, Choshu was isolationist and wanted to expel all foreigners. This put the two great clans at loggerheads.

All these pent-up hatreds exploded in March 1860, when the shogun's chief counsellor was assassinated by twenty samurai outside the shogun's palace in Edo (later renamed Tokyo). Disarming his bodyguards at the Sakurada Gate, the killers dragged the counsellor from his carriage, threw him down in the snow and hacked off his head. Murdering the most powerful man in Japan next to the shogun himself was part of a Satsuma plot to bring the crisis to a head. But the shogun, a boy of 16, took desperate steps nobody had foreseen. After centuries of snubbing emperors, the shogun came to Kyoto to pay a courtesy call on Emperor Komei, promised to drive out all foreigners, and agreed to consult nobles and clan leaders about reorganizing the government. Emperor Komei was so surprised and pleased that he reciprocated by giving the shogun his sister in marriage, tying the two families together. This unexpected alliance between the powerless emperor and the hated shogun caught all the conspirators off-guard. Without realizing it, Emperor Komei had doomed himself. He was expendable, because he had a son who could be substituted as the new Son of Heaven. And events were about to be overtaken by the politics of brute force.

In August 1864, hotheaded Choshu marched its troops to Kyoto and rushed the Hamaguri Gate of the imperial palace, planning to 'rescue' Emperor Komei from 'corrupt elements' and hold him hostage until the shogun expelled all foreigners. Bullets flew around the low palace roofs and through its thin walls of sliding panels, giving 11-year-old Crown Prince Mutsuhito a sharp first taste of combat with something other than toy swords. As the battle raged, the prince fainted, less from fear than from excitement. When the fight ended,

Choshu was repulsed, at terrible cost. All around was smoking ruin. Burned to the ground were eighteen of the noble mansions surrounding the imperial park, and forty-four of the great pavilions of provincial domain lords. Beyond in the city itself many small homes had been burned, along with Shinto shrines, Buddhist temples, popular theatres and the hovels of the poor.

Satsuma's warriors now temporarily sided with the shogun–emperor alliance and Choshu was repulsed. Because the clans were murderous rivals, Satsuma had to block a premature Choshu victory, even if it meant post-poning a change of regime. This defeat threw Choshu into great confusion. The shogun commanded Lord Mori to present himself for punishment, but Mori wisely refused. So the young shogun had to mount a punitive campaign against the rebel stronghold. Gathering and equipping an army took months, during which there was frenzied conspiracy behind the scenes. Both sides sought to buy all the Western guns they could.

Aside from the few foreign traders isolated in Nagasaki, who were closely watched by the shogun's spies, the primary gun-merchant in Japan was the Satsuma clan, who dominated the black market in illicit arms. To assure the defeat of the shogun's forces, other clans secretly brokered a deal in which Satsuma helped Choshu obtain all the rapid-fire weapons it wanted in return for huge payments in rice and money. Western agents in Shanghai sent guns by steamship and trained Choshu men in their use. Choshu and Satsuma were persuaded to put aside their rivalry and to join forces temporarily, to concentrate on overthrowing the regime. Well-placed palace nobles joined the conspiracy in return for a leading role in the next government. A secret alliance was formed of twenty-three domains, led by Satsuma, Choshu, Hizen and Tosa. Soon they would be cheating furiously, but the pact would last long enough.

A well-educated young samurai involved in the plot wrote a message to the British chargé d'affaires explaining the dramatic turnabout: 'Hitherto there had been a great number of stupid and ignorant persons in our provinces, who still adhered to the foolish old arguments. They were unaware of the daily progress of the Western nations . . . being like the frog at the bottom of the well. But lately they have learnt . . . The eyes and ears of the stupid having thus been opened, the question of opening the country to foreigners . . . has become clear . . . and there is very little difference of opinion on the subject.'

The fate of the shogun was sealed. Heavily armed men from Choshu and Satsuma moved into positions around Osaka and Kyoto. In June 1866, when the shogun's army set out to punish Choshu, they were ambushed and easily defeated. The humiliation was too much for the young shogun. His spirit broken, he died the following month. His widow, the sister of Emperor Komei, shaved her head and entered a Buddhist convent.

With the country at risk of plunging into deeper chaos, Emperor Komei again dismayed the rebels by opposing all schemes to end the shogunate by force. This doomed him. In December 1866, still young at 36, Komei was stricken suddenly by smallpox and died in torment two weeks later. Many believed he was murdered with a handkerchief contaminated with the virus, killed by court nobles who wanted to clear the way for a new regime built around his son. Japanese historians identify Iwakura Tomomi as the man most likely to have arranged the murder. When the new government later took shape, Iwakura was named vice-president of its ruling State Council.

Mutsuhito was 14 when his father died, and he inherited fear. In a court drunk on intrigue, his survival was in doubt. With all the rumours of poison, he was afraid to eat or drink. He was haunted by nightmares provoked by his father's sudden death and the palpable dread in the palace. His grandfather noted that: 'He has mysterious visions . . . Every night, a monkey appears before him and torments him.' His mother confided: 'In this age which has become so degenerate . . . the Court is everywhere filled with devils and [we are so] frightened and terrified that I am overcome with grief. If [my son] is not a particularly sagacious emperor, he will never be able to solve the problems within and without . . . I know of nothing to do but to pray.'

Months passed before his fate was settled. A new Tokugawa shogun resigned in November 1867. His generals were defeated, and the regime disintegrated. On 2 January 1868, troops of the Satsuma, Tosa, Hiroshima, Echizen and Owari domains, led by Saigo Takamori, Okubo Toshimichi and Iwakura Tomomi seized the gates of the imperial palace. By letting through only those nobles and councillors opposed to the shogunate, they succeeded in having the new boy emperor proclaim the Meiji Restoration. It was grandly declared that the whole country had now 'submitted to rule by the emperor'.

This was not the case at all, as Great Britain's envoy to Japan, Sir Harry Parkes, discovered two months later when he set off to meet the new emperor at the first audience ever given to Westerners by an emperor of Japan.

All details were arranged in advance for Parkes and his French and Dutch counterparts. The British translator was assured that while the young emperor had never spoken to a Westerner before, he would have a prepared speech. As the British contingent approached the Kyoto palace, escorted by Satsuma and Higo warriors, they were set upon by two rogue samurai who sprang out of an alley with drawn swords. Nine Britons were wounded before one of the assailants was beheaded and the other captured. Apologies were made, and the Parkes audience was rescheduled. When it took place three days later there were surprises of a different kind.

Entering a hall in the palace grounds, Parkes and his interpreter, A. B. Mitford, found the young emperor seated on a dais under a canopy. A slightly lower dais was ready for Sir Harry. Emperor Mutsuhito made a startling impression. 'His complexion was white,' Mitford noted, 'perhaps artificially so rendered, his mouth badly formed, what a doctor would call prognathous [protruding], but the general contour was good. His eyebrows were shaven off, and painted in an inch higher up. His costume consisted of a long black loose cape hanging backwards, a white upper garment or mantle and voluminous purple trousers.' His cheeks were rouged, his lips were painted red and gold, and his teeth were blackened in the traditional Japanese court manner – a long way from the elegant, bearded monarch of later years.

In a whisper, Mutsuhito asked about Queen Victoria, apologized for the murderous attack three days earlier, stumbled through the first sentence of his prepared speech, then lost his place in the text. Jumping in to cover the awkward moment, a young aide named Ito Hirobumi (of whom we shall hear more) read the English translation of the whole speech. In reply Sir Harry praised the emperor for establishing a strong government and adopting the system of international law, and thanked him for the gracious reception. All agreed it was a successful audience, despite the botches. The physical cosmetics were soon abandoned, although the political cosmetics remain in place.

It was easier for foreign nations to acknowledge the new monarch than it was for Japanese. After eight centuries of military rule, most of them did not know there still was an emperor. They only had been conscious of rule by the shogun. Outside of Kyoto, people had long ago ceased to be aware that the imperial house existed, so it was necessary to reintroduce the emperor to the people, and make him an icon again. The strategists behind the new regime launched a vigorous promotion campaign. If Japan's new strongmen were to remain invisible, the emperor had to be conspicuous. To become an effective figurehead, he had to be put on display. This involved a certain falsification. As Professor Carol Gluck put it, when he was taken out of the closet the emperor was deliberately 'enveloped in an aura of symbolic meaning' that had not been practised for over seven hundred years.

Venturing outside Kyoto for the first time in April 1868, Mutsuhito, now 15, climbed into a palanquin and was borne off to nearby Osaka for his first glimpse of the blue water and lush green crags of the Inland Sea. He saw six new steamers belonging to wealthy domain lords, reviewed soldiers, and had a great day. The public was told the emperor had left Kyoto at the head of his army to put down a few die-hard rebels in the east, but that was only to inflate his image as a military leader. His next journey was a permanent move to the shogun's administrative capital at Edo. While Kyoto had been the imperial capital since 794, it was not suitable as a home for the new government because Japan's new strongmen wished to distance themselves from the intrigues of the old aristocracy, and to make certain that everyone saw the emperor taking the place of the shogun. The great castle of the Tokugawa shoguns at Edo was redecorated as a new home for the imperial family. This move was announced as an imperial decision, but Mutsuhito had nothing to say in the matter. The term 'imperial decision' meant the emperor gave his nod to something already decided for him.

The royal move began on 4 November 1868, and took twenty-two days. A procession of 1,000 soldiers, 2,300 attendants and 1,000 wagons moved 12 miles a day up the old Tokaido road, which hugs the edge of pine-forested mountains as it winds north along the Pacific coast. The procession was led on horseback by Prince Arisugawa, a member of the larger imperial family who had actually taken part in the suppression of rebels. At each of the fifty-two way-stations, local people pros-trated themselves, pressing their foreheads to the soil. The chanting of 'Miya-sama, Miya-sama' (Lord Prince) during this trip provided Gilbert and Sullivan with the text for their chorus in the operetta *Mikado*. Mutsuhito spent most of the trip sipping sake in his palanquin, watching the scenery from behind fine silk-gauze curtains. His counsellor Kido Takayoshi was determined that the emperor would see 'his' subjects for the first time. Although Mutsuhito remained hidden, he saw rice-farmers, porters, fishermen, shopkeepers, peasant women – a true cross-section of ordinary people and their way of life. This was the first time in 2,000 years that an emperor had crossed the mountains to eastern Japan. Though the trip was made to remove the emperor from the conspiratorial aristocracy in Kyoto, word was put out that he really wanted to be closer to the scene of rebel suppression.

Six months later he returned to Kyoto briefly to be married. His bride, Princess Haruko, was not beautiful at first sight because of her irregular features, but she always struck people as ravishingly pretty because of the force of her personality. At 18 she was two years older than Meiji, but she was so tiny that she looked like a child, less than five feet tall and delicately boned. Her father was Prince Ichijo Tadaka, from one of the five regent families whose pedigree went back a thousand years. Her mother was a Fujiwara.

The court's move to Tokyo was of profound significance, both as a break with the past and because the emperor was seen taking up residence in the great fortress of the shoguns. This gave him credibility as a ruler, although in fact he was only window-dressing. One of his first important visitors in Tokyo was Prince Alfred, Duke of Edinburgh, who arrived in 1869 as a Royal Navy captain aboard the HMS *Galatea*. The British legation said people were 'wildly excited' because Alfred was the first foreign royal ever to visit Japan. He was put up at the Hama Goten palace, specially redone in Western style with ponderous Victorian furniture rushed from Hong Kong that clashed with the exquisite Japanese decor. Alfred's visit posed delicate problems. Anyone admitted to the emperor's presence had to undergo Shinto rites to cleanse him of evil influences. But it would be rude to imply that the duke needed cleansing. So Shinto priests in white robes and black caps took up positions outside the palace to wave their magic wands in the direction of the duke without him noticing. This time the emperor would adopt modern etiquette and abandon the ancient customs dear to the hearts of traditionalists, including the rouge, lipstick and blackened teeth. At earlier audiences, diplomats had protested having to stand while the emperor sat, so from then on Mutsuhito also stood. It would never do to let the envoys sit in his presence. However, as the Duke of Edinburgh was of royal blood, he would be permitted to sit with the emperor as an equal.

When Alfred entered the audience hall with his entourage, he found Mutsuhito dressed in a stark white Shinto priest's robe and a black lacquered hat with a tall pennon. In 1869, he was not yet the Westernized monarch of later photographs, when he would look like the star of a Viennese operetta, but this was a dramatic change from the first audience with Harry Parkes. After formal greetings were exchanged, Mutsuhito invited Alfred to stroll in the garden. Before the visit ended, the duke gave the emperor a diamond-studded snuff box. It was the first of many friendly meetings over the years with British and German royalty. Harry Parkes conceded that there had been a 'remarkable improvement' in relations. 'Three or four years ago the foreigner entering [Tokyo] watched, with well-grounded distrust, the movements and forbidding aspect of every armed Japanese; but on this occasion . . . they acted as if they were receiving foreign friends instead of traditional opponents.' At 17 the Meiji emperor still seemed awkward and unsophisticated. But without court make-up he had a swarthy, masculine face with an intense look under his own bushy brows. His long black hair was plastered down in Victorian style with camellia-oil pomade. His face was only lightly talced to relieve the darkness of his skin. At five feet seven inches he was stocky and solid by Japanese standards. Close observers noticed that he moved with a slight jerkiness or hesitation, which was much more pronounced decades later in his grandson, Hirohito. Despite being divine, the Meiji emperor had a number of these small personal afflictions that humanized him, making him a truly sympathetic figure. Even as an adult he continued to be haunted by nightmares, feared drowning, and hated ships and the sea.

The Meiji emperor was becoming an international celebrity, but very little could be learned about him with any certainty. Aside from a few military reviews and infrequent audiences with diplomats, Mutsuhito's life was one of pampered inactivity and deep secrecy. Most of his time was spent sipping sake, watching sumo wrestlers or inspecting his stable of horses. If he was not running things, who was?

Traditionally, Japanese strongmen and power-brokers take extraordinary pains to disguise themselves and their ambitions. It would be gauche and dangerous to do otherwise, for to have their ruthlessness revealed would defeat the whole purpose. After being excluded too long from decision-making, the coalition of conspirators who put Mutsuhito on the throne was ruthlessly aggressive. But they were extremely careful to manoeuvre in the background, while the emperor provided window-dressing. They did not restore power to the throne, but only went through the motions of doing so. To be more precise, they restored a certain kind of implicit power to the throne, but kept executive control for themselves. Mutsuhito became head of state, but not head of government. In itself, this was an historic change, for many centuries had passed since emperors were allowed even to be figureheads. During the Meiji coup, real power simply was transferred from one backstage clique to another, from the shogun's faction to a faceless group of new oligarchs. The Japanese people did not participate, nor did the emperor, except ceremonially. The throne was exploited to provide an aura of divine legitimacy, and to hide the fact that members of the new ruling coalition were continually cheating and trying to destroy one another. This clever deceit was so artfully contrived that most people were convinced it was real. Even within the State Council and among the power-brokers themselves, the deceit was maintained so effectively that in a few short years it became dogma, and the idea of Japan being ruled by the emperor became accepted as holy writ. It was suicidal to challenge this, or to point out that it was myth, and by the early decades of the twentieth century even the power-brokers and the emperor himself were addicted to its maintenance.

It was not always so. The leaders of the Meiji coup were senior agents of the Satsuma, Choshu, Hizen and Tosa clans. Most celebrated were Japan's Three Great Heroes: Kido Takayoshi ('the Pen'), Saigo Takamori ('the Sword') and Okubo Toshimichi ('the Despot'). All from samurai families, they had entirely different natures. Kido was the youngest and most charismatic, born in 1833 the son of a wealthy doctor in Choshu. After an elegant education, he was sent to the shogun's capital to be Choshu's eyes and ears. An eloquent speaker and a gifted writer, he earned the nickname 'the Pen'. He was not a good spy because he was so preoccupied by his own thoughts that he often overlooked undercurrents and was caught off-guard. Once he had to flee for his life, helped by his quick-witted and faithful geisha, Ikumatsu. A play based on this adventure became a hit during his lifetime, and Kido was so popular that his rivals began looking for ways to destroy him.

Saigo, 'the Sword', was a bear-like man with a big

heart, at two hundred pounds and nearly six feet towering over most Japanese. Born in Satsuma to a family that served as bodyguards for Lord Shimazu, everything he did was epic in scale. His tragic flaw was sincerity, which made him susceptible to manipulation by more ruthless men like his fellow clansman Okubo. It was Saigo who led the force that seized the gates of the imperial palace in Kyoto and brought about the change of government. He became minister of war in the new government and was immensely popular with militant samurai.

The third hero, Okubo, 'the Despot', was a back-room manipulator. Frail as a boy, son of a Satsuma bureaucrat, he was not up to the sweaty ordeal of swordplay, but like his father he had a head for numbers and a knack for organization. Starting as an assistant in the clan archives, he had access to secret information about all the leading men of Japan and their enemies. Promoted to tax collector, he sharpened his instincts for milking victims. Okubo matured into a brilliant but ruthless autocrat who thrived on intimidation and extortion. He was completely lacking in popular appeal, but was all the more dangerous for that.

These three exceptional men had a broad education in Western subjects and were well prepared for the challenge facing Japan. Yet as all revolutionaries learn, consolidation of power and the creation of a government are vastly more complex than simply killing the old guard and seizing control. Victory devours her young.

Following the Restoration, the new State Council left practical matters largely to these three men, to put down resistance, to gain control of the national treasury and to work out a new form of central government that would put Japan on an even military and economic footing with the West. They rarely consulted Mutsuhito. When they did, it was only to have him issue Imperial Rescripts, through which they ruled by decree. More than a decade would pass before Japan had a written constitution. After putting down small outbreaks of armed rebellion, their next concern was to consolidate military and police control, so nobody could challenge the new order. Then came financial consolidation, beginning with the seizure of all the vast assets of the Tokugawa family, who over the centuries had gained direct or indirect control of most of Japan's land and wealth. Some of this confiscated wealth was turned over immediately to the ruling families of Satsuma, Choshu, Hizen, Tosa and lesser partners in the coalition, to reward them for backing the coup.

Kido was active in setting up new government structures, replacing the old hereditary domains with a new system of prefectures and governors, purging the old chain of command and introducing a fresh one with new people in control. Saigo was promoted to general, in charge of reorganizing the armed forces and creating a national army of conscripts to replace the private armies of hereditary samurai. Okubo, as minister of finance, occupied himself with confiscating assets, underwriting the government and the army and laying the foundation of a private fortune for the imperial family, which was seen as the only way to make it completely insensitive to the blandishments of conspirators.

At the same time, these three men were deeply involved in the re-invention of the emperor. Kido, the romantic, thought the Meiji emperor should be a wise and moral example, an enlightened and accessible monarch in touch with the problems of humanity. Saigo, the big-hearted samurai, thought the emperor should be a reincarnation of Japan's ancient warrior-sage king, a man on horseback leading his country to wealth and prosperity through military might and foreign conquest, at the head of an army that loved him. Okubo, the manipulative despot, believed the emperor's job was to look, eat, think and dress like a Western monarch, while leaving the real business of government to a handful of supremely talented bureaucrats like himself, who knew how to knock heads together, squeeze wallets and get things done.

While they had profound differences, all three believed that Japan must be run exclusively by the elite. Ordinary Japanese had never been allowed to participate in government, so that was not at issue. When democracy was discussed, what was meant was a synthetic democracy, intended to impress the outside world with Japan's modernity but really contrived by and for the power elite. As they had no concrete idea how to proceed, and were continually at each other's throats, these strongmen set up a number of governmental organs that rose and fell in rapid succession. The highly visible emperor was used to hide their quarrelling and in-fighting behind the throne. Yet that was not enough. Because the Meiji Restoration was done by brute force, followed by smoke and mirrors, it had to be reinforced by the creation of practical political and administrative organizations that would be held together by the new myth of Japan's unique and divine imperial tradition. This was the great age of nationalism, and all patriotic Japanese were expected to get behind the national agenda, to build a powerful state.

Meanwhile, they had to rescue Mutsuhito from himself. His private life was a dizzy swirl of beautiful women, feasting and drinking, and afternoons exercising his horses. Although married, he still had three hundred ladies-in-waiting, and five principal concubines. As he entered his twenties, his days passed playing Go, writing poems and joining friends in Japanese-style football in which the object was not to win but to keep the ball in the air – symbolic of Japanese life as a whole. As a gourmand he had no peer. He drank everyone under the table. Each meal was preceded and washed down by many bottles of the finest French wines. Dessert consisted of strolling past his ranks of ladies, dropping a hanky in front of his choice for the evening. From these romps came fifteen children, not one by Empress Haruko. His drinking parties were extremely popular and, like those of the celebrated Heian Court a thousand years earlier, often turned into drunken carousing with the court ladies. Wine was poured for each guest according to rank. They were expected to recite a poem or sing a song before raising the cup or glass to their lips. In drinking games, the losers downed a 'cup of defeat'. On more than one occasion, Mutsuhito could not get to his feet and had to be carried to his quarters. Hangovers were eased by quiet mornings in the gardens of the imperial palace, where he patiently bred a different flower, the Japanese iris, *I. kaempferi*. His advisers noted all this with growing alarm and took radical steps to correct the problem.

In a surprise move, all palace management was put under a new Imperial Household organization, divided between Inside and Outside. The Outside was responsible for protocol, audiences, court appearances, public appearances, financial affairs including imperial estates, and the public image or 'transcendental dignity' of the emperor. The Inside managed daily life, palace staff, tutors, valets, aides, equerries, chamberlains, ladies-in-waiting, and looked after the well-being of the emperor

78

and his family. It was also responsible for concealing the emperor's personal opinions (and any other indiscretions) from the public. Centuries earlier, shoguns had posted watchdogs in Kyoto to keep an eye on emperors and courtiers. The new Imperial Household combined all these functions, including watchdog duties, under the supervision of conservative chamberlains.

A keening arose immediately from the ladies-in-waiting. They were the traditional intermediaries between the emperor and the outside world. This privilege had been acquired only after generations of effort, and was not to be surrendered casually. But the State Council blamed the ladies for encouraging Mutsuhito's frivolous life, his drinking parties, his exquisite fatigue and his lack of serious attention to matters of state. Unwisely, the ladies even denied General Saigo an audience. Incensed, the general took action, and a new man was put in charge of the Inside who – on Saigo's orders – dismissed all 300 ladies-in-waiting, brought in samurai to be the emperor's personal staff and instituted a new regime of manly sobriety. Japanese are tolerant of drunkenness, but self-restraint is a cardinal virtue. Mutsuhito was in no position to protest. In any case he admired Saigo, and was in awe of him.

But Saigo's great personal influence over the emperor now took a curious turn. Late in 1871, State Council Vice-President Iwakura (the man thought to have poisoned Mutsuhito's father) left Japan with forty other officials, including Kido and Okubo, for a two-year tour of Europe and America to acquaint themselves with Western government and industry. Their shopping list was long and complicated. To catch up with the West, Japan needed more than just a modern army and navy. It needed technology, factories, commercial know-how, financial systems and new forms of administration that could be seen as modern while protecting the status quo.

During their absence, Saigo had the emperor to himself, so he spoke of what troubled him deeply. There had been intense debate about how to reorganize the military. Privately, Saigo conceded the need for a modern all-conscript army, but he could not bring himself simply to abolish Japan's traditional samurai forces. In doing so, tens of thousands of hereditary samurai would then be made redundant. Without income, many of them would be impoverished and become dangerous to the new order. Samurai were more than mere soldiers. Their code had shaped Japanese life for a thousand years. Forfeiting that tradition could be a fatal mistake. Many samurai were already sulking and rebellious. In Saigo's mind Korea was the solution to the problem.

The two countries had a long history of meddling in each other's affairs. Korea had repeatedly refused to recognize the new Meiji government, a gross insult requiring action. Saigo convinced the emperor that an invasion of Korea would redress the insult, while giving great numbers of samurai something to do and a cause worth dying for. When fighting ended, there would be fewer samurai. Those left could be given jobs in conquered Korea. Saigo had a plan to go to Korea as a special envoy, ostensibly to settle the current dispute, and to behave so outrageously that it would provoke his own murder, justifying a declaration of war. Nothing would please him more than to give his life for his emperor and country. He pressed his case so hard that Mutsuhito gave in and approved Saigo's secret plan on 18 August 1873, just before Kido and Okubo returned to Japan with the rest of the Iwakura mission at the end of their two-year tour of the West.

Shocked, they all ganged up on Saigo and persuaded the emperor to withdraw his endorsement of the scheme. Saigo was humiliated and resigned from the State Council, returning to his childhood home in Satsuma to lick his wounds and play with his dogs. It was not that his rivals were opposed to military adventures, or to the conquest of Korea. But each man had his own plan to develop Japan into a great power and was not prepared to alter his agenda. Moreover, the Korea issue provided a rare opportunity to destroy Saigo.

It was Okubo, the manipulator, who contrived Saigo's downfall. During his travels in Europe with the Iwakura mission, Okubo had been impressed by Prussia's strongman, Otto von Bismarck, who manipulated the kaiser like a hand-puppet. Okubo now saw himself as Japan's Iron Chancellor. Taking advantage of a cabinet reshuffle following Saigo's resignation, he moved to gain personal control of the entire government bureaucracy. He switched portfolios from finance minister to home minister, which put him in charge of the national police and secret police. The army might control the country, but the secret police controlled the army. Okubo clearly was no longer interested in sharing power. His ruthlessness offended even the urbane Kido, who also resigned in disgust from the State Council but hung around at court making himself a thorn in Okubo's side.

There it might have remained, with Okubo as an invisible dictator hiding behind the throne, had not Saigo been the kind of man he was.

In disgrace, Saigo became a symbol for disgruntled samurai all over Japan. He opened a private military academy in Kagoshima, and twenty thousand samurai enrolled. To government spies this looked like a private army assembling. From Okubo's perspective, samurai were swaggering bullies and troublemakers. Early in 1876 he withdrew their right to carry swords. A flurry of small rebellions broke out in response. Saigo was thought to be behind them. Then Okubo abolished the hereditary stipends upon which most samurai survived. This proved to be the last straw.

At the end of January 1877, while Saigo was on a hunting trip in the mountains, Okubo sent assassins to Kagoshima to lie in wait for Saigo's return. Saigo's disciples discovered the plot and reacted angrily, storming the arsenal and arming themselves. Saigo hurried home and agreed to lead a rebellion. In a last display of feudal glory, his samurai army headed for the capital, banners flying, to present their grievances. A new all-conscript national army of sixty thousand men came to meet them, led by Choshu's General Yamagata Aritomo, who had succeeded Saigo as minister of war.

While fighting raged, Kido, depressed by this turn of events and bitter about Okubo's growing tyranny, persuaded the emperor to ride with him through the streets of Tokyo to inspire the population. The weather was cold and rainy, and Kido did have a history of heart trouble and a touch of tuberculosis, but neither man showed ill-effects afterwards. Yet a few weeks later Kido mysteriously contracted what appears to have been meningitis – 'brain fever', it was called – and died just shy of his forty-fourth birthday.

Civil war raged for six months. By late spring Saigo and his samurai were suffering disastrous reverses. In September, he returned to Kagoshima with a few hundred men for a last stand on a hill above the city. On 24 September, General Yamagata's troops attacked. Saigo was mortally wounded. By prior arrangement one of his men gave him the *coup de grâce* by beheading him.

As agreed, the head was washed and sent to Yamagata, who took it in his hands and said: 'Ah, your face looks so serene. Because of you I have not been at ease for half a year . . . you were one of the greatest heroes of our land . . . What a pity that this should be your fate.'

Saigo had played a crucial role in the Meiji coup, which ushered in a new Japan. For many Japanese, he has remained a symbol of the heroic past, for others a talisman of convulsive nationalism. The emperor honoured Saigo's family with a patent of nobility. In Saigo's papers was found this poem of warning:

> I do not mind the bitter cold of winter;
> What fills my heart with fear is
> The cold hearts of men.

With Kido and Saigo dead, only one of the Three Great Heroes remained. On the morning of 14 May 1878, as Okubo's carriage approached the imperial palace, six samurai fell upon it with drawn swords. Okubo raised his hand to ward them off, but the blows were so violent his hand was sliced off and his head was cleaved in two. As the assailants vented their rage, his body was cut to pieces. The assassins were from Satsuma, the domain that had given birth to both Saigo and Okubo. Keeping the ball in the air as was his duty, the Meiji emperor at once conferred the highest rank upon the ghost of Okubo, elevating his sons to the nobility.

With the death of the Three Heroes, a second generation of strongmen moved forward to take their place. One would become the emperor's dearest friend and drinking companion.

CHAPTER 2

BISMARCK'S MOUSTACHE

'Ito is my drinking companion!' Emperor Mutsuhito declared one day. Early in the Meiji Restoration he could still make such genial revelations without electrifying the Household minions responsible for his transcendental image. That would soon change, and the emperor would once more be put above the clouds – or, as the Japanese say, 'enshrined alive'. The regime behind the throne also grew remote. After the deaths of the Three Heroes, the strongmen who succeeded them became wary, and sought ways to fend off rival oligarchs and dangerous liberals. This new generation of councillors was called the Genro, or elder statesmen. Part of Japan's modern mythology is that these were public-spirited men who put national interest ahead of self-interest, and created a democratic, constitutional government. On closer inspection this is no more true of the Genro than of the Three Heroes.

Foremost among the Genro were Ito Hirobumi, the drinking companion, and General Yamagata Aritomo, who had mused sadly while holding in his hands General Saigo's freshly severed head. Mutsuhito's personal relations with them are revealing. It was Ito who completed the job of glorifying the emperor. It was

Yamagata who caged him up again. They were volcanic men, and ruthless rivals who did all they could to undercut each other and gain absolute control for themselves and their cliques. Even when they appeared to collaborate they were secretly cheating, so the government system they created was deeply flawed to favour manipulation by power cliques. No checks and balances were built in, no referendum was possible, and most people were excluded from the political process. For this basic flaw Japan has paid a terrible price. The system remains flawed to this day.

Of the two, Ito was by far the more appealing. He was the emperor's alter ego, a lusty, egocentric, moon-faced man of great intelligence, vivacity and sexual appetite. As a young *Sonno Joi* firebrand in 1862 he had taken part in the torching of the British legation. Then he travelled overseas, making repeated trips to America and Europe, listening carefully to Prussia's Otto von Bismarck. Back in Tokyo, he became the emperor's spokesman and proxy. Mutsuhito experienced the world through him. Ito's genius as a negotiator and administrator made him one of the movers and shakers of modern Asia. It was chiefly Ito who designed Japan's new government, then justified it with a constitution that seemed modern and democratic.

Ito's influence over the emperor was based on personal affinity. He was only eleven years senior, so he and Mutsuhito bonded as if they were brothers. A stimulating companion, Ito would stay up late in the emperor's bedroom, the two men dressed in kimonos, downing bottle after bottle of claret. Mutsuhito often gathered his favourites to talk about the rise and fall of Western states, the ebb and flow of dynasties, the battles that changed history, but only Ito broke palace rules. He always had a cigar in his mouth. When a servant reminded him not to smoke in the corridors, Ito explained that only cheap cigars produced sparks, and kept his lit. (Later he got the emperor's permission to smoke in the halls.) A sensualist, the only thing he liked more than wine and cigars was a good woman. As a young rebel, he once dodged the shogun's policemen by hiding in the pit of a latrine while his beautiful concubine hoisted her skirts and squatted with her bare bottom over the opening. For that bold act he married her. She was tolerant of his visits to inns and brothels. From a bouquet of butterflies he would single out a pretty waitress or entertainer, and bully the others into leaving. Then, in his cups, he would croak his favourite song: 'Drunk, my head pillowed on a beauty's lap; sober, grasping power to govern the nation.'

Like many Japanese, Ito was harsh to subordinates but meek before higher authority. This was his manner towards the Mori family, the Choshu lords who sponsored his education and backed his career. As a child he and his parents – poor farmers – were adopted by a childless samurai. The boy was so exceptional that he was sent to a Choshu academy run by the famous dissident Yoshida Shoin. After helping burn down the British legation, Ito and two other young samurai were smuggled abroad by a Scottish trader named Thomas Blake Glover, who had a factory at Nagasaki and ties to Jardine Matheson. Glover wanted to help the radicals destroy the shogun, and had a high opinion of Ito's sharp intelligence. In England Ito and his two comrades learned all they could about Western law and modern weapons.

Returning to Japan in 1864, Ito helped negotiate the secret pact between Choshu and Satsuma that finally toppled the shogun. He then became the young Meiji emperor's English-language interpreter, which gave him personal leverage in the palace. In 1871, he joined the Iwakura mission for its tour of Europe and the United States. During the tour, Ito became convinced that Okubo 'the Despot' had the best grasp of what must be done to give Japan effective government. He became one of Okubo's most effective lieutenants and succeeded him when he was assassinated in 1878, taking over the Home Ministry where he became Japan's new strongman, controlling police and patronage. Perhaps what made Ito so much more appealing and human than Okubo was his love of alcohol. In his youth he drank three or four gallons of sake each day, went to sleep as late as 4 a.m., and was out of bed promptly at 8 a.m. In later years doctors warned him to avoid whisky, so he drank claret by the case. Not only did this endear him to the Meiji emperor, it set him apart from rivals like General Yamagata, who were too paranoid to risk losing control with alcohol.

A chamberlain said, 'I was deeply impressed that in so many matters the emperor agreed to whatever Ito proposed.' Especially when he proposed a toast. Ito could rise flush-faced at any banquet and, to the horror of nobles to right and left, call for three cheers for the emperor. Their friendship was lifelong. In 1905 Britain's ambassador Sir Claude MacDonald observed at a banquet: 'The imperial princes . . . treated [Mutsuhito] with marked deference, but . . . Ito . . . seemed to speak on absolute terms of equality and cracked jokes which made this direct descendant of the Sun roar with laughter. It was a great revelation to me and one which pleased me very much for though a Mikado he seems very human.' Such intimacy was rare at court, all but unheard of in the past, and provoked intense jealousy.

The austere Yamagata, who never relaxed, openly questioned whether it was prudent for the emperor to bestow such trust on any individual, implying that he might be led astray by unscrupulous companions. However, it was Yamagata – not Ito – who proved to be the serpent.

For the Genro, consolidating personal power came first, government later. The 1868 palace coup was not a grassroots revolution. Power only transferred from one elite group to another, although control did then shift from clique to clique. At first the coalition was dominated by the Satsuma, Choshu, Hizen and Tosa clans, but Hizen and Tosa soon were squeezed out of most top jobs and spoils. Satsuma got the upper hand, then lost control because of the fatal quarrelling of Okubo and Saigo. By default, Choshu gained the dominant position and clung to it tenaciously, dominating Japan till the end of World War II, when most of those the Allies executed as war criminals were Choshu men.

Ito and Yamagata were both Choshu. Their personalities were opposite – one brilliantly outgoing, the other brilliantly secretive – but both were domineering. Their first concern was to disarm the clan's enemies, then to block any interference by rival Genro or politicians. Both men despised political parties as disease organisms that could destroy the state. Western ideas of government as an expression of 'the will of the people' they frankly regarded as a political lie. Under their influence, the emperor learned to share this elitist view, which was not uncommon elsewhere in the world during the nineteenth century. The biggest danger was posed by other members of their coalition, rival oligarchs who were now being excluded from spoils, patronage and leverage. Leaders of the Hizen and Tosa clans in particular were angry about being elbowed aside. Hizen's leader was so furious that in 1874 he raised a private army and fought the government for two months before being killed. So the original coalition that staged the coup was being reduced dramatically to a handful of survivors. Other challenges were political, not military. Instead of cooperating, the Genro improved their own positions, built loyalty nets, tricked each other and played king-of-the-castle.

Their greatest challenge came from former samurai who were excluded from the division of spoils. These men were joining political parties and pushing for a constitution and parliament. This was done for their own leverage, not on behalf of ordinary Japanese. The new politicians were seeking to weaken the State Council and loosen the grip of the Genro. One leading agitator was Itagaki Taisuke, an oligarch from Tosa who was excluded from power by Ito and Yamagata. He fought back by organizing other disaffected samurai into the Patriotic Party and petitioning the emperor for a national parliament. The moment Ito and Yamagata invited him back into the government, Itagaki obligingly folded up his political party. Whereupon Ito and Yamagata turned against him again. So Itagaki resigned once more, founded the Liberal Party of rural landowners and pressed anew for a parliament. Today's ruling Liberal Democratic Party is an evolution of Itagaki's nineteenth-century creation.

The same path was taken by Okuma Shigenobu, an oligarch from Hizen who was squeezed out of his post as finance minister by one of Ito's phoney 'reforms' in 1880. This was actually a dispute over the division of the Tokugawa shogun's vast assets, which had been seized following the 1868 coup. As soon as Okuma resigned, Ito cancelled the reform. The following year Okuma organized the Constitutional Progressive Party, made up mostly of urban business leaders, and lobbied for a parliament.

Okuma and Itagaki were wildly popular and charismatic public figures. Playing upon the Japanese public's craving for a voice in government, and the demand of many financial and commercial groups for political leverage, they built political parties based on opposing rural and urban interests that wanted a bigger voice. It was no longer possible simply to have Okuma or Itagaki murdered. They were so popular that their murders could incite popular rebellion.

Ito outfoxed both Okuma and Itagaki by having the emperor issue an edict calling for the drafting of a constitution and the creation of a legislature, while ensuring that he, Ito, their chief enemy, got the job. Researching and writing a constitution would take time. Ito's constitution would sound modern and democratic, but the delay would allow him to reorganize the government and make it impervious to popular involvement and democracy itself. Duplicity would be institutionalized by his constitution. The democratic baby would be suffocated in the crib, using its own swaddling clothes.

Although Ito – like Yamagata – was alarmed by the idea of democracy, he realized that Japan could not remain aloof for ever from 'subversive' Western influences. Japanese students and intellectuals were excited about ideas from France, England and America, such as social democracy, political pluralism, land reform, organized labour, intellectual freedom and free markets. Many Japanese wanted the right to participate in their government. The Genro, as agents of conservative landowners and urban financiers, felt comfortable only with Prussian politics, which were less permissive. In 1882–3, Ito and other members of a constitutional study mission spent months in Berlin listening to scholars like Rudolf von Gniest and Lorenz von Stein, who convinced them that the Prussian constitution and methods of operation provided the best model for Japan. Ito had long conversations with Bismarck that impressed him deeply. Ito was so taken with the Iron Chancellor that he began to dress and act like Bismarck, and grew a similar moustache.

The concepts of human rights and individual liberty had never existed in Japan, only that of duty. Japan never experienced a social revolution, nor did its new leaders want it to. Despite periodic efforts at reform (including briefly giving women limited rights to inherit property, later retracted), wealth was tightly held by a small ruling group and changed hands grudgingly. The idea that Meiji Japan transformed itself overnight into a modern state is pure propaganda. No country is more conservative, politically rigid and socially static, and when there is no alternative to giving an inch, the inch given is very small indeed. Within one generation Japan did transform itself into a world power militarily, accompanied by astonishing industrial and financial development, but politically it took refuge in a rigid Prussian system that was modern only in costume. Bismarck made sure that none of Prussia's democratic institutions could seriously challenge his autocratic rule. Ito's Japan would look similarly modern; its structure would have a democratic façade, but the windows and doors would be nailed shut. There would be an elected assembly, the Diet, where politicians could blow off steam, but they would be controlled by an executive responsible only to the emperor, who could never be challenged because he was divine. The emperor, in turn, would have his decisions made for him by a group of advisers, the State Council, ruled by the dominant clique. The leader of this clique would guide the emperor in the same way that Bismarck guided the kaiser.

There was no disagreement from the conservative Mutsuhito. As the constitution was being drafted, Ito had him issue decrees that put into law the central concept of ultimate loyalty to the emperor. One of these, the Imperial Rescript on Education, was a strict code of ethics that transformed a generation of Japanese into true believers. It called on all subjects, from childhood, to 'be filial to your parents, affectionate to your brothers and sisters . . . bear yourselves in modesty and moderation; . . . advance public good and promote common interests; always respect the constitution and observe the laws; should an emergency arise, offer yourselves courageously to the State'. The slightest deviation from this code meant personal disloyalty to the emperor, which was blasphemous, and suicidal. Given the fact that during the previous eight centuries most Japanese did not even know there was an emperor, this was an extraordinary turnabout. Yet the new dogma of emperor worship was so powerful, so draconian and so effectively driven home that by the end of the nineteenth century most Japanese thought this had been absolutely true throughout 2,500 years of unbroken rule by the Yamato dynasty.

Constitutions are intended to replace secrecy with transparency, but Ito's did the reverse. It did not provide a legal framework for future organs of government. It rationalized organs already in place. Extralegal instruments of power that could not be justified, such as the ruling State Council, were disguised. Borrowing from Britain, the State Council was quaintly renamed the emperor's Privy Council and set apart from the government, while the leader of its strongest clique became lord privy seal, the emperor's senior private adviser. Supervision of the armed forces, which General Yamagata was not prepared to submit to any kind of civilian review, was also set apart. An Imperial Rescript decreed that Japan's military would be answerable only to the emperor himself, bypassing the government bureaucracy and the future legislature. Thus both the Privy Council and the military became autonomous, above the law. Here was a decision the throne would come to regret, because the military became a separate, self-contained regime, and in practice no emperor who followed dared to challenge the high command casually. So long as Yamagata was in charge this was not a problem, as he was a man of extraordinary self-restraint, but his military heirs would exercise the power without the restraint.

The toothless Diet and the Meiji Constitution were set up not to facilitate popular power but to prevent political parties gaining serious influence. Still, the ability of party leaders to enact legislation favouring their own special-interest groups caused bribery and bid-rigging that was already skewing Japan's economy. Politicians, while they could not hire and fire bureaucrats and judges, were able to promote them and to see that they received lavish rewards indirectly. This became the benchmark of Japanese politics then and now, and added to the institutional corruption that permeates the entire system. Top bureaucrats blocked any initiative that did not benefit these cliques of power-brokers. The bureaucrats' most ingenious fraud was to deny that they exercised any power whatsoever. Like Shinto priests, they were merely performing, as Japan scholar Karel van Wolferen puts it, 'the right rituals and ceremonies to sustain the natural order . . . motivated by a selfless desire to serve the emperor and thereby the nation, for the benefit of the entire Japanese family'.

Although Ito's constitution only put authoritarian rule in democratic costume, it did at least imply unprecedented human rights, before putting them out of everybody's reach. A parliament, no matter how toothless, was both enlightened and progressive. It could be seen as a step in the right direction, and some day the people of Japan might actually get it to function on their behalf. In a sense, Japan's democracy was no more of a sham than Bismarck's moustache on Ito's face. Neither the moustache nor the democracy was fake. They were just Japanese.

Ito, like his predecessors, was consumed with reinventing the emperor. It was Ito who decided that to win international respect Japan needed a truly magnificent emperor. According to a Japanese biographer, he was 'hopelessly enthralled' by solemnity and pomp. He saw evidence all over the world of the human craving for majesty. He picked up where Okubo and Kido left off. Kido had overseen the emperor's education, arranging for scholars to give him instruction in Confucianism, European political thought and the German language. Okubo, on the other hand, had a fit when he learned that the emperor wore traditional court dress to inaugurate the first railway line in Japan, linking Tokyo to the foreign community at Yokohama eighteen miles away. Okubo was painfully conscious of appearances, and always wore Western clothing himself. Having grown up in the age of Abraham Lincoln, he wore a dark business suit with a stovepipe hat, and was the first Japanese to appear at court with a Western haircut. He built himself a mansion in the Paris style of Napoleon III, filled it with French furniture and rode to his office each day in a grand British carriage. He insisted that the emperor completely abandon Japanese clothing except for Shinto ceremonial functions where he would not be seen by foreigners. He also made sure that Mutsuhito's long black hair was shorn, and had him cultivate a moustache and spade beard in the style of the Victorian royals. On ordinary days, the emperor must wear an Austrian field marshal's uniform as commander-in-chief. To review the fleet, he must dress as an admiral. After work, he must wear a frock coat. (In private, Mutsuhito still preferred a dark tunic with baggy scarlet pants.) Only when it came to ponies did Okubo admit defeat. He could never get the emperor to ride a horse with the upright bearing of a modern major general. Mutsuhito just slouched over the pommel like a warlord.

Despite these arbitrary Western fashions, which he affected in good grace, Mutsuhito was at heart an un-reconstructed traditional Japanese. Most of the imperial palace was decorated in Western furnishings, but his private chambers were traditional Japanese. He never stopped jotting *waka* poems on the backs of envelopes that arrived bearing messages of state. When he read for pleasure, he preferred the amusing treacheries of China's classic *Romance of the Three Kingdoms*. He accepted the need for Japan to compete with the West, but he insisted on preserving tradition, ceremony and rituals. When he arrived at a party staged by one of the princes, he was appalled to see Japanese men and women ballroom dancing in European evening dress. He exclaimed, 'What is this?', and stalked out.

It was Kido who first persuaded the emperor to get out and meet his subjects, taking a grand tour of Japan's north in 1876. For eight weeks, Mutsuhito – now the Meiji emperor – rode through many prefectures in palan-quins or in carriages, visiting shrines, reviewing soldiers, decorating scholars' tombs and meeting throngs of common people who crowded the streets for the occasion and pressed their foreheads against the dirt. Mutsuhito marvelled at the scenery, stayed in hotels, attended fairs, watched horse breeding and silk reeling, went to paper mills and iron foundries, and listened to local officials. He had his guards shoot ducks and fire at flocks of crows. He paused to see naked fishermen hauling a net up a beach, and seemed 'mightily pleased to see things just as they are'. His chamberlains were distressed that the emperor preferred to do all these things while reclining, and it was not easy to get him to mount his horse or walk on foot. Watching performances of plays and farces, he put away so much sake that they worried 'the emperor might go too far in his merriment'. Clara Whitney, daughter of an American professor, once saw him costumed in French military dress. 'His hat was ornamented by a luxuriant ostrich plume . . . His face was . . . very good-looking . . . However, he seemed very tired as if he wished the people would not stare at him so hard.'

For long periods, the emperor preferred to remain out of sight in his private apartments. Japanese were told that he was a painstaking, studious monarch, with a good memory. His tutors thought otherwise. Said one: 'At present the sovereign's wisdom is not yet extensive and his benevolence is not yet comprehensive.' On good days he rose at 6 a.m. for breakfast followed by visits to his family. At nine each day court physicians examined him and urged him to spend more time riding or walking in the garden. He met advisers till lunch, when he ate sushi and sashimi washed down with green tea, then returned to his office till six. Evening meals were large, with chicken soup, vegetables, grilled fish and claret. He must have known he was being exploited, but his ministers went through the motions of involving him, briefing him, asking his approval. There may have been times when he regretted losing the seclusion of Kyoto, but there is no evidence that he resisted his glorification.

He was continually encouraged to be grand by Ito, who adorned himself like a child posing before a mirror. Ito loved to dress in ribbons and medals and strut around, and wanted the emperor to do the same. Later, when he became Viceroy of Korea, Ito designed a uniform with tasselled epaulettes and gold braid, and took the salute of his palace guard. His mind was equally ornate. Mutsuhito said that when Ito came to visit, 'You need to brush up on your Chinese classics.' Famously vain, Ito harped on his achievements until listeners became glassy-eyed. He believed Japan's salvation rested on his shoulders alone, and that other people were stupid. This brutal frankness made him seem to be without guile, compared to men like Yamagata who always hid their feelings. Ito wrote poems under the pen name Spring Field, an allusion to his own fecundity. One goes, 'At work in my fine mansion, draining three cups of wine, I have as my friends all the Great Heroes of the nation.' He so admired the Three Heroes – Saigo, Kido and Okubo – that he built a shrine at his seaside villa with a tablet praising them for sweeping away the militarism of the past. 'To whom does the mantle pass?' the tablet asked, and answered: 'At long last . . . our Prince Ito has . . . enlarged the bounds of civilized government.'

Liberals and other outsiders did everything they could to separate the emperor from the Genro and to put the throne above politics, so the government could be criticized, challenged and changed, if not necessarily overthrown. But Ito had foreseen this, and identified

Mutsuhito with every aspect of government.

To undermine opposition, Ito and Yamagata continually sought to identify the more effective opposition leaders and, if bribes would not work, offered them jobs in the bureaucracy. Or, if all else failed, elevation to the peerage. This lay behind the creation of a new peerage system, which raised the Genro themselves and many of their contemporaries to high rank. Ito and Yamagata both became princes. The recipient of a bribe never tired of putting out his hand, whereas peerage bound a noble to the throne permanently. Ito was never known to accept cash bribes but he was not above paying them, and Yamagata was expert at indulging human weakness. Both men became very wealthy on modest government salaries. Ito received many gifts that were not necessarily bribes. Yamagata had multiple income sources.

Not everyone was cowed or taken in. A Japanese politician complained, 'There are people who always mouth "loyalty" and "patriotism" and who advertise themselves as the sole repositories of these qualities, but what they actually do is hide themselves behind the throne and fire at their political enemies from this secure ambush. The throne is their ambush. Imperial rescripts are their bullets.'

Traditionally, an empress was hidden from view. But Ito encouraged Empress Haruko to become a public figure. Everyone was impressed by her poise, verve and intelligence. She was an accomplished poet. She was picked to be empress in part because her father had backed Choshu during the 1868–9 power struggle. Soon after her wedding, five young girls chosen to be educated in America came for an audience, Haruko's first visit with daughters of samurai. Seven-year-old Tsuda Ume said the girls knelt down before a heavy screen, 'through which we could see nothing, even if we had dared to raise our bowed heads, but behind which we knew was seated the sacred presence'. Haruko gave each a length of red silk and some court cake said to be a panacea for all ills.

Several years later, the screen began to lift. At a lawn party for diplomats, Clara Whitney saw Haruko at close range and gushed, 'She was little, oh, so little, dainty with high aristocratic features and a very full underlip. She was powdered very highly . . . and wore her hair in that peculiar flat court fashion with a long well-oiled tress falling down her back.' When Britain's Princes Albert Victor and George came to Japan in 1881, they were entertained at the imperial palace. Mutsuhito was in full uniform, 'dark blue tunic with heavy gold braid . . . Although . . . not thirty years old . . . a much aged look about the face . . . The empress in cheerful and genial manner then tried to begin a conversation. Eddy [Prince Albert] asked her to accept two wallabies which we had brought . . . from Australia . . . The Empress seemed very much pleased.'

By then she had stopped blackening her teeth. Whatever she wore, she had the knack of making herself seem exquisite, even in Western gowns and jewels that Ito ordered for her. One gown, trimmed with sable, cost $20,000. The wife of a British diplomat recalled that 'her dark eyes [were] full of life and intelligence . . . Her gown of rosy mauve brocade had only one ornament – a superb single sapphire worn as a brooch.'

Japanese were equally pleased with her transformation into a modern empress. A young aristocrat noted, 'She looked beautiful to us in . . . Western costume, her bonnet trimmed with a large white ostrich feather and a veil, her hands sheathed in long white kid gloves . . . Sometimes she smoked her golden pipe, respectfully offered by a young lady-in-waiting, who filled it each time from a gold lacquered tobacco box. Every time she accepted her pipe, she lifted her veil to smoke it.' Smoking was widespread among men and women.

Haruko's education was in traditional etiquette, how to compose poetry, to walk and dress correctly, to remain invisible. Historically an empress was important only for political leverage; it did not matter (except to her own parents) if she bore no children, as any child fathered by the emperor could be the next in line. After an invisible start, Haruko gradually emerged to participate in official functions and to play an increasingly active role in charities and education. Ito, who found women fascinating, was much involved in remaking the empress. She took to the role of modern monarch with enthusiasm and aplomb, enjoyed her liberated role, and was refreshingly open and friendly.

Empress Haruko sponsored the Japanese Red Cross when it was admitted to the International Red Cross in 1886, another sign that Japan was being accepted into the international community. She began a tradition of volunteer work by upper-class women. Clara Whitney spoke for many when she burbled, 'The empress is exceedingly intelligent and is so anxious to cultivate virtue and good deeds that she has collected all the notices of good deeds and qualities among her subjects . . . and has published them in three volumes as an incentive to great exertions . . . It is considered a mistake in His Majesty, the Mikado, that he does not confide matters of state to her, as she is fully capable of understanding and assisting in any political matters.' Clara's parents had friends in the American legation who were privy to diplomatic gossip.

During those years of unprecedented public exposure,

the emperor and empress often left the palace to be entertained at the homes of leading nobles and favourite ministers. They arrived with a flock of princes and chamberlains. One evening at the Western-style Matsukata mansion began with a stroll through the garden and a paddle around the pond, followed by performances of Satsuma music and dance, all climaxed with a sumptuous Western-style banquet. In appreciation the emperor would present his host with a vase, scroll or painting, a set of silver sake cups with the imperial crest and a thousand yen in cash to cover expenses.

It was Ito who asked Empress Haruko to preside over the new girls' school for nobility, the Peeresses School, opened in 1885. One of its first teachers was Tsuda Ume, back from college in America. Her father was a Christian and she became a Quaker, as did many other influential Japanese women in those decades. The school's revolutionary curriculum, modelled on progressive women's colleges in the United States, included foreign languages, mathematics, science, ethics, both Japanese and Western comportment and gymnastics. Nevertheless, Tsuda was depressed by the fate of her pupils after graduation. She wanted them to be Japan's leaders. Although by birth they were the most fortunate of children, all were doomed to be legal nonentities, chattels of fathers, husbands and dreaded mothers-in-law. The idea of educating Japanese women, which electrified educators and missionaries alike in the nineteenth century, washed over the Peeresses School like a wave over a rock in a woodcut by Hokusai – only an illusion.

Japan craved to be modern but feared its effect on tradition. In Berlin Bismarck had assured Ito that without Christianity Japan would never be a truly civilized land. Ito's interest in Christianity, however

101

abstract, alarmed his critics. They suspected him of urging the emperor to convert – an accusation he hotly denied. But Ito was so alarmed he asked Tsuda Ume, the teacher, to move out of his household, where she had been living since her return from America. He said it would be better if he did not 'keep in his house a Christian girl'. So while one hand gave, the other took away.

In 1894 when the imperial couple celebrated their twenty-fifth wedding anniversary, an American woman complained: 'It gives a shock . . . to learn that he celebrated the twenty-fifth anniversary of his marriage to the empress by adding another concubine to his harem.' This was not true. Mutsuhito did father two additional daughters after that date, but both were born to Lady Sachiko, who had been an official concubine for many years and bore him eight children in all. It was his responsibility to produce at least one surviving heir, preferably a robust one, but this he only just achieved. It is not easy to read a genealogy, but the details are revealing: Empress Haruko bore no children. Of the five official concubines, Lady Mitsuko gave birth on 18 September 1873 to Meiji's first son, who died the same day. Lady Mitsuko died four days later. Lady Natsuko (1856–73) gave birth on 13 November 1873 to a daughter who died the same day. Lady Natsuko died the next day. Lady Naruko (1855–1943) gave birth to three children, a girl in 1875 who died the following year, a son in 1877 who died a few months later, and in 1879 another son, who survived and became the next emperor, Yoshihito. Lady Kotoko (1855–1944) gave birth in 1881 to a girl who died of meningitis, and another girl in 1883 who also did not survive her first year. Lady Sachiko (1867–1947), although the most successful at child-bearing, lost two boys and two girls to meningitis, and only then had four girls who survived and, as we will see, married the four most important princes in Japan. Taken all together this is a sad catalogue, with tragic hidden consequences that only surfaced later.

When one boy and four girls did survive, Empress Haruko formally adopted them. This did not mean she became intimately involved, for noble women left children to wet nurses and tutors.

As to Haruko's private life with the emperor, we have no clue, but there is no hint of discord. At diplomatic dinners where they were scrutinized by practised eyes, the two behaved with affection and respect. Professor Stephen Large, the eminent Cambridge scholar who has written much about the emperors, notes that 'though she bore no children, he reportedly visited her apartments nearly every day in what was a companionable relationship'.

Ito, the lover of pomp and magnificence, had glorified the throne and made certain that Japan's emperor and empress were acknowledged as modern monarchs of international stature. It was his rival Yamagata who decided that they were being overexposed, and reversed the trend. The artificial flowers remained in place, to be dusted off when needed. But the party was over.

Ito's fatal disadvantage was his inability to delegate responsibility even to his own lieutenants, so there were severe limits to how far he could extend his network and protect himself. Yamagata, on the other hand, was so covert by nature that he could not read a speech in public without being paralysed by stage fright, but he knew all about networking. While Ito was furiously busy enhancing the emperor and empress, writing the constitution and setting up government agencies, Yamagata was busy spreading his invisible web throughout Japan, using the army, the police, the secret police and the underworld. As the new prime minister and one of the two most powerful Genro, by 1889 Yamagata was running the country day to day, succeeding Ito as the new strongman.

'Yamagata is my soldier,' the emperor declared. Truth to tell, he was afraid of Yamagata, as was everyone else. When the general came to the palace, Mutsuhito dressed in his best uniforms. Their meetings were awkward and uncomfortable. Where Ito was colourful and fun-loving, Yamagata was austere, humourless, bloodless. Dry severity was the essence of his style. As a born secret policeman he was completely unable to accept anything but rigid authoritarian rule. A thin man with thin lips and a thin attitude, he wore a brush moustache and had magnificent cheekbones, the carved ivory face of a Buddhist hermit sniffing something vile on the breeze. He was Japan's version of a Prussian superman, with none of Ito's appetites. Yamagata disdained pleasures of the flesh and was abnormally in control of himself and his surroundings. While Ito was drinking and cavorting with the emperor, Yamagata was methodically extending his influence into all sectors of Japanese life. His one weakness was a nervous stomach. He was devoted to his wife, and gave all his spare time to landscaping his splendid garden. Had he been reckless and charismatic, he might have made himself shogun, but he was a grey man of icy severity, balanced, patient and rational. Rather than admit to a miscalculation, or a mistake, he would evaporate from view and pick up the strings later. This ability to vanish made him seem faultless, when he was only calculating and elusive. Because he was a super-patriot, his cunning and manipulation seemed to be in the very best of causes. It was Yamagata who built Japan's modern police state and military machine, while he created for himself a vast loyalty net through jobs, patronage and bribes. As he was remote, he preferred the emperor to be remote. Yamagata had his own idealized samurai values, and intended to reintroduce them to Japan.

His family in Choshu were impoverished low-ranking samurai, so as a boy he had been snubbed by everyone and excluded from school. He was entirely self-taught. With nothing else to do, he hung around police head-quarters acting as a gofer and informer. Most of what he learned came from listening to the police, which shaped his values and his future as Japan's grand inquisitor. After both parents died, his grandmother raised him. According to Yamagata, she was so devoted that she drowned herself to advance his career by getting out of his way. In 1863 he was put in charge of Choshu's ex-perimental – and unsuccessful – irregular militia of farm boys, street rabble and roughneck merchants, armed with Western guns. On the eve of the shogun's downfall, he was one of many young men sent out to spy on the changing situation, and in Kyoto became acquainted with the heroes Saigo and Okubo. After the coup he and Saigo's younger brother travelled abroad, visiting England, France, Belgium, Holland, Prussia and Russia. Like other Japanese he was deeply impressed by Prussia's martial spirit. On his return he became a deputy to General Saigo, helping to build a conscript army. In the vacuum following Saigo's angry resignation, Yamagata took his place as army chief. This became his career pattern – taking over posts vacated by Saigo, Okubo, Ito and others, replacing their appointees with his loyalists, gradually spreading his web of patronage and moving into an unassailable position. He was so low key that his presence was hardly noticed until his nets were all in place.

Succeeding Saigo as army chief, he got the military in line. When there was a small mutiny within the Imperial Guard in 1878, Yamagata blamed it not on the real cause – short pay – but on the spread of poisonous liberal ideas from the West (how could loyal Japanese strike over short pay?). Several officers and nearly fifty men were executed by firing squad to make this point. Yamagata warned all soldiers against ever joining any sort of political organization, or expressing political ideas of any kind unless they were ultranationalist. To make it stick, he created Japan's first military police, the *kempeitai*, with secret agents throughout the ranks, chosen for being zealots.

Succeeding Ito as head of the Home Ministry, Yamagata replaced his predecessor's national police chiefs with his own iron men. To head the Tokyo police he chose Mishima Michitsune, soon known far and wide as Chief of the Devils. Japanese were easy to intimidate because they had been obliged to spy on each other for centuries, and always had to be wary of their neighbours and even their own families. In the 1600s shoguns had introduced the Hoko system of neighbourhood associations where one member of each household was responsible for the thoughts and behaviour of the entire family. From every ten homes, one person was chosen to bear responsibility for everyone in that group. From every hundred of these people one was chosen, and so forth. They were held to blame personally for the behaviour and opinions of everyone beneath them, so thousands of citizens became hostages of the state to guarantee the submission of the whole society.

Yamagata ran his personal loyalty web the same way, so senior police chiefs and underworld bosses alike owed personal loyalty to him. Yamagata's loyalty, in turn, was to the idea of the throne, not to any single occupant. The throne was Japan, not a personality. And Japan was his garden to cultivate.

Yamagata's police state was all-pervasive. Public meetings were permitted only if they met severe restrictions, so there was no forum of any kind for political discussion. State employees including teachers and bureaucrats were forbidden to take part in political meetings. Journalists were gagged by self-censorship. To blot up activists he encouraged all kinds of patriotic societies expressing intense loyalty to the throne or devout obedience to superiors. Although he backed a law prohibiting secret societies, Yamagata encouraged all manner of secret organizations, paramilitary forces and underworld gangs, so long as they were ultra-nationalist. Behind harmless groups like the Women's Patriotic Society was a paramilitary cult known as the Genyosha (Black Ocean), founded by Toyama Mitsuru, a follower of General Saigo who transferred his loyalties to Yamagata after his release from prison for his role in Saigo's rebellion. Toyama became Japan's leading underworld middleman, feeding the egos of men who dreamed of conquest and looting on the Asian mainland and making available to Yamagata an endless supply of bullies and assassins. Yamagata's web also included the Yamaguchi Gumi (Yamaguchi Group), gangsters based in Yamaguchi Prefecture, the new administrative name for Choshu. He used gangs to harass political organizers and labour demonstrators. Later he used them to soften up Korea and Manchuria in advance of invasion by the Imperial Army.

107

So long as Yamagata was alive these underworld forces were kept in line, and Japan's military machine remained under tight control, because Yamagata's greatest concerns were at home. His enemies were political parties and any other groups demanding more freedom or a piece of the pie of power. Yamagata was no more generous in sharing power than was Ito.

'Insincerity is everywhere apparent,' he said, 'with the driving motive now to make money. Those without self-discipline are impudently boastful and conceited, readily resisting officials. Furthermore, the foreign word "freedom" is mouthed without any understanding of the principle of freedom. Respect and love for superiors and kindness towards others have disappeared; infatuation with fashions and thoughtlessness are now common.' Written laws are easy to evade, he said, a poor substitute for the inbred sense of communal responsibility of farmers and lords on Japan's great rural estates, which he idealized. In recent centuries, he said, most samurai had neglected this tradition. But not the Mori family of Choshu, which was exemplary. These days, the high no longer felt responsible for the low, and the low no longer showed respect. Instead of recognizing this as another stage of Japan's social evolution, Yamagata saw it as a virus from the West.

Yamagata took a similarly dim view of the wearing of Western fashions. Japanese men now wore bowlers, and Japanese women for the first time wore panties. (Since the construction of Western-style multi-storey buildings, there had been some fires where women were trapped upstairs. Rather than climb out of a window and down a rescue ladder, which would flash their private parts to those below – the most shameful thing conceivable in Japan – some women chose to burn to death. More practical women decided instead to adopt panties.) To Yamagata, such innovations were symptomatic of a disease that would destroy tradition and damage the grip of the great families.

As chief adviser on military matters, Yamagata's aim was to expand the army to seven divisions, for future conquest on the Asian mainland. He emulated the Prussian high-command structure of Count Helmuth von Moltke, hero of the Franco-Prussian War. A staff college was set up in Tokyo, and Berlin was invited to send instructors. When the job was offered to Major Klemens Wilhelm Jakob Meckel, he hesitated: 'To tell the truth, I cannot live without Mosel wine. If I do not have it with dinner I cannot sleep at night.' Fortunately his vintner agreed to ship thousands of cases to Japan. Meckel, a tall, beet-faced, mutton-chopped holder of the Iron Cross, ranked Mosel just ahead of German opera as one of life's necessities (in retirement he composed an opera of his own). Four years younger than Yamagata, he was a kind, even-tempered man with a phenomenal memory that served him well as a teacher of military history, but left him gravely short of intuition. He arrived in Tokyo in March 1885 and was given a red-brick cottage copied from the Berlin suburbs, with a horse and carriage at his disposal. He had the dual role of staff-college lecturer and adviser to the general staff. Japanese were impressed by his teaching and his wine consumption. On duty he was a stern taskmaster, but after hours he moulted into civilian clothes and relaxed. Prussians were popular in Tokyo. Japanese considered the German Junker class to be their doppelgängers – a crude Western form of samurai. Germans had helped write Japan's constitution; a German was a chamberlain in the palace; Tokyo University school of medicine was staffed by

German doctors; and a German physician looked after the imperial family. Until Meckel arrived, the only staff-college teachers were Japanese trained in France and Germany, who grasped little of mass tactics and logistics. Meckel, lecturing through an interpreter, astonished them with his encyclopedic knowledge of tactics, logistics, military history and organization. His Franco-Prussian War maps and battle plans fascinated the Japanese. Samurai never fought as groups, only as individual knights supported by pages and footmen with pikes, or sometimes as small, fast-moving units of cavalry and archers. Germany's industrial-age logistics, mass tactics and mechanized procedures entranced Japanese officers, who became ardent converts. Meckel's audiences included top men from the War Ministry and general staff, the Imperial Guard and the Tokyo garrison.

The army Meckel wanted Japan to build was for use in Korea, Manchuria, Siberia and China. He talked about problems with landing points, positions to be occupied, transportation and supply. His excited pupils went off to develop war games. Yamagata's new conscript national army gave Japan a means to empire, and in the late nineteenth century a colonial empire was the mark of a civilized nation. Bismarck had told them: 'When large countries pursue their advantage they talk about international law when it suits them, and they use force when it does not.'

Meckel was in Japan for only three years. When he left, he saw that the emperor's personal seal was missing from the imperial message of thanks. Meckel sent the message back, demanding the seal, plus an upgrade to his Order of the Rising Sun. He got both, but left a bad taste. Soon his pupils were saying, 'Japan was a military nation before she ever heard of Germany.'

After Meckel left there was a fateful development. In 1891 Russia's Crown Prince Nicholas was sightseeing in Kyoto on the last leg of a grand tour of Asia, riding in a rickshaw, when a policeman saluted him, drew his sword and attacked him. The future czar escaped with minor cuts around the neck, but the Japanese government was shocked. One prince and two doctors hurried to Kyoto, and the Meiji emperor followed the next day. Against the advice of chamberlains, Mutsuhito accepted Nicholas's invitation to lunch aboard a Russian warship. The lunch passed without incident, but there were troubles to come.

Japan was now ready for a military adventure. She had the government, industry, navy and army to do what she wished. The czar's decision to build a trans-Siberian railway fed fears that Russia would seek a warm-water terminus in Manchuria or Korea.

It was Yamagata's position that Japan had to defend not only a line of sovereignty around its territory, but a much broader line of advantage. Korea and Manchuria were part of it. Japan's security depended on preventing them from falling under the control of a third country. To do this, Japan might have to absorb Korea. Access to its iron and coal resources would be good for Japan's new industries.

Compared to Russia, China was not a serious threat to Japan, but their competition for influence in Korea was causing tension. At Yamagata's instigation, terrorists from Black Ocean and a similar secret society called Black Dragon provoked so much trouble in Korea that Japanese troops had to be sent to calm things down. When Korea asked China for help, Japan sank a Chinese troop ship and drove Chinese forces out of Korea, seizing south Manchuria for good measure. To obtain a ceasefire, China had to give Japan the island of Taiwan.

This unexpected military success amazed the West. Germany, Russia and France demanded that Japan return south Manchuria to avoid 'destabilizing' the Far East. With no allies, Japan had to comply. Then Britain, unhappy with the meddling of her European rivals, signed a treaty with Japan in 1902 to go to its aid militarily if it became involved in a war with more than one foreign power. To its great surprise, Japan found itself with a friend and ally for the first time – and a powerful ally at that.

When negotiations with Russia over rights in Manchuria and Korea broke down in 1904, Japan launched a surprise attack in Manchuria, severely damaging the Russian fleet at Port Arthur. Fighting raged for a year and a half. Following Meckel's advice, the Japanese fought by the book, with infantry advancing in close formation through barbed wire in the face of artillery and machine-guns. There were 60,000 Japanese casualties. Yamagata was pushing for a ceasefire when Czar Nicholas rashly sent his Baltic fleet to Asia. It was totally destroyed in the Battle of Tsushima.

Japan emerged from the Russo-Japanese War with control of Korea and south Manchuria. Yamagata was triumphant. President Theodore Roosevelt offered to broker the peace in return for a secret accord. Japan could have Korea if the United States could have the Philippines.

Ito was sent to Korea as Japan's reluctant viceroy. He was bullied into it. When he initially resisted plans for seizing Korea and Manchuria, Black Ocean boss Toyama and three beefy thugs arrived at Ito's front door in Tokyo where Toyama shouted, 'I don't know whether there is going to be a beating or not.' According to the official history of the secret society, Toyama's conversation with Ito that day 'determined the decision for war'.

The great Ito's time had now passed and his days were numbered. Japan now belonged to Yamagata. Half a century earlier, Ito had been the right man in the right place at the right time. His Choshu masters had given him the job of stage-managing the emperor, of conjuring up the administrative organs of the new Japan and of making them look modern and democratic. He had done all this and more. Thanks to Ito's stagecraft, the new state looked dynamic, and the imperial family gained domestic adoration and international stature. But his showmanship also cloaked the intrigues of Yamagata and others who were only interested in personal power. They despised Ito's sophistication, his Western ideas, his endless talk, his grandly negotiated solutions. They perceived that Japan had no real friends in the world, only enemies. They wanted to turn the clock back. They arranged for Ito to be sent as proconsul to Korea, where he would be a very large target.

As an old man, Ito had lost his elasticity and even his sense of humour. In his dealings with Korean officials he was overbearing. Yamagata arranged for the Black Dragon boss, Uchida, to be on Ito's staff, accompanied by a large contingent of thugs. Secretly financed from army funds, Uchida's thugs murdered 18,000 Koreans during the next three years under the pretext of suppressing rebels. Disgusted by Yamagata's meddling, Ito resigned as proconsul in 1909. But as his enemy intended all along, Ito was widely seen as Korea's oppressor.

On a trip to Manchuria that winter to ease tension with the Russians, Ito arrived in Harbin on a cold, blustery morning under snow clouds. Before descending from the train, he put on a greatcoat, then stepped down to greet the Russian finance minister. Shots rang out behind him and Ito crumpled. Fifteen armed Koreans had been allowed on to the platform by Yamagata's security men. When Ito was told the identity of his young assassin, his last words were, 'What a fool!'

In Japan, Ito's murder was used to rouse popular support for Korea's annexation. His body was taken back to Tokyo where he was given a state funeral.

The emperor took his best friend's death badly. His own health was failing. Five years earlier, Mutsuhito had been diagnosed with diabetes, signs of kidney failure and uremic poisoning. Some Japanese sources say he also had cancer. Gossip attributed his fatigue to heavy drinking, but he would not change his habits. His steps faltered. After 1906 he rarely left the palace, and he may have suffered a stroke in 1908. Ito's murder finished him.

'I am alone now,' Mutsuhito said. 'Prince Ito was the only man with whom I could discuss state matters as an equal.' His chamberlains watched him disintegrate. In July 1912, during graduation ceremonies at Tokyo University, the Meiji emperor suddenly complained of feeling tired and short of breath. In his palace bedroom eighteen days later, he died. He once told a Household minister, 'All of you have the expediency of resignation, but We, We have no expediency.'

CHAPTER 3

THE TRAGIC PRINCE

The Meiji emperor's one surviving son, Yoshihito, became Japan's 'tragic emperor' under the reign name Taisho. The real nature of his tragedy has been obscured by caricature and overstatement. Little was ever written about him except mockery, as if a deliberate effort was made to erase him from history. Most historians concentrate on Hirohito, or Mutsuhito, the Meiji emperor, glossing over Yoshihito if they mention him at all. What is said is negative. He was too little, too delicate, too stupid, too vain, too self-indulgent, too crude, too sexual, too drunk, too demented, a comic parody. False contrasts are drawn between the boy and his father – false, because the image of Meiji is as exaggerated one way as that of his son is the other. So much effort was expended to glorify Meiji that whoever followed would inevitably seem small, and his flaws would be amplified where Meiji's were hidden. On closer study, Yoshihito turns out to be surprisingly different from the caricature.

As a child, he was already found wanting. On a visit to the Peeresses School, when he was eight years old, a teacher noted: 'The poor little fellow seemed quite bewildered, . . . I fear he won't amount to very much, from all accounts.' Half a century earlier the same was said about

Meiji – his mother worried that he would not make the grade, and others called him a frail, effeminate child. While we cannot put much stock in either childhood appraisal, bear in mind that apprehensions about Meiji's competence, tantrums and drinking continued for decades, although his image-builders tried to hide them.

Yoshihito's problem was medical, and began at his birth on 31 August 1879. His mother, imperial concubine Lady Naruko, was 24. Eldest daughter of a court noble, she had lived in the palace since she was 13, when she joined the household of Dowager Empress Eisho, widow of Emperor Komei. The dowager was impressed by her, so the following year Naruko was designated an imperial concubine. Her job was to bear children, but her first two died, the boy of 'water on the brain' and the girl from 'brain fever'. Both deaths were, in fact, caused by meningitis, or inflammation of the brain lining. Little was understood about meningitis in the late nineteenth century. It was endemic in Japan and nearly always fatal to infants, unless treated by antibiotics, twentieth-century drugs. By the time she was pregnant with her third child, Yoshihito, a lady-in-waiting said Lady Naruko was in an 'hysterical state' fearing for her baby. When the infant emerged he was thought to be stillborn, but after frantic work by the midwives he was howling. During the next three weeks Yoshihito was seriously ill with meningitis, contracting the infection from the birth canal, or from his swaddling clothes.

Everyone was surprised when the boy recovered. To put him in a different environment, he was taken to the home of his great-grandfather, Lord Nakayama, who now had a mansion in Tokyo. Nakayama had raised Meiji as an infant and was now 70 but still vigorous. Yoshihito remained with him till he was seven. Japanese

116

sources say that as a child he was easily frustrated, with tears and tantrums daily, but this is precisely what was said of his father. The big difference was Yoshihito's volcanic energy. He wore everybody out. Today he would be called hyperactive, with a short attention span, boundless energy and needing little sleep. As he matured, Yoshihito's restlessness became pronounced. Erwin Baelz, the German doctor who looked after the imperial family, said this was a result of meningitis.

He was no longer sickly, however. Many who observed him as a child remarked about his sunny, effervescent disposition. One relative, Princess Nashimoto, observed that 'in contrast to Emperor Meiji, Emperor Taisho was a friendly, lighthearted person'. Later, Emperor Hirohito also remembered his father being conspicuously happy in his youth. Yoshihito's childhood valet, Bojo, said he was neither haughty nor arrogant, but 'an amiable person with a commoner-like demeanour'. Meiji's childless Empress Haruko had great affection for her adopted son; a diplomat reported, 'one hears of his paying her visits pretty constantly'.

He was the first crown prince ever taught to dress himself and tie his own shoelaces. After having so much difficulty raising Meiji, and putting up with his lifelong tantrums and indolence, there was no tolerance of Yoshihito's failings. If he was not a good poet, or much of a thinker, at least they could make him physically active. Nothing could have pleased a hyperactive child more, so he thrived on outdoor activities and grew very strong.

He was tutored with a small group of noble playmates at the Aoyama palace, which was his first residence as crown prince. When he turned eight he was sent to the Peers School where the competitive atmosphere might stimulate his intellectual curiosity. Two years later Lady Fraser, wife of the British ambassador, wrote that 'the education of [the crown prince] is the most notable tribute to European ideas yet paid by this country. The little prince is ten and . . . [looks] rather delicate . . . He has a fine pale face, and piercing dark eyes . . . his own people say that he is strong and healthy, fond of outdoor exercise, and already well-trained in fencing and single-stick [*kendo,* sparring with bamboo staves] . . . the prince takes cold baths, eats meat, and will have no women to wait on him.'

He did have difficulty reading and writing. As a hyperactive child, he had problems sitting still, and in handling the rote memorization that is essential to mastering an ideographic language like written Japanese. Once, illness kept him out of school for a year. Palaces were not insulated and had no heating aside from cooking stoves, so they could be very cold, and Yoshihito (who took cold baths anyway) often got bronchitis. He finally graduated from elementary school at 14, and after a year of middle school was tutored by experts at the palace. There he was taught the basic Chinese classics, Japanese literature and history, world history and politics, economics, basic French and other subjects. His ability to write *kana*, the simplified script used by most Japanese, improved and he began to enjoy composing *waka* poems.

His academic shortcomings were obvious to outsiders as well. When Britain's envoy Sir Claude MacDonald met him in 1912 he noted: 'Intellectually [he] is generally supposed to be somewhat wanting, and that is certainly the opinion the casual observer would arrive at after some moments' conversation.'

Meiji did little to encourage his son; their relationship was remote and formal. A servant said that whenever the boy visited his father and bowed low, the emperor nodded but said not a word throughout. 'Emperor Meiji was a man of few words,' he added, but most children of the nobility were ignored completely by their fathers. One of Meiji's daughters once exclaimed, 'Believe it or not, I met my father on the eve of my wedding for the first time in my life. He didn't even recognize me. He asked me who I was and where I was from!'

The crown prince and his companions passed their leisure hours with archery, football, kendo or rowing on palace ponds. Sometimes Meiji watched at a distance, never exchanging a single word with his son. Fishing was Yoshihito's favourite sport during summers at the imperial seaside villa in Hayama. His love of the ocean shore was in contrast to his father's hatred of the sea. He passed on his interest to his sons and grandsons, some of whom became marine biologists.

His playmates were the heirs of the Iwakura and Saigo families. They stayed with him twenty-four hours a day, living in the same palace and going to the same country estates. He was not treated with particular reverence by them or by his attendants. All slept in the same quarters, and when they felt cold at night, they got up and took Yoshihito's extra blankets. In a dark bath house they tried to scare each other by recounting horror stories. When they wanted to exclude Yoshihito from some private activity, they hung a big *daikon* radish on the door. The crown prince hated the phallic vegetable and wouldn't pass it to enter the room.

One of his no-nonsense tutors was Major Tachibana, who taught sports and swordsmanship. He put lead weights in the ends of his bamboo training swords and kendo staves so his pupils 'saw stars every time he struck us'. He gave the crown prince strenuous swimming lessons. Wearing only red loin cloths, Yoshihito and his comrades were rowed offshore where the major threw them overboard. This was repeated until the gasping and exhausted prince learned to swim a few metres by himself. They did this twice a day all summer. To them, the major was 'a virtual demi-god'. From this it is clear that Yoshihito really was not the weakling he was later made out to be. No sickly sole heir to the throne would have been so roughly handled. Contrast this to the utterly passive life of Meiji.

Curious about life outside and restless in the palace among so many chamberlains and ever-present guardians, Yoshihito would slip out of the villa in Hayama and wander by himself, often visiting the old farmhouse of the Uematsu family. Uninvited, he would enter their living room and make himself at home. Whenever they saw him coming they prepared tea and cakes, and looked after him.

It was not unusual for Yoshihito to be seen in the countryside or at the seaside as he hated Tokyo and left it whenever he could. In 1902, when he was 23, the American-educated Quaker teacher Tsuda Ume saw the crown prince at the shore and remarked on his easygoing manner. 'He bowed to us most pleasantly, and seemed pleased. He was dressed in simple costume, and with very few attendants. He walks all around the shore . . . and talks to the village people, and he is much loved around here.' He stopped to watch fishermen at work, often buying their entire catch of bream. Yoshihito felt suffocated by court protocol and was desperate to escape. Dr Baelz noted in his diary: 'I was summoned to examine the crown prince . . . during the last fortnight there has been a rapid and extensive loss of weight. This suggests somewhere or other a latent tuberculosis process may be going on. His face is rather too lean, but the muscles of the chest and shoulders are like those of a wrestler . . . As a relic of the meningitis from which he suffered in early childhood, the crown prince is morbidly restless and lacks the power of concentration. These disorders have now assumed the form of a craving for travel. Above all, he has taken a dislike to Tokyo.' Dr Baelz grasped that while the problem had medical origins, it was more political than medical.

In 1906, following Japan's victory in the Russo-Japanese War, Yoshihito had the Akasaka palace rebuilt in European rococo style as his new residence. An immense two-storey pink marble building, the new palace looked like 'the offspring of the mating of . . . Versailles with Buckingham Palace'. Rooms were furnished with replica Louis XV antiques. Meiji referred to it as his son's 'French house'. Yoshihito was merely following a fashion established earlier by Okubo and others who emulated France in style and Germany in arms.

In his twenties Yoshihito grew a handlebar moustache that he waxed in the style of Kaiser Wilhelm II, whom he admired. (This was one of many things later used to make Yoshihito seem ridiculous, for during World War I and afterwards the kaiser was mercilessly lampooned by French, British and American propaganda.) There are interesting parallels between Wilhelm and Yoshihito. The kaiser was born with a withered left hand and some historians saw this as a clue to his behaviour, for despite his disfigurement he had to live up to the image of a great Prussian warrior. He overdid it, and was seen as both bombastic and irresolute. Yoshihito's birth defect was not a withered hand but something similar, yet invisible to his critics.

To assuage his restlessness, the crown prince was sent on trips around Japan, visiting factories, schools, farms and mines. His father, gloomy and withdrawn, rarely left the palace, so between 1902 and 1912 Yoshihito travelled throughout the islands and even visited Korea, trips heavily reported in the press. By all accounts he behaved normally and made a good impression. He clearly enjoyed getting out of the imperial cage and appreciated the changes of scene. In Tokyo he often visited the barracks of the Konoe Regiment, to which he was attached for military training, drinking and eating with officers and men. 'This food', he said, 'is good enough for soldiers and I, too, am a soldier.' It was partly this common touch that doomed him to be reviled and ridiculed by his elitist peers.

Kawahara Toshiaki, a journalist who has written several books about the family, says he 'must have hated being compared to Meiji, who was larger than life'. In one way he greatly outdid Meiji – when he became the father of four comparatively healthy sons, all born by his own wife, all of whom grew to maturity and lived full lives, and had strong affection for their father. However else he was said to be deficient, he secured the imperial line rather well. More than a little credit was due to a fortunate choice of bride.

Under the new Imperial Household law, drafted by Ito, an emperor or a crown prince had to marry someone from a branch of the imperial family, or from the Five Regent Families of the Fujiwara clan (Konoe, Ichijo, Kujo, Nijo or Takatsukasa). Emperor Komei married a Kujo, Meiji an Ichijo. Failing that, the bride had to be from the Seika families, the next tier of the old nobility, or as a last resort from a princely family in the newly created Meiji Restoration peerage. After a number of other candidates were considered, Princess Sadako was chosen. A daughter of Prince Kujo Michitaka, she was born in Tokyo on 25 June 1884. Her paternal aunt was Dowager Empress Eisho. Yoshihito and his bride were legally cousins, but there was no close blood tie, which improved their chances of having healthy children.

As an infant, following traditional practice, Sadako had been sent away from home so she would not grow up in hermetic isolation surrounded only by children of other nobles. The Okawara family, which was chosen to raise her, were silk-farmers in the village of Koenji, in Gumma Prefecture north-west of Tokyo. Sadako was brought up in a rustic setting on their farm, nursed and raised by the silk-farmer's wife, who happened to be a Quaker, as were many other silk-farmers in the area.

Christianity had been introduced to Japan in the sixteenth century by Catholic priests travelling on Portuguese ships trading at Nagasaki. A large Christian population developed on the southern island of Kyushu, including farmers, fishermen and rich families of the dominant Satsuma clan. Convinced that these Japanese Christians were conspiring with the Portuguese, the Tokugawa shogun banned Christianity in 1639 and expelled the Portuguese traders. Anyone who defied the shogun's ban was crucified. Most Christians went underground, learning to be invisible. Shinto, Buddhism and Confucianism had coexisted in Japan for many centuries, but Christianity was seen as foreign and subversive. After the Tokugawa shoguns were overthrown in 1868, the new leaders of Meiji Japan allowed the country to open up gradually to the outside world and to Western ideas. In the closing decades of the nineteenth century, Western missionaries began to arrive again. Least conspicuous of the Christian sects was the Society of Friends, the

Quakers, who had no churches, preachers or litany. Their low profile appealed to Japanese, who were passing through a period of violent ultra-nationalism. Militant Japanese were quick to attack anyone they thought was unpatriotic or had foreign loyalties. So the Friends gradually developed a strong, nearly invisible following in Japan, including many intellectuals and powerful members of the nobility. It was vital to be seen as Japanese first, Christian second. Except when you were in the company of foreigners, when you were Christian first, Japanese second.

At the age of six Sadako was taken from her Quaker foster family, brought back to Tokyo and sent to the Peeresses School. Seven years later she was chosen as Yoshihito's bride, when she was 13 and he was 18. Sadako spent two years learning court etiquette before the marriage. Many years later her daughter-in-law, Princess Chichibu, said, 'I had heard that the Empress [Sadako] . . . received a rigorous training from . . . ladies-in-waiting who had served at court for a long time.' Such training began with how to walk. 'It was considered indecorous to let one's shoes show when walking. One had to move gracefully, with elegance. And one had to learn how to put on ancient ceremonial robes and how to deport oneself in them. And when required to stand in attendance, one had to remain absolutely motionless for no matter how long.' The American Quaker educator Elizabeth Vining, who was close to Sadako in later years, said she was chosen 'because of her brilliant mind and sterling character, though early photographs . . . show her to have been pleasing in appearance too'. As the prospective bridegroom, Yoshihito neither saw Sadako nor any photograph of her. In a photo taken around 1912, when she was 28, she looks much more poised than either of her predecessors, Dowager Empress Eisho or Empress Haruko. Her oval face had well-modelled features, dark eyebrows and prominent ears neatly camouflaged by an upswept hairstyle – pretty but not a conspicuous beauty.

Before their marriage, Yoshihito again was sick with bronchitis and lost weight. Meiji, who otherwise could not be bothered, fretted over the health of his son. His concern came from the requirement of imperial succession. At last, the groom was declared fit. Dr Baelz said that Ito and other senior advisers to the throne thought it would be improper for Taisho 'to touch any other woman before his marriage'. If he went to his wedding a virgin, in later years he was ridiculed for being a womanizer, though his marriage seems to have been genuinely happy.

They were married in May 1900, and the Belgian envoy's wife reported what little is known about the Shinto ceremony. 'Their marriage took place in the Imperial shrine in the palace grounds at eight in the morning. Both bride and bridegroom were dressed in ancient court dress, but only Japanese were present and only two people outside the family witnessed the actual ceremony behind the curtain of the holy of holies . . . [Then] they changed into Western-style court dress and decorations and presented themselves to the emperor and empress.' Later that afternoon the diplomatic corps went to the palace to pay their respects to the emperor, empress and newlyweds. 'The bride', reported the Belgian, 'looks full of life and strength, and she possesses a pleasant and intelligent face.'

After the honeymoon, Dr Baelz often saw the crown prince and princess. 'The prince looks well and strong. He is much more lively and vigorous than he used to be.

There is something very attractive about the princess.' Sadako and her husband got along very well. She loyally and vigorously defended him no matter what happened, particularly against the manipulative Yamagata. She always spoke fondly and with respect of Yoshihito, saying his nature was 'to feel a strong sense of responsibility and whatever he did, he was very earnest'.

Sadako also proved she was up to her primary task, the production of male heirs. One year after their wedding, on 29 April 1901, she gave birth to Michi (Hirohito – the Showa emperor). A year later, on 25 June 1902, she produced Atsu (Yasuhito – Prince Chichibu). Two and a half years later on 3 January 1905, she delivered Teru (Nobuhito – Prince Takamatsu). Ten years later, on 2 December 1915, came Sumi (Takahito – Prince Mikasa). It had been generations since an empress had achieved such a feat.

By custom, the children were taken away from the parents. Dr Baelz was told that in the past this was to prevent fathers and sons from allying together to overthrow the shogun. 'The crown prince's son has been put under the care of [an] elderly admiral . . . The poor crown princess was compelled to hand over her baby, which cost her many tears. Now the parents can see their child only for a brief period once or twice a month. The reasons brought forward in support of what has been done are utterly worthless. It is said that the princess's ladies-in-waiting are all old maids who understand nothing about children.' In 1902, after her second son was taken away, Baelz noted that Sadako was 'the unhappy Japanese princess'. Three years later, in March 1905, Baelz said Sadako and Yoshihito 'are now allowed to have their children with them in their own house'. The antique regulation by which they were deprived of

126

their children had at last been dropped. It was dropped because of Sadako's diligent pressure, one of the qualities she possessed that would infuriate men at court.

Thereafter the parents and children had much more contact than had been the case for centuries, an unusual intimacy. Sadako and Yoshihito, an unpretentious young man, played vigorously with their first three boys, organizing games of hide-and-seek and 'catching tails', in which each child had a white handkerchief tied to his belt at the back of his trousers and they would all try to grab each other's tail, which made the children squeal with laughter. (Japanese sources do not reveal whether the emperor and empress also wore these tails, but it seems likely.) A significant change from Meiji. Yoshihito could not resist showing off his sons to Dr Baelz, who remarked: 'His paternal delight in these little ones is most touching.' The eldest, Hirohito, recalled that when his father was crown prince, 'he was very cheerful and lively . . . . [But] after he ascended the throne everything became very rigid and restricted.'

There remains one unresolved family mystery. Japanese journalist Kawahara said he discovered that Sadako's last childbirth produced twins. 'According to Shinto doctrine, twins are unclean. For the emperor's wife to produce them would be a terrible omen.' Kawahara claims that the Imperial Household spirited one of the twins, a girl, out of the palace and hid her in a nunnery in Kyoto for the rest of her life, where he said he interviewed her before she died.

At Meiji's death in 1912, Yoshihito became the Taisho emperor. Often in recent years he had stood in for his ailing father, acting informally as regent while Meiji became more ill and remote. So there is no reason why 1912 should mark any change in his activities or responsibilities.

Yoshihito had already shouldered the responsibilities. However, four years later in 1916, Sadako saw a great alteration in her husband. He became withdrawn, depressed, tired, and went rapidly downhill from there. Yoshihito's behaviour became unpredictable, puzzling or bizarre. During parades, or while reviewing troops, we are told that – despite being an excellent rider – he would fall off his horse, or strike soldiers impatiently with his riding crop. On one occasion we are told that he leapt from his horse and embraced a foot soldier. Another story says that when he was about to read a prepared speech before the assembled parliamentarians in the Diet, he rolled up the speech and used it as a telescope, 'causing great consternation'.

The truth about this dramatic change in his health remains a state secret. However, most sources agree that 'soon after his birth he contracted meningitis, which was to affect his health in later life'. How could childhood meningitis cause a mature and vigorous man to fall apart?

Meningitis causes inflammation of the delicate linings of the brain and of the spinal column. When he was born, Yoshihito had bacterial neonatal meningitis. Mortality among babies can be as high as 80 per cent, and those who survive can suffer lifelong disabilities. Bacteria attack the middle of three protective layers enveloping the brain and spinal cord, producing different types of damage. This may show in different ways, including the hyperactivity and short attention span conspicuous in Yoshihito. The brain damage can remain unnoticed for years, then in times of stress suddenly manifest itself in odd behaviour, which may resemble dementia. In the early years of the twentieth century, little was known about these delayed symptoms.

Yoshihito had managed things reasonably well as crown prince, better in some respects than his father, but when he became emperor the stress increased sharply for certain significant reasons, mostly having to do with the malignant influence of Yamagata. He coped with it by chain-smoking, drinking and (some say) pursuing women. These were things his father had done with considerable celebrity. Because of the changed circumstances that accompanied the decline of Ito and the rise of Yamagata, what seemed kingly in Meiji was made to seem weak and pitiful in his son. The flamboyant Meiji Restoration heroes – Saigo, Kido, Okubo and later Ito – had encouraged Meiji's appetites because they needed his endorsement to make their power seem legitimate, and his cooperation in their murderous power struggles against rivals and against each other. By the time Yoshihito became emperor, these men were all dead, and the humourless, puritanical Yamagata was pre-eminent. Growing up in the palaces under Yamagata's austere martial influence was like growing up in the police state beyond their walls: repressive, severe, heavily stylized, the opposite of what Yoshihito craved. Nobody dared to mock Yamagata, but it was open season on Yoshihito. This is odd because Yoshihito was a Son of Heaven while, by the standards of the Japanese nobility, Yamagata was only an upstart from the paddy fields who still had 'duck feet' – splayed toes typical of wet-rice farmers.

Some critics portrayed Yoshihito as a drunken libertine, like the degenerate Shogun Ienari, and claimed that he provoked his own insanity. As always, there is some truth in the rumours. But not much. Consider the sex lives of father and son. Politician Hara Kei noted in his diary that there were many things about Yoshihito that people did not like, among them his affairs. Yoshihito is said to have taken to bed any court lady who happened to be passing. However, it was commonplace historically for emperors to have many bed partners. In addition to Empress Haruko, Meiji had been supplied with five official concubines and 300 ladies-in-waiting. Over many years, he and Ito were rumoured to have rounded off their drinking bouts with various courtesans. And yet the practice of providing emperors with official concubines stopped suddenly after Meiji. Taisho was a virgin at the time of his wedding. Here is a double standard at work. If no one mocked Meiji's prodigious sexual appetite, why should Yoshihito's seem excessive? Once, when Yoshihito asked Yamagata to bring a woman, the general curtly replied, 'No, Your Majesty, that cannot be done.' The source of this story, however, is Yamagata himself.

As for Yoshihito's alleged alcoholism, drinking is such a part of Japanese male culture that it is difficult to see how he acted out of the ordinary in this respect. Kido tells us that Meiji drank hugely and on many occasions his advisers worried that 'he might go too far' (meaning to die of alcohol poisoning). After their wedding, Sadako was effective in setting limits for Yoshihito. It is said that he would sneak into the palace pantry and down a cup of sake, warning the servants to 'keep it secret from my wife'. Ito was Meiji's drinking companion, downing gallons of sake and claret each day, but Yoshihito could not drink even a cup of sake with Yamagata.

In these anecdotes lies the probable explanation – the difference in style brought about by the fall of Ito and the rise of Yamagata.

Yamagata was, in short, a power-freak. He preferred to glorify the throne but to diminish the monarch. It served his purpose to have everyone believe that the new Taisho emperor was incompetent, alcoholic and degenerate. A man who employs assassins does not hesitate to employ character assassination. Japanese were now so thoroughly indoctrinated in the new concept of the emperor as a divinity that it was suicidal to criticize Meiji or, later, Hirohito. So it is inconceivable that there could have been so much backbiting about Taisho if it were not being encouraged by Yamagata and his clique.

When Yoshihito became emperor, Yamagata tightened the screws, stress increased sharply and Yoshihito – his nervous system weakened by childhood meningitis – began to buckle under the strain. He hated protocol, preferred to break out and go his own way, and often did the unexpected or unconventional. As a mildly eccentric and unpretentious young man with a common touch, he was unpredictable, defiant, irrepressible – the opposite of the kind of person Yamagata wanted on the throne. He resisted Yamagata, and was stubborn enough and headstrong enough to continue resisting when anyone else would have become frightened and caved in. So it became necessary for Yamagata to undercut the emperor by spreading the word that he was insane and incompetent, degenerate, drunk, feeble and stupid. Only Yamagata could get away with such a campaign of lese-majesty, because he controlled the armed forces, the police, the secret police and – importantly – the underworld. Japan's outlaws are typically superpatriots, and as such would be the first to strike at anyone critical of the emperor. Anyone but Yamagata would have been committing suicide. The campaign to ridicule Yoshihito took hold and became the conventional wisdom, so that even today this is the prevailing image of Yoshihito, although it is largely untrue.

Yamagata's control was not universal, however, and many opponents were trying to weaken his grip, including Empress Sadako. Disparate factions were struggling against his police, underworld and military web. Among those allied against him were the powerful Satsuma clan who had been forced to give way to Choshu. Senior people in the imperial palace were resisting Choshu's domination. Their success depended upon the throne – the Taisho emperor – being able to resist Yamagata's deceits and manipulations. The current privy seal, General Oyama Iwao, a Satsuma man, was a vital buffer against Yamagata. A cousin of the famed General Saigo, strongly Western-orientated, he had become minister of war in 1880 before Yamagata attained the same position, and thus had seniority in army and government service. His brilliant and attractive wife, a Vassar-educated Christian, was part of the inner circle of Dowager Empress Haruko and Empress Sadako, all opposed to Yamagata. Then late in 1916, General Oyama died of old age and was replaced as privy seal by a Yamagata man, Baron Matsukata. (Matsukata was from Satsuma, but he always took Yamagata's side in power plays.) With General Oyama gone, the young emperor faced Yamagata's pressure without any buffer. This is likely to be what really caused such sudden and severe stress that the emperor's weakened nervous system was overwhelmed.

Yoshihito's behaviour was not always lunatic, sometimes just disturbingly informal for an emperor. When ministers and councillors came for an audience, he would grab a fistful of cigarettes from a box and say, 'Thanks for all your efforts. Now, here, have a smoke!' It was his nature to break tension with such disarming gestures. When he felt like it, he would burst into song or recite poetry. It pleased him to have his Imperial Guards perform martial music in the garden or to watch them play tug-of-war. In the age of Ito this would have prompted chuckles. In the age of Yamagata it was evidence of insanity.

The emperor was not unaware of what was being said behind his back. But he was truly powerless. By September 1918, he had become extremely withdrawn, depressed and passive. At the opening of parliament that December he was too tired to attend. The nerves running down the small of his back and into his legs began to give him pain. In the last seven years of his life, his depression was nearly unbroken, like the last years of Meiji. At the end of 1919, he suffered a complete breakdown, aggravated by a stroke. His speech was affected, his memory faltered and he walked with a dragging step. Empress Sadako moved him to the seaside villa he loved and attended him constantly. Except for brief, infrequent appearances in Tokyo, they remained at the country villas in Hayama, Numazu or Nikko. Later, people said he had always been in ill health, a weakling from start to finish, but the record of his active childhood and vigorous youth simply does not agree.

After reigning for seven years, not unusual in historical terms, the Taisho emperor was retired in 1919 and his eldest son, 18-year-old Crown Prince Hirohito, took over his father's duties, becoming regent three years later. In December 1925, Yoshihito suffered another stroke and collapsed in his bathroom. A chamberlain heard him fall and rushed in to find him on the floor. The next December he suffered a final stroke, contracted pneumonia, and died in bed at his beloved Hayama palace at the age of 47.

When the Taisho emperor died, it was time for a

realignment of power-brokers around Crown Prince Hirohito. Of the original Genro who had quarrelled among themselves since the 1870s, only Yamagata was left, with his protégé Prince Saionji, a second-generation Genro. But Dowager Empress Sadako caught them off-guard. She was still a young woman and outlived her husband by twenty-five years, through the bitterness of World War II and the Allied occupation. During those decades, she had unique influence. Her leverage had increased on the death of Meiji's Empress Haruko in 1914, which left Sadako the ranking imperial woman. Then, because of the illness of her husband, decisions about family matters fell more and more under her control. Prime ministers, privy councillors and Imperial Household ministers found themselves dealing with a person they could not cajole or wheedle with bribes, alcohol or geishas.

Sadako was a woman of courage, intelligence and strong character. As empress and later as dowager empress she was a discreet, vital force in imperial affairs for four decades. This derived from two things. Visibly, she was Hirohito's mother, the mother of one of Japan's longest-reigning monarchs, in a culture where a mother's power and authority over her son can never be over-estimated. No one but Yamagata dared to interfere with her, and eventually he paid the price. Although she was from one of the top five families of the Fujiwara clan, she had been raised by Quakers, and surrounded herself at court with Quakers and other Christians, permanently altering the power equation there. What is significant is not their Christianity, but that Sadako expanded her circle of influence through people who were outside the Shinto and Buddhist traditions, introducing a different point of view and very different networking.

134

In the nineteenth century any Japanese girl fortunate enough to be educated had to avoid 'contamination' by Christian attitudes. Bismarck had told Ito that Japan would never be great until it embraced Christianity. Although Ito was careful not to expose himself to criticism as an exponent of Christianity, his wife and daughter were tutored by a Japanese Quaker. Later, his daughter was sent to a Canadian Protestant mission school in Tokyo. Ito discreetly encouraged the Meiji emperor to issue an edict of religious toleration in 1873, which ended the long prohibition. After that, Christianity spread quickly, fed by a new wave, mainly Protestant, moving through networks of trade, commerce, industry, banking, education and foreign travel. By the middle of the twentieth century there were still relatively few Christians in Japan – only half of 1 per cent of the population in 1945 – but many of them were members of the ruling elite, whose wealth and education gave them greater influence than their numbers suggest.

When Sadako was sent to the Peeresses School at the age of six, there were Christians and Quakers on the teaching staff. Although they were prohibited from teaching Christian doctrine, they had indirect influence and related stories of model Christian women in the West, such as Joan of Arc and the mother of George Washington. Many of Sadako's classmates, who became her lifelong friends and confidantes, were Christians. In particular, Sadako's friendship with Nabeshima Nobuko led to an astonishing variety of Christian connections throughout the Japanese government and power structure. This included senior and mid-level diplomats in the Foreign Ministry, at Japanese embassies in England and America, and a close bond with Alice Perry Grew, the niece of Commodore Perry and wife of

America's longtime ambassador to Japan, Joseph Grew. Sadako's network came to include major foreign bankers and Western business interests, who benefited from direct links to the imperial palace.

There can be little doubt where Sadako herself stood, although great tact and discretion had to be exercised during a period when Yamagata's military clique was increasing its grip on power. Sadako frequently read the New Testament. A translation had been available since the 1870s. Prior to the Pacific War 145,000 copies of the Bible were distributed in Japan annually. Her youngest son, Prince Mikasa, would teach at a Christian university in Tokyo. Sadako personally chose a Quaker schoolgirl to be her second son's bride. Many of her inner circle were Christians. From the 1930s on, the Imperial Household was headed by Christians personally selected by her. And at the end of her life, there was consternation when the Imperial Household was obliged to carry out her wishes for what was delicately described as a discreet 'non-Shinto' private burial service in addition to the traditional Shinto funeral ritual. Her second son, Prince Chichibu, absolutely forbade Shinto rites at his own funeral.

Sadako and Yamagata were very different people, and they were on a collision course from which she was to emerge triumphant.

CHAPTER 4

THE CAGED BIRD

Of Sadako's four sons, the first born was the least imposing physically. While of average height for a Japanese at five feet six inches, the young Hirohito was frail, nearsighted, stooped and awkward. Already he showed signs of developing a twisted spine that would lead to a humped shoulder, and as a child he sometimes moved about with an uncertain hop like a fledgling bird tumbled too soon from its nest. As his little brother Prince Chichibu put it, 'When he falls down, he doesn't know how to get up!' Tutors prevented him from doing anything dangerous, such as jumping off a foot stool. When he fell down, aides rushed to his side. When he tried to join other children jumping off a low garden wall, his guardians were there to catch him. This was in sharp contrast to the robust training his father the Taisho emperor received, repeatedly being pitched into the sea for swimming lessons.

In each generation the Imperial Household reversed the practice of the previous one, because the outcome was always troublesome. Meiji was too coddled, Taisho too unrestrained. After going to so much trouble to convince Japanese once again that the emperor was divine, they were disappointed by Meiji one way, Taisho another, and were trying to find the right combination with Hirohito. To avoid the rebellious indolence of Meiji and the unconventional rebellion of Taisho, the Imperial Household constantly supervised Hirohito, giving him a lifelong dependence on mentors, advisers and counsellors for guidance in all matters. This reassured Yamagata and his protégé, Prince Saionji, that they would have less difficulty with this emperor, and gave a false impression of consensus, so important to Japan. As consensus was only an illusion, this put the Son of Heaven at a great disadvantage, for when it came to personality he was neither here nor there.

The object was to create an emperor who could be seen to participate in collective decision-making, but who did not dip his oar in the water in a way that might provoke one clique or another with unpredictable consequences. It was very delicate, very delicate indeed. When he in turn became the emperor's top private counsellor, Prince Saionji never let Hirohito forget this lesson. Saionji's lifelong concern was to preserve the throne's ambiguity. This does not mean that Hirohito was kept uninformed of military and other crucial decisions, as many people have subsequently asserted, but it does mean chamberlains of the Imperial Household were fully occupied preserving the ambiguity of his role in decision-making. On those few occasions when we do know that Hirohito acted entirely on his own, as in putting down the 1936 Young Officers' uprising, he was remarkably peevish.

The collective diligence of the Imperial Household produced some impressive results. Aside from one or two revealing lapses, Hirohito showed no appetite for extramarital affairs, consumed only small amounts of alcohol and rarely flew into rages. He was remarkably constrained and disciplined. He bottled up whatever

138

dismay or anger he felt at the independent actions of his ministers, his generals and his brothers. He carefully avoided saying anything outrageous, and rarely revealed his personal feelings. His few outbursts as a mature man were reserved for private conferences with his brothers, when there were accusations and weeping all around. Oversupervision made him painfully self-conscious and, like Taisho, he developed a lifelong craving to escape his keepers, even for a day. 'I am like a caged bird,' he often said wistfully.

He was born eleven months after his parents were married, arriving at 10.10 p.m. on the night of 29 April 1901, while his father was away at the seaside villa of Hayama. There were no health problems. Before the infant was three months old he was transferred to the home of Count Kawamura, while his mother wept bitterly. His father and grandfather had agreed that the 60-year-old Kawamura – a Satsuma member of the Privy Council – was the right man to safeguard the heir to the throne. When Hirohito's brother, Prince Chichibu, was born a year later, he also joined the Kawamura household, so it is both useful and revealing to contrast these two boys then and later. A retired admiral, Kawamura was one of those in the Privy Council generally opposed to the dominant Choshu clique of Yamagata. He was trusted to keep the boys out of Yamagata's clutches.

Given the high infant mortality rate among princes, it was an assignment of national importance. Kawamura had three wet-nurses take turns feeding the boys every two hours and fifteen minutes, while he followed them around 'like a shadow follows the substance'. His wife, daughter and nieces helped.

In those days, the wealthy Shimazu family of Satsuma were giving special attention to the education of their children, and had hired a British governess, Ethel Howard, who earlier had taught the children of Kaiser Wilhelm II. Kawamura interviewed her about her methods and was moved by her humanistic approach, her 'fostering of an independent spirit, a feeling of gratitude, and of a sympathetic heart'. So he was guided by her techniques in raising Hirohito and Chichibu.

Thanks to the proliferation of newspapers, the childhood of Hirohito and Chichibu aroused much interest in Japan, and Kawamura gave interviews. 'Children – especially in upper-class families – are apt to have likes and dislikes about food. Special attention has been paid to keep the two little princes free from this bad habit. Owing to this they often fretted and became peevish. This is quite natural to children of this age.' When Hirohito was given food he disliked, he threw down his chopsticks and exclaimed, 'I won't eat that.' The old man looked at him thoughtfully, and said, 'If you don't like it, you don't have to eat it. But you will be served no more food.' With that he whisked it away. After a stunned silence, the prince sobbed, 'I'll eat it, I'll eat it!' Kawamura turned his face away, tears welling in his eyes. He said the prince never again complained about meals.

One day Kawamura's patience gave way to the incessant refusal of the boys to cooperate. Drawing himself up, he said gravely, 'I have got weary of staying with Your Imperial Highnesses. Now, let me go away from you.' Hirohito began to weep. Loneliness was strong punishment. Fear was another form of discipline. One of the babysitters gave all the children nightmares. Hirohito told Chichibu he awakened from these bad dreams with a hand clutching at his heart.

Eventually, rewards and punishments had their effect,

and by all accounts Hirohito learned to suppress his wants, likes and dislikes in favour of cooperation. According to his valet, even while playing 'catching tails' with his brothers and friends, he 'always played strictly according to the rules, never employing any of the little tricks that were possible in this game'.

The boys were encouraged to play samurai, and for this Hirohito had a white rocking horse with its mane tumbling over its eyes, called Snow White. A baby photo shows him in a white lace dress and riding gloves, sitting proudly astride the wooden charger. In later years he gave the same name to his favourite real horse, but the Imperial Household reversed its name in English to White Snow, for reasons of transcendental dignity.

Recalling Hirohito's puckish expression as an old man, and his gnomic posture, it comes as a surprise that he was such a handsome child. His valet – Kanroji – described his 'wide, intelligent forehead and limpid, tranquil eyes set below thick eyebrows'. Chichibu's face was broader and more angular, with 'eyes and mouth that indicated he had a mind of his own'. Chichibu recalled that when he got carried away on his own rocking horse, Hirohito would rush to his side crying, 'Dangerous, dangerous.' If Chichibu coveted his sibling's toys, Hirohito gave them to him, knowing that his brother would then quickly lose interest. His mentors encouraged this habit, known in Japan as 'winning by losing', with interesting historical consequences. Hirohito's generosity stopped short of giving Chichibu the throne, although many people wished he had.

On Kawamura's death, the two princes were returned to their parents at Aoyama palace where a kindergarten was organized with five other boys, all sons of peers. The kindergarten consisted of three rooms divided by sliding doors, with tatami mats on the floor and cushions strapped to the pillars so the children would not get hurt. Each month they had a day trip somewhere. Hirohito always asked to go to the zoo, the start of his interest in biology.

When he was seven he was moved to the Peers School, where he was joined the following year by Chichibu, then by the third brother, Prince Takamatsu. Dean of boys at the Peers School was rotund Ishii Kunji, nicknamed the Log. He loved sake, but his sense of responsibility kept him from drinking alcohol while the crown prince was at the school. When the boy graduated, the Log announced, 'I have ten years of drinking to make up for.' Some students lived in a dormitory, but the three princes walked each day from Aoyama palace. The head of the school, General Nogi, found it painful watching the crown prince button his coat or tie his shoes because his hands fumbled and he was nearsighted. He could not wear glasses because the Imperial Household refused to acknowledge any flaw. Many of Hirohito's problems arose from such innocent causes. His muscles and nerves did not agree. His uncertain gait was part of this, called ataxia, and had been apparent in his grandfather as a child. Predictably, Hirohito was poor at callisthenics. Years later, when he took up golf, his first drive lofted the ball into the woods. Endless frustration made him philosophical, even whimsical. As he matured, he hid his awkwardness, but curvature of the spine – scoliosis – gave him a hunched shoulder and left him stooped. By the late 1940s he was three inches shorter than in his youth.

General Nogi was forbidding but kind. A stickler for cleanliness, he washed his own underwear each night. He also taught swordsmanship. Older boys were given real swords and made to slaughter pigs, to end any fantasies about samurai assaulting living flesh. In the old days, young samurai had trained by hacking at the bodies of executed criminals.

Nogi's real passions were skiing and mountain-climbing. He was a sponsor of Japan's first Antarctic expedition. So it was to his delight that the second son Chichibu, unlike the clumsy Hirohito, was an avid sportsman, and particularly enjoyed rock-climbing and skiing. These skills enabled him to join in outdoor activities with others that would normally be denied a prince of the blood. Equally good with an oar, Chichibu sculled along the coast at Hayama while his older brother walked the beach, searching tidal pools for marine specimens.

There was only one sport Hirohito really loved – sumo wrestling. As a boy he learned to push opponents out of the ring. Sumo has everything to do with remaining upright, keeping feet firmly on the ground. This became his lifelong passion. One of the few photographs ever published showing Hirohito grinning broadly was taken when he was nine, sumo wrestling with a tutor. Sumo never interested Chichibu at all.

The two princes slept in the same room, together day and night, until the death of their grandfather, Meiji, when Hirohito became crown prince and went to live alone at the Togu palace. This isolation became especially difficult for Hirohito, whose pensive nature made it difficult to cultivate friends. Chichibu's memoirs speak of his brother with affection, recalling bits of conversation. Had they only been samurai, life would have been different.

MY BROTHER: I like simple ways, but our position makes it difficult.

ME:	That's right. We can't do what we want.
MY BROTHER:	Even nobles can't . . .
ME:	Being nobles wouldn't help. We would have to be samurai.

Unlike Hirohito, who was intensely shy, Chichibu was confident and outgoing, cheerful, amiable and with a certain dash. He had been his grandfather's favourite. There were always rumours that Meiji or Taisho, or this clique or that, preferred to see Chichibu on the throne. Such rumours recurred in the 1920s, 1930s and 1940s. Whenever there was a crisis, it was whispered that Prince Chichibu might do this, or go there, and the outcome might turn on him. He was his mother's favourite as well. Family sources said she was 'extremely fond' of him.

A special high school was created for the brothers, called the Crown Prince's Learning Institute, overseen by Satsuma's famous Admiral Togo, hero of the Battle of Tsushima Strait in which he virtually destroyed Russia's Baltic fleet. The institute was in a wood-framed Western-style building at the Takanawa palace. It was decorated with maps and filled with lab equipment and natural-history specimens. The only decorations were pots of flowers raised by Hirohito. For seven years, he and five other boys studied there with routines like those of a British boarding school. Days began at 6 a.m. with breakfast, followed by a brisk twenty-minute walk. Lessons started at eight. After lunch and study hall, late afternoons were given to baseball, tennis, gymnastics, riding and swordsmanship. After supper there was another brisk walk before leisure time and bed. Hirohito spent this free time keeping a diary, which he had begun in the sixth grade using cheap student notebooks. Except for a few very brief fragments, these have been kept secret by the Imperial Household to this day. Because he had no aptitude for music, arts, crafts and composition, the subjects were downplayed. These were anyway not manly, and concerted effort was made instead to shape Hirohito to a military mould. Hirohito was introverted, unsmiling, overly meticulous. His mentors, mindful of Yamagata, gave the crown prince vigorous lessons in horseback riding and military science, plus a little French. Most Japanese children studied English, but French was still the international language of diplomacy and aristocracy. Later, he was taught some English, but was never fluent.

As Hirohito matured, worries increased about his posture and nearsightedness. The trees on the south side of his palace were cut down so he could see the ocean, and he was encouraged to stare at it to exercise his eyes. Instead his vision became weaker. Doctors favoured glasses, but the Imperial Household remained firmly opposed. How could the Son of Heaven wear spectacles? Even so, Hirohito's aides presented him with a pair to use in private. All the brothers except Takamatsu ended up wearing glasses. To correct his posture, a special chair was made so he could sit upright with his forearms flat on the armrests, his chest forward. He was to do all his reading here with his book on a raised, upright stand. No crown prince in generations had been subjected to such methodical and relentless control.

Ironically, many of the anxieties about Hirohito were misplaced. Chichibu did seem to be a better specimen, graceful, coordinated, urbane and athletic, but despite an extraordinarily adventurous career he spent the last years of his life as an invalid and died of tuberculosis before his fifty-first birthday. Hirohito, for all his disabilities, would live to the grand old age of 87, alert until the last months.

He was being prepared for the great solitude of the throne. Every Saturday, he visited his parents at the imperial palace. Once a week, his brothers came to see him. The rest of the time he had only the companionship of chamberlains, aides, valets and military men. One of his few indulgences was an occasional film.

On 3 November 1916, after his father's condition sharply deteriorated, Hirohito was officially declared crown prince to prepare for the succession. There was immediate speculation about who would be his empress. As had been the case for 'generations unbroken', he had no say in the matter. A number of eligibles were pictured in the press. There were more than a dozen candidates. Empress Sadako had used her periodic visits to the Peeresses School to look for prospective brides for her sons. After initial review by the Privy Council, only three girls remained. Matchmaking always reveals stress lines around the throne, even to this day. One girl was Yamagata's favourite, the favourite of Choshu. The other two, favourites of Sadako and Taisho, had links to three of Choshu's enemies, Aizu, Hizen and Satsuma. The silent struggle over which girl would be chosen lasted five years and was unusually vicious even by Japanese standards, with scurrilous leaks to the press, nasty insinuations, vile slander, and even threats of ritual suicide. It became a final power struggle between Empress Sadako and Yamagata.

As Japan's current strongman, his web extending through the military, police, secret police, courts, business, bureaucracy and underworld, Yamagata had incomparable leverage even in semi-retirement. A measure of his power was that he was 'not permitted' to retire. This charade meant that nobody was going to get rid of him easily. His grip on the palace and the government was maintained through proxies he had spent decades working into place. During the reign of Meiji, Yamagata was forced to take a back seat to Ito, the great impresario of the Restoration. After Ito's violent death, Yamagata's control of Taisho was frustrated by the young emperor's unpredictable nature and stubborn resistance to manipulation, supported by partisans of Satsuma and other clans opposed to Choshu. It must be remembered that Japan had an ancient tradition of strongmen going to extraordinary lengths to neutralize, isolate, badger, remove or murder reigning emperors, often accomplished by replacing them with compliant juveniles like Hirohito. And by his own admission, Yamagata had driven his own grandmother to suicide. So, when Yamagata was at last successful in driving Taisho around the bend, it became crucial to establish control over Hirohito by marrying him to a girl with the right loyalty ties, a practice that had been raised to a fine art in Japan over two thousand years. If Yamagata's nominee became the next empress, the Choshu military clique would control access to the palace and domination of the throne. Equally it became just as important for his enemies to prevent them doing so, by installing their own rival bridal candidate.

Yamagata's choice was Princess Ichijo Tokiko from the Fujiwara bride-pool of Five Regent Families. Meiji had married an Ichijo.

Naturally, Hirohito's parents had influence over whom their son would marry, but the sham of consensus neutralized this influence and made intrigue unavoidable. They needed as many allies as possible, so a devious strategy of their own was devised and they nominated two girls. First choice was Princess Masako, daughter of Prince Nashimoto. This girl was Sadako's favourite and the niece of her closest childhood friend, her Christian schoolmate Nabeshima Nobuko. The girl's parents were from the Aizu and Hizen clans, whose hatred of Choshu was absolute. On the principle that the enemy of my enemy is my friend, this made them very good friends of Satsuma.

Their fallback candidate was Princess Nagako, eldest daughter of Prince Kuni Kuniyoshi. In Leonard Mosley's popular biography of Hirohito, he says that Nagako's father was 'one of the most amiable rascals in the Japanese aristocracy', who had sired a total of eighteen children, nine of them by his wife, another nine with concubines. Actually the rascal was her grandfather, not her father. Her father had a good reputation to protect, as we will see. In 1916, when she was short-listed as one of the candidates for next empress, Nagako was only 14. Her first visit to the palace had been at the age of nine, when she accompanied her mother to pay a condolence call at the death of Emperor Meiji. That day the little girl only bowed and blushed, saying not a word, but she made a lasting impression on Empress Haruko, who asked for her photograph. During the last years of Haruko's life a warm friendship developed between her and the young princess. So it was Haruko who first broached to Sadako the idea that this girl would make a good bride one day.

An attractive, serious girl, she had a large number of Japanese Christian friends, which was an advantage to Sadako's network. As to Nagako's personal beliefs, we cannot be any more certain than with Sadako herself, for members of the imperial family are never officially identified as Christians. Any suggestion that the emperor

148

or members of his immediate family might be Christian, or even half-Christian, would inflame Shinto and Buddhist fanatics.

Opinions again polarized into 'Open' and 'Closed' camps: those who favoured opening to the outside world, and those committed to isolation, the 'frogs in the well'. Yamagata was adept at manipulating both groups in order to try to diminish Empress Sadako's influence over the court and the future of the imperial family.

Yet Empress Sadako was also a capable strategist. She had carefully built her own influence at court. Her friends described her as 'charming, vivacious, low-voiced', but always alert and intense. When she asked questions, her fingers continually turned in her lap. Nobody could spend time in the palace without becoming aware of her force and influence. The Imperial Household organization was gradually infiltrated by her agents. Sadako refused to be intimidated by its chamberlains, nor did she allow them to control every detail of her life. (They even sought to decide the conduct and duration of her private audiences with friends.)

One observer, Dr Koizumi Shinzo, said Sadako was 'a wise and thoughtful woman, and a wonderful judge of men. It was natural that many of our leading personages, especially Count Makino and Baron Shidehara, had sought opportunities to talk with her.'

Not everyone admired her. Prime Minister Hara, a Yamagata man, complained bitterly about the problems he was having because of Emperor Taisho's 'incapacity' and Empress Sadako's growing influence. Hara was not from Choshu, but married a Choshu girl, after which he shifted to Yamagata's clique. Hara became so irritated with the empress and her Christian allies that he huffed: 'Recently it has got to the point where one must do

149

everything through the empress, and I am very concerned about the abuses this might lead to in the future.'

Before a decision could be made about which of the girls would be Hirohito's bride, the Peeresses School had to give detailed accounts of the candidates' education, and the head of the Imperial Household paid repeated visits to their homes to investigate every detail of their lives, while palace doctors poked and prodded every inch of their bodies. Nothing negative was discovered.

By 1917, Yamagata had gathered enough support to overrule the choice of Sadako's favourite, Princess Masako. While his own candidate was from the Five Regent Families of the Fujiwara, he objected to Masako because she was not. This was only a technicality, but it was easier to gather consensus on a technicality than it was for anyone to admit to their real motives. Masako was married instead to the crown prince of Korea, in an attempt to assuage the bitterness between the two countries.

Yamagata was equally opposed to Princess Nagako for a number of reasons. First, she was Sadako's choice; second, her mother was part of the enemy Shimazu family of Satsuma; and finally, her paternal grandfather had been a bitter adversary of Choshu, backing the wrong side in the Meiji Restoration. He was pardoned in 1875 and eight years later his family – Kuni – was grafted on as a part of the imperial family. Unless Yamagata could find some other basis to dismiss her candidacy, he would have to swallow the bitter pill.

In January 1918, when Yamagata was briefly away from Tokyo, Sadako and Taisho quickly concluded a private betrothal agreement with Nagako's parents. Before Yamagata returned, Nagako's engagement to Hirohito was announced. For once, the general was caught completely off-guard. When he heard what had been done, he was furious, and redoubled his efforts to find an excuse to destroy the girl. Meanwhile, he fumed that the engagement was arranged behind his back. He had not been 'advised of the negotiations' nor given a chance to 'offer his objections' before it was announced. For the moment, the best he could do was to characterize the engagement as 'unofficial'.

As she was now Hirohito's fiancée, Nagako spent the next two years being tutored in court lore, protocol and etiquette. During that period she met Hirohito socially several times, but it could hardly be called a courtship.

Meanwhile, Yamagata launched a counteroffensive, leaning hard on Taisho, pressing him to retract the engagement and finding ways to increase pressure on the throne. Taisho bore up until November 1919, when he suffered his first massive stroke. Hirohito, who was 18, took over ceremonial duties.

Taisho's stroke was the opportunity for which Yamagata had been waiting. There was no way to be sure how long Taisho would survive as an invalid. Prince Saionji, Yamagata and Prime Minister Hara waged an energetic campaign to have the emperor officially retired and for Hirohito to be named regent. Instead of hiding the emperor's decline, as had been the case with Meiji, Yamagata saw to it that the newspapers carried frequent reports of Taisho's increasingly feeble condition. Next, Hara and Yamagata agreed on a division of power: 'Politics are the government's responsibility and the court is the Genro's.' The prime minister would make daily political decisions, while Yamagata and Saionji would decide court strategy and manipulate Hirohito through Baron Nakamura, the Choshu head of the Imperial Household. To make sure that Prime Minister

Hara knew that members of the imperial family were off-limits to him, Yamagata warned him not to visit the palace too frequently.

Next to having Hirohito named regent, the most important item on Yamagata's palace agenda was the forthcoming marriage. The engagement could still be reversed if something negative could be discovered about Nagako or her family. With Yamagata's entire web searching, something could turn up. It did. At the end of 1920, newspapers excitedly reported a 'grave court affair' – a struggle 'between a few dozen influential men at the palace and in the high bureaucracy'. Journalist Morgan Young called it 'a sordid struggle on the steps of the throne'.

Yamagata disclosed a devastating genetic weakness in Nagako's family – on the Shimazu/Satsuma side. Yamagata's family physician, Dr Hirai, had discovered an article in a medical journal written by a specialist in heredity, discussing colour blindness in the Shimazu family. On the basis of this article, Yamagata declared that Nagako's ancestors had been colour-blind, clear evidence of genetic flaws in her lineage. While not explicitly saying so, he made it clear that the Sons of Heaven had enough biological problems already.

Without consulting the emperor, the empress or the crown prince, Yamagata sent messengers to Nagako's father, Prince Kuni, appealing to his patriotism, requesting that he withdraw his daughter from consideration because of the genetic dangers to the imperial line. Backed by Prime Minister Hara and Baron Nakamura, he said everything possible must be done to protect the purity of the imperial bloodline. To ensure that Prince Kuni would not suffer unnecessary hardship because of this change of plan, Yamagata sent along a couple of Choshu nobles who promised the prince a large financial settlement once the engagement was called off.

Enraged, Prince Kuni sat down and wrote a long formal memorandum to Empress Sadako: 'I . . . took every possible step to check into the matter of colour blindness in our family before accepting the royal offer, and came to the conclusion that the trait was virtually negligible . . . There are only two situations which I feel would make it imperative to cancel my daughter's engagement to the crown prince. First, if their majesties the emperor and the empress or the crown prince himself deemed it better that way. Second, if I were convinced that the marriage would inevitably bring weakness to the imperial line. Herein enclosed your majesty will find a complete set of scientific findings about the nature of the colour blindness in our family and its transmissability. I . . . beg your majesty to check into the matter and favor me with imperial advice.'

In fact, the authoritative medical report did not even speak of 'colour blindness' but only of 'colour weakness'. Yamagata was found to be exaggerating.

While waiting for a reply from Empress Sadako, Prince Kuni threatened to bring down the curtain on the whole sordid episode in very dramatic style. Writing to Prince Fushimi, who also opposed the marriage, Nagako's father coldly reviewed the situation: 'It was the imperial house itself that asked for my daughter's hand. If the engagement is to be broken, it should be done by the imperial house. And I'd like to add that if that comes to pass, I shall be forced to answer the insult to me and my family by first stabbing Nagako to death, and then committing suicide myself.'

He asked Prince Fushimi, 'Is this idea sanctioned by Their Majesties the Emperor and the Empress? Or is someone making noise to annoy us?'

Word of Prince Kuni's warning spread quickly. Prime Minister Hara said he was outraged by Kuni's 'surprisingly rude behaviour'.

When this news reached the outlaws of the Black Ocean Society they were electrified. To everyone's astonishment, Toyama Mitsuru's thugs turned against Yamagata, who had been their patron and co-conspirator for decades. All over Japan, Black Ocean henchmen passed out pamphlets in the streets, giving the broad outlines of Yamagata's backstage machinations. One source said it was Hirohito's tutor in ethics who got the Black Ocean boss aroused by pointing out that Yamagata was showing 'disrespect' for the throne. Toyama hired crowds of students to shout 'Death to Yamagata' and 'Nakamura insults the emperor'. Yamagata's magnificent villa and gardens had to be ringed by armed guards. Possibly Satsuma called in some private debts as well from this paramilitary organization.

Most observers expressed surprise that the incident exploded as it did. One Japanese source even asserts that Yamagata was 'fond' of Princess Nagako and was 'very sorry' to have discovered the bad news about her genes. How unfortunate that the girl's father had the bad taste to announce his plan to disembowel the two of them, to expiate the shame. Japan's 'pure blood' fanatics (Yamagata among them) were outdone by the 'shame' fanatics. In a society where getting caught is the worst possible crime, shame fanatics have a certain advantage. Prince Kuni's warning that he would kill his daughter and then commit suicide gave anti-Choshu partisans just what they needed. Journalist Morgan Young was baffled: 'It is incomprehensible why Yamagata, who was all-powerful, ever allowed the struggle to take place.' He overlooked some evidence from Yamagata himself. In December 1920 the general had written to Prince Kuni about his distress over the engagement. While the letter was twelve feet long, the essence of the quarrel was explained in a few brush-strokes. 'The fact is that the engagement was arranged, so to speak, behind our back. If we had been advised of the negotiations, we would have been able to offer our humble point of view beforehand.'

Bent on revenge, Yamagata had now gone too far. A stain of such magnitude was too much even for the old spider. His ally, Baron Nakamura, head of the Imperial Household, had to resign in disgrace to take the blame for his master's gaffe. This cost Yamagata his senior agent in the palace, a great victory for the anti-Choshu alliance. Pouring salt in the wound, they arranged for the baron to be replaced by Satsuma's urbane Count Makino.

One of Yamagata's oldest enemies, political party leader Okuma, declared: 'As for Prince Yamagata, it is incumbent upon him to resign all the public offices he holds, to say nothing of renouncing his treatment as a Genro, so as to apologize to the emperor and to the nation. Otherwise it would be impossible to placate the nation, which feels high resentment against his attitude.' (The forthright Okuma was fond of saying that he had many scars on his body, but none on his back.)

On 10 February 1921, newspapers carried a palace announcement that no changes would be made in the wedding arrangements for Crown Prince Hirohito. Soon afterwards, Yamagata wrote a letter to the throne beginning with the traditional deceit, 'I am merely a soldier.'

He begged to be released from all his official positions, and asked for permission to give up his court rank and princedom, and all his decorations. Empress Sadako let him squirm for several months. In late May 1921 Yamagata had a formal audience with the failing Emperor Taisho, who coldly handed him a written message rejecting his resignation. His part in the affair was excused and his positions and honours, and his loyalty, were officially confirmed. (A good example of 'winning by losing'.) The empress, and the emperor he had sought to humiliate and destroy, had outfoxed him and then forgiven him – the ultimate put-down. It was Yamagata's last visit to the palace.

His public virtue restored, but his personal chagrin complete, Yamagata died the following winter. In the longer term nobody could stave off the military takeover of Japan that he had set in motion since the 1890s, but in the course of the next three decades, Sadako and her more enlightened circle would remain the dominant force inside the palace, and she would live to see Choshu's top generals go to the gallows in 1945.

CHAPTER 5

OUT OF THE CAGE

While the Yamato court was preoccupied with the Hirohito betrothal struggle, Europe was engaged in the bloodiest war in history, radically altering the balance of world power. After World War I, the United States – which joined the fray only near the end but profited greatly as arms merchant and financier – emerged with the resources to influence global diplomacy in a way Britain previously had. This power shift had a profound and little-understood impact on Japan because it damaged the crucial links that had existed for a long time between Tokyo and London.

Britain had played a significant backstage role in the Meiji coup, and had been the first nation to recognize the legitimacy of the new emperor and the Restoration government in 1868. British merchants had supported the young radicals and the clans plotting to overthrow the shogun. There were secret arms sales, alliances and loans. Over subsequent decades many British royals had visited Tokyo, including the Duke of Edinburgh in 1869, Princes Albert and George in 1881, the Duke of Connaught in 1890 and his son, Prince Arthur, in 1906, when he conveyed the Order of the Garter to the Meiji emperor. There had also been royal visitors to Japan from Russia and Germany, but not as many, and their visits were clouded by quarrels over zones of influence in North Asia. At the start of the twentieth century Britain was anxious to counteract the new alliance of France, Germany and Russia, both in Europe and in Asia. This would be easier if Britain had a strong ally in Asia, and the result was the Anglo-Japanese Alliance of 1902. This alliance was of great importance to Japan's international stature and gave the impression that Britain was Japan's only real friend in the world. True enough.

Equality with the West had been one of the goals of the Meiji era. In the nineteenth century the Western powers had all been involved in gunboat diplomacy, in which one would use force to penetrate a part of Asia and the rest would rush in demanding similar privileges. Asia became a patchwork of European colonies and spheres of influence, which America joined when it seized the Philippines from Spain in 1898. Japan was determined to avoid the same fate.

No Asian nation was considered worthy of respect until Japan's surprising emergence as a military force at the beginning of the twentieth century. Her diplomats had to broker deals to make Tokyo an equal partner in what the West called the Great Game. The overriding foreign-policy goal was to become a member of one of these powerful coalitions, both to protect Japan from predators like Russia and to guarantee diplomatic and economic support in the pursuit of Japanese commercial or territorial ambitions on the Asian mainland. Britain was the first choice as an ally because of her support during the Meiji Restoration and because of the many similarities that existed between the two offshore island nations, their royal families and some of their traditions.

For Britain as well, there were many reasons why an

alliance with Japan made sense, not least being that her far-flung empire was increasingly difficult to defend alone. The Anglo-Japanese Alliance bound London and Tokyo to assist one another in safeguarding their respective interests in North Asia. As part of the package, Britain bolstered Japan financially during the difficult period of the Russo-Japanese War of 1904–5 and kept other countries from becoming involved. When the Japanese Navy defeated the Russian fleet in 1905, Britons cheered. Aside from trouncing Britain's leading rival in the Great Game, most of the victorious Japanese fleet had been built in England. When Tokyo needed loans in the years that followed, these were underwritten by British financiers, sometimes with participation by American colleagues. Japan went on the gold standard, and 300 British-trained Japanese were given the job of organizing a sound banking and financial system for Japan. The alliance was renewed after the Russo-Japanese War and again in 1911 after Japan's annexation of Korea, demonstrating that Britain endorsed both events.

World War I gave Japan a chance to enhance her international prestige further. Largely because of the Anglo-Japanese Alliance, she entered the war on the Allied side. Her navy patrolled the Indian Ocean, protecting Australia and New Zealand. She sent a cruiser and fourteen destroyers to the Mediterranean to escort Allied shipping there. Japanese ships guarded the great Europe-bound convoy of troops from Australia and New Zealand. Japanese forces helped keep order in Singapore, Hong Kong and Shanghai while Britain's manpower was occupied in Europe. Japanese troops occupied German possessions in the Pacific and the German naval base at Tsingtao.

After World War I this exclusive alliance began to be

challenged by America. Washington claimed that Britain had been let down because Japan had not sent troops to join in the ground war in Europe, and pointed out that Japanese companies had taken advantage of Britain's war-preoccupation to penetrate its commercial markets all over East and Southeast Asia. Just as everything that happened in Asia during the nineteenth century was deeply influenced by British meddling, everything that happened in Asia during the twentieth century would be influenced by American meddling.

The United States now had great economic clout and was in a position to steer world events. Thanks to its massive war loans, war production, agricultural production and general exports, the Great War had made the US the biggest creditor nation in the world. Everyone owed America money, except the Japanese. A tired, demoralized and nearly bankrupt Britain was faced with a choice between American and Japanese goodwill. Britain's huge war debts, most of them owed to America's House of Morgan, gave the United States tremendous financial leverage. With all these war profits, Morgan Bank was looking closely at investment opportunities in Japan, so its influence was being felt in London, Tokyo and Washington.

Washington recognized that the British Empire was beginning to weaken in Asia, and saw all the commercial advantages this could present to American enterprise in the future. Britain tried to get America to join as a third party in the Anglo-Japanese Alliance, which could have had historic consequences. But America and Japan were now the world's two biggest naval powers. America saw Japan as its great future rival in the Pacific, and was determined to break the Anglo-Japanese Alliance.

This situation called for an extraordinary act of diplomacy. In 1921, it was decided to send Crown Prince Hirohito on an image-building tour to Britain (and more or less incidentally to Western Europe as well). London would be his main destination, where it was hoped that his visit, an unprecedented gesture, would encourage the British government to resist US pressure to end the alliance.

No Japanese emperor or crown prince had ever travelled further than neighbouring Korea, which Hirohito's father had visited briefly in 1907 while he was still crown prince. There had been plans for Meiji to make a European tour in the early 1880s, but the proposal was blocked by conservatives at court, aghast at the idea of a Son of Heaven being contaminated by immersion in alien cultures. In any case, Meiji's grand tours of Japan had shown him to be an unhappy tourist, unable to hide his boredom and restlessness. He might have done no better in Europe. Although Taisho was invited to tour the United States, doctors said his health was not up to it. Unlike Meiji, the outgoing Taisho probably would have been an amiable guest, but at the time Japan did not want to jeopardize its vital economic and military links with Britain by getting too cosy with America.

Hirohito's visit to London was opposed by the army's ultranationalist Control Group who were gaining leverage in Tokyo, forging secret alliances with banking and industrial cliques. The rise of such ultra-nationalist groups was isolating the Anglophiles in Japan's Foreign Ministry just at a point when their influence was crucial to preserving the alliance. Among these were the diplomats Yoshida Shigeru and Matsudaira Tsuneo. They had both served in London, forming lasting friendships with senior British government officials and leading members of British society, who shared their commitment to continued friendship between the two countries.

Hirohito's journey was to last six months. In addition to England, Scotland and France, he would visit Belgium, the Netherlands, Italy and the Vatican. A last-minute invitation from the United States was turned down to make it perfectly clear that Japan favoured its bond with Britain.

The crown prince set out from Yokohama on 3 March 1921, aboard the cruiser *Katori*, escorted by the cruiser *Kashima* – both British built – accompanied by a cloud of equerries, military officers, valets, instructors and interpreters. In his personal entourage was his 56-year-old cousin Prince Kanin Kotohito, a strikingly handsome man, moustached, fit and well tailored. Prince Kanin's appearance was so un-Japanese that in France he often passed for a Parisian. Also there was Hirohito's 65-year-old political adviser, American-educated Count Chinda Sutemi who had been ambassador in London between 1916 and 1920 and had attended the Versailles peace talks. The crown prince's chief aide-de-camp was 53-year-old Nara Takeji, the personal choice of Empress Sadako. Others in the entourage included Count Makino, who would be the principal civilian adviser to the throne until the end of 1935. He was a tall, slim, nervous, thin-lipped man of 59 and spoke excellent English, having spent eight unhappy years as a boy studying in the United States. In 1919 he also had been at the Versailles peace talks. Another in the retinue was Okamura Yasuji, an agent of the army's Control Group and one of its most manipulative trio, who called themselves the Three Crows.

In each port of call, Hirohito went ashore bracketed by bodyguards, two bulletproof vests always at hand. Despite the warnings of a Shinto priest the voyage passed without incident. After a courtesy call at Okinawa, all stops along the way – Hong Kong, Singapore, Colombo, Aden, Suez, Port Said, Malta and Gibraltar – were British, and thanks to the Anglo-Japanese Alliance the crown prince received a warm welcome at each, with 21-gun salutes and formal welcoming ceremonies. Hirohito passed days at sea swimming in a pool on deck and was judged to be an excellent swimmer. He practised golf, teeing off into the Indian Ocean in preparation for British fairways. His courtiers were terrified that he might make a gaffe at Buckingham Palace, or a gaucherie at the Elysée Palace, so he was coached daily in the peculiarities of British etiquette, and the mysteries of French wine and cheese. Hours were spent at tables spread with linen, silver and crystal, explaining banquet protocol and teaching Hirohito how to wield a knife and fork in the British and continental styles.

During a stop at Malta he saw his first opera, Verdi's *Otello*. He also visited a cemetery where seventy-seven Japanese crewmen were buried after their frigate was sunk while escorting an Allied convoy in World War I.

Then there was a panic about his wardrobe. Yoshida, first secretary at the embassy in London, hired a master tailor from Savile Row and rushed him to Gibraltar to measure the crown prince from top to toe. The tailor then hurried home to oversee the cutting and stitching of a complete wardrobe to be ready when the *Katori* reached Portsmouth. Nobody thought a British Army dress uniform would be needed, therefore one had to be hastily made up later so that Hirohito could become an honorary field marshal in the British Army. (The honour was withdrawn in 1941 when Japan attacked Britain's Asian colonies.)

In the meantime, Hirohito let his schoolboy crewcut

grow out. He had to be ready for appearances at the House of Commons, receptions and dinner parties, visits to British banks, to Oxford, Cambridge and Edinburgh universities, to country estates, castles, golf courses and trout streams. Along the way he was to become a Knight of the Garter.

His French was fairly good, and his English was improving, but when the *Katori* arrived at Portsmouth on 9 May 1921, where he was welcomed ashore by the Prince of Wales, he was too shy to speak English. This was all the better, for it enabled the official interpreters to filter whatever he said. The royal party took the train to London, where they were welcomed at Victoria Station by King George V and rode in horse-drawn carriages to Buckingham Palace along a route lined by cheering throngs.

For three days Hirohito was a guest of the Windsors at the palace. The first evening began with a gala banquet unmatched for splendour since before the Great War. There were 128 people at the table. In his toast, King George recalled his own visit to Japan with his brother Albert in 1881, when they were graciously entertained by Emperor Meiji and Empress Haruko.

The Japanese naval attaché in London, Admiral Takeshita Isamu, who served as one of the interpreters during the tour, reported that Hirohito's remarks were composed and forceful, carrying throughout the spacious hall. 'He mixed freely with the guests, his British hosts as well as us Japanese, a pleasant smile constantly on his lips. It would be difficult for anyone in Japan to imagine how intimate he was. No matter what the title or position of his interlocutor, the crown prince never lost his composure or was at a loss for words. One could not help but think that, after all, there were

2,500 years of imperial blood flowing in his veins.'

Yoshida Shigeru described Hirohito's reception as 'extraordinary'. The crown prince had been given 'respectful affection' by all levels of British society, high and low, he said, which he attributed to 'his inborn beautiful characteristics, [his] simple and natural naiveté, [and his] virtue of modesty'. He said Hirohito greeted the Windsors as if it were 'a meeting of relatives'.

The gregarious informality of the Windsors – compared to severe Japanese etiquette – was something for which no amount of tutoring could have prepared the crown prince or his entourage. They were dumbfounded when King George sauntered into Hirohito's suite at breakfast time, wearing only trousers, an open shirt, braces and slippers, and clapped the crown prince on the back.

'I hope, me boy,' he said, 'that everyone is giving you everything you want while you are here. If there is anything you need, just ask. I'll never forget how your grandfather treated me and me brother when we were in Yokohama. I've always wanted to repay his kindness.' Chuckling, he added, 'No geishas here, though, I'm afraid. Her Majesty would never allow it.'

Hirohito was touched. 'I was deeply pleased at the time because King George spoke to me as if I were his son.' Many friendly conversations followed that gave him 'a first-hand knowledge of English politics'. He also noticed the obvious affection of the British people for their monarch.

Lord Curzon, the foreign secretary, gave a luncheon for the crown prince at Carlton House Terrace, followed by a performance by the ballerina Anna Pavlova (described by the Japanese as 'a dancer from France'). Curzon later praised Hirohito's 'intelligence, amiability, dignity of demeanour and anxiety to please', while Prime Minister Lloyd George called Japan a 'steadfast ally'. All these events occurred with a heartiness and clamour that was completely alien to Japanese social life, at least among the aristocracy. Despite the bruised sensibilities of some of his own retinue, Hirohito fared remarkably well and was universally acclaimed by his hosts.

After the third day at Buckingham Palace, the royal visit ended and the Japanese moved to Chesterfield House as guests of the British government. Next came a round of social and ceremonial events laced with sightseeing, and Hirohito wore his new uniform of honorary British field marshal to Sandhurst, Aldershot and Camberley. On a visit to Oxford he watched a regatta, and at Cambridge he toured the library and received an honorary doctorate of law. In London, he spent an hour sitting for a portrait by Augustus John, a painting now in the imperial palace in Kyoto. The painter noted that Hirohito had an unruly cowlick, which his valet kept trying to pat back into place.

On 19 May he took the train north to Edinburgh, where he received another doctorate and stayed at Holyrood Palace, before moving on to Blair Castle in the Highlands as the guest of the Duke of Atholl. At tiny Scottish villages that had never before set eyes upon a gentleman from Japan, Hirohito was greeted – as his official diarists recorded – by 'lovely country lassies' who adorned him with garlands of flowers. It was a brilliant stroke, giving the Japanese an utterly incongruous taste of the rural good life, far away from the anxious ceremony of London.

Blair Castle was the centrepiece of a huge estate. There was time to stroll the glens and to fish. Miles Lampson, who helped organize the tour for the Foreign Office, concluded that one of the highlights of the Scottish leg was 'when we inducted the crown prince into the gentle art of snouking [sniffing out] salmon'. At a banquet the night before Hirohito's departure, members of leading English and Scottish families in the area mingled freely with their servants, and with the estate's shepherds and farming families, who came with their wives and children. Wine and whisky flowed, bagpipes wailed and rich and poor drank, sang and danced together, climaxed by the duke's musicians playing the Japanese national anthem, *Kimigayo,* on bagpipes.

Although Hirohito did not join in the dancing, he seemed to enjoy the evening hugely. The sight of the duke dancing with a village woman, and the duchess dancing with a rough farmer, inspired one of the retinue to exclaim: 'A genuine democracy without class distinction!' For a caged bird, this was an astonishing and refreshing change from imperial Japanese protocol and Hirohito spoke enthusiastically of 'How nice it would be if the [Japanese] imperial family could do something like this, to get into direct touch with the people.' Visiting shipyards in Glasgow, the crown prince was startled to discover that the workers would not bow, but insisted upon shaking his hand. As the visit to Scotland came to an end, the Duke of Atholl sent Hirohito off with a good supply of single malt to mellow his return home.

Although the fate of the Anglo-Japanese Alliance still was undecided, the visit was judged a grand success. For the first time, a Japanese royal had become an international media celebrity. *The Times* of London called Hirohito 'a modest and gentle prince', and went on: 'One of the Crown Prince's greatest assets . . . is his striking resemblance both in person and character to his grandfather the great Emperor [Meiji]. This resemblance has been the subject of much comment during the last two or three years when, owing to the ill-health of the Emperor [Taisho], the Crown Prince often took his place at the reception of foreign ambassadors and other court functions. It is related that many of the court dignitaries were moved to tears by the striking resemblance of the Crown Prince's appearance and deportment to that of his grandfather.'

His own advisers were surprised. Hirohito was so poised there were even rumours that it was really a stand-in. Hearing these reports, the Prince of Wales (later King Edward VIII) remarked to Hirohito that this was the first time he had ever been in the presence of 'a ghost', someone who seemed to be there but actually was not there.

Japanese newspapers and magazines fed their readers a steady diet of tour news. A women's magazine published a special issue with minute details of Hirohito's engagements, essays by Japanese officials in his retinue, maps and numerous photographs. The Japanese people were solemnly assured that their crown prince had carried it all off with dignity and confidence.

One of the small mysteries remaining from Hirohito's European tour persists to this day. According to a Western biographer, 'There are still rumours in Japan that during part of his tour he disappeared from official ken for at least twenty-four hours and sampled the entertainments provided by British geishas.' This is alleged to have taken place at the instigation of the Prince of Wales while Hirohito was staying at Buckingham Palace. The gist is that late one night, while his retinue slept soundly, Prince Edward spirited Hirohito out from under their noses and took him off to one of London's more exclusive brothels. This seems highly unlikely, given the obsessive security concerns of his Japanese entourage, and may owe more to the erroneous popular image of Prince Edward as a bon vivant.

If Hirohito had such an experience, it is far more likely to have occurred on the private leg of his tour in Paris, when he was in the company of his playboy uncles, Prince Higashikuni, Prince Asaka and Prince Kitashirakawa.

Aside from a grand luncheon at the Elysée Palace given by the French president, and a reciprocal banquet at the Japanese Embassy, this visit to France was private. He toured Versailles. When he took a ride on the Paris Metro he was reprimanded by a conductor for trying to squeeze into an overflowing car. 'I had a good scolding,' he recalled wryly years later. Unlike Britain where he was dependent upon interpreters to fill in the details, Hirohito was able to speak and read French with some fluency, so the Gallic reprimand was savoury. On exiting from the Metro, he pocketed his ticket instead of throwing it away, and still had it at the time of his death in 1989.

He spent much of his time in France in the company of his three uncles. Princes Asaka and Higashikuni were half-brothers, Kitashirakawa a cousin. Power clusters in Japan are based often on same birth years, same school and so on, but this trio were more fortunate than most. Born the same year, they had been students together at the Peers School, then had gone together to the military academy in Tokyo, gained commissions in the Imperial Army, and each married a daughter of the Meiji emperor. As dowries the princesses brought great wealth and large tracts of land. Asaka and Kitashirakawa built mansions in Takanawa, the southernmost section of Tokyo, overlooking Tokyo Bay. Higashikuni built an art-deco palace outside Yokohama.

Originally, they had been a quartet. Prince Takeda Tsunehisa had married the fourth of Meiji's surviving daughters. However, Takeda had died in 1919. His son would become a favourite of the other three, and play an important role in World War II.

The trio had come to Paris in 1920. Higashikuni is said to have quarrelled with the Taisho emperor and been sent abroad to get him out of Tokyo, and his two pals joined him. They made a pretence of being attached to the Japanese Embassy as military attachés and of being part-time students at France's St Cyr military academy, but they were only having a good time. Instead of military uniforms, these good-looking young men sported bowler hats, moustaches and suits cut to the latest Paris styles. There was no shortage of cash, and all three had powerful handbuilt Bugatti roadsters or touring cars. Princess Fusako, the wife of Kitashirakawa, had come with him. They settled into a leased mansion facing the Bois de Boulogne. Princess Fusako furnished it lavishly and filled her wardrobe with Paris fashions. They were quickly welcomed into the balls and galas of high society, and did not neglect low society, making frequent visits to dives and brothels. Prince Asaka's wife was expecting their fourth child and reluctantly stayed behind in Japan. Prince Higashikuni and his wife were not fond of each other, so she was happy to remain in Tokyo. In Paris he kept several stunning European mistresses, roared around drinking absinthe with them and regularly made the gossip columns in items of scandal.

Princes Higashikuni, Asaka and Kitashirakawa took the crown prince to dinner at La Perouse, where – to the revulsion of his aides – Hirohito ate snails. Dining out in

Paris like this he judged to be the climax of his trip. One night he appears to have gone with Higashikuni to what was then the most famous brothel in the city of love – the Sphinx – inspiring the rumours that persist to this day. But no certain evidence has turned up in any French archive; those at St Cyr were destroyed by US bombing in World War II.

There were many smaller pleasures. In Amsterdam, Hirohito strolled through the galleries of the Rijksmuseum, lingered before the Rembrandts, and watched the cutters at a diamond factory. He ate fettuccini with Italy's King Victor Emmanuel and talked with the Pope. Then he took the train to Naples, visited the ruins of Pompeii, saw that Mount Vesuvius was no match for Fujiyama, and boarded the cruiser *Katori* for the two-month voyage home. Prime Minister Hara wrote in his diary: 'The trip was a huge success and the imperial family and Japan will benefit from it in the future.'

It was, however, not as great a success as was hoped. Under mounting pressure from the United States, in June 1921, while Hirohito was still in Europe, Britain buckled and agreed not to renew the Anglo-Japanese Alliance. Many Britons expressed grave concern and the Japanese were shocked. Winston Churchill later remarked that terminating the alliance created 'a profound impression in Japan and was viewed as the spurning of an Asiatic power by the Western world. Many links were surrendered which might afterwards have proved of decisive value to peace.' Suddenly, not only was Russia – now the Soviet Union – a fearful enemy, but Britain too was seen by Japan as a perfidious power. America's undermining of the alliance was downplayed in the decades that followed, but this was the first in a series of unfortunate developments that would lead ultimately to the Pacific

War. Tokyo was left isolated and friendless, without any allies until the conclusion of the Tripartite pact with Germany and Italy in September 1940.

Less obvious was the impact this reversal had on the influence in Japan of many cosmopolitan, pro-British (and pro-American) members of the elite, including thousands of Japanese who had studied or travelled abroad. Britain's encouragement had been vital to their efforts to make Japan more open and less xenophobic. The alliance had given Japan worldwide stature, and tipped the diplomatic balance in favour of those who sought to solve problems by negotiation rather than by force. Another slap in the face to the Japanese had occurred at the Versailles peace talks when a clause declaring racial equality was rejected after heavy lobbying by yellow-peril jingoists from the United States and Australia.

In Tokyo, the hand of the army Control Group was immeasurably strengthened when the Anglo-Japanese Alliance ended, and before Hirohito got home the first dynamic steps were put into motion to prepare for war against the West. Princes Higashikuni, Asaka and Kitashirakawa numbered among their circle some of Japan's most conspiratorial army officers. Two of the Three Crows were already serving as military attachés in European capitals, and after they were joined by the third Crow – Okamura from Hirohito's entourage – they met secretly at Baden-Baden to plan for the day when they would return to Japan to help complete the army's rise to absolute power and wage total war on the West. With cooperation from Japan's *zaibatsu* conglomerates, secret military installations were begun under industrial cover in the American Philippines, the Dutch East Indies and elsewhere, including underground complexes that doubled as mining operations, all-weather airstrips on isolated plantations and submarine pens carved out of coastal mountains with naval gun emplacements overlooking the South China Sea. Only now has evidence emerged that this was set in motion in 1921 when the Anglo-Japanese Alliance ended, two decades before Pearl Harbor.

Despite the diplomatic setback, the European tour was exhilarating for the crown prince, as his brother Prince Chichibu confirmed: 'Apparently some people feel that since [Hirohito] was brought up in confined circumstances, he does not much mind living a caged existence. This is not my view . . . [His] feelings are evident in a letter I received from him: "England gave me my first experience of personal freedom." . . . It is my belief that [he] was quite dissatisfied with his restricted life within the Imperial Palace.'

Hirohito told Chichibu, 'I knew freedom as a man for the first time in England.' Again and again he returned to the bird image. 'My life up until then was like that of a bird in a cage.' This trip to Europe, he said, had 'allowed the caged bird to fly'. He later told his aide General Honjo Shigeru, 'I enjoyed my freedom when I went on a tour of Europe. The only time I feel happy is when I am able to experience a similar feeling of freedom.'

Chichibu experienced the same freedom when he went abroad three years later. But life for the third brother, Prince Takamatsu, was far more restricted, as he revealed in private musings to his diary: 'I can never have the freedom I crave.' The difference in age between Hirohito and Chichibu was only fourteen months. They had a bond that was not shared with Takamatsu, who was nearly two and a half years younger than Chichibu.

Takamatsu never got on well with Hirohito. In later years, Hirohito criticized Takamatsu for 'making problems' and 'for his lack of respect for authority'.

Although Hirohito and Chichibu kept diaries, these were kept secret by the Imperial Household. For this reason we know little about their personal views except as interpreted by third parties – advisers, companions, bystanders, or the discreet memoir published by Princess Chichibu in the early 1990s. In the case of Prince Takamatsu, however, his diaries were discovered in a warehouse in the 1990s and were published in Japanese by his widow over the protests of the Imperial Household. In them we find a surprising self-portrait of the third prince, a young man filled with anger, defiance and self-doubt. At 16, while Hirohito was abroad, he wrote: 'When I asked a military aide why he always follows me he said that Principal Suzuki had ordered him to accompany me, even into the classroom. At this I began to weep. As the class was about to start I had to pull myself together. It seems that wherever I go inside the school they will follow me. Why can't I be trusted to walk on my own? When the aides are here they have to follow the Principal's orders. In the long run there is nothing for it but for me to do what I want to, regardless of them. I can't give them orders myself. It really is awful. So from now on I shall have no sympathy for them.'

On a separate sheet in the diary for 1929 he wrote: 'I cannot understand why it is imperative for the imperial family to serve in the military. In the first place why is an imperial family necessary? I can't help thinking that the imperial family is not needed. Because Japan is a country ruled by a "line of emperors unbroken for ages eternal" perhaps a Crown Prince is necessary to ensure the succession, and I can't deny that it is desirable to have some

174

people in reserve, however that doesn't mean that there have to be countless such "reserves". No one has yet calculated the number scientifically, I imagine. I think maybe one or two. If you think about it that is the only reason I have to occupy the position of royalty. I am not saying that I am worthless as a member of the imperial family but I don't think that simply living as a spare is enough. The whole existence, the whole duty of the spare is just to exist and to do nothing bad. Having plenty of virtues and knowledge is also a mandatory requirement for the spare. So you could say that the imperial family is a purely internal thing, not an active one. In some senses I acknowledge that, but at present the education of the imperial family takes no account of the current state of affairs. At least, they haven't been given the opportunity to find out.' As to being a spare, he said that 'no other occupation is so ridiculous'.

These fragments are typical of the outpouring in Takamatsu's diaries, showing him to be an intelligent, compassionate and complex individual, who suffered much from the stifling atmosphere of the imperial family and the severe regimentation imposed upon every tiny aspect of his life by the minions watching and reporting his every twitch. Indeed, the Japanese police state that was evolving was never more neurotic than where it applied to its imperial hostages. Takamatsu must have been acutely jealous of the relative freedom enjoyed by his older brothers while he was only 'a cockroach living in the mountains'. But Takamatsu would soon see that even Hirohito's freedom was illusory.

When Hirohito first returned to Tokyo the change in him was conspicuous. The Japanese press predicted that he would 'banish all caution' in bringing the imperial house closer to the people. He came dangerously close to

175

doing just that. He began by going to the races, and he went out at night to the bland nightclubs of the Japanese aristocracy. He ate ham and eggs for breakfast, gobbled chocolates and played golf in plus-fours. He never lost this taste for Western clothes. After the tour, he quit wearing Japanese clothes altogether except for ceremonial occasions, and had his private rooms in the palace done over in European style.

He was made prince regent in November 1921 and the following month decided to throw a homecoming party for himself at the Akasaka palace, inviting all his old friends from the Peers School. Thanks to the generosity of the Duke of Atholl, there was plenty of single malt at hand. He initiated the festivities by announcing, 'For the next two hours, please forget that I am crown prince. Let us not stand on ceremony.' His young companions let out a cheer and started celebrating. They played the phonograph records he had brought back from London and Paris, drank a lot, and were soon as relaxed as possible, towards the crown prince as well. Palace chamberlains were appalled and horrified. Afterwards, Hirohito was so sharply rebuked by Prince Saionji that he never again took such a risk of informality.

He did, however, play the role of genial imperial host when, six months later, in April 1922, the Prince of Wales arrived in Japan for a state visit as part of a round-the-world voyage on the cruiser *Renown*. He was welcomed as an official guest. Hirohito suggested a game of golf and they went off to the greens dressed alike in plus-fours. Hirohito managed to hit the ball only after several wild swings. To rescue his host from loss of face, Prince Edward said, 'By design, I developed a disastrous hook.' Edward was then taken on a tour of Japan, travelling westward from Yokohama to Kyoto, Nara and

Kagoshima, where he resumed his voyage. Wherever he went, his unconventional manner caused a stir among the Japanese. But the Imperial Household minions were not amused.

Their fears of loose living by Hirohito were confirmed when word reached the palace of a terrible tragedy in Paris. On April Fool's Day 1923, Prince Asaka, Princess Fusako and her husband Prince Kitashirakawa were in a violent car crash. They had gone for a day's drive to Calvados in Kitashirakawa's Bugatti touring car with the cloth top down. He insisted on driving himself, his French chauffeur, Victor Daliat, sitting in the front passenger seat. Prince Asaka and Princess Fusako were in the back seat with the princess's lady-in-waiting, Elizabeth Sauvy, the granddaughter of France's General Tisseyre. At 4.30 p.m., after a long liquid lunch in Deauville, they were hurtling homewards down a two-lane road in Normandy, between rows of huge white-trunked sycamore trees, near a village called Farrière-la-Campagne, about 145 kilometres (90 miles) west of Paris. Prince Kitashirakawa pointed out with delight that the speedometer showed they were doing 120 kilometres per hour (75 m.p.h.), a very high speed on such a narrow road under any circumstances. They were behind a slower car and the prince decided to pass, turned the wheel a bit too far and crashed head on into the massive trunk of a sycamore. The wreck flipped over. Both Kitashirakawa and the chauffeur were killed instantly. Prince Asaka was thrown clear but suffered multiple fractures of his left leg and a broken chin. Princess Fusako was critically hurt with both legs broken, a kneecap smashed and a deep wound in her head. Mademoiselle Sauvy had a fractured right knee and was in shock. The other motorist stopped immediately and dragged her from the car, and she helped him extract the others.

For three weeks Prince Kitashirakawa's body lay in state at the Japanese Embassy in Paris, surrounded by wreaths and Shinto offerings of carp, rice, poultry, vegetables and water. Then it was shipped home to Japan for cremation. Princess Fusako and Prince Asaka remained in a Paris hospital for more than a year. Prince Asaka's wife, Princess Nobuko, sailed for France to take care of him. When they had recovered enough to travel, she and Prince Higashikuni escorted them back to Japan, and the curtain came down on imperial shenanigans.

CHAPTER 6

YAMAGATA'S GHOST

In the late summer of 1923 following the automobile accident in France, Hirohito and Nagako were busy preparing for their wedding, scheduled for November. There was more to celebrate than a wedding, because this was the end of nearly seven years of infighting at court to block the marriage and to keep Choshu in control. Yamagata was gone at last – or so it seemed. Then, on Saturday, 1 September 1923, Yamagata's ghost got in a last word when the devastating Kanto earthquake struck. Hirohito and his fiancée were not injured, but Tokyo was reduced to rubble. It would have been graceless to celebrate a wedding so soon after such a catastrophe.

Just before noon on that day, shops and offices were closing for the weekend. The new Imperial Hotel, designed by Frank Lloyd Wright to withstand earthquakes, was preparing for a gala opening. Weekend crowds were gathering at beach resorts and in Tokyo's Ginza entertainment district. Fifty miles south of Tokyo, the earth suddenly split open along the Sagami Bay fault and for the next five minutes violent jolts shook the great Kanto Plain like a dirty rug, shattering buildings in Tokyo and Yokohama. Next came a murderous tsunami,

36 feet tall, which lashed the coast. Then followed a yellow cloud that grew quickly into a huge billowing mass of dust, rising from thousands of collapsed buildings. Tens of thousands of homes, built out of wood and paper to flex in ordinary quakes, splintered in this monster, and burst into flame as stoves and braziers overturned, igniting straw mats and rice-paper screens. As the fires spread, the city of Tokyo became a single blaze. More than the earthquake itself, the fire wreaked havoc, incinerating many square miles of congested housing, while refugees fled in panic before walls of flame, converging on the banks of the Sumida River. The flames followed, igniting wooden bridges, roasting alive tens of thousands of people huddled along the river banks. Great plumes of flame twitched overhead. Thousands fled into the waters of Tokyo Bay, where they were engulfed in new flames as 100,000 tons of fuel gushed from burst tanks at Yokosuka naval base. Firestorms raged through the night. By Sunday morning more than 300,000 buildings had vanished and two-thirds of the city was reduced to smouldering ashes. Aftershocks continued. On Monday morning, dazed survivors began sifting the debris for the remains of relatives. Over 140,000 people were lost from an urban population of 1.5 million. Property damage came to 2 per cent of Japan's total national wealth. Two million people were homeless.

When the quake struck, Hirohito was at work in the imperial palace downtown. He is said to have remained perfectly calm, the only one who did not rush outside for fear the palace walls would collapse. His chamberlain, Kanroji, stayed with him. While some palace outbuildings were destroyed by the ensuing firestorm, behind its broad moat the imperial palace itself was one of the few places secure from the inferno.

Typically, the resilient Japanese are quick to rebuild their lives after quakes. This time there was a frenzy of mob violence that lasted for two weeks. The magnitude of this disaster quickly exhausted emergency supplies of food, water and shelter. Government efforts at fire-fighting were inadequate to the point of criminal neglect. To avoid shame, officials diverted attention towards Korean and Chinese residents and Japanese leftists. Rumours were spread that Koreans were lighting fires, looting houses, raping Japanese women and committing murder. It was a perfect opportunity for the extreme right to provoke violence against immigrants and leftists. As in the past, the police and secret police exploited the media to reinforce the rumours. Martial law was proclaimed and the army mobilized. An invasion from Korea was rumoured. As a precaution, all Koreans were to be killed, and paramilitary groups that had been Yamagata's favourite weapons took to the streets. One Tokyo newspaper said the government had ordered the killing of Koreans, and claimed that Koreans and social-ists were plotting rebellion inside Japan. Mobs caught, beat or killed anyone suspected of being Korean, Chinese or socialist. With police and army complicity, the vigi-lantes surged through poor districts and murdered thousands whose poverty implied they were leftists. People who looked Korean or spoke Japanese with an accent were slaughtered with clubs or spears. There were 80,000 Koreans in Japan at the time, and the atrocities against them are documented. A soldier boasted: 'Our cavalry was excited with this bloody ceremony and started the main Korean hunting that evening.'

During the firestorm, when a well-known socialist tried to lead a crowd to safety in the moated grounds of the imperial palace, he was arrested by the secret police and strangled to death on the spot. His wife and little son were also strangled. Some 1,300 'known socialist malcontents' were jailed.

Eventually the government called a halt to the reign of terror, but insisted that Koreans had provoked the riot and rampage.

When order was restored, Hirohito toured the ruined city. In army uniform he rode on horseback through the Ginza, through districts of rubble and through Ueno Park, where the zoo's animals survived unscathed. He invited the homeless to shelter in the park, and gave money to quake victims. In Imperial Rescripts he expressed sympathy, and postponed his wedding to show compassion. His future sister-in-law and her family, whose mansion had been destroyed, set up temporary living quarters in a sewer pipe while their home was rebuilt. Problems were not over, for the Kanto Plain is Japan's biggest agricultural region, and many farms were damaged. Warehouses had collapsed and burned. That winter, even the elite ate tapioca, and canned beans donated by the United States.

America provided more than beans. Jack Morgan sponsored a $150 million loan package for earthquake reconstruction (an enormous sum in those days) and, in doing so, bought himself a piece of Japan's future. The House of Morgan had become involved in Japan nearly half a century earlier during the Meiji Restoration, when the bank was first established by Jack's father, J. Pierpont Morgan.

Morgan could easily handle giant loans. The United States had come out of World War I with a lot of excess capital generated by wartime business. Morgan Bank in particular profited when it became the major purchasing agent for the British Army and Navy and for the French government. During the war, Morgan handled $3 billion in commercial transactions, netting $30 million in fees. Then there was a $500 million Anglo-French loan for which Morgan demanded a steep 6 per cent interest, while generously waiving all other fees. Before the war was over, Morgan had arranged over $1.5 billion in credits. With this leverage, and the decline of Britain's dominance of international finance, the House of Morgan became the world's most influential bank, 'America's premier foreign lender', and the sage of Wall Street. This tremendous economic clout had the result of moving the House of Morgan into the political arena of foreign policy, making the firm virtually an extension of the US government. As the bank became a global player, it turned its attention to Asia and sent Thomas Lamont to survey the scene.

A Harvard man, Lamont had risen quickly to vice-president of Bankers Trust, where he came to the attention of Jack Morgan. In 1911, he became the youngest partner in the House of Morgan. During World War I he arranged the financing and purchasing of American supplies for France and Britain. After the war, he negotiated Germany's reparations payments. Lamont had natural talent as a diplomat, able to make himself seem sympathetic to all sides, but he was just as good at beguiling himself. Nowhere was this more evident than in his mistaken assessment of Japan.

In 1920, with the blessing of Commerce Secretary Herbert Hoover and the Department of State, Jack Morgan sent Lamont to Asia to look for clients and opportunities. China was in turmoil, divided among warlords, crippled by strikes, noisy with student protests against the Treaty of Versailles, which seemed to give Japan control of Germany's sphere of influence in China.

183

Lamont was repelled by China and the Chinese, disgusted by their blatant corruption and the bribes demanded by everyone from beggars to warlords. 'The Chinese', he said, 'have never become a nation . . . Corruption is decried . . . yet almost invariably practiced, and with shamelessness at that.' He concluded that the political instability and the culture of corruption made China a poor investment risk, and recommended that Morgan Bank make no loans to China.

Japan was another matter. While Lamont saw the Chinese as slovenly, unwashed and degenerate, he saw the Japanese as clean, brisk, efficient and arrow-straight. He thought of Japan as the Britain of Asia. Like America, Japan had prospered during World War I, and had major gold reserves. The US was Japan's best customer, and Japan was becoming an important market for US exports. During his visit, Lamont was entertained by the cream of Japan's financial elite, the Mitsuis, and the Iwasakis of Mitsubishi. He was dazzled by their magnificent homes and splendid gardens, and was persuaded that these were hospitable liberals, eager to open their country to new influences. He was taken in by the surface cleanliness and calm of Japan, and believed that it was just as tidy and well scrubbed on the inside. What he failed to see was Japan's deeply hidden structural corruption.

'Corruption in Japan', says Karel van Wolferen, 'is legitimatized by its systematic perpetration. It is so highly organized and has become so much a part of the extra-legal ways of the Japanese system that most citizens or foreign residents do not recognize it for what it is, but accept it as "a part of the system".' Corrupt Japanese did not put their hands out for small change like the crude

Chinese because they got all they wanted through an intravenous drip.

During the Meiji Restoration economic oligarchs became intricately tied to Japan's political strongmen and the bureaucracy they created to run the new government agencies. Back in the 1870s, to give the nation a vigorous industrial base, the Genro poured the huge confiscated assets of the Tokugawa shoguns into new factories, railways and commercial enterprises. These were then privatized very selectively. To keep the national assets and the wealth they generated in the right hands, these companies and industries were clustered in four conglomerates, or *zaibatsu*, headed by relatives or intimates of the Genro. Each *zaibatsu* was a self-contained commercial empire, with its own mines, workers, factories, banks, insurance companies, ocean fleets and export agencies. They were modelled on the long-established Mitsui family commercial empire, which had underwritten the military regime of the Tokugawa shoguns and which had survived the power shift by switching its allegiance to the Meiji regime. These four new *zaibatsu* were Mitsubishi, Sumitomo, Yasuda and Iwasaki. Of the original Meiji Genro, Ito was closely tied to Mitsubishi, Inouye to Mitsui, Okuma to Iwasaki, Yamagata to Sumitomo (his protégé Prince Saionji was the brother of the head of Sumitomo). Early in the twentieth century a second layer developed with such upstart *zaibatsu* as Nissan, which would play a leading role in financing the rise of the militarists.

What bound the strongmen, the conglomerates and the bureaucracy together were networks based on kinship, marriage, school ties, bribes, rigged bids and sweetheart deals that enriched them personally as they developed Japan into a modern industrial economy. So close was this to a mirror image of America's wealthy elite, of which he was part, that Lamont failed to see the corruption, or thought nothing of it because it was so perfectly groomed. Scandals did occur when rival strongmen provoked them, but these were hastily swept under the tatami mat and some scapegoat took the fall to shield the real culprits. (The spectacle of corporate leaders and government ministers sobbing openly as they admit their shame is a set piece of comic theatre in modern Japan.) No effective measures have ever been taken by Japanese governments to rein in the nation's financial overlords, or genuinely to reform the financial system, for the simple reason that this would be tantamount to collective suicide.

Lamont spent the next several years trying to arrange a major business loan to Japan. The Bank of Japan wanted $30 million to develop the South Manchurian railway. American industrialists resisted such offerings. They wanted to put their money into Japan itself, not into Japanese ventures on the Asian mainland that would be in competition with American ventures. When the Kanto earthquake struck, however, reconstruction loans proved to be exactly what these investors wanted. The House of Morgan made a $150 million loan structured with thirty-year sinking fund bonds and a 6.5 per cent coupon. A further £25 million loan was offered by Morgan Grenfell, the London syndicate. Lamont was now satisfied that the Japanese government would be Morgan's 'permanent client'. This happened, but not in the way Lamont expected.

The last pulse of the Kanto earthquake was felt in late December 1923 when a shot was fired at Hirohito as he passed in a motorcade through Toranomon. The bullet missed him but wounded a chamberlain. The gun was fired by Nanba Daisuke, son of a conservative Diet member from Choshu, but, given the polarization of politics in Japan, the secret police found it convenient to spread reports that Nanba was a communist. Before this question could be resolved one way or the other, he was executed. Afterwards, there was widespread speculation that the assassin had been encouraged by Japan's ultra-right, who wanted to frighten the imperial family into a life of complete seclusion, making them easier to control by restricting all access to the throne. Since coming home from his European trip, Hirohito had made it known that he favoured a more open relationship between the throne and the Japanese people. This alarmed his guardians, and Yamagata protégés running the secret police used Nanba's attack as an excuse to intensify security around Hirohito, isolating him even more from public contact. As his youngest brother Prince Mikasa affirmed, Hirohito's life 'entirely changed after the Toranomon Incident'. So much for populism.

In other ways, his life changed for the better. On 26 January 1924, he and Nagako were married at last. Crowds gathered outside the palace to shout *'Banzai'* (long life). Chamberlain Kanroji said people saw the wedding as 'a bright and hopeful event in otherwise gloomy and pessimistic times'. The Shinto ceremony unfolded at the family shrine in the palace, with bride and groom in ancient robes. Holding the polished bronze sacred mirror before him, Hirohito looked deep into it and announced to his 123 imperial predecessors that he was taking a bride. Present in the brilliant sunshine were 700 guests, princes and princesses, court and government officials, in traditional costumes or military uniforms. There was a bloom of court ladies in kimono;

others in dresses of European style. No foreigners were invited. Among the guests was Black Ocean godfather Toyama, Japan's leading ultra-right patriot. As the couple drove to the Akasaka palace through streets lined with soldiers, schoolchildren broke the prescribed silence to cheer. A national holiday was proclaimed. Public entertainments and costumed processions were staged to lift spirits.

Among the wedding presents were several 'pillow books'. Certainly the bride was chaste; as to Hirohito, some claim that his father had sent him a geisha when he turned 16. Possibly his uncle Higashikuni did take him to the Sphinx in Paris. If not, pillow books were needed. For a society that places so much emphasis on the diligent instruction of children, sex education was ignored. Proper families provided 'pillow books' or 'bride books' filled with erotic scenes so that newlyweds could learn about sex 'the same way they learn to plant a garden'. Hirohito and Nagako proved to have green thumbs, but it would take them a long time to produce a boy. Their first child was born on 6 December 1925, a girl. The following year Taisho suffered his second stroke, succumbing to pneumonia. Hirohito became emperor. As he had not yet fathered a male heir, Prince Chichibu remained next in line. In February 1927, the palace was excited to discover that Nagako was carrying another child. Born in September 1927, this too was a girl. As Prince Takamatsu wrote in his diary: 'A princess . . . Oh, bother. What a shame it was not a boy.' Once there was a male heir, the pressure would decrease on 'spares' like him.

Prudently, Dowager Empress Sadako set herself the task of arranging another marriage, this time for her favourite son.

Prince Chichibu was an impressive figure, tall and slim. He climbed mountains, played tennis, spoke fluent French and English, and had studied abroad before taking up a career in the army. Unlike Hirohito, he did not live a captive existence. Idealistic fellow officers could talk to Chichibu, and he could say what he wanted, providing he made sure he was not overheard. He seemed genuinely concerned about hungry farmers and the oppressed. Like his father Taisho, Chichibu insisted on being treated the same way as his fellow officers, rejecting special privileges. Admiringly, his comrades said he was 'a heavy drinker who never got drunk'. Secret policemen kept an eye on him around the clock. Many young army and navy officers thought Chichibu would be a much better emperor than Hirohito, so he became their champion. Although Chichibu was not con-spiratorial by nature he was passionate about reform, and there is evidence that he encouraged at least two violent plots against the ruling elite during the murderous 1930s.

It is unlikely that he ever considered himself a serious contender for the throne. He had no appetite for that terrible life, neither the stamina nor the commitment. He was indulged by his mother in a way Hirohito had never been. Chichibu preferred to remain the debonair and engaging prince, enjoying all the perquisites of being heir-presumptive, one breath away from the throne.

Early in 1925, still a lieutenant in the infantry, Chichibu left Japan for a sojourn abroad, free from official duties. For sixteen months, he had lessons from an English tutor, climbed the Swiss Alps, played tennis and golf, rode horseback, went to the cinema, shopped, danced, attended dinner parties and enjoyed the role of a well-heeled playboy, though under close supervision by his equerries. After that he settled down to life as an undergraduate at Magdalen College, Oxford, becoming a familiar figure with books under his arm, slouching by in the rough sports clothes favoured by the students. He hoped to spend at least a year at Oxford, studying modern British history, politics and economics, but after only two months was called home because of his father's final illness. He left England expecting to return in a few months. But he was away for more than ten years.

The journey home with his guardian, Baron Hayashi, was by way of the United States because that was the shortest route. Three days out of England, a cablegram reached the ship announcing his father's death. In New York, the prince was met by Japan's ambassador to Washington, Matsudaira Tsuneo. A cheerful, moonfaced, roly-poly golf enthusiast, he took Chichibu to Washington for a break before continuing by train to California. President Calvin Coolidge invited him to the White House for a thirty-minute chat. Because of his mourning, there was no official socializing. His stay with the ambassador's family was relaxed. Mrs Matsudaira – Nabeshima Nobuko – was his mother's dearest friend and her niece had been Sadako's first choice to marry Hirohito. Compared to most Japanese aristocrats, who were still frogs in the well, the Matsudairas were cosmopolitan and sophisticated. Before coming to Washington they had served at the embassy in London, and they were part of the core group of Japanese diplomats who favoured solving problems by negotiation. Their children, including eldest daughter Setsuko, 17, were enrolled at the Quaker Sidwell Friends School, one of Washington's best private schools. As Setsuko will become a major character in the imperial family, we must pause to consider the happy life she would be asked to abandon.

Sidwell Friends was popular with diplomats who pulled strings to enrol their children to gain the lifelong connections that came with the curriculum. Charles Lindbergh had gone to Sidwell, as had many other famous Americans. At the school, Setsuko's English developed a plangent southern accent. She won tennis tournaments, learned to dance and stood out even among the exotic faces on embassy row. A family friend at the State Department, Joseph Grew, who could rarely find two words to say what could be said in twenty, described her as 'really lovely'.

Setsuko was as different from young Empress Nagako as Chichibu was from Hirohito. Born at Walton-on-Thames while her father was third secretary at the embassy in London, Setsuko became a lifelong Anglophile. She was only mildly impressed by Prince Chichibu's celebrity. Several years earlier they had met in Tokyo, when Empress Sadako invited the Matsudairas to the palace before their posting to Washington. The prince had not spoken a word to her. Wryly, Setsuko recalled: 'My first impression of His Highness the Prince was the sparkle of his glasses and his fine, tall figure.'

On their second meeting, in Washington, he did speak to her, asking her about school and what sports she enjoyed. From his time abroad, he did seem more mature, but she was not swept off her feet. About to graduate from Sidwell Friends, she looked forward to college in America. Marriage only happened to older girls, and romance only in Hollywood. She was a realist.

The prince left Washington by train the next day and reached Yokohama in mid-January 1927. A few months later, following the birth of Hirohito's second daughter, Dowager Empress Sadako sent a secret emissary to the embassy in Washington, her friend the US-educated

Count Kabayama. He had instructions to persuade Ambassador and Mrs Matsudaira to consent to the marriage of Setsuko to Prince Chichibu.

Although he bore a strong resemblance to Humpty Dumpty, Matsudaira was an exceptional man with an epic history. He was the fourth son of a famous rebel, Matsudaira Katamori, former domain lord of the Aizu clan, who was one of the leaders of the alternative nine-teenth-century movement to ally the emperor and the shogun rather than eliminate the shogun entirely. Early in the game, Aizu warriors helped Satsuma troops repel Choshu's attack on the imperial palace in Kyoto, which Meiji had witnessed as a boy of 11. This earned the Matsudaira family the undying hatred of Choshu. When the shogun was defeated, the domain lord withdrew to his stronghold at Wakamatsu Castle in Aizu to resist his Restoration enemies. After a long and bitter siege, the castle was stormed and Matsudaira faced charges of treason. Though on the losing side, he had always been loyal personally to the emperor, so in short order his family honour was restored, the Aizu clan was pardoned and the Matsudairas resumed their place among Japan's privileged elite.

Fresh out of Tokyo University, Setsuko's father joined the Foreign Ministry and began a steady rise to the top. After serving as a young diplomat in China, he returned to Tokyo to run the Foreign Ministry bureau handling relations with Britain and America, and was named ambassador to Washington. Eventually he would become the top civil servant in the Foreign Ministry, and would be chosen to head the Imperial Household during World War II.

The Matsudairas were dismayed by the idea of their daughter marrying Prince Chichibu. For all the prestige attached, a royal wedding entailed severe restrictions for the bride. The atmosphere of the embassy became dark and bleak. Nothing was said to Setsuko. While she continued her usual activities, her parents and Kabayama talked late into the night. Unable to persuade the parents, the count returned to Tokyo. Setsuko was surprised when he returned some weeks later, stony-faced. Once again he and her parents talked late into the night. Next day, Kabayama sent for her, and told her he had come as the emissary of the empress dowager to persuade her to become Princess Chichibu. 'I was speechless. My head went quite blank, and I sat there stiff and tense.' Her parents had already voiced every excuse – lack of noble title, the family stigma as Restoration rebels, their daughter's lack of restraint. But Kabayama's renewed assault weakened their resolve. They left the decision to Setsuko. She made her own excuses. Then she fled to her room, refused to eat and cried for three days.

She was distressed because of what marriage means to a woman in Japan. She would be leaving a privileged position in her own family to become a subordinate member of her husband's family. Even under the best of circumstances this was a depressing prospect. Worst of all, as a royal her life would come under the control of the Imperial Household and its meddlesome chamberlains. There would be a suffocating ritual of etiquette that would end her independence and isolate her from her own family. Her parents would have to address her in stylized honorifics. Household rules would cut her off completely from personal friends. She would have to live 'above the clouds', prevented from having any contact with normal people. Setsuko had her own dreams, of living a free life as an enlightened woman of the world. How could she give up these dreams to become a hostage?

When she was exhausted by three days and nights of weeping, she capitulated. If this was her destiny, there was no point fighting it. Count Kabayama went back to Tokyo.

There were numerous formalities. As Setsuko had no title, she was adopted by her uncle, a viscount. Rushed back to Tokyo following her graduation from Sidwell Friends, she was given a crash course in palace etiquette, supervised by the dowager empress herself. Brides usually had years of preparation. Setsuko got a three-month immersion course. In a foretaste of what was to come, she was warned not to bring to the palace any jazz records or other Western things.

On her wedding day, 28 September 1928, a date judged auspicious by numerologists, she was awakened early for the long process of coiffing and dressing. Thick camellia-oil pomade was combed into her hair, which was arranged in a heart shape with a hip-length tress down the back. The dresser came next. Over a purple silk under-kimono, she helped Setsuko put on a pleated purple divided skirt that 'seemed to be made for a giant, my feet coming where the giant's knees would be, and the rest trailing a long way behind'. In all she wore twelve layers, the full costume weighing 16 kilos, or 35 pounds.

She was conveyed to the wedding ceremony in a horse-drawn state carriage of imperial maroon colour. Crowds lined the way, waving tiny rising-sun flags, a demonstration organized by the Imperial Household. Nothing spontaneous was permitted. When she reached the Kashikodokoro sanctuary in the palace grounds, Prince Chichibu was waiting and the two exchanged bows. She was led to a dressing room where a three-pointed coronet was placed in her hair, and she was given a cedar-wood fan symbolizing modesty. Flutes and mouth-organs sounded the beginning of the Shinto ceremony, and a priest intoned a prayer to the gods. Bearing a sceptre, Chichibu preceded her, taking a seat on the right facing the altar. Setsuko took a seat on his left. Speaking the ancient court language, Chichibu announced to the gods, 'At this auspicious time on this auspicious day, we conduct this ceremony of marriage before Thee. We solemnly vow that henceforth and for evermore we shall live together in mutual love and fellowship.'

After sipping sacred green tea, Chichibu and Setsuko rose to leave, and the silence was shattered by a single cannon booming a salute of twenty-one blasts. A procession of guards with imperial standards preceded their coach out of the gate and across the Niju Bridge over the moat. Mounted cavalry in white-plumed helmets led the way to Chichibu's palace in Akasaka, as crowds along the route shouted 'Banzai'. They were met by his four aunts, the daughters of Meiji – Princess Asaka, Princess Higashikuni, Princess Takeda and the recently widowed and badly scarred Princess Kitashirakawa. A banquet followed, photos were taken, then Setsuko retired to her new boudoir, where she was stripped and had the pomade washed from her hair, a 'dreadful ordeal' because soap and benzine got in her eyes. Quickly her hair was arranged in Western style, and she put on a European gown. Over her right shoulder and diagonally across her breasts went the sash of the Order of the Sacred Crown, First Class, fastened with a diamond brooch. A diamond tiara was placed in her hair, and she was again ready for photographs. Chichibu joined her in front of the cameras, in the dress uniform of an infantry lieutenant, holding a plumed hat.

When the portraits were done they returned to the imperial palace to pay their respects to Hirohito and

Nagako, then went to the dowager's palace, where Sadako welcomed them happily. It was evening when they returned to Akasaka palace and Setsuko was helped into a black kimono embroidered with ocean waves and gold and silver cranes. Chichibu's youngest brother, 13-year-old Sumi (Prince Mikasa), a cadet in military prep school, came to pay his respects. Huge crowds had gathered outside, and on impulse Chichibu went to thank them. To be spoken to personally by a member of the imperial family was unprecedented. The crowd was stunned, and broke into thunderous applause and wave after wave of '*Banzai*'.

A few weeks later, 26-year-old Prince Chichibu entered the military academy. For the next three years, he bent over his homework from supper till after midnight. When Setsuko tried to distract him, he explained: 'There are lots of my classmates who have to do the same work in cramped quarters with an infant bawling its head off. Here am I working in quiet, palatial surroundings, so I've little to complain of.'

To compensate, after midnight they went roller-skating through the upstairs corridors of Akasaka palace. At first the servants thought the noise was thunder. On weekends, they played tennis on the palace grounds, and had a squash court installed for rainy days. Although Setsuko had been warned not to bring jazz records in her trousseau, the prince had his own collection and knew how to dance.

Any anxieties Setsuko had about her mother-in-law proved to be unfounded. The dowager showered her with gifts and designed clothes for her. The Chichibus visited her often to screen Hollywood films, including *Merry Widow*, *Tom Sawyer* and Marlene Dietrich in *Morocco*. The dowager came to their palace for

American lunches and British tea. No similar bond would ever exist between the dowager and the wives of her other three sons. Protocol stifled friendship with Hirohito and Nagako. As time passed, the brothers grew farther apart. Informal contact between them practically ceased. Setsuko was surprised on the rare occasions when Chichibu and Hirohito had a friendly conversation.

Later Setsuko learned that the dowager secretly hoped their marriage would 'bring England, America and Japan closer together'. The dowager was 'concerned about Japan's future as a world power and her relations with other countries'. She hoped that important foreign visitors would see Prince and Princess Chichibu as representative of the new Japan. The Chichibus were urbane, informed, cosmopolitan, sophisticated and had a flair for informality. Regrettably, they were still vastly outnumbered by the frogs in the well.

Despite the success of his British tour, Hirohito was uneasy and reserved among foreigners. He and Nagako lived an austere private life that was virtually friendless, remaining inaccessible even to family members. When the dowager started an Imperial Family Social Club, with a guest speaker followed by drinks and dancing, Hirohito and Nagako never attended. The emperor rarely drank anything alcoholic. For her part, Empress Nagako suffered all the constraints imposed on empresses in the past. Japanese women, it is said, know freedom only before the age of seven and after the age of 60.

Palace sources described Hirohito's marriage as one of 'attentive intimacy' and 'a beautiful thing to see'. In summers the couple took short holidays at the beach palace, but their strolls by the water's edge were accompanied by a dozen chamberlains. In Tokyo they spent

197

idle hours reading, or strolling through the gardens. The Great Lawn was contoured with flowers and trees. Hirohito could identify all of them. They stopped at ponds to feed wild ducks, cranes and swans, which came to greet them. One black swan, in a parody of Japan's oligarchs, always flapped and hissed to scare rivals away. Nagako loved music, played the piano, sang and listened to records with Hirohito. She had a passion for ping-pong, which he was too awkward to play, but he would watch. The palace had a nine-hole golf course and many afternoons they played a round by themselves. To please him, she had learned the game during their honeymoon but did not enjoy it. When Nagako wasn't there, the swans and the chamberlains watched the emperor making his way alone around the greens, club in hand.

Because Hirohito's passion was marine biology, a 1600-square-foot laboratory was built at the palace and his old biology tutor was enlisted to oversee the facility. At the beach in summer, Nagako helped him gather tiny creatures from the tidal pools. Dressed in a white kimono, she strolled the sand slowly, passing the emperor a collecting net or holding a specimen tube. On snowy days in winter, the emperor and one of the younger chamberlains would spend an hour or two skiing on the low slopes of the palace grounds. It is unlikely that he and Nagako ever went roller-skating in the palace. Yet, instead of one caged bird, there were two.

As their daughters arrived, they became a source of unrestrained pleasure. From palace ponds Hirohito collected tadpoles for the girls to see. Hide and seek was a favourite game. The emperor often became so absorbed in the games that chamberlains had to interrupt to get him back to business. They made sure no photos of family play appeared in the press.

The girls were raised in separate quarters joined to those of their parents by a long corridor, an improvement over the complete isolation of the past. Empress Nagako visited the nursery to feed them, to sing lullabies and was even known to change nappies. Her efforts were not appreciated by the Household staff, who wanted no interference. They said she would encourage her children to become too high-handed and naughty.

When they had been married just over three years, their six-month-old second daughter, Princess Sachiko, developed 'an inexplicable illness' (described by some sources as pneumonia) and died six days later. Early in 1929, Nagako became pregnant again, and another daughter, Princess Kazuko, arrived that September. According to a Japanese biographer, shortly after this birth, the empress was informed by a court lady that she, Nagako, was under 'Yamagata's curse' and would never bear a son. In March 1931, when the whole nation waited again for the double-siren signal from the imperial palace – one blast for a girl, two for a boy – the siren sounded only once for the arrival of a fourth daughter, Princess Atsuko.

In earlier times, the problem would have been solved by adopting the son of a relative, or fathering a son by an official concubine. Hirohito was the first male heir born to an empress – rather than to a concubine – in more than 150 years. Japanese sources claim that a decision was made behind Hirohito's back to revive the concubine option. Count Tanaka Koken, 'the most ardent protagonist of the "other woman" movement, talked his face blue in support of his argument to anyone he thought had influence with the emperor'. Tanaka was in his eighties and had been president of the Peers School and minister of the Imperial Household, so he knew the ropes. He is said to have picked three very pretty girls and turned over a portfolio and photo of each, asking a chamberlain to make a presentation personally to the emperor. According to this source, Hirohito flatly refused. He is said to have told Empress Nagako that he was not worried if the throne were to pass to one of his brothers, or their descendants. During the decade from 1921 to 1931, Hirohito had begun a fundamental trans-formation in his outward persona from aspiring young playboy to absent-minded professor, a role that made him seem aloof from all the conspiracy, bloodshed and upheaval to come.

Outside the palace things were grim and getting grimmer. Ten years had passed since Hirohito assumed his father's duties, years in which man and nature conspired against Japan. The terrible damage of the Kanto quake was nothing compared to what loomed ahead. Japan's great experiment of opening up to the West was suffering severe setbacks. The racial rebuff at Versailles and the collapse of the Anglo-Japanese Alliance discouraged progressive Japanese, feeding the fears of the isolationists and the appetites of the extreme right. Ancient paranoia deepened and society entered what Japanese call 'the dark valley'. Diplomatic failure and growing economic crisis provoked conspiracies at home and Japanese Army intrigues on the Asian main-land. Spurned by the West, Japan felt cornered and compelled to go its own way militarily. Russia – now the Soviet Union – might be seen as the immediate threat, but Britain and America were now viewed as untrustworthy friends and probable future enemies. Tokyo became defiant, inward-looking and aggressive. Already having seized Korea, the army stepped up its intrigue and bullying in Manchuria and north China.

Eclipsed were those who favoured friendly relations with the West. Even before World War I, yellow-peril agitation and fears of a Japanese invasion of California had featured prominently in American newspapers. White politicians, labour leaders and journalists nourished this hysteria. By 1924 the US had tightened its exclusion laws forbidding Japanese immigration. Meanwhile, a China lobby was taking shape that sought to 'rescue' China by tying it to American evangelism. The prospect of converting millions of heathen Chinese to Christianity was promoted in American magazines and newspapers, while the same press warned of the danger of Japanese attack. Ludicrous as both prospects seemed, they had an intoxicating effect.

Japanese may be acutely sensitive to image in their daily lives, but they have little knack for damage control in international relations. Inept handling of Japan's image in the 1920s provoked bad press everywhere. Continued Japanese bullying did not help. The campaign to bully China into becoming a Japanese protectorate, to 'save it from Russia', caused outrage, especially in Washington. This encouraged the China lobby to launch a new crusade portraying China as righteous and Japan as evil. Forgotten was Washington's backing of the Japanese takeover in Korea, in return for Japan endorsing America's annexation of the Philippines.

Industrially, Japan seemed to be booming in the 1920s, but this was an illusion. Prosperity was enjoyed by the elite only – thanks to their exclusive control of wealth and the carefully cultivated corruption at all levels of government. Rural Japan did not prosper, nor did job-hunters who streamed in from the countryside, adding to unemployment in the cities and reducing the workforce available on farms. At the time of the Meiji Restoration, Japan's population had been 30 million. By the end of Hirohito's first decade, it was 65 million. Employers manipulated workers with feudal techniques and cultural values. Each company claimed to be a family, with a caring boss who always knew best and who would look after everyone in return for intense loyalty. His responsibility did not include fixing the squalor in which workers lived and toiled. On an island near Nagasaki, Mitsubishi had a huge coal mine where prisoners, outcasts, dispossessed farmers and indentured labourers from Korea and Manchuria lived and died as virtual slaves. Throughout Japan, thousands of girls as young as 11 toiled in wretched conditions. Labour protests and efforts to organize social-welfare movements were brutally suppressed. The left never got off the ground in Japan. In universities, some young Marxists attracted attention, but most of them were from wealthy families and quickly outgrew their infatuation with social equality. The Japan Communist Party was founded in 1922, but collapsed during the next ten years because of fratricidal squabbling.

In what seemed to be an extravagant democratic gesture, universal male suffrage was granted in 1925, giving the vote to Japanese farmers, tenants and industrial workers. But Japan's government rarely gave anything with one hand without taking it away with the other. In the same year a harsh Peace Preservation Law was also passed, making it a crime punishable by death to criticize the emperor in any way, directly or indirectly, which included criticizing his government. This made the emperor unassailable, and also made the power-brokers hiding behind the throne unassailable because of the pretence that they were only carrying out the emperor's orders. The law effectively blocked candidates of the left from gaining seats in the Diet, because if they criticized the imperial system in any way, or the government, they were arrested.

Three years later, in 1928, the law was strengthened. It became a capital crime to agitate against private property or speak against government policy. Anyone talking about or even thinking about changing the system faced death or life in prison. As a safeguard against the spread of dangerous thoughts, defendants in such cases were denied the right of trial by jury. Education Minister Hatoyama, who opposed jury trials under any circumstances, was a champion of these draconian measures. He wanted to purge any primary- or secondary-school teacher who had 'dangerous thoughts'. He sought the dismissal of a law-school professor from the faculty at Kyoto University for criticizing the relegation of women to an inferior social and legal status and for defending Tolstoy's notion that society is as responsible for crime as the individual criminal. Hatoyama defined liberty as 'a freedom to do what you should do and not what you should not do'. Later, Hatoyama was forced to resign his ministerial post when he was charged with 'receiving and paying bribes, selling honours, evasion of income taxes, and falsification of stock ownership statements' for himself and his wife. (Hatoyama did not vanish from the political scene because of this scandal. In 1954, after the US occupation ended, he became Japan's prime minister.)

Before Hatoyama suffered his brief spasm of embarrassment, he and his cabinet colleagues arranged for the public deification of the emperor. In November 1928, Hirohito had his formal enthronement in Kyoto. Four days later he was deified as the direct descendant of sun goddess Amaterasu. The ceremony, a late-nineteenth-century contrivance based on vague Shinto mythology, was to remind Japanese that Hirohito was a true god and the shadowy figures behind his throne, such as Hatoyama, were his high priests.

Deification did not reduce Japan's growing domestic crisis. Problems were not solved by executing the people who drew attention to them. The elite complained that society was becoming too bourgeois, merchants too powerful, youth too vulgar. Taxicabs and dance halls were competing with tea ceremonies and geishas. In Ginza nightclubs, girls wore short skirts and bobbed hair, and there were chorus lines on stage. But the real crisis was much deeper.

Two years before the Wall Street Crash in 1929, panic hit Tokyo. The Japanese banking crisis of 1927, just like the Japanese banking crisis of the late 1990s, had everything to do with systemic corruption and sweetheart deals. Vast sums of money were lent by Japan's biggest banks to business concerns run by the same men or their relatives and friends. Other powerful families did the same thing, creating a false impression of prosperity. The banks did not secure these loans, because in sweetheart deals it would be embarrassing to insist on security. The banks then failed to audit their own conduct. With so much easy money and no supervision, businesses expanded recklessly. As years passed without any payment of interest on the loans, the banks suffered a liquidity crisis and began to haemorrhage. To stop the collapse of the banks in 1927, the government forked out 2 billion yen in emergency loans, but only to ease the pain of the privileged people who had caused the problem. Of 1,422 banks in Japan before the 1927 crisis, more than eight hundred went bust. (Seventy years later, Japan's banking fundamentals remain largely unchanged.)

When Wall Street crashed in 1929, nearly half of Japan's small and medium businesses went under. From 1929 to 1931, exports fell by 43 per cent by value. Prices of farm produce fell 50 per cent, crippling rural families.

In the countryside, Japanese agriculture had been failing for a decade. Most farmers could not own their land and had to forfeit most of their production to landlords and tax collectors. Land reform was long overdue but highly unlikely. Farmers had to augment their income by putting more effort into silkworm production. Rice farmers made up to half their income on silk. The silk trade depended entirely on the US market, so the collapse of the American silk market in 1929 brought disaster to Japanese farmers. Unable to pay rent or taxes, farmers were forced off their lands, and by 1930 Japan was starving. Massive unemployment was joined by famine. Whole rural villages died of hunger and urban workers joined breadlines. Once again desperate families sold children into brothels. Home Ministry documents show that in six prefectures of north-eastern Japan, 60,000 girls were sold into slavery in 1934 alone. Lucky ones were sold to geisha schools, but most went to brothels or became slaves of restaurant owners who forced them into prostitution. In Japan as a whole during the 1930s, 200,000 girls were being sold by their families each year.

After so thoroughly fouling their own nest, the ruling elite turned once again to Tom Lamont and Morgan Bank. Lamont arrived in Japan during the banking crisis of 1927 to see what he could do to help his friends. While there, he met Emperor Hirohito and was awarded the Order of the Rising Sun. When he returned to New York, Lamont got busy on Japan's behalf. By 1931, Morgan had floated new bond issues totalling $263 million for Japanese borrowers. Morgan's original Kanto earthquake reconstruction loans were followed by a 1930 loan to Tokyo for debt refunding, and a guaranteed loan in June 1931 to Japan's electric utility in Taiwan. Morgan also reorganized a $25 million bank credit to the Yokohama Specie Bank for currency stabilization to help Tokyo get back on the gold standard.

While ultra-nationalists insisted that the Great Depression was a plot by Western racists, the bursting of the banking bubble momentarily revealed the hidden corruption within Japan's ruling elite. Instead of looking for ways to reform the system and put the damaged nation in order, the leading cliques were preoccupied with arresting and executing critics and quarrelling among themselves.

There were now three broad groups playing musical chairs. The ultra-nationalists and their military allies wanted to get rid of Japan's troublesome politicians and to nationalize the great concentrations of commercial wealth, bringing all control into the grip of a single iron hand. Simultaneously they wanted to create an overseas empire by military conquest the way the West had done in the previous century.

The left, such as it was, wanted social revolution to rescue poor farmers and workers from their desperate plight, as well as an end to the fake emperor system with its 'evil' elite hiding behind the throne.

In the middle was a third group of educated elite, linked to wealth by family ties, who wanted to keep the existing system intact. They were flawed by their reluctance to reform the system, because they, too, were profiting from the status quo. Self-sacrifice has never been a quality particularly prized by the Japanese elite.

They believed that the economic crisis could be overcome by cooperation with Britain and America, and by investing the nation's resources in underdeveloped areas of Japan like northernmost Hokkaido and in the new mainland colonies of Korea and south Manchuria. They feared the military and its reactionary allies, but they feared the tiny left even more. This middle group included Dowager Empress Sadako and Prince and Princess Chichibu.

These three groups were on a collision course. All three claimed to be dedicated to reforming Japan's corrupt system, but the first priority was to eliminate their rivals. While they conspired against each other, the system remained unchanged and the crisis worsened.

In a country where genuine democracy was considered deviant behaviour, assassination and terror became the national sport of the 1930s.

CHAPTER 7

EVIL SPIRITS

On the heels of Prince Chichibu's marriage, the third imperial brother, Prince Takamatsu, was chafing to play a more active role. After graduating from the Naval Academy in 1925 as a second lieutenant, he spent three years at the Torpedo School, Aviation School and Gunnery School. He was restless to get on with whatever life he was to be permitted by the humourless guardians of the throne. After years spent envying his brothers their foreign travels, he was told he could go abroad in the spring of 1930 to spend fourteen months in Britain and Europe, the United States and Canada. However, a condition was attached. First he must be married. The grand tour would be a honeymoon, a reward for enduring the marriage. We can only guess what he felt at this twist as certain volumes and passages of his recently discovered diaries are missing. The entry soon after his eighteenth birthday did show that he had deep misgivings about his sexual orientation. 'I feel no love for the opposite sex. Am I really homosexual? If so I won't find a partner, homosexuality is taboo.' Had he not been Hirohito's brother, this would have been less difficult. As the perceptive Japan-watcher Ian Buruma explains, homosexuality was never regarded as a sickness or criminal deviation, so long as social rules like marriage were observed: 'For many centuries homosexuality was not just tolerated, but was actually encouraged as a purer form of love . . . this was part of the warrior tradition: gay lovers made good soldiers, or so it was hoped.'

In the 1920s the Windsors, on whom the Japanese imperials so liked to model themselves, had to cope with the 'open secret' of the homosexual love affairs of George, Duke of Kent, youngest surviving son of Queen Mary and King George V. The duke was handsome, natty and articulate. Like Prince Takamatsu, the handsomest of Japan's royal brothers, George also held a commission in the navy. The biggest difference was that George was so far down the line of succession that he could behave as he wished. His affair with the playwright Noel Coward was an open secret and the two were often seen in gay nightclubs in full make-up. King George once remarked, 'Men like that shoot themselves.'

We do not know if Dowager Empress Sadako was aware of her son's yearnings, but little escaped her notice. The girl she chose to be Takamatsu's wife was stunning, the most beautiful royal princess of that generation. At 19, Princess Kikuko was six years younger than Takamatsu. Like him, she was a fashionable dresser, always in the latest styles. A photograph taken soon after their February 1930 wedding shows her in coquettish flapper style in a sleeveless, drop-waist sheath with long white gloves and ostrich plumes in her bobbed hair. Her selection as his bride was fraught with the usual conspiracies. Allegations were made that there was a history of insanity in her family. Indeed, she was famous for her temper. On her mother's side, Kikuko was from the Arisugawa family, one of the Four Princely Houses that often intermarried with the imperial family. On her father's side she was descended from the Tokugawa shoguns. A gullible Western journalist later wrote that it was 'a love romance'. They had known each other since infancy, he reported, and 'it had been understood from the time they were children that one day they would marry'.

Two months after the wedding, they set off on the world tour. While it was labelled a honeymoon, as Takamatsu was both a prince and now a captain in the Imperial Navy there were official engagements at every stop. They arrived in England in June. Prince Takamatsu was uneasy when he saw the cheering mob lining the route to Buckingham Palace, but Kikuko was in her element. At a state banquet that evening, wearing a gown of silver lamé, the princess was 'the focus of all eyes'. On behalf of the emperor, Prince Takamatsu presented the Order of the Rising Sun to King George. This was all intended to put the best possible light on a new naval limitation agreement just concluded in London, setting a new ratio of warships for each of the signatories. Although this treaty was more generous to Japan than the earlier Washington Naval Treaty, it provoked bitter opposition in Tokyo. Takamatsu was one of the moderates, strongly opposing naval expansion. He hoped this agreement would end the arms race between Japan and the West, 'for the mutual good of the whole world'. Takamatsu was a consistent critic of the war party in Japan.

The couple then spent six weeks in Paris before returning to Britain 'incognito' to enjoy the autumn, duplicating parts of Hirohito's itinerary in Scotland. They wintered in Lisbon, Seville, Rome, Athens and Ankara. Then they were off to New York. When the *Aquitania* arrived in the Hudson River, newsmen swarmed aboard and Takamatsu gave a cordial interview in the smoking lounge. The *New York Times* told readers: 'The prince speaks English, but he explained half apologetically that he was not very clever in its usage in conversation and spoke through interpreters. He had no official message for America . . . [but] "I look forward to seeing all of the things which make for the greatness of America and to meeting many of its prominent people . . . I have long read and studied books on America."' The couple enjoyed skiing, the paper said, and the princess played piano and sang, and they could dance but did not do so. Takamatsu was described as 'a slim, smiling youth' and Kikuko a 'delicate and piquant beauty'. The prince's equerries were alarmed by so many questions about his private life.

Tom Lamont and the House of Morgan had arranged a ticker-tape parade. Fifty thousand people cheered the motorcade down Fifth Avenue, which was preceded by an escort of prancing cavalry. When they reached Washington, DC, they were greeted at Union Station by President Herbert Hoover. At a state dinner in the White House that evening they were joined again by Tom Lamont, one of Hoover's most important political and financial backers. The next evening, Japan's ambassador gave a reception for 2,000 guests at the Mayflower Hotel, followed by an intimate dinner for fifty that included Hoover's army chief of staff, General Douglas MacArthur, who would play a pivotal role in determining the future of the imperial family at the end of World War II.

Hirohito cabled Hoover to thank him for the warm reception accorded to his brother. Hoover cabled back saying the newlyweds had 'completely won our hearts'. Finally, the couple headed home aboard the liner

Chichibu Maru, reaching Tokyo in June 1931.

Twelve months later, in June 1932, Joseph Grew, the man chosen by Hoover (and backed by Lamont) as America's new ambassador to Japan, was given a remarkably warm welcome to Tokyo. Since Commodore Perry's famous display of naval force in Tokyo Bay in 1853, future generations of the Perry family had enjoyed exceptional prestige in Japan. The current generation was Grew's wife, Alice Perry Grew. She was the commodore's pretty great-grandniece. Alice spoke Japanese and knew everybody who mattered from Hirohito's mother down. Her father, Thomas Sergeant Perry, was a Boston scholar. Her mother was a Cabot, at a time when this meant unrivalled social and spiritual connections, famously caricatured by the American poet John Bossidy: 'And this is the good old Boston/ The home of the bean and the cod/ Where the Lowells talk to the Cabots/ And the Cabots talk only to God.' During the last three years of the nineteenth century the Perry family had lived in Tokyo while Alice's father taught English literature at Keio University, the first private university in Japan. Many of Japan's future leaders were students there at the time. Alice became fluent in Japanese and socialized with girls from the Peeresses School. Her closest chum was a demure Japanese Christian called Nabeshima Nobuko, who introduced Alice to another girl who became Empress Sadako, the mother of Emperor Hirohito. Nobuko's daughter became Princess Chichibu. In this way, Alice's childhood connections would tie Joseph Grew directly into the imperial family.

Grew's family also had longstanding ties to Asia. They were Boston bankers who helped underwrite the opium clipper ships of Russell & Company and were linked to the great Yankee merchant clans of Forbes, Delano and

Roosevelt. The wealth and virtue of these families was already secure. What was left to boys like Joe Grew was to measure up. He went to Groton and on to Harvard where he worked with Franklin Roosevelt on the staff of the *Crimson*. After graduation in 1902, Grew's family sent him on a world tour. Hunting ibex in the Pamirs, bears in Kashmir and tigers in China, he paused briefly then in Japan and returned to Boston with twenty-two pieces of luggage and a valet named Suzuki. The trip gave Grew a taste for exotic places, and he craved a stint in the foreign service. Strings were pulled. Meanwhile, he met Alice at a party.

'What really bowled me over and caused me to ask her to marry me was the vision of her standing on her hearth at home in a gaily coloured Japanese kimono.' Suzuki played cupid, carrying flowers and notes to Alice, chatting happily with her in Japanese. Although Grew had been drilled in European languages at prep school, he was nearly deafened by an illness and could never learn Japanese. He only heard you speak if you raised your voice, which added to the impression that he was remote.

Before their wedding, Grew was offered a job as a consular clerk at the US Embassy in Egypt. In those days diplomacy was not a civil service but an informal affair. Friends of the president, political donors and out-of-work politicians were given foreign posts where they were helped by clerks and attachés. Many diplomats were wealthy amateurs, who took along as secretaries young men of independent means like Grew. He was offered only $600 a year to start, but money was not a problem. He married Alice in 1905 and they sailed for the Nile. Over the next few years he used family channels to press President Theodore Roosevelt for a better assignment. From Egypt they went to Mexico and Russia before finally winning a coveted post in 1908 at the embassy in Berlin. In those perfumed days before the Great War, Berlin nightlife was supremely elegant. The Grews lived well, with cars, servants, wine and chamber music, mixing with Germany's best. Most days Grew was only at the embassy chancery for several hours. His day began with two hours of piano practice, then a stroll up the Tiergarten to the chancery. Evenings were a round of soirées.

Berlin's caste system was much like Boston society, and diplomacy was conducted at luncheons, teas, dinners and dances. His deafness kept him from hearing what was going on outside a small circle of aristocracy. He avoided politicians, artists and intellectuals, and had no contact with the man in the street. Instead, he cultivated one or two journalists who could tell him what was being said by the lower orders. But he was a good manager. He loved detail. As first secretary he took it upon himself to shop for the ambassador's cornflakes. He had a prodigious memory, and worked his staff hard.

In Berlin society he knew everybody's name, what everyone drank, what games they played and to whom they were related, but he was completely astonished in 1914 when World War I broke out. Grew loved Germany and he was an unrestrained champion of the German cause. His letters home and his reports to the State Department were full of praise for the German government, army and nation, so he was taken aback by the curt rebuttals from his family, who let him know he was out of touch. It came as a shock that – as he put it – he had swallowed German propaganda, 'hook, bait and sinker'. He thought, as many Germans did, that Russia, Britain and France had contrived the war because they were jealous of Germany's success and prosperity. Washington saw it differently.

America was not yet involved in the war militarily but she was deeply involved financially, bankrolling the Allies, selling food, consumer goods and *matériel* to the belligerents while also giving aid to the suffering people of Europe regardless of nationality, a combination of profit and charity that appealed to her puritan nature. One of Grew's jobs at the embassy was to oversee Herbert Hoover's relief programmes in Germany. The future president was a 'modest millionaire', a Quaker who had made his fortune as a mining engineer in Asia and could now devote himself to enlarging his fortune and doing good work around the world.

When the United States did enter the war in April 1917, Grew and the rest of the embassy staff quickly left Berlin. Back in America, he tried to correct his pro-German image by going on a Liberty Bond whistle-stop sales tour, speaking to 24,000 people in eleven days. Now he described the Germans as licentious barbarians and international criminals.

The end of the Great War took Grew to Versailles where again he was thrown together with Herbert Hoover and joined Hoover's core group of wealthy American conservatives. The two men cultivated influential Japanese delegates, including Prince Saionji and Count Makino, the senior advisers to the Japanese throne. During the 1920s, Grew was posted to London where he met Ambassador Matsudaira, whose wife Nobuko was Alice's childhood friend.

Back home, Grew helped Hoover in his 1928 Republican presidential campaign, rallying support from financial circles in Boston, Philadelphia and New York.

Hoover was president when Wall Street crashed the following October, and was blamed for it by the Democrats. Although he served only one term, losing the 1932 election to Franklin Roosevelt, Hoover made strategic appointments that would resonate long into Japan's future, including General Douglas MacArthur as US Army chief of staff and Grew as the new US ambassador to Tokyo.

Despite the Great Depression, Japan remained the most important Asian market for American goods. Preserving and expanding American commerce in the Pacific was part of Grew's new job in Tokyo. Hoover, Morgan, Lamont and other Republicans preached the doctrine that national economies linked together by private enterprise would stabilize the world. In Asia and the Pacific, trade privileges could be used as carrot and stick to ensure cooperation, peace and prosperity. In their view, Roosevelt's New Deal Democrats were nascent Bolsheviks. In this, their attitudes were surprisingly similar to those of Japan's elite, who regarded all liberals as Bolsheviks.

Grew was related by marriage to the House of Morgan. Although he was raised an Episcopalian, Joe's maternal grandmother was a Quaker. One of his cousins, Jane Norton Grew, had married Jack Morgan. In Japanese eyes this made Joe Grew a member of the great Morgan *zaibatsu*. In Tokyo as in Boston, multi-generational ties between families implied interlocking directorships that created solidarity at home and extended economic influence overseas. Thanks to their family ties, both Joe and Alice would be cultivated by the most elegant members of Japan's elite, the tycoons discreetly financing the growing power of the army.

The Grews were going to Japan at a very dangerous

time. In 1930, a group of officers fatalistically calling themselves the Cherry Blossom Society – because the blossoms live such a short time – began plotting to overthrow the civilian government. They wanted to bring an end to political party cabinets and to install an army regime under General Ugaki, but the plot fizzled out when Ugaki refused to participate. That November, a young assassin shot Prime Minister Hamaguchi at Tokyo railway station.

This was only one in a series of spectacular political murders during those years carried out largely by Japanese military officers and their friends. Some assassinations were intended to push Japan into conquest on the Asian mainland. Other murders were committed by young army idealists who believed they had to rescue the emperor from 'evil' advisers. It all began in 1928 with the assassination of the Manchurian warlord Chang Tso-lin, his train blown up by Japanese officers. Evidently Hirohito had no advance knowledge of this plot, but once he learned that his army had carried out the murder to create an opportunity to seize Manchuria by force, he showed no anger. Although his role was kept hidden for decades, he personally sanctioned a cover-up of the assassination. As one Japanese scholar points out, by approving the cover-up the emperor forgave an act of terrorism and indulged the army in its insubordination, encouraging officers to take matters into their own hands again. The stage was thus set for murders, bombings and conspiracies that gradually enabled the army to expand its control on the Asian mainland, without interference from Tokyo.

The warlord's assassination was intended to provoke his Manchu troops into attacking Japanese units, allowing Japan to intervene in force and grab Manchuria.

But this took three more years of provocation to bring off. Lieutenant-Colonel Ishihara Kanji carefully planned the Manchurian Incident of 1931, a phoney attack blamed on Chinese soldiers that enabled Japan to seize all of the 440,000 square miles of Manchuria. Again, Hirohito's role was kept secret until the publication in 1990 of the diary of his chief military aide at the time, which has the following entry for 22 September 1931, three days after the start of the incident: 'At 4.20 p.m. Chief of Staff Kanaya had an audience with the emperor and asked the emperor to approve the dispatch of the mixed brigade [to Manchuria from Japan's army in Korea]. I received the emperor's comment that although this time it couldn't be helped, [the army] was to be more careful in the future.' In a subsequent entry, the aide says: 'When I asked His Majesty for his thoughts on how to punish the army chief of staff and the Kwantung Army commander [in Manchuria], it seemed as though, ulti-mately, the former will receive no more punishment than the warning he got the other day from the emperor. As for [the Kwantung Army] commander, the emperor intends to dispose of the matter with a light punishment.'

Japan's attack was no surprise. Even many Westerners thought that the seizure of Manchuria was the only way Japan could recover from its social and financial crisis. They argued that Manchuria was an ideal source of food and raw materials to fuel Japanese industry. Western financiers like Tom Lamont supported the takeover and neatly blamed China for provoking it. In public, President Hoover denounced the Japanese takeover, but he supported it in private. Manchuria became Japan's puppet, 'ruled' by Emperor Pu Yi.

Hirohito's main worry was that the army's actions in Manchuria might provoke economic sanctions or war with America and Britain. The emperor asked his advisers if the navy and army were prepared 'in case we are subjected to an economic embargo or if we open hostilities with the Great Powers'. Ten more years would pass before that happened. But his aide's notes reveal that as early as 1931 Hirohito believed that war with the West was likely if his army continued its aggressive moves on the mainland. Because he did not intervene forcefully, and let the perpetrators off with mild scolding, he sanctioned their conduct. He was not a passive bystander, and praised the army for 'cutting down like weeds large numbers of the enemy . . . I deeply appreciate their unswerving loyalty.' The shattered glass of the twentieth century reflects more than one image of Hirohito.

The only real opposition to the Manchurian takeover came from Chinese citizens who boycotted Japanese exports, which fell an average of 90 per cent in 1932. In Chinese cities, Japanese were beaten up or murdered. In Shanghai, portraits of Hirohito were paraded with paper daggers stuck through his heart. Here was an opportunity not to be missed. Japanese provocateurs posing as Buddhist monks provoked a quarrel with a Shanghai mob and two 'monks' were slain. At the time, Japan's navy was responsible for policing her commercial interests in Shanghai and there were a number of well-armed Japanese vessels in the Whangpo river. Knowing that reinforcements were already on the way, the Japanese admiral in Shanghai dispatched his marines and mobilized some of the city's 30,000 Japanese residents. Immediately fighting broke out with the Chinese Nineteenth Route Army camped outside the city. Soon there were 50,000 Japanese troops in Shanghai. Random gunshots were succeeded by artillery barrages and aircraft strafing and bombing runs. Large parts of the city were flattened. Thousands of Westerners watched the carnage from the relative safety of the International Settlement, so where Japan's unseen actions in Manchuria had been applauded, its conspicuous brutalities in Shanghai were denounced. Tom Lamont lamented that the Japanese blunder (the blunder of being observed) would make it 'impossible to arrange any [further] credit [for Tokyo], either through investment or banking circles'. Ambassador Yoshida said the assault on Shanghai had been a 'grave miscalculation'. There would be many others.

Shortly before the Grews arrived in Japan in 1932, a group of young military officers calling themselves the Blood Brotherhood murdered Finance Minister Inoue and Baron Dan, the director of Mitsui, Japan's biggest *zaibatsu* conglomerate. Their declared motive was to save Japan from 'evil' influences. Then, on 15 May 1932, while Alice and Joe were in the mid-Pacific, 78-year-old Prime Minister Inukai was slain by officers who disliked his resistance to army expansion in Manchuria and were angered by his efforts to make peace with China. On a bright blue Sunday afternoon the killers arrived at the prime minister's residence in taxicabs, burst in with drawn pistols and shot down police guards. A bodyguard urged Inukai to escape, but the grizzled old man refused. 'I want to see these people. If I meet them and have a talk, they will understand.' He invited the killers into his office, sat down behind his desk and offered them cigarettes, taking one himself. As he did so, two young men shot him in the head, point blank, then ran from the room. A terrified maid found Inukai stunned but alive, sitting at his desk, holding his bleeding head in his hands. He asked her to light the cigarette still in his lips. 'Call back the young people who were here a moment ago,' he said. 'I want to talk with them.' That evening he died. The same day, attempts were made to bomb Mitsubishi Bank and Tokyo police headquarters, and to kill Count Makino.

When Inukai was slain, Prince and Princess Chichibu were watching a track and field competition. On their return, they found their palace swarming with police. 'We were greatly alarmed,' the princess wrote later, 'and the prince left immediately for the palaces of the emperor and the empress dowager.' There, he quarrelled with Hirohito. (It was said only that he 'behaved badly'.) Chichibu shared the view of many young officers that there was urgent need for reform. He argued that the prime minister's killers were not radicals or communists but idealists driven to action by the increasingly desperate circumstances of the Japanese people. They revered the emperor and sought to increase the power of the throne by ridding the palace of corrupt and evil advisers. Hirohito disagreed across the board.

As boys the brothers had shared idealistic impulses and Hirohito had envied King George's popularity. But the reality of life in Tokyo was different. A Japanese emperor's relations with his people were less like those of a king than a pope. After ten years of conditioning, Hirohito reflected the complacent attitude of his elderly senior advisers, who regarded the reform movement as dangerous and its members as radical leftists who would destroy the existing balance in Japan and put the throne in jeopardy. So this 1932 quarrel between Hirohito and Chichibu neatly defines the opposing sides of a monumental clash of wills that would cause crisis after crisis in Japan for the next two decades and beyond, to the end of the twentieth century. It is crucial to see this dispute clearly.

221

The officer corps were the key players, divided into two cliques. One was a group of naive young radicals called the Imperial Way faction because of their idealization of the throne. Many of these young officers were personal friends of Prince Chichibu, and he was increasingly their champion. They completely accepted the dogma of the Meiji Restoration; they believed in the sacred role of the emperor and were convinced that the reason the system did not work was because the emperor was being manipulated by evil advisers. They were prepared to use violence to purge the government of these evil men, to clear the way for much-needed social reform and to rescue Japanese society from its deep malaise. They wanted to nationalize wealth to improve the desperate lot of farmers and workers who made up the majority of Japan's population. This alarmed their potential supporters among the more moderate elite, who had no intention of forfeiting their own wealth, and who regarded any form of social welfare as Marxist. To be sure, the young officers were radical right, not radical left, but the elite saw any form of radicalism as deviant behaviour. Tragically, what doomed the young officers in the end were their earnest motives. Their absolute sincerity made people uneasy, including the emperor.

The other clique was a circle of tough opportunists at headquarters called the Control Group, who were patiently and steadily moving Japan towards military dictatorship. They were manipulating and inflaming the young officers and using them as puppets to eliminate troublesome civilian politicians like Inukai. Most army generals pretended to be aloof from both factions. They spoke sagely of reform but, like Yamagata had, secretly accepted bribes or stipends from big business and yearned to become leading members of the ruling elite.

Increasingly, the young officers suspected they were being manipulated, but they were so passionately involved that they could not draw back from the brink.

The Control Group's solution for Japan's economic problems was not the institutional reform needed to get rid of systemic corruption, but the creation of a Japanese colonial empire on the Asian mainland, followed by total war with the West. Leaders of the Control Group differed only over whether to strike north into Soviet Siberia, south into China, or to remain content for the moment with the colonies of Korea, Manchuria and Taiwan. In any case they wanted larger military budgets and a free hand on the mainland. They inflamed the young officers by stoking their craving for immediate action, encouraging them to plot coups and murders and to dream of a new restoration which would put everything right by 'returning' all power to the sacred emperor.

The young officers did not want total war. 'It is obvious', said one of them, 'that Japan's relations with Russia, China, Britain, and the United States are now so strained that any careless step on Japan's part may throw our divine country into the abyss of war and annihilation.'

If the young officers could get a coup started, they hoped some colonels of the Control Group would join them, perhaps a few generals as well. Their hero was General Araki, a dashing fanatic who excited young admirers by blaming all Japan's problems on corrupt civilians around the throne. When he became army minister, General Araki permitted officers to wear swords for the first time since the samurai rebellions of the nineteenth century, and this privilege greatly enhanced the army's swagger at a dangerous moment.

223

Most Japanese were confused about who were the real villains. Murdered government officials were described by their killers as 'evil men'. General Araki praised the killers as 'pure and naive young men' who sincerely believed they were acting 'for the benefit of Imperial Japan'. Putting aside for the moment the question of whether the victims were really evil, to what extent were the killers idealists?

About half the young officers were from poor rural families. They came to the military academy in the 1920s, a period of severe inflation, rice riots, the destruction of the Kanto earthquake, the collapse of many Japanese banks in 1927, followed by the Wall Street Crash and the Great Depression. Ambitious and intelligent, they were dismayed at the inability – or unwillingness – of one civilian government after another to improve the situation. They realized that Japan's small ruling elite was not seriously interested in the plight of the poor majority. Most of the enlisted men under their command came from starving farm families, and every week they had to deal with frantic soldiers whose sisters were being sold into prostitution. The failure of the civilian government to turn the situation around made them disenchanted with the system. Japan's elite was implacably selfish, senior advisers around the throne were evil because they did nothing, and the country was disintegrating socially and morally.

One young officer spoke for the rest when he wrote in his diary: 'Look around! See what has become of our beloved country . . . The Genro have usurped the powers of the emperor. The ministers behave in a shameful way. Look at the Diet. Are these men responsible for the affairs of state? . . . The ruling clique makes the same mistakes in foreign affairs, internal policies, the economy, education, and in military affairs . . . it has brought Japan to the brink of disaster.' Unless they did something urgently, Japan was doomed.

The Meiji Restoration had not really changed the feudal status quo, it had only 'repainted the signs', as the Japanese put it. An elite addicted to wealth and status was afraid to give ordinary Japanese more than cosmetic democracy. For a thousand years, it was the policy of emperors and shoguns to keep people ignorant, and to keep taxes high enough so families had to struggle to survive, because this kept them fully occupied and harmless.

The young officers imagined Hirohito to be fundamentally good and pure, and believed he was being manipulated by treacherous advisers and disobeyed by them. They trusted Hirohito because nobody else could be trusted. Never did they guess that they could not trust him either. They could not trust him because (as they would discover) he was a party to the fraud, and he would resist vigorously any attempt to alter the status quo. Prince Saionji and others had spent years tutoring Hirohito to abandon youthful idealism; when Saionji or other advisers were given explicit verbal orders by the emperor, they often chose not to obey because his orders were 'not written down'. From their perspective, they did this to avoid problems, so decisions could go forward by consensus. They urged Hirohito to keep in mind the British constitutional monarchy, to remain vague, to make only delphic pronouncements that could be interpreted to suit the occasion. The less he used the throne's real power, the more its magic could be held in reserve.

Although the emperor was commander-in-chief, the young officers knew first-hand that he was frequently disobeyed by generals and colonels in Manchuria. The high command, while professing absolute loyalty to the throne, was scathingly critical of Hirohito in private. They detested his scholarly nature, his vagueness, his expressions of concern for the welfare of ordinary soldiers fighting in Manchuria. They despised his awkwardness. Those who had observed the emperor at close range mocked his bent posture and the audible click made by the joints in his neck and shoulder when he turned his head. They believed he would never produce a male heir. They said he spent too much time playing mahjong with Empress Nagako. A persistent idea in the 1930s was that it might be necessary to replace Hirohito. Some generals thought he was mediocre and should abdicate. In 1933 his chief aide heard that certain generals were 'questioning the sagacity of His Majesty'. The Cherry Blossom Society said they might have to 'threaten the emperor with a sword'. But if Hirohito stepped down, next in line was Prince Chichibu, a less predictable young man, and ally of the young reformers. This worried the old guard.

As a student in the Tokyo military academy following his marriage, Chichibu from the outset showed strong sympathy for the reformers. They explained to him the desperate plight of rural farmers. He visited jailed soldiers who had deserted to try to help their families. Years later, in 1947, Chichibu still expressed similar views: 'Those who now comprise the ruling class, the politicians and new business magnates, should examine well their behaviour, so that their way of life may fit the general condition of the people.'

When he graduated from the academy, Chichibu was posted to the Third Regiment in Tokyo, under the overall command of barrel-chested General Yamashita, who started life as a poor farm boy and genuinely sympathized with the reformers. As a captain, Chichibu was smack in their midst. He told a lieutenant, 'I agree with your idea about the necessity to reform Japan. Please regard me as your comrade.' One of his closest friends was the leading reformer Captain Ando Teruzo, son of a professor at Keio University. Chichibu's affability made him as popular with these young men as he was anathema to the old guard. He insisted upon being treated like them, rejecting all royal privileges except the right to keep his own adjutant. This adjutant once remarked that Chichibu was sympathetic to the Cherry Blossom Society coup plot in 1931. The following year, as we have seen, he quarrelled with Hirohito about the need for reform after the murder of Prime Minister Inukai. Thereafter, Chichibu was kept under close surveillance by the secret police. In another coup plot in 1933, the conspirators planned to replace Hirohito with Chichibu. To distance him from these troublemakers, the palace had Chichibu transferred to the general staff headquarters where he would be under the nose of the older Control Group. At a regimental farewell party, there was much talk of the need for action, and his friend Captain Ando said: 'Prince Chichibu, please ask the emperor to issue us his direct command.' Chichibu snapped: 'Don't be a fool, do you think this is an easy thing to do?' He understood that his older brother was comfortable with the very counsellors the young officers wanted to eliminate. Despite his transfer to headquarters, spies reported that Chichibu continued to meet privately with his comrades. He kept in touch through his adjutant, and obtained copies of reform tracts that were in private circulation. One year later, however, Hirohito remarked that his brother had begun to 'improve' and no longer supported every wish of the reformers.

At this moment a curious thing happened. Prince Konoe, a gifted statesman who was more open to innovation than most, proposed that Prince Chichibu succeed the elderly Count Makino as lord keeper of the privy seal, which would have made the reform-minded Chichibu the emperor's senior adviser. The suggestion was squashed immediately by Prince Saionji, who said it would give Chichibu too much power. We can only speculate how this might have altered the many tragic subsequent events. In this top position Chichibu might have been able to steer events in the direction of reform, or he might have been turned into a defender of the status quo.

When the Grews disembarked at Yokohama in June 1932, calm had returned to Tokyo. After the mildewed embassy of Ankara, Turkey, they were delighted by Tokyo's new US ambassador's residence and chancery, rebuilt after the Kanto quake. The embassy sat on a low wooded hill overlooking downtown Tokyo. Money had been lavished on bronze doors, teak staircases, walnut panelling, a ballroom and a banquet hall. An ideal place to entertain old friends. The Grews began a round of entertainment that would go unbroken for ten years. They had lots of competition, for there were now over thirty foreign missions in Tokyo. Old friend Count Makino warned them that things were changing in Japan 'in these days of military domination' and that he and their mutual friends the Matsudairas, and his son-in-law Ambassador Yoshida, had much less influence than previously.

Eight days later the Grews were presented to the emperor and empress at a palace lunch for twenty-four, including Makino, the Chichibus and the Matsudairas. Alice sat at Hirohito's left, Joe on Nagako's right.

Although Alice spoke Japanese, for reasons of protocol her conversation with Hirohito was conducted in court Japanese through Count Makino. A lady-in-waiting interpreted for Grew, and he found Empress Nagako a perfect hostess, eliciting 'pretty nearly the whole story of our lives'.

On 23 December 1933, Alice woke Joe at 7 a.m. when the palace siren wailed to announce an imperial birth. One minute for a girl. Then it sounded again. A male heir – Tsugu no Miya Akihito – had arrived at last. This was Nagako's fifth pregnancy, after nearly ten years of marriage. At a palace party celebrating the birth, the Grews found the emperor and empress 'beaming'. Hirohito even asked Grew about his black dog, Sambo, who had become a celebrity after being rescued from the palace moat.

The Grews were more cautious than Sambo about immersing themselves. As in Berlin on the eve of World War I, they restricted their contacts to the elite, so there was a limit to what Grew learned on the eve of World War II. Because of the repercussions to his sympathy for the German militarists, Grew was rigidly hostile to Japan's militarists, reporting regularly on the cancerous growth of army power. His main sources were the civilians Matsudaira, Makino and Yoshida, team players no matter what they said, and the Chichibus, whose sympathy for reform switched on and off. Grew never tried to comprehend the life of the other 90 per cent of Japan, the workers, farmers, soldiers and shopkeepers. He regarded the empress dowager's circle as his most important source of information. They were the most cultivated people in Japan. And the least likely to know what was really going on.

The man Grew trusted most was Count Makino, who

229

headed most lists of 'evil men' around the throne. He had first met Makino at Versailles, and thought of him as 'a really great gentleman'. Makino was the son of the Meiji Restoration hero Okubo, the 'Despot', who had ruthlessly undermined General Saigo and then been assassinated himself in 1878. Educated in America, he first served as Japan's ambassador to Italy and to Austria. After Yamagata's death, Makino had become privy seal, the senior official adviser to the emperor, and the top Satsuma man at court. (Prince Saionji of Choshu was the senior unofficial adviser.)

Makino was the leading exponent of the pendulum theory, explaining to Grew that power in Japan swung from left to right. Until recently it had swung left in favour of international cooperation, he said, but now it was swinging right towards 'xenophobic nationalism'. The flaw in this theory was that in Japan there was no left, only right – no tick, only tock. What Makino portrayed as dynamic swings from extremism to moderation and back were only drawing the sword out, or sliding it back in its sheath.

Another confidant was Princess Chichibu's father, Grew's old friend from London and Washington. The Matsudairas spent so much time with the Grews that the chancery staff joked they were permanent residents of the embassy compound. At this point Matsudaira was a senior official of the Foreign Ministry, soon to become head of the Imperial Household.

Grew's other favourite was Ambassador Yoshida, who as a young diplomat in 1921 had arranged Hirohito's London wardrobe. Son of a geisha, he had been adopted by a wealthy businessman, who died in 1887 leaving the 11-year-old a millionaire many times over. Wealth made Yoshida less anxious to please than most Japanese, so he became pushy, abrupt and tenacious. After joining the foreign service in 1907, he married Count Makino's beautiful eldest daughter, Yukiko, his exact opposite. Artistic and sensitive, she had attended a convent school in Tokyo, studied violin in Vienna and was fluent in German and English. Their marriage was a disaster. Yoshida said he always spoke to her in English because 'if we speak Japanese we invariably start quarrelling, but my English isn't good enough for quarrels.' She was a great asset in London because she charmed British society. In Tokyo, she was one of Alice's dearest friends.

The Grews might as well have brought Boston with them. The Makinos, Yoshidas and Matsudairas were just like the Saltonstalls, Sedgwicks and Peabodys, all blandly certain that the pendulum would swing back their way any moment. They believed they were all striving for peace, and reassured each other that Hirohito was a liberal pacifist. If Grew had accidentally met some Japanese fanatics, he might have made a valuable discovery. For, as historian Nakamura Masanori affirms, there really was little difference between moderates and fanatics. They were not divided over fundamental policy, only over lesser considerations of strategy and timing. Grew was waiting for a change that would not come.

In December 1933 General Araki, who foreign observers expected to be Japan's new shogun, surprised everyone by retiring suddenly on grounds of ill-health. He was getting out of the way of a more dangerous man, General Nagata Tetsuzan, a leader of the Control Group and one of the three conspiratorial military attachés who called themselves the 'Three Crows' and who had met secretly at Baden-Baden in the 1920s to plan total war against the West. This change in personnel put one of the toughest of the hardline militarists into direct confrontation with the young reformers. One month after Tetsuzan became the new head of the Military Affairs Bureau, a staff report predicted that by 1935 or 1936 there would be 'an extraordinary political disturbance' – the young officers would strike, and the army must be ready to seize the opportunity. Nagata was already scheming to entrap the young officers when they made their move. In November 1934 military police arrested a group of young plotters. The plotters were inflamed and set up for betrayal by Captain Tsuji Masanobu, an ally of General Nagata.

Now that the flamboyant General Araki was out of the way, the young officers hoped to get support from another of their heroes, General Mazaki, the reform-minded head of military education. But the Control Group persuaded the emperor that Mazaki was a dangerous influence. Here is the first clear signal that Hirohito did not favour the reformers even though they wanted to give him supreme power and greater control of government. In fact, he did not want more power, and was convinced that his survival depended upon the preservation of the status quo. The young officers who worshipped him were doomed in advance.

Frightened by the reform movement, Hirohito transferred Mazaki to the Military Council, where he was powerless on a back shelf. This infuriated the young officers, who misunderstood who was behind Mazaki's transfer. They concluded that General Nagata was their deadliest opponent. In mid-August 1935 a brave man, Lieutenant-Colonel Aizawa Saburo, walked into Nagata's office, drew his sword and impaled the general like a moth to his office door. The head of the Tokyo military police was in the office and claimed he had tried unsuccessfully to intervene. Calmly, Aizawa walked down the hall to the office of a friend to await his arrest. In the corridor he encountered General Yamashita, who shook his hand and said, 'Thank you.' Aizawa had disposed of one of Japan's more sinister figures.

Nagata's murder and the court martial of his killer brought the whole issue to a head. Hirohito told his war minister: 'These young men have gone too far. I want you to take stern measures to put an end to it.' It was decided to transfer the First Division – one nest of conspirators – to Manchuria early in 1936. If they were ever going to act, it must be before their ship sailed. As a precaution, Prince Chichibu was transferred to the 31st Regiment on the north tip of Honshu, sixteen hours away by train. Rarely was an imperial prince stationed outside Tokyo, so Hirohito doubtless approved the transfer. Professor Stephen Large notes, 'By 1936 Chichibu represented the most potentially dangerous penetration of the court by radical restorationism. The army rebels may have had no definite plans to put him on the throne, but they did not discount this possibility.' Before leaving for the north, Chichibu told one plotter, 'Before you do something, please inform me in advance.' To another he said, 'In case you stage an uprising, come to welcome me at the head of your men.' They took these as words of encouragement and concluded that the emperor's brother would back them or lead them. When the time came, however, they failed to alert Chichibu in advance.

Their uprising was set for the last week of February 1936, just before the regiment was to sail. The young officers showed their manifesto to General Yamashita, who approved it. 'If you intend to act,' he told them, 'the sooner you do it the better.' A month before the coup, they also revealed their plot to the war minister, General Kawashima, who implied his support by a gift of expensive sake. General Count Terauchi, who became army minister two months later, remarked that if all those who supported the rebels were to resign, there would not be enough high-ranking officers left to take their places. The young officers even had the support of the military police, whose job normally would be to suppress them. The Control Group did nothing to block the coup, so confident were they of capitalizing on it. The failure of the rebels would discredit everyone associated with reform.

This lack of opposition should have alarmed the plotters, but they were young. Above all, they trusted Emperor Hirohito to support them, once he was liberated from the evil men holding him hostage.

They planned to kill three chief villains: Prince Saionji, Count Makino and army Inspector General Watanabe Jotaro. Makino and Saionji were on the list because they manipulated the emperor and did not use their immense personal fortunes to ease the suffering of the people. Both men heard of the plot. Makino, who was ready to retire, chose this moment to go and was succeeded as privy seal by the former prime minister, Viscount Saito.

Four other targets were added to the list: the new privy seal Viscount Saito, Grand Chamberlain Suzuki, elderly Prime Minister Okada and Finance Minister Takahashi. At the last minute it was decided to spare Prince Saionji, because he usually decided who would be the next prime minister. The plotters thought they could force Saionji to appoint General Mazaki, their candidate, to the job. Knowing all about their plans, the old fox arranged to take refuge at the home of his local police chief.

Leading businessmen heard of the plot and, to protect themselves, gave money to the plotters. Several tycoons, including the new head of Mitsui, fled Tokyo just before the coup. Palace security was so tight that at new year celebrations in January 1936, Joe Grew wondered why he was unable to convey his best wishes directly to the emperor and empress. There was no luncheon, not even a champagne toast. Something was afoot, though he was the last to know what.

Heavy snow fell on 25 February and Hirohito spent hours skiing in the garden with a young chamberlain. At the American Embassy that evening the Grews threw a dinner party followed by the movie *Naughty Marietta*. Among the guests was 78-year-old Viscount Saito, the new privy seal, now marked for death. He was enchanted by Jeanette MacDonald playing a princess captured by singing pirates. The party broke up at 11.30.

After midnight, the men assigned to kill Count Makino left the First Regiment barracks by car for the mountain resort where Makino was staying. When they reached the mountain resort, police in Makino's house wounded their leader. In the resulting confusion, Makino escaped with his grandchild (the daughter of Ambassador Yoshida) and a nurse. Bullets missed Makino but hit the nurse.

At 2 a.m. other young officers awakened their soldiers and told them for the first time of the planned action. Ammunition was issued and they set out on foot or by truck. At 5 a.m. one group reached the home of Finance Minister Takahashi, smashed the gates and shot the old man in his bedroom. Others forced their way into the home of Viscount Saito, sleeping soundly after the movie, and shot him dead. At 6.30 a.m. others arrived at the home of Inspector General Watanabe, pushed his elderly wife aside and riddled him with pistol and machine-gun slugs. When Captain Ando's group reached the home of 69-year-old Grand Chamberlain Suzuki, he tried to reason with them, but they shot him anyway. Badly injured, he later recovered, and served as prime minister when Japan surrendered at the end of the Pacific War.

At the official residence of Prime Minister Okada, three hundred rebel soldiers forced their way in shooting. Okada's quick-thinking brother-in-law hid the kimono-clad prime minister in a snow-covered garden shed where the old man began to shiver violently. The attackers mistook the brother-in-law for the prime minister and shot him dead. While they were celebrating his death, Prime Minister Okada crept back into the warmth of the house where two frightened maids hid him in a closet beneath dirty laundry. Later that day a clever neighbour spirited him out of the house disguised as a grief-stricken mourner.

Aside from the guards at these houses, no police were seen anywhere in downtown Tokyo. The rebels occupied police headquarters without resistance. A contingent sent to seize the palace gates did gain entry but was soon forced to leave, failing in their mission to isolate Hirohito.

By 10 a.m. on the twenty-sixth, the 1,400-man rebel force controlled a square mile of Tokyo south of the palace, including the Diet, War Ministry, general staff headquarters, government offices, embassies and a hotel full of foreign guests. Banners were unfurled with the slogan *Revere the Emperor, destroy the traitors*, and streets were blocked with barbed wire and sentries. No move was made against them. The rebels were courteous to pedestrians and helped foreigners move out of the Sanno Hotel to safety.

Several young officers went to see General Kawashima, the war minister who had given them sake, and handed him their manifesto: 'Recently, evil and selfish people have encroached upon the authority of the emperor, caused utmost misery to the people, and brought humiliation by foreign powers upon our country. These rascals . . . [have made] the imperial army into their private force, [and] usurped the emperor's right of supreme command . . . It is obvious that Japan's relations with Russia, China, Britain and the United States are now so strained that any careless step on Japan's part may throw our divine country into the abyss of war and annihilation.' They wanted full powers restored to the emperor, but left it up to the Son of Heaven to decide what should be done to rescue Japan.

Rebel Captain Yamaguchi alerted his father-in-law General Honjo, the emperor's chief aide-de-camp, that the rebellion had begun and asked for his help. Honjo rushed to the palace at 6 a.m. to see the emperor but Hirohito had already been awakened by a chamberlain, and was angrier than anyone had ever seen him. 'So they have finally done it,' he said. He demanded that the 'mutineers' be crushed at once. Honjo was dismayed to hear the emperor use such a word. His own son-in-law was one of them. Hirohito declared that anyone deploying soldiers without his authorization was a mutineer – although by this definition the entire Kwantung Army in Manchuria had been in full mutiny for years. He told Honjo, 'They have killed my advisers and are now trying to pull a silk rope around my neck . . . I shall never forgive them, no matter what their motives are.'

237

But this was not the first time Hirohito's advisers had been murdered, and neither Saionji nor Makino had bothered to warn the other victims. As to pulling a 'silk rope' around his neck, Hirohito was clearly frightened of what would happen if the reformers' demands were met, altering the status quo.

War Minister Kawashima arrived, read Hirohito the rebel manifesto and to his credit suggested setting up a strong cabinet to reform the country, but Hirohito still insisted that the mutineers be crushed. As this was only a verbal order, General Kawashima ignored it and waited to see what unfolded.

There were many high-level meetings but nothing was decided. Most officials were evasive, waiting to see if the tide was going in or out. The Supreme Military Council endorsed the rebels' goals but not the uprising itself. This was a crucial distinction, for ultimately what was used against the rebels was that they had involved regular army soldiers. Everyone could express pious support for reform, then crush it on a banal technicality.

This was exactly what the Control Group wanted. By the second day, it had won Hirohito's approval to bring in two divisions from outside the city to put down the rebels. Meanwhile, the navy moved warships into Tokyo Bay in case the emperor needed help or the Control Group became reckless and attempted to stage its own coup.

Hirohito's patience, so flexible during the Manchurian conspiracies, now snapped. Two days had passed since he had given explicit orders to crush the 'mutiny' and nothing had been done. He told his chief aide that if the army did not act at once, he would personally assume command of the Imperial Guards Division and deal with the rebels himself.

There was fear at court that if Prince Chichibu came out in support of the young officers, many powerful men would 'fall like an avalanche' into the reform camp and the rules of the game would suddenly change. Prince Asaka, Prince Higashikuni and other princes were ordered not to meet with anyone at all until further notice. Higashikuni, hoping to be named prime minister by the rebels at any moment, got roaring drunk.

When news of the rebellion reached Chichibu far to the north, he immediately asked permission to go to Tokyo. His division commander phoned Prince Takamatsu for instructions. A moderate in all things, Takamatsu was utterly opposed to the radical reform movement and wanted to keep Chichibu out of it and far away from Tokyo. Senior court officials regarded Takamatsu as a rational person who understood current issues 'extremely well'. He never saw himself as a candidate for the throne, so he remained unusually calm during crises. Takamatsu instructed the division commander to refuse Chichibu's request.

Without permission, Chichibu left the base at 1 a.m. on 27 February and boarded a train for the sixteen-hour trip to Tokyo. Prince Takamatsu hurried north by train to intercept his brother and was at the station in Omiya when Chichibu's train pulled in. They spent the rest of the trip south arguing. When they reached Tokyo's Ueno Station, imperial guards bundled Chichibu into a limousine. He was driven to the imperial palace where he talked first with General Kawashima and General Honjo, then was taken to see the emperor and was effectively neutralized. Although Chichibu favoured radical reform, the reversion of power to the throne and a purge of cynical elements in the army, the chief concern of Hirohito and the rest of the imperial family that day was the possibility that they would be assassinated if they resisted the Choshu-dominated Control Group. Fear overcame altruism and won the argument. After the rebellion, Hirohito remarked, 'Prince Takamatsu is the best. Prince Chichibu has behaved much better [this time] than [during] the May 15 [1932] Incident.' However, as a precaution, Chichibu was not allowed to leave the imperial palace.

Once everyone accepted the Control Group's logic of using the unauthorized deployment of troops as a technicality to put down the revolt, consensus emerged. Everyone was off the hook. No painful decisions needed to be made about reform. The young officers could simply be rounded up and shot.

Hirohito signed an order instructing the army to evict the rebels from the downtown area and return them to their units. Written orders could not be ignored. On the morning of 28 February, the young officers were told that even their revered emperor was against them. They were told of Hirohito's signed order, and that they must obey or be killed. Their response was poignant. They asked the emperor to order them to commit suicide, thus making their deaths an act of ultimate obedience to their emperor. Hirohito refused.

With tears in his eyes, General Honjo informed the young men that if they wished to commit suicide, the emperor expected them to do so on their own. Prince Chichibu tried to intercede by sending his own emissary to his comrades with a personal request that the officers 'act gallantly' – send the soldiers back to barracks and commit group suicide. At 5 p.m. military police began arresting rebel sympathizers elsewhere in the city. Tanks appeared in the city centre, ready for a showdown next morning. At sunrise no resistance was offered. The ordi-

Unhappy Monarch: Japan's Meiji emperor Mutsuhito was the unfortunate tool of power cliques that overthrew the shoguns in 1868. After 800 years in eclipse, the imperial family were put on stage to dazzle and mystify ordinary Japanese. Empress Haruko (*inset*), seen here in traditional costume, was to enjoy dressing in Paris gowns and jewels, and dazzled foreign diplomats and Japanese alike.

Stage Manager: brilliant statesman Ito Hirobumi was the shrewd impresario who groomed the Meiji emperor as a modern monarch. A ruthless political operator, he used the emperor's magical authority to keep an autocratic grip on power. Ito had real affection for Meiji, and the two spent many nights drinking till dawn.

Army Strongman: General Yamagata Aritomo (*second from left*) undercut Ito and forced the Meiji emperor to live like a caged bird. His army protégés led Japan into the Second World War and catastrophe.

Imperial Family: entering the twentieth century, Meiji's family
was decimated by mysterious illness. Most of the emperor's children
died in infancy of meningitis, known at the time as 'brain fever'.
His only surviving son, the future Taisho emperor, is pictured
in the centre of the group.

Breaking the mould:
the Taisho emperor was
informal and spontaneous.
His behaviour alarmed
anti-democratic forces
at court.

Samurai in silks: as her husband
came under relentless attack,
Empress Sadako fought back,
rallying powerful southern clans
against General Yamagata's
devious clique. She outfoxed
Yamagata and destroyed him.

Boys and Playboys: future Emperor Hirohito (*left*) and two of his three brothers give no hint of the extraordinary careers ahead. Third eldest Prince Takamatsu (*centre*) became a naval officer and harsh critic of the militarists. Second eldest Prince Chichibu (*right*), urbane and international, became a champion of reform.

Travelling Circus: Crown Prince Hirohito visited London in 1921 as a guest of King George V. At a banquet in Mansion House he shares honours with Edward, Prince of Wales. Only in Paris did Hirohito let down his guard, going out on the town with three uncles to ride the Metro. One uncle, Prince Kitashirakawa (*inset*), died on a country lane in France when his Bugatti hit a tree at high speed.

Choice of the Militarists: scolded for his reckless behaviour abroad and at home, Hirohito settled down to an obedient routine as the figurehead of Japan's oligarchs and militarists, gradually becoming one of them. Here he wears his costume as chief Shinto priest.

Empress of the Sunrise: Hirohito's Empress Nagako was a pretty girl and an attentive mother, but she was gradually stifled and warped by the obsessive supervision of the Imperial Household Agency.

Love and War: Prince and Princess Takamatsu (*left*) dazzled London as Japan's most glamorous couple, partying the night away in flapper style, while the prince held forth in full naval dress uniform.

Thunder in the Palace: on the eve of the China War, Prince and Princess Chichibu (*above and above right*) rollerskated through the corridors of their palace residence after midnight. Servants thought it was thunder. Chichibu traded his life of leisure and went off to war in China (*right*), becoming the secret overseer of Golden Lily, Japan's programme to loot the conquered countries.

Raping Asia: Japanese troops invade Manchuria (*top*); Hirohito's playboy uncle Prince Asaka (*centre right*, with General Matsui) orders the Rape of Nanking, to teach 'our Chinese brothers a lesson'; Japanese troops use Chinese civilians for bayonet practice at Nanking (*above*) while Golden Lily removes 6,000 metric tons of gold from China's capital; as bombs fall on Pearl Harbor (*right*), the USS *Shaw* explodes.

Treasure Ship: the 453-foot, 9,138-ton *Huzi Maru*, built in Japan in 1937, was repainted to disguise its identity, with giant red crosses to protect her from attack by Allied planes and submarines. Here she rides high in the water in the Philippines after unloading a cargo of thousands of metric tons of gold bars in bronze boxes. This photo was taken from a fishing pirogue by OSS agent John C. Ballinger, whose men tracked the gold to a cave and watched the Japanese hide it. Among treasures recovered since the war is this one-ton gold Buddha from Burma (*left*), recovered from a cave in the Philippines by amateur treasure hunter Rogelio Roxas (*below*). The Buddha was subsequently hijacked from Roxas by President Marcos, and Roxas murdered before he could testify at a US court in Hawaii. But the court awarded victims of the Marcoses $25 billion. A Swiss court says the Roxas Buddha is now in a bank vault beneath Zurich airport. (Photos courtesy of his son, Gene Ballinger.)

nary soldiers returned to their barracks. The young officers chose to surrender, planning to make use of their court martial to explain their motives.

Hirohito had foreseen this wrinkle, so he ordered a quick, secret court martial. Thirteen officers and four civilians were condemned to death, the rest to prison terms. There were no pardons. On 12 July the condemned were executed by firing squad. Several shouted, 'Long live the emperor!' Captain Ando shouted, 'Long live Prince Chichibu!'

It was General Count Terauchi who emerged as the front man of the army-controlled cabinets that followed the 1936 revolt. Under the pretext of purging the army of reformers and other deviants, the general staff and the Control Group gained dictatorial power. By warning that there could be further rebellions if the army did not get the budgets it wanted, the generals got bigger budgets.

Completely missing the nuances and the undercurrents, Grew cabled Washington that the failed uprising was staged by 'young fascists' who had slain a number of 'prominent men' who were, of course, his friends.

The stage was now set for army domination of Japan, and for a decade of total war.

With all the duplicity, many Japanese were left completely baffled by the 1936 uprising. They could not decide whether the reformers were wrong or right. General Ugaki, Japan's governor-general in Korea, understood it all too well. He grumbled sourly, 'How disgusting it is to watch these rascals, holding in one hand the matches and in the other the water hose, setting fire and putting it out at the same time, inciting the pure young officers, pleading their cause and then claiming credit for having put them down.'

241

Indeed, as Ugaki's comment reveals, there is no better illustration of the emptiness of Japan's imperial myth than the cynical way in which its most ardent supporters were cut down in 1936. After being raised to believe in a divine emperor, they saw that the emperor was routinely deceived and manipulated by his own senior advisers and military officers. Yet when they tried to overthrow these 'evil men' and to restore power to their beloved emperor, the emperor himself sided with the evil men. Tragically, the whole set-up was a fraud, the emperor himself was in on the fraud, and the last thing the emperor really wanted was to be deprived of the evil men upon whom he depended. If these young reformers were so naive as to take the imperial myth seriously, they were very dangerous indeed, and must be exterminated.

No one was more stunned by this discovery than Prince Chichibu, who had sympathized with the reformers, encouraged them, felt great pain for the downtrodden and desperate in Japan, and might have been a dynamic leader where Hirohito was only a compliant pawn. The last thing Japan's power elite wanted on the eve of World War II was a dynamic emperor.

A decade of treachery had ended on a suitably deceitful note, and now a decade of conquest and looting would begin.

CHAPTER 8

WITH THE PRINCES AT WAR

Our memories of the Pacific War fix on certain dramatic events – such as the surprise attack on Pearl Harbor in 1941, or the fall of Singapore soon afterwards. We remember the military violence but we forget that there was a parallel economic war that was equally catastrophic. We remember the damage, but forget what inspired it. In 1936 Japanese military planners were deeply divided about what to do. Some wanted to attack the Soviet Union and to take control of lightly populated Siberia with its vast resources which, added to those of Korea and Manchuria, would give Japan all it needed to feed its industry and its stomachs, while creating a buffer against communism. Another advantage was that many Western leaders at the time would have welcomed such a blow against Stalin.

In the spring of 1937 when Prince and Princess Chichibu sailed to England to attend the coronation of King George VI, opinion was still sharply divided over whether Germany or the Soviet Union was the greatest menace to civilization. In London, Japan's Ambassador Yoshida – heir to a huge fortune – found himself in complete accord with Neville Chamberlain, Sir Samuel Hoare and other members of the Cliveden Set who favoured an alliance with Hitler against Stalin. Old money and old aristocracy, the Windsors included, feared that the Bolsheviks would line them all up against the wall, as they had the Romanovs. In America this view was shared by such wealthy conservatives as Herbert Hoover and Charles Lindbergh. The Republican Party was considering a MacArthur/Lindbergh presidential ticket that was strongly anti-communist and keenly pro-German. On Wall Street, Tom Lamont's friends never forgave the Bolsheviks for defaulting on Russia's huge Western loans. Executing blue bloods was one thing, not paying overdue bills another.

Ambassador Yoshida told Britain's leaders that Japan's elite was alarmed by the growing menace of communism in China, in Manchuria and even within the Japanese Army. According to Yoshida, the Control Group was secretly Stalinist and intended to turn Japan into a central bureaucratic dictatorship like that in Moscow, and had already done this in Manchuria under the guise of a centralized war economy. Yoshida sought an anti-Soviet coalition of Britain, America, Japan and Germany. At the time, this did not seem farfetched to anyone in London or New York who worried about the future. Many Western strategists saw Japan as an important ally.

Prince Chichibu's mission was to mend fences, encourage a new Anglo-Japanese Alliance and advance this anti-Soviet coalition. It was Japan's last chance to reach an accommodation with the West before that hope was finally dashed by another rash military 'incident' in China, contrived by Japan's Kwantung Army. Chichibu wanted Japan to concentrate on developing Manchuria and Korea. If the Kwantung Army could not be restrained, he preferred to see it strike north into Siberia.

However, all-powerful financial cliques in Japan were secretly pushing the Control Group to strike south instead. If the army conquered China and Southeast Asia, that would provide Japan with huge existing commercial markets, great economic assets and industrial base, vast quantities of government and private treasure that could be expropriated and immediately accessible natural resources that were already being exploited by Western colonialists. We now realize that, to an astonishing degree, the Pacific War was motivated by calculated strategic greed rather than simply uncontrolled militarism. Or, to put it another way, it was rash militarism underwritten by greed. In the future this will become even more obvious as we uncover the long-hidden economic side of Japan's conquest, and its carefully orchestrated looting of a dozen conquered countries. With that kind of inducement, how could the army resist? In Tokyo there was a lot of lofty discussion of expelling Western imperialists from Asia, and Japan's plans for development of an East Asian Co-Prosperity Sphere, but when push came to shove it was systematic looting carried out at gunpoint.

Had Japan only remained content with Manchuria and Korea, the West was prepared to live with the arrangement and to let those territories become a permanent part of Greater Japan. When the Manchu puppet emperor Pu Yi was enthroned in 1934, Prince Chichibu attended the ceremony as Hirohito's proxy. In April 1936, Pu Yi visited Hirohito in Tokyo and was given a lavish reception by the Chichibus and by Dowager Empress Sadako.

Real power in Manchuria was in the hands of the Kwantung Army and its underworld allies, overseen by General Tojo Hideki, head of the secret police, who kept dossiers on every Kwantung officer. Its economy was managed top to bottom by the newly formed Nissan *zaibatsu*, brought in because the army had bungled the job. A young bureaucrat, Kishi Nobusuke, was chosen to straighten out the mess, and Kishi enlisted Nissan, which was headed by his uncle. Nissan moved its headquarters to Manchuria, and soon made itself and the army very rich. The Kwantung Army became financially independent of Tokyo, able to act without budgetary restraint, peer review or government interference. Tojo became its chief of staff, on his way to becoming prime minister of Japan. This was thanks in large part to Kishi, under whose deft management total investment in Manchuria reached $1.1 billion by 1939, developing iron and coal mines, timber and opium. There were 900,000 Japanese civilians in Manchuria. Compared to hard times in the Home Islands, life in Manchuria was luxurious, with plenty to eat and much to do. Such extraordinary success stimulated the Kwantung Army's appetite to seize more territory. China was certainly more tempting than Siberia.

On 7 July 1937 – while the Chichibus were trying to win support in London – the Kwantung Army set off another phoney incident, this time at the Marco Polo Bridge outside Peking, where an unidentified man shot at Japanese soldiers, allowing them to open fire on the Chinese defenders. The incident quickly escalated to full invasion and a China War that bogged down nearly a million Japanese troops for eight years. The Japanese commander promised 'to chastise the outrageous Chinese'. Many predicted it would be over quickly. 'Crush the Chinese in three months and they will sue for peace.'

The start of the China War nullified what goodwill the

Chichibus had earned in Britain. There were howls of protest in Washington. Invitations to Norway and Sweden were withdrawn. Only the pragmatic Dutch went ahead with a luncheon Queen Wilhelmina threw for the Chichibus. One of Holland's best customers was Japan's Imperial Navy, which depended on oil supplies from the Dutch East Indies. But American embargoes would soon stop that.

From Holland, Prince Chichibu travelled alone to Nuremberg to meet Adolf Hitler. Tokyo and Berlin had signed an Anti-Comintern Pact the previous year, mostly for its propaganda value. It did not have the ugly connotation of later years, as both Britain and America were still on amicable terms with Germany and were both supporting Franco's fascists in the Spanish Civil War. The high command in Tokyo thought a visit from an imperial prince would boost relations with Germany. Over lunch at Nuremberg castle, Hitler launched a scathing attack on Stalin that personally repelled Chichibu.

After that, their visit a complete failure, the prince and princess headed home, bypassing the United States and taking ship from Vancouver. As they crossed Canada by train, President Roosevelt was making veiled threats that economic 'quarantine' would be one way of dealing with the 'epidemic' of Japanese aggression. Although public opinion was aroused, Roosevelt was not yet able to invoke sanctions because of a strongly isolationist Congress and the powerful Wall Street pro-Japan lobby. Morgan Bank and a number of other major American corporations were anxious to protect their large investments in Japan, Manchuria, Korea and Taiwan.

By the time the Chichibus got home on 15 October, Shanghai had been under bloody siege for over two months and Japanese forces were preparing to launch an all-out offensive on the capital city of Nanking. Contrary to the impression created by postwar propaganda, dozens of imperial family members, including Hirohito's brothers, uncles and first cousins, served on active duty at the front in Manchuria, China, Southeast Asia and the Pacific islands.

Prime minister then was 46-year-old Prince Konoe, a brilliant but erratic man, a student of philosophy and law who was fluent in German and English. His personal style was informal, and he refused to follow court ritual when dealing with the emperor. Where others sat rigidly in Hirohito's presence, Konoe sprawled and spoke like a family member. Like Chichibu, he had been sympathetic to the young reformers in the 1930s, and he had tried unsuccessfully to get Chichibu the post of privy seal, the emperor's top adviser. Konoe warned Prince Saionji, uselessly, that 'Civilian leaders must carry out the necessary reforms if they wished to impede the political rise of the military.' He also argued that rich nations must share territories and resources with 'late-comers' like Japan – ideas first voiced by one of President Woodrow Wilson's advisers. (One proposal was to give the huge island of New Guinea to Japan for development as a colony.) Konoe said the Versailles peace treaty was cynically designed to protect the Anglo-American power bloc. This made him favour closer ties to Germany, which had also suffered acutely under the Versailles treaty. He defended the Kwantung Army's activity in Manchuria in the early 1930s as 'action taken solely for national survival'. If Japanese diplomats could not negotiate what Japan needed, the army must do it by force. Hirohito expressed similar sentiments: 'The military stood up under such circumstances, shouldering the frustrations of the nation [and] freeing the state from deadlock.'

Originally the army promised to stop its conquest at China's Yangtze river. When it crossed the Yangtze and surrounded Nanking, an inner circle of senior Japanese diplomats launched a secret peace initiative, involving a massive bribe, which Generalissimo Chiang Kai-shek was preparing to accept. But the Japanese general staff learned of the deal and blocked the initiative. For reasons that remain unclear, at this delicate moment Hirohito sent his eccentric uncle Prince Asaka to take command of the forces surrounding Nanking.

It had taken a year for Prince Asaka to recover from the multiple fractures he suffered in the 1923 car accident in France that killed his playboy cousin Prince Kitashirakawa. Asaka's wife nursed him back to health in Paris, and when they returned to Tokyo early in 1926 it was with the idea of starting over. He was given command of the Imperial Guards Division, responsible for the security of the imperial family, largely a ceremonial post. Asaka's splendid Takanawa palace had been destroyed by the Kanto earthquake, so while a new palace was being planned they went to the town of Karuizawa – a sprawling resort being developed by the wealthy Tsutsumi family – where they built an Edwardian villa and began throwing sumptuous parties. This made the resort fashionable and was the start of a lifelong friendship between Prince Asaka and the Tsutsumis, which would bind the Tsutsumis to the imperial family in surprising ways.

When Prince Asaka's new Tokyo palace was done, visitors were astonished by its garish and expensive neo-Greco kitsch – big glass angels, baroque ornamentation, mosaic floors, marble fireplaces, mirrored doors, huge porcelain urns. The princess, one of Meiji's four

249

surviving daughters, took to wearing only Paris gowns. Like characters from Scott Fitzgerald, the Asakas showed everyone how to foxtrot, tango and drink. It was too much for the princess. Six months later, she died suddenly at 44. Prince Asaka never recovered. There were no more parties. He soured, grew thin and grey, drank even more heavily, and became known as 'the nasty one'. Emperor Hirohito criticized Asaka for having a chronic bad attitude, and may have given him the Nanking assignment to redeem himself.

If so, Hirohito was tragically mistaken. Prince Asaka personally ordered the massacre of a totally defenceless population, in one of history's worst atrocities. After the Rape of Nanking, any prospect of peace was destroyed.

The commander of the Yangtze region, General Matsui Iwane, had tuberculosis and was in bed with high fever at his headquarters in Suchow when Prince Asaka and his retinue arrived to take charge of Nanking. Matsui knew Asaka's reputation and was afraid that the prince would ruin everything, so he issued a set of moral guidelines for all officers and men. The bulk of the Japanese Army would remain outside the city limits and only certain disciplined battalions would enter the capital, so that the Japanese Army – in Matsui's words – would 'sparkle before the eyes of the Chinese and make them place confidence in Japan'. He told his officers explicitly, 'Let no unit enter the city in a disorderly fashion . . . Let them be absolutely free from plunder . . . prevent unlawful conduct.'

Nanking had been abandoned to its fate by Generalissimo Chiang who – characteristically – withdrew his army and left the civilian population undefended. Chiang had to keep his army intact to maintain himself in power. When Prince Asaka learned that Nanking was surrounded, defenceless and ready to surrender, he told aides, 'We will teach our Chinese brothers a lesson they will never forget.' He issued orders under his personal seal, saying: 'Kill all captives.'

The Rape began on 13 December 1937. On that day, Japanese troops began to enter the city, followed by tank corps, artillery and truckloads of infantry. Said an American who was one of many foreigners to witness the ordeal: 'Complete anarchy has reigned for ten days – it has been a hell on earth.' Western missionaries helplessly watched grisly spectacles. Over many days whole households of women, from grandmothers to little girls, were raped repeatedly in front of their families. In all, more than 20,000 women and girls were gang-raped. Male prisoners were taken to ponds and machine-gunned. Others were tied together, drenched with petrol and set ablaze. Some 20,000 Chinese men of military age were marched out of the city and used by Japanese infantry for live bayonet practice, while officers practised beheading. Three months later when spring rains came and temperatures rose, many thousands of decomposing bodies emerged from shallow graves around the city.

The Western press reported the Rape of Nanking in detail. Prince Asaka was not a faceless militarist but a senior member of the imperial family personally dispatched to Nanking by Hirohito. He was recalled to Tokyo but was not disciplined. In his diary, Joe Grew wrote that 'the appalling atrocities in Nanking have blemished the Japanese escutcheon in a way which has given foreign nations a new conception of the traditional *Bushido* and honour of Japan. Japan's reputation can never recover.'

After World War II, in the rush to exonerate the imperial family from any implication of wartime guilt, comparatively innocent men would claim responsibility for Nanking and other atrocities. General Matsui, who spent the duration of the Rape in his sickbed at Suchow, sick in spirit as he was in body, was bullied and coerced after the war to claim responsibility for the Rape of Nanking and was hanged for it, while Prince Asaka escaped punishment of any kind and lived to a ripe old age. At his war crimes trial, observers noted that Matsui's testimony was confused and contradictory, but that was because he was forced to mouth the guilty phrases to shield the imperial family.

Attacking cities south of the Yangtze committed Japan to war beyond its means and helped plunge it into the abyss. Japanese forces were carrying out the Three Alls policy: 'Burn All, Kill All, Seize All.' Prime Minister Konoe had offered to buy peace with Generalissimo Chiang for 100 million yen, and then had second thoughts, for peace might be interpreted 'as an admission of Japan's underlying weakness' and could 'inflict a major blow to Japanese morale'. Any compromise with China, he said, 'would create financial panic in the Japanese money market'. Prince Chichibu's rejoinder was, 'How much longer [will] Japan's financial strength . . . last anyway?' Keeping 700,000 soldiers in China was costing $5 million a day. Grew likened the China War to Brer Rabbit's struggle with the Tar Baby: 'The more fiercely the Japanese forces thrashed the Chinese, the more firmly [they were] attached . . . to their victim.' Soldiers were told to forage for what they needed to survive, a euphemism for looting. The army was paying its own way by going into business, looting financial assets, extorting money from rich individuals, robbing temples and museums, seizing agricultural products, running gambling casinos and brothels and marketing heroin and other drugs, in addition to hoarding strategic materials like copper wire. Commanders constantly sought new ways to squeeze resources from the occupied territories. They were more predatory and systematic than any plague of locusts.

In the Home Islands, people were already living with strict rationing, and the national debt skyrocketed. Reserves of raw materials and foreign currency vanished. Late in 1938, the emperor gave the Bank of Japan seventy solid gold art objects and urged others to donate. While he contributed gold, other princes of the blood found ways to do their part through the looting of newly conquered territories.

In previous centuries Japan had often invaded and looted Korea, but the first documented instance of strategic, systematic Japanese looting in modern times was in 1900 when Allied forces lifted the so-called Boxer siege of the legations in Peking. While British, American, German, Russian and French forces were celebrating their successful storming of the imperial capital, the Japanese Army secretly entered the Forbidden City through its back gate and removed all the most important treasures, all the gold bullion in its tunnel complex and all the imperial archives. These were spirited away immediately to Tokyo. Five years later when Japan gained control of Korea as a protectorate (with full annexation in 1910), the army's systematic looting was expanded to an entire country and everything valuable in Korea, including priceless paintings and ceramics, was taken to Japan where all but a few items remain to this day despite the repeated demands of Korean governments and individuals. When Japan then seized Manchuria in 1931, the same methodical looting was carried out under the control of the senior Japanese intelligence officers,

Colonel Doihara (the 'Lawrence of Manchuria'), and Colonel Ishihara. Over the next six years, these methods were refined by economic boss Kishi and secret police chief Tojo. Both in Korea and Manchuria, a deliberate effort had to be made to control the looting and to ensure that the bulk of the treasure remained in the hands of Japan's ruling elite, otherwise it would have to be siphoned off quickly by the army, the underworld, and greedy entrepreneurs. To achieve this, imperial princes were put in charge of a secret financial operation code-named Golden Lily, a name chosen by Hirohito from a poem he had written. As conquests continued, Golden Lily grew into an increasingly elaborate organization, with financial experts heading teams of accountants and its own smelting factories where looted gold and other precious metals were melted down and recast into bars for onward shipment to Japan.

Prince Takeda Tsuneyoshi was made chief resident financial officer for the Kwantung Army. The favourite nephew of Princes Asaka and Higashikuni, he was a handsome young man who after the war became closely identified with Japan's Winter Olympics. Others said to be involved were Prince Asaka Takahito, Prince Asaka's son, and the son of Prince Kitashirakawa who had died in the car wreck in France. It is hard to say why so many princes became engaged in this economic aspect of conquest, except that it could be seen as more elegant – less ugly, less violent, less hazardous, requiring more brains and imagination. Well-educated princes could tell themselves that they were doing this to enrich Japan, no matter how the war came out, and they would benefit personally without getting their hands too bloody. In the meantime it was far more exciting to extort money from canny Chinese bankers, businessmen and crooks than it was to bomb, shoot, stab, bludgeon and rape.

When Japanese armies invaded China in 1937 and expanded their control southward, Golden Lily was conducted as a parallel financial campaign. Loot was amassed in every form imaginable and trucked north to Manchuria and Korea for onward shipment to the Home Islands.

Prince Chichibu became involved in Golden Lily at an early stage. During the Rape of Nanking in December 1937, he appears to have been sent to Nanking with Prince Takeda to keep an eye on army looting. His presence at Nanking has never been admitted officially, but in later years he was tormented by nightmares that he attributed to gruesome atrocities he observed there. Some 6,000 tons of gold bullion was said to have been amassed in Nanking, a combination of government treasure, bank holdings, the personal hoards of small gold bars that rich Chinese preferred over all other forms of wealth and gold melted down from jewellery and ornaments taken from ordinary individuals. Early in 1939, Prince Chichibu was sent to the South China Sea to observe the Japanese invasion of Hainan Island and the low-lying Spratley Islands off Vietnam, conquests that put their forces only 700 miles from Singapore.

His next trip in midsummer 1939 took him to the disputed Manchuria/Siberia border. A strike north into Soviet Siberia was still very much a possibility, and there were large numbers of Japanese troops along the frontier, engaging in skirmishes with Red Army units. At one point Soviet and Japanese frontier troops fought for possession of a barren hill on the border, but the Soviet Air Force gave the Japanese such a drubbing that after two weeks they agreed to a settlement. Then another skirmish began more or less by chance near Nomonhan on the border of Outer Mongolia. This quickly developed into fierce warfare, with the first large-scale tank battles in military history. It was one thing to butcher dejected and helpless Chinese whose Nationalist government left them undefended, another entirely to cope with motivated Soviet armour, aircraft and ground troops who would be shot by political commissars if they retreated. For eight months, May to December 1939, Japan and the Soviet Union fought a major undeclared war on the bleak plains of Mongolia. At first the Kwantung Army played down the dispute, hoping it would end quickly. Prince Chichibu was not so optimistic. He spent two weeks there in June urging commanders not to enlarge the Nomonhan affair. The US consul in Harbin said Chichibu was trying to restrain the Japanese 'from pursuing the [Russians] into Mongol territory'.

Chichibu's recommendations were ignored. The Kwantung Army believed the Soviets would stick to defensive actions because Moscow tricked them by sending fake orders to frontier posts. Meanwhile, Stalin secretly sent his best commander, General Georgyi Zhukov, with the First Army Group including 35 infantry battalions, 20 cavalry squadrons, 500 aircraft and 500 nimble T34 tanks, far surpassing anything the Kwantung Army could muster. Remembering Nanking, this time it was Stalin who ordered Zhukov to teach the Japanese 'a lesson they would never forget'.

By the end of August 1939, Zhukov's Russian and Mongol forces had encircled and completely wiped out the entire twenty-third division of the Kwantung Army. The Japanese suffered more than 50,000 casualties in a single protracted battle, the worst defeat they had ever experienced. This sharply discouraged them from further probes into Soviet territory and caused their strategy to veer southwards.

Scholars still hotly dispute whether Japan used biological weapons at Nomonhan. Historian Alvin D. Coox rejects the assertion as 'leftist' propaganda, but a Japanese chemical warfare expert interviewed by the *Asahi* newspaper in 1989 said Nomonhan 'was definitely the first use of biological warfare by the Japanese army'. According to Japanese sources, when the battle started going badly, it was decided to contaminate Russian water supplies with typhoid. Thirteen soldiers took three days and nights to reach a river where they dumped more than 225 litres of a gelatinous culture of typhoid pathogens. Coox asserts that even if the event did occur, it was badly conceived because typhoid germs poured into a river would disperse and become ineffective. No outbreak of typhoid was reported. Yet the history of biological and chemical warfare is filled with episodes in which people in the field bungle the use of such poisons. Other activities of Unit 731 were more effective.

Unit 731 was the brainchild of Ishii Shiro, a 1920 graduate in bacteriological research from Kyoto University. He was intrigued by European use of chemical weapons in World War I, and persuaded General Araki to back a scheme to develop Japan's own poisons. Officially, as in other countries, the programme was described as defensive. Unit 731 was established in Manchuria in 1933. Headquarters were built at Ping Fan, outside Harbin, with other facilities at Changchun. (Later, as Japan extended its control over most of East Asia, biological experimentation centres were set up in Peking, Guangzhou and Singapore.)

Several princes were linked to Unit 731, and knew of

its biological warfare experiments. Prince Takeda, as chief financial officer of the Kwantung Army, frequently visited Ping Fan where he was known by his nom de guerre, Colonel Miyata Tsuneyoshi. Takeda decided who would be permitted to visit Ping Fan or its satellites. Prince Higashikuni toured Ping Fan with Takeda. (Since returning from Paris in 1926, Prince Higashikuni had served as a division commander and chief of air force headquarters. In 1937, soon after the China War began, he was made chief of all military aviation. The following year he was sent to north China as commander of the Second Army.)

Chichibu attended lectures by Colonel Ishii in Tokyo. The colonel was known personally to Hirohito. One of his inventions was a purification device that turned urine into drinking water, and he showed this to Hirohito, offering him a glass of the finished product. The sources do not say whether Hirohito drank or was amused. How much the emperor and his brothers knew about experiments on POWs cannot be demonstrated because many of Unit 731's archives were destroyed by the Japanese at the end of the war and the rest were confiscated by American intelligence services who wanted the information for their own chemical and biological warfare agenda. At General MacArthur's orders, the activities of Unit 731 were kept secret even from the war crimes tribunal.

Another who was familiar with Ping Fan was Hirohito's youngest brother, Prince Mikasa. Although only in his early twenties, he often visited the front. Born in 1915, Mikasa was the least like his three siblings in temperament. His schooling was much the same, and climaxed with Military Staff College, graduating in 1941. He would hold staff positions in post-Rape

Nanking and elsewhere in China, with the rank of major, and would serve in the air force. Like Hirohito and Chichibu, his eyesight was poor and he wore glasses. But he was much more outspoken than they in his condemnation of army conduct. In 1943 he wrote a long secret critique of the behaviour of Japanese soldiers, which was circulated in the highest echelons, then destroyed, and only by luck (good or bad depending on your point of view) was a single copy discovered in the Diet archives in 1994. In postwar interviews Prince Mikasa recalled seeing films in which 'large numbers of Chinese prisoners of war . . . were made to march on the Manchurian plain for poison gas experiments on live subjects', and others were 'tied to posts in a wide field [and] gassed and shot. It was a horrible scene that could only be termed a massacre.'

Despite Japan's atrocities in China and its annexation of Manchuria, the United States reacted mildly. From the perspective of big business in the late 1930s, much would be lost if America went to war. Top US firms like General Electric had big loans in Japanese utilities and substantial direct investments. More personal links cannot be ignored. Secretary of War Henry L. Stimson had strong ties to Morgan Bank, and Ambassador Joseph Grew was a relative and close friend of Jack Morgan.

After the 1939 disaster at Nomonhan, Japan's general staff decided that if total victory in China was not achieved within the year, troops would be withdrawn gradually from south China and repositioned in north China as a shield against the Russian and Chinese communists. However, when Hitler launched his spring 1940 blitzkrieg into the Netherlands and France, Tokyo's thinking changed again. Control Group strategists like Colonel Tsuji Masanobu advocated a massive strike into the South Seas to seize all Southeast Asia before negotiating peace with the West from a position of strength. This idea of gaining a position of relative strength was dangerously seductive. Over the next eighteen months Japan, America, Britain, Italy, Germany, Russia and France concluded secret deals, alliances and treaties – not to avoid the coming war, but to put them in positions of 'relative strength'. Tokyo signed a treaty with Bangkok that enabled it to send military units to Siam. Believing that Russia, Britain, China and America would combine against her at any moment, Japan allied herself with Germany and Italy, then concluded an agreement of neutrality with Moscow, imagining that this would relieve her of her biggest enemy. A similar pact existed between Germany and Russia, but would soon vaporize.

In April 1941, President Roosevelt signed a secret executive agreement with Britain and the Netherlands agreeing to go to their defence if their colonies in Asia were attacked by Japan. Such an agreement bound the White House without the knowledge or approval of Congress. After this secret agreement was signed, Churchill, who was desperate to get America into the war, declined to provide the air or ground reinforcements urgently requested by his top commanders in Singapore and Malaya, sending only token naval reinforcements, which left Singapore a sitting duck. In Malaya, British officers warned of imminent Japanese attack but their appeals for help were ignored.

In July 1941, Tokyo signed a treaty with the Vichy French government, allowing Japanese troops to occupy northern Indochina. With troops in Siam and Indochina, it was obvious that Japan was preparing for a strike. Roosevelt now exercised the economic quarantine he

260

had been threatening since 1937. All Japanese assets in the US were frozen, and all American trade with Japan was stopped. Britain and the Netherlands followed suit. This included an embargo on all oil shipments to Japan, primarily from the Dutch East Indies. Washington said the oil embargo would be lifted if Japan agreed to get out of Indochina, out of China and out of her Axis pact with Germany and Italy. (Nothing was said about getting out of Manchuria or Korea, but the Japanese mistakenly thought this was expected of them. Foolishly, nobody assured them otherwise.)

Still looking for a negotiated solution, Prime Minister Prince Konoe proposed a face-to-face meeting with Roosevelt in the mid-Pacific. Initially, FDR seemed enthusiastic, but Secretary of State Hull served as a spoiler, claiming to be suspicious of the idea. Konoe, realizing he had played his last card, resigned in mid-October 1941. Others who favoured a negotiated settlement left government with him. His resignation led to intense debate about who should succeed him. Konoe favoured Prince Higashikuni, but Hirohito said privately that Higashikuni had 'weak opinions from start to finish'. Plus, the situation was now dangerous for the imperial family – 'If an imperial prince made the decision for war or peace, the act might bring the "wrath of the people" upon the imperial family.' Instead, Hirohito sanctioned the choice of War Minister Tojo, the former head of secret police in Manchuria. Higashikuni was put in charge of home defence headquarters.

By the eve of Pearl Harbor, Prince Chichibu is said to have retired from the general staff for medical reasons. In 1940, only in his late thirties, he had been diagnosed with tuberculosis. TB was endemic in the world at that time, as common as athlete's foot. Many officers continued to serve throughout the war despite the illness. According to his wife's memoirs, Chichibu withdrew to a country estate at the foot of Mount Fuji, where they lived quietly without seeing anyone for the next three and a half years. On the pretext of the dangers of contagion, Chichibu did not visit Hirohito again formally until late in 1945, when he became involved in the postwar rescue of the imperial family.

While Chichibu was supposedly recovering at his country estate, Prince Takamatsu was playing the devil's advocate. Takamatsu had long ago decided that his eldest brother indulged in self-deception, and he came as close as anyone could to confronting Hirohito with uncomfortable realities. According to General Honjo's diary, 'Takamatsu seems not to have had as close a relationship with the emperor as did Prince Chichibu . . . Right up to the outbreak of the Pacific War, [Takamatsu] shared the apprehension that prevailed among some middle-ranking naval officers about the plan to strike at Pearl Harbor. Evidently he conveyed these sentiments to the emperor when he met with him on November 30, 1941.'

Propaganda aside, the plan to attack Pearl Harbor was not a well-kept secret. Nearly a year ahead of time, in January 1941, Ambassador Grew picked up unsettling rumours: 'There is a lot of talk around [Tokyo] to the effect that the Japanese, in case of a break with the United States, are planning to go all out in a surprise mass attack on Pearl Harbor.' Grew reported this to Washington, along with rumours of a similar planned strike at Singapore. If Grew knew, then many others knew. Meantime, American code-breakers cracked the Japanese diplomatic code using a decoding device called 'Magic' and were able to read the diplomatic messages

Tokyo sent to Japanese officials all over the world. Magic machines were sent to London, Singapore and the Philippines, but not to army or navy headquarters in Honolulu. By November 1941, alerts of imminent Japanese attack were being circulated to US commanders in the Philippines and Panama, but in Hawaii neither General Walter Short nor Admiral Husband Kimmel was alerted.

In Washington there were frantic last-minute attempts by some Japanese diplomats to stop what was 'already inevitable'. One of them was Terasaki Hidenari, an intelligence officer and first secretary at the Washington embassy. Joe Grew thought 'Terry' Terasaki was a man of reason. Terry had attended Brown University, was fluent in English, married Gwen Harold from Tennessee and had a nine-year-old daughter, Mariko, who looked Japanese but was thoroughly American. Terry was well connected; his older brother Taro was head of the American Bureau at the Foreign Ministry in Tokyo and dealt often with Grew until he resigned with Prince Konoe in mid-1941.

Terry was a classic pacifist, desperate to prevent war because he was convinced that Japan would be obliterated. His personal mission was hopeless, not only because Japan was committed, barring unlikely concessions on both sides, but also because Secretary of State Hull was stonewalling. Roosevelt had already secretly committed the White House to war if British and Dutch possessions in Asia were attacked. So, while Roosevelt played the public peacemaker, Hull remained implacable.

Terry, the loyal Japanese who loved America, was stuck in the middle, as shown by his diary entries just before Pearl Harbor. On 26 November, the embassy received another ultimatum from Hull. America required the immediate abandonment by Japan of all territories she had acquired by force since 1935. (By this measure Manchuria, Korea and Taiwan were not in jeopardy.) Japan must not only withdraw from China and Indochina, but support Generalissimo Chiang's regime in China and abrogate the Tripartite Pact it had made with Germany and Italy. In return America would lift oil embargoes, unfreeze Japanese assets and work towards a favourable trade treaty. Hull rejected Japan's counter-proposal of withdrawal from China and Indochina in twenty-five years. In reply, Tokyo instructed Ambassador Nomura to reach a more acceptable accord by midnight of 30 November. He was not told that this deadline was imposed because the Japanese fleet would then be committed to the Pearl Harbor attack. But Terry, as an intelligence officer, knew what was coming.

On the evening of 26 November, Terry wrote, '[Special Envoy] Kurusu called me to a private room . . . "We are desperate. We have no choice . . . I am thinking to have Mr Roosevelt send a wire to the Emperor. That might stop the war." He told me, "Can't you somehow manage to achieve it?"' (Kurusu, like Terasaki, was married to an American and had three children, one a son in the Japanese Air Force who would die in a dog-fight over the Pacific.)

Kurusu cabled Foreign Minister Togo, saying, 'I am trying to have Mr Roosevelt send a telegram to the emperor. Do you think that would help the situation? This war might endanger the life of the emperor. We have got to stop it.' He also wired Privy Seal Kido: 'I sent a very important telegram to [the foreign minister]. Don't fail to see it.' Both Kurusu and Terry genuinely believed that the emperor could intervene to halt the attack.

Terry approached President Roosevelt through Stanley Jones, a Methodist missionary with personal access to FDR. Jones saw the president on 3 December, and Roosevelt said, 'I was thinking the same thing, that is, to send a wire to the emperor. I talked to my advisers and all agreed. Therefore, I am going to send a wire of my own initiative . . . please tell the Japanese patriot to feel relieved.' The bad news was that it took three days for the State Department to draft the brief message, which was only sent at 7.40 p.m. on 6 December, curiously using slow commercial telegraph. American radio stations were informed of the telegram that night and were told it was 'a bold gesture of peace' from Roosevelt. Ambassador Grew first heard about it not from the State Department but from a commercial shortwave news programme. The telegram reached Tokyo at noon on what (because of the international dateline) was already Sunday 7 December in Japan. Delivery was only made to Grew at 10.30 p.m. that night. He went directly to Foreign Minister Togo and asked for an urgent audience with the emperor. Togo said, 'Give me the telegram. It is too late to have audience with the emperor.' Togo called Princess Chichibu's father, Matsudaira, now head of the Imperial Household, who said it was 'a political matter, not a ceremonial matter' and that Togo should phone Privy Seal Kido. According to Kido's diary: 'At 12.40 a.m. . . . . Togo telephoned me to consult about the treatment of the personal telegram from President Roosevelt to the emperor . . . I advised him to consult the Premier [General Tojo] as regards to its diplomatic effect and procedure.' Four hours passed before Kido and Foreign Minister Togo arrived at the palace to see the emperor. By that time, as long planned, Pearl Harbor was under attack. Japanese planes flying from aircraft carriers far to the northwest appeared suddenly over Honolulu with a dawn assault that took local army and navy commanders completely by surprise. The air raid, intended to cripple the US Navy in the Pacific by destroying the heart of the fleet at Pearl Harbor, did no such thing. The vital American aircraft carriers had all put to sea ahead of time, and in a few short months would play a crucial role in the Battle of Midway, reversing the course of the war and putting Japan on the defensive. But Pearl Harbor signalled the end of intrigue on both sides and the beginning of open hostilities. It also marked the beginning of massive, highly organized Japanese looting throughout Southeast Asia, and the meticulous collection and inventory of the treasure. Plundering on this multinational scale had never been seen before in human history. But in the chaos of conquest few individuals were in a position to observe more than isolated incidents of extortion, and the cruelties were so horrific that they obscured the underlying economic motive.

As Privy Seal Kido approached the palace over a hill, he saw the first glimmer of sunrise in the east. 'I thought it was symbolic of the destiny of this country now that we had entered the war against the USA and England . . . At 7.30 a.m. I met the premier, the chief of the Army general staff and the chief of the Navy general staff. I heard from them a great news relative to the success of the surprise attack on Hawaii. I saw the emperor at 11.40 a.m. and talked until 12. I was very much impressed by the self-possessed attitude of the emperor on this day. The Imperial Proclamation of war was issued.'

In 1946 Hirohito told Terry he did receive Roosevelt's appeal and if it had arrived a day earlier 'he would have stopped the attack'. Hirohito thus conceded to an intimate that it had been in his power to halt the attack.

One other enduring question is whether Pearl Harbor really was a surprise. Evidence is emerging that political and military leaders in Britain and America knew precise details in advance and allowed the attack to proceed. Yoshida believed that Churchill was working hard behind the scenes to provoke war. On 10 November, Churchill declared in a speech that if war broke out between the US and Japan, Britain would declare war on Japan 'within the hour'. Yoshida said: 'In order to crush Nazi Germany . . . Great Britain was prepared to do almost anything to draw the United States into war.'

While the US was reading Japanese diplomatic messages, Britain had cracked the Japanese naval code JN-25. According to British sources, Churchill had full advance notice of the Pearl Harbor attack. In Cairo, US Army attaché Colonel Bonner Fellers was told by British Air Chief Marshal Sir Arthur Tedder that he had seen a secret signal on 6 December that Japan would strike at America within 24 hours.

Many sources maintain that Roosevelt also had fore-knowledge but avoided informing his commanders in Honolulu. According to this scenario, the 'surprise' attack on the 'day of infamy' was the only way Roosevelt could provoke the isolationist Congress into the war. Churchill wrote, 'It was . . . a blessing that Japan attacked the United States and thus brought [her] into the war. Greater good fortune has rarely happened to the British Empire.'

Among conspiracy theorists there is a parallel argument that while Roosevelt wanted Japan to attack Pearl Harbor, Churchill wanted them to overrun Singapore. British officers sent a stream of intelligence reports to London pleading for weapons and manpower on the Malay peninsula, to block an expected landing party, but

Churchill did not respond. When the Japanese Army did attack and found the back door wide open, they moved swiftly south towards Singapore, while other Japanese forces struck at Burma and Sumatra, Hong Kong and the Philippines. Singapore fell in February. On 9 March 1942, resistance collapsed in Java. Bataan surrendered on 9 April and the rest of the Philippines fell on 6 May. Two months earlier, General MacArthur had already escaped from Corregidor in Manila Bay by submarine, vowing, 'I shall return.'

In Washington, Roosevelt and others later regretted that MacArthur had not been left behind to clean up his own mess. As US Army chief of staff under President Hoover, MacArthur had been a sabre-rattling Republican with a monumental ego and presidential ambitions of his own. In the 1930s, Roosevelt had been only too glad to get rid of MacArthur by sending him to the Philippines as America's field marshal, with responsibility for the war-readiness of 22,000 American troops and 8,000 Filipino soldiers.

When Japan invaded the Philippines on 22 December 1941, two weeks after Pearl Harbor, nobody was prepared, despite the advance warnings. During the invasion, MacArthur never went anywhere near the front, relying on staff officers to keep him informed. He made one brief visit to the Bataan peninsula, remaining as far as possible from the enemy. Dwight Eisenhower, who had worked closely with MacArthur in the Philippines in the 1930s, wrote in his diary in January 1942 that MacArthur was 'as big a baby as ever. But we've got to keep him fighting.' On 3 February 1942, Eisenhower wrote again that it 'looks like MacArthur is losing his nerve'. At this point, MacArthur received half a million dollars from President Quezon as an award for his 'magnificent defence' of the islands. More than one scholar has called this an outright bribe; at the very least, MacArthur violated US military regulations by accepting it. Although President Roosevelt knew about the award, he made no moves to stop the payment or to force MacArthur to return the money.

Historian Ronald Spector concluded, 'At this point, MacArthur might justifiably have been relieved.' Australian historian Gavin Long observed: 'MacArthur's leadership in the Philippines had fallen short of what might have been expected from a soldier of such wide experience.'

Instead of being relieved, MacArthur became a hero and a legend in America. Fed by MacArthur's clever public-relations staff, the US press published breathless accounts of his exploits as 'The Lion of Luzon'. Walter Lippman wrote of his 'vast and profound conception'. President Roosevelt awarded him the Medal of Honor for the 'heroic conduct of defensive and offensive operations of the Bataan Peninsula'. In these early days of frightening military reversals, Roosevelt needed a war hero and MacArthur was the only general defending the only American turf in Asia. General Marshall, chairman of the Joint Chiefs of Staff, and President Roosevelt decided they had no alternative but to award MacArthur the Medal of Honor, to rescue him by submarine from his doomed command, and to have him take charge of a new American force in Australia. MacArthur took the award seriously, as something he uniquely deserved, and continued to manipulate the press for image-building throughout the war. It is not difficult to see why the Japanese found him, during the postwar occupation, to be the perfect patsy.

Five months after Pearl Harbor, Japan controlled most

of East Asia. Despite its tactical success, the occupation was a disaster. It was intended to rescue Japan from economic collapse by gaining control of Southeast Asia's oil and other raw materials, but it failed to do so. The Japanese Army discovered that the region's resources were controlled by ingeniously manipulative overseas Chinese. With centuries of experience of undermining bureaucrats, conquerors and local tyrants, the Chinese became a terrible drain on the war machine, weakening Tokyo as the Allied counterattack gathered momentum.

Japanese corporations took over Chinese, Dutch, British and American firms, tried to exploit strategic resources, and set up monopolies in commodities. Mitsui's monopoly of salt and sugar, and Mitsubishi's of rice, drove Chinese merchants out of business. Malayan tin production and Indonesian tea cultivation collapsed. Regional racketeers created a booming black market. The result was unemployment, inflation, hunger and hoarding. Prices shot up. Famine spread across East and Southeast Asia and rice became as precious as gold. The conquerors had no choice but to go into partnership with Chinese rice-smuggling syndicates. Japanese banks moved in to rescue (or exploit) the situation. Lotteries, brothels and gambling clubs were started to lure black money out of hiding. Japanese officers became personally involved with local gangsters, profiteers and drug lords.

Because of the failure of its economic strategy, Japan's financial rape of Asia became more important than its military conquest. Loot and plunder became the only way Japan could stay afloat and continue to finance the war. Across China and then Southeast Asia and the Malay archipelago, banks were looted; directors and accountants forced to reveal financial records of clients;

clients arrested and extorted; factories stripped; churches, mosques, temples, pagodas denuded of priceless relics, gold leaf peeled from stupas; art removed from museums and wealthy homes. Most of this was acquired by Golden Lily, which melted everything down to bars and ingots, except for some priceless art objects and the solid-gold Buddhas, which represented a thousand years of accumulated wealth for the leading sects in Vietnam, Laos, Cambodia, Siam and Burma. Masses of jewellery were confiscated, the gems prised out and the gold or silver melted into bars. Gold looted from Burma, Cambodia and Sumatra was collected at Ipoh in the Malay peninsula, a major tin-mining centre, where it was melted down and recast at a factory owned and operated by overseas Chinese. A Hokkien black-marketeer named Wu Chye-sin ran the factory for the Japanese in return for a percentage of the loot. There were similar operations in Kuala Lumpur and Singapore. When the gold was recast in uniform bars, they were marked with the Chinese character for gold, the British name for the country of origin and a number of five-pointed stars indicating their purity. These markings enabled Golden Lily accountants to keep track of the provenance of the gold and its fineness.

Until the end of 1942, this treasure was accumulated in Rangoon, Penang, Singapore and Jakarta, then shipped by sea to Manila for trans-shipment to Japan. There was no overland route by way of China until the brief success of Operation Ichigo in late 1944. The merchant ships used were painted to resemble hospital ships, one of which – the *Awa Maru* – was sunk by an American submarine anyway, in fairly shallow water just off the coast of China. (By international agreement, hospital ships are supposed to be immune to attack.)

Warehouses along the Manila Bay front became clogged with bullion and oil drums full of gems and coins. A 35-mile-long tunnel, half as wide again as a loaded army truck, was dug by POWs so that this loot could be trucked from the bay front to the old Spanish military forts on the eastern perimeter of Manila, where there were catacombs available to hide it. The tunnel is still there, although most Filipinos are unaware of it.

According to numerous Japanese sources, Prince Chichibu's 1940 medical retirement was a cover. They claim that Hirohito appointed Prince Chichibu the new head of Golden Lily in 1940 with Prince Takeda as his deputy, and assert that from 1941 to 1945 they travelled widely throughout the occupied territories, to China, Hong Kong, Vietnam, Laos, Cambodia, Burma, Malaya, Singapore, Sumatra, Java, Borneo and the Philippines, overseeing the collection of treasure and its shipment to Japan using the fake hospital ships to avoid Allied attack. Prince Mikasa is also said to have paid a number of visits to his brother in the Philippines, so while nobody has alleged that he had any direct involvement in Golden Lily's activities, perhaps he was aware of them. Prince Takamatsu, according to these sources, did not take part.

When the US submarine blockade became effective early in 1943, and the war turned increasingly against Japan, a huge quantity of looted treasure was still in the pipeline, unable to move beyond the Philippines. According to Japanese sources, Prince Chichibu moved Golden Lily's headquarters from Singapore to Luzon, the northern island of the Philippines, where he devoted two and a half years to inventorying and hiding the treasure in carefully engineered vaults, tunnels, bunkers and caves at 172 'imperial' sites. (There were many other sites for which the army was separately responsible.) According

KEY

⊠	trucks of gold bullion	◎	staircase
▪	gems (oil drums of loose diamonds)	⊙	mill stone
⊠	solid gold buddhas	○	vent tube

Prince Chichibu's map of a war loot burial site in the Philippine's resembles a child's stick figure. The tunnel was dug by POWs under an army base at Teresa in Rizal, south-east of Manila, and is one of 172 sites where billions of dollars' worth of stolen gold, platinum, diamonds and solid-gold Buddhas were hidden after Allied naval blockade made it impossible to ship the loot on to Japan. Loaded trucks were driven into the tunnels and the entrances sealed with POWs still inside, buried alive to prevent them from revealing the location. A copy of the waxed paper maps was left in the islands with the prince's valet who hid them until 1974, when President Marcos seized them and began recovery efforts with Japanese partners. Marcos brought in Nevada mining engineer Robert Curtis who, with Japanese help, decoded the maps.

The position of the flag – flying to the left or right – indicates whether the map should be reversed. The three circles to the left of the flag mark vent tubes. To confuse, the ideographs mix old and new styles. The symbols at the top reveal the location at Teresa. Those below the flag identify it as Project No. 5. Those by the cross at the left are phonetic for 'tractors' (to-ra-ku-ta-a). Those by the X-filled squares under the clock say 'trucks' (to-ra-ku). Below this, gems are shown as dotted squares. The centre ideographs identify solid-gold Buddhas on trucks. The spiral to the left of this is a staircase. The circle at the right is a huge millstone Curtis found when he excavated the site in 1975. At bottom left, Chichibu marked the site as worth 777 billion yen in 1944 values. Curtis said his team removed $8 billion worth of gold (in 1975 values) for Marcos from half of Teresa, not counting Buddhas and oil drums of loose diamonds.

Marcos subsequently turned his attention to other sites, and the other half of Teresa remains untouched to this day. He ordered his men to shoot Curtis, but Curtis had already photographed all 172 maps, sending the copies to his wife Yolanda in Nevada, and hid the originals. With Curtis dead, Marcos would be unable to recover the maps. That night Curtis burned the originals on his hotel balcony and the next day left the Philippines by plane.

Many sites have now been emptied, but most treasure-hunters fail because they cannot decode the clocks on the maps, which reveal compass bearing, depths and other secrets. (*Map courtesy of Robert Curtis.*)

to Japanese who participated, a second inventory team in Luzon was headed by Asaka's son, Prince Asaka Takahito. The Japanese hoped that they would be able to arrange a cease-fire that would allow them to hold on to the Philippines, essentially annexing it, so that they could recover the war loot at their leisure. If they were unable to annex the Philippines, they reasoned that they could still recover the treasure gradually under a variety of covers – which is essentially what did happen after the war. Having gambled and lost, it was essential not to forfeit the plunder, which would be needed to rebuild Japan.

In the last year of the war, Japan also hid large quantities of bullion at sea, deliberately scuttling ships including the cruiser *Nachii,* sunk with all hands in Manila Bay by a Japanese submarine that then machine-gunned all the Japanese crew members who came to the surface. The gold aboard the *Nachii* was recovered from its hulk in the late 1970s by President Marcos.

The Japanese sub *I-52,* a cargo vessel the length of a football field, was attempting to deliver two tons of gold worth $25 million to the Nazi sub base at Lorient, France, when it was sunk in mid-Atlantic by a US Navy plane. It has now been located and a recovery operation is under way. Other bullion shipments were made by sub to Europe and South America, and deposited in overseas branches of Swiss banks.

For decades after the war, the existence of this hidden treasure was regarded by many as sheer fantasy. It served Japan's purpose to have people think so, while recovery efforts went on secretly. But in the 1990s courts in America and Switzerland concluded that billions of dollars of gold were indeed looted by Japan and hidden in the Philippines. In 1997 a team from Japan's Asahi

Television was led to a mountain cave in the Philippines where they examined 1,800 of these bars, worth $150 million, and drilled core samples that confirmed their provenance. They were some of the bars minted in Ipoh. The gold, hidden by Golden Lily during the war, had been discovered in a cave by barefoot Igorot hillpeople, who were afraid to sell it for fear they would be victimized. A Manila contact had informed Asahi in the hope of bypassing the Filipino gold market and dealing directly with Japan. Sources at Asahi Television said they were discouraged from doing a full investigation because of fear of reprisals by Japanese extremists.

There is growing evidence confirming that Prince Chichibu was indeed in the Philippines during this period, heading the treasure effort. But a full and detailed study of Golden Lily must be the subject of another book. In Tokyo in the 1950s, after Chichibu's premature death from TB, a member of the imperial family confided to a foreign visitor that the army had amassed over $100 billion in treasure, and much of this was hidden in the Philippines, where 'it will take a century to uncover'. He confirmed that Chichibu was in Luzon for two and a half years, escaping to Japan by submarine early in 1945. The involvement of the imperial family in such activities has never been acknowledged in Japan, although in recent years it has been widely discussed in private.

Nazi war loot got more attention because of the powerful postwar Jewish lobby which was able to mount an effective, coordinated campaign for which there was no Asian equivalent. Both wars had horrific consequences. Six million Jews were killed by the Nazis but as many as 30 million Asians died as a result of Japan's aggression, 23 million in China alone. The scale of Japanese plunder overshadows Nazi looting in terms of numbers, and remains officially denied.

Attention in the West remains curiously fixated instead on Hirohito's role in waging the war as if this were a matter of profound significance. Many scholars argue that the emperor wanted an early peace and made this wish clear to Tojo in February 1942: 'I assume you have given full consideration to not losing any opportunity of ending the conflict. It is undesirable to have it prolonged in vain . . . I [also] fear that the quality of our troops will decline if the war is prolonged.' Yet no matter what happened, Hirohito did not sue for an early peace. Victories fed a desire for more victories, setbacks made it necessary to recapture the advantage before going to the negotiating table. So both victories and setbacks required more victories.

The first great setback was the Battle of Midway in June 1942. After that, Prince Takamatsu concluded that the war must be ended as soon as possible. Hirohito disagreed and told him so. But as the turning tide began to rip, Hirohito groped urgently for better footing – the deployment of more air power at Guadalcanal and a new offensive in New Guinea. The worse things became, the more determined he was to gain an advantage. In a secret memo written after the war, he said: 'I wanted to strike the enemy just once, anywhere, and quickly obtain the chance for peace.' It did not happen.

There was a secret 'peace faction' of former prime ministers, diplomats, court officials and members of the imperial family identified with Dowager Empress Sadako's circle. One plan was for Prince Konoe to move to Switzerland with aides like Terasaki Taro to negotiate secretly with the Allies. Konoe was startled by the idea, but willing to give it a try. Yoshida then presented the plan to Privy Seal Kido, but Kido's response was tepid and the matter died there.

Members of the peace group were old money who saw the status quo slipping away. Peace was needed to preserve what was left of traditional Japan and their place in it. Surgical assassination of Prime Minister Tojo and other hardliners was beyond them. Other than sending peace feelers through Swiss bankers, they concentrated on persuading Hirohito to replace Tojo with an army hero. This hero would then purge the Control Group, after which Japan could sue for peace. Yet nobody could sway Hirohito from his conviction that the armed forces could and should gain the advantage before negotiating, and he considered Tojo essential for that. In November 1943 he told Prince Takamatsu: 'It is said that Tojo is no good, but who would be better? If there is no one better, is there no alternative but to cooperate with the Tojo cabinet?'

In April 1944, as defeats multiplied, Prince Konoe changed his mind about Tojo and told Prince Higashikuni that Tojo should remain as prime minister till the war was lost so all blame could be pinned on him. Konoe had learned of secret talks between Joe Grew and Japan's ambassador to Switzerland, Kase Shunichi. Grew assured Kase that America believed the retention of the emperor was Japan's only safeguard against a communist coup after the war. To salvage the imperial family, they would need Tojo to take the blame for the war. Konoe told Higashikuni: 'Americans [have] little knowledge of the imperial family or how the imperial institution worked in Japan'. Sadly, the war was dragged out for over a year more because of these two obsessions: the need for a military advantage before negotiating, and the need to preserve Tojo as a scapegoat to divert blame from the emperor.

After the loss of Saipan in June 1944, giving the US an air base from which to strike Japanese cities easily, matters began to come to a head. General Honjo, the emperor's aide, said: 'Prince Takamatsu was drawn into [the] plan to remove Tojo from office and end the war. The prince began to bring "disturbing sounds" into the imperial court against the wishes of Lord Privy Seal Kido and the emperor. Takamatsu and Hirohito had frequent arguments. After a particularly heated argument again about Tojo, Takamatsu told His Majesty that no information aside from what he is given by the government ever comes to his attention. The emperor said that this was not so. It seems that he does not approve of members of the imperial family discussing political affairs with him.' Dowager Empress Sadako – who had always been against the war – was drawn into the fray to influence Hirohito to end the war. Prince Higashikuni even considered enlisting Empress Nagako, but that was vetoed by Prince Takamatsu because 'if it is mishandled, it could cause serious [domestic] problems'.

Hirohito's continued refusal to sue for peace justified more radical moves within the palace. Prince Takamatsu, Prince Higashikuni, Prince Mikasa and Prince Konoe were the prime movers. Prince Chichibu, who was still in the Philippines, may also have been involved because he apparently made several quick trips back to Japan by plane during this period. On 8 July 1944, it was secretly agreed by members of the family that Hirohito should be forced to abdicate in favour of his son, 10-year-old Crown Prince Akihito, with Prince Takamatsu as regent. Prince Higashikuni would replace Tojo as prime minister, and peace moves would begin at once. When word of this reached Hirohito by way of Privy Seal Kido (a perpetual spoiler), he suddenly deserted Tojo, who resigned on 14 July. From this, one conclusion seems inescapable – that to Hirohito the war was less important than the preservation of his position.

Because of the many procedural difficulties imposed by consensus, removing Tojo was only a first cautious step. War continued for thirteen more months. When General Koiso Kuniaki took over from Tojo as prime minister, neither Hirohito nor Privy Seal Kido gave him explicit written orders to pursue a strong peace initiative. So he did not. Hirohito had eliminated the immediate threat to his own rule, but he was still waiting for a great victory, his *tennozan*, the epic battle that would shift the advantage back to Japan. With *tennozan* in mind he backed the biggest naval engagement in history, the Battle of Leyte Gulf in October 1944. As Hirohito rationalized after the war: 'If first we attacked at Leyte and America was forced to withdraw, then we would probably be able to find room for compromise.' Echoing Hirohito, Prime Minister Koiso said in a radio address, 'If Japan wins on Leyte, we win the war.' Japan lost. The admiral commanding the fleet hid in his basement in Tokyo during the entire battle, communicating orders by radio.

By February 1945, it was being predicted in Tokyo that the Allies would invade the southern island of Kyushu by June and the main island of Honshu by September. Prince Takamatsu, the most pessimistic and clear-headed of the princes, thought it would come even sooner.

The peace group around Yoshida had been pressing Prince Konoe for some time to make a direct personal appeal to Hirohito. They drafted a memorandum for him

279

to use. The latest Japanese setbacks in New Guinea gave them an opening, so a palace meeting was arranged for 14 February 1945. By now Prince Konoe was becoming obsessed with the fear of communist revolution in Japan. At his private meeting with Hirohito, Konoe read the memo. He warned the emperor that unless Japan ended the war soon, a communist revolution would destroy the imperial family. The capitalist system, the class structure and the imperial house were all in jeopardy. Konoe explained: 'The majority of our professional soldiers come from below middle-class families, and their circumstances make them receptive to communist doctrine. Communist elements seek to lure the soldiers to their side with the claim that [the imperial family] and communism can stand side by side. It is now clear, I think, that the Manchurian Incident and the China War and their expansion into the Great East Asia War were deliberately plotted by this [communist] group within the military.' He was referring to the Control Group. It may seem bizarre that the hardline fascists of the Control Group were being labelled communists, but not if one keeps Stalin in mind. Fifty years earlier, General Yamagata had seen 'democracy' in strikingly similar terms. It was his classic right-wing argument that anything less than far right meant far left. Democracy and communism were two heads on the same snake. Indulge one, you got both.

True, the war was releasing pent-up revolutionary tendencies everywhere in Asia. Communists and other radicals were gaining ground in Korea, China, Indochina, Burma, Malaya and Indonesia. Prince Konoe argued that unless the Control Group was ousted quickly, Japan's inevitable defeat would be followed by social upheaval, the fall of the Yamato dynasty and an end to all they revered. The only recourse now was to install as prime minister one of the army heroes identified with the prewar Imperial Way movement, someone admired throughout the military. (Ironically, this would fulfil the plan that the young officers had tried and failed to carry out in the reform uprising of 1936, which Hirohito had stymied.) Only such a military hero would be acceptable to enough of the armed forces to enable the complete purge of the Control Group. General Ugaki would have been their first choice, but he refused to come out of retirement, so they had settled on General Mazaki, the champion of the young officers in 1936.

Hirohito was aghast. He had despised Mazaki in 1936, still despised him, and nothing could persuade him to allow the Imperial Way reformers into the leadership. It remains one of the great enigmas about Hirohito that he feared the naive, misplaced idealism of the reformers more than he did the disasters visited upon Japan by the Control Group. Since the Meiji Restoration the divine position of the emperor had depended heavily on contrived mythology and mystification – smoke and mirrors – so the passionate support of the emperor by the Imperial Way faction was clearly an obsession with falsehood and fantasy. It may be that Hirohito was frightened and repelled by their extreme devotion to him. To let true believers into the palace might lead to unforeseeable consequences. Nobody is more wary of religious fanatics than the object of their devotion.

If peace was arranged now, Prince Konoe predicted that the United States would not destroy the imperial house, but would keep it in place. He said the influence of Joseph Grew and other anti-communist Americans would ensure this.

Konoe should have stopped at this point, while there

was some hope that Hirohito would agree to these dramatic changes. Instead, he unwisely let it slip that Hirohito also would have to abdicate in favour of his son and retire to a Buddhist temple in Kyoto, as so many other emperors had in the past. It is astonishing that Konoe, one of the brightest princes, could have been so imperceptive about Hirohito. The emperor grew silent, brooding over this latest twist. He would make no immediate decision. The audience was over.

After this inconclusive meeting, Prince Takamatsu became furious at Konoe, Yoshida and the peace group for their incompetence in putting the case to Hirohito. Takamatsu accused them of 'running around' without a concrete strategy.

Eleven days later, while Hirohito continued to vacillate, US aircraft began napalming Japan's highly flammable cities. Nearly 200,000 died in Tokyo alone. By 10 March, nearly 2 million more were homeless in Tokyo. The raids stepped up and Osaka, Nagoya, Koriyama, Shizuoka and Koizumi were devastated. Hirohito's silence continued.

In late March he made a decision: 'Since the army and navy are willing to fight the decisive battle of Okinawa, now is not the appropriate time to stop the war.' During nearly three months of fighting on Okinawa, 110,000 Japanese soldiers and 150,000 civilians died. American dead numbered 12,000 with 36,000 wounded. While the battle raged, Roosevelt died and Harry Truman became president. On 7 May 1945, Germany surrendered unconditionally. This gave Hirohito another opportunity to call a halt. He had maintained that he could not abandon his German allies by seeking a separate peace. 'Having given a firm promise to Germany not to make a unilateral peace, I did not, for reasons of international trust, want to discuss peace before Germany did. Therefore I [wanted] Germany to be defeated as quickly as possible.' Nevertheless, after Germany's unconditional surrender, Hirohito delayed his own decision another three months.

A little more than two weeks after the German surrender, during another napalm raid on Tokyo, the imperial palace compound was set ablaze. Some two dozen buildings were destroyed, including the main palace and the palaces of Dowager Empress Sadako and Crown Prince Akihito. Empress Nagako became hysterical, although they were safe in a bunker beneath the imperial library. Hirohito was said to be relieved that he could now be seen to share the misery of his people. In these latest fire-bombings half a million more Japanese civilians were killed, and 13 million more were made homeless.

On 26 July, the Allies issued the Potsdam Declaration demanding Japan's unconditional surrender. In Washington, where Grew was now an undersecretary of state, he urged the White House to give the Japanese a clear idea of what was meant by unconditional surrender. 'The greatest obstacle to unconditional surrender . . . is their belief that this would entail the destruction or permanent removal of the emperor and the institution of the throne.' Grew meant to reassure the elite, whose privileged position depended upon the continuation of the dynasty, with the emperor as its front man.

After much wrangling, the Allied ultimatum made the following guarantee: 'The occupying forces of the Allies shall be withdrawn from Japan as soon as objectives have been accomplished and *there has been established in accordance with the freely expressed will of the Japanese people a peacefully inclined and responsible government*' [authors' italics]. There was no explicit guarantee of preserving Hirohito on the throne or even of preserving the dynasty. So, instead of replying to the Potsdam Declaration, Hirohito's imperial council remained silent. This convinced the Allies that they would end up having to invade the Home Islands.

On 6 August Hiroshima was hit by the war's first atom bomb, causing the death of 140,000 more Japanese. Hirohito's council still made no move. Three days later, Nagasaki received the second atom bomb, and another 80,000 died. The previous day, the Soviet Union had entered the war against Japan. There was a secret agreement between Stalin and the other Allies that Moscow would enter the war three months after the defeat of Nazi Germany. Not knowing this, the peace group in Tokyo had initiated desperate attempts to have Moscow broker a peace deal. Stalin, who hoped to take Japan's northern islands as his prize for entering the war against Japan, blocked the initiative. President Truman, General Marshall and General MacArthur did not believe that the atomic bombing of Japan was going to end the war. All three wanted to have Soviet participation in assaulting the Home Islands. They did not want heavy casualties borne exclusively by American troops. Japan had a deep primal fear of Russia and there was no doubt that Soviet invaders would include Mongol units like those at Nomonhan, probably under the command of the same General Zhukov. The prospect of Soviet troops inspiring a communist revolution in Japan caused profound dread among the elite in Tokyo.

Hirohito spoke at a late-night imperial conference on 9 August: 'I have given serious thought to the situation prevailing at home and abroad and have concluded that continuing the war can only mean destruction for the nation and prolongation of bloodshed and cruelty in the world.'

Next day, Tokyo notified Washington that it accepted the Potsdam Declaration 'with the understanding that the said declaration does not comprise any demand which prejudices the prerogatives of his majesty as a sovereign ruler'. President Truman and the new secretary of state James Byrnes were opposed to making any unequivocal public commitment because polls showed that 70 per cent of Americans favoured Hirohito's execution or life-imprisonment for his part in the war. A deft reply from Byrnes gave implicit assurance: 'The ultimate form of government of Japan shall, in accordance with the Potsdam Declaration, be established by the freely expressed will of the Japanese people', implying that the emperor system could remain if the Japanese people wished. This reply was sent through Swiss channels on behalf of the United States, Britain, China and the Soviet Union.

On the morning of 14 August, Japan was bombarded a different way. Thousands of leaflets fell with a translation of the Japanese government's acceptance of the Potsdam Declaration and Byrnes's note of clarification. Privy Seal Kido saw one and was 'stricken with consternation'. The cat was out of the bag. Fearing this 'leak' could provoke a military coup, he rushed to Hirohito and a conference was arranged that morning. Hirohito spoke: 'I have studied the terms of the Allied reply, and I have come to the conclusion that they represent a virtually complete acknowledgment of our position.' Later that day, he recorded a radio broadcast. That night, an army unit tried to seize the palace and destroy the recording. They failed.

Next morning the recording was broadcast. It was

Hirohito's first speech to his people, his voice high-pitched and reedy. Instead of speaking ordinary Japanese, he spoke court dialect, which few could understand. This was an unnecessary reminder that he was still 'above the clouds'. The words 'defeat' and 'surrender' were avoided.

'To our good and loyal subjects: After pondering deeply the general trends of the world and the actual conditions obtaining in our empire today, we have decided to effect a settlement of the present situation . . . the war situation has developed not necessarily to Japan's advantage . . . Having been able to safeguard and maintain the structure of the imperial state, we are always with you, our good and loyal subjects, relying upon your sincerity and integrity.'

Soon afterwards Prime Minister Suzuki – sworn in a few months earlier – made his own radio broadcast. After thanking the emperor for making 'the sacred decision to end the war in order to save the people', Suzuki said, 'The nation sincerely apologizes to His Majesty [for the way the war has ended].' Prince Higashikuni echoed these sentiments when he publicly called for national repentance. 'It was His Majesty himself who, in deference to the spirits of the imperial ancestors, decided to save millions of his subjects from privation and misery and to pave the way for an era of grand peace . . . Never before have we been moved so profoundly as by this act of boundless benevolence. With tears of overwhelming gratitude we can only offer our humble apologies for having caused His Majesty so much anxiety.'

CHAPTER 9

THE EXORCISTS

Two days after Japan's surrender, Hirohito's restless uncle Prince Higashikuni got his lifelong wish and became prime minister. He had been angling for the top job since the 1920s but was always blocked by palace advisers who distrusted his readiness to change direction with every breeze like a rice-paper carp swimming upstream on a flagpole. Hirohito had said it was dangerous for a prince to be prime minister when war broke out as this could incriminate the dynasty if the war went wrong. Now that peace had come the throne wished to collect as much credit as possible. Soldiers and civilians would cooperate more readily if the top bureaucrat was a prince, implying the imperial sanction of all orders. Prince Asaka, the butcher of Nanking, was sent to China to make sure army officers in the field obeyed orders to surrender. Prince Takeda was sent to Manchuria to do the same, and to make sure all treasure piled up there and in Korea was quickly shipped to Japan.

There was a flurry of activity in government and military offices all over Japan. Skies were brown from the burning of sensitive documents. Crates of weapons and ammunition were buried where they could be recovered quickly. Soldiers stripped off uniforms and dressed as poor farmers. All of this was illustrative of a state of mind in which Japan was not admitting defeat but was making a strategic withdrawal to fight another day. Many Japanese still insist they did not lose the war. Militarists and their financial backers were just going under deep cover. The Allies had made it clear in the Potsdam Declaration that they intended to prosecute Japanese war criminals. In Germany detailed archives were captured and used as evidence, but in Japan the evidence vanished. Germany's Nazi leadership was purged after the war, but Japan lost only a handful of generals and admirals who took the fall to save the rest.

Billions of dollars in gems, gold bullion and other precious metals were lowered on to the sea bed offshore, or sealed in bomb shelters, their entrances filled and giant bamboo planted to discourage casual digging. The hospital ship *Tenno Maru* (formerly the Dutch freighter *Opten Noort*, captured in Indonesia) arrived at Yokosuka Naval Base loaded with casualties from fighting in the Philippines, and 2,000 metric tons of gold bullion put aboard by Golden Lily. This was one of the six merchant vessels painted as hospital ships on the orders of Golden Lily, which had served as the main transports for gold bullion. A few days later, the *Tenno Maru* and its gold bars were moved to Maizura Naval Base where more treasure was taken aboard. Then the ship was sailed into the bay at night, her captain and twenty-four-man crew murdered, and the ship scuttled by opening its Kingston valve. It was recovered only in 1987 in a secret operation where, according to participants, Australian salvage specialists were brought in by the Japanese. Another hospital ship, the *Awa Maru*, hurrying home along the China coast in April 1945 with VIP families, 40 metric tons of gold bullion, 12 metric tons of platinum, 150,000 carats of diamonds and large quantities of titanium and other strategic materials, was sunk accidentally in heavy fog by a US submarine, whose skipper said he thought she was a warship. Japan hotly protested her sinking but never admitted to her having war loot aboard.

In the Japan Alps, trucks carried mysterious loads into old mine-shafts and hauled heavy cargoes into the recently completed imperial bunker at Matsushiro near Nagano, the future Olympic Village 110 miles north-west of Tokyo. During the last ten months of the war, some 10,000 Korean slave labourers dug a 10-kilometre tunnel complex there under Mount Minakami. This was to be the emperor's hideout and army headquarters in case the Allies invaded Japan. There was more than 60,000 cubic metres of underground space in a chess-board grid of tunnels big enough for the largest trucks. There was room for all government agencies, and even for the Peers School. When the Allies did not invade and the war ended in surrender, branch tunnels became a convenient repository for Golden Lily, like the mountain vaults of Swiss banks.

Not everything went undersea or underground. Four tons of opium and heroin worth over $6 million 1945 dollars were discovered by US occupation patrols in the rafters of a warehouse in Nagano.

Long before Japan surrendered, America decided that the occupation would be exclusively under its control. Unlike Germany, where each Allied power established a military government to rule its own occupation zone, Japan had only an American zone, and the existing civil government was used to facilitate Washington's occupa-tion policy. On the day Japan surrendered, President Truman appointed General MacArthur as Supreme

Commander Allied Powers (SCAP), with the concurrence of Britain's Prime Minister Attlee, Stalin and Chiang Kai-shek. For the next six years, MacArthur would exercise virtually unchallenged power over 83 million Japanese. As Supreme Commander, he ignored the eleven-nation Far Eastern Commission, which became only a toothless forum. Moscow, London and Canberra protested in vain. MacArthur was in a unique position to inflict reform on a country that urgently needed it, but instead he delivered the Japanese people back into the hands of the same men who had led them into the 'dark valley'. This unfolded gradually, but it was programmed to happen that way all along. There were two schools of thought in Washington about what should be done in Japan. Liberals wanted reform pushed through, while conservatives wanted the reforms aborted, the emperor kept on his throne and the government and financial system restored to its rightful owners. MacArthur's personal mission was to pretend to carry out Washington's liberal reforms, while actually doing the reverse and fulfilling the conservative agenda.

Aside from a remarkably successful US-backed land reform, which went ahead before it could be blocked (proving that real change could occur), little else was done. The rest was cosmetic. There was no break with the past. Demilitarization was supposed to begin with the arrest of significant military leaders, followed by the round-up of business and financial leaders who had underwritten the war and profited from it. However, under MacArthur the arrest of these men was only temporary. Some did spend a year or two in Sugamo prison as indicted war criminals awaiting trial, but most of them were soon back on the street, running for election to head a government that was remarkably like the one just 'defeated'. The imperial family, which had participated in the war on many levels, from the Rape of Nanking to the looting of Golden Lily, evaded all responsibility, and the emperor himself was totally exonerated in a process of exorcism carried out secretly by MacArthur's staff. For these reasons, postwar Japan, unlike Germany, did not develop a functioning democracy.

The emphasis was not on reform but on continuity. During seven years of occupation, 1945 to 1952, the same Japanese ruling elite that had run the country since the Meiji Restoration was expected to purge itself, slap itself on the wrist and democratize itself. This harked back to the insistent theories of Tom Lamont and Joe Grew that Japan's civilian elite were free of China's endemic corruption. Japan's bureaucrats, financiers, industrialists and imperial family were inherently good, and had simply been overwhelmed by the evil militarists. As Grew assured President Truman, it was just a question of cutting out the cancer of militarism and then letting nature take its course. Critics groaned at the disingenuous naiveté of such expectations.

During the first two years of occupation, call it SCAP-1, there was a rush of democratic activity. Hopes were raised as new ideas swept the countryside. The long-overdue land reform changed Japan from a nation of tenant-serfs to a nation of small landowners. There were also grand plans for the dissolution of the great *zaibatsu* conglomerates; for banking reform; for payment of significant reparations to the raped populations of a dozen ravaged countries; for educational reform; for the promulgation of a genuine constitution that would make the political system truly answerable to the Japanese people. However, in less than two years

MacArthur was backsliding on reforms and backsliding on the punishment of war criminals. During the remainder of his term, call it SCAP-2, he did a complete turnabout, banning all labour demonstrations in Japan and cancelling the right to strike. There were many other dismal consequences. Before the ashes of Hiroshima and Nagasaki were cold, men opposed to reform of any kind regained control in Tokyo and resumed their former monopoly of wealth and power.

To see how this happened, we must go back to the first manipulations. On 19 August, four days after the surrender, a team of sixteen Japanese officials flew to Manila to talk with MacArthur's staff, work out details for the formal surrender ceremonies and get the measure of the Americans. MacArthur remained in seclusion, letting his staff handle the horse trading. One of the first discoveries the Japanese made in Manila was that very few Americans knew anything about Japan, or spoke any Japanese, or had any appetite to learn. They wanted to get the job done as quickly as possible and go home. A few days after the Manila meeting, the Japanese Foreign Ministry hastily set up a new Central Liaison Office to handle all matters relating to the US occupation. It was the brainchild of Foreign Minister Shigemitsu and his canny, Amherst-educated right-hand man Kase Toshikazu. Kase was listed as the personal secretary of all Japanese foreign ministers since the 1930s, but in reality he was a senior civil servant and gentleman secret agent of the old school. Before Pearl Harbor, for example, he had been secretary to Foreign Minister Matsuoka, travelling with him to Berlin and Moscow as the man in the background who made the foreign minister look clever. Americans loved Kase. Bonner Fellers described him as 'a very dear friend of mine . . .

closer to the emperor than anybody'. Just before the war broke out in 1941, Kase had succeeded Terasaki Taro as chief of the first section of the American Bureau in the Foreign Ministry. Like the Terasakis, he was an intimate of the Grews. After Pearl Harbor, when the Grews were confined to the US Embassy until their repatriation, Kase conveyed messages between them and Prince and Princess Chichibu.

As intended, the new liaison office in Tokyo made everything temptingly simple for the Americans, providing a single channel for all business between SCAP and the Japanese government. Directives from SCAP were conveyed through the liaison office, all official appointments were arranged by it, all important documents were translated by it. And it had branches throughout Japan to handle all liaison between local SCAP teams and local Japanese civil authorities. This gave Kase and his staff crucial advantages over SCAP by acting as a shock absorber, filter and go-between. SCAP directives could be (and were) delayed, manipulated and interpreted to Japan's advantage. Hard information moving towards the Americans could be cushioned or massaged so that SCAP liked what it heard. Kase was a master spin-doctor, an expert at mystification. He understood the Americans and had many wild cards tucked up his sleeves. His liaison office also served as an intelligence agency, developing secret dossiers on all US officials in Japan, containing their intimate secrets, idiosyncrasies, indiscretions, vulnerabilities, conflicts and rivalries.

Among those dragooned into the liaison office was Terry Terasaki, who had tried frantically to get Roosevelt to send a personal cable to Hirohito in time to stop the attack on Pearl Harbor. Like Kase, Terry was fluent in English and at ease with Americans.

On 2 September, the official surrender ceremony took place aboard the USS *Missouri* in Tokyo Bay. Tarnished by having to sign the document, Shigemitsu resigned immediately and was succeeded as foreign minister by Grew's old friend Yoshida. That evening, Bonner Fellers and Kase had a private dinner together to talk about all the international pressure to try Emperor Hirohito as a war criminal. During the war, when Joe Grew held secret talks with Japan's ambassador to Switzerland, Grew had given assurances that America would not prosecute Hirohito and promised that he would be kept on the throne. Grew did this in full knowledge that his position was backed by some of the most powerful men in America, in politics and in high finance. It was now up to Fellers and Kase to see that Grew's assurances were carried out.

Next, Kase sent Foreign Minister Yoshida to see Fellers, and they talked long after midnight. Kase, Yoshida and Fellers were in the process of hatching a plan to rescue Hirohito from all blame for the war, and to re-establish him as the model monarch of a new, democratic postwar Japan. There were two basic problems to be solved. First, it had to be demonstrated that Hirohito's true peace-loving nature had been deceived and overwhelmed by the all-powerful militarists, as if he had been possessed by their evil spirits. Next, he had to be exorcized of these evil spirits and set free, to resume his rightful place as Japan's liberal pacifist monarch. To facilitate the exorcism, Yoshida offered to assign someone from the Foreign Ministry to act as special liaison between Fellers and the palace. Soon afterwards, Terry Terasaki appeared at SCAP headquarters in the Dai Ichi Life building and introduced himself to Fellers.

According to Fellers and to Terasaki's wife Gwen, the two men had never met before, and were surprised to find they were related by marriage. (Fellers's great-great-grandmother was a Harold from Tennessee.)

'Really!' said Fellers. 'This is the most astonishing thing I ever heard of, Mr Terasaki. I think we must be some kind of cousins-in-law!'

Cousins or not, they became close collaborators, although Terry remained uneasy about the intense cynicism and ruthlessness he saw in Fellers. Each day thereafter Terry was picked up at his home by a maroon imperial Rolls-Royce – he called it 'the cement mixer' because it was so massive and ponderous – and driven to the palace where his job was to advise Hirohito on all his dealings with MacArthur and Fellers. During the next five and a half years, Terry became privy to the most delicate secrets of the emperor and of MacArthur, including many that were kept secret until after Hirohito's death, and others so sensitive they may never see daylight.

Originally, Terry had shared the hope of Japan's prewar 'liberal' elite – that the evil militarists would be removed from power because moderate statesmen still had the ear of the emperor. At the right moment they and the emperor would bring the country back to a democratic course. When they discovered that the emperor preferred to keep the militarists in office, the 'liberals' adjusted their views to fit. Terry could not adjust. Although he had known that Pearl Harbor was coming, he was devastated by it. His health and spirit collapsed. Repatriated to Japan with other diplomats, he and his wife and daughter spent the war in desperate conditions, watched by government spies, often going hungry. When his diaries were stolen he lived in dread that his efforts to stop the war might be discovered. Now Terry – one of the many unintended victims of the war – found himself responsible for rescuing the emperor from punishment. He was not sure he could do it. Terry was only a year older than Hirohito, but in all other respects they were light-years apart, at opposite extremes of the ideological scale. Court formalities were a terrible strain, so while he worked hard at the palace Terry's health did not improve. Once he collapsed with fatigue, and Hirohito had to help him on to a couch. In time, however, their relationship became more relaxed and friendly. With great awkwardness, Hirohito once slipped Terry five thousand yen to help make ends meet in inflation-ridden Tokyo.

Other members of the imperial family did not want Hirohito to remain on the throne. They blamed him for dragging the war out at least two years longer than necessary, and for all the additional deaths, destruction, chaos and suffering that that had entailed. They were very uneasy about the ambiguous deal being arranged between the palace and MacArthur. Anxious discussions took place within the family. On 15 September, Prince Chichibu, who had not been seen in the palace since 1940 on the pretext of dangers of contagion from TB, came to see his brother, wearing the uniform of a major-general. Prince Higashikuni and Prince Takamatsu both argued that Hirohito should abdicate immediately in favour of 11-year-old Crown Prince Akihito. Prince Chichibu could be regent, they said. But Hirohito had other plans.

This was not the family's first crisis meeting on abdication. During the war they had also discussed it. Prince Mikasa later told a meeting of the Privy Council that his eldest brother must accept responsibility for Japan's defeat. Prince Higashikuni leaked to the press that

296

'many' members of the imperial family wanted Hirohito to abdicate. According to one source, Hirohito said it would be 'easier' for him if he did abdicate, but none of his brothers was capable of being regent. Chichibu was sick, Takamatsu 'pro-war' and Mikasa too young.

Nothing could be decided by the family anyway. Under the terms of the occupation, they took orders from SCAP. Word came that MacArthur wanted to see Hirohito. The message was passed from Fellers to Terry to Hirohito. The emperor must make an appearance at the US Embassy to pay his respects to the general. Palace officials were horrified at the implications. But the meeting, described in the prologue to this book, took place on 27 September 1945. The widely circulated story that MacArthur exonerated the emperor at their very first meeting is sheer propaganda. MacArthur was in the priceless position of being able to extort whatever he wished. Being the kind of man he was, he was none too subtle in holding Hirohito's feet to the fire. Fear of criminal prosecution made Hirohito uniquely vulnerable to manipulation and exploitation. He was informed that if MacArthur chose to let the Allies have their way he would face public trial with the likelihood of hanging – the Soviets favoured a firing squad – unless he collaborated intimately with MacArthur, making the general's tenure as proconsul in Japan a grand success. In which case Hirohito's collusion would be kept secret from everyone. Later that day Fellers wrote to his wife, describing a conversation he had with MacArthur immediately after the meeting. 'The emperor fears you will punish him,' Fellers said. MacArthur said, 'Yes. Yes. He's prepared to take it. He feels he is liable to lose his neck.'

Having warned Hirohito personally, MacArthur put

297

Fellers to work saving the emperor. The emperor was now their hostage, so they had to keep him on the throne, to benefit from the leverage. Unlike earlier episodes of 'capture the emperor' this time he was the hostage of an alien power. The imperial family understood this, and recognized that the only way to remove MacArthur's yoke was to get Hirohito to abdicate. Crown Prince Akihito, having been a child during the war, would not be vulnerable to the same extortion. Family interests aside, many Japanese said then and later that it would have been better for the country if Hirohito had accepted blame and abdicated, to put war guilt behind all of them.

MacArthur had to prevent abdication at all costs. He needed a frightened Hirohito, who would agree to be made over as a humble democrat. The more democratic the emperor looked, the better MacArthur, who still entertained presidential ambitions, would look. Making secret use of Hirohito would assure his success as America's proconsul in Japan. The American public would only see the carefully staged image of MacArthur as a father figure guiding Hirohito to Western democracy.

MacArthur was not alone in profiting from Hirohito's cooperation. Washington bureaucrats and politicians, Wall Street financiers, Japanese bureaucrats, gangsters and business magnates, all had a stake in the emperor's neck. The throne still had a magic cachet that could be used to achieve a variety of special effects.

On 2 October 1945, Fellers neatly summarized the argument in a one-page memo to MacArthur: 'It would be a sacrilege to entertain the idea that the emperor is on a level with the people or any governmental official. To try him as a war criminal would not only be blasphemous but a denial of spiritual freedom . . . It is a fundamental American concept that the people of any nation have the inherent right to choose their own government. Were the Japanese given this opportunity, they would select the emperor as the symbolic head of the state. The masses are especially devoted to Hirohito . . . They know he is no puppet. They feel his retention is not a barrier to as liberal a government *as they are qualified to enjoy* [authors' italics] . . . In effecting our bloodless invasion, we requisitioned the services of the emperor . . . therefore having made good use of the emperor, to try him for war crimes, to the Japanese, would amount to a breach of faith . . . If the emperor were tried for war crimes the governmental structure would collapse and a general uprising would be inevitable . . . there would be chaos and bloodshed. It would necessitate a large expeditionary force with many thousands of public officials. The period of occupation would be prolonged.' This memo was not written to change MacArthur's mind, only to provide him with a summary to use when he communicated with Washington. Bonner Fellers was only one of a number of exorcists carefully put into place by Joe Grew and Herbert Hoover. In the 1930s, Fellers had developed a reputation in the army as a Japan expert, though he had only a superficial knowledge of the country and, like Grew, never learned the language. As a student at Earlham, a Quaker college in Indiana, he befriended two Japanese co-eds and became fascinated by their culture. Later, as an army officer, he wrote a treatise on the mentality of Japanese soldiers.

When he was on MacArthur's staff in the Philippines in the 1930s, Fellers made frequent trips to Japan where he became friends with Ambassador Grew. Fellers knew former president Hoover through both MacArthur and Grew. He made much of their being Quakers, and struck up a correspondence with Hoover that lasted the rest of his life. Hoover used Fellers to convey ideas to MacArthur, and MacArthur used Fellers to push his presidential nomination in the Republican Party hierarchy. In 1939, Hoover received a letter from Fellers praising a potential Republican presidential ticket of MacArthur and Lindbergh. 'I know that President Roosevelt not only respects . . . MacArthur's ability, but he also *fears* him.' Hoover agreed, and told Fellers, 'If MacArthur should come home at the right time, he can sweep the country.' In 1942–3, when Grew was repatriated from Japan and working at the State Department, Fellers returned to Washington from a two-year stint as army attaché in Cairo, where he had earned a brigadier general's star observing Rommel's desert campaign and the Nazi invasion of Crete. Arriving in Washington, he was told to report directly to the White House. There Roosevelt personally rewarded Fellers by putting him to work in America's intelligence service, the OSS (Office of Strategic Services). One of his jobs was to coordinate with Grew on future plans for Japan. Grew often brought Hoover in on these planning sessions, where the exorcism of Hirohito was first conceived.

As president, Herbert Hoover had showed little interest in foreign policy. This changed a few years after he had lost the presidency when in the late 1930s war loomed again in Europe. He then took an active role in policy debates, and in 1938 went to Germany to confer with Hitler. Like most conservatives, Hoover was more alarmed by Stalin and the communist menace than by Hitler and the Nazis. In his eyes, there was nothing to choose between Nazi Germany and communist Russia. If pressed to choose, he would not have chosen Russia. From his early days in Asia as a manager of mines in Manchu China, and from his participation at the

Versailles peace talks, Hoover knew many Japanese leaders personally. He had been visited at his California home by Prince Konoe and pro-Nazi Foreign Minister Matsuoka, who both shared Hoover's fear of Russia and his contempt for Wilsonian pacifism.

Hoover wanted conservative, anti-communist Japan to be America's political, commercial and financial ally in Asia. Tokyo would be the Asian base for the Republican Party and its Wall Street supporters, leaving degenerate China to Roosevelt's New Deal Democrats. This plan was spoiled by Pearl Harbor. But now that the war was over it could be reactivated, without the militarists. The exorcism of Hirohito was one of the rituals needed to put Hoover's Asian strategy into practice. Once the emperor was freed of any war taint, the Japanese government would be magically cleansed. Japan's financial and industrial machinery could be up and running again as a bulwark against communism.

Thus the exorcism of Hirohito was ultimately a joint effort of Grew, Hoover, Fellers and MacArthur. Tom Lamont would have been more active a participant but he was an old man now, in poor health. On the Japanese side the key liaison men were Yoshida and Kase, working through Terry Terasaki. All shared the same gospel: 'Retention of the emperor as the only safeguard against Japan's conversion to communism.'

As Grew explained it to new president Truman, 'The idea of depriving the Japanese of their emperor and emperorship is unsound for the reason that the moment our backs are turned (and we cannot afford to occupy Japan permanently) the Japanese would undoubtedly put the emperor and emperorship back again. From the long range point of view the best that we can hope for in Japan is the development of a constitutional

301

monarchy, experience having shown *that democracy in Japan would never work*' [authors' italics].

The exorcism had to be kept secret because countless Americans, Britons, Australians, not to mention all the former POWs, combatants and victims of other countries, would have been outraged to discover what was going on. Reflecting widespread public attitudes in 1945, the US Congress had just voted unanimously that Hirohito should be tried as a war criminal. Of course, Hirohito was well informed of Western outrage. His own family wanted him to step aside in favour of his son, Crown Prince Akihito, because Hirohito's bad press gave the Allies a way to bring pressure on the imperial family, pressure that could be exerted to achieve a multitude of ends. But Hirohito refused to listen to them, refused to abdicate and – despite later efforts to portray him as unassuming and retiring – clung tenaciously to the throne the way he had clung tenaciously to the prospect of victory. Although there are recorded instances of his being kind to certain aides and to his empress, and even of his weeping with his brothers during family quarrels in the 1930s, he showed no sign of sympathy towards victims of the war and was singularly determined to cling to power.

The process of exorcism was engineered by Fellers and Japanese-language expert Max Bishop, a Grew protégé now assigned to MacArthur. To discover the true nature of Hirohito's involvement in the war, they first conducted a series of secret interviews with Japanese officials and indicted war criminals at Sugamo prison. Once they assembled all the facts, they could sanitize each incriminating bit of evidence in turn, discrediting and suborning witnesses in the process if necessary.

There were several ways they could alter the facts. For

302

example, anyone who might testify against Hirohito either had to change his testimony or face persecution and ruin. When Fellers discovered something negative about Hirohito, he literally set about destroying the source. Naturally Prince Konoe was intimately informed, and when Fellers heard what Konoe had to say about Hirohito's guilt, he denounced the prince as 'a rat who's quite prepared to sell anyone to save himself, and even went so far as to call his master the emperor "the major war criminal".' Thereafter, Fellers, Bishop and MacArthur took an intense dislike to Prince Konoe and, with no further justification, added his name to the list of war criminals to be prosecuted. One of the few statesmen who had tried to talk Hirohito into seeking an early peace, and who had earlier volunteered to go to Switzerland to arrange secret peace talks, Prince Konoe now was blackballed by the Americans and hounded to despair in a vicious campaign of backbiting and innuendo. He was informed (falsely) that his name had now been moved to the top of the list of war criminals, and that he faced imminent arrest and imprisonment. On 16 December 1945, he was found dead in his home. Most sources quote him saying he would not submit to the indignity of trial. The official ruling was suicide, but scholars Meirion and Susie Harries, among others, believe that Prince Konoe was murdered. They offer compelling evidence against suicide. For one thing, Generalissimo Chiang wanted Konoe's name removed from the list of potential war criminals. Konoe was not on the British list. American sources indicate that Konoe was, in fact, never a serious candidate for trial. Joseph Keenan, who became head of the Tokyo tribunal, regarded Konoe as a 'confidential informant' of the greatest importance. Yet as the Harrieses note, 'There

303

was no shortage of people at every level of the Japanese government who would have preferred Konoe not to testify.' Other crucial witnesses also died conveniently before the trials commenced. Two of Prince Asaka's staff who carried out his orders at the Rape of Nanking died suddenly of 'heart trouble' at the end of 1945, before the trials got under way.

In the midst of this witch-hunt, Washington sent instructions to MacArthur to 'proceed immediately to assemble all available evidence of Hirohito's participation in and responsibility for Japanese violations of international law'. Instead, MacArthur's team was frantically erasing the trail. MacArthur then received a curt reminder from the Joint Chiefs of Staff to get serious about collecting evidence against the emperor, because 'the United States government's position is that Hirohito is not immune from arrest, trial and punishment as a war criminal . . . when the occupation can proceed satisfactorily without him, the question of his trial will be raised.'

Despite such explicit orders from the Joint Chiefs, MacArthur would not permit the emperor to be indicted, to appear as a witness, or even to be interviewed by prosecutors. How was America's top military officer in Japan able to evade and ignore direct orders from Washington?

Few people understood this as clearly as the American statesman George Kennan. Washington had demanded and received 'dictatorial powers' in Japan, he said, then made the mistake of making MacArthur the dictator. This gave MacArthur such independence that the State Department and War Department lost all control. The general, Kennan said, 'asked for guidance' only when he 'felt a need for cover of higher authorities in some awkward or disagreeable decision for which

[he] did not want to accept exclusive responsibility'.

'Not only was it difficult to tell [MacArthur] what to do, but it was not always easy to find out what [he] was doing . . . MacArthur would not even hear of State Department advice . . . Americans who would have protested violently at the first sign of paternalism or arbitrariness at home . . . found it . . . entirely in order . . . wholly admirable and inspiring . . . that an American commander should exercise wholly autocratic power [in Japan], untrammeled by legislative controls.' When he was supposed to be America's chief agent of democratic change, MacArthur was doing things the Japanese way, in the high-handed manner of a shogun. He ignored his own government entirely, and instead listened to special-interest groups that had his ear for other reasons, among them big-money Republicans who were crucial to his eventual presidential bid.

MacArthur was practised at smoke and evasion. On 25 January 1946 he sent a secret telegram to Army Chief of Staff Dwight Eisenhower, vigorously protesting any idea of putting the emperor on trial. Citing 'investigations' conducted by SCAP he lied blatantly: 'No specific and tangible evidence has been uncovered with regard to [the emperor's] exact activities which might connect him in varying degree with the political decisions of the Japanese Empire during the last decade. I have gained the definite impression from as complete a research as was possible to me that his connection with affairs of state up to the time of the end of the war was largely ministerial and automatically responsive to the advice of his counselors . . . If he is to be tried great changes must be made in [America's] occupational plans . . . His indictment will unquestionably cause a tremendous convulsion among the Japanese people the repercussion of which cannot be overestimated. He's a symbol which unites all Japanese. Destroy him and the nation will disintegrate.' In that event, MacArthur said, he would need a million US soldiers and hundreds of thousands of civilians to administer the occupation. The cost to America would be staggering.

Having Hirohito abdicate in favour of his son – the option favoured by most of the imperial family – was not even mentioned.

Although Eisenhower personally detested MacArthur and distrusted him, the decision was not in his hands. The Truman administration was alarmed by MacArthur's shrill telegram and, with strong parallel lobbying in Washington by Hoover, Grew and others, began discouraging attempts to have Hirohito prosecuted. However, he might still be obliged to testify as a witness, and could incriminate himself and others. Both MacArthur and Fellers used this to keep pressure on the emperor.

There was a collective frisson in the palace on 23 February 1946 when General Yamashita was hanged in the Philippines for war atrocities. Since then, it has been widely agreed that Yamashita was railroaded by a kangaroo court as MacArthur's revenge against the man he blamed for his embarrassing difficulties in retaking the Philippines. Later, when Yamashita's superior officer was tried in Tokyo, he was acquitted of the same crimes at MacArthur's direct instigation, though his overall responsibility theoretically was greater.

Also targeted along with Yamashita was General Homma, the amateur playwright and mild-mannered former aide to Prince Chichibu, a favourite of the dowager empress. He was shot by a firing squad in the Philippines for atrocities carried out by his subordinates in the Bataan Death March during the conquest of the country, although it was acknowledged that Homma had completely lost control of his men. Princess Chichibu recalled, 'We, who knew so well what a gentle warrior he was, could do nothing to help him. Nothing but bow our heads, silently, towards Mount Fuji, and say a prayer.'

It was not lost on the imperial family that both Yamashita and Homma were singled out for victimization by MacArthur personally. Such selective justice was coming ever closer to the intimate circle of the palace.

Meanwhile, MacArthur's staff launched a public-relations campaign to improve Hirohito's image in America. Starting in February 1946, the emperor was put on the public-relations circuit, promoting his new image as a great pacifist, touring Japan and shaking hands with the people. SCAP made the emperor and his family pose for news photographers, and soon they appeared in American newspapers and magazines, looking like shy mid-western farmers. Shutters clicked while Hirohito bounced his grandchildren on his knee. His daughters were shown peeling vegetables, preparing humble meals and doing the washing-up.

Behind the scenes, Fellers and MacArthur employed simple intimidation. All Japanese officials and military officers were expected to take the line that responsibility for the war lay exclusively with the government and the military; the emperor was not in any way to blame. Fellers had a private talk with Admiral Yonai Mitsumasa, a former prime minister and navy minister. 'I am not an emperor worshiper,' Fellers said. 'Therefore, whether the imperial system would exist 15, or 20 years from now in Japan or what will personally happen to the emperor himself does not concern me.

However I am aware that the emperor is the best supporter of the Allied occupation. Under the present circumstance, as long as the occupation continues, the imperial system should be retained.' Then he added: 'It is extremely disadvantageous to MacArthur's standing in the United States to put on trial the very emperor who is cooperating with him and facilitating the smooth administration of the occupation.'

He gave Yonai this advice: 'The best strategy would be for the Japanese side to prove the emperor's innocence. The best occasion, it seems to me, would be the Tokyo trials, which are soon to start. It would be best to blame all responsibility on Tojo.'

Tojo, the wartime prime minister and minister of war, had been arrested on 11 September 1945. Learning that he was on the first list of war criminals, Tojo tried to shoot himself in the heart but narrowly missed, and had since been in Sugamo prison hospital. Fellers ordered Admiral Yonai to tamper with this most important witness. 'I want Tojo to say that he was going to force Japan to go to war with the United States no matter what; even if the emperor had opposed it at the conference. Would you ask Tojo to say it?'

'I am in complete agreement with you,' Yonai replied. He sent an aide to Sugamo prison hospital to give Fellers's message directly to General Tojo. The aide said Tojo replied: 'Tell Yonai not to worry. The reason I continue to live, despite the shame, is to prove exactly that point.' (Many people were puzzled why Yonai himself evaded prosecution, because he had been deeply involved in looting and the shipment of war loot, but that is explained by his readiness to conspire with Fellers in tampering with a key witness. As former navy minister, Yonai knew a lot about Golden Lily, and about the looting carried out by Japanese underworld figures under navy cover. He had powerful friends.)

MacArthur's final list of war criminals was remarkably short. Of 300 investigated, only 28 actually appeared before the Tokyo Tribunal. They were charged with leading the 'criminal, militaristic clique' from 1 January 1928 till 2 September 1945, and with conspiring to plan and wage the war. Many also faced charges of violating international agreements about treatment of prisoners of war, and committing inhumane acts against civilian populations.

There were eleven judges, one from each Allied nation. Chief prosecutor was Joseph Keenan, an American. In the three years the trials lasted, the primary motive changed from retribution to political expediency. The Allies arbitrarily granted immunity to a number of men who had been high on their lists. For example, Britain decided not to prosecute a Japanese naval officer who was charged with machine-gunning 600 British prisoners who were trying to stay afloat after their ship was sunk. Occupation collaborators like Admiral Yonai were excused. On MacArthur's orders not a single bit of evidence about the biological warfare section – Unit 731 – was revealed to the tribunal. The Japanese scientists and their grim secrets were absorbed into America's secret chemical and biological warfare programme.

Although Hirohito's name was not on the trial list, MacArthur, Fellers, Grew, Hoover and others still worried that he might be implicated by defence lawyers, leading to his trial at a later date. How could they prepare in advance for all contingencies?

Fellers had a long chat with Terry Terasaki and laid his cards on the table, much as he had done with Admiral Yonai. Fellers urgently wanted nothing less than

309

complete written proof of the emperor's innocence, in the form of a secret affidavit from Hirohito. Fellers gave Terry a question: 'As my investigation progressed, it became clear that the emperor himself personally forced his militarists into accepting the terms of the Potsdam Declaration. Then the next question is, if the emperor had the power to stop the war even before Japan was invaded, why did he permit it to start in the first place?'

Terry relayed the question directly to Hirohito. 'Firstly I asked his majesty the following question: "It is common knowledge both here and abroad that you were highly instrumental in terminating the war. But the question everybody in Japan as well as abroad is asking is why did you not exercise the same power at the time the war started?"' The emperor replied: 'Let me explain my reason.' He started to explain to Terry alone. Later in his monologue they were joined by other aides and a palace stenographer.

The emperor's monologue grew into a series of secret official dictations. Despite being in bed with the flu, on 18 March 1946 Hirohito began explaining and rationalizing his involvement in the war. The emperor lay in bed wearing white quilted pyjamas. The questions his aides posed to him originated with Fellers, although some later came to Fellers from Herbert Hoover. The secret dictation went on for weeks, then was compiled into one document, which was kept secret for the next forty-four years until it was discovered in 1990 after Hirohito's death. Ironically, in this document created exclusively to vindicate him, to make him seem un-informed, peace-loving and selfless, Hirohito showed himself to be well informed, belligerent and self-serving. Without using notes, he talked from memory. The stenographer also kept personal notes: 'One wonders why it was necessary for his majesty to talk so urgently [when he was so sick]. Since there are people who question his war responsibility in view of the trial it was necessary for us to write down his majesty's frank thoughts as soon as possible.'

On 13 April 1946, the Soviet Union's prosecution team arrived in Japan, making everyone in the palace nervous. Moscow still demanded that the entire imperial family be tried and executed by firing squad. As a precaution, early in the dictation process, Hirohito ordered Terry to give an English translation of the monologue to Fellers, to be kept secret and used only if necessary.

Three weeks later, when the Tokyo Tribunal began its first hearings, Fellers had a series of long discussions with Herbert Hoover, who was in Japan ostensibly looking into the matter of providing food and humanitarian aid to starving Japanese. Before coming to Japan, Hoover had written to Fellers warning him to be careful because the State Department was sending 'a bunch of communists and fellow travelers' to Japan to meddle in SCAP policy. Fear of direct and indirect 'communist' intervention in Japan was one of Hoover's favourite topics. During their conversations in Tokyo, Fellers brought Hoover up to date on the secret dictations at the palace. 'Hoover was tremendously gratified . . . [to know] that information from the emperor, explaining his position during the war and in forcing the peace, is being prepared.' They discussed how best to use the monologue. Fellers noted, 'Because of American bitterness [against the emperor] Mr Hoover said that material from the emperor would not be as effective now as a little later. He would use it, however, the moment an emergency justified.' Fellers gave Hoover a copy for that purpose.

Hoover also made a number of points that he wanted Hirohito to include in his monologue. Two days later, Fellers passed on everything Hoover had told him to Terry, along with the message that 'an emergency might still arise'. Further dictation continued until 1 June 1946, when Fellers was satisfied that all Hoover's concerns were addressed. Meanwhile, Hoover lobbied defence attorneys to make sure their clients said nothing to implicate Hirohito.

These additional sessions of monologue were translated for Fellers and Hoover. In the Fellers Papers at the MacArthur Memorial Library in Norfolk, Virginia, there is an untitled page of typescript dated 'Tokyo, 18 June 1946' with Fellers's handwriting at the top: 'Hirohito and Hoover Very Important'. It appears to have been dictated by Hirohito exclusively for an American audience:

Since the scourge of war came to the Orient, I have spent many hours in anguish and in meditation. I have endeavored to assess the cause of the tragic course of my people which has resulted in our national humiliation and led us to the very brink of destruction. As time passes, it is becoming increasingly clear to me that we have suffered from a deficiency of moral responsibility. We have unhappily deceived ourselves. We have believed that the people from the West were our sworn enemies who sought to destroy our national polity and enslave our people. We lost the war. The enemy occupied our land with his Armies. But these Occupation forces have neither destroyed, nor enslaved us. Rather they have built and emancipated. They have exhibited qualities of tolerance, justice, and compassion to a degree heretofore unknown among my people. I am led to conclude that this enlightened attitude of our former enemies is a quality worthy of emulation. I therefore enjoin my people to study diligently these spiritual values in hope that we may achieve salvation through strengthening the moral fiber of our race.

There was another reason for Fellers's urgent efforts to conclude the secret dictation to everyone's satisfaction. Since October he had known that he was being squeezed out of the army. Someone in the War Department had discovered what he was doing and was removing him from Japan. His enemies did not stop there. They also demoted him from brigadier general to colonel. Technically, his thirty years of service were up. But there were other reasons. George Marshall, chairman of the Joint Chiefs of Staff, and Army Chief of Staff Dwight Eisenhower were both determined to break up MacArthur's clique in Tokyo. Demobilizing military officers was a useful device. The moment it became technically possible to 'demob' General Fellers, they did so, removing one of MacArthur's key men. As Fellers's daughter explained: 'Jealousy, intrigue: I know too much to say it didn't exist; too little to fairly record it.' Fellers left Japan in such a hurry that he did not attend a personal farewell audience with Hirohito arranged by Terry Terasaki. When Fellers reached Washington, Herbert Hoover got him a job with the Republican National Committee, planning the 1948 presidential campaign. MacArthur still hoped to be on the ticket. His place on MacArthur's staff was taken by Colonel Laurence Bunker.

Still worried, Hirohito began another series of dictations for Herbert Hoover in July 1946 that continued for three more months. Not until November 1947 was the decision finally made that the emperor would not testify at the trials. This was imperative, because under cross-examination it was always possible that he might inadvertently blurt out something embarrassing, incriminating himself and damaging his value as MacArthur's main asset in Japan. General Tojo was fully programmed to assume all the blame. He took the witness stand the following month. There was one close call when he forcefully declared that 'no Japanese subject . . . would dare act against the emperor's will'. MacArthur and his men froze. Tojo was clearly stating that he could only have conducted the war with the full approval of Hirohito. Hastily, Judge Keenan appealed to former Privy Seal Kido, himself a defendant, to get Tojo to revise his testimony. At the next session, Tojo corrected himself, saying that the war had come about 'because of the advice given by the High Command' and that 'the emperor consented, though reluctantly, to the war'. He added a flourish, saying that the emperor's 'love and desire for peace remained the same right up to the very moment when hostilities commenced, and even during the war his feeling remained the same'.

There were many such examples of confused and contradictory testimony from the defendants as, one by one, they exonerated not only the emperor but his entire family. General Matsui, unfairly charged with responsibility for the Rape of Nanking, which was personally ordered by Hirohito's uncle, Prince Asaka, gave a confused and jumbled testimony. In the end, though, he accepted all responsibility for the Rape.

At last, the emperor was off the hook. Terry wrote to

Fellers in Washington in December 1947: 'The emperor asked me to express his deep appreciation for all you have done for him.' (Fellers never went back to Tokyo, but in 1971 he was discreetly awarded Japan's Order of the Sacred Treasure, Second Class, at a private ceremony in Washington.)

The Tokyo Trials ended in April 1948. Seven more months passed before sentences were announced. During this nervous period, Fellers heard that Hirohito was again being pressed to abdicate. He wrote anxiously to Terry.

'There is frequent mention of the Sire's abdication in the American press . . . [This] would be considered a victory for all communists and especially the Russians, who hold it is naive to claim that Japan can be democratized so long as the emperor remains on the throne. *His abdication would be a blow to the MacArthur occupation as the general's success has made the very best use of the emperor's prestige and personal leadership* [authors' italics]. His abdication, especially if it coincided with the announcement of war crimes punishments, would, in the eyes of the world, identify the Sire as one of the military clique. This of course is absolutely untrue. It would reverse public opinion in this country which is beginning to turn to the impression that the emperor was *not* responsible for the war. Abdication would fix the Sire's place in history as one who sympathized with the war criminals and, as a gesture of his sympathy for them, gave up his throne.'

Now that he was out of the loop, Fellers did not realize that the threat of abdication was merely a device being used to pressure MacArthur into modifying certain of the sentences, in a form of plea bargaining. When the sentences were announced on 12 November 1948,

Hirohito sent a letter to MacArthur saying he was not going to abdicate after all.

Only seven men were sentenced to hang. They were General Tojo, General Itagaki who oversaw the Manchurian Incident, secret agent General Doihara Kenji who served in China and Manchuria, General Muto Akira who served in the Philippines and Dutch East Indies and General Kimura Heitaro who served in Burma. General Matsui and Hirota Koki, a civilian, were both sentenced to hang for their 'responsibility' for the Rape of Nanking. Hirota had been foreign minister at the time and was nowhere near Nanking. Prince Asaka was never put on trial, eluded any form of punishment, and lived in great comfort in his palace, playing golf nearly every day, dying in bed at the age of 93. Not a single prince was brought to trial. Not one person involved in Golden Lily was ever prosecuted, or even accused.

Of those who did hang, the majority were men from Choshu. No Satsuma men were hanged. Traditionally, Satsuma had favoured navy careers, while Choshu favoured army careers. Some historians hold that the navy conducted itself more honourably in the Pacific War than did the army, which was involved in more grisly atrocities. But it is a matter of record that the navy used six fake hospital ships to transport war *matériel* outbound, war loot homebound. And a number of times the navy carried out its own atrocities – notably in the scuttling of the cruiser *Nachii* in Manila Bay with a major cargo of gold bullion aboard. On that occasion a Japanese submarine sank the *Nachii* with a torpedo fired broadside and then the sub's gunners machine-gunned the *Nachii*'s crewmen when they bobbed to the surface.

So when most of those hanged for war crimes were Choshu men, this was really the payoff for the bitter feud that had persisted from the early days of the Meiji Restoration to the horse trading in postwar Tokyo. Here at last was Empress Sadako's revenge on the protégés of General Yamagata.

The name Choshu was stricken from maps as well, when the region was renamed Yamaguchi Prefecture after the war. It is, however, famous as the home base of one of Japan's biggest underworld organizations, the Yamaguchi Gumi, a hangover from the secret networks of General Yamagata.

Many of the powerful families of prewar days, like the Mori family of Choshu, continue to be rich and powerful, as are the many clans of Satsuma. They have shifted their identities, donned new costumes and now are seen as captains of industry. Yet they remain the leaders of the old financial cliques and – along with some new faces – are still the secret rulers of Japan.

One of those who did not hang, but served time in prison for his role in the war, Privy Seal Kido, the emperor's closest wartime adviser, later wrote a note to Hirohito: 'No matter how one looks at it, the emperor bears responsibility for losing this war. Therefore . . . when a peace treaty is signed . . . I think it is most proper for you to take responsibility and abdicate for the sake of your imperial ancestors and for the nation . . . If you do not do this, then the end result will be that the imperial family alone will have failed to take responsibility and an unclear mood will remain which, I fear, might leave an eternal scar.'

Hirohito ignored the advice.

Knowing MacArthur's flair for theatre, it was predicted that he would choose the seventh anniversary

317

of Pearl Harbor as the date for carrying out the executions. But this plan was foiled by an unexpected defence appeal to the US Supreme Court. Although the appeal was turned down, the anniversary date had already passed. Instead, MacArthur ordered the hangings to be carried out on 23 December 1948 – the fifteenth birthday of Crown Prince Akihito. The crown prince cancelled his birthday party.

The perfidious legacy of the exorcists survives to the present day. In July 1999 prime minister Obuchi declared Hirohito to have been the 'man of the century'.

CHAPTER 10

UNCLEAN HANDS

While Hoover, Fellers and MacArthur were secretly exorcizing the emperor, SCAP-1 investigators were supposed to be taking a hard look at Japan's elite, to punish those who had been wicked during the war and to 'democratize' Japan's society and economy for the future. First, Japan had to purge itself of ultra-nationalists whose names were on a long list of dangerous people – many of them politicians and militarists – who were to be excluded from taking part in the new postwar government. Second, America declared that there must be a major redistribution of wealth in Japan. This was intended to correct many of the same gross inequities that had been the target of the young officers in the 1936 uprising, thwarted by Hirohito himself. Many SCAP-1 advisers previously had worked for President Roosevelt's New Deal and were planning to engineer similar radical programmes in Japan. America blamed the exclusive concentration of economic power in the big *zaibatsu* conglomerates for creating the autocratic conditions in which militarism flourished without check. This incestuous cartel of special-interest groups, created by the Meiji Genro, had grown into a huge machine to feed the elite, the military, the bureaucrats, the tame politicians and underworld godfathers.

One of the chief objectives of the occupation was to root out the venality of the existing system. SCAP-1 was going to try to level the playing field by removing the long list of 'evil men' from power, dissolving the biggest conglomerates and banks which provided them with their monopoly on wealth. SCAP would introduce a new system of government based on a new constitution with built-in US-style checks and balances, with public oversight, accountability and referenda. It was an idealistic and ambitious agenda. Optimists in Washington and Tokyo viewed these reforms as nothing less than revolutionary. Japan's society would be completely changed by them, the way rural life in Japan was being changed by the American-led land-reform programme.

This revolution did not happen. It failed because some powerful Americans and some powerful Japanese wanted it to fail. After getting off to an awkward start, they quickly sorted out their differences and made common cause. Together they sabotaged SCAP-1 and turned it into SCAP-2 – a parody of reform that put everything back the way it was, under the same 'evil men'. A number of cosmetic changes were made, like doing over Emperor Hirohito as a 'constitutional monarch' dressed in the same rumpled style as President Truman, and business resumed as before.

Joe Grew had been preparing the way for this reversal for some time. In 1944 he said, 'To try to graft full-fledged democracy on Japan, as some of our people would like to do, would certainly lead to chaos in short order.' The following year he warned, 'From what I know of the Japanese, an outright democracy with an elected president would bring about political chaos.'

Because memories of the war were still fresh in America, MacArthur at first moved cautiously and made himself seem to be the champion of America's liberal agenda. Many of SCAP's early pronouncements, issued in his name, had a liberal, populist vocabulary. This made MacArthur seem uncharacteristically fair-minded. He still had one eye fixed on the 1948 presidential campaign in America. If he wanted the backing of the Republican Party, he had to carry out the very different agenda for Japan laid on him by the party's money men, who communicated with MacArthur through Hoover and Grew. No one in Washington could force MacArthur to do anything about civil liberties. George Kennan said MacArthur had a 'flealike agility' that enabled him to resist any demands from Washington to get on with the democratization process.

In retrospect, one may regret that Japan was not made more answerable to its own people when America had the chance, but that would have taken time, patience, tax-dollars and will-power. Paraphrasing the senior State Department adviser in postwar Tokyo, liberal George Atcheson, there were a long solution and a short solution. The long solution would probably be better, and would lead to the Japanese people having more say in their own government. But under the circumstances, the short solution was more likely. He was right. The start of the Cold War in Asia and Europe distracted those who might have worked miracles in Japan. Meanwhile, counter-revolutionary Americans and Japanese manipulated the reform agenda to their own ends. The mood of the world was swinging from fear of fascism to fear of communism. It was easy to fan fears of communism taking over Japan and in the process to suffocate all legitimate criticism, dissent, protest and opposition.

Nowhere was deceit more conspicuous than in SCAP's investigations of the finances of Emperor Hirohito, the imperial family and the *zaibatsu* elite. Ethics can be argued, but here we are talking hard fact and cold cash.

MacArthur sabotaged the process by tying SCAP's hands. He limited SCAP investigators to the emperor's visible domestic wealth, completely ignored his huge foreign holdings and turned a blind eye to persuasive evidence that much of the throne's gold bullion and other liquid assets were carefully hidden or moved offshore in the closing months of the war, while palaces and other real estate were conveyed to the wealthy Tsutsumi family and others for safe-keeping.

Washington declared that 'the property of the imperial household' was to revert to the state – meaning the people of Japan. To this end, SCAP investigators were instructed by Washington to carry out a meticulous audit of the imperial family's entire wealth. Instead, MacArthur ordered Hirohito's own financial advisers and accountants in the Imperial Household to prepare a self-audit listing only the emperor's domestic holdings as of late October 1945. According to this self-audit, Hirohito's domestic assets, excluding art treasures and palaces, totalled only 1.6 billion yen, or about $100 million (1945 dollars). This figure, they said, included his 'income' from all his farms and country estates, vast tracts of forest, scores of major corporations, bonds, currency and gold bullion. The self-audit was rich with minor details about how much Hirohito had earned in 1944 from his timber reserves, but it did not include the value of the forests themselves or the land on which they grew. The imperial family were the biggest landowners in Japan, much of it conveyed directly to the throne when the Tokugawa shogunate collapsed, and in terms of value they ranked as one of the world's greatest land-owning entities.

Also not included in the self-audit were all manner of undeclared or hidden assets, in Japan and in overseas accounts. When SCAP investigators passed this audit up the line, they noted sourly, 'No representation as to accuracy is made by this Division.'

After the occupation ended, Japanese experts recalculated the emperor's domestic wealth – not counting palaces, land or art treasures – at well over 66 billion yen or $4 billion (1945 dollars). Most independent estimates agree with this figure. Contrast this $4 billion to the $100 million offered by the Imperial Household self-audit.

Where did all the imperial wealth come from? Since the Meiji Restoration, some of Japan's best financial brains had worked to maximize its growth. In keeping with Bismarck's advice to make the emperor so rich he would be above bribes, 10 per cent of shares in leading Japanese corporations and banks were conveyed to the throne, along with a similar percentage of their annual profits. Over three generations, this multiplied prodigiously. Specifically, Hirohito owned nearly one-fourth (22 per cent) of the stock in the Yokohama Specie Bank, Japan's official foreign-exchange bank, known today as the Bank of Tokyo. He also held large stock portfolios in twenty-nine conglomerates, including the Mitsui, Mitsubishi, Sumitomo and Yasuda *zaibatsu,* which profited richly from producing weapons, aircraft and munitions for the Japanese Army, and doing business in occupied territories. These tax-free imperial earnings were reinvested all over the world. In 1942, on the basis of information he gathered from bankers and economists, John Gunther had ranked the imperial family as 'the third or fourth biggest capital enterprise' in Japan. By this measure, the family came just after Mitsui, Mitsubishi and Sumitomo, but ahead of Yasuda, and far ahead of lesser 'new' *zaibatsu* such as Nissan.

Similarly huge were Hirohito's foreign assets. These included major investments in Western banks, manufacturing and property – and also gold bullion, platinum and silver held under various covers in the vaults of banks in Switzerland, Sweden, the Vatican, Portugal, Argentina, Spain, Britain and the United States. The House of Morgan, while a commercial bank, also handled private investment portfolios for the supremely rich. Tom Lamont had spent much of his professional life enriching Morgan's Japanese clients, one of whom was the emperor.

In January 1944, anticipating an American invasion of the Home Islands, Privy Seal Kido called together Japan's leading investment bankers who were financial advisers to the throne. On their recommendation, most of the throne's immediate liquid assets were conveyed to Swiss bank branches in Tokyo and credited to numbered accounts in Switzerland. The same Swiss banks already held, on Hirohito's behalf, investment credits denominated in the currency of Nazi Germany, and during 1944 these were converted into 'clean' currencies of neutral countries. It was reported that some imperial bullion was sold to wealthy Chinese, and the hard currencies obtained were credited to Zürich. There were also reports that some quantities of war loot were sent to South America on Japanese cargo submarines and deposited at Swiss banks in Buenos Aires.

Even after the Imperial Household's comic self-audit in October 1945, Hirohito's declared domestic assets were not frozen by SCAP for nearly another month. By the time SCAP officers got around to having a look for themselves, the emperor's stock and bond certificates, and his gold and silver bullion held in the Yokohama Specie Bank, had vanished. Bank officials explained that all their records had been destroyed by American fire-bombing (a useful excuse in those days). As for gold or silver, they knew nothing about any bullion.

By then all the emperor's bullion that was not already secured in Swiss vaults in Tokyo was tucked into the mountain bunker near Nagano. Paul Manning, a war correspondent trusted by MacArthur, many years later stated flatly that 'General MacArthur was aware of the emperor's missing gold and transferred currencies, but chose to ignore them'.

Ultimately, SCAP made the extraordinary announcement that the emperor, after paying back taxes and other 'penalties', had only $42,000 in cash left to his name, roughly what a small-town American businessman in 1945 might have saved towards his retirement. It was declared that from then on Hirohito would receive a tax-free annual salary equivalent to $22,000. To make sure everyone appreciated the emperor's humility, the Japanese press reported that Hirohito was going to sell the family jewels and his collection of ancient Japanese art to buy food for the common people. One article said the emperor was donating 10 million feet of timber to rebuild homes destroyed by Allied bombing.

So that America could not confiscate the palaces and real estate of other members of the imperial family, many of these were 'sold' to the Tsutsumi family, friends of the imperial family who had made their fortune in railways, department stores and property speculation following the Kanto quake. The Tsutsumis were buying up 'excess' imperial palaces at what were said to be 'fire sale' prices.

The impression was given that this had to be done because the dynasty was desperately strapped for cash. Prince Takamatsu and Prince Chichibu were even said to have been 'reduced by financial pressure to selling their personal and household belongings, even empty whisky bottles'. Princes Higashikuni, Asaka, Takeda and the family of Kitashirakawa also made such deals. However, they were not obliged to move out of their palaces even after having 'sold' them. Prince Asaka continued to live in his palace for the remainder of his very long life. The Tsutsumis were on their way to becoming one of the world's richest families and would enjoy unparalleled leverage in Japan for the rest of the century, thanks to their imperial connections.

In short, the overwhelming impression was created that Japan was bankrupt, and the dynasty penniless. Indeed, the war did exhaust Japanese industry and raw materials, but most top management of banks and corporations had personal wealth that remained hidden and intact. Most *zaibatsu* had participated in the looting of conquered countries and helped in running the wartime drug trade on the mainland. An estimated $3 billion was made in the heroin trade alone, in which drugs grown and processed under army supervision in Manchuria were sold throughout China and Southeast Asia with the help of the *zaibatsu*.

Within days of the surrender, but before the occupation actually began, corporate directors anxious to obliterate any record of their close ties to the military and of wartime profits ensured that all incriminating paperwork was hidden or burned. Their top executives were shifted to obscure rural offices where they assumed the temporary guise of underlings. With feudal loyalty structures still operative, there was no danger of staff turning bosses in. The Finance Ministry hastily paid bills owed to defence industries on wartime contracts. One such contract in the last days of the war netted future prime minister Tanaka Kakuei an effortless $73 million profit.

There were other prominent men who had also accumulated great personal fortunes during the war. The most famous figure in Japanese organized crime, godfather Kodama Yoshio, spent the war supervising the looting of strategic *matériel* and the distribution of drugs. Kodama first worked with the army in Manchuria and China, then was given the rank of rear admiral by the navy minister, Admiral Yonai (who helped General Fellers suborn General Tojo). In this guise, Kodama travelled throughout East and Southeast Asia, making free use of naval vessels for the repatriation of loot and reputedly keeping the platinum and the best gems for himself.

Then there was Golden Lily, which was dedicated only to so-called 'imperial' loot – plundered treasure that was collected, inventoried and set aside for the imperial family. If Golden Lily did hide considerably more than $100 billion worth of this treasure in the Philippines, then the claim of postwar insolvency is rather suspect.

During the closing months of the war, American guerrilla forces operating in the mountains of Luzon observed Japanese Army units hiding truckloads of very heavy small boxes in caves. They captured and interrogated Japanese soldiers and learned that the boxes contained gold bars. When the war ended, MacArthur's G-2 General Charles Willoughby and other intelligence officers backed secret recovery operations that netted huge sums, according to some of the American officers who participated. The gold was slipped into the market cautiously to avoid affecting world gold prices. These recoveries continued intermittently over the years. One such effort involved America's John Birch Society, a virulently anti-communist organization named after an American who was killed by Maoist forces during the Chinese civil war. In the mid-1970s, the society lent nearly $500,000 to an American treasure-hunter to finance a recovery in the Philippines, promising to help him launder up to $20 billion of the recovered gold. (The society seemed to believe that it was perfectly correct to break American laws regarding the illegal laundering of money, providing it was done to finance anti-communism.) Colonel Laurence Bunker, a close friend of General Willoughby who took over from Bonner Fellers as MacArthur's chief aide, personal secretary and spokesman from 1946 until his retirement in 1952, was a charter member of the John Birch Society.

Because none of this was revealed to the war-crimes tribunal, to the American people, to the Japanese people, or to Japan's victims in other countries, serious questions are raised of ethics and fraud.

When MacArthur first arrived in Japan in 1945, the Joint Chiefs of Staff ordered him to arrest key business figures. The directive said, 'You will assume that any persons who have held key positions of high responsibility since 1937, in industry, finance, commerce, or agriculture have been active exponents of militant nationalism and aggression.' MacArthur immediately ordered the arrest of one of the emperor's uncles, Prince Nashimoto, who was said to have joined a plot to prevent Hirohito from announcing Japan's surrender. He was the only member of the imperial family to be arrested for any reason and the only one to die in poverty. SCAP also arrested several senior *zaibatsu* officials, including the chairman of Mitsubishi, which had been Japan's primary arms maker, and the managing director of Mitsui, the oldest *zaibatsu*.

Soon afterwards, it was decided to tell MacArthur about $2 billion in gold bars that had been sunk in Tokyo Bay in the closing days of the war. The gold had been flown from Korea to Tokyo by the Japanese Air Force on the instructions of Prince Takeda. The small gold bars were then placed in bronze boxes and submerged in the bay. In April 1946 the Central Liaison Office informed SCAP of the gold and asked if it could be raised and placed in the central bank 'for the common good of the Japanese people'. MacArthur approved, saying his mission in Japan was to 'return the nation to solvency'. President Truman was informed about this recovery. One plan was to ship the gold bars to America for safe-keeping and as security against outstanding loan payments to groups like Morgan Bank. Instead the gold was kept in Japan. At the same time, perhaps coincidentally, Prince Nashimoto, the Mitsubishi chairman, the Mitsui managing director and three other top Japanese business leaders were quietly released from Sugamo prison and all charges against them were dropped.

This was only one of many such coincidences during the occupation. Substantive reports of huge sums of money being transferred back and forth around the Pacific during that period coincided with groups of 'Class A War Criminals' being released from Sugamo with all charges dropped. Generalissimo Chiang Kai-shek drew up several lists of Japanese he thought should be arrested, and others he thought should not be arrested. In what some might regard as clear indication of collusion or extortion, names were moved from one list to the other. When godfather Kodama turned over half of his declared fortune to SCAP, he walked free, as did his good friend and cellmate, future prime minister Kishi Nobusuke, the wartime vice-minister of munitions and the financial brains of Japan's Manchurian exploitation.

After more than half a century, SCAP documents relating to these mysterious payments have yet to be made public. When a Japanese official was asked who was behind the apparent connivance between the Imperial Household and MacArthur's headquarters, he raised his hands above his head and clapped. 'Now, tell me, which hand made the noise?'

In October 1946, Joseph Keenan, chief of the war-crimes tribunal, announced that after prosecuting the militarists he planned a second trial that would prosecute businessmen. This provoked a ripple of fear through the elite, but it never came to pass. This intended purge of business leaders was detailed in a secret directive to SCAP from the Far Eastern Commission (FEC) in Washington, a task force charged with planning the occupation of Japan. The secret directive, known only as FEC-230, was designed to break Japan's huge conglomerates into smaller corporations and put in place anti-monopoly laws that would prevent their re-establishment. This would end the monopoly profits the *zaibatsu* had been squeezing from captive Japanese consumers since the 1870s. It was also meant to re-inforce political freedom by diluting the wealth the elite used to corrupt politicians through bribery and kick-backs.

Imprudently, the American bureaucrats who drafted FEC-230 foolishly overlooked the vested interests of major US banks and corporations that had made huge prewar loans and investments in Japan. Morgan Bank had provided Japan with many loans, including one of $150 million to rebuild Tokyo after the Kanto earthquake, and the Japanese government had defaulted on repayment of all these loans at the time of Pearl Harbor. Many other US corporations had major prewar stakes in Japan in the form of loans and direct investments. At the end of 1941, American investment accounted for three-quarters of the total foreign capital in Japanese industry. The largest single direct investment, nearly half of the total, was by General Electric, one of the Morgan extended family. GE held 16 per cent of the paid-up capital of Tokyo-Shibaura Electric, a firm linked to the Mitsui *zaibatsu*. Other large investments had been made by Associated Oil in Mitsubishi Petroleum, by Westinghouse in Mitsubishi Electric, by Owens-Libby in Sumitomo, by American Can in Mitsui, and so on. After the war these US corporations were owed reparations, royalties and loan payments totalling more than a billion dollars. They were determined not only to recover their investments but to resume their profitable business operations in Japan. If Japan's biggest conglomerates were broken up, this would impact directly on their American partners. If the directors and owners of these *zaibatsu* were condemned to death or to long prison terms, the new management might well argue that they were not responsible for debts incurred under a previous criminal military dictatorship. If efforts to introduce democracy to Japan miscarried and led to a socialist or communist takeover, past experience with Soviet Russia showed that such debts would never be honoured.

This new rationale was taking hold in Washington and being echoed in Tokyo, thanks to careful orchestration. Japanese government spokesmen said that SCAP was persecuting businessmen not because they had committed war crimes, or acquired their wealth by illegal means, but because they had been successful. 'We find it difficult to understand how this can be democracy . . . the empire's key financial and industrial figures, the men we need most to provide a sound business development upon which real democracy must rest, are being condemned without trial, merely because they were businessmen.' The old guard in the Diet (echoing Joe Grew) predicted 'chaos and confusion' and communist revolution in Japan if these purges went ahead.

In Washington, a group known as the Japan Crowd encouraged these reversals of SCAP policy. Joe Grew was their spokesman, guided by Herbert Hoover as well as Tom Lamont, who had raised a generation of investment bankers to share his view of China as a corrupt place and Japan as a nation of fiscal self-discipline. After the war, Grew retired from his post as undersecretary of state and moved to Wall Street, where he became the leading lobbyist of the Japan Crowd. By 1947, America's Republican Party was in full resurgence. Democrats were on the defensive. SCAP reforms were being aborted and all talk of purges and retribution in Japan was silenced. Grew and the Japan Crowd prevailed because Mao's success in China and communist challenges in Korea, Vietnam, Indonesia and elsewhere alarmed even liberal politicians, persuading them of the need to build an Iron Triangle of Japan, Taiwan and Korea.

Conservative American business leaders were usually careful to denounce monopolies and cartels in principle, but they successfully fought off any effort to break up Japan's conglomerates in practice. Grew and his colleagues made all the right democratic noises about reforming postwar Japan, while working energetically behind the scenes to block all efforts at reform. These men believed that the best hope for the future Pacific economy lay in reviving prewar trade patterns, with America again becoming Japan's biggest trading partner. Japan had the only massive industrial base in Asia. Once its financial elite were fully restored to positions of control, Japan would become an industrial bulwark against further expansion of communism in Asia. The time frame was urgent.

Grew also became co-chairman of a new lobbying group, the American Council on Japan (ACJ). The ACJ was a political action committee set up by wealthy American conservatives immediately after the war to lobby Washington and to fight the initiatives on reforming Japan that were being championed by liberals – whom the ACJ scathingly referred to as 'New Deal Democrats' and 'communist fellow travellers'. The ACJ was backed by *Newsweek*, the magazine founded in 1937 by Averell Harriman and others. (Harriman's brother was a *Newsweek* director.) The magazine championed the Wall Street view of Japan's future. ACJ's chief organizers were Harry F. Kern, *Newsweek*'s foreign editor; Compton Pakenham, the magazine's Tokyo bureau chief; and James Lee Kauffman, a New York lawyer who had taught at Tokyo University between 1913 and 1919 and had served as an attorney in Japan for General Electric, Standard Oil, Westinghouse, Ford, National Cash Register, Otis Elevator and Dillon Read. Kern was a personal friend of the Harrimans, and Pakenham had grown up in Japan and – as one critic put it – 'looked upon most indicted war criminals in Tokyo as [his] childhood playmates'. After the war, Kern and Kauffman were both given high honours by Hirohito.

Grew's co-chairman at the ACJ was another member of the Hoover circle and a former ambassador to Japan,

William Castle. Descended from one of Hawaii's plantation-owning grandee families, Castle had been an undersecretary of state during Hoover's presidency. Grew's right-hand man at the ACJ was Japan-born career diplomat Eugene Dooman, who had worked with Grew at the State Department during the war. Their self-proclaimed mission was to correct SCAP 'excesses' – to reverse America's early efforts to punish, reform and democratize Japan.

In the summer of 1947, Kauffman visited Tokyo on behalf of Dillon Read and made a personal assessment of the Truman administration's secret plan for the break-up of the *zaibatsu*. The secret FEC-230 documents were then leaked to *Newsweek* by Undersecretary of the Army William Draper, in civilian life a senior partner of Dillon Read. In December 1947, while America was gearing up for its presidential election campaign, *Newsweek* began a series of articles denouncing SCAP-1. The magazine accused SCAP of running amok and exceeding its authority. SCAP was trying to impose 'an economic theory which has . . . no counterpart anywhere else in the world. It is not communistic but it is far to the left of anything tolerated in this country.' *Newsweek* went on to warn American taxpayers that this plan posed grave dangers to their wallets. 'Japan is costing the American taxpayers millions of dollars a year.' Breaking up the *zaibatsu* would 'weaken the Japanese economy to the point where the maintenance of Japan would become a continual charge on the American taxpayer'. It was vital, Pakenham said, to get Japan back on track and make it 'a fertile field of American capital'.

In the US Congress, the attack was led by Republican Senator William F. Knowland, a wealthy Californian newspaper publisher who charged that vital information about US policy in Japan was being hidden from the American people. He said SCAP policy was 'contrary to American standards of decency and fair play [and] not in conformity with our own political, moral, or economic standards'. Foreshadowing the witch-hunts of Senator Joseph McCarthy, Knowland insinuated that FEC-230 had been concocted by communists in the State Department.

Herbert Hoover had earlier warned Bonner Fellers that the State Department was sending 'a bunch of communists' to Tokyo, along with some 'fellow travellers'. At the time Fellers was very busy suborning General Tojo and other key witnesses. Hoover was living in an apartment at the Waldorf Astoria Hotel in New York City, where he met regularly with Grew, Kern and the others. He encouraged them to attack SCAP, while at the same time secretly giving advice to MacArthur and Fellers, and passing questions to Hirohito. During this whole period, Hoover continued to lead MacArthur to believe that he had a serious chance of being nominated as the Republican presidential candidate or, at the very least, vice-president.

This made MacArthur acutely sensitive to *Newsweek*'s charges that SCAP was pursuing goals that were virtually communistic. In a fury, he expelled Pakenham from Japan, then was obliged to backtrack and let him return, under pressure from his Republican friends in New York City. When Senator Knowland then made his inflammatory charges in the Senate, MacArthur became apoplectic with rage, but there was nothing he could do. While he could ignore the White House, the Pentagon and the State Department, he could not offend the men who would decide his presidential chances. Accordingly, MacArthur halted all further punitive moves by SCAP, weeded out the remaining liberals and New Dealers from its ranks, turned SCAP-1 into SCAP-2, and followed the prophylactic course dictated by those who held his future in their fists.

The death-blow to reform came soon afterwards. In February 1948 the American government sent two Wall Street bankers to Japan to decide whether liberal reforms should go ahead or not. The outcome was predictable. The Draper–Johnston mission – led by banker Percy Johnston and Undersecretary of the Army William Draper – spent two weeks in Japan, then announced its recommendations. Draper knew little about Japan but, as he was on leave from his position as a vice-president of Dillon Read, it was only natural that he was anxious to protect its investments and those of related firms. Earlier, he had made a name for himself by rescuing German industry from the 'excessive zeal' of US occupation forces in Europe. Percy Johnston was chairman of New York's Chemical Bank, which had longstanding ties with Mitsui Bank. So this was like sending foxes to inventory the hen house. What Japan really needed, they said, was not to be punished for waging a merciless war, but to be restored to economic power as quickly as possible. The Japanese themselves could not possibly have said it better.

Of the original list of 325 Japanese companies that were to be reorganized, only 20 remained on the Draper–Johnston list. No Japanese banks were to be restructured. The ambitious American plan to reform Japan's economy and government was suffocated in the cradle in less than three years.

As a precaution, the great *zaibatsu* banks did change their names for a while. Mitsubishi Bank temporarily became Chiyoda Bank, Sumitomo Bank became Osaka

Bank, Yasuda Bank became Fuji Bank, and so on. (The boom brought about by the Korean War, 1950–3, quickly returned them to profitability, and made it possible to resurface their carefully hidden assets without attracting attention. Prime Minister Yoshida called the Korean War 'a gift from the gods'.)

Japan's incest of business, politics, bureaucracy and outlaws ensured that preserving any one of the four guaranteed the survival of them all. The initial American purge directive of 4 January 1946 had removed from eligibility for postwar political office anyone who had played any part in promoting Japanese aggression or militant nationalism. This included all military officers, heads of overseas business organizations, colonial officers and leaders of ultranationalist organizations. Some 220,000 persons were declared ineligible to hold public office in the new Japan. Washington believed that if these people were purged, new democratic voices would take their place.

Nascent labour movements formed in 1946 began noisy demands for reform. MacArthur, after first encouraging such political freedoms, reversed his opinion in 1947–8 and decisively crushed the Japanese labour movement, labelling it a dangerous threat to economic recovery. Anyone who became politically active in organized labour or other radical postwar political movements was called a Marxist. The purge mechanism, intended to remove ultranationalists from public life, was redirected at socialists, labour activists and other leftists. In July 1948, MacArthur intervened personally to avert a general walkout by Japanese railway and communications unions, and followed that with a law prohibiting all government employees from striking.

Because he needed the wartime civilian bureaucracy to run the day-to-day business of government after the war, MacArthur left the bureaucracy intact. Japan's bureaucracy had its roots in the former samurai class, so they practised clique loyalties and aligned themselves with oligarchs who could assure their promotion or with special-interest groups who rewarded them more directly with kickbacks. Because no effort was made to reform it after the war, Japan's unreconstructed bureaucracy became the new centre of power.

After promising Japan a new constitution, something had to be contrived. At first, MacArthur ordered the Japanese to write their own, but when he saw the results he decided to have it done by his own staff. They were given only three guiding principles: the emperor system would be preserved, the Japanese would formally repudiate war as an instrument of foreign policy, and certain feudal vestiges of the old nobility – like the peerage system – would be eliminated. This constitution was drafted in six days by MacArthur's old friend General Courtney Whitney, a former Manila lawyer and businessman, who was helped by a team of SCAP legal experts. When Whitney presented his hasty draft to Japanese officials, he told them, 'If you are not prepared to sponsor a document of this type, General MacArthur will go over your heads to the Japanese people. But if you will support a constitution of this kind, General MacArthur will support you.'

Yoshida consented to the constitution only when he was directly ordered to do so by Emperor Hirohito and because MacArthur had promised that this would guarantee the emperor's safety. The idea of being subjected to any kind of national constitutional referendum so horrified Hirohito and Yoshida that they decided to make the best of it. Being shrewd men, the Japanese recognized that Whitney's text was full of holes and subject to a broad range of interpretations when it was finally – as MacArthur put it – 'presented by the emperor to the Japanese people'. Historically, constitutions are drafted by the people or their representatives, as a way of defining and restricting the authority of their government. MacArthur preferred that this constitution would be handed down to the people by the emperor, like the Meiji Constitution before it. As MacArthur's biographer William Manchester noted, it would be conveyed from the emperor to the people by 'the handpicked Tojo Diet' left over from before the surrender. Reporter Mark Gayn observed sourly in March 1946 that 'the new constitution is being passed on to the Japanese by unclean hands'. MacArthur retaliated by banning Gayn from Japan.

Although the constitution was written by his own team, MacArthur publicly praised Japan's government for 'such an exemplary document which so coincided with his own notion of what was best for the country'. The constitution did make a pretence of stripping the emperor of political authority, but he had never really had that, so this was done more for the international audience. More importantly, by endorsing a continuation of the imperial institution, MacArthur and Whitney wittingly or unwittingly breathed new life into the very octopus SCAP had been charged to dismember. The emperor was obliged to renounce his divinity, which he did in January 1946 in a statement drafted by SCAP and approved by MacArthur, but this was such an abstraction as to be completely meaningless.

By preserving the throne, MacArthur, Hoover, Grew and the others gave conservative Japanese politicians back the very device they had used to hoodwink the

Japanese public since the Meiji Restoration. The emperor was a magic wand, and whenever the wand was waved it distracted people from what was really happening.

Before the war, any criticism of the Japanese government was interpreted as an insult to the emperor, punishable by death. After the war, no matter what SCAP said, the emperor continued to serve as the chief priest of Shinto and was still popularly regarded as sacred. Conservative politicians hammered home the argument that the emperor remained the head of the Japanese family. Thus any criticism of his government was still an insult to the emperor, the father of the country, with dire consequences. During the 1946 election campaign, the Liberal Party ('liberal' in name only) let it be known far and wide through campaign posters and rhetoric that a vote against them was a vote against the emperor himself. This stirred such deep and fearful resonances that the Liberals easily won.

By the end of 1951 all but a few of the 220,000 people purged for their involvement in the war had been exonerated, had their pensions restored and were allowed to resume life as if there had been no war. In 1952, when Japan's sovereignty was fully restored, the few remaining on the list were de-purged. A number of them immediately returned to senior economic advisery posts, while others resumed their jobs in the police and defence forces. In the October 1952 general elections, 139 individuals recently freed from detention were elected to parliament.

When the occupation ended in 1952, all Japan's leftists were back in prison, reform was a dead issue and hopes for democracy were again on the back shelf. Japan was quietly bringing its hoard of gold bullion out of hiding. By not forcing the elite to play a leading role in the reform of the Japanese system, America had allowed them to sabotage the very idea of reform. America's oligarchs had rescued Japan's oligarchs. Although it was absurd to see the Pacific War as only a minor historical aberration, they were intent upon restoring things in Japan as they were before the war. George Kennan said: 'We had purposely relieved our erstwhile opponents of every shred of responsibility for what was now to come.' The elite simply tucked the bitter pill in their cheek to spit it out the moment the Americans were gone.

Given a priceless opportunity, the American occupation had done little to change Japan. What was intended to be a victory of Western democracy over Japanese fascism became a struggle between American liberals and American conservatives, with many casualties. One of them was George Atcheson, the senior State Department adviser in Japan. Although he was resigned to 'the short solution', he had his enemies, more than he knew. Repeatedly, he and his liberal colleagues and friends were harassed by MacArthur's hard-core rightwingers: General Whitney, General Willoughby and Colonel Bunker. Atcheson had been friends with Terry Terasaki and his wife and daughter since 1941 when Terry had tried frantically to stop the attack on Pearl Harbor. In Tokyo after the war, Atcheson saw a lot of the Terasakis and, realizing how desperately poor they were, he took them packages of foods and other gifts from the embassy store and the US Army post exchanges. Inevitably, US military police or G-2 agents would then appear, arrest Terry and search his house for 'stolen American goods'. This was the kind of harassment the MacArthur team was good at, a form of 'friendly fire'. In August 1947, when MacArthur's inner circle was making the final turnabout from SCAP-1 to SCAP-2, George Atcheson decided he had to go back to Washington personally to report to the secretary of state and the White House what was afoot. He gathered several members of his staff together and set out by government plane across the Pacific, bound for Honolulu. After passing lonely Johnston Island but well short of Hawaii, the plane that had been fully fuelled mysteriously ran out of fuel and went down. One of the survivors said that, as the plane fell, Atcheson shrugged, shook his head sadly and said, 'It can't be helped.'

When news of the crash reached Terry Terasaki in Tokyo he was stunned. In a daze, he went to the shore of Sagami Bay and, tears in his eyes, walked fully clothed into the sea, to immerse himself for an hour with his friend Atcheson and all the other victims of the war, whose hopes had now died twice. Once when they were trampled by the oligarchs of Japan, and then when they were trampled by the oligarchs of America.

CHAPTER 11

JAPANESE GOTHIC

Hirohito's heir, Crown Prince Akihito, was born in the Year of the Rooster, which in 1933 meant the Water Rooster, intellectual, scientific, solemn, introverted, observant, cultured, with lots of energy and initiative to get things done, but just as ready to turn inward if thwarted. While still an infant he was placed in the custody of the Imperial Household organization and kept in the palace nursery apart from other babies. As a young mother, Empress Nagako had often visited her daughters in the same nursery, but she came under such criticism for spoiling them that by the time her son arrived she accepted the inevitable and came to see him less frequently. He grew accustomed to being alone in a crowd. At the age of three Akihito was taken away completely from his parents to live in a separate palace with his chamberlains, nursemaids, doctors and tutors. In contrast to the bright and aggressive Dowager Empress Sadako who waged and won a long, hard battle to have closer contact with her children, Empress Nagako accepted the separation from her son without protest. Rather than resist the will of the chamberlains, and the deliberate isolation of the emperor and empress, she grew increasingly remote and austere,

343

surrounded by a retinue of aristocratic ladies whose exclusive interest was backbiting. Lovely as a young bride, Nagako became shrivelled and transformed by the behaviour of these court ladies, and gradually became one with her gossipy claque.

Left to the chamberlains, Akihito was given the same humourless upbringing as his father. He emulated his father's interest in marine life, peering at carp in palace pools, netting colourful specimens and handling live lobsters, watched over constantly by two ladies-in-waiting, a chamberlain and a doctor. Aged six in 1939, with Japan already at war in China, he was sent to the Peers School, headed by retired Admiral Yamanashi. There he was a typical Water Rooster – lonely, wary, withdrawn, friendless. Chubby and dark, his schoolmates called him Chabu Chan ('brown pig').

During the later stages of the Pacific War, he and his classmates were moved outside the city. He did not see his parents again for nearly two years, returning to the palace only in the autumn of 1945, after the bitter surrender. A letter from his father explained to him the disaster of the war: 'Our people believed in the imperial state too much and despised Britain and the United States. Our military men placed too much significance on spirit and were oblivious to science . . . They could only advance, but had no knowledge of withdrawal.' On the day of surrender, Akihito wrote in his diary, 'I think I must study harder from now on.'

Initially SCAP did not make any direct demands on the Imperial Household concerning the young crown prince and his education. When Akihito returned to Tokyo, Admiral Yamanashi hired Reginald H. Blyth, an Englishman long resident in Japan, to teach the boy English. Yamanashi was an Anglophile, Blyth a Japanophile, and the two had been friends for many years. They were a curious pair of social outsiders. A rational man, Yamanashi's career in the navy had come to an early end because he favoured arms limitation, which made him unpopular with his more aggressive colleagues. He had resigned and joined the Peers School. Blyth had begun his sojourn in Asia decades earlier, as a teacher of English in Korea, where he fell in love with, and married, a Japanese woman. He planned to take Japanese citizenship but the war intervened. Like others in his situation he was interned for the duration in the mountains near Nagano. When the war was over, he came to Tokyo looking for work as a language expert and was delighted to be offered a job tutoring the crown prince. His delight was premature.

Blyth's appointment annoyed General Bonner Fellers and Colonel Larry Bunker, who thought they should have had first crack at inserting an American in this influential post. To them, the occupation was strictly an American affair. They could not block Blyth's appointment because both Blyth and Admiral Yamanashi were doing favours for SCAP, but they could outflank this eccentric Limey. Finding the right American took time, but by late 1946 Akihito and his siblings began to receive their English lessons not from Blyth but from Elizabeth Gray Vining, a 44-year-old Quaker widow. Blyth remained in the palace but was completely upstaged and made to feel like an extra thumb.

As Vining explained, 'Someone in the upper echelons of the occupation had indicated to someone on the Japanese side that . . . the crown prince should have a more democratic education.' Behind this bit of gloss is yet another episode of MacArthur's men tightening their talons on the imperial family. It happened this way: early in 1946 a mission of US educators headed by Dr George Stoddard, superintendent of education in New York State, visited Japan to advise SCAP-1 on reforming education in Japan. Fellers arranged for Stoddard to see Japanese Quaker educator Kawaii Michiko, who had gone to college with Fellers in Indiana. She was an intimate friend of Sekyia Teizaburo, a high palace official who had already opened many doors for Fellers. It was agreed to enlist the support of Dowager Empress Sadako, and to inform Emperor Hirohito that MacArthur preferred to have the crown prince tutored by an American.

Accordingly, at an imperial reception for the Stoddard mission on 26 March 1946, the emperor suddenly turned to Dr Stoddard and asked him if he could find an American to tutor his son. Such a 'spontaneous' request made it appear that Hirohito had initiated the idea, but he was being manipulated again. A few days later Stoddard met privately with Admiral Yamanashi and Terry Terasaki, and learned that Hirohito had specifically requested the tutor be an American woman, aged about 50, 'a Christian but not a fanatic', and someone without any prior experience in Japan.

There was strong opposition to this. Admiral Yamanashi was hostile to the idea of an American becoming a palace insider in this way. Many Japanese conservatives who sat with him on the council overseeing all arrangements for the crown prince were furious. As for Blyth, he freely expressed his opinion that any American coming to fill such a position would only be a publicity seeker and self-aggrandizer. MacArthur pretended to have 'doubts' because of the possibility that this was 'a cynical political move' on the part of the Japanese to make it appear that they were more eager to learn about democracy than they actually were. Such was his sense of humour. Having set up the whole thing in advance, this was only unabashed grandstanding.

Once back in America, Stoddard chose Vining. A year younger than Hirohito, she worked for the Friends Service Committee and was the author of a number of books for young readers, mostly inspirational histories of famous Quakers like William Penn. Stoddard knew about the Quaker network in Japan and in the imperial palace. He knew that his choice of a mature Quaker woman would meet with Dowager Empress Sadako's approval. Stoddard passed on Vining's dossier to Fellers, and he gave it to Gwen and Terry Terasaki. (Terry was then fully occupied with the emperor's burdensome monologue.) Gwen thought this was a good choice because Vining had known personal tragedy when her husband of less than five years was killed in a car accident. 'I am sure she will understand in her quiet way the sorrow of others. And the Quakers hate war and always have.'

Admiral Yamanashi consulted his imperial overseers, and they grudgingly accepted. Later, when Vining proved to be a great success, Hirohito took full credit, remarking: 'If ever anything I did has been a success, it was asking Mrs Vining to come here.'

Vining arrived in Tokyo in October 1946. Although she was just another employee of the Imperial Household, SCAP gave her a commandeered Western-style house for her exclusive use, furnished with Louis XV antiques from the Akasaka palace and Western beds bought for the Prince of Wales's visit in 1922. She was provided with a Japanese Quaker secretary, a housekeeper, a maid, a maintenance man and a chauffeur. Whenever anything needed fixing they simply called the

Imperial Household. Vining described her relations with the palace as 'delightfully homely'.

She was to teach the emperor's children English, democracy and Western culture. At the time, Akihito and his siblings were attending the Peers and Peeresses Schools on campuses which had been army barracks, at Koganei in the outskirts of Tokyo. The roofs leaked and there was no heat, little electricity and only crude wooden desks. The children were not much better off. Japan's very rich aristocracy were taking pains to look poor, even when their families owned millions of dollars' worth of property, and this showed most conspicuously in the way they dressed their children. Even the emperor's children seemed carefully threadbare. It would have been foolish to dress them in silks. Such a game was made of this pretence that when he was demobbed and went back to Washington, Fellers sent Sears mail-order catalogues to Emperor Hirohito, filled his orders and had the goods sent to his former military aide at SCAP in Tokyo, who passed them on discreetly to the palace by way of Terry Terasaki.

Although the Imperial Household groaned at the very idea, Akihito and his schoolmates were disarmed when Vining gave them American-style nicknames to avoid having to use court honorifics. Crown Prince Akihito became Jimmie, a sister became Patricia. Such was the humble key to democracy. During the four years she tutored Akihito, he undeniably experienced an upbringing unthinkable in his father's childhood. He associated freely with Japanese, British and American schoolboys, moved about with minimum escort, shared a dormitory cell with a roommate, cleaned up after himself, cleared dishes from communal dining tables, learned to play bridge and Monopoly, and at Vining's suggestion read *Gone with the Wind*. She made a lasting impression on him, and kept careful and detailed diaries during her stay. Later, at Hirohito's suggestion, she would write three books and numerous articles about her experiences with the family.

Vining was a frequent guest in the palace, welcomed to informal chats by Dowager Empress Sadako. On these occasions, Sadako always wore a black floor-length silk shirtwaist dress, in the fashion of the late 1890s. She was now in her late fifties. Since the death of Emperor Taisho in 1926, the dowager had brought only one other Westerner into her midst, Alice Perry Grew. Vining found Sadako 'still an impressive and influential figure in Japanese life', intensely concerned about the fate of her family, especially her grandson. Interestingly, the French journalist Robert Guillain also drew the conclusion that Hirohito's mother was one of the most powerful individuals in the palace in the immediate postwar years. 'An intelligent, enlightened woman,' Guillain said, 'her influence remained strong.' (Just as Fellers used the Quaker network to meddle in palace affairs, the dowager used her Quaker web to meddle back.)

Soon Vining also found herself giving English lessons to many adults in the imperial family, including Empress Nagako and her brother-in-law, Prince Takamatsu. She found Princess Takamatsu to be charming and vivacious. The prince and princess were among the most visible royals during this period, travelling the country and attending charity balls to raise money for war-damage repairs. Prince Mikasa, Hirohito's outspoken youngest brother, also took English lessons from Vining. An unpretentious man, Mikasa came to her house driving himself in a tiny Japanese car, or taking the train and

349

walking from the station. She described him as having the dowager's bird-like profile and something of her personality. 'His mind was very open and keen and I was always much interested in his frank and uninhibited comments on affairs.' Since the turn of the century, when Dr Erwin Baelz had been the family physician, no other Westerner had so regularly penetrated the inner sanctum of the Imperial Household. None has since.

Journalist John Gunther, another Quaker, became close to Vining while she was in Tokyo and wrote articles about her. '[She] entered upon her task with humor, dignity, common sense, and an earnest sense of the goal at stake . . . A Quaker, she believes in virtue. And virtue, together with much else, is what she taught.'

From the beginning she often found herself in trouble with the chamberlains of the Imperial Household. She was most at odds with Crown Prince Akihito's grand chamberlain, Hozumi Shigeto, an elderly lawyer, Confucian scholar and connoisseur of Japanese art, literature and drama, who was considered an 'outstanding liberal', especially when it came to women's rights. In 1946 he was 67, and the most influential man in the crown prince's retinue. A small, rotund man with a moustache and spectacles, he spoke excellent English, but was always evasive. Vining found this frustrating. When she tried to talk with him about the crown prince he would laugh and change the subject.

Although her classes with Akihito were supposed to be private, chamberlains were always present and it was months before she was permitted to be in a room with him alone. The cocoon surrounding Akihito was eye-opening. His affairs were managed by a group of chamberlains, called Togushoku (the Board of the Eastern Prince), with further guidance from an advisory council. Mrs Matsudaira Tsuneo, mother of Princess Chichibu and childhood intimate of the dowager, was on this advisory board. Even on solitary walks along a beach, the crown prince was trailed by seventeen attendants. 'He seemed unable to answer for himself without seeking their help.' Vining blamed this on the chamberlains, who wanted the prince to become dependent on them. 'Chamberlains . . . went with him everywhere and told him what to do at every turn, breathing out fears that he might make some mistake.'

At least five chamberlains were with him around the clock: watching him eat, correcting every mistake before it could be committed, and anticipating every want before it could be expressed. All of the chamberlains were university graduates and two spoke very good English. One, a former secretary to Prince Konoe, had accompanied him to visit Herbert Hoover in California in the 1930s. Another was a Christian. They were suspicious of Vining, but eventually she won them over. Her favourite was 30-year-old Toda Yasuhide, tall and athletic, who had been wounded at the time of the surrender when palace guards tried to seize and destroy the recording of the emperor's surrender broadcast.

As much as Vining wanted to change the system and to unwrap the cocoon swaddling Akihito, she was blocked at the highest levels, even after expressing her views frankly to Hirohito and Nagako. 'It was always on my mind and heart that the crown prince should not be kept apart as much as he was from his family, especially his parents and his younger brother. It seemed to me unnatural and a great waste of opportunity for deepening his understanding and widening his heart. The compartmentalization of an intelligent, conscientious, affectionate family seemed to me an indefensible

351

deprivation in the life of a boy who should have had and might have had the best of everything.' But everyone resisted her ideas about the imperial family living together.

Although isolated from his family, Akihito was put on public display for the first time in January 1947. Over seven days he visited temples, schools and colleges, a fish hatchery, a lotus farm, a weather station and an archaeological museum. He climbed a mountain, saw folk dances and watched a swimming exhibition. Wherever he went crowds gathered. Vining was impressed with his composure, and sympathetic to his plight: 'He was learning fast that an imperial prince belongs not to himself but to the public [but it] was difficult discipline after all the years of being protected from the public gaze.'

Tension between Vining and the palace bureaucrats eased in the spring of 1948 when Matsudaira Yoshitami retired as the emperor's grand steward. This Matsudaira had studied at Oxford and spoke excellent English, but was a stern traditionalist who had been in the Imperial Household since he was a childhood playmate of Emperor Taisho. The new grand steward was another Quaker, Tajima Michiji, already in his sixties, a former president of Showa Bank. In his youth Tajima had been a protégé of Dr Nitobe Inazo, a well-known Japanese Quaker educator who had married a Philadelphia Quaker and brought up two imperial princes who were farmed out to him. Vining said Tajima 'brought with him a fresh breeze, and some doors which had been closed blew open'. With Tajima's appointment, Professor Koizumi Shinzo was put in charge of Akihito's education. Koizumi was born in Tokyo in 1888 and educated at Keio University, where Alice Perry Grew's father once taught. He was then sent abroad to study in London, Berlin and Cambridge. He taught economics at Keio and became its president in 1930. Vining first met the professor in March 1948. Although she knew that Koizumi had been badly burned during the American napalming of Tokyo in 1945, she was unprepared for the terribly scarred and crumpled man who now confronted her. A handsome tennis champion as a young man, he was now permanently lame, his face seamed with scars. In order to sleep, he had to tie a silk scarf over his lidless eyes. His only son, a young lieutenant in the navy, was killed in the war.

Before this appointment, Koizumi was not a part of the imperial court. It took all of Tajimi's powers of persuasion to convince him to take the job. Vining learned that Koizumi was now responsible not only for the education of the crown prince, but for the direction of his life in every detail. He became Akihito's closest confidant and counsellor. Just as his great-grandfather Meiji had gravitated to Ito, Akihito needed someone other than court chamberlains.

Koizumi understood Akihito's predicament: 'His only defect is that he is the crown prince.' As Ito Hirobumi once remarked, 'It really is very hard luck to be born a crown prince. Directly he comes into the world he is swaddled in etiquette, and when he gets a little bigger he has to dance to the fiddling of his tutors and advisers.' Koizumi condemned the court's hidebound traditionalism, especially the excessive grovelling of the ladies-in-waiting.

Bonner Fellers once told Vining, 'You're going to get credit some day for the first Christian emperor of Japan.' She replied, rather hotly, 'Not at all. I'm only going to teach him English and that's all.' Vining was as good as her word, carefully avoiding manipulating her position, but General MacArthur played both sides of the street. Official SCAP policy, handed down by Washington, was that in Japan there would be strict separation of church and state. One objective was to eliminate the influence on the throne of State Shinto, which many Westerners had labelled a religion of war. But MacArthur personally craved to convert Japan, speaking of 'the hope and belief I entertain that Japan will become Christianized'. It is impossible to say whether this was genuine, or more of the grandstanding typical of him as an aspiring presidential candidate. In 1946 he told American church leaders that it was 'necessary to replace the old Japanese religion with Christianity' and urged them to send missionaries to Japan. MacArthur insisted that 'Democracy and Christianity have much in common, as practice of the former is impossible without giving faithful service to the fundamental concepts underlying the latter'. The Hellenic Greeks would have disagreed. More important to MacArthur was the fact that Christianity was an antidote to atheistic Marxism. American educators without church credentials were barred from Japan during the first two years of the occupation.

Missionaries were given extra-legal privileges including army transport, the right to make purchases at subsidized American military base stores and the right to use US Army postal service mail-boxes. MacArthur personally asked the American Bible Society to send 10 million Bibles to Japan. The Bibles arrived on military ships, freight paid by American taxpayers. While at first there did seem to be an outburst of Christian conversions, it soon became apparent that many of the converts were out of work and had nothing better to do than attend church meetings. As to the brisk sales of Bibles, they were printed on paper that was a perfect substitute for high-priced cigarette paper. English-speaking Japanese made jokes about Holy Smoke.

According to William P. Woodward of the religious-affairs section of SCAP, there was persistent public speculation that Emperor Hirohito was going to become a Christian. 'How the story first got started that the imperial family was interested in Christianity is difficult to say, but from the time the members of the Protestant delegation had audiences [with the emperor] in November 1945, there was a constant stream of outstanding Christian leaders who met the emperor.' A Japanese Christian gave instruction to Empress Nagako, and the president of Tokyo University predicted that Hirohito would convert.

Some of these rumours were started by Bonner Fellers. In May 1946 he wrote privately to Hoover that a 'Christian lady-in-waiting' from the palace had told him that 'the emperor and the empress both have been reading the bible daily'. Fellers added that 'recently the Empress Dowager remarked, "What this country needs now is Christianity."' Once he was retired from the US Army and working for the Republican National Committee in Washington, Fellers was stating publicly that: 'The throne favours Christianity. The empress dowager reads the bible and prays . . . the emperor himself leans towards Christianity . . . it would be surprising indeed if the crown prince does not accept Christianity.'

Woodward maintains that nobody at SCAP 'ever did anything directly or indirectly to assist or encourage the active proselytizing of the higher echelons of the government, the Imperial Household or the emperor [but] it appears that MacArthur did discuss the issue with

Hirohito. And that the emperor once offered to make Christianity the state religion of Japan. MacArthur turned down the offer saying "no nation must be made to conform to any religion".' The conversion of the emperor, MacArthur added, would only lead to charges of 'outrageous cynicism'. In fact, the emperor did not publicly convert and, according to Woodward, there is 'no evidence that any private change took place either'. Hirohito once told an Australian correspondent for the *Melbourne Sun* that he had no intention of converting. Nonetheless, rumours continued to circulate and it was reported that Hirohito was anxious for Akihito to come under Christian influence. Akihito later described himself to Vining as 'a scientist and an agnostic'.

The one public convert in the imperial family was also the most questionable. On 17 December 1951, Hirohito's uncle Prince Asaka, who had triggered and personally oversaw the atrocities of the Rape of Nanking, was baptized a Roman Catholic in ceremonies in Rome. A Japanese Catholic bishop officiated at the ceremonies.

Vining had been in Japan for nearly four years before she finally persuaded MacArthur to meet the crown prince. MacArthur set the following rules: 'I don't want anybody else here – except you, to make him feel comfortable.' Once she had MacArthur's agreement, Vining broached the matter with Tajima at the palace. He had no objection, and thought it would be a valuable experience for the crown prince to meet MacArthur. Hirohito was pleased with the idea, but stipulated that there should be no publicity until afterwards. When Vining finally asked Akihito about it, he was character- istically noncommittal. He made no comment but 'looked interested and thoughtful'.

The meeting took place one evening in June 1950. There was no escort. Akihito made the trip to SCAP headquarters at the Dai Ichi Life building in Vining's car. Everything possible was done to avoid drawing public attention.

As they drew up, Colonel Bunker came out and opened the car door. She presented him to the prince, and they went in, the honour guard saluting as they passed. Akihito signed the guest register, then was taken into MacArthur's office.

MacArthur shook Akihito's hand and said, 'How do you do, sir. I am glad to meet you.'

Akihito replied, 'How do you do, General. I am glad to meet you.'

MacArthur led him to a sofa and drew up chairs for Vining and himself, lit his pipe and began talking. They discussed school and sports, with MacArthur typically dominating the conversation. After twenty minutes, the general handed the crown prince a box of candy and bid him farewell. Later Colonel Bunker phoned Vining and said, 'I thought you'd like to hear that your charge passed his examination with flying colors. The general said immediately when he came out that he was very favorably impressed – the prince had poise and was charming and attractive.'

Akihito had only one rival in Tokyo and that was MacArthur's own son, Arthur MacArthur IV. Biographer William Manchester put it in reverse: 'Arthur's only real peer was Crown Prince Akihito.' Indeed, the young MacArthur was always indulged and coddled like a crown prince and behaved with premature arrogance. The two boys met once and were photographed together, but the photos make it clear that they were hostile. Although every effort was made to make it seem that the MacArthur family were intimates of Japan's imperial family, that was far from the case. Emperor Hirohito and Crown Prince Akihito were the only members of the core imperial family whom the MacArthurs ever met, and they were effectively hostages.

Vining's perceptions of Akihito are much more telling. In her daily diary entries she described him as 'cautious and self-effacing'. When asked if he ever wished to be an ordinary boy, Akihito replied, 'I don't know, I've never been an ordinary boy.' Once when Vining asked her pupils what they wanted to be when they grew up, one said 'a writer', another 'a gentleman'. Akihito replied, 'I shall be emperor.'

Professor Koizumi's assessment of Akihito was frank: 'He is by no means an exceptional young man. But he will do. He is sincere, takes his responsibilities seriously, and he is a good thinker even if the process is sometimes painful. He is the product of his upbringing. Like other members of the imperial family, he has lived a cocoon-like existence, with little knowledge of people and events in the outside world. He has too many servants but he lives simply. His great handicap is that all his life things have been spoon-fed to him, including education.'

By 1949 there were long discussions about Akihito's university options. Vining, Koizumi, Tajima and Mrs Matsudaira considered whether he should study both in England and the United States. They decided that some travel would be a good idea. In the end, the hazards outweighed the benefits. Although Akihito would make a world tour in 1953, he would not be allowed to attend a foreign university. When Akihito finished junior high school, Vining left Tokyo, in December 1950. The occupation officially ended in April 1952, and seven months later, in an elaborate Shinto ceremony, Akihito was declared of age and formally named heir apparent to the throne of Japan.

The ceremony should have occurred a year earlier, but was delayed by the unexpected death of Dowager Empress Sadako. At 66 she succumbed to a sudden heart attack in June 1951. When he heard the news, Prince Chichibu, her favourite, was overwhelmed with grief. Although she was unquestionably a lifelong Christian, and had left instructions for her funeral ceremonies that were described as 'troublesome' for the bureaucrats of the Imperial Household, her funeral was turned into a national Shinto pageant. There was a Shinto state funeral in Tokyo, where half a million people watched the funeral procession wind through the streets. Her body was then interred next to the remains of the Taisho emperor at the imperial mausoleum in Tama, west of Tokyo.

This was one of the first manifestations of what Professor Murayama called the reassertion of 'the pathology of the ultra-right' that followed the end of the American occupation. Shinto rituals were one way in which the imperial family's status could again be manipulated by politicians and bureaucrats. These 'ancient' rituals, actually contrived by Ito Hirobumi during the late nineteenth century, had the effect of mystifying the imperial family, and with them the government. Critics like Murayama were very much aware of the magical power these rituals conveyed. The magic had been used cynically by the Genro and the militarists. Now it was to be wielded once more, this time by bureaucrats and politicians. With the end of the occupation, the ruling elite once again intended to veil the throne in elaborate Shinto rites. The moment the Americans were gone, a senior adviser at the imperial palace acknowledged that arch-conservative politicians and lobbyists were again pulling the strings from behind the scenes. Sociologist Fujitana Takashi asked: 'How is it that despite the withering of aura and belief, and regardless of the recent de-mystification of the nation and the monarchy, so many people still act as if they believe in the dominant narratives of the nation that were created in the Meiji era?'

Ito's smoke and mirrors were back in fashion.

By now Akihito had outgrown the 'brown pig' stage and matured into a slender, good-looking man, with more strength of character in his face than any other prince since Meiji. Soon after his investiture as crown prince, it was announced that he would represent his father at the coronation of Queen Elizabeth II. Along the way he would visit the United States.

He spent six weeks in London, Edinburgh, Oxford and Cambridge. At the coronation his presence was judged utterly correct. The summer was spent visiting kings and heads of state in Spain, France, Italy, Belgium, Holland, Germany, Denmark, Norway, Sweden and Switzerland. In America, a dinner was given by the Japan Society in New York, with John Foster Dulles, Joseph Grew and John D. Rockefeller among the hosts. One who did not attend was General Douglas MacArthur. During the Korean War, MacArthur had been appointed commander of American forces on the peninsula, perhaps in part to keep him away from the American political stage. In Korea he had continually disobeyed orders from Washington, provoking President Truman to fire him from his command. Herbert Hoover and other Republican Party barons also had turned their backs on the man whose dreams of the White House they had long and rather cynically encouraged. His old enemy, Dwight Eisenhower, was now America's new president. Licking his wounds in private, MacArthur declined polite invitations to see the crown prince during his visit, and did not extend any invitations in return. Akihito stayed at the modest Philadelphia home of Elizabeth Vining, then went west to spend some days at the Rockefeller ranch in Wyoming.

When he returned to Japan, Akihito resumed his studies while Professor Koizumi and others turned their attention to finding him a bride. Early rumours had suggested that his bride would be Princess Kitashirakawa Hatsuko, granddaughter of the playboy prince who had been killed in the crash of his Bugatti near Deauville in 1923. Her own father had died in a military plane crash in 1940 when he was on active duty in Manchuria. Professor Koizumi and other members of a committee screened hundreds of candidates, starting with all the eligible girls at the Peeresses School, now renamed Gakushuin University. Empresses Sadako and Nagako had both been students there when they were selected, so it was assumed that the bride would come from the blooded aristocracy. However, by March 1958 the search was widened to include other leading girls' schools. Heading a list of candidates submitted by the Sacred Heart Convent in Tokyo, a bridal incubator for more cosmopolitan members of the postwar elite, was Shoda Michiko. She was a star on its track and field team, called the 'antelope' because of her speed and grace. A flawless English speaker, she was bright, intellectual, natural, forthright and charming – a refreshingly original young woman compared to the rigidly correct automatons bred by the elite as the future mothers of their progeny.

Akihito and Michiko had met on the tennis courts the previous summer. In their first encounter she and a partner had soundly beaten Akihito and his partner in a doubles. In the more urbane atmosphere of Japan in the 1950s, the crown prince was allowed to entertain friends at his holiday residence in Karuizawa, formerly Prince Asaka's summer retreat. He gave an occasional dance party there, and made certain Michiko was included.

Although Michiko was technically an approved candidate, she was very much a dark horse, stubbornly unconventional and individualistic, even down to having curly hair in a country where most hair is straight. Her parents were both world travellers and Christians, qualities that were frowned upon by the frogs in the well. More troublesome still, Michiko was a commoner. The term is hardly accurate, as she was the pampered daughter of a very wealthy manufacturer, and therefore qualified as a member of the ruling elite. But her family were not part of the ancient aristocracy, or even the newer Meiji peerage. However, in 1955 the Nisshin Flour Milling Company, her father's noodle business, was the largest enterprise of its kind in Asia, with annual sales of $93 million.

Most important historically, it was Akihito himself who had put her name forward. And he would have it no other way. When the engagement was announced there was strong negative reaction from hard-core conservatives. Even Mrs Matsudaira Tsuneo, Princess Chichibu's mother, originally opposed the match. Extremists, who preferred the bride to be chosen from the House of Fujiwara, threatened to murder every member of the Shoda family.

Grand Steward Usami Takeshi finally went before parliament to defend the decision, reminding them of the folly of 'excessive intermarriage' among persons of the imperial line. He added that the choice was 'in keeping with the new Japan'. The president of the parliament and most powerful man in the ruling Liberal Democratic Party, Kishi Nobusuke, raised an issue: 'The imperial family follows Shinto, but the Shoda family is Christian. Does anyone see a problem there?' Usami Takeshi replied: 'It is true that her family is Christian, and the school that she attended is Catholic, but Michiko herself has not been baptized. I imagine that she can convert to Shinto.'

Even Professor Koizumi had reservations about Michiko. He wrote to Elizabeth Vining: 'Her non-aristocratic birth (although of an old family of good name) has of course made us hesitate, but after every possible consideration we have decided. It is not only His Highness's but our choice too.' Koizumi's hesitation may actually have been out of sympathy to Michiko, for he knew what she could expect from the Imperial Household chamberlains' 'tradition-encrusted ways'. Many nobles – they still thought of themselves as nobles, even though the nobility had been terminated by SCAP – were horrified at the thought of paying the necessary deep ritual obeisance to a commoner empress. Even those most anxious to break with the rigid past were worried about fatally damaging the institution of the throne by introducing the tiniest flaw. Once commoners could be empresses, where would it all end?

To pacify these critics, the Imperial Household assured everyone that the royal marriage was not just a tennis-court romance, but had been prearranged long in advance. This was not true, but sounded good. Yes, the crown prince had not been allowed to take his pick of all the maidens in the nation, only of the daughters of the super-rich. Despite being an avid tennis player, he was

363

allowed to play tennis only with people who were carefully vetted. So, to some extent, every girl he met was appropriate. But some were more appropriate than others. Furthermore, with at least five chamberlains constantly hovering around him, he could never engage in a romantic fling, and showed no inclination to do so. More importantly, Michiko was his choice.

After being formally presented to the emperor and empress, Michiko gave a television interview. Asked what she liked most about Akihito, she said, 'I was attracted most by his integrity and sincerity. From my heart I can trust and respect him.' She added, 'I should like to consult with the crown prince in everything about our future. I should also like to do my best to improve myself, with the advice and help of other people.' The interview was not spontaneous, of course. All questions were submitted to the Imperial Household in advance. They composed Michiko's answers and she memorized the text. Akihito's former school principal, Admiral Yamanashi, noted that her public presence showed 'dignity, frankness, wisdom and above all . . . gentle, easy grace'. She charmed all observers. Professor Koizumi went one step further: 'The people's enthusiasm for Miss Shoda was stormy – or, better, explosive.' Her public popularity was dangerous, for it stirred deep jealousy within the imperial family, especially among its women. One of Michiko's former teachers once remarked to her sourly: 'Your only defect is that you have none.'

A few would be invented. Empress Nagako's claque would take care of that.

When the wedding took place in April 1959, part of the ceremony was conducted before television cameras for the first time. Professor Koizumi was anxious that the imperial family get a face-lift, and this was the chance to bring two of its most attractive members into public view. Empress Nagako was furious that Michiko's wedding coach was pulled by six white horses, two more than had been allocated for her enthronement in 1928. Millions of Japanese watched on flickering black and white sets purchased for the occasion. As usual, the public made a game of guessing the total value of the wedding gifts, estimating them to be worth between 200 and 300 million dollars. (It is known that for the wedding of one of Hirohito's nieces in 1983, presents totalled $140 million, so for the wedding of the crown prince himself an estimate of double that was considered reasonable.) It is worth noting that these estimates of the value of wedding presents amounted to many times the emperor's net worth as reported to SCAP by the Imperial Household self-audit just a few years earlier.

As had been the case for Sadako's funeral and Akihito's investiture, the wedding ceremony was deliberately cloaked in Shinto mystification.

The young couple became instant media celebrities. 'Proudly touted', as Professor Irokawa remarked, 'as part of a prosperous Japan, a magnificent accessory and symbol to be admired.'

Akihito was easy to like and admire. Unlike his father, he was an excellent horseman, an enthusiastic tennis player, drove his own car, played a number of musical instruments and liked both classical music and jazz. He spoke fluent English, drank and smoked in moderation, and kept informed of world affairs through his own private channels. Although shy and habitually wary as any good Water Rooster would be, he had a polish and easy sophistication unmatched since Meiji. For her part, Michiko was also an athlete and a musician, urbane and cosmopolitan, as modern as it was possible for a

Japanese girl of her wealth and status to be in the late 1950s.

Straight away the young couple got down to the business of having a family. The following year their first son and Akihito's presumed heir took up residence in a new imperial nursery within the couple's new private dwelling on the imperial grounds. Before their wedding, Akihito had promised Michiko that their children would not be taken away, and would live with them. He was as good as his word. First-born Prince Naruhito was followed five years later by Prince Akishino, and in 1969 by Princess Nori.

Despite the outward appearance of family bliss, however, life in the great within was already being made extremely difficult for Michiko. From the moment of the wedding, rumours of strife between Michiko and her mother-in-law, Empress Nagako, made the rounds. Michiko's own ladies-in-waiting were handpicked by the Imperial Household, and owed their status and loyalty to Empress Nagako. Ladies at court regarded Michiko as 'a little upstart' who would always be an outsider. Instead of a companion and friend, the 24-year-old bride was assigned a 60-year-old chief lady-in-waiting, Makino Sumiko, the daughter of a baron. She was a virago, part of the old prewar court. Two other slightly younger women were also assigned to Michiko, one of them widely regarded as Nagako's personal spy. All the efforts of Michiko and Akihito to have the troublemaker removed came to nothing.

Michiko was always disarmingly frank. She wondered aloud in front of palace staff why her mother-in-law disliked her so much. Others pointed out that even if Empress Nagako did not personally encourage the behaviour of the ladies-in-waiting, she did nothing whatever to stop it. The sense of being completely power-less, even in the most intimate of circumstances, was corrosive.

Immediately after the end of the occupation in the 1950s, profound intolerance once again returned to Japan. Michiko was 'suspected' of indoctrinating her children with Bible stories. She was criticized for the length of her gloves, for breast-feeding her children, and not least for cutting a glamorous figure that eclipsed other ladies in the palace. After less than four years of marriage, the ebullient crown princess suddenly retired from view, suffering from nervous exhaustion and 'deep sadness'. Officially it was announced that she had gone into hospital because of 'great mental strain'. She was pregnant at the time, and her doctors insisted that the pregnancy be terminated. Later, there were similar episodes, and at one point she collapsed and was unable to speak. This profound malaise was far greater than could be attributed to any ordinary domestic problem. The intrusive and invasive living arrangements in the palace, and the caustic troublemaking of her mother-in-law and of her reptilian ladies-in-waiting, gradually reduced the crown princess to a mere shadow of her earlier vibrant self. She always held herself in rigid check, but the strain was clearly visible in her eyes.

Even Akihito's sisters followed their mother's lead in doing everything possible to make Michiko feel un-welcome. Princess Takako snapped: 'If Miss Michiko thinks that just because she's got a commoner's back-ground she can reform the imperial household she is very much mistaken.' This vicious backbiting and harassment became so notorious that it would cause great problems in the future, when it came time for Akihito to find brides for his own sons.

Akihito supported Michiko in every possible way, but there was a limit to what he could do. Empress Nagako was nothing if not implacable, and her coven of court ladies had nothing better to do than sharpen their nails. Akihito found small ways, which were extremely significant to the Japanese public, especially when they observed the royal couple holding hands in public. No one appreciated the magnitude of this gesture more than Michiko.

By contrast, it appears from her own statements that the ageing Emperor Hirohito was a warm presence in Michiko's life. 'The emperor was so generous and accepted me as I was. I was guided by him. I was reared by him.'

During the nineteen years from 1952 to 1971, Hirohito was rarely seen in public. After the death of Empress Mother Sadako, the Household Agency fell back into traditionalist hands. The Americans were gone and hardline Japanese conservatives were again firmly in power while their front men posed as democrats. Keeping the imperial family under wraps was the job of the Imperial Household organization. Its prewar bureaucracy of 10,000 individuals was reduced to 1,100 by SCAP, but the Imperial Household was never made accountable to the public. One of their main jobs was to police the public image of the royals. Occasional slip-ups occurred.

For example, there was panic in the Imperial Household in 1951 when Prince Mikasa, Hirohito's youngest brother, the most original and precedent-breaking of Sadako's four sons, told the Japanese press that he had been horrified to learn that 'Japanese soldiers had used living Chinese prisoners for bayonet practice'. He was immediately attacked by Tokyo's right-wing

Shogun meets Emperor: America's postwar viceroy in Japan, General
Douglas MacArthur, carefully staged this photo of his first meeting
with Emperor Hirohito. Although the emperor wore full diplomatic
dress, with top hat and tails, MacArthur greeted him in casual dress
with his collar open and hands on hips.

New Image Makers: as part of MacArthur's secret deal, Brigadier General Bonner Fellers (*above left*) arranged to whitewash Hirohito and save him from the gallows. Dressed like President Truman in baggy clothes and rumpled fedora, Hirohito posed for cameras planting rice in the palace garden (*above*). Fellers arranged for wartime prime minister General Tojo (*left*) to take all the blame for Pearl Harbor and the Pacific War. Prince Konoe (*below*) and other Japanese leaders who would not cooperate in this deception died in mysterious circumstances.

American Meddlers: former US president Herbert Hoover (here disembarking at Atsugi Air Base near Tokyo) led the secret American right-wing campaign to rescue Hirohito in return for financial and political advantages in postwar Japan. Hoover was part of a circle of wealthy American bankers and industrialists led for many years by Thomas Lamont of Morgan Bank (*below*). Hoover's choice for US ambassador to Japan in 1932 was Joseph Grew (*right*).

Unclean Hands: thanks to the secret manipulations of Hoover, MacArthur and Fellers, many of Japan's bloodstained wartime leaders escaped punishment to start a new political party – the LDP (Liberal Democratic Party). Financial brain behind the LDP was Kishi Nobusuke (*above left*). Party boss Hatoyama Ichiro (*above*) advocated beheading all critics of the regime. Bribery expert Tanaka Kakuei (*left*) showed the LDP how to buy off the postwar bureaucracy. Takeshita Noboru (*below*) remains LDP kingmaker today, despite being forced to resign as prime minister because of bribery scandals.

New Generation: one year after the Pacific War ended,
Hirohito and his family posed for the American media.
Twenty-seven years later, in 1973, another generation joined
the group (*below*). Seated, left to right, are: Crown Princess
Michiko, Crown Prince Akihito, Hirohito, Empress Nagako,
and Prince and Princess Hitachi. They are watching little
Princess Nori, future Crown Prince Naruhito and his younger
brother Prince Akishino play bagatelle.

New Emperor: free of wartime taint, Crown Prince Akihito emerged as a very different monarch. Part of the credit is due to his American Quaker tutor, Elizabeth Gray Vining (*below*). She took charge of Akihito when he was still 'Chabu Chan' ('Brown Pig') – the nickname given to him by his schoolmates at the Peers School (*above and left*).

Twilight of the Royals: Japan's imperial family has long modelled itself on the House of Windsor, but at the start of a new millennium both institutions are under scrutiny. The royal visit to Britain of Hirohito and Nagako in 1972 (*above*) was marred by bitter protests from war victims. In May 1998 the visit of Emperor Akihito and Empress Michiko (*right*) provoked similar demonstrations. The new Crown Prince Naruhito and Crown Princess Masako (*below*) face an uncertain future.

Imperial Fan: Emperor Hirohito was a lifelong fan of Mickey Mouse and other Disney characters. As a child he called his hobby horse Snow White (the Imperial Household Agency told outsiders it was called White Snow). When he made a state visit to America in 1975, Hirohito insisted on visiting Disneyland in California, where he signed Mickey's guestbook and purchased a Mickey Mouse watch, which he wore for the rest of his life. Hirohito died in 1989 and was buried with his Mickey Mouse watch still on his wrist.

press, who complained that he was providing ammunition for communist propaganda. The prince startled everyone with a second interview: 'I was very happy to read the criticism of my statement. I was happy because this was the first time I ever received such candid criticism. I have been used to flatterers . . . It is really wonderful, to me, to be criticized.'

There were still many arch conservatives in Japan who regarded his brother, Prince Chichibu, as 'the Red Prince', because he had supported the reform movement of the young officers in the 1930s and had been sympathetic to the plight of the downtrodden. Chichibu's role as head of Golden Lily during World War II was kept so secret that, ironically, he never got the credit he richly deserved for fuelling Japan's rapid postwar economic recovery.

In the spring of 1945 Chichibu had returned to Japan by submarine from the northern tip of Luzon, coughing up blood. His tuberculosis had been aggravated by the tropical climate and by recent weeks spent trekking overland to the coastal rendezvous, while General Yamashita fought his delaying action in the mountains. He was also suffering from malaria. In Japan, Chichibu was hospitalized, then moved back with Princess Chichibu to his country estate at Gotemba below Mount Fuji.

During the occupation, Prince and Princess Chichibu became darlings of the Western press. They were both fluent English speakers, they were a photogenic couple at ease with foreigners, a perfect example of the elegant humanity of the imperial family. Once while Princess Chichibu posed for photographs, the prince made everyone smile with the revelation that he was a big fan of Al Capp's comic strip, *L'il Abner*. But Chichibu's recuperation was a failure. After the death of Dowager

Empress Sadako, he went into sharp decline and died of tuberculosis on 4 January 1953, at the age of 50.

When news came that Chichibu was dying, Emperor Hirohito tried to leave the palace at midnight to visit him a last time (presumably to make peace with him) but was blocked by chamberlains. They did not block his departure the following morning because by then they knew that Chichibu was dead. Still, they prevented the emperor from attending his brother's funeral. Tokyo newspapers charged that the Imperial Household was back to its old tricks. 'Many Japanese', one said, 'are now trying to kick overboard everything forced on them during the occupation. The most conspicuous is an attempt to make the emperor a demigod again.'

Prince Takamatsu prevented the Imperial Household from overriding his brother's last wishes. There was only a simple funeral ceremony in which Chichibu's aides took the places normally filled by Shinto priests, his funeral bier was carried by thirty-four friends – all commoners – the imperial orchestra was obliged to play Beethoven, Grieg and Tchaikovsky, and for the first time the body of a Japanese imperial prince was cremated. In subsequent decades, Princess Chichibu became Japan's goodwill ambassador to Europe and North America. She made repeated visits to Britain and was honoured by Queen Elizabeth. When Prince Charles and Princess Diana went to Tokyo in 1990, they visited Princess Chichibu. She had known Charles since he was a pre-teen and he called her his 'Japanese grandmother'. She died in 1995 just weeks before her eighty-sixth birthday, having successfully avoided the worst strains and ordeals of imperial family life.

The black curtain of the Imperial Household was also lifted slightly in January 1966 when Crown Prince

Akihito's 42-year-old brother-in-law, Takatsukasa Toshimichi, was found dead with a nightclub hostess. The husband of Akihito's older sister, Princess Kazuko, he was a descendant of the Tokugawa shoguns and his father was chief priest of the Meiji Shrine. When they were married, Emperor Hirohito and Empress Nagako had broken with tradition and attended the ceremony. Japanese magazines were full of pictures of the newly-weds at home with the smiling princess cooking and being domestic. After the princess had a miscarriage, she was unable to have other children.

Like many Japanese salarymen, Takatsukasa, who worked in a museum, often passed his evenings in Tokyo nightclubs drinking with pretty hostesses. He became a regular at the Isaribi Club, always in the company of hostess Maeda Michiko. On 26 January 1966, after a long evening of drinking, he and Miss Maeda went to her apartment, conveniently only a few hundred yards from his own home. When he failed to report to work at the museum the next two days, his boss alerted the authorities. Police came to Miss Maeda's apartment where they found Takatsukasa and his lover dead from carbon monoxide poisoning. Officially, the deaths were called 'accidental', caused by fumes from a defective heater. But Tokyo gossips made it out to be a lovers' suicide. A grand chamberlain was quoted in the Tokyo press as saying, 'It is unbelievable. Takatsukasa and his wife seemed to be so happy.' A friend said Takatsukasa might have been depressed by the ordeal of being married into the imperial family.

Each member of the family responded to the ordeal differently. In all Akihito had five sisters and one brother. One, Princess Sachiko, died as an infant in 1928. First-born Princess Shigeko, who married Prince

371

Higashikuni's eldest son in 1943, had three sons and two daughters, then died of cancer in 1961 at the age of 35. Third-born Princess Kazuko married a son of Prince Takatsukasa. Fourth-born Princess Atsuko married Ikeda Takamasa, a millionaire rancher and son of a marquis. Akihito's only brother Prince Hitachi, born in 1935, spent his life waiting in the wings, doing good works. He married Hanako, a descendant of the Mori family of Choshu, who were still rich and influential. Finally, there was the baby of the family, Princess Takako, who made catty remarks about the crown princess. She married an aristocratic banker, Shimazu Hisanaga. Like royalty anywhere they were a mixed bag.

In 1971 Emperor Hirohito and Empress Nagako briefly reappeared in public to make a world tour. During the farewell ceremonies at Haneda Airport, broadcast live on Japanese television, Hirohito and Nagako moved down the line of well-wishers, greeting each in turn. When Empress Nagako came to Crown Princess Michiko she ignored her and moved on to Akihito. In Japan, a snub of this magnitude is like having someone urinate on you in public.

Half a century after his first visit to England as a youth, Hirohito during this world tour was again entertained by the House of Windsor, receiving the Order of the Garter from Queen Elizabeth II. War memories intruded. There had been no public declarations of remorse by the throne or, more importantly, by the Japanese government. If Western capitals were expecting a formal apology in 1971, the Household Agency was not prepared to let Hirohito utter it. In Denmark and the Netherlands there were anti-Japanese demonstrations. In England, angry protesters dug up and destroyed a sapling Hirohito had just planted.

In 1975 they made another foreign tour, this time to the United States, and were a public-relations triumph. President Gerald Ford and other politicians provided the warmest of welcomes, and the emperor laid a wreath at the Tomb of the Unknown Soldier, speaking of 'that unfortunate war, for which I am profoundly saddened'. The highlight of the trip for Hirohito was a visit to Disneyland, where he acquired the Mickey Mouse wristwatch that remained part of his imperial regalia ever after.

Life changed after the war for other royals as well. Not necessarily for the worse. Hirohito's uncle Prince Asaka, who was 'retired' after the atrocities at Nanking in 1937, went into business with the Tsutsumis, who were on their way to becoming the world's richest family. Asaka sold various of his palaces and properties to the Tsutsumi holding company called Seibu, which protected them from being confiscated by the Americans. The deal allowed him to continue to live in his palaces until his death, so his life of luxury continued unchanged. An enthusiastic golfer, Asaka was paid by the Tsutsumis to design the O-Hakone golf course. He died in 1981 at 93.

Prince Higashikuni was also on the list of men who might be purged by SCAP, and this made him nervous. So, like Prince Asaka, he took the precaution of selling his palaces to the Tsutsumis for safe keeping. (The Tsutsumis were benefactors to other members of the imperial family as well, also acquiring the palaces of Prince Takeda and Prince Kitashirakawa.) To emphasize how 'poor' he was, Higashikuni acquired a dressmaking business and a second-hand shop. For good measure, he set up his own religious sect, but it was soon banned by SCAP because of its blatantly ultra-right leanings.

Higashikuni remained on the blacklist for seven years. When the Americans finally left, he quietly resumed his playboy life, dying in January 1990 at the ripe old age of 102.

By contrast, Hirohito's surviving brothers, Prince Takamatsu and Prince Mikasa, lived quietly and attracted little attention. Takamatsu involved himself in cultural activities and served as president of the Japanese Red Cross. Occasionally, he gave interviews to the press. In 1976 he told the leading Japanese magazine *Bungei Shunju* that after the Battle of Midway in June 1942, 'I expected no victory.' Diagnosed with lung cancer, he died in February 1987 aged 82. His diaries, discovered in a warehouse after his death, and published at the insistence of his widow over the protests of the Imperial Household, revealed a man deeply pained by the absurdities of Japanese society and the birdcage role of the imperial family.

Prince Mikasa, the youngest and most refreshingly original of the four brothers, spent his postwar years as a scholar. Enrolling in Tokyo University, he studied archaeology, the Middle East and Semitic languages. For many years he taught on the faculty of Tokyo Women's Christian College, and was a visiting professor at the University of London. He and his wife had five children and eight grandchildren. Periodically, Mikasa would let slip a flash of extraordinary insight into the dark side of World War II, such as his long-suppressed essay on the horrors of Japanese Army atrocities he had witnessed personally.

By 1987, Hirohito himself was found to have terminal duodenal cancer, though the nature of his illness was kept from him. Less than two years later, he died on 7 January 1989, to be succeeded by Crown Prince Akihito.

Old ways die hard in Japan, where it can still cost your life to speak aloud. Drunks worry that they might make unpatriotic remarks while in their cups. More than forty years after the war, the mayor of Nagasaki, Motoshima Hitoshi, mildly criticized Hirohito's role in the war. He said only that the emperor (then 87 years old) bore *some* responsibility for World War II, 'as do all of us who lived in that period'. He added: 'I taught recruits to die for the emperor.' The mayor immediately received death threats, including bullets mailed to him, and shots were fired through his City Hall windows.

'If I had said what I said before the war,' the mayor observed, 'I think I would have been assassinated. So I think we are making progress.'

He spoke too soon. On 18 January 1990, one year after the death of Hirohito, the mayor was shot just above the heart by a member of an extremist group called the Righteous-Minded Academy. He was the first politician to be shot in Japan since World War II.

Part of Japan had moved into the high-tech future, but part of it was still stuck in the samurai past. The transition to a more modern Japan, and a more modern emperor, was not going to be easy for either. Japan's powerful gatekeepers would see to that.

CHAPTER 12

INVISIBLE MEN

In the last decades of the twentieth century, Japan looked to many people like a rich, healthy industrial society quaintly ruled by a Shinto emperor. But this was only a façade. While Emperor Hirohito grew old and Crown Prince Akihito waited patiently in the wings, Japan's financial oligarchs used the ruling Liberal Democratic Party (LDP) to undermine the constitution and completely corrupt the postwar government. In Japan, bribery became banal. Nothing could happen without bid-rigging and bribes. So much black money was in circulation from war loot, and property prices became so inflated by built-in bribes, that a bubble economy developed like a great abscess. Although during this period Hirohito seemed to be only a constitutional monarch like the Windsors, playing no visible role in the corruption, it would not have been possible without his collusion, as we shall see.

Hirohito coexisted comfortably with the LDP king-makers, as he had coexisted comfortably with the wartime militarists, because both the militarists and the kingmakers were just tools of the financial elite that had always controlled the throne – a single inbred family, above the law. Although Hirohito seemed to hold himself aloof, and to be preoccupied only with marine specimens, microscopes and Petri dishes, there were many filaments tying the throne to the LDP and the oligarchs. For example, the chief financial bulwark of the imperial family after the war – the supremely wealthy Tsutsumi clan – was also the chief financial bulwark of the LDP, and the primary backer of LDP kingmaker Takeshita Noboru. (Tsutsumi Yoshiaki once remarked, rather modestly as it turns out, 'When I speak, about a hundred politicians jump.')

During his forty-four years on the throne after the war, Hirohito's traditional position as the divine icon of the state still made any public criticism of the regime implicitly sacrilegious, and therefore extremely hazardous. Those who spoke out against corruption and collusion were denounced as communists and jailed. As time passed, opposition politicians grew silent, accepting hush-money from the LDP and becoming addicted to these bribes. Only after Hirohito's death in 1989 did the mask of god slip, exposing a regime so carelessly corrupt that it could no longer sustain its gross appetites.

This is not the first time Tokyo has been in serious trouble. Three times in the last 150 years, Japan has gone through convulsions to become a world power, only to bungle it – under Meiji, under Tojo and under Japan Inc. Why does this happen? What keeps going wrong?

The underlying issue is always power, which ultimately turns on wealth. If you dig beneath the opaque surface, financial leverage was always pre-eminent in Japan, as far back as Lord Soga in the fifth century, who grew richer than anyone else by acquiring a monopoly on imports from the Asian mainland. From Lord Soga to the Meiji Restoration, few emperors or shoguns were ever fully in charge – real power was exercised by their in-laws and counsellors, who used their excessive wealth to undermine adversaries and to control events behind the scenes. Japan's modern militarists – the progeny of General Yamagata – sustained themselves the same way, by secret alliances with financial cliques. Although Japan Inc. now has gone high-tech, power is still exercised behind the scenes by the same type of financial cliques, with the same ulterior motives of personal power and greed, using the same backroom deals and influence peddling. This corrupts the system and demoralizes and damages the country, the same way incest damages a family's genes and causes birth defects.

In today's power equation, the only thing that has changed from the past is that instead of sharing power to some extent with shoguns, samurai or militarists, the postwar financial cliques share power with nobody. Not with the emperor, who is only a magic wand, and not with elected politicians, who are only hand-puppets. Financial cliques are the most powerful forces in modern Japan. And they no longer have any serious rivals, no natural enemies. Remember, these cliques include not only financiers, bankers and heads of corporations, but underworld bosses. So invisibility is imperative. In their interlocking directorships, it is common for a member of one financial clique to be a member of several others. Distinguishing between the cliques is tricky, even for well-informed Japanese. If one set of bankers, financiers and gangsters meets each Tuesday in private rooms at a particular Tokyo restaurant and calls itself the Four Heavenly Kings, several of them will meet with a different set at a tea house on Thursday but call themselves the Twelve Divine Generals – or some other fanciful sobriquet from Asia's pantheon of magic immortals. This is how their networking controls Japan at all levels of industry and society. Marriages among them further strengthen these alliances.

What keeps Japan's financial elite – and their army of militant disciples – separate from the other 90 per cent of Japanese people is their exclusive right to play crooked games with the national wealth. Since the trivializing of World War II by Hoover, MacArthur and others who let Japan escape punishment, money has replaced bullets, but Japanese still denominate bribes and election costs in terms of 'bullets' (a 'bullet' is 100 million yen, or roughly 800,000 dollars). These days, instead of bribing militarists, Japan's money cliques use the LDP to bribe the government bureaucracy.

The good news is that fear of ultra-nationalist violence is diminishing. The death sanction remains implicit in Japan, but is fading. The pretence of racial superiority and national consensus has frayed around the edges. With communism in collapse, the far right can no longer use fear of the far left to ward off social revolution and expect to be taken seriously.

The bad news is that corruption has become universal, reckless and out of control – so reckless that the oligarchs have fouled their own nest. As a result, Japan's economy is in a severe crisis, which affects profits. Never having reformed anything before, the oligarchs do not know how to proceed. Reform is to them such a repugnant idea that there is serious doubt whether they can fix their banking system and save Japan from Russian-style economic collapse. Even to admit that they have the power to reform frightens them. In Japan, a saying goes, it is better not to admit anything. The last thing powerful men in Japan want is for anyone openly to acknowledge their power, because that would make them vulnerable to scrutiny. It is when they forget this lesson that they get into serious trouble.

The invisibility of Japan's 'invisible men' is based on the ancient money-lenders' axiom: 'All trouble comes from the mouth.' In the 1930s, author John Gunther was fascinated by them. 'I had not been in Japan 20 minutes before I heard a strange use of the word *they*. *They*, I was told, had decided . . . recent changes in policy; *they* had decided that the country should do this and not that. *They* had arranged the appointment of the . . . prime minister.'

Although greed has always been a fundamental force in Japanese society, as it is everywhere, its existence there is disguised, hidden and denied to a remarkable degree. In Japan the key to success is the *invisible* exercise of self-interest, whether you are a financier, a politician, a gangster or a bureaucrat. General Yamagata, the spider who wove much of this web together in modern times, was always careful to characterize himself as only a simple soldier. This is the Japanese way.

Today, the government of Japan still actively supports the invisible exercise of power. Accountability is almost non-existent. It was not supposed to be that way. The postwar political system was supposed to be visible, accountable and answerable to the people. The bureaucracy was to be a meritocracy immune to blandishment and bribery. The judiciary was to exercise strict accountability over any politicians, bureaucrats or businessmen who attempted to subvert the new system.

This presupposed that Japan would operate in a rational way, like urban traffic in which vehicles share junctions, crossroads and roundabouts without crashes or 'road rage'. By accepting certain rules of the road, different groups in the new Japan would alternate in political power as they do in Europe or North America.

Each group would lose power only temporarily, so opposing groups would be willing to accept supervision from the voters, the bureaucracy, the courts and the media.

In such a rational system, everyone submits to the rules because the rules apply equally to all, including those temporarily in power and those temporarily out of power. This levels the playing field. However, during the US occupation, Japan's oligarchs successfully dodged a rational political system, and kept power exclusively to themselves by setting up single-party rule dominated by the LDP.

Using black money provided by the oligarchs, the LDP skilfully subverted smaller parties with huge sums of black money, addicting them to bribes. Rather than a rational transfer of power from party to party, the LDP held on to power exclusively for decades. During that period, there was only the transfer of financial leverage from one kingmaking faction to another. Although these LDP factions have their own headquarters, sources of funds, candidates for prime minister, shadow cabinets and so forth, they all adhere to the same ultra-conservative policies typical of Japan before World War II. On key votes, all these LDP factions cooperate to keep the party in exclusive control of Japan. Money provides the superglue. And the Japanese people are left without any political counterbalance, and without any means of scolding the LDP.

The inside story of the LDP is truly eye-opening. It was established after the war with huge infusions of black money from Japan's ultra-conservative underworld, drawing on secret stocks of war loot. Since then, acting for the oligarchs, the LDP has used massive quantities of black money – much of it from the underworld – to buy off the bureaucracy, the judiciary and commercial rivals. This has been revealed in the Japanese press during a number of spectacular scandals over the decades that have rocked the LDP to its foundations, putting the party briefly into eclipse in the mid-1990s. But the LDP penetrates so deep into the organic tissue of Japanese life, and owns so many people, that it has regenerative power like the monster in the film *Alien*. Cut off all its heads and all its tentacles, pour acid over it, burn it, blast it, radiate it, and it will be back an hour later in a new manifestation.

One scholar called the Japanese legal system the rule *by* law, rather than the rule *of* law. This means that the law is used to block ordinary people from getting anything done, while the elite remains above the law, exempt from all the rules that frustrate everyone else. The elite avoid trouble in advance by backroom conciliation, or deal-making outside the rule of law. This occurs among all four components of the elite – bureaucracy, politicians, big money and the underworld – who resolve their disputes in advance and out of sight *before* they provoke embarrassment. So rarely does trouble erupt into the open in Japan that the appearance of consensus is maintained to an extraordinary degree. This is why everything seemed so calm in Japan during Emperor Hirohito's last three decades. He kept the bland mask in place, while bureaucrats, politicians, money cliques and underworld colluded happily in 'the Japanese Way'.

Whenever disputes *are* exposed to public scrutiny, a scapegoat is quickly chosen by the same process of conciliation; he weeps before the news cameras, resigns his post and goes off to enjoy the retirement he was guaranteed in return for taking the blame. Finance ministers typically take a dive several times in the course of their careers. These periodic exposures of 'the evils of the system' have a cathartic function, taking the place of genuine reform. The system never changes, and scandal does not mean that a power-broker loses his leverage for long. His brief exposure to the light only temporarily reduces his power, like a vampire weakened by the flame of a torch before he slips back into his crypt. A perfect example was LDP kingmaker Takeshita Noboru, whose vanity led him to come out of the closet and assume the post of prime minister, only to be embarrassed into resigning in 1989 by the sensational 'Recruit' scandal. In this scandal a real estate firm of that name provided unlisted shares to politicians and bureaucrats, including Prime Minister Takeshita, enabling them to make huge profits reselling the shares on the open market. This led to the temporary collapse of the LDP. But after three years of confusion, in which other political parties tried and failed to find a wooden stake big enough to drive into its heart, the LDP revived and Takeshita resumed his kingmaking from behind a lightproof black curtain. He is still there a decade later.

This lack of sunlight provides the septic environment suitable for the structural corruption adored by Japanese fixers. Corruption is such a familiar part of the system that only in rare moments like the Recruit or the Lockheed scandal does it attract much public outrage. Japanese propagandists claim that such scandals are the exception, and that their nation is held together by ancient traditions, racial homogeneity, imperial legacy and a virtuous bureaucracy. In fact, the scandals reveal a tightly controlled, highly sophisticated system of corruption with the sole purpose of keeping the national wealth inside a very small circle, excluding all others.

Although most Japanese feel that their politicians do not represent them in any way, LDP politicians have made themselves useful as doorkeepers and pimps. In return for lavish campaign contributions they act as intermediaries and bagmen between financial cliques and government bureaucrats. In this way, they create the illusion of democracy. In Japan 'democracy' simply means that bribes are funnelled through elected politicians rather than paid directly, as they were in the days before 'democracy'.

How did Hirohito figure in all of this? During the first post-surrender election campaign, in 1946, Liberal Party leader Hatoyama Ichiro had made it clear that any vote against the Liberal Party (precursor to the LDP) was a vote against the emperor – implicitly invoking the death sanction. Although (officially) the emperor had ceased to be sacred, Hatoyama hammered home the argument that Hirohito remained the head of the national family. Most Japanese remembered that in 1925 Hatoyama was the education minister who backed the death penalty for even the vaguest insult of the emperor. So in 1946 they got the message loud and clear.

Hatoyama's Liberal Party ('liberal' referring only to its bribery) was financed by a huge grant from Japan's top underworld godfather, Kodama Yoshio, just before Kodama was put in Sugamo prison as a class-A war criminal. Using intimidation and unlimited underworld funds, the Liberal Party won an easy victory. Hatoyama was then fingered by enemies, who explained to the Americans what kind of person he really was, and General MacArthur had no choice but to lock him up for the duration. This cost Hatoyama his chance to be Japan's first 'elected' postwar prime minister. Before going to prison he arranged for Joe Grew's old friend Foreign Minister Yoshida to take over the Liberal Party, to serve as prime minister in his place.

When the Americans left in 1952, Hatoyama was free to resume politics. He and his underworld allies started the Democratic Party as a rival to his old Liberal Party, and quickly toppled Yoshida from office. Hatoyama assumed the prime minister's post himself in 1954. With more funding from godfather Kodama, Hatoyama then merged the Democratic Party with the Liberal Party and other factions to create the Liberal Democratic Party (LDP), which Japanese are fond of pointing out is not liberal, democratic or a party. Since then, the LDP has ruled Japan for the remainder of the century, over four decades, with just the one brief interruption during the Recruit scandal.

In 1954, Prime Minister Hatoyama and his LDP cronies immediately set about their appointed task of seducing Japan's postwar government. Because the US occupation had needed help to run Japan day by day, the government bureaucracy had been allowed to continue functioning undisturbed after the war. It was not restructured, and was the only part of the prewar machine to survive completely intact, acquiring much of SCAP's authority and cachet along the way. By the time the occupation ended, the bureaucracy in Tokyo was the single most powerful arm of the Japanese government, a kingdom unto itself. In theory alone was it a meritocracy. The bureaucrats cleverly enlarged their power by creating byzantine rules that completely immobilized society. Nothing could be done in Japan without first paying bribes to bureaucrats to obtain permission to bypass the rules. The layers upon layers of regulations so typical of Japanese life are there for a purpose: only the richest and most powerful can get anything done, using bribery. Well-placed bureaucrats allow certain individuals, companies, politicians, gangsters or financiers to bypass the rules in return for promotions, bribes or their guaranteed transfer into top executive posts after retiring from the government.

Film director Itami Juzo explained, 'Unlike politicians, bureaucrats cannot be voted out of office. We may be unhappy about the bureaucrats, but . . . we are powerless to influence this [bureaucratic institution], no matter how poorly it serves us.'

To say that the oligarchs and the LDP seduced the bureaucracy is not entirely accurate. The bureaucracy could not get its clothes off fast enough, and was an enthusiastic and vigorous partner in bed. It set up the simple ground rules by which it could be corrupted. The rest was easy for the LDP.

To see how it works, all we have to do is examine the amazing careers of three LDP kingmakers. Each one began his career as an 'invisible man'. Then each materialized in front of our eyes and self-immolated, like Takeshita, because his inflated ego would no longer permit him to remain in the background. The three kingmakers we have chosen for this purpose are Kishi Nobusuke, Tanaka Kakuei and Kanemaru Shin. They are not the only mischievous LDP politicians, but their stories form a single thread that is easy to follow. Together with underworld godfather Kodama and party-founder Hatoyama, these were the great political vampires of postwar Japan. They (not the emperor) had the last word in picking prime ministers and allocating cabinet posts. No prime minister from 1946 to 1993 held his job without the blessing of one of them.

Kishi personally bridged the prewar and postwar epochs, going from deal-making for the Kwantung Army in Manchuria to deal-making for Japan Inc. without breaking stride. His story is an object lesson in the cross-dressing of high finance.

Physically, he resembled a salamander. Born Sato Nobusuke in 1896 in Choshu (now called Yamaguchi Prefecture), he was so quick-witted and clever that he was adopted by a paternal uncle bearing the Kishi name. His brothers stayed at home and used the Sato name. One brother, Sato Eisaku, became a postwar finance minister and LDP prime minister. Eldest brother Sato Ichiro became an admiral.

After Tokyo University, Kishi Nobusuke got a job in the Ministry of Commerce and Industry filing policy papers and correspondence, which gave him insider information. During the Great Depression his star rose quickly when he showed rich investors how easy it was to gobble up and loot small firms that were going under. He became a wizard in the creation of cartels and trusts. Japan's seizure of Manchuria in 1931 gave him his big chance. He was sent there to investigate industrial possibilities. He made friends with General Tojo, chief of the secret police in Manchuria, and showed Tojo how the army could squeeze private shareholders out of the state-controlled South Manchurian Railroad Company (SMRC). The SMRC had all the rights to exploit Manchu railways, harbours, ports, mines, oil, hotels, transport and communication, and was already one of the largest capital-resource units in the world. Fortuitously, the president of the SMRC was Kishi's uncle by marriage. Kishi showed his uncle how the SMRC could greatly increase its profits if the Kwantung Army and the Japanese underworld used state terror to bring Manchuria into submission. (In other words, Kishi promoted the use of terror and extortion to advance the Japanese Army's wealth in Manchuria.) He was able

387

to arrange for army-controlled Manchuria to enjoy the most modern administrative skills by bringing in one of Japan's most successful new *zaibatsu,* Nissan, which was headed by another of Kishi's uncles. By putting his two uncles together with General Tojo, Kishi wove together the interests of politics, army, business and gangsters, in a way that would have deeply impressed Hitler and Stalin. Manchuria under Kishi also became the prime source of heroin in Asia. He made the Kwantung Army so rich that it could act independently of Tokyo, and could go off to start the China War on its own. Thanks in large measure to Kishi, General Tojo was such a success that he became the Kwantung Army's chief of staff and eventually Japan's wartime dictator. So we have Kishi to thank for many things.

During the war Kishi was promoted to minister of commerce and industry in Tokyo, and also served Tojo as vice-minister of munitions. After Japan's surrender, Kishi was jailed in Sugamo prison on charges of looting China and Manchuria, theft of private assets and enslaving thousands to work in factories and mines. On the eve of his arrest, Kishi received a telegram from a crony: 'Americans aren't likely to convict and execute you so advise don't do anything rash.' (Don't admit to anything.)

In Sugamo prison, Kishi mingled with a who's who of politicians, businessmen, bureaucrats and outlaws. Among his cellmates were underworld godfather Kodama and the extremist future founder of the LDP, Hatoyama, who favoured beheading all political opponents. So Sugamo prison was a finishing school for scoundrels. During the war, Kodama, the most famous of Japan's tattooed outlaws the *yakuza*, had made billions sidetracking war loot, and in 1945 was the richest man in Japan after the emperor. Kodama had already paid for the founding of the Liberal Party, and now he offered to found another party for Hatoyama, if Hatoyama agreed to let Kishi handle all the finances. Hatoyama would be leader of the new Democratic Party, but Kishi would be the money man and backroom deal-maker. They agreed, and Kodama turned over millions of dollars to set up a slush-fund. This was only a drop in the bucket. SCAP estimated Kodama's worth in 1945 to be $13.5 billion (probably only a small portion of the actual total). Kodama only admitted publicly to having $200 million, and generously offered to give all of that to SCAP to split between America's friend, General-issimo Chiang Kai-shek, and the Counter-Intelligence Corps (CIC), a forerunner of the CIA. When Washington secretly accepted Kodama's offer, Kodama and Kishi were quietly released from Sugamo and were never prosecuted for their leading roles in the dark side of the war. The American CIC was so appreciative of this $200 million bribe that Kodama was later hired as an expert on Red-bashing during the Korean War. He remained on the CIA payroll until the Lockheed scandal in the 1970s.

After his release from Sugamo, Kishi – backed by Kodama's black money and using Hatoyama's well-oiled political network – established himself as one of Japan's first great postwar kingmakers. Meanwhile, his brother Sato Eisaku had risen to be chief secretary to Prime Minister Yoshida. When the new Liberal Democratic Party came into existence, it was able to buy a substantial majority in the Diet, thus preventing tiny rivals from ever coming to power. Having bought control of parliament, the LDP could claim that it was Japan's supreme moral authority next to the emperor.

So long as he remained in the background, Kishi's power was unchallenged, but when he let his friends (or his enemies) encourage him to become prime minister (1957–60), he got into trouble immediately. His call for the rearmament of Japan provoked violent protests in Tokyo. Embarrassed, he resigned. Behind the scenes once more, he remained a leading fixer for years thereafter, but in gradual decline. This should have been a lesson for others like him. It was and it wasn't.

One of his protégés was ready to step into Kishi's shoes. Tanaka Kakuei was a more robust and charismatic man. Born in 1918 with dirt already under his nails, Tanaka never finished high school. His father was a bankrupt cattle broker. Poor as he was, Tanaka was a charmer with a head for numbers. Taking a draughting course at night school, he got a job as a draughtsman, errand-boy and part-time accountant at a Tokyo architectural firm. There he met Viscount Okochi Masatoshi, boss of a conglomerate called Riken Group, which was scooping up money from wartime military contracts. (During the Pacific War, Viscount Okochi was an adviser on ordnance production, while Kishi was vice-minister of munitions; there was therefore a direct link between them.)

The viscount took a huge liking to the garrulous young Tanaka. He set Tanaka up for life by arranging for him to marry a rich divorcee, rescuing her from an impossible social situation in Japan. The divorcee, Sakamoto Hana, was seven years older than Tanaka, but she was also the daughter of a very wealthy and grateful man, the ailing owner of a construction company. As part of the marriage deal, Tanaka inherited his father-in-law's company. He renamed it Tanaka Construction, and in only four years, while most Japanese were losing everything in fire-bombing, Tanaka became a dollar millionaire many times over, on his way to becoming one of the richest men in Japan. Viscount Okochi saw to it that Tanaka won hugely inflated military contracts. These included building underground complexes for the defence of Japan in case of Allied invasion, which then became vaults for war loot and hidden documents. Early in 1945, Viscount Okochi was ordered to transfer a piston-ring factory to Korea to put it out of the range of American bombers. Okochi gave the job to Tanaka, who received a $73 million voucher as payment in advance. Learning privately of the emperor's decision to surrender – inside information passed to him privately by Kishi and Okochi – Tanaka hurried to a Japanese bank in Korea where he had a friend, and cashed in his voucher for some of Golden Lily's gold bars, walking away with a fortune. The war's end made it unnecessary to move the piston-ring factory, so he was paid $73 million for nothing. In the confusion, he did not have to account for it.

Tanaka spent some of this windfall on an $80,000 contribution to the new Liberal Party, which launched him on his political career. By 1947, he had won a seat in the Diet. Barely a year later, he was arrested for taking a bribe. He ran his second election campaign from jail and won. Cleared of the bribery charge, he went on to a brilliant political career corrupting the very bureaucrats who had ordered his arrest.

Tanaka recognized that bureaucrats were the biggest source of money in postwar Japan, because they determined which construction companies were awarded fat public-works infrastructure projects. So he devoted himself to cultivating bureaucrats. When his patron Kishi became prime minister in 1957 he made Tanaka minister of posts. In Japan, rather like in Britain, the postal system is also a national bank, providing postal giro accounts for millions of citizens. The postwar government had introduced a Fiscal Investment Loan Plan that allowed bureaucrats to dip into this huge postal savings system and use the funds entirely at their discretion. In effect this gave the government a second annual budget, but one that could be used in ways that did not require Diet approval. Tanaka's tenure as minister of posts endeared him to all manner of bureaucrats who enriched themselves by dipping into the giro, stealing the savings of ordinary people. These bureaucrats could be counted on to return Tanaka's favours.

Tanaka's flair for creative accounting attracted so much admiration that in 1962 the high-school drop-out was named minister of finance in the Ikeda government, a post he held for three years. Normally, the Ministry of Finance is run by career bureaucrats. But Tanaka took personal control of all central-government subsidies for local governments, and all national and local expenditures for public works. (Japan's national and local governments spend about $400 billion on public works each year, making this an immensely lucrative scam.) Thanks to Tanaka, construction companies enjoyed a boom in government business, and became the single biggest source of kickbacks to the LDP slush-fund.

The incest between the LDP and Japan's building contractors is built on rigged bids. Before a construction company can bid on a public-works project, it must first grease a powerful politician. All nominated contractors meet in advance to decide which one will get the job, and what the winning bid should be. All the contractors know they will get to work on a government project sooner or later so they cooperate in rigging the bid. Rival

392

bidders set their bids well above the designated winner. There are laws covering the formal authorization of contractors, but bureaucrats play along. The committee that picks the winning bid also plays along. For a big public-works project like a highway, the politician responsible for securing it may get a kickback of 1 billion yen (roughly $8.3 million) from a single company.

Bribes aside, senior bureaucrats get their ultimate reward by knowing they can retire to a top post in private industry, with a fat salary and stock options, for doing nothing but playing golf. Opposition politicians do not protest because many of them are trying to get elected with the help of building contractors. Also, the LDP is the biggest source of bribes to its political opponents. Japan's Socialist Party has been completely neutered by its dependence on LDP bribes.

Tanaka did so many favours, and allowed so many fat cats to get around currency controls, that his personal wealth grew at an astonishing rate. He became a king-maker in his own right, choosing cabinet ministers from his own faction. The Tanaka faction became the largest in the LDP. His key lieutenants were Takeshita and Kanemaru.

If Kishi invented money politics in postwar Japan, it was Tanaka who brought bribery to perfection. He then carried it to the international stage when he headed the Ministry of International Trade and Industry (MITI), which worked with Japanese corporations to expand their global clout dramatically. Then, in 1972, aged 54, his ego got the better of him, and Tanaka came out from behind the curtain to become Japan's most colourful prime minister of the twentieth century. This broke the rule of invisibility. Barely two years later he was forced to resign under a cloud.

A team of Japanese investigative journalists published an exposé of Tanaka's corruption, causing such a storm that he had to claim ill-health and step down as prime minister. He was not prosecuted, and after a few months it looked like he would be able to continue as kingmaker behind the scenes the way Kishi had. But in February 1976, the US Senate Foreign Relations Committee began hearings in the Lockheed bribery scandal, the biggest foreign bribery case in Japan since Germany's Siemens bribed the Japanese Navy in 1914. It emerged that Lockheed had paid huge bribes to Japanese executives and government officials – including the prime minister – to secure sales of its new airliner to All Nippon Airways (ANA) in preference to planes from Boeing or McDonnell-Douglas. More embarrassing for the Americans, the pipeline for these giant bribes was godfather Kodama, acting on behalf of the CIA.

Since 1958, Kodama had been on a fat retainer from the CIA and from Lockheed. He had also arranged for Japan to buy 230 Lockheed F-104 Starfighters.

Tanaka was arrested in July 1976, and indicted for accepting $2 million in bribes from Lockheed. While the trial dragged on for seven years, Tanaka chose three prime ministers. Godfather Kodama's own trial ended prematurely when he became ill. He died in January 1984. Tanaka was convicted in October 1983, fined $4.4 million (not a big sum for him) and sentenced to four years in prison. He had spent over $8 million on his defence. With typical bravado he ran for re-election to the Diet that December and was returned for the fifteenth time. He remained Japan's most powerful politician until February 1985, when he suffered a cerebral haemorrhage. He died in December 1993.

Tanaka's backroom partner and successor, Kanemaru

Shin (1914–96), never made the mistake of becoming prime minister, although he did go as far as deputy prime minister before pulling back. He wisely remained a back-room manipulator, ranked as Japan's number-one fixer. Son of a sake brewer, the young Kanemaru became a courier for the gangsters and shady businessmen who carried out Kishi's economic plans in occupied Manchuria and north China. After World War II he reappeared as one of Kishi's bagmen, distributing large sums of money in bribes and kickbacks. He came out of the woodwork slightly in 1958, when he was elected to the Diet while Kishi was prime minister. In all, Kanemaru was re-elected to the Diet twelve times, but he always remained an invisible man. Tanaka once appointed him minister of construction, but Kanemaru wisely kept out of sight.

Kanemaru looked after the secret financial side of the LDP. When huge building contracts were to be opened for bids, Kanemaru would canvass prospective contractors who were big contributors to the LDP. By colluding with cabinet ministers and top bureaucrats, Kanemaru would fix it so the contract would be awarded to the company of his choice. The winning contractor kicked back 2 or 3 per cent of the gross to Kanemaru, and also donated millions of dollars to the LDP slush-fund, much of it kept in cash in several wall-safes at Kanemaru's home.

He understood greed better than most men. Instead of fighting the LDP's political opponents, he bought them. But in 1992 Kanemaru began to lose it. Whether out of fatigue, indifference or arrogance, he became careless, allowing the public to get a glimpse of the role gangsters played in LDP operations. The Recruit scandal exposed the LDP's payoffs to politicians, bureaucrats, businessmen and gangsters, ultimately forcing the resignation of Prime Minister Takeshita and the near collapse of the LDP. Kanemaru avoided any personal taint from the Recruit scandal or earlier scandals. His downfall was caused by the next one – the Sagawa parcel-delivery scandal. In August 1992, prosecutors revealed that Sagawa's boss had confessed to paying Kanemaru half a billion yen (over $4 million) just before the 1990 general election. Sagawa had also passed $4 million in bribes to the LDP through Kanemaru. It emerged that, over the years, Sagawa alone had spent billions of dollars on influence peddling. Where did a parcel-delivery company get such money? The scale of payoffs was so monumental that the Japanese public became spellbound. Next came the revelation that Sagawa was closely tied to businesses run by Japanese gangsters in occupied China during World War II. The difference between it and other courier services lay in what was delivered in the parcels. Dark vestigial memories of the rape of Asia, of plunder, of gangsters and secret police, of POWs buried alive to guard vaults of gold bullion, and of princes and politicians who never were punished, caused a wave of national revulsion. On 27 August 1992, Kanemaru resigned as deputy prime minister and as head of the old Tanaka faction of the LDP. He was fined a mere $1,820 – equal to a major Tokyo traffic fine – without even being interviewed by the prosecutors. In November 1992, he checked into a hospital, hoping in this time-honoured fashion to dodge further prosecution.

Three months later he was arrested on charges of tax evasion. Thanks to spy satellite interception of microwave telephone conversations, details of his secret life had been assembled painstakingly by enemies of the LDP. In a raid on his home, Japanese tax authorities found a hoard worth $51 million. This included 220 pounds of tiny gift-size gold bars, cash and money orders. In the spring of 1996, before Kanemaru's trial was concluded, he died, and all charges were dropped.

Another player in this unfolding drama was Ozawa Ichiro, a protégé of Kanemaru and Takeshita, who showed so much promise that he was secretly cultivated by Washington. Just before the LDP crisis that led to Kanemaru's downfall, Ozawa retired suddenly from the LDP claiming heart trouble. Journalists later speculated that Ozawa was removing himself to a safe distance because he knew what was coming. Soon afterwards, the scandals broke, leading to the downfall of Kanemaru, the near downfall of Takeshita, and the police raid on Kanemaru's house that clearly involved elegant electronic surveillance available only to the American National Security Agency. It looked like a palace coup designed to dislodge the LDP and – for optimists – to open up Japanese politics. A little later, Ozawa miraculously recovered from his political illness and emerged as a leader of the 'opposition' to the LDP. He started his own Liberal Party (one of the least liberal in Japan), and received outstanding media coverage from America. To his credit, Ozawa has since remained free of any taint of corruption, although he was a deft moneyman and backroom intriguer.

The collapse of the LDP did inspire hope of a change, but it was shortlived. Tragically, neither Ozawa nor any other opposition leader was able to take advantage of this golden moment. There was a scramble to form new parties, and new leaders played musical chairs. But nobody had the machine or the deep pockets to take the place of the LDP. After decades of addiction to LDP hard candy, most opposition politicians were toothless. Even the Socialists had become dependent on LDP handouts. So before too many months had passed, the LDP was back in power, and Takeshita was again its top king-maker.

Can anything be done to stem this gross abuse of power? Only a draconian revision of the political system and implementation of harsh new laws can stop such corruption. That's not likely to happen unless the oligarchs themselves get behind it, out of self-interest.

Today, the deepest pockets in Japan belong to the Tsutsumi family, who have been one of the main supports of the LDP since its founding. They have been doing big favours for the imperial family since the 1920s. In the 1980s the head of the family, Tsutsumi Yoshiaki, was estimated to have a personal fortune of some $22 billion, the world's largest private fortune before Bill Gates topped it in the 1990s. (However, the way wealth is reported in America and the way it is hidden in Japan would imply that Gates still has a way to go before he really surpasses Tsutsumi.)

The Tsutsumis, to whom much of the imperial family's palaces and real estate were conveyed during the occupation, are said to own one-sixth of the entire landmass of Japan. They got their start in the chaos following the great Kanto earthquake of 1923. Founding patriarch Tsutsumi Yasujiro had tried to get rich during World War I, when Japanese firms made a lot of money in Asia while the Great Powers were preoccupied in Europe. But the ships Tsutsumi bought were sunk. The Kanto earth-quake, however, caused so much destruction that a building boom followed, financed by foreign loans from Morgan and other banks, and Tsutsumi Yasujiro made his first fortune in property speculation and development during the recovery. He was elected to parliament in

1924 as a supporter of the extremist Hatoyama. In the late 1920s Tsutsumi made desirable properties available to Prince Asaka, Prince Higashikuni and other imperial princes, enabling them to build stylish new residences, while tying them to the Tsutsumi clan. During the rise of the militarists in the 1930s Tsutsumi expanded into stores, supermarkets, railways and property speculation. He was one of those who benefited from young Kishi's early moneymaking scams.

At the end of World War II, Tsutsumi was on the Allied list of war profiteers to be purged, and whose web of corporations must be dissolved. How he managed to escape purging, and to preserve his corporations intact, remains a mystery. But he came out of the war with the right connections and seemingly limitless resources, making continual acquisitions of choice property while everybody else seemed to be stumbling around looking for food and firewood.

At the end of the war, while Emperor Hirohito and everyone else in the imperial family were trying to appear bankrupt, Prince Asaka sold his opulent neo-classic country villa to the Tsutsumi family. They tucked it into their hotel chain and renamed it the Sengataki Prince Hotel, but kept it reserved as the emperor's unofficial summer palace. Prince Asaka also sold his main palace to the Tsutsumis, but never moved out.

Other imperial princes also sold their palaces to the Tsutsumis. They were rich men, and had been rich all their lives, but now SCAP cut them off from their lifetime stipends. Each imperial prince was given a huge golden handshake (Prince Asaka personally received $800,000). But each prince also faced a hefty tax bill, payable in October 1947. Tsutsumi Yasujiro, a personal friend to each of them, came to the rescue, bought their palaces and mansions, and relieved them of their tax burdens as well. There was no competitive bidding. In all, Tsutsumi bought the Tokyo palaces and mansions of all eleven families of collateral princes who became commoners in 1947 when SCAP ended the nobility. Other rich Japanese also purchased imperial properties during this period of transition, but not one remotely approached Tsutsumi in the scale and depth by which he bound and obligated the imperial family to the Tsutsumi clan.

This was only the start of his buying spree. Much of the real estate amassed over eight centuries by the Tokugawa shoguns, confiscated from them in 1868 and transferred to the imperial family, ultimately ended up in the Tsutsumi portfolio after World War II. The Tsutsumis are uniquely powerful politically as well. Tsutsumi Yasujiro was one of Hatoyama's biggest backers when godfather Kodama's underworld money and Kishi's brains were used to combine the Democratic Party and the Liberal Party into the LDP. Re-elected to the Diet for the twelfth time, Tsutsumi was named speaker of the house in 1953 just in time to help propel Hatoyama into the prime minister's post the next year. When Yasujiro died, his son Yoshiaki took his place as one of the biggest backers of the LDP, benefiting from the rigged public-works deals arranged by Kishi, Tanaka and Kanemaru. Tsutsumi's Seibu Group grew to include over one hundred companies in Japan, with six overseas subsidiaries and forty-five affiliated foreign companies.

Because they own or control so much of what was once imperial property, the Tsutsumis occupy a unique position of leverage with the dynasty. The historical precedents for this go back to the Sogas and the

Fujiwaras over the last fifteen centuries. History has come full circle. Unlike the Sogas and the Fujiwaras, there have been no marital ties so far between the Tsutsumis and the dynasty. But that could change. The young heir to the great family fortune, Tsutsumi Masatoshi, was considered the most likely future husband for Crown Prince Akihito's only daughter, Princess Nori. Born in 1969, she was educated entirely in Japan. As the only imperial princess of her generation, she was a catch. She met Tsutsumi Masatoshi during a holiday at the Tsutsumi resort of Karuizawa. But Masatoshi seemed disinterested, devoting most of his time to skateboarding. Ordinary Japanese called him 'wild', 'useless' and 'utterly lacking in social grace'. But as the son of one of the richest men in the world and of the most powerful man in Japan, such things could be overlooked. The Tsutsumi family were often splashed by scandal of a very superficial kind. In a country where mistresses are commonplace, especially among the rich, Tsutsumi men were famous for showing off their lovers in public. Masatoshi's father was the son of a concubine, and enjoyed heavily publicized liaisons with Japan's most beautiful screen stars.

From a public-relations viewpoint, the difficulty for the imperial family was not mistresses but the embarrassing fact that the Tsutsumis were one of the most prominent sources of money for the LDP at a time when the LDP was repeatedly exposed for bottomless corruption, ties to the underworld and the rape of Asia. It was said that Masatoshi's father held the entire LDP in the palm of one hand. Since he held so much imperial property in his other palm, one could not escape drawing conclusions about these interlocking relationships, including the throne.

Surprisingly, for one of the world's richest men and his family, the Tsutsumi clan remains practically invisible. Nobody talks about them, their name rarely appears in print outside Japan, and then only in connection with sport. As Japan's most powerful oligarch, Tsutsumi Yoshiaki would logically appear in the excellent nine-volume *Kodansha Encyclopedia of Japan* published in 1983. But he is not mentioned in it once. There are two brief entries on his Seibu Group and railways, but neither entry mentions a Tsutsumi by name.

Invisible men, as we have seen, try to remain invisible. When Kishi, Tanaka and Kanemaru stopped being invisible, they fell from grace. The same could happen to the Tsutsumis because of a different scandal, over allegations of bribery in the Olympic Games. In 1988, Tsutsumi Yoshiaki decided that Japan would host the 1998 Winter Olympics, and the Olympic City would be Nagano – in the mountains north of Tokyo near the huge Matsushiro underground imperial bunker where so much of the war loot was said to have been hidden. He was a senior member of the Japan Olympic Committee, and the most influential figure in Japanese sport. At the time, Nagano was a dingy, old-fashioned town three hours by slow train from Tokyo. Property around the town was dirt cheap. Its only tourists were hardy zen pilgrims visiting its ancient temple, Zenkoji, and a small stream of Koreans who came quietly to mourn relatives who died excavating the imperial bunker. Quietly, Tsutsumi began acquiring properties in the adjacent Shiga Highlands, a vast plateau covered with spiny yellow gorse and dotted with pine-forested peaks. When he had bought most of it, Tsutsumi began building large modern hotels and golf courses in the valleys, bull-dozing the forested hills to make ski runs. Meanwhile, he had himself named chairman of the Japan Olympic Committee. He cultivated the chairman of the International Olympic Committee, Barcelona banker Juan Antonio Samaranch, entertaining him at the New Takanawa Prince Hotel, built on land that once had been part of the estate of Prince Kitashirakawa. The friendship blossomed when Tsutsumi allegedly contributed $13 million to Samaranch's pet project, the Olympic Museum in Lausanne, Switzerland. The Japanese press added two and two and realized that 'If the government constructs a . . . bullet train line and highways for the sake of the Nagano Olympics, the value of [Tsutsumi's] golf courses, ski grounds and hotels scattered all over Nagano Prefecture will go up . . . [and] his company [will] benefit the most from the Nagano Olympics.'

In June 1991, Nagano was chosen for the 1998 Winter Olympics, beating Salt Lake City, Utah, in what we now know was horse trading with lavish bribery. During the three years of lobbying for the games, Tsutsumi's Japan Olympic Committee spent more than $16 million wooing all the right people. But that was peanuts compared to the $10.5 billion in public money that was then spent creating the Olympic facilities and infrastructure. Local governments in Nagano Prefecture dug deep into their pockets, while Tsutsumi and other entrepreneurs took out huge loans and went on a binge building Western-style accommodation. An expressway was blasted through the mountains at great cost, and a sleek new bullet train reduced travel time from Tokyo to only 90 minutes. As usual, big chunks of this money were kicked back by contractors to the LDP, and the usual payoffs were made to senior bureaucrats for government approvals. Also, as usual, the bidding on each project was rigged in advance, so that sweetheart deals were cooked to perfection.

Everyone involved in the Nagano infrastructure made immense profits. The Winter Olympics themselves were deemed a great success. But during subsequent months the International Olympic Committee was shaken by scandal involving numerous cities, including Nagano. There were demands for Samaranch to resign. In February 1999, when the Tsutsumis staged a party to celebrate the first anniversary of the Nagano Olympics, the most prominent celebrity invited was Princess Nori, still unmarried at 30. Beforehand, the Japan Olympic Committee blandly let it be known that it had burned all the financial records for Nagano – in another episode of 'the Japanese Way'.

With Japan in meltdown, facing economic collapse, and with politicians unwilling to castrate themselves, it is up to the oligarchs to save the day. Japan's oligarchs – supremely wealthy and powerful men like Tsutsumi Yoshiaki – must have an economic system that works to their advantage. You cannot go on pillaging a country for ever. If Japan's economy crashes, such men stand to suffer enormous losses. Out of self-interest, eventually, they may be forced to push through effective reforms. They can no longer count on their faithful servants in the LDP, who have become an international joke. Japan's bureaucracy has been debased by total absence of accountability. As for Emperor Hirohito, he must have been intimately informed of what was going on in the LDP and in his own government during the 1950s, 1960s, 1970s and 1980s, but there is no evidence that he ever did anything to interfere with the spread of corruption. Doubtless he could easily have made his displeasure known, to Tsutsumi Yoshiaki, that intimate friend of the imperial family. But Hirohito has now gone beyond the reach of guilt.

What of his son Akihito? Was there any hope that Japan's imperial family might at last rise to the occasion, and lead the way to genuine reform?

CHAPTER 13

ECLIPSE OF THE SUN

In 1986, Japan's latest maroon Rolls-Royce, with Crown Prince Akihito aboard, came to a halt before a red traffic light in downtown Tokyo, and proceeded only when the automatic signal changed to green. Hirohito's maroon Rolls-Royce is said to have stopped for a red traffic light only once during its entire career, when there was heavy contrary traffic one day in 1945 on his way to the fateful first meeting with General MacArthur. There was no traffic now, so Crown Prince Akihito was the first to obey this simple rule of the road. In the weeks that followed, the event was much discussed, like reading oracle bones. Moderates cited it as a refreshing example of Akihito's upbeat egalitarianism. Conservatives denounced it as an attempt to denigrate the imperial image. Cynics joked that Akihito was sending a message to 'stop' money politics.

What the incident really demonstrates is that the imperial family, being hostages, can only exercise influence indirectly. Whether such gentle leverage makes any difference is another question entirely. Not since Prince Chichibu in 1936, and Prince Takamatsu in 1945, has the family shown any real defiance of the status quo, and both of them were quickly neutralized.

Social revolution is easy for Westerners to champion, but too much for most Japanese to contemplate. In a country where democracy and liberalism were long condemned as forms of communism, there is a sad history of broken heads and strangled hopes. If changes must be initiated from the top down, this means from the oligarchs, not from the royals. Japan is more than a one-party dictatorship. It is a one-class dictatorship by a financial elite evolved from the clan lords of previous centuries. Their rule by manipulation, intimidation and corruption is as complete as that of the Stalinists in Russia and Eastern Europe – themselves a variant form of oligarchs. Oligarchs only make changes in order to remain in control. There are lessons for Japan in Eastern Europe. Even the Stalinists ultimately suffocated their own roots.

Japan's imperial family has been neither brave nor honest. In 1989, when Hirohito died, he had reigned for sixty-eight years, if you include his time as regent, and was Japan's longest-reigning historical monarch. For the last forty years of his life he presided vaguely, complacently and absentmindedly over a stunning economic transformation that made Japan the second most powerful industrial economy on earth. But as we have seen, he also presided over the complete degeneration of Japan's political and administrative system through runaway greed, to reach a humiliating impasse at the century's end.

We can hope that his death marked the beginning of the end of a merciless, mercenary era, but that may be overly optimistic. His funeral was – like Hirohito himself – a study in deceit and contradictions. President Ronald Reagan, true to form, eulogized Hirohito for his 'truly heroic role' in bringing an end to World War II, while

New Zealand's defence minister said that Hirohito 'should have been shot or publicly chopped up at the end of the war'. The head of an Australian veterans' league said, 'Going to his funeral would be like going to the funeral of the devil.' South Korean students threw fire-bombs at the Japanese Cultural Centre in Seoul to protest statements that war had broken out 'in spite of Hirohito's wishes'.

It was Prime Minister Takeshita (already up to his tiny ears in bribery scandals) who sombrely intoned that 'Hirohito was a pacifist who resolutely brought to an end the war that had broken out in spite of his wishes, out of a determination to prevent further suffering of his people, regardless of the consequences to his own person'. The Japanese media, like a Greek chorus, shamelessly repeated this lyric of 'the selfless sovereign' who had suffered deep privation and humiliation for the sake of his people.

Many humble Japanese did not agree. Tominaga Shozo, who served for five years as a soldier in China, protested that the little people of Japan always get stuck with the guilt and the blame. 'The real war criminals', he said, 'were the emperor, the cabinet ministers, and the military commanders. Small fish like us weren't war criminals.' Another veteran, Azuma Shiro, said he was outraged by Hirohito's behaviour. 'We went to war for him, my friends died for him, and he never even apologized.' Then he added: 'They turned the emperor into a living god, a false idol . . . Because we believed in the divine emperor, we were prepared to do anything, anything at all, kill, rape, anything . . . But you know we cannot say this in Japan, even today. It is impossible in this country to tell the truth.'

There was even duplicity surrounding Hirohito's

funeral ceremonies on the palace grounds. While State Shinto had supposedly been outlawed by the postwar constitution, Hirohito remained chief priest of the cult, which still claimed 108 million adherents. So there were two funerals – the first a Shinto affair, all flutes, smoke and mirrors to thrill the ultra-nationalists, and the second a drab 'modern' government ceremony without Shinto priests, for the benefit of more urbane Japanese and the outside world. To satisfy critics, the two ceremonies were separated by a curtain that was lowered when the Shinto segment ended. Many people took umbrage at this evidence of the way in which the government perpetuates the same old fraud, and simply drops a curtain over it to look modern. In a significant departure, the new emperor – Akihito – invited to the funeral as a guest of honour the mayor of Nagasaki who had publicly faulted Hirohito for his war responsibility. (It was a year later that the mayor was shot by a right-wing fanatic.)

A one-ton casket – some joked that it might be gold rather than lead – conveyed Hirohito's body through Tokyo's dingy commercial zone, past the glitzy Honda showrooms, to a huge hemispherical burial mound at the Musashi Imperial Cemetery. In ancient times, members of an emperor's entourage were entombed with him to attend to his happiness thereafter. Hirohito was accompanied only by a simple microscope which he had used for fifty years, a list of all-time great sumo wrestlers, a number of scientific articles he had written and a few other personal effects, which we will remark on later.

In keeping with the tradition of fraud, it was announced that Hirohito left an estate valued only at slightly over $13 million. Critics said this represented what was left in the petty-cash drawer, after the rest of his worldwide holdings had been dispersed among his heirs and shared out among the oligarchs. The funeral costs were officially declared to have been over $74 million. To those familiar with Japan's accounting methods and bid-rigging, there was nothing odd about spending $74 million on a funeral.

When Akihito then assumed the throne, there were equally elaborate Shinto ceremonies, staged like kabuki. As emperor, Akihito tried to nudge Japan gently in positive directions. His public style was refreshingly informal. He and Empress Michiko easily did many things that Hirohito and Nagako would never have dared. They were photographed performing a graceful foxtrot. On a visit to handicapped children, they knelt to talk with them. Akihito refused to use the ancient court language. He spoke colloquial Japanese in public, which Hirohito never did. His voice was reedy, like his father's, with a slight lisp, but his manner was straightforward and modest. He cut the number of his security police, his food tasters and the officials required to see him off at airports and train stations. He cut the heavenly umbilical, and came down from the clouds. 'I find it natural', he remarked, 'that the imperial family should not exist at a distance from the people.'

There is no comparison between the two men. Hirohito turned from a sympathetic child into a devious and often malignant adult. In the 1930s, inflated with victory, he lent his prestige to ruthless military and financial conspiracies on the Asian mainland, and personally thwarted any reform efforts at home, including those of his own brothers. He favoured men who were profoundly corrupt and gloated when his armies cut down enemy forces 'like weeds'. In this, it is true that he was influenced by the ultra-nationalists around him, but when he had a chance to displace them in 1936 and 1945 he refused. We cannot lose sight of his intense egotism (demonstrated by his blocking of any reforms that might have jeopardized his cosy position), his jealousy of his brother Prince Chichibu and his refusal to consider stepping aside before, during or after World War II, despite the pleas of his own family. Then there were his repeated prolongations of the war in the hope of achieving a face-saving victory (at the cost of the lives of hundreds of thousands of his own people), and his refusal to admit to any guilt whatever. In his mind there was no correlation between his interests and whatever suffering they inflicted on the rest of humanity. The image he projected in later decades of a wry, stoop-shouldered, whimsical old gnome with a twinkle in his eye is misleading. He presided over the China War, the Pacific War, the looting of a dozen countries and the postwar restoration of the same corrupt politicians and self-centred oligarchs who had oppressed Japan and led it into catastrophe. In all of this, he provided the imperial mask that hid Japan's real intentions, not so much from the outside world but from the people of Japan. This is the nub of their complaint against Hirohito – that he misled them.

To remain in power, he then connived with MacArthur, Hoover and others, to an extent that may not be fully known for many more years. During the 1980s, when he was rarely to be seen except on a distant balcony, he continued to provide cover for the LDP money machine.

Unlike his father, Emperor Akihito is sincere. While this sincerity makes him a much more sympathetic figure, it does not add to his political power, nor does it enable him to champion dynamic reform. Just the opposite is true. His sincerity weakens him among the power elite. It is a lesson of Japanese history that the emperor is only as strong as the strongmen who back him. They regard sincerity as a weakness. So Akihito's sincerity puts him at a disadvantage. He is a better constitutional monarch, and a better human being, but he has forfeited his father's leverage. As the anecdote about the traffic light demonstrates, he is powerless to influence events except by moral example. In Japan, moral example goes only so far.

America contributed to Japan's predicament while claiming to be saving it from communism. Because of the secret exoneration of Hirohito by MacArthur's men, and the reverse course of SCAP after 1947, the Pacific War was trivialized and victory was turned to deceitful ends. Half a century later, Japan still has not confronted and exorcized the very real ghosts of World War II. They will not go away. In 1990 both Akihito and Prime Minister Kaifu apologized to South Korea for Japan's long occupation. In 1993, Prime Minister Hosokawa personally apologized to all of Asia. And after hiding themselves away for fifty years, women who were forced into prostitution as 'comfort women' for the army were loudly demanding compensation.

In May 1998, when Emperor Akihito and Empress Michiko spent four days on a state visit to Britain, they were welcomed with all the splendour that the House of Windsor could muster, and Akihito received the Order of the Garter, Britain's highest rank of chivalry. But their visit aroused nationwide protests from former British prisoners of war and civilian internees who had been 'guests' of the Japanese Army. The protesters were demanding a full official apology for the war from the emperor, and additional monetary compensation from the Japanese government.

Everywhere Akihito and Michiko went in England and Wales, protesters gathered, a Japanese flag was burned and backs were turned to insult the imperial couple who, of course, were only children during the war. Red-gloved veterans raised their hands as a silent reminder of the 'bloody hand' of Japanese conquest. While the protesters acknowledged that Akihito was only 11 when the war ended, his presence in Britain rankled. One veteran snapped, 'You wouldn't think about inviting Hitler's son here, would you?' A former Japanese ambassador to London did not help matters when he said to the press: 'People who are very highly educated and broad in outlook think towards the future and not to the past. But of course there are people who demonstrate. They are in their rights, but not the elite people of society.' He added that for most Japanese these British protests were insignificant, because the Japanese were only interested in the upcoming football World Cup.

In his speech at a state banquet at Buckingham Palace, Emperor Akihito said, 'The empress and I can never forget the many kinds of suffering so many people have undergone because of that war . . . our hearts are filled with deep sorrow and pain.' Veterans objected that this was only a statement of personal regret and not an 'official' apology. Prime Minister Tony Blair countered, saying that such an apology had been given by Japan's Prime Minister Hashimoto on his visit to Britain earlier in the year. Queen Elizabeth had faced a similar problem on a visit to India in 1997 when Indian protesters demanded that she make an official apology for British imperialism and the bloody massacre of Indians in the city of Amritsar seven years before she was born. She was unable to do so because this is not within the constitutional prerogatives of the British royal family. If it was inappropriate for the queen to apologize for the Amritsar massacre, why should Emperor Akihito apologize for World War II? In both cases, an official apology could only come from the respective governments. Collectively, Japan's government still refused to do so. Akihito is powerless to force a genuine apology from his government, powerless to silence the catcalls from the LDP.

The second demand of the protesters was that Japan should now pay every surviving British war-internee £14,000 in additional compensation. They argued that a great injustice had occurred when the British government agreed in 1951 that Japan would pay only £48 to each military prisoner of war and £78 to each civilian internee. Many of these people had spent more than four years in concentration camps working as slave labourers. Prime Minister Tony Blair, practising damage control, stood firm and said that the issue of compensation was 'settled by treaty fifty years ago'. Simon Jenkins, columnist for *The Times*, sided with Blair and added that this was all that Japan could have possibly paid at the time because Japan was 'bankrupt'. Or so we were led to believe.

When Singapore fell, Japanese forces took 50,000 British servicemen prisoner. Of these, one in three died in captivity, often in the most brutal circumstances of starvation, beatings and beheading. Allied servicemen captured by the Germans suffered a mortality rate of one in twenty-five. While Germany has paid some £30 billion in compensation and reparations over the years, and continues to pay, the Japanese have paid only £2 billion, and that grudgingly. In 1993 international jurists in

Switzerland ruled that women who were forced to be sexual slaves of the Japanese military during World War II deserve at least $40,000 each as compensation for their 'extreme pain and suffering'. There were 139,000 of these 'comfort women' – Australians, Dutch, Eurasians, White Russians, Koreans, Chinese, Burmese, Indonesians, Malays, Filipinos, Taiwanese, Vietnamese, Cambodians and Laotians, as well as Japanese – most of them minors between the ages of 14 and 18, and about 40 per cent of them are still alive today. The £14,000 demanded by British internees is less than half that amount per person. Some thought Japan should be happy to settle its longstanding guilt – half a century later – for such a trifling sum. But this only includes the British detainees. There are hundreds of thousands of other Allied detainees, not to mention millions of Asian detainees who might then demand similar compensation. If that should come to pass, Japan might have to pay out $100 billion or more. Whatever Japan ended up paying would, in fact, be a mere pittance for a nation that recovered amazingly quickly from its alleged bankruptcy, and now ranks as the world's second-richest economy. The half-century since World War II was very generous to Japan, and very stingy to its victims. The increased value of Golden Lily's war loot since 1945 would more than cover the bill.

In November 1998, a Tokyo court turned down an appeal from 20,000 British, New Zealand, American and Australian former internees for compensation of $22,000 each. Arthur Titherington, head of one of the British internees associations, was furious when he emerged from the Tokyo court. 'They are lying bastards!' he exclaimed. 'There is no justice in this country.' The Canadian government was so appalled by the ruling that

Ottawa said it would compensate Canadian victims from its own treasury.

What is the truth? Many Japanese politicians, particularly in the LDP, still state flatly that Japan did not lose the war. Do they know a few things we do not? A Japanese scholar put it in the form of a zen riddle, or *koan*: 'If a robber steals $100 billion and successfully hides the money before he is captured and jailed, and then is released after seven years for "good behaviour", did he fail or did he succeed?'

By this Oriental logic the Japanese military lost the battles, but Japan's financial elite ultimately won the war. If Hirohito refused to apologize to his own people for losing the war, could that be because he knew the war was not really lost?

Nazi loot, some of which was traced and recovered after the war, continues to be the subject of controversy to this day in litigation with Swiss banks that handled the loot for the Third Reich. But no serious effort has ever been made to trace and restore to its rightful owners Japan's loot from a dozen conquered countries and colonies. This is curious. Aside from China, the biggest losses due to Japanese looting were suffered in the former colonies of Britain, France and the Netherlands and in the American Philippines. After the war, all of Asia was in turmoil, preoccupied with independence struggles. Ultimately Burma, Malaya, Singapore, Laos, Cambodia, Vietnam, Indonesia and the Philippines became independent nations. Their new governments were fully occupied with survival. There was no Pan-Asian equivalent of the worldwide Jewish lobby to fight for the recovery of lost private assets.

While it is commonly believed in the West that there is only some 130,000 metric tons of gold in circulation and much of that has already been worked into jewellery, the gold market is extremely secretive about how much gold really exists. Nobody has any idea how much gold was privately held in Asia when the Japanese conquest began. Asians never trusted governments or banks, and for thousands of years kept their hidden wealth in small gold bars. The Japanese Army understood this and was brutally efficient in inducing captive populations to part with all they had. Terror was applied in many ways, sometimes with extortion rather than violence. When Hong Kong was conquered by the Japanese, residents were forced to hand over all their property, including money and jewellery, in exchange for Japanese scrip. Today, 3,500 of these families are asking the Japanese government to redeem the scrip – now worth $10 billion. In today's money this represents slightly less than $3 million per family. So far their case has been heard fifteen times in Tokyo courts, but remains unresolved.

In time we will have answers to such haunting questions, as new investigations of war looting reveal the secrets. As China's Prime Minister Zhu Rongji has said in another context, 'Historical facts cannot be covered up by anybody. The truth will always come out.'

Surprisingly, the demand of wartime internees for a renegotiation of their compensation is fully recognized by the terms of the 1951 settlement. According to the treaty, the British government is entitled to renegotiate compensation if any other government received larger payments for its citizens. Both Burma and Switzerland (not even a belligerent) negotiated compensation packets worth fifty times that accepted by the British government. When this was pointed out in the mid-1950s, the Tory government decided not to apply for a re-adjustment because of Japan's 'perilous' economy. In

417

today's money, the compensation paid to Burmese and Swiss citizens would be worth about £40,000 – considerably more than the detainees are asking, and more than the international jurists recommended be paid to 'comfort women'. For that missed chance should they blame the Tories or the widespread – but false – notion that Japan was 'bankrupt'?

The issue of Japan's compensation is still very much alive in America as well. One month before Emperor Akihito's 1998 visit to Britain, Congress passed a resolution, inspired by Iris Chang's seminal book on the Rape of Nanking:

Whereas the government of Germany has formally apologized to the victims of the Holocaust and gone to great lengths to provide financial compensation to the victims and to provide for their needs and recovery; and Whereas by contrast the Government of Japan has refused to fully acknowledge the crimes it committed during World War II and to provide reparations to its victims: Now, therefore, be it Resolved by the House of Representatives (the Senate concurring), That it is the sense of the Congress that the Government of Japan should –
1. Formally issue a clear and unambiguous apology for the atrocious war crimes committed by the Japanese military during World War II; and
2. Immediately pay reparations to the victims of those crimes, including United States military and civilian prisoners of war, people of Guam who were subjected to violence and imprisonment, survivors of the 'Rape of Nanking' from

December, 1937, until February, 1938, and the women who were forced into sexual slavery and known by the Japanese military as 'comfort women'.

What Congress failed to comprehend is that the Japanese government's handling of reparations and compensation was the result of sly gerrymandering during the American occupation. At the end of 1945, while SCAP investigators were peering into empty Japanese bank vaults, President Truman dispatched Edwin S. Pauley, a rich oil man and one of the conservative oligarchs in the Democratic Party, to make an assessment of Japan's ability to pay reparations to the countries it had looted and destroyed. When Pauley had been chairman of the Democratic National Committee in 1944, he had backed the conservative Truman as Roosevelt's running mate, pushing leftist Henry Wallace off the ticket. Accordingly, Truman valued Pauley highly, and called him a tough negotiator who could be 'a real son of a bitch'. Perhaps, but he was a pushover for the Japanese financial cliques.

In one sense, Pauley must have been a miracle-worker. It took him less than two days to assess the economic situation in Japan. He noted that SCAP had indeed traced some Japanese assets hidden in Sweden, Switzerland and Argentina, but concluded that these 'belong principally to the *zaibatsu* or families controlling large financial combines. They do not constitute a large sum and none, so far as is known, is in the name of the imperial family.' If Pauley was not stupid – and nobody has ever suggested that he was – how could he reach such an astonishing conclusion? Why was Pauley interested only in treasure openly identified with the imperial family? Why would he brush aside treasure belonging to 'families controlling large financial combines' as if Japan's oligarchs had nothing to do with the war? What led him to believe that treasure identified with the imperial family would be found lying around waiting to be confiscated by the Allies? Did he really believe that Japan's two millennia of extraordinary wealth had simply evaporated? Did he know nothing about the looting of Asia? Was he really uninformed about the OSS agents and US Army officers who were at that moment emptying several mountain caves in the Philippines of gold bullion hidden by Golden Lily and the Imperial Army?

We refer here to a major recovery of Japanese war loot carried out in Luzon between 1945 and 1948. Severino Garcia Santa Romana, a Filipino-American OSS officer and later an officer in the CIA, under the direct field supervision of the CIA's General Edward G. Lansdale, oversaw the recovery. Documents show that this massive recovery of war loot was known to OSS chief General William Donovan, to General MacArthur, to Brigadier General Fellers and to Herbert Hoover, and later to CIA Director Allen Dulles and his deputies, so it was probably known to President Truman. We must assume that Truman's close associate Pauley was also aware of it when he went to Japan.

The Santa Romana recovery – the first of its kind – came about in the following manner. In the closing months of the war, American OSS officers fighting alongside Filipino guerrillas observed a heavily laden Japanese hospital ship unloading bronze boxes at Subic Bay. A convoy of army trucks carrying the cargo was tracked into the mountains where guerrillas watched Japanese soldiers carry the remarkably heavy boxes into a cave. When the Japanese sealed and disguised the cave entrance and left, the guerrillas – including one American OSS major – opened the cave and discovered that the boxes contained gold bars. They then resealed the cave. After the war, Santa Romana was assigned by Generals Donovan and Lansdale to empty the cave secretly. Documents show that no attempt was made to return this bullion to its rightful owners, or even to set up a fund to benefit victims of the war. Instead, the gold bullion was deposited by Santa Romana in 176 bank accounts in 42 countries, and became the basis of the CIA's 'off the books' operational funds during the immediate postwar years, to create a worldwide anti-communist network. This was done by distributing gold certificates to influential people, binding them to the CIA. One single account in General Lansdale's name at the Geneva branch of Union Banque Suisse, documents show, contained 20,000 metric tons of gold. It is only one of many. Here is a clear precedent to the secret accounts set up by Colonel Oliver North during the Iran–Contra arms conspiracy of the 1980s, which were trivial by comparison.

Some of the bullion accounts that Santa Romana squirrelled away were set up for his own private use, with gold bars that he sidetracked during the recovery process. These accounts still exist in New York and elsewhere, and they are the object of numerous legal actions by people claiming to be Santa Romana's heirs. But there is a lot more gold still in the ground in the Philippines, yet to be recovered.

Documents also show that one of the big gold-bullion accounts set up by Santa Romana was in the name of General Douglas MacArthur. Other documents indicate that gold bullion worth $100 million was placed in an account in the name of Herbert Hoover. Both men were deeply involved in rescuing Emperor Hirohito, and suborning witnesses at the Tokyo war-crimes tribunal. What does this suggest?

It suggests that Washington's declarations about Japan being bankrupt in 1945 were highly disingenuous, to say the least, a point that should not be lost on the US Congress, or on those many thousands of Pacific War and China War victims still seeking compensation and restitution.

We do know that a few weeks after arriving in Japan, Pauley was informed of the $2 billion in gold bullion hidden in Tokyo Bay. Surely he could not have been unaware that palaces and other property of the imperial family were being conveyed to the Tsutsumi family and others to avoid confiscation?

Yet, in a miraculous epiphany, Pauley concluded within 48 hours of his arrival in Tokyo that Japan was a 'shattered empire', which could not even pay its fair share of the expenses for the American occupation, let alone contribute anything to rebuild Asia. Pauley said if Japan were forced to pay big reparations, of the sort Germany had to pay at the end of World War I, she would have nothing left to rebuild her own ruined economy – and communists would eat her for lunch. Largely on the basis of Pauley's assessment, when the bill for war reparations was finally handed to the Japanese government, it came to only about $1 billion. If this had actually been divided among the next of kin of the 20 million people who died as a result of Japan's aggression, each might have received just over $30. Most of them got zero.

In the immediate postwar scramble for reparations, the Japanese *zaibatsu*, including the wealthy families towards whom Pauley was so sympathetic, and who (like postwar prime minister Tanaka, for example) had profited enormously from the war and hid their profits, submitted their own claims for compensation for *wartime damage to their armaments factories*. These claims came to more than $5 billion, and many were paid. Compare that to the $1 billion paid to victims.

Instead of cash payments to conquered countries, Japan was ordered to send industrial equipment. Even these token reparations were suspended by Washington when the equipment was claimed as collateral for bonds issued before the war by American firms including Morgan Bank and Dillon Read, who were at the head of a long line of US corporations with big prewar investments in Japan. By the early 1950s, Japan owed Morgan nearly $600 million in unpaid interest, penalties and principal just for the 1924 earthquake loan. This did not include other huge sums for other loans that Morgan, and members of its extended family, had made before 1940.

In 1951, an official from Japan's Ministry of Finance arrived at Morgan headquarters at 23 Wall Street, saying, 'I have come to honor my signature.' At this time no Japanese bureaucrat had the power to make such a statement. Japan was still an occupied country and nothing of this sort could have been said without the explicit approval of General MacArthur. In any event, the official went on to say that Japan had not defaulted on a loan in two thousand years. Refinancing and servicing was arranged through Smith Barney and Guaranty Trust. Smith Barney had already joined the Morgan family when it suffered financial reversals during the Depression, and Guaranty Trust had been a Morgan 'ward' since the 1920s. Thus Morgan not only benefited by getting its loans repaid, but by having its subsidiaries collect commissions for restructuring the same loans. In the end, there was nothing fair about the way Japan's (acknowledged) postwar resources were allocated. People who were physically the victims of Japanese brutality were completely upstaged by big corporations that commandeered all the money made available.

In short, the Japanese government and the imperial family have not told the whole truth, nor did America encourage them to do so – just the opposite. And this is the crux of the problem for Japanese born since the war. They know they have not been told the full story, but they have been raised not to ask questions.

Some Japanese people are familiar with Golden Lily because they, or their fathers and uncles, took part in the looting and hiding. In recent decades, some have participated in recovering loot hidden in the Philippines or Indonesia. But most Japanese are mystified by news of such 'vile deeds'. As a Tokyo businessman told us, 'We cannot presume that nothing of the sort ever happened. The Rape of Nanking did take place. And how could that rape go without looting? We must now ask where those stolen treasures went.'

The most sensitive issue up to this point in time – the criminality of Hirohito – is gradually fading, ceasing to be of any interest to younger generations. Few of them have personal experience of war atrocities, but inherited from their parents dark memories of the war. As the businessman went on to say:

'If we tried to reason with our parents today about such disturbing evidence, we would never be allowed to enter their home again. Why do older generations reject such things? They want to forget the nightmare that tortured them for decades. They do not want their inter-

424

pretation of history to be revised. They were in the war, but it would be harsh to force them to be responsible for the barbarism committed by their own army. They simply reject the idea that they were accomplices. Their attitude towards the emperor is one of self-defence, rather than awe or deference.'

Since the war, he said, the Japanese have been controlled by cunning media, financed and manipulated by oligarchs and politicians. Education has been crafted so that attention would not be focused on such subjects.

'We ordinary people all sense it,' he said, 'but who cares? The generation born in the 1950s and early 1960s went through education that taught nothing but the impossibility and absurdity of war. Textbooks described the war as a campaign into Eurasia, which ended in a disappointing result, only because the plan was implemented recklessly. We never understood that the military's deeds violated humanity, or that their disgraceful activities tormented many nations, from which we should at least draw moral issues. We were not taught to possess an eye to see how things developed, how they worked, and what was the core of the problem. I think this was why we were never made to realize the magnitude of the crime. Something wrong happened in the past. It was an act of some idiots. But it's OK now, and has nothing to do with us. Now that we've got the most pacifist constitution in the world, we are not to brood on the past. Remorse? Why should we feel remorse?'

Why indeed? In Germany, the acceptance of moral responsibility for the Holocaust has been crucial to the growth of a rational democracy. Films about the grimmest aspects of the Holocaust can be shown at the Berlin Film Festival to audiences that can accept responsibility for the past as an essential part of dealing with the future. Japan, by denying the past, has denied the future. By refusing to acknowledge guilt or to compensate its victims, the Japanese government has institutionalized a lie, which is continually being reiterated. So Tokyo has no moral authority, and its posturing is a joke. This has created a predicament for her own people, for those who do not understand the past may be doomed to repeat it.

But the Japanese people are not alone in evading responsibility for war crimes and looting. America clearly played a deceitful role in postwar Japan with respect to war crimes, war loot, war poisons and war reparations. In recent years, Washington has joined in the outcry about Swiss banks sitting on Nazi loot, but remains silent about its own collusion with Tokyo and the question of American banks sitting on Japanese loot. The two issues should be linked, because expressions of outrage over Nazi behaviour, without similar expressions of outrage about Japanese behaviour, simply perpetuate a grotesque political lie. The twist is that Tokyo knows such admissions would be embarrassing to Washington, so collusion continues, with one shielding the other.

What, then, is the fate of the dynasty? While Emperor Akihito tries to present a more human face, this has achieved little. If the emperor no longer wants to be the tool of the oligarchs, what is he there for? Has he any role to play in Japan's future? If he wishes to represent the people, what if they no longer care? While 75 per cent of Japanese feel only contempt for their politicians, 80 per cent are said to be satisfied with the current emperor and empress, at least as token monarchs. But nobody seriously expects the royals to lead the way. The more

Emperor Akihito and Empress Michiko try to identify themselves with change, the more they are isolated from the people by their guardians, who fear change.

Change comes with glacial slowness in Japan. As recently as the late 1960s, when Emperor Hirohito took a bath in the provinces, the local aristocracy lined up in formal dress to bathe in the same water. Older generations of Japanese still believe that if they look directly into an emperor's face, they will be blinded. Shinto rituals continue to reinforce these notions of supernatural power. The mirror of the sun goddess is still in use. Some of the elite believe in such magic, while others make purely cynical use of Ito Hirobumi's brilliant nineteenth-century stagecraft.

The new crown prince, Naruhito, may not be entirely comfortable with the cut of his straitjacket, but he shows no sign of wanting to be a champion of social revolution. Any similarities between him and the young Prince Chichibu are superficial.

True, Naruhito did start with a clean slate. He grew up in close proximity with his parents in the Togo Gosho palace, specially built for them. Yet life in a 45-room mansion with dozens of staff is a far cry from the cubicles of Tokyo salarymen, where as many as three generations are crammed into tiny spaces with minimal plumbing. But Crown Prince Naruhito's childhood was a great change from tradition nonetheless.

By comparison with the caricature of Meiji by Sir Harry Parkes, of Taisho by Sir Claude MacDonald and of Hirohito by Morgan's Thomas Lamont, Naruhito is a robust young man with even features, some might even say nice-looking. He went to Oxford, as did his brother Akishino, the first children of a Japanese emperor to attend school abroad since Prince Chichibu spent a term at Oxford in 1925. There were similarities between Naruhito and his great-uncle in their love of sports, wine, music and literature, and speaking English. But with the much greater openness and sophistication of modern Tokyo, people in Japan expect Naruhito to be very urbane and cosmopolitan – which they say he is not.

Naruhito did experience a different life at Merton College, Oxford, taping his own windows shut against chilly English weather, doing his own laundry. But while he had no difficulty using a credit card, his critics at home point out that he never mastered the washing machine.

When he returned to Tokyo and took up his responsibilities as crown prince, he did denounce the shooting of Nagasaki's Mayor Motoshima. To older generations of Japanese this may have seemed audacious, but the gesture was regarded by younger critics as yesterday's green tea, which should be poured down the drain.

Naruhito is easily upstaged, as in 1990 when 24-year-old Prince Akishino beat him to the altar, marrying Kawashima Kiko, a 23-year-old graduate student in social psychology. Princess Kiko was fluent in German and English, and had spent six years in Philadelphia, while her father taught economics at the University of Pennsylvania. She had also lived with her family for a while in Austria. The newlyweds moved into a Western-style two-storey house built for them on the imperial palace grounds, so they were not obliged to leave their shoes at the door. When they promptly had two daughters, the infants were not taken away by Imperial Household chamberlains. This comparative relaxation had its cost. Their privacy was invaded by Japanese gossip columnists who artfully denied rumours that Prince Akishino, a marine biologist, had fallen in love with a Thai expert on catfish. In a press conference to which he was accompanied by Princess Kiko, he called the reports of this love affair 'entirely untrue'.

It was unusual for the younger brother to marry and have children first. But Crown Prince Naruhito's first choice for his future empress, Owada Masako, took a long time making up her mind. A beauty by any standards, she was ambitious and bright, with a strong individualistic streak. Masako was a commoner, the daughter of a wealthy, high-ranking official of Japan's Ministry of Foreign Affairs. She had lived as a child in the Soviet Union and the United States when her father was posted abroad. In 1985, she graduated with honours from Harvard and then attended Tokyo University. She planned to join the Foreign Ministry, where a career was ready and waiting for her thanks to her father's prominence. The ministry sent her to England to prepare for a role as a trade negotiator.

Although the crown prince was relentless in his courtship of her, Masako was equally relentless in resisting. To become crown princess meant giving up her own career. This was the same crisis faced by Matsudaira Setsuko in Washington in the late 1920s, when she was courted by Prince Chichibu. But seventy years later it was made worse by the fact that, at the millennium, many young Japanese women at last had a chance to excel in professional careers.

Japanese say there was more to Masako's footdragging than mere reluctance to spend the remainder of her life as a palace hostage. Part of the problem, they insist, was Crown Prince Naruhito.

'Robust he may be,' a Tokyo business executive explained, 'but far from handsome, and we have never heard that he is intelligent. His English is poor, despite having attended Oxford, and although he plays the viola he does not play it well. He is a dull, banal, average man, lacking any sort of sophistication. When the royal marriage was announced, public reaction was to sympathize with the bride, for everyone knew that she could not turn it down despite herself. We think he does not deserve her, and she does not deserve her hardships in the palace.'

Foreigners may see the crown prince and princess on television or in person and find them an appealing couple, compared to what is left of the West's motley royals, but cosmopolitan Japanese regard this as a joke, and 'a particularly bad joke at that'. Japanese have outgrown their rulers.

No young Japanese woman can refuse to become empress. The best Masako could do was to exact Naruhito's promise to 'protect' her from the Imperial Household organization, a tall order. Like Empress Michiko, who has been the target of continual abuse from the old aristocracy, Masako was criticized from the outset for being wilful and individualistic. She was said to be 'brazen enough to talk more than His Imperial Highness' and 'probably no different from those girls who have no class and no manners – the types who grew up abroad'. Such a person, a saying goes, has 'forgotten how to wear a kimono'. Her troubles were only beginning.

They were married in June 1993. Six years later they still had no children. Elements in the Japanese press began to suggest that the rules of succession should be modified to allow a female to sit on the throne, in case the only heirs available were Prince Akishino's daughters. The Imperial Household clamped down so tight on the crown princess that she was kept in a bell jar, unable to act or speak freely. The international press began carrying stories calling Masako 'the silently suffering princess' who was being kept in isolation by 'old traditionalists'. Journalists who once marvelled at her vivacity began to speculate that the future empress of Japan was just another painted doll costumed in silks, 'simplistic' and 'one-dimensional'. Afraid that this negative image might stick permanently among foreign audiences, the Imperial Household grudgingly authorized a special news conference for Masako to 'speak her mind freely'. Her remarks were careful, contained and impersonal: 'I should think that all the foreign media coverage is an indication of keen interest in which Europeans and Americans hold Japanese society today, given Japan's growing stature in the world and the changes currently taking place in this society.' She might be speaking her mind freely, but only after every word and nuance was thoroughly masticated and regurgitated by the Imperial Household. Even so, the press conference set a precedent, the first sign of change in the protocol-obsessed palace. With any luck Masako would prove to have the same tenacity that enabled Dowager Empress Sadako to survive suffocation and gain some control.

The royals were not foremost on Japan's agenda. By 1999, what had been one of the world's richest and most deceitful governments, secured in its bad habits by preying upon a great pool of personal savings, found itself like a drunk salaryman up a blind alley, vomiting up the feast. More was needed than a stomach pump. Too much bingeing, incest, greed and corruption is not healthy, even for predators.

Until recently, Japan was respected for its economic might. Today it is feared for its economic weakness. The difference lies in the growing universal recognition of fraud. Japan's industrial superiority, like its politics, was

431

based on incest among banks, companies, bureaucrats and the underworld. Such links may be expedient, but they involve financial inbreeding that eventually corrupts the organism. This incest is not new. Today's banking crisis is identical to the banking crisis of the 1920s. Nothing was done to reform the system then, and nothing serious has been done this time.

The International Monetary Fund and economists the world over wait for the government in Tokyo to 'do something about it', for otherwise the Japanese crisis could pull the whole global economy down into deep recession. But to fix the system would require changing the rules by which Japanese banks operate, and that would spoil the sweetheart deals that keep corruption alive in Japan. Any politician or government minister who tried that would be committing suicide. Furthermore, at this point Japan's economic crisis is mostly hurting the middle class, the upstarts, the *nouveaux*. Big money thinks it can ride it out. The oligarchs *know* they can ride it out. As an American robber baron once said, 'In a recession, money returns to its rightful owners.'

However, the situation is different now in important ways. The people of Japan are no longer completely in the dark. Information that was once unobtainable now proliferates with dish antennae and websites. The Japanese have had a strong taste of intellectual freedom and personal liberty, and the genie will not go back in the bottle.

Some restructuring is inevitable because the crisis will not go away. Male unemployment in Japan is now higher than in America. If the calculation were done in Japan the way it is done in Britain or America, that rate would be nearly double. By April 1998, a record 17,500 businesses in Japan had gone bankrupt, exceeding the number of start-ups. Japan's all-important pension funds were at risk. In a study of twenty-six top Japanese companies, the assets in their pension funds covered only 60 per cent of the projected benefits. Among those with shaky pension funds were Mitsubishi, Mitsui, Toshiba and Sony. Frightened by all this bad news, Japanese consumers cut their spending even further. Many stopped putting their savings in postal giros because of the revelations of the LDP's abuse of postal savings. They were hiding their money under the tatami mat, or investing it more securely overseas, which was now easy to do. Nobody in Japan wanted a Tanaka, a Kishi, a Kanemaru or a Takeshita dipping into precious private savings to top up the LDP slush-fund, or to bail out banks on the brink of collapse because they had loaned too much money to the *yakuza*, the tattooed outlaws of Japan's underworld.

Japan's banks had gone on a binge of reckless lending during the 1980s when property speculation sent prices sky-high. When the bubble of speculation burst in the early 1990s, the stock market fell nearly 60 per cent, and property prices fell 80 per cent (giving some idea of the grossly inflated valuations). Borrowers defaulted on their loan repayments and the banks were left holding bad paper, and properties whose deflated values would not cover outstanding loans.

In late 1998, a modest estimate from the Finance Ministry said there was a total of $548 billion of these bad loans. It was acknowledged that at least $235 billion of them were made to the *yakuza*, or to organizations tied to the *yakuza*. However, the *yakuza* represent only a small part of Japan's outlaws. Many men in politics, bureaucracy and business are *above* the law, although

433

they do not have tattoos or severed fingers.

The problem is much worse than the Finance Ministry admits because the bad-debt figures are based on un-audited self-assessments by the insolvent banks. The ministry made no demands for an independent audit. Some analysts think the real amount of bad loans may be $1 trillion, not including Japan's bad-loan exposure elsewhere in Asia.

Because of the insolvent banks, Japanese companies can no longer get unsecured loans at near-zero interest. They must turn to capital markets where Japanese and foreign investors demand higher returns and greater accountability, both alien concepts to traditional Japanese banking practices. Many more businesses will not be able to pay market rates and will go bust. Bankruptcies will continue, and unemployment will grow. To survive, some Japanese companies are already having to merge with foreign firms. Of the big car companies, Mazda management was taken over by Ford, while Nissan merged with Renault. Smaller businessmen do not have this kind of leverage.

Ultimately, the real test is whether Japan's oligarchs are prepared to bare their bellies, take out the short sword and cut out the rotten parts, allowing the healthier organs to heal. So far only one big bank, Hokkaido Takushoku, has been closed, along with some insignifi-cant smaller ones. Both the Finance Ministry and the Bank of Japan steadfastly maintain that no other big institutions are insolvent. Foreign observers find this absurd. Western governments say Japan must let the insolvent institutions collapse, and reform the rest. Instead, the LDP pushes scheme after scheme to bail out all the banks – solvent and insolvent – without reforms, oversight or regulations. This is how drug addicts prefer to deal with addiction. Injecting more rescue capital rewards bad habits, bad owners, bad managers and the outlaws, whose bad loans will never be repaid. Foreign investors are afraid of buying up Japanese loans – even those discounted to a rock-bottom 10 per cent of their paper value – because in nearly 40 per cent of the cases they would have to collect from the *yakuza* underworld. And the *yakuza* send empty coffins to foreign executives as 'house-warming' presents.

America fudged its way out of the 1980s savings-and-loan crisis in only three years. Japan's LDP is trying to do the same. Some 75 trillion yen was pumped into 'emergency' public works between 1992 and 1995, benefiting the LDP's favourite construction companies. The excuse was that Japanese consumers would be reassured by the government's example, and would begin to spend their own money again. But Japanese consumers are no longer so easily fooled. More than half the rescue money financed tunnels leading nowhere. So much of Japan has been paved over, there is no place left to pour cement.

Like a crippled supertanker, Japan is coming slowly to a halt.

No longer able to deceive, the LDP has become a turnstile. Finance ministers and prime ministers come and go with increasing speed. When Prime Minister Hashimoto was replaced in July 1998 by Obuchi Keizo, the world was informed that Obuchi was 'picked by party boss Takeshita Noboru who had been young Obuchi's mentor since Obuchi entered the Diet in 1963'. This was not reassuring, as Takeshita – the prune-faced LDP kingmaker – was part of Japan's problem. So low was public opinion of Prime Minister Obuchi that the Japanese media labelled him Takeshita's 'goldfish shit'.

Was this only an eclipse of the sun, which would pass?

Could the Japanese people, voting with their savings by refusing to spend them, change the way things are done and bring about long-awaited reforms? Was a quiet social revolution at last under way? Many well-informed Japanese think it is too late. One scholar says the problem is that 'the interests of the most influential clique become the interests of the nation as a whole'. Reform cannot come, he says, in a nation where there is only 'vertical' equality – where everybody at the top is equal, and everybody on each lower rung is equal to others on that rung. In Japan the whole object is to rise as far as possible, then hold on to your social and financial position for ever.

If serious reform again proves impossible, the LDP clearly hopes that Western governments and the IMF will intercede, propping up Japan's corrupt system as they did Indonesia's.

Could the imperial family, with its new human face, sway things in favour of reform and transparency? Emperor Akihito has earned some public trust by demonstrations of sincerity, breaking with tradition in a number of small but meaningful ways. But nobody believes that Akihito will startle his guardians by declaring himself in favour of sweeping reforms.

In an age when all we expect of royals is that they do not drool in public, few Japanese anticipate any demonstrations of courage from Crown Prince Naruhito either.

'Americans were right', a Japanese scholar says, 'in assuming that preserving the monarchy was the only way out of national misery after the war. If the monarchy was destroyed, our parents and grandparents would have had to kill themselves. Who would then reconstruct the country? But what was true after the war is no longer true. We are now out of that misery, long since, and not obliged to revere the monarchy. We would not mind if they decided to disband and go away.

'Some say the existence of the emperor has been invaluable as the symbol of the Japanese nation; that he represents national identity, and brews a sense of love towards our own country. Don't give us that. What do we know about what they do day-by-day? Do we know about them as much as we know about Princess Di and Prince Charles? They are invisible. There is a lack of dearness towards the royals. We have grown up caring less and less about them. We are damn sure that before we become a republic we need far better politicians than we have had so far, but our monarchy is not the reason to avoid becoming a republic.

'We think very little of the emperor. We feel no need of him. Yet there is no debate about ending the imperial family. Why? Because we lack a clear sense of direction. We as a nation do not think about where we should go and how. Because of inertia and lack of will-power, we leave those questions to future generations. We hardly talk about such things. Foreigners do not ask, because they think we are deeply patriotic and that would offend us immensely. Not at all.

'We are currently in turmoil with a rotten system, politically and economically. Our society is changing, but not because we have designed that change after deep thought. We must contemplate the long way we have come since the Meiji Restoration, and develop a new agenda in which we review, strategically, our future way in the international community.'

If Japan could hold a referendum to make the royals answerable to the people rather than to the oligarchs, the emperor and the crown prince might have something more than a ceremonial role in the theme park of the future. But that is highly unlikely. Meanwhile, people under 60 are resigned to the royals, mildly curious about their private lives, but do not take them more seriously than they do baseball players, or cartoon characters. They care no more about the monarchy today than they did in the eight centuries preceding the Meiji Restoration 150 years ago. The Yamato dynasty has come full circle, from insignificance, to insignificance.

Maybe that is why so many past emperors abdicated to spend their lives more happily in monasteries. There are also monasteries of the mind. In 1999, Dowager Empress Nagako was living in total seclusion, apparently suffering from Alzheimer's and remembering little of the twentieth century, a blessing of sorts. Resting inside the Musashi mausoleum, Hirohito is as unrevealing and equivocal as ever, adorned with his favourite possessions. Among them the Mickey Mouse wristwatch he purchased when he crossed the Pacific to visit Disneyland, the kingdom of Mickey – his only true rival.

NOTES

It may seem that the Japanese people are completely uninterested in their recent political and social history, particularly the 1930s and 1940s. However, the truth is that they are simply starved for information about their past. Because the elite control the writing, research and teaching of Japanese history, it is not unusual for today's high-school students to ask, 'Did we win the war?'

Japanese historians and journalists have been vigorously discouraged from investigating their own modern history. As some put it, the study of history in Japan stops with the Meiji Restoration. Bills passed by the Diet in the mid-1920s made it a serious crime to criticize the government. Gagging of government critics intensified during the war years. The gag was removed, briefly, during the first few months of the occupation in 1945. Since then, silence again has become the rule, so for most of the last three generations, Japanese have not been able to learn (or even think) about their modern history, their emperors or their invisible oligarchs.

The hunger of the Japanese to know more about their past was never made clearer than in 1990 when Emperor Hirohito's secret memoirs of World War II were discovered among the papers of his aide Terasaki Hidenari.

These papers, edited by Terasaki's daughter Mariko Terasaki Miller, were published by *Bungei Shunju sha* under the title *Showa Tenno Dokuhakuroku (The Emperor's Monologues)*. More than 140,000 copies were sold within the first few months of publication.

Scholar Herbert Bix took a particular interest in these documents and published two articles: 'Emperor Hirohito's War' and 'The Showa Emperor's Monologue and the Problem of War Responsibility'. In these, Bix translates certain portions of the monologues. Other portions of the Terasaki transcripts were translated by Terasaki himself in the late 1940s and passed on to Brigadier General Bonner Fellers. We found these extracts among the Fellers Papers at the MacArthur Library. Other extracts of the monologues were included in a documentary broadcast by NHK in Tokyo on 15 June 1997, as 'The Showa Emperor's Two Monologues' (in Japanese).

In the notes that follow, readers will see citations to The Emperor's Monologues. As no single source is complete, our citation refers (unless otherwise specified) to all three sources, for simplicity's sake. What the people of Japan crave to know about their own history is to be found in such bits and pieces all over the place. It is only a question of diligently searching out the pieces and assembling them in a coherent form, which is what we have attempted to do in this book.

PROLOGUE: EMPEROR MEETS SHOGUN
25   Details of Hirohito's first meeting with MacArthur were drawn from a variety of sources that do not always agree. These include Kawahara, *Hirohito and His Times*; Kanroji, *Hirohito: An Intimate Portrait*; Crump, *The Death of an Emperor*; Manchester, *American Caesar*; Toland, *The Rising Sun*; Large,

Emperor Hirohito; articles by Bix in our bibliography; Irokawa, *The Age of Hirohito*; the Papers of Bonner Fellers; and the accounts of Dr Egeberg and Faubion Bowers.

25   A trusted English-language interpreter. According to Bix, the translator at the first Hirohito–MacArthur meeting was Okumura Katsuzo. Mariko Terasaki Miller told us her father was also present. Faubion Bowers claimed he was there as well, but that the general deferred to Hirohito's choice of translator.

26   'If you call' is from Toland, *Rising Sun,* which gives details of Hirohito's angry interview with Sugiyama.

27   The immediate postwar conditions in Japan are described by Robert Shaplen, *A Turning Wheel,* and Irokawa, *Age of Hirohito*.

27   MacArthur had been in Japan only one month. According to Fellers, MacArthur's secretary, the occasion of their arrival in Japan could have been another massacre, like that of 'Custer at the Little Big Horn'. From Fellers's letters to his wife, MacArthur Library.

29   Despite the unusual secrecy. Transcripts of the first meeting are still classified top secret in Washington and Tokyo. The first page of a letter Fellers wrote to his wife that day is in the MacArthur Library. Evidently Fellers revealed more than the US government wished to be known.

29   Our information on Fellers came from primary sources and interviews: correspondence and phone interviews with his daughter, Nancy Fellers Gillespie, who died in late 1998, and his papers at the MacArthur Library and at the Hoover Institute. We were also aided by Fellers's associate, Bruce Merkle. We learned other details during a week-long visit to our home by Mariko Terasaki Miller; her father, Terasaki Hidenari, was the Imperial Household liaison between SCAP and Hirohito.

30   Of MacArthur's notion that Hirohito was fluent in English: Fellers wrote to his wife on 27 September 1945 that MacArthur told him: '[The Emperor]

understands English and understood readily every-thing which I said.' Fellers Papers, MacArthur Library. MacArthur's mistake was revealed in Egeberg's recollections cited in our bibliography. We conclude that he confused Hirohito with Prince Chichibu.

30   Aide Faubion Bowers describes the photo session with the emperor for the *New York Times*.

31   Hirohito smoking a cigarette. Bowers says: 'The morning of the meeting . . . The General asked me if the Emperor smoked. I answered yes. As a student in Japan before the war, I had once received a packet of cigarettes, gold-embossed with the imperial 16-petal chrysanthemum crest – given out as a souvenir at an imperial garden party. MacArthur took my Lucky Strikes and Zippo lighter and put them in his pocket.' Because the palace gave out gift packs of cigarettes, Bowers assumed that the emperor smoked. See Bowers in our bibliography.

31   'I bear sole responsibility' is from MacArthur, *Reminiscences,* 1964. Interpreter's notes made no mention of Hirohito accepting responsibility. For different versions of Hirohito's war responsibility see Toland, *Rising Sun*; Large, *Emperor Hirohito*; Manning; Buruma, *Wages of Guilt*; the Cooks' *Japan at War*; Irokawa, *Age of Hirohito*. His acceptance of guilt is contradicted sharply by Hirohito's secret memoir, The Emperor's Monologues.

34   For discussions of Hirohito as a victim of Tojo and the militarists, see Toland, *Rising Sun*; Joseph Grew's two memoirs; articles by Bix; Dower, *Empire and Aftermath;* Nakamura Masanori; Buruma, *Wages of Guilt*; and news stories that appeared at Hirohito's death and at the time of his son's accession. Unpublished personal papers of participants like those of Joseph Grew at Harvard's East Asian Institute, the Fellers Papers and the papers of Herbert Hoover shed light on the tortured logic used to support this myth.

34   Hirohito's ultimate decision to continue the war. Fellers said it was a quirk in Hirohito's personality

that made it 'impossible for him to yield'. See 'Bonner Fellers: Japan Background', Fellers Papers, MacArthur Library.

35   How Asaka evaded punishment is in Iris Chang, *The Rape of Nanking*; Michael Montgomery; Toland, *Rising Sun*. See later chapters of this book.

36   Photograph of MacArthur and Hirohito. Bix discusses the controversy in his articles. See also Nakamura Masanori.

38   Of Terasaki Hidenari: Mariko Terasaki Miller gave us many details of her father's life and her memories of him and that difficult time in Tokyo, when she was a young girl. Her mother Gwen Terasaki wrote a memoir, *Bridge to the Sun*, which became a Hollywood movie. Some Terasaki letters are in the Fellers Papers, MacArthur Library. Other details of Terasaki come from a tape of the NHK broadcast on The Emperor's Monologues, provided to us by Bruce Merkle.

38   Watanabe Yuri and Kawaii Michiko are both discussed by Liebenthal (see the bibliography).

39   Alice Perry Grew's grandfather was Matthew's brother Oliver Hazard Perry, the American naval hero of battles on Lake Erie in the War of 1812. Some background of Alice's girlhood in Japan and her aristocratic connections can be found in the book compiled by Edwin Robinson and cited in our bibliography.

40   Grew–Morgan connections come from Heinrichs, and from Chernow, whose *House of Morgan* is outstanding.

40   Grew's impressions of the Japanese elite are from his two memoirs in our bibliography, and his personal correspondence and unpublished diaries at Harvard's East Asia Center. See also Nakamura Masanori, and Dower, *Empire and Aftermath*. What Grew failed to see is identified by Chalmers Johnson and Karel van Wolferen as Japan's 'structural corruption'.

40   Scattered facts about Sadako can be found in the works of Ponsonby-Fane, Stephen Large, and

443

Elizabeth Vining. Other details about her family genealogy came from Hamish Todd.

41 For the history of Japan and the Yamato dynasty before 1868, Sansom's three volumes are highly recommended. As a financial adviser to the British Embassy in Tokyo, Sansom had a rare comprehension of financial politics.

45 Japanese scholars such as Irokawa point out that the Meiji Restoration was no revolution, and 'it was made to appear that the emperor ruled'. See also Professor Carol Gluck's *Japan's Modern Myths* and the excellent, groundbreaking study by Professors Ramseyer and Rosenbluth.

46 Meiji's indolent lifestyle. Gluck describes Meiji's contrived public image. Perceptions of the real Meiji are found in the diaries of his advisers, especially Kido Takayoshi, in our bibliography.

46 Imperial Household details are from Titus, *Palace and Politics in Prewar Japan*. Few institutions are so secretive.

46 Taisho's image as a buffoon was the creation of Yamagata Aritomo. Those who fell for this disinformation campaign include Leonard Mosley (see the bibliography), but it has been repeated carelessly for decades. Mosley is often ridiculed by scholars, who go ahead and cite him as a source anyway.

46 On the modern police state see Tipton, *Japanese Police State: Tokko in Interwar Japan*.

47 Hirohito as weakest, least promising prince. Details of Hirohito's infancy and youth are from memoirs of Kanroji, Irie, and the 1940 article by Taguchi.

48 Nothing was done to ease the desperation. Irokawa Daikichi speaks bitterly of the famine and enslavement of girls and women in *The Age of Hirohito*.

49 Golden Lily. Only the vaguest mentions of Japan's looting of Asia from 1931 to 1945 appear in general histories of the war. Compare this to the massive literature on Nazi looting. Iris Chang touches only briefly on the issue at Nanking, where some 6,000 metric tons of gold in all were believed to have been

444

looted by the Japanese. Our information has been assembled over twenty years and involves confidential Japanese and Western sources, who fear being murdered if they are identified. One reason why evidence of the involvement of the imperial family in looting is surfacing only now is explained by Bix: 'Unlike in Germany, where the Allies confiscated enormous amounts of top-secret government documents and conducted their war-crimes trials on the basis of that evidence, most of the top-secret wartime records of the leaders in Japan were either deliberately destroyed in the weeks before MacArthur's arrival, or else falsified or hidden, leaving wartime memoirs and oral testimony' as the basis for much of what has been learned since about Japan's role in the war. Burning all documents is referred to sourly by journalists (and even by Japanese officials) as 'the Japanese Way'. A similar situation confronts investigations of corruption in the selection of Nagano as the site for the 1998 Winter Olympics; this investigation is hampered by the fact that the Japanese Olympic Committee burned all its records, describing the act as 'the Japanese Way'. Because Japan obscured her wartime record during the lifetime of Emperor Hirohito, it is only since his death in 1989 that the façade has begun to crack. See Brackman, *The Other Nuremberg*, and Bix, 'The Showa Emperor's "Monologue"'.

49   Prince Chichibu's involvement in Golden Lily. A number of Japanese and other sources have told the authors that Prince Chichibu headed Golden Lily between 1941 and 1945, and have identified other princes as working with Prince Chichibu. These sources include Japanese and Filipinos who participated in placing war loot in numerous elaborate sites in the Philippines, onshore and offshore; in the inventory of the loot before the sites were sealed and disguised; and in the subsequent recovery of loot from many of these sites. Several of these sources have undergone lie-detector tests, stress analysis tests and

hypnosis. The authors conclude that they are telling the truth, but our investigation continues and will be reported in detail in a sequel to this volume. The authors have direct personal knowledge of the existence of the war loot, and the recovery of massive quantities. But the full scope of the princes' participation is still to be measured.

49   On the gold Buddhas, see Bruppacher, Guyot, Lucas.

49   Japanese hospital ships. Roger Dingman talks about the fate of one of these hospital ships, the *Awa Maru*, and mentions reports of looted treasure aboard. But he does not attempt to resolve the 'rumours'.

50   Gold bullion sunk in Tokyo Bay is from Manning.

51   There was never a formal investigation of Japan's looting. America was so anxious to keep Japan from going communist after World War II that Washington blocked other Allies' demands for an inquiry, and shielded Japan from any potentially damaging investigations. See our postwar chapters for details.

CHAPTER 1: REINVENTING THE EMPEROR

53   Details about Meiji in this and other chapters come from many sources. We used Japanese sources whenever possible. See the articles of Yonekura Isamu, the diaries of Kido Takayoshi, the books of Oka Yoshitake, Stephen Large (particularly *Emperors of the Rising Sun*), William Griffis, and Carol Gluck, and the very accessible *Kodansha Encyclopedia*.

53   Perry's fleet arrived on 8 July 1853.

53   Details of Perry's visit are in Arthur Dudden's *The American Pacific*.

54   Emperor as divine hostage is discussed by Ramseyer, Gluck and Sansom.

54   On the danger of being divine, see Sansom Vol. 3, p. 235. The use of emperors as a political shield also comes from Sansom.

55   Our genealogy of the imperial family comes from an unpublished family tree painstakingly compiled by Hamish Todd, curator, the British Library Oriental

& India Office Collections. We were fortunate to be given access to this document, the only accurate source in English. There is a website with a genealogy (geocities.com/Tokyo/Temple/3953/) but use it with caution.

56   Emperor Komei's children. Details are few. An early Western scholar who studied the Japanese royals, Ponsonby-Fane, combined anecdote with genealogical details, and included rare portraits and photos.

56   Materials about Lord Nakayama are from Yonekura Isamu, 'The History of the Imperial Family', *East*, Vol. 12, No. 1, January 1976, p. 16.

56   Wet nurses. Feeding infants whenever they show hunger is still the fashion. When Japanese grow up they rank second to Americans in snacking.

56   Meiji's tantrums and bad temper even as an adult are mentioned in Large, *Emperors of the Rising Sun,* p. 20. Tantrums were not confined to Japanese royals. Queen Elizabeth I was famous for her rages. One courtier said he 'would rather be in Calcutta' than be the target of the queen's rage.

57   Meiji's love of swords. He collected over three hundred masterpieces of Japanese swordmaking, some gifts from General Saigo. For colourful personal details of Meiji and his day, see Griffis, *Mikado*, pp. 309–10.

57   The wagon and Meiji's excursion are in Griffis, *Mikado,* p. 90.

57   Women around Meiji. Details of the role of women in the palace are found in Titus, *Palace and Politics in Prewar Japan.* See Thomas, *Modern Japan,* for accounts of the fierce character of ladies-in-waiting.

58   The hygiene practised by the ladies is in Griffis. Details of cotton masks and restrictions about how to thread a needle are from Hamish Todd.

58   Even imperial nutrition was poor. See Ivan Morris, *The World of the Shining Prince,* and Charles Dunn.

59   Emperor Komei's poem is in Griffis, *Mikado,* p. 95.

59   Sansom tells of the lack of food imports even during famines.

60   'For more than ten years' is from Katsu Awa, in Sansom, Vol. 3, pp. 237–8.

60   'Exhausted voluptuary' is from Sansom, Vol. 3, p. 208. Ienari died at 69 in 1841, and was succeeded by one young shogun, then another, who was in power when the shogunate was overthrown.

61   Cannibalism, uprisings and spies in the bath house are from Sansom.

62   The emperor concept became all important. Ramseyer, p. 17 and notes.

62   Komei's unexpected strength is in Ponsonby-Fane, *The Imperial House,* p. 123.

63   Mori's secret slush-fund. Sansom, financial attaché at the British Embassy, mentions this secret Choshu treasury.

64   The chief counsellor who was assassinated. Discussions of Il Naosuke are in *Encyclopaedia Britannica, Kodansha Encyclopedia* and articles by Yonekura Isamu. His assassins were ronin from Mito and samurai from Satsuma. The murder was 'especially savage', Thomas, *Modern Japan,* p. 49. For the need to get rid of him, see Beasley, *The Rise of Modern Japan,* p. 39.

64   Politics of brute force. The extraordinary peace of the Tokugawa era was permanently shattered and the 'physical force politicians' took control of events. Griffis, *Mikado,* pp. 285–6, uses the term to describe politics by assassination in the 1880s, but brute force was a major element in Japanese politics from the 1850s to 1945. In the 1990s, as we shall see, a Japanese mayor was shot when he merely said that Hirohito bore 'some' responsibility for the war.

64   The plan to 'rescue' Komei. This account of the attack on the palace in the hope of kidnapping Komei is from Griffis, *Mikado,* pp. 113–15. An American educator hired by the Restoration government in the 1870s, Griffis said he 'heard the story of this battle from the lips of . . . men, who took part in defending the Palace'. The incident is mentioned briefly in 'Reign of Meiji', *Fortune,* July 1933. Four clan officials

	involved were sentenced to death, and three Choshu field commanders were obliged to commit suicide. Hackett, p. 34.
64	Meiji fainting is from *Kodansha Encyclopedia,* Vol. 5, p. 153.
66	'Frog in a well' is in a letter of 5 April 1865 to Chargé d'Affaires Winchester, probably from witty Ito Hirobumi. See Accounts & Papers, LXXVI (1866), p. 457, British diplomatic records. The image is from the ancient Chinese tunnel-vision proverb: 'The frog in the well thinks the sky is round.'
66	Fate of Komei's sister. Yonekura, *East,* Vol. 11, No. 10, December 1975, p. 24.
66	Circumstances of Komei's death are in Griffis, *Mikado,* p. 122. 'Melancholy fever' was how Thomas said contemporary sources identified the fatal illness, p. 50. According to Thomas, 'Bergamini goes so far as to allege suicide or murder, referring to the famous statesman Iwakura as Komei's "assassin".' In fact, Japanese sources say murder is a strong possibility, and name Iwakura. Rumours spread throughout the court that the emperor was poisoned. These rumours are even included in the cautious *Kodansha Encyclopedia.* 'Some claimed that the court had not compromised sufficiently with the Shogunate and thus the emperor was killed; others claimed that the emperor had proven an obstacle to the overthrow of the Tokugawa and thus had to be eliminated.' So the attribution to Bergamini by Thomas is intended to make it seem outrageous, which is misleading. Bergamini is everybody's favourite whipping boy. See also Yonekura, *East,* Vol. 11, No. 10, p. 24.
66	Iwakura, the man thought most likely to have arranged Komei's murder, was close to the manipulative Satsuma oligarchs. Here we refer specifically to Japanese author Irokawa Daikichi, *Culture of the Meiji Period,* p. 252. Iwakura was from a family of court nobles and after the Restoration became one of Japan's most powerful leaders. By the late 1870s he was the de facto head of the government.

67   'He has mysterious visions' and descriptions of Meiji's fears are from Yonekura, *East*, Vol. 12, No. 1, p. 17. According to Yonekura, Meiji suffered a nervous disorder in the months following his father's death.

67   'In this age' from Meiji's mother is in Yonekura, *East*, Vol. 12, No. 1, p. 17.

67   Parkes's audience with Meiji. Details of the first audience are from Mitford, Lane-Poole, Satow, Fujitana, Griffis, and Brown's 'Kido Takayoshi and the Young Emperor Meiji', p. 3.

68   The plan for Meiji to make a speech is described in Satow, p. 358.

68   The attack on the Parkes party is described in Satow, p. 358. Mitford's account identifies Nakai. Satow remembered: 'Nakai brought the head of the other man back with him, and kept it by his side in a bucket as a trophy; it was a ghastly sight; on the left side of the skull a terrible triangular wound exposed the brain.'

68   The description of Meiji's appearance is by Mitford quoted by Fujitana.

68   Meiji's black teeth are mentioned in 'Reign of Meiji', *Fortune*, July 1933. Blackening of teeth was a practice followed by the nobility. Scraps of iron were soaked in tea or sake and this 'mouth rinse' had the effect of blackening the teeth. It appears to have been effective in warding off tooth decay, at least this is what some physical anthropologists have concluded from dental remains.

69   Reintroducing the emperor to the people. Gluck's *Modern Myths* argues that the notion that Japan's imperial traditions date back to the fifth century BC is a fabrication. Like Ramseyer, she sees the emperor as an icon.

69   'Enveloped' is from Gluck, *Modern Myths*, p. 73.

69   Meiji's first excursion was described by Griffis, *Mikado*, p. 138.

69   Working on Meiji's military image is from Gluck, *Modern Myths*, p. 74.

70	'Imperial decision.' One of Meiji's advisers claimed it was Meiji himself who made the final choice. Thomas, *Modern Japan,* p. 45, says Kido records the choice of Tokyo as the new capital as a result of 'imperial decision'. All this means is that Meiji gave his nod to a decision made by the oligarchs.
70	The royal move. The Tokaido road scene and the court's move, and chanting, are from Gluck, *Modern Myths*, p. 74. There are also references in Gibney, *The Pacific Century,* p. 80, and in Brown, 'Kido Takayoshi and the Young Emperor Meiji'. See also Kido diaries and the article by Addis.
71	About Meiji's bride, Princess Haruko. Her full name was Ichijo Haruko (1850–1914). Details of her life are few. We found bits in *Kodansha Encyclopedia* and *Japanese Biographical Encyclopedia*. Eyewitness accounts are from Clara Whitney, from the two-volume collections edited by Ian Nish, and from Satow, Griffis, and Ponsonby-Fane. Hamish Todd provided her genealogy.
71	The significance of moving into the shogun's castle is discussed by Thomas in *Modern Japan*, p. 45.
71	Details of Prince Alfred's visit are from recollections of Mitford, the secretary of the British legation, later Lord Redesdale, quoted in Nish, Vol. 2. Recognition from a foreign power, especially the number-one power in the world at the time, was of great importance for Japan's new regime.
71	The problem of 'cleansing' Prince Alfred is in Griffis, *Mikado*, p. 159.
72	Griffis mentions the snuff box.
73	Meiji's preference for pampered inactivity was one of the major concerns of top men like Kido; see his diaries.
74	Kido, Saigo and Okubo. When the decision was taken by Satsuma, Choshu and their allies to oust the shogun and make the emperor sole head of state, many leading samurai were slain or found wanting, but these three survived to carry out the plan. See Hall, *Japan: From Prehistory,* p. 270.

74	Kido's family lived in great comfort in a mansion. There were two doors to a doctor's office – one for the samurai and one for ordinary patients. Kido's father blended traditional Japanese medicine with Western medical practices and was instrumental in pushing his son to study Western ways. Details of Kido's early background and his father's profession come from Sidney Brown. See also the essay on Saigo in Ivan Morris, *The Nobility of Failure*. There is good material in annotations to Kido's diaries.
75	Saigo had been close to Emperor Komei.
75	Okubo material is from Oka, *Five Political Leaders*, Hackett, Nakamura Kaju, and Thomas.
75	Okubo, Saigo Kido and Ito all had Western-orientated education. See Hall, *Japan: From Prehistory*, p. 269.
75	The new State Council was headed by two court nobles – Sanjo Sanetomi, allied with Choshu, and Iwakura Tomomi, allied to Satsuma. See Hall, p. 271.
76	Making the imperial family impervious to blandishments and bribery was suggested to Okubo and Ito by Germany's Iron Chancellor, Otto von Bismarck.
78	Meiji's drinking parties. In *Shining Prince*, Morris describes palace drinking parties in tenth-century Japan, descriptions which still applied in the nineteenth century. 'Drinking parties were extremely popular. Wine was poured for each guest in turn according to his rank; often people were expected to recite a poem or sing a song before raising the cup to their lips. There were several drinking games, in which the losers were obliged to drink the "cup of defeat", and these frequently turned into drunken carousals.' Much the same ritual is practised today by Japanese business executives. Concern about Meiji's voluptuous lifestyle was voiced frequently by Kido in his diaries.
78	Reorganization of the Imperial Household with Inside and Outside is from Titus, *Palace and Politics*.
79	Saigo's new regime of manly sobriety. Among the exemplary samurai installed at the palace were

Takashima Tomonosuke, Shima Yoshitake and Tamaoka Tesshu (Tetsutaro). *Kodansha Encyclopedia.*

79   Iwakura mission. This was not the first time Japanese missions had been to the West. 'The process of Westernization began early. The shogunate in 1860 had sent a mission of 80 samurai officials to the United States to ratify the commercial treaty. A second shogun embassy traveled to England, Holland, and France in 1862. In 1863 Choshu secretly sent five of its young samurai to England. In 1865 Satsuma sent 19 men abroad.' See Hall, pp. 267–8.

80   There are many sources on Saigo's plan for Korea. The most accessible is the 'Saigo' entry in *Encyclopaedia Britannica.*

82   Details of Saigo's rebellion are in Hackett's biography of Yamagata. Hunter also was consulted.

82   *Kodansha Encyclopedia* calls Kido the 'conscience of the cabinet'. Although there is no firm evidence of Okubo provoking Kido's death, that cannot be ruled out, given Okubo's ruthless nature. Kido's death is described in notes to his diaries. 'Brain fever' can mean meningitis, a big killer of adults throughout the world even today.

83   'Ah, your face'. Yamagata's farewell to Saigo is from Hackett, pp. 80–1.

83   Gibney in *The Pacific Century* mentions the patent of nobility for Saigo's family. In the end, it seems that Meiji was deeply affected by the death of his great general. According to Yonekura, 'Soon after the rebellion, when the emperor gathered the Court ladies to have them compose *waka* poems in memory of Saigo Takamori, he told them: "Do not slander Saigo on account of his offense. Do not disgrace the great achievements he made in the restoration by merely considering his rash and reckless acts of late."' Yonekura, *East*, Vol. 12, No. 1, pp. 23–4.

83   Saigo's poem is in Morris, *The Nobility of Failure,* p. 231.

83   Okubo's murder is in Griffis, *Mikado*, pp. 277–8, and *Kodansha Encylopedia*.

CHAPTER 2: BISMARCK'S MOUSTACHE

84   'Ito is my drinking companion'. Quoted in 'Reign of Meiji', *Fortune,* July 1933. The article contains many anecdotes about the Meiji emperor (Mutsuhito).

84   On closer inspection. Professors Ramseyer and Rosenbluth remark: 'We think some of the "facts" of Japanese history as scholars traditionally understood them are not facts at all. All too often, in Japanese history scholars have used implausible hypotheses to explain phenomena that never occurred.' They conclude that 'as a symbol the imperial house was highly manipulatable and effectively indeterminate'. They closely examine Japan's power politics in the early twentieth century, and the ruthless competition between oligarchs like Ito and Yamagata. An emperor is a useful icon in the hands of oligarchs, whose modern incarnation, as we shall see, are financiers, political dealmakers like Kishi and Takeshita, and outlaw godfathers like Kodama.

84   Our portraits of Ito and Yamagata derive from many sources. Oka Yoshitake's *Five Political Leaders* contains a well-rounded portrait of Ito. Nakamura Kaju is valuable. Ramseyer challenges the conventional wisdom. Beasley's works provide details of Ito, Yamagata and contemporaries. Others include Griffis, Satow, Fujitana, Titus, and Gluck. Yamagata's chief biographer is Hackett, who drew extensively on Japanese-language sources.

85   Ito and Meiji's companionship is described in 'Reign of Meiji', *Fortune,* July 1933.

86   Ito's smoking dispensation is from Oka's *Five Political Leaders,* p. 24. Oka also gives details of Ito's love of wine and women. In the letters of Tsuda Ume edited by Furiko Yoshiko *et al.*, there are details of Ito's marriage and his mistresses.

86   Oka is the source for Ito's evenings out and favourite

song. See pp. 36–9. Ito's switching from harsh to meek is also from Oka.

86 Ramseyer says Ito and the others went to England at the invitation of an agent of the Hong Kong traders, Jardine Matheson.

87 Controlling police and patronage. For Ito's role see Oka, and Hackett. Hackett says Yamagata found out that 'behind the scenes the Mitsubishi interests are giving monthly financial support to Okuma'. Hackett, p. 100.

87 'I was deeply impressed' is from Oka's *Five Political Leaders*.

87 'Ito seemed to speak' is from MacDonald in Nish, Vol. 1, p. 144.

89 Ramseyer describes Itagaki's effort to strike back at Yamagata and Ito.

90 Okuma is portrayed in Oka's *Five Political Leaders*. See also Ramseyer.

91 Many sources describe Ito's fascination with Bismarck. See Oka, *Five Political Leaders,* pp. 8–9.

91 According to Richard Storry, 'There can be little argument that what the Germans did was to confirm Ito in the convictions he already held – namely that in the Constitution the powers of an elected assembly should be tightly controlled and restricted by an executive responsible, not to the assembly, but to the Sovereign Ruler of the country.' Storry, *Modern Japan*, p. 116. Among those who helped Ito draft his constitution was Herman Roessler, a German adviser to the Foreign Office in Tokyo.

91 The notion that Meiji was a 'liberal' is another bit of window-dressing contrived by Ito. 'From the outset, Ito's constitution was open to a variety of conflicting interpretations that no amount of political bargaining or accommodation could hope to resolve.' Oka, *Five Political Leaders*, p. 12.

92 About the constitution. In Hackett, p. 116, an over-enthusiastic Japanese contemporary hails the promulgation of the constitution as the 'Third Restoration'. Professor Irokawa Daikichi of Tokyo

University points out that most of the nearly thirty draft constitutions prepared by popular rights figures outside the government began with precisely the same reference to the imperial line being 'unbroken for ages eternal'. This clearly shows that the regime's efforts to give itself divine legitimacy through the emperor were a success. Irokawa, *Culture of the Meiji Period*, p. 256.

92 The Rescript on Education is in many sources, including Gluck's *Modern Myths*, and Hackett, p. 133. 'A copy of the rescript, together with portraits of the emperor and his consort, was kept by every school in a secure place, often a small shrine, and was brought out on national days to be read to all pupils. Its prestige was great among all Japanese, and it amounted to an insurance policy taken out by the oligarchy, to shield them against any waves of liberalism that might sweep over Japan in the future.' See Storry, *Modern Japan*, pp. 119–20.

93 The toothless nature of Ito's constitution and the way in which the idea of participatory government was manipulated by the oligarchs and to silence critics are examined by Ramseyer.

93 Karel van Wolferen in *The Enigma of Japanese Power* explores the role of Yamagata in the subversion of electoral politics.

94 'Hopelessly enthralled' is from Oka, *Five Political Leaders*, p. 19.

94 Meiji's education. 'For instruction in moral and political philosophy he was put under charge of the scholarly Nagazane Motoda.' See *Kodansha Encyclopedia*. Griffis also talks about Meiji's education, as do Kido's diaries.

94 This railway line was an experimental one that gratified the foreign community who desired quick travel from Tokyo to the treaty port. The line was opened by Meiji on 14 October 1872. See Checkland for the ceremonies, pp. 48–9. Gluck says, 'In the popular iconography of the Meiji period two ubiquitous images gradually emerged as symbols of civilization:

the monarch and the locomotive.' *Modern Myths*, p. 101.

94 Okubo's fascination with the West is in Pyle, *Modern Japan*, p. 86.

95 Meiji's preference for Japanese clothes is in Griffis, *Mikado,* pp. 303, 164. Meiji's style on horseback is from p. 301.

95 Meiji was a traditional Japanese. An American teacher who observed him said he always remained 'a Japanese of Old Japan'. Griffis, p. 93. His traditionalism is discussed by Yonekura, *East* Vol. 12, No. 1, p. 27.

95 Meiji's poetry writing is from Yonekura, *East,* Vol. 12, no. 1, p. 27. His love of Chinese novels is from *Kodansha Encyclopedia.*

95 'What is this' is from Yonekura, *East*, Vol. 12, No. 1, p. 27.

96 'Mightily pleased', other details of the royal progress and 'Might go too far' are from Kido's diaries.

96 'His hat' is from Whitney's diary, pp. 85–6.

96 Kido was worried about Meiji's isolation and withdrawal. Kido's diaries, especially Vol. 3.

96 'At present' is from Kido's diaries.

96 Meiji's daily routines are noted in Kido's diaries, Vol. 3, p. 468, More on Meiji's personal habits are reported by Griffis, *Mikado*, pp. 300–6.

97 Oka talks about Ito's uniform, his vanity and love of personal ornament. *Five Political Leaders*, p. 22.

97 'You need to' is from Oka, *Five Political Leaders,* pp. 22–3.

97 Both *Kodansha Encyclopedia* and Oka mention Ito's being long-winded, especially when fascinated by his own stories.

97 Examples of Ito's self-love are in Oka, *Five Political Leaders*, pp. 16–18.

97 It was made to seem that Meiji had a personal role in every decision. This results from the concept of *Kokutai,* Japan's 'national essence'. Here was something from the mystical past, not based on a social contract but an ancient immutable bond between the

457

emperor and the people. See Irokawa, *Culture of the Meiji Period*, pp. 256–7.

98   Hackett is the first to admit that Yamagata subscribed to the politics of bribery, while maintaining that Yamagata never accepted bribes himself. But we know from other scholars that Yamagata received income from a number of sources and became very wealthy. He collected full salaries from all of the various government and military positions he held simultaneously.

98   'Imperial rescripts are their bullets' is quoted from Diet member Ozaki Yukio shortly after the death of Emperor Meiji. In Mosley, pp. 24–5.

98   Haruko's poetry. There are only fragments in the histories about Empress Haruko. Her writing of 30,000 *waka* poems is noted by Ponsonby-Fane. Griffis adds other details, as does Tsuda Ume in her letters edited by Furiko Yoshiko *et al*.

98   'Through which we could see nothing': details from Tsuda Ume. See her biography by Barbara Rose, and her letters, edited by Furiko Yoshiko.

99   The description of Prince Albert's visit, of Meiji and Empress Haruko, is from Nish, Vol. 2, p. 85.

99   Tsuda Ume described the empress's luxurious attire. See Furiko Yoshiko *et al*. (eds), *The Attic Letters*, p. 274.

99   'Her dark eyes' is from Fraser, p. 17.

99   'She looked beautiful' and Haruko's smoking her little pipe is from Baroness Ishimoto's memoir, p. 63. Tobacco smoking was widespread in Japan, though it had been outlawed by the Tokugawa shoguns four hundred years earlier. Tsuda Ume was proud to note that 'The empress looked very well in foreign dress'. Furiko Yoshiko *et al*. (eds), *Attic Letters,* p. 256.

100   On Haruko, the Red Cross and upper-class ladies, see Haru Reischauer, p. 100. Haruko's favourite charity was the Tokyo Jikeiin Hospital, which she visited for twenty-five years, providing winter clothing for each invalid, and toys and candy for the children. Like Santa Claus she only came one day each year, but for

the entire day greeted everyone without exception, although members of her entourage fainted from exhaustion. See 'Reign of Meiji', *Fortune*, July 1933.

100 'The empress is exceedingly intelligent' is from Whitney's diary, p. 201.

101 The account of imperial visits to their noble subjects is based on Haru Reischauer's memoir, *Samurai and Silk*, p. 102. Haru was the wife of the American ambassador to Tokyo, Edwin Reischauer. Haru was from the old Japanese elite, her grandfather being Matsukata Masayoshi (1835–1924), one of the Genro, who served for many years as finance minister.

102 It would be better for Ito if he did not 'keep a Christian girl'. See Rose, p. 69. Tsuda Ume wrote in more detail: 'All the papers and everywhere are so much against him for his favorable policy to Christianity and scores of enemies are formed on that account. It will be politic in him, as he is not really so favorable to Christianity as they say, if he did not keep in his house a Christian girl.' See Rose, p. 69.

102 'It gives a shock' is from Montgomery, p. 222.

102 Precise details of Meiji's concubines and their offspring are from the genealogy of Hamish Todd and from *Meiji Tennoki*.

103 'She bore no children' is from Large, *Emperors of the Rising Sun*, p. 20.

104 'Yamagata is my soldier' is from 'Reign of Meiji', *Fortune,* July 1933. This is also the source for some examples of Meiji's discomfort in Yamagata's presence.

104 Hackett makes a virtue of Yamagata's austerity.

104 Hackett notes Yamagata's ability to escape blame. 'He was careful not to move ahead recklessly when the prospects for advancing were slim . . . he had the faculty of appearing and disappearing most skillfully, never being caught holding the bag.' Ramseyer mentions Yamagata's failure as a man of action. He was most effective in the shadows.

105 Yamagata's family. Hackett says Yamagata traced his ancestry to one of the branches of the Minamoto clan in the ninth century, as did many others.

105   Hackett is the source for Yamagata's early life as a revolutionary and spy. He quotes the suicide note of Yamagata's grandmother: 'If an old woman like me leans upon you, your resolution will become enervated. I, therefore, go to the other world, so that you may concentrate your mind and devote your life to the clan service.' Others say this is apocryphal, but Hackett quotes Yamagata himself as saying, 'She committed suicide that I might not be fettered by family ties.'

105   Hackett says Yamagata liked Prussian attitudes and found Paris fey.

106   'Chief of the Devils' is from Hackett.

107   No political discussion was permitted. Hackett quotes Yamagata: 'The executive power is of the Imperial prerogative, and those delegated to wield it should stand aloof from political parties and be guided solely by considerations of the general good.' Hackett, p. 112. See also Tipton for the evolution of the Japanese police state.

107   Information about Toyama Mitsuru and his secret society comes from Montgomery, Axelbrook, and Kaplan and Dubro.

108   Yamagata's attitudes towards political parties are covered in Hackett, van Wolferen and Ramseyer.

108   'Insincerity' is from Hackett, p. 93.

108   The anecdote about the department-store fire comes from Edward Seidenstucker, professor emeritus of Columbia University, in *Tokyo Rising*.

109   Details about Major Klemens Wilhelm Jakob Meckel come from Ernst Presseisen, and the Harrieses, *Soldiers of the Sun*.

110   'When large countries' is Bismarck from Pyle, *The Making of Modern Japan*, p. 98.

110   After leaving Japan, Meckel remained another eight years in the German Army, becoming quartermaster general, then at 54 retired to raise dogs and write his opera. When he married the divorced American heiress Carmela de Ripley, his former colleagues in

the high command were displeased. See Presseisen, pp. 126–7.

110 'Japan was a military nation' is from Iwasaki, 'The Working Forces'.

111 Line of sovereignty, line of advantage. Hackett quotes Yamagata: 'If we wish to maintain the nation's independence among the powers of the world . . . it is not enough to guard only the line of sovereignty; we must also defend the line of advantage.' Hackett, p. 138.

111 The importance of Korea and Manchuria to Japan is discussed in many books. See Pyle, *Modern Japan,* p. 137.

112 Japan's quandary as a modern nation without allies in the era of imperial power politics became an overriding concern of her foreign policy until World War II. See Pyle, *Modern Japan,* p. 138.

112 Battles between Japan and Russia at Port Arthur. See the Harrieses, *Soldiers of the Sun.* Also Cowley, *Experience of War,* p. 238. Among thousands of Japanese soldiers sacrificed in these battles were two sons of General Nogi Maresuke, later a teacher of Hirohito and his brother Prince Chichibu. At the time of Meiji's death, Nogi and his wife committed ritual suicide to join their emperor. Some people, however, believe that Nogi and his wife were murdered at the instigation of Yamagata. Gluck, *Japan's Modern Myths,* gives a good description of Nogi and details of his death.

112 Ito was reluctant to go to Korea. It would take him away from the centre of power and make him vulnerable. Oka, *Five Political Leaders,* p. 17.

112 'Beating' is from Montgomery, p. 187.

113 That Ito was 'overbearing and menacing' are words used by Oka, *Five Political Leaders.*

113 Uchida's and Yamagata's thugs are from Montgomery, p. 210, and the Harrieses, *Soldiers of the Sun,* p. 99. See also Axelbrook.

114 'What a fool!' The assassin was tried for murder in February 1910 at Lushun regional court, sentenced to death and executed. Oka, in *Five Political Leaders,*

461

takes it at face value that Ito was murdered by a Korean dissident. We disagree. Montgomery, p. 210, maintains that Uchida arranged the murder by a Korean member of Black Dragon. See Axelbrook.

114   On the plan for the annexation of Korea see Montgomery, p. 210, and the Harrieses, p. 99. Black Dragon's Uchida used links with a Korean organization called Iichinhoe. At Uchida's prompting, Iichinhoe presented a petition to both Korean and Japanese authorities in December 1909 calling for the merger of the two countries as the only way to protect Korea from predatory Western powers. Beasley, *Japanese Imperialism*, p. 90.

114   Details of Meiji's declining health are from a variety of sources including 'Reign of Meiji', *Fortune,* July 1933. In *Emperors of the Rising Sun,* Large says Meiji was suffering from diabetes by 1904, had Bright's disease, and after 1906 rarely left the palace. Mention of cancer is from *Japan Biographical Encyclopedia.* Griffis talks about Meiji's health problems, p. 308. Meiji's faltering steps are in Yonekura, *East*, Vol. 12, No. 1, p. 28.

114   'I am alone now' is from 'Reign of Meiji', *Fortune,* July 1933.

114   After Ito's death, said historian Oka, 'the sovereign noticeably entered old age'. *Five Political Leaders*, p. 25. 'No expediency' is from Yonekura, *East,* Vol. 12, No. 1, p. 27.

CHAPTER 3: THE TRAGIC PRINCE

115   Our portrait of Taisho is really not 'revisionist' when you consider that all this information has been there all along but was ignored in favour of the malignant caricature put about by the character assassins. How easy it was to write off Taisho as an oaf.

115   Taisho was called 'the tragic prince' by Kawahara, in *Hirohito and His Times*, p. 44.

115   'When [Taisho] is mentioned, it is usually in very unflattering terms'. Large, *Emperors of the Rising Sun*, p. 77. 'The fact that by the time Meiji died, intense interest in

the monarchy had made the office of emperor "public property" meant that Taisho would be subject to growing public scrutiny and his flaws would be widely known sooner or later, if not at the very beginning of his reign.' Large, *Emperors of the Rising Sun,* p. 118. While we agree in part with this point, Yamagata clearly had a hidden agenda in exaggerating and distorting Taisho's flaws to the public.

115   'Poor little fellow' is from Tsuda Ume. See Furiko Yoshiko *et al.* (eds), *The Attic Letters*, p. 265. Taisho was eight years old at the time, having celebrated his birthday six weeks earlier.

116   By late summer 1878, Meiji's empress had not produced a child, and his four offspring by his official concubines had all died in the cradle.

116   Taisho's mother. Yanagiwara Naruko was the eldest daughter of court noble Yanagiwara Mitsunaru. Ponsonby-Fane provides the name of Komei's empress, Eisho. Hamish Todd gives Naruko's dates as 1855–1943.

116   Naruko's first two children died. From the *Meiji Tennoki* we know the son was hydrocephalic, the daughter died of 'brain fever'.

116   Naruko's hysterical state was described in a book by Yamakawa Michiko, a lady-in-waiting at court. Lady Yamakawa said the infant was at first thought to be stillborn. See Hosaka.

116   Large says Taisho had meningitis at three weeks. Cases of newborn meningitis are usually contracted from the birth canal. Neonatal meningitis is described in great detail in *Manson's Tropical Diseases.*

116   Kanroji Osanaga, later Hirohito's chamberlain, gives many details about the early years of Taisho, as he does the early years of Hirohito. Other details of Taisho's birth and infancy came from Hamish Todd, and Large, *Emperors of the Rising Sun.* See also the diary of Dr Erwin Baelz, the German physician to the imperial family during Taisho's lifetime.

117   Taisho's hyperactivity. Medical researchers say hyperactivity can be due to low-level brain dysfunction,

damage so slight it does not register in tests, the result of trauma such as meningitis producing lesions on delicate linings protecting the brain. See *American Medical Association Family Medical Guide*, 'hyperactivity', p. 687. Kanroji speaks specifically of Taisho's restless nature, as does the German physician, Dr Baelz.

117   Erwin Baelz was born in Swabia in 1849. A Japanese official travelling abroad in 1876 was treated by the young Baelz. At the time, Westerners were coming to Japan in great numbers as advisers. Baelz was initially hired for a two-year term as professor of medicine at the Imperial Medical Academy in Tokyo. He fell in love with Japan and remained most of the next thirty years, marrying a Japanese. His diary was published through the efforts of his son. His Japanese patients were famous men – Iwakura Tomomi, Yamagata Aritomo, Inoue Kaoru and others. In 1889 when Okuma's leg was ruined by a bomb, Baelz was on hand to advise Japanese surgeons.

117   Taisho's sunny disposition is from Princess Nashimoto, quoted in Large, *Emperors of the Rising Sun,* p. 88, and Kawahara, *Hirohito and His Times*, p. 44. Bojo's comments about his good nature also are in Large, *Emperors.*

117   'Paying visits' is in Fraser, p. 108.

117   Packard mentions Taisho learning to tie his shoes and dress himself. When Emperor Pu Yi, the last emperor of China, found himself a prisoner at the end of World War II, he had no idea how to tie his shoes or button his shirt.

118   'The education' quote is from Fraser, p. 41. Large talks about Taisho's difficulties reading and writing in *Emperors of the Rising Sun.*

118   Baelz often comments on Taisho's lung problems. At one point he was thought to be suffering from tuberculosis.

118   His valet Bojo Toshinaga judged Taisho's poems to be mediocre. Large, *Emperors,* p. 85.

118   'Intellectually [he] is generally' is in Nish, Vol. 1, p. 142.

119   'A man of few words' is in Kanroji, p. 21.

119   The anecdote about Meiji not recognizing his own daughter comes from the Japanese biography of Hirohito's empress. See Koyama, *Nagako: Empress of Japan*, p. 70. The princess in question was probably Meiji's tenth child.

119   Taisho's love of fishing is in Koyama, p. 46.

119   Names of his playmates are in Kanroji, p. 30. Horror stories are from Large, *Emperors,* p. 85. The radish story is from Kanroji.

119   Major Tachibana is in Kanroji, pp. 30–4. After giving us this picture of Taisho's strenuous workouts, Kanroji says in the next breath that Taisho 'never had a robust physique'. Others said he was stocky and strong.

120   The anecdote about the Uematsu family is from Kawahara, *Hirohito and His Times*, p. 44.

120   'He bowed' is from Tsuda Ume. See Furiko Yoshiko *et al.* (eds), *The Attic Letters*, p. 386.

120   Large mentions the bream in *Emperors.*

120   'I was summoned' is from Baelz's diaries.

121   'The offspring' is from Large, *Emperors,* p. 89.

122   'This food' is in Large, *Emperors,* p. 87.

122   Finding a suitable bride. In 1891 the chief chamberlain was given the task of finding someone suitable for Taisho. Each month he invited prospective candidates to play with the emperor's daughters and give him a chance to observe their deportment. From this process Princess Sachiko, only daughter of Prince Fushimi Sadanaru, emerged as the favourite. The emperor and empress paid a visit to her father and reached agreement. However, in 1898 Sachiko became ill with appendicitis. Although she made a complete recovery, court officials saw a medical report about 'watery noises' in the right side of her chest. This might have an adverse effect on the imperial line. The list of candidates was reviewed and

the future Empress Sadako was chosen. See *Meiji Tennoki.*

123   Details of Sadako's family come mostly from Hamish Todd. See also Ponsonby-Fane, who includes photos of Empress Eisho, who died in 1897.

123   Elizabeth Vining, tutor to Crown Prince Akihito, became intimate friends with Empress Sadako. Sadako told Vining of her childhood, fostered by a family of well-to-do silk farmers, many of whom were Christians and, indeed, Quakers. Haru Reischauer said that by the 1870s in Gumma Prefecture 'silk and Christianity' were synonymous. Hamish Todd provided the Okawara family name of her foster parents. Letter to the authors, 18 November 1997.

124   'It was considered' is from Princess Chichibu's *The Silver Drum: A Japanese Imperial Memoir,* pp. 74–5.

124   'Brilliant mind' is Vining in *Return to Japan*, p. 32.

125   Large in *Emperors* mentions how Taisho's health was often kept secret from Meiji. Baelz's remark of 'improper' is from his diary.

125   Descriptions of Taisho and Sadako's wedding are from the Belgian ambassador's wife quoted in Mosley, pp. 1–2.

125   'The prince looks well and strong' is from the Baelz diary, p. 144.

126   'To feel a strong sense' is from Large, *Emperors.*

126   Dates for Taisho's children come from Hamish Todd's genealogy.

126   Custom of separating imperial infants from their parents is from the Baelz diary, p. 248.

126   'Unhappy princess' is in the Baelz diary, p. 240.

127   'Catching tails' is from Kanroji, p. 16.

127   Taisho's 'Paternal delight' is in the Baelz diary.

127   'He was very cheerful' is a quote from *The Honjo Diary*, p. 185.

127   Kawahara's charges appeared in *The Economist*, 7 December 1996. He may have the sequence wrong. In December 1904 Baelz wrote that Sadako was 'expecting the birth of another child [Takamatsu], the fourth in five years'. This would mean a pregnancy

between Prince Chichibu and Prince Takamatsu, ending in a miscarriage in 1903–4. Baelz, p. 329. Hamish Todd has found no trace of the twin-birth in any of the records he can access.

128   Baelz often refers to Taisho's deterioration during this period.

128   Many of these rumours of Taisho's ill-health and bizarre behaviour were spread by Yamagata through his web to the Japanese press. The report of rolling up his speech in parliament cannot be verified.

128   Kawahara, *Hirohito and His Times,* p. 44, said Taisho contracted meningitis shortly after birth. Hamish Todd is precise, saying the illness struck at three weeks old. Letter to the authors, 16 November 1997.

128   On meningitis we consulted *Manson's Tropical Diseases, Atlas of Tropical Diseases, Medline, AMA Family Medical Guide,* Garrett's *The Coming Plague* and *The Encyclopaedia Britannica.* Meningitis is common in winter when people cluster and thrives in poor hygiene: lack of bathing, lack of clean clothes, shared towels, handkerchiefs. It can kill in less than 24 hours. Humans are the reservoir. In Britain in the late 1990s several young adults died despite medical intervention. Dr Charles Fattal, a French expert on brain damage, told us brain lesions provoked by neonatal meningitis can cause grave problems many years later, with adults suffering progressive loss of abilities similar to Taisho's.

130   Taisho's 'womanizing'. Hara's reports are in Large, *Emperors,* p. 89.

130   'No, that cannot' is in Large, *Emperors,* p. 89. Hackett does not mention such unsavoury details. Of course, the source of the story is Yamagata himself.

130   Kawahara in *Hirohito and His Times* tells the anecdote of Sadako trying to limit Taisho's drinking. Taisho drank much less than Meiji or Ito. Details of Taisho's pastimes come from Kawahara, *Hirohito and His Times*, p. 44. See also Large, *Emperors,* chapter 2.

131   Further deterioration of Taisho's health is noted by A. Morgan Young, *Japan under Taisho*, p. 176. Also Large, *Emperors,* pp. 96–100.

133   Taisho's final illness and death are from Kawahara, *Hirohito and His Times*, p. 42.

135   Tutor to Ito's wife and daughter, Tsuda Ume wrote of her experiences. See Furiko Yoshiko *et al.* (eds), and the biography by Rose. Haru Reischauer, in *Samurai and Silk*, mentions the Canadian school, p. 231.

135   Information about Christians in Japan is from Lawrence Wittner. By 1945, Sadako was one of some 300,000 Japanese Christians in Japan.

135   For information on Christian faculty members of the Peeresses School see Rose, p. 70, and the memoir of Ishimoto Baroness Shidzue.

136   On Sadako's religious convictions, Vining says Sadako read the New Testament almost daily, but quickly adds that Sadako 'was not a Christian'. When we spoke with General Fellers's daughter, Nancy Gillespie, she laughed aloud at a question about what Vining's statement meant. Gillespie said her father had no doubt that Empress Sadako was a Christian.

136   The translation of the New Testament is mentioned by Haru Reischauer in *Samurai and Silk*.

136   Wittner gives the statistics about Bible translations.

CHAPTER 4: THE CAGED BIRD

137   Of Hirohito's 'hunchback', Kanroji says the 'emperor appears to be stooped because of an unusual amount of muscle on the shoulders'. Scoliosis, a form of curvature of the spine, sometimes causes a hunched shoulder. Visitors remarked that vertebrae in his neck clicked when he turned his head.

137   Anecdotes of Hirohito's overprotective upbringing are from Taguchi, and Kawahara, *Hirohito and His Times*, p. 16.

139   Details of Hirohito's birth and placement in foster care are from Taguchi, Kanroji, and Kawahara. Taguchi and Kanroji tell of the old admiral

summoned by Taisho to learn that he must look after the baby. Kanroji says Hirohito was turned over to the admiral on 7 July 1901, p. 151.

139   Anecdotes of the admiral and the young princes are from Taguchi.

140   Details on Ethel Howard are from Hamish Todd, from the introduction to a Japanese edition of Howard's book, *Japanese Memories* (published in English in London in 1918 under her married name, Bell).

140   'Fostering' is from Kanroji, who gives Howard's three principles.

140   'Children – especially in upper-class families' is from Taguchi.

140   'I won't eat' is from Kanroji, p. 19.

140   'I have got weary' is from Taguchi.

140   Kanroji tells of Hirohito's nightmares, and the recollection of Chichibu.

141   'Always played strictly' is from Kanroji, p. 16.

141   'Winning by losing' is from Taguchi.

141   The kindergarten set-up is in Kawahara, *Hirohito and His Times*, p. 15.

142   The zoo anecdote is from Kanroji, p. 24.

142   'Ten years of drinking' is in Kanroji, pp. 44–5.

142   Hirohito's fumbling is in Kawahara, *Hirohito and His Times*, p. 16.

142   The problem of eyeglasses is in Kanroji, p. 27.

142   Kanroji talks of Hirohito's poor coordination, difficulty with sports and 'posture', pp. 26–7.

143   Hacking pigs and criminals are from Haru Reischauer, *Samurai and Silk*.

143   Nogi's passion for alpine sports is in *Samurai and Silk*, pp. 301 and 305. Chichibu's love of sports is from *Silver Drum*, p. 121.

143   Kanroji tells of Hirohito's passion for sumo, and includes a photo of the young prince wrestling. Chichibu's disinterest in wrestling is noted in *Silver Drum*.

143   Togu palace: see Kanroji, p. 23.

143	Chichibu and Hirohito's exchange on freedom is from Kanroji, p. 42.
144	The personality differences between the two brothers are often remarked upon. Nogi was alarmed by Sadako's preference for Chichibu. In *Silver Drum* (p. 180) Princess Chichibu says her husband had 'such a specially close relationship with his mother'. Also Koyama, p. 87; Kawahara, *Hirohito and His Times*, p. 16.
144	Hirohito's secondary education and details of Takanawa palace school are from Taguchi. Kanroji says Hirohito began a diary at this time, p. 41. Meiji also kept a diary, the mark of an educated man. The diaries are still top secret.
145	Hirohito's serious nature is from Kawahara, *Hirohito and His Times*, p. 16.
145	Hirohito's eyeglasses and special chair are from Kanroji, p. 27.
145	Chichibu was born 25 June 1902, died 3 January 1953. Hirohito was born 29 April 1901, died 7 January 1989.
146	Hirohito's restricted social life is in Taguchi, and Kanroji, p. 41.
146	Initial selection of bride candidates for Hirohito is in many sources. See Kawahara, *Hirohito and His Times*, pp. 9, 26 (mentions photos on p. 10). *Japan Biographical Encyclopedia* gives details of Nagako's selection and says that she was formally chosen consort on 17 January 1918. Her biographer Koyama talks about her candidacy. Three prime candidates is from Hamish Todd, letter to the authors, 15 December 1997.
146	Yamagata's favourite was Ichijo Tokiko from one of the 'five collateral families' – the Konoe, Ichijo, Kujo, Nijo and Takatsukasa. Todd letter to the authors, 18 November 1997. Todd: 'Miss Ichijo has been wrongly identified by several authors (British and Japanese) as Ichijo Asako, but this is an incorrect reading of the ideograph of her name. When she was not chosen for Hirohito, she was married to another

imperial prince, Fushima no Miya Hiroyoshi, who died in the late 1930s of wounds sustained in the China War.'

146   Taisho and Sadako's first choice was Princess Masako (father's full name Prince Nashimoto no Miya Morimasa O). Masako's father was, in fact, a half-brother of Nagako's father, and half-brother of Prince Asaka and Prince Higashikuni. This made Masako and Nagako paternal first cousins. At the end of World War II, Prince Nashimoto was the only member of the imperial family imprisoned for war crimes; see our later chapters.

148   Aizu connection: Princess Chichibu talks about this in *Silver Drum*. General Oyama's Vassar-educated wife, Princess Oyama, was also from Aizu. There was a strong Aizu influence in the palace inner circle. See Kuno Akiko, *Unexpected Destinations: The Poignant Story of Japan's First Vassar Graduate*.

148   Nagako was the parents' second choice. Her mother was seventh daughter of Prince Shimazu Tadayoshi of Satsuma. Mosley scrambled up the relationships. Hamish Todd's genealogy sorts them out.

148   Haruko's role in choosing Nagako. Details concerning Nagako, Meiji and Haruko come from Koyama, pp. 11–14, and Hamish Todd.

149   'Frogs in the well' was Ito's view of ignorant xenophobes (see p. 66). They hated Empress Sadako and her urbane circle and saw them as disloyal to Japan because they included so many 'Western devils'. One 'devil' was the personal physician of the rich Shimazus, Baron Doctor Takaki Kenkan, who had studied at St Thomas' Hospital in London, a centre for Quaker doctors blocked from other institutions because of their religious convictions. When Russia's Crown Prince Nicholas was wounded in Kyoto in 1891, Dr Takaki was sent by Emperor Meiji to attend him. His daughter-in-law was an English interpreter for Empress Sadako. Another 'devil' was General Oyama's widow, Satematsu, one of five Japanese girls sent to America with Empress Haruko's blessing in

the early 1870s. See Kuno, p. 81, Vining, and Haru Reischauer.

149   Our source for these descriptions of Sadako is Vining, *Windows,* pp. 157–9, and *Return to Japan,* pp. 33–4. For other positive appraisals of Sadako by Japanese see Nakamura Masanori, p. 123. Dr Koizumi is quoted in Vining's *Return to Japan,* p. 34. While Shidehara was Japan's ambassador to Washington in the 1920s, his children attended Quaker-run Sidwell Friends School, seedbed for cosmopolitan Japanese. See *Silver Drum,* p. 30.

149   Prime Minister Hara had worked for a newspaper founded by Ito, had been consul in Tientsin and was esteemed by Ito. Oka, *Five Political Leaders,* pp. 88–9. Hara's quote is in Kawahara, *Hirohito and His Times,* p. 35.

150   The physical examination of Nagako is in Koyama, p. 20.

150   On Princess Masako. Masako and Princess Chichibu were maternal first cousins. After Yamagata's death Sadako was able to arrange the marriage of her second son to Masako's first cousin, Setsuko. Masako's marriage to the crown prince of Korea was ridiculed because of extreme Japanese prejudice towards all things Korean. Princess Chichibu mentions Masako and her husband fondly in *Silver Drum.* They owned land in central Tokyo, formerly belonging to the Kitashirakawa family, and lived in an elegant French Gothic residence filled with priceless antiques. After World War II, they sold it to land developer Tsutsumi Yasujiro who turned it into the Akasaka Prince Hotel. See Havens.

150   Nagako's paternal grandfather was involved in a plot during the Meiji Restoration and later pardoned: Hackett, p. 335, Note 122.

151   For Yamagata's gripe that he was stabbed in the back and not 'advised of the negotiations', see Koyama, p. 32.

151   Nagako's biographer, Koyama, refers to this period

of intense private schooling. Hamish Todd calls it 'the princess school'.

151   'Politics are the government's responsibility' is from Hara's diary as quoted by Hackett, p. 333, an entry dated 22 September 1920.

152   Yamagata's warning not to visit the palace too often was noted by Hara in his diary, an entry dated 13 October 1920, quoted by Hackett, p. 333.

152   'Grave court affair' is from Hackett, p. 335.

152   'A sordid struggle' is from Young, p. 227.

152   Crump, *Death of an Emperor,* tells the anecdote about Dr Hirai.

152   Yamagata's efforts to block the engagement because colour-blindness ran in Nagako's family are discussed in Hackett, Crump, and Koyama.

153   The plan to buy off Prince Kuni is mentioned by Crump, p. 87. Prince Kuni's angry counterattack is from Koyama, pp. 30–1.

153   Hackett concedes that Yamagata got it wrong. 'Prince Kuni was encouraged in his position when the court physicians pointed out that "color weakness" rather than "color blindness" was the more accurate term.' See Hackett, pp. 336–7, Note 130. Prince Kuni's rebuttal and threat, 'It was the imperial house', is from Kawahara, p. 27.

154   'Is someone making noise to annoy us?' is from Koyama, p. 24.

154   'Surprisingly rude behavior' is in Kawahara, *Hirohito and His Times,* p. 27.

154   Yamagata's fear of Black Ocean is in Hackett, p. 337, and Crump, p. 87.

154   Hackett's biography of Yamagata rarely admits to any flaws in his subject. 'Charges and countercharges swirled around the court and the highest levels of the government. And a wide variety of explanations were offered for the cause of the conflict. One view held that Yamagata was determined to prevent an alliance between the court and the Satsuma family . . . Another explanation [cited] scheming people in the household of Prince Koya . . . [or] a consequence of the rivalry

473

among scholars hoping to be selected to tutor Nagako . . . Other explanations were rumoured . . . but none satisfactorily answered the question of why the issue was raised when it was.' The very dark side of Yamagata is the reason why.

155 'It is incomprehensible' is from Young, p. 227.

155 'The engagement was . . . behind our back' is in Koyama, p. 32.

155 'As for Prince Yamagata' is quoted by Hackett, p. 339. Okuma's biographer, Idditti Smimasa, describes Okuma as a statesman who ran a newspaper and discussion club, and was a popular speaker. Okuma helped Tsutsumi Yasujiro get his start in the Diet and business. See Havens for more.

155 No scars on his back is from Idditti, p. 414.

155 The 10 February 1921 announcement is in Hackett, p. 338. Kawahara *Hirohito and His Times* says Nagako's selection was made in 1918, but Hirohito was not told of the decision for two years. No two sources agree about this engagement.

155 'I am merely a soldier' is from Hackett, p. 340. Hackett does not see the wonderful irony here.

156 Yamagata was let off the hook officially. Hackett, p. 340.

156 Yamagata died 1 February 1922.

CHAPTER 5: OUT OF THE CAGE

157 The visits of British royals to Japan 1869–1906 are in Nish, Vol. 2.

158 For further discussion of Anglo-Japanese ties, and meddling by Washington, see *Kodansha Encyclopedia*; *Encyclopaedia Britannica*; Beasley, *Japanese Imperialism*; Elphrick; Paul Kennedy, *Rise and Fall of the Great Powers*; Buckley; and Coox and Conroy.

159 When Tokyo needed loans. Among financiers involved were Britain's Sir Ernest Cassel and America's Russian-Jewish emigré, Jacob Schiff.

161 Large mentions plans for a Meiji trip abroad and reasons why it never came off. *Emperors,* p. 27.

161   Taisho's foreign trip was ruled out because of ill-health: Baelz was recalled from Germany to offer his opinion on the crown prince's health. See his diary.

162   Nish, Vol. 2, 'Crown Prince Hirohito in Britain', is excellent on details.

162   Nara Takeji remained a figure in the palace as Lord Steward to Sadako. See Large, *Emperor Hirohito and Showa Japan*.

162   Three Crows are in Montgomery, Shillony, *Revolt*, pp. 43–4. Okamura was one of three military attachés who met secretly at Baden-Baden in 1921 and decided to fight Choshu domination of Japan's army, creating a clique of supermen. The other two were Obata Binshiro and Nagata Tetsuzan.

162   Anecdotes from Hirohito's sea voyage come from Kawahara, *Hirohito and His Times;* Kanroji; Nish, Vol. 2; and Gunther.

163   Wardrobe problems are from Dower, *Empire and Aftermath*, pp. 50–1, and Nish, Vol. 2.

164   Admiral Takeshita Isamu's role is in Nish, Vol. 2, p. 209.

164   'He mixed freely with the guests' is quoted in Kanroji, pp. 85–7.

165   'Extraordinary' and other Yoshida remarks are in Dower, *Empire,* p. 52.

165   'I hope, me boy' is from Mosley, p. 57. While Mosley is eccentric, even scholars regularly cite his works. See Large, *Emperors,* p. 218, Note 17.

165   Details of Curzon's reception come from Crump, p. 89.

166   For the cowlick, see Augustus John's *Chiaroscuro.*

166   The Scottish sojourn is from *The Times*, 3 March 1921, and Nish.

167   'A modest and gentle prince' and other quotes in this paragraph are in *The Times.*

168   Rumours that the young man in London was a stand-in are in Kanroji, p. 85.

168   Media coverage of Hirohito's trip is in Large, *Emperors,* p. 109.

168   'There are still rumours' is from Mosley, p. 61.

168   Edward's image as a Don Juan does not bear scrutiny. He was sent on four tours between 1919 and 1924, covering 55 countries. When Hirohito arrived in England, Edward was nearing breakdown and made no secret of his boredom, but he was no rebel, sublimating with alcohol instead. Women were available, but he looked to them for solace, not sex. See Spoto.

169   Hirohito's Metro ride is reported erroneously in most accounts of his trip. It was said that he kept his ticket instead of surrendering it to a ticket collector, but in the Paris Metro tickets are thrown away at the exit. In the case of Hirohito, he simply kept his. There was no ticket collector.

169   The mansions of Prince Asaka and the others are from Downer, pp. 104–6. Havens adds a bit. Details of their highlife in Paris come from French journalists. But we are the first to remark upon the special nature of this quartet, and its extraordinary influence on twentieth-century Japan, from Paris to Nanking, Golden Lily and the Nagano Olympics.

170   Mosley talks about dinner for 'four'. We believe the party comprised Hirohito and his uncles. Kanroji also mentions the snails.

171   'The trip was a huge success' is Hara, in Large, *Emperors,* p. 110.

171   'A profound impression in Japan' is quoted in Thomas.

173   Kanroji has the quotes: 'Apparently some people feel', 'I knew freedom as a man', 'A bird in a cage'.

173   Hirohito's remarks to Honjo are in Honjo's diary.

173   'The freedom I crave' is from Hugo Gordon's article in the *Daily Telegraph*.

174   'When I asked a military aide' is from *Takamatsu no Miya Nikki* (*Diaries of Prince Takamatsu*). Translations were specially made for us by Hamish Todd.

175   'No other occupation is so ridiculous' and 'A cockroach living in the mountains' are from Hugo Gordon's article.

175   Hirohito's swinging new lifestyle on his return to
        Tokyo is from Kanroji.
176   Hirohito's 'wild' party is discussed in Kawahara,
        Hirohito and His Times, and Large. It might have
        comforted Hirohito if he had known that he was not
        alone in his royal chagrin. When Queen Mary decided
        to learn some of the new jazz dance steps, King
        George walked in on a lesson. He rebuked her so
        completely that she never tried dance lessons again.
        See Spoto. Of course, Prince Saionji had been a wild
        libertine in his own youth.
176   Large, *Emperor Hirohito*, p. 25, mentions the golf
        hook. Kawahara, *Hirohito and His Times,* p. 38, tells
        of the hostile reception of the Imperial Household.
177   Details of the April Fool's Day accident of Prince
        Kitashirakawa, Prince Asaka and Princess Fusako are
        from *Le Matin,* 2 April 1923, the *Japan Weekly
        Chronicle,* 5 April 1923, the *New York Times* and
        The Times.

CHAPTER 6: YAMAGATA'S GHOST
179   Hirohito's wedding date was originally set for
        November 1923. See Kawahara, *Hirohito and His
        Times*, p. 40.
179   Details of Kanto earthquake of September 1923 are
        from Walker, *Earthquake*.
180   Economic devastation by the earthquake is from
        Chernow, *House of Morgan*, p. 234.
180   The emperor's calm reaction is from Kanroji, pp.
        102–3. Young (p. 310) confirms that some buildings
        in the palace grounds were ruined by the quake, but
        he does not say whether by tremors or fire.
181   Thomas talks about the backlash against Koreans.
        There was a very long history of bad blood towards
        Korea, which was now enslaved by Japan. In 1919,
        students in Korea declared their country independent
        from Japan. Demonstrations throughout the penin-
        sula caught Japanese occupation forces off guard. To
        cover their surprise, the army reacted with extreme
        violence, killing some 8,000 Korean demonstrators

and wounding 46,000 others. Korean communities in Japan seethed with hatred. See Cheong Sung-hwa, *The Politics of Anti-Japanese Sentiments in Korea*.

181   Details of brutality to Koreans come from Young; Irokawa, *The Age of Hirohito*; Montgomery; and Thomas. 'Our cavalry was excited with this bloody ceremony' is in Thomas, pp. 139–40.

181   Killing of socialists comes from Montgomery, and Young. Laying the blame on socialists comes from Thomas, pp. 139–40.

182   Princess Chichibu's memoir tells us about the sewer-pipe residence; the detail about tapioca and beans is from Haru Reischauer.

182   Haru Reischauer speaks of a 200 million-yen loan. Chernow, p. 236, speaks of a $150 million loan, concluded February 1924. The global role of the House of Morgan is nicely evoked in Chernow, particularly his chapter 10.

183     $1.5 billion in credits: Chernow, p. 209.

183   Details of Lamont are from Chernow, E. Lamont's *Ambassador from Wall Street*, articles in the *New York Times*, and Thomas Lamont's memoir, *Across World Frontiers*.

183   Chernow talks of Lamont's China trips, pp. 230–1. The quotes are from Lamont's memoir, *Across*, p. 241.

184   That Morgan must refrain from loans to China is in Lamont's memoir, *Across*, p. 262. Lamont's first visit to Japan is described in his memoir, and by E. Lamont in *Ambassador*.

184   'Corruption in Japan.' Structural corruption is a term used by Karel van Wolferen and by Johnson; see *Japan: Who Governs?*, p. 184.

186   Among the men who most impressed Lamont in Japan was General Yamagata, the canny police snoop who rose from extreme poverty to great wealth and power by taking multiple incomes (and exquisite gifts) behind the screen. 'Mr Lamont,' said the general, 'my two axioms are: with China peace and trade; with America friendship, always friendship,

478

and commerce as well.' For a 'simple soldier' the old spider had a surprisingly good grasp of the importance to Americans of hearty smiles and bonhomie. See Lamont memoir, p. 259. Van Wolferen is one of the few modern Japan-watchers to appreciate the malignant influence of men like Yamagata on Japan's current predicament.

186   The earthquake loans, and some problems Lamont encountered with potential American investors, are described by E. Lamont. 'Permanent client' is from E. Lamont, p. 196.

186   Details of the 'assassination attempt' on Hirohito come from many sources. Montgomery says Nanba Daisuke was from Choshu. See also Irokawa, *Age of Hirohito*, and Stephen Large's two books.

187   'Entirely changed after the Toranomon Incident' is from Irokawa, *Age of Hirohito*, p. 9.

187   Description of Hirohito's wedding is from Koyama; Kawahara; Irokawa, *Age of Hirohito*; and Young.

188   Toyama was a wedding guest: Montgomery, p. 274.

188   'The same way they learn to plant a garden' is in Ruth Benedict, *The Chrysanthemum and the Sword*, p. 283.

188   Dates and names of Hirohito's children come from the genealogy of Hamish Todd.

188   'A princess . . . Oh, bother' is from Takamatsu's diary for 10 September 1927, translation by Hamish Todd.

189   Some characterizations of young Prince Chichibu come from the *New York Times*, 25 December 1926. See also recollections from Princess Chichibu's *Silver Drum*, and the obituary of Princess Chichibu in the *Daily Telegraph*, 1 September 1995. Kanroji touches on the differences between Chichibu and Hirohito.

189   Chichibu was 'a heavy drinker who never got drunk', Shillony, pp. 99–100.

189   Chichibu indulged by his mother. General Nogi, who taught the boys, expressed concern about Sadako favouring Chichibu. *The Honjo Diary*, p. 51.

189   Details of Chichibu's travels are from the *New York Times*, 25 December 1926, and *Silver Drum*.

190   Details of the Matsudaira family are from *Silver Drum* and the memoir of Gwen Terasaki, *Bridge to the Sun*. Her husband, Terasaki Hidenari, was one of Matsudaira's protégés. Nish, Vol. 1, has an essay on Matsudaira.

190   For her years in Washington, Princess Chichibu is the best source. See *Silver Drum*. We were also helped by Sidwell Friends' alumni office.

191   That Princess Chichibu was 'really lovely' is in Grew's memoir, *Ten Years*.

191   'My first impression' is from *Silver Drum*, p. 23.

191   Count Kabayama's wife was the daughter of Admiral Kawamura, first foster-father of young Hirohito and Chichibu. See *Silver Drum*, pp. 57–8.

192   History of the Matsudaira clan is from Nish, Vol. 1, and *Silver Drum*.

192   The dismay of Princess Chichibu's parents is very clear in *Silver Drum*, including the quote, 'I was speechless.' Royalty was suffocating.

194–6   Princess Chichibu says in *Silver Drum* that she was warned against bringing jazz records to the palace. Details of her wedding ensemble and the ceremony are in *Silver Drum*, pp. 77 and 100. 'There are lots of my classmates' is p. 113. Rollerskating, squash court and films are all from *Silver Drum*.

197   The isolation of Hirohito and Nagako from the rest of the family is noted by Princess Chichibu and by Kanroji.

197   'Bring England, America and Japan closer together' and 'concerned about Japan's future' are from *Silver Drum*, pp. 104–5.

197   'Attentive intimacy' and 'a beautiful thing to see' are in Kanroji, p. 107.

198   The bird stories are in Kanroji, pp. 106–7. Ping-pong and piano playing are in Kawahara, *Age of Hirohito*, p. 141. Grew noted that Prince and Princess Chichibu were excellent ping-pong players. Of the royals Grew met, he found only the Chichibus completely amiable and relaxed.

198   Golfing is from Kanroji, pp. 105–6, 141, and

Koyama, p. 57. Kanroji said Hirohito seemed very lonely when he played golf without his bride.

198   The biology lab and Nagako's participation are from Kawahara, p. 42, and Kanroji, p. 107. Details of Hirohito playing with his children also come from Kanroji.

199   Koyama is the source for Nagako's nurturing of her children and for the criticism she endured for her maternity. See Koyama, p. 70.

199   Hamish Todd gives the death date of Princess Sachiko as 8 March. Others say 7 March.

199   Nagako's biographer Koyama is the source for 'Yamagata's curse' and subsequent wasted efforts to interest Hirohito in a mistress.

199   First heir born to an empress. Hamish Todd says Hirohito was the first male heir born to an empress since Emperor Momozono in 1758.

199   Count Tanaka, leader of the 'other woman' movement, is from Koyama. That Hirohito had nothing to do with them is discussed in Koyama, pp. 80–7. Koyama observes that Hirohito was said not to care about the succession.

201   There are many places where yellow-peril jingoism is discussed. See Dudden among others.

201   'Save it from Russia'. See Elphrick, pp. 16–17.

202   Thomas devotes pp. 153–4 to the problems of the poor in Japan.

202   Gibney, *Pacific Century,* has Mitsubishi mines and child labour, p. 100.

202   Ineptitude of the communists is described by Thomas, p. 155.

202   Komei Kato's cabinet in 1925 passed the Peace Preservation Law.

202   Bix talks of the danger of criticizing the government in the 'Showa Emperor's Monologue'. Tipton's book surveys the police state in Japan.

203   On strengthening the Peace Preservation Law, see Tipton, Thomas, Bix.

203   'A freedom to do what you should do' is from Dower, *Empire and Aftermath*, pp. 250–1.

203	Dower mentions the scandal that unseated Hatoyama, and also describes Hatoyama's postwar role: *Empire and Aftermath*, pp. 249–52. Hatoyama is also discussed by Bix, and Kataoka Tetsuya.
204	Ginza and glitz are from Richard Storry, *History of Modern Japan*, p. 167.
204	Sweetheart deals. For example, the Matsukata family (future in-laws of US Ambassador Edwin Reischauer), one of the most influential, obtained huge loans for its own personal interests. They took 50 per cent of the big loans and 30 per cent of the total lending of the Fifteen Bank. See Tamaki, pp. 152–3. For more on Matsukata and international finance, see Nish, Vol. 1, pp. 120–32.
205	The figure of 800 banks going bust comes from Tamaki, *Japanese Banking,* p. 158.
205	Irokawa, *Age of Hirohito*, describes the impact of the Wall Street Crash on Japan. Beasley discusses this in *Japanese Imperialism*.
205	The plight of the silk farmer and Japan's inability to feed itself are in Thomas.
205	Data on females sold into slavery are in Irokawa, *Age of Hirohito*, p. 8.
205	Lamont met Hirohito and described his audience. 'The emperor . . . clothed in military attire . . . [was] a young man of medium Japanese size with heavy eyebrows and rather protruding lips. He had a pleasant and cordial expression . . . he gave me a cordial handshake.' E. Lamont, pp. 233–4.
206	For the loans see E. Lamont. Tom Lamont pulled strings whenever possible, staying in close touch with Grew and arranging for Prince Konoe to take lunch with J. P. Morgan aboard his yacht while watching the Harvard–Yale crew races. Lamont also arranged for Konoe to visit Herbert Hoover in California. Like other financiers east and west, Lamont imagined that 'moderates' would prevail over 'extremists' and Japan's aggression on the mainland would be halted. See E. Lamont, p. 414.
207	Looking to Korea and Manchuria. See Irokawa, *Age*

of *Hirohito*, pp. 12–14, and Beasley, *Japanese Imperialism*.

207   The growing partisanship and the coming collision is well covered in Dower, *Empire and Aftermath*.

CHAPTER 7: EVIL SPIRITS

208   Details of Takamatsu's early years come from his diaries, *The Honjo Diary*, newspaper articles and information provided to us by Hamish Todd.

208   'I feel no love for the opposite sex' is from Takamatsu's diary, 20 February 1923. Translation by Hamish Todd.

209   'For many centuries homosexuality': Buruma, *Behind the Mask*, p. 129.

209   Spoto, pp. 194–5, gives the details and the king's reaction.

209   The allegation of insanity in Princess Takamatsu's family is mentioned by Hane in his translation of *The Honjo Diary*, p. 29.

209   Princess Takamatsu's temper was affirmed by Hamish Todd. On her mother's family we have Todd's genealogy and his memo of 18 November 1997. The Four Princely Houses: Arisugawa, Fushimi, Katsura, Kan'in.

210   'A love romance' is a phrase from the *New York Times*, 11 April 1931.

210   'Focus of all eyes' is from the *New York Times*, 11 July 1930.

210   On the Takamatsus in London see the *New York Times*, 27–8 June 1930.

210   For Prince Takamatsu as a moderate, see Hane's introduction to *The Honjo Diary*, pp. 51–2. He was one of the first in the imperial family to press Hirohito to bring a speedy end to the war against the United States.

210   'For the mutual good of the whole world': the *New York Times*, 28 June 1930.

210   For more royal itinerary see the *New York Times*, 18 November 1930 and 18 January 1931. Interviews and quotes are from the *New York Times*, 11 and 15

April 1931. Details of the reception in New York and Washington are the *New York Times*, 11, 12, 16 and 17 April 1931.

211   Hirohito's cable was in the *New York Times*, 19 April 1931.

211   'Completely won our hearts' is the *New York Times*, 24 April 1931. At this time Terasaki Hidenari was in the Japanese Embassy in Washington, DC. According to his daughter, Mariko Terasaki Miller, there was a dead silence at the dinner party. The Takamatsus could not relax, nor could their hosts. 'It was a real Quaker meeting,' said Mariko.

212   The Grews arrived in Japan on 6 June 1932. See Grew's *Turbulent Era* and *Ten Years in Japan*. We also read Grew's unpublished letters and diaries at Harvard's East Asian Institute. His biographer is Waldo Heinrichs.

212   *Kodansha Encyclopedia* identifies Alice as Commodore Perry's great-grandniece. (Her great-grandfather was Matthew's brother Oliver Hazard Perry, hero of battles on Lake Erie in the War of 1812.) Her fluency in Japanese is widely affirmed.

212   Dower calls Keio University 'a citadel of nascent capitalists' where founder Fukuzawa extolled 'the patriotic virtues of economic man'. See *Empire and Aftermath*, an excellent read.

213   Grew's early life and his Japanese valet, Suzuki, are from Heinrichs.

213   'What really bowled me over' is from Grew, *Ten Years,* p. 26.

214   Grew's total lack of contact with the lower orders is from Heinrichs, p. 14. How Grew misread the German situation is clear in Heinrichs, pp. 20–1.

215   'Modest millionaire' is how Hoover's biographer Nash described him. In 1914 his fortune was modestly estimated to be between $1 million and $10 million. There is a critical biography waiting to be written about Herbert Hoover and his role as back-room manipulator of the Republican Party from 1932 to 1964.

215   Heinrichs, p. 33, documents Grew's quick turnabout on Germany.

215   Meeting with Japan's elite at Versailles is in Grew, *Ten Years*, p. 26.

216   For background on Grew's Quaker grandmother, see Heinrichs, p. 4.

217   The complexity of the situation in Japan in the mid-1930s leading up to the crisis of 1936 is discussed by Shillony in *Revolt*. Other interpretations of these events include Maruyama's. See also Lesley Connors, and Large's article on the imperial princes. Grew's papers and memoirs provide zero insight. Implications of the revolt are still poorly grasped. Many problems the young officers attempted to redress in 1936 still exist today, and are still being dodged.

217   The assassination of Chang Tso-lin was planned by Colonel Komoto Daisaku. Hirohito's army minister, Shirakawa Yoshinori, was confronted by the problem of whether or not to punish the colonel. In a secret memo that came to light only decades later, Hirohito said: 'According to what I heard, Komoto said that if he was put before a court-martial and interrogated, he would have revealed everything about Japan's plot. So, I understand that the military court-martial was cancelled.' From The Emperor's Monologues.

217   As one Japanese scholar points out. Chimoto Hideki, cited in Bix, 'Showa Emperor's Monologue'. Bix and others, including the Australian government, concluded that Hirohito had 'ratified' the Manchurian Incident and thereby encouraged other rogue military actions. See The Emperor's Monologues.

218   'At 4.20 p.m.' The source was Nara Takeji; see Bix, 'Showa Emperor's Monologue', pp. 342, 343. Also for 'When I asked His Majesty'.

218   Hoover's private support of the Japanese takeover of Manchuria is mentioned in the Harrieses, *Soldiers of the Sun*.

219   'Cutting down like weeds' is in Bix, 'Showa Emperor's Monologue', p. 344.

219   When Japan invaded Shanghai in 1932, the new Japanese 'concession' was administered by an organ called the Shanghai Northern District Citizens' Municipal Maintenance Association, set up by the Japanese military and run by the Chinese Green Gang mafia. 'This government, in fact, was nothing more than a glorified extortion agency whose main administrative function was to run gambling houses, opium divans and brothels.' See Brian Martin, p. 151.

220   Details of Inukai's assassination and his quotes come from Oka, *Five Political Leaders of Modern Japan,* and Shillony, *Revolt.*

221   The attacks on Mitsubishi, etc., are noted by Gunther.

221   'We were greatly alarmed' is in Princess Chichibu's memoir.

222   The young men in the Imperial Way faction were radical right, not radical left. They admired religious mystic Kita Ikki, who advocated suspending the Meiji Constitution and nationalizing 'excess' wealth. Enemies characterized them as Marxists to panic the establishment.

222   See Shillony, *Revolt,* for a discussion of the Control Group, and Toland. Corruption of the 'pure' military is discussed by Shillony, p. 24.

223   'It is obvious' is from Shillony, *Revolt,* p. 217.

223   General Araki's young admirers were known as the Imperial Way faction because Araki sprinkled his statements with 'imperial' this and 'imperial' that, and his followers favoured restoring all power to the emperor. Most were young southerners from prefectures once called Hizen and Tosa, which together with Choshu and Satsuma had carried out the Meiji Restoration. They felt destined to lead a new restoration. They earnestly believed that 'evil men' around the throne had usurped the emperor's power; killing them would fix Japan's problems. One was a son-in-law of General Honjo, head of the Kwantung Army in Manchuria, who after 1933 was Hirohito's military aide. Such connections shielded them from the secret police. See Shillony, *Revolt.*

224   The poverty of the young officers and their men is mentioned in Shillony, *Revolt*; in *Silver Drum*; and in Irokawa, *Age of Hirohito*. Thomas describes the suffering of many in Japan at the time. Irokawa and Shillony say the regime was not interested in helping the poor, preferring to let them all die.

224   'Look around' is from Shillony, *Revolt*, p. 15.

225   Fully occupied and harmless. For a discussion of this feudal standoff, see Sansom, the outstanding British historian of Japan. Ignorance and poverty were tools of suppression.

226   Scathing criticism of Hirohito. The army used the word *bon'yo*, mediocre. See Shillony, *Revolt*, p. 102.

226   'Questioning the sagacity of His Majesty' is from Shillony, *Revolt*, p. 103.

226   Nishida Mitsugi was in the same academy class as Prince Chichibu and succeeded in approaching Chichibu in the gardens when he was not accompanied by his guardians. In his diary, Nishida wrote: 'What I was looking for was not merely the support of an Imperial Prince, but a way to reach through Prince Chichibu the highest person in Japan, the Emperor.' Shillony, *Revolt*, pp. 241–2.

226   'Those who now comprise' is Chichibu in Shillony, *Revolt*, p. 99.

227   'I agree' is in Shillony, *Revolt*, p. 98. For Chichibu's common touch, see Shillony, *Revolt*, p. 99, and Kanroji. Much is made of this by his wife in *Silver Drum*. For Chichibu's sympathy with the Cherry Blossoms, see Shillony, *Revolt*, p. 100.

227   In the Shimpeitai Affair of 1933, plotters intended to replace Hirohito with Chichibu, and make their uncle, Prince Higashikuni, prime minister of a reform cabinet. The plotters thought Chichibu more 'resolute' and Hirohito too 'absent-minded'. See Shillony, *Revolt*, p. 108.

227   'Don't be a fool' is from Shillony, *Revolt*, p. 100.

228   Saionji's fear of Chichibu is discussed by Shillony, *Revolt*, p. 107. See also Large, 'Imperial Princes and Court Politics'.

228   Before his murder, Inukai had ordered a new Lincoln automobile, which arrived after his death. Grew was offered the use of the car until his Cadillac arrived by ship weeks later. Grew, *Ten Years,* p. 17.

228   Heinrichs describes the remodelled embassy, p. 192.

228   Grew reports Makino's warning in *Ten Years*, p. 33.

228–9   The party with Hirohito and Nagako, and the 'story of our lives' quote are from Grew, *Ten Years*, pp. 16–17.

229   'Beaming' is from Grew, *Ten Years*, p. 122.

229   Sambo's adventures are in Grew's *Ten Years.*

229   Grew's distance from reality in Japan and his reliance on Sadako's Westernized advisers are discussed by Nakamura Masanori in *The Japanese Monarchy: Ambassador Joseph Grew and the Making of the 'Symbol Emperor System'.*

230   'A really great gentleman' is Grew, in Nakamura Masanori, p. 43.

230   Makino is well described by Dower, *Empire and Aftermath,* as are many other 'moderates' at court. See pp. 231–4.

230   The pendulum theory is discussed in detail in Nakamura Masanori, and Dower, *Empire and Aftermath.*

230   The best biography on Yoshida is Dower's *Empire and Aftermath.* Yoshida's own memoir is opaque and self-serving.

231   'If we speak Japanese' is in Mrs Yoshida's memoir, *Whispering Leaves,* p. 28.

231   Assuming Hirohito was a liberal pacifist: see Nakamura Masanori.

231   The other two Crows were Obata Binshiro and Okamura Yasuji. See Shillony, *Revolt*, pp. 43–4.

232   'An extraordinary political disturbance' is in Shillony, *Revolt,* p. 39.

232   The Tsuji detail is from Shillony, *Revolt,* p. 45. For Tsuji's extraordinary career during the Pacific War, see Seagrave, *Lords of the Rim.*

233   'Thank you' is from Shillony, *Revolt,* p. 53.

233   Prince Chichibu's transfer was made in August 1935.

Shillony points out it was rare for an imperial prince to be posted outside the Tokyo region. It is certain that Hirohito personally approved Chichibu's transfer.

233   Shillony says Yamashita endorsed the young officers' manifesto.

233   Prince Chichibu's remarks, *Hirohito*, p. 67. See also Large, *Imperial Princes and Court Politics*, *Japan Forum* Vol. 1, No. 2, October 1989.

235   Shillony, *Revolt,* pp. 92–3, remarks on big business contributions to the military.

235   Grew complained about the chill reception. 'I had to be received by the Grand Master of Ceremonies of the Empress in order to request him to express to her Majesty the New Year's good wishes of the diplomatic Corps.' *Ten Years,* p. 162.

235   Hirohito skiing on the palace grounds is from Irie.

237   'Recently, evil and selfish people' is in Shillony, *Revolt,* p. 147.

237   'So they have finally done it' is from Kanroji, p. 125.

237   'They have killed my advisers' is from Shillony, *Revolt,* p. 173.

239   'Fall like an avalanche' is from Connors, p. 169.

239   Higashikuni's binge is from Large, 'Imperial Princes and Court Politics', p. 261.

239   Takamatsu understood 'extremely well' is from Hane's introduction to *The Honjo Diary*, p. 52. A religious cult claimed that Takamatsu was the successor to the southern court of the Ashikaga period, which they saw as the true dynastic line. See *The Honjo Diary*, p. 50.

239   Connors is one source for the material on Chichibu's activities.

240   The imperial family fear of Choshu is in Connors, p. 171. We touched on this earlier regarding the animosity of Taisho and Sadako towards Yamagata. That Taisho's sons were fostered by a Satsuma admiral furthers the case.

240   'Prince Takamatsu is the best' is from Shillony, *Revolt,* p. 100.

241   'Long live Chichibu!' is in Large, 'Imperial Princes ...',
       p. 262.
241   In March 1936, a month after the rebellion, Marquis
       Kido asked Chichibu to stop criticizing Hirohito. A
       year later, in spring 1937, War Minister General
       Count Terauchi complained of secret meetings
       between Chichibu and young officers. In 1941
       Terauchi had overall command of the invasion of
       Southeast Asia. Many historians think he was only a
       front for the Control Group.
241   'How disgusting it is' is from Shillony, *Revolt*, p. 203.

CHAPTER 8: WITH THE PRINCES AT WAR
243   Yoshida's inheritance is from Dower, *Empire and
       Aftermath*.
244   A MacArthur/Lindbergh ticket is backed by Bonner
       Fellers in letters to Herbert Hoover. Fellers Papers,
       MacArthur Library.
244   Yoshida's tortured argument is in Dower, *Empire*,
       and echoed by Prince Konoe in his famous memorial
       to Hirohito presented in February 1945.
245   Princess Chichibu describes her husband as
       Hirohito's proxy at the coronation of Pu Yi, in *Silver
       Drum*, p. 122. Pu Yi's visit to Tokyo is in Honjo's
       diaries, Pu Yi's autobiography, and *Silver Drum*.
245   Tojo's secret files are from Dan Kurzman, p. 126.
246   Many details of Kishi come from Kurzman's book,
       and conversations with the authors at the
       Washington Post. See also Chapter 12 of this book.
246   The involvement of Japanese bureaucrats, military
       and *zaibatsu* in the drug trade in Manchuria, China
       and Southeast Asia is widely reported. See the
       Harrieses, *Soldiers of the Sun*, Jonathan Marshall,
       Brian Martin.
246   The good life in Manchuria is from the Cooks' superb
       Japan at War.
246   'Chastise' and 'Crush' are from Toland, *Rising Sun*,
       pp. 51–2.
247   Chichibu's visit with Hitler is in *Silver Drum*.

247 Roosevelt's threat of 'quarantine' is from Toland, *Rising Sun*, p. 53.

248 Konoe's relaxed, almost irreverent attitude to Hirohito, and sympathy for the reformers, is from Oka's biography, *Konoe*.

248 'Civilian leaders must carry out the necessary reforms' is in Oka, *Konoe*, p. 36. Konoe's view of the Versailles treaty is from Oka. For Konoe's militant attitudes see Large, 'Imperial Princes and Court Politics'.

248 'The military stood up' is from The Emperor's Monologues.

249 Aside from being a career army officer, and playboy intriguer, Asaka was devoted to golf. His palace and life after the car accident are in Downer, pp. 106–7. See Havens for business arrangements between Princes Asaka, Higashikuni, Takeda and Kitashirakawa, and speculator Tsutsumi Yasujiro and his son Tsutsumi Yoshioki.

250 Hamish Todd said Prince Asaka was widely regarded as 'the nasty one'.

250 Theory that Hirohito gave Asaka the Nanking assignment as a chance to redeem himself: Large, 'Imperial Princes and Court Politics', argues that Asaka was in disgrace for having been involved, however obliquely, in plots against Hirohito of the early 1930s. Iris Chang also speculates on the reason Asaka was assigned to Nanking. For background on General Matsui Iwane see Iris Chang; Toland, *Rising Sun*; the Harrieses, *Sheathing the Sword*.

250 'Sparkle before the eyes of the Chinese' is Matsui quoted by Iris Chang.

251 'Kill all captives' is from Iris Chang. She mentions an argument that the orders were not necessarily issued personally by Asaka but this is specious, as no aide would give such orders without his master's instruction.

251 'Complete anarchy' is from the Harrieses, *Soldiers of the Sun*, p. 222. For details of atrocities, Iris Chang provides many in her excellent book. Brief summaries

can be found in Time-Life's *Rising Sun*; Toland, *Rising Sun*; the Harrieses, *Soldiers of the Sun;* and the Cooks' seminal work, *Japan at War*. You will find no such accounts in Japanese history books. Even in the 1990s, the Japanese government still refused to acknowledge the Nanking atrocities in full, and Japanese politicians still pointed out that there had been earlier rapes of Nanking, including one by China's Manchu rulers during the Taiping Rebellion of the mid-nineteenth century. Japan's Ambassador to the United States (Saito) denounced Iris Chang's book as 'groundless', like neo-Nazi assertions that the Jewish Holocaust was imaginary.

251 'Appalling atrocities' is a rare insight from Grew, *Ten Years*, p. 249.

252 The railroading of Matsui as a war-criminal scape-goat for Asaka is treated in a number of sources: Montgomery, pp. 394–8; the Harrieses, *Soldiers of the Sun* and *Sheathing the Sword*; Toland, *Rising Sun*, pp. 56–7; and Iris Chang. Another man hanged to shield Asaka was Hirota Koki, Japan's foreign minister at the time of the Rape. No imperial princes were punished for war crimes, and only one was briefly jailed for unrelated activities. Prince Asaka made 'spiritual' amends by joining the Roman Catholic Church in 1951. For Hoover's and MacArthur's duplicity in all this see the next two chapters. All the other men convicted for war crimes during the Rape of Nanking were later released by the Japanese government.

252 'How much longer' is in Calvocoressi *et al*., p. 809.

252 Tar Baby metaphor is from Calvocoressi *et al*., p. 809, and Grew.

253 Hirohito's donation of trinkets is from Gunther, *Inside Asia*, p. 16.

253 For Japan's looting of Beijing in 1900, see Seagrave, *Dragon Lady*.

253 Japan's looting of Korean treasures is from James Sterngold's article in the *New York Times*.

253 Looting of Manchuria is in Bix, 'Japanese

492

Imperialism and the Manchurian Economy 1900–1931'. See also Beasley, *Japanese Imperialism*; the Harrieses, *Soldiers of the Sun*; Iris Chang; Kaplan and Dubro; Jonathan Marshall; Brian Martin; Martin Booth, *The Dragon Syndicates*; Seagrave, *Lords of the Rim*, *The Marcos Dynasty*. See also the second note for page 219 of this book.

254   Prince Takeda's assignment in Manchuria is from Sheldon Harris, *Factories of Death*.

254   Japanese who participated in hiding the loot insist that Asaka's son was one of the princes engaged in Golden Lily work in the Philippines; the sources cannot be named because of fear of extremist reprisals in Japan.

255   Knowledgeable gold traders and those involved in successful recoveries of war loot in the Philippines agree that Japan looted approximately 6,000 metric tons of gold from Nanking. (Authors' interviews.) Iris Chang, p. 161, gives the following account: 'Soldiers were permitted to mail back to Japan some of their booty, but most goods were confiscated and concentrated for official use. Warehouses filled rapidly with rare jade and porcelain, artwork, rugs and paintings, gold and silver treasures. In late December the Japanese began to heap stolen goods on the wharves for transport back to Japan. The Japanese used acetylene torches, pistol shots and hand grenades to blast open vaults in banks.' See second note for page 49, on Prince Chichibu.

255   A Filipino who spent three and a half years as a valet attending Prince Takeda and Prince Chichibu around the clock testified that they often had trouble sleeping because of nightmares they attributed to atrocities they witnessed at Nanking. The valet did not know what Nanking was.

255   Princess Chichibu gives amazingly few details of her husband's activities in the 1930s. 'Prince Chichibu left Japan in connection with the attack on Canton [sic]' – her history and geography are fuzzy. If, as she says, Chichibu was in the South China Sea in January

1939, this meant attacks on Hainan Island and the Spratleys. Canton had fallen the previous year. She said, 'He lived aboard a warship for some time.' See *Silver Drum*, p. 141.

255 An exhaustive treatment of Nomonhan is by Alvin Coox.

256 'Pursuing the [Russians] into Mongol territory' is in Coox, p. 255.

257 Nomonhan 'was definitely the first use of biological warfare by the Japanese army' is from Professor Tsuneishi Keiichi, in Gold, *Unit 731 Testimony,* p. 66. Iris Chang discusses the bigger picture during the war years from 1942. 'We now know that Japanese aviators sprayed fleas carrying plague germs over metropolitan areas like Shanghai, Ningpo, and Changteh, and that flasks of disease-causing microbes – cholera, dysentery, typhoid, plague, anthrax, and paratyphoid – were tossed into rivers, wells, reservoirs and houses. The Japanese also mixed food with deadly germs to infect the Chinese civilian and military population. Cakes laced with typhoid were scattered around bivouac sites to entice hungry peasants; [bread] rolls syringed with typhoid and paratyphoid were given to thousands of Chinese prisoners of war before they were freed.' Chang, *Rape of Nanking*, p. 216.

257 The mission with the typhoid jelly is from Gold, pp. 64–6.

257 Isshi Shiro and chemical warfare is from Gold, and Harris. See also the Harrieses, *Soldiers of the Sun*, Gomer *et al.*

258 Prince Takeda's pivotal position in the financial side of World War Two. '[Takeda] was the Kwantung Army Chief Financial officer and as such, he handled the monies allocated to all the biological warfare stations in Manchuria. He visited Ping Fan frequently. His most important responsibility as a staff member was to determine who would be granted permission to visit Ping Fan and the satellite facilities. When the commander-in-chief of the Kwantung

Army, or his immediate subordinates, visited Unit 731 laboratories, Takeda personally escorted them on their tours.' See Harris, *Factories*, p. 143. Harris is also the source for Prince Mikasa's visits. It was Japan's Kwantung Army, of which Prince Takeda was chief financial officer, that then struck south into China, eventually engaging in the Rape of Nanking. Prince Takeda was then attached to the staff of General Count Terauchi, the overall commander of Japanese armies that overran Southeast Asia, and was identified in each of these countries with Terauchi. When General Terauchi later moved his headquarters to the Philippines, Takeda also was based there.

258   Takeda's nom de guerre is given in Sheldon Harris as Miata. Hamish Todd says the spelling should be Miyata and we have followed his guidance. Memo to authors of 1 June 1998 from E. Murray.

258   Biographical details on Higashikuni come from his obituary in *The Times, Japan Biographical Encylopedia,* Shillony, Downer, Hamish Todd.

258   Chichibu attending biological warfare lectures and the urine experiment are both from Sheldon Harris, p. 144.

258   How the chemical/biological warfare was kept from the war crimes tribunal by General MacArthur is discussed by Roling and Tribunal Judge Cassese in *The Tokyo Trial and Beyond*. See also Brackman, Gomer *et al.*, Gold, and Sheldon Harris.

258   Princess Chichibu says Mikasa went to the front. See *Silver Drum,* p. 150. Photographs of Mikasa in uniform at the front are in several books he wrote, which have been published only in Japan. It is generally accepted that Mikasa was assigned to post-Rape Nanking, but he is said to have made a number of trips to the Philippines as well. It is not alleged that he had any direct involvement with Golden Lily's operations.

258–9   Some of Mikasa's military career details come from Hane's introduction to *The Honjo Diary,* from Princess Chichibu, and from Hamish Todd.

259 Mikasa's condemnation of Japan's atrocities appeared in a story published in *The Times*, 7 July 1994. He had actually spoken out against this conduct *during the war*. The copy of his document, rediscovered in 1994, was the source of the *Times* story. However, we also found a short article in the *New York Times* of November 1951 in which Mikasa expressed dismay over the Japanese Army's conduct.

260 Japan's pact with Germany and Italy. Hirohito later commented: 'The Navy had been against war with the Soviet Union all the time, and the Army was against it also, but rather for the reason that the Army was not ready.' See The Emperor's Monologues.

260 The secret alliances and promises concluded by the United States, Great Britain and the Netherlands in the months immediately preceding Pearl Harbor are discussed by Elphrick. Hirohito also discusses this situation from Japan's point of view. See The Emperor's Monologues.

261 Japan's moves in Southeast Asia were discussed by the emperor. According to Hirohito, 'the Imperial conference succeeded in stopping war against the Soviet Union, but decided to invade south French Indo-China'. From The Emperor's Monologues.

261 That Higashikuni's opinions were 'weak opinions from start to finish' is from The Emperor's Monologues.

261 'If an imperial prince' is from The Emperor's Monologues.

261 Princess Chichibu says her husband retired for medical reasons. At the war's end, however, he was still in uniform and promoted from colonel to general, which is curious indeed for an invalid confined to his bed throughout.

262 'Takamatsu seems not to have' is from *The Honjo Diary*, p. 52.

262 'There is a lot of talk' is from Grew, *Ten Years*, p. 368.

263 The way in which the American command in Hawaii was kept singularly ignorant of events was first touched upon by Toland in *Rising Sun* and has since

496

been explored by many authors. See, for example, Elphrick.

263   Terasaki 'Terry' Hidenari. Details about the Terasakis are in Gwen Terasaki's memoir, *Bridge to the Sun*. We learned other details first-hand from Terasaki Hidenari's daughter Mariko Terasaki Miller.

264   After the war, Terasaki gave a copy of some of his recollections to Bonner Fellers, who was then in Tokyo serving as MacArthur's military secretary. These can be found in the Fellers Papers at the MacArthur Library. The last-ditch efforts on the part of Terasaki and Kurusu and their dialogues are from the papers cited above; some details are also from *Bridge to the Sun*.

265   Both Toland, *Rising Sun*, and Elphrick look at the dithering in Washington during the days just before Pearl Harbor.

265   The events and delays in Tokyo concerning the telegram are covered in the diaries of Kido Koin. Kido's diaries were translated as evidence for the war-crime trials in Tokyo. Copies of pages of these transcriptions are in the Fellers Papers at the MacArthur Library. See Schaller, *Douglas MacArthur*, p. 55. Toland, *Rising Sun,* says the version given to the tribunal was incomplete and inaccurate. A text of the Roosevelt telegram is contained in the *Department of State Bulletin*, Vol. V, No. 129, 13 December 1941.

266   'I thought it was symbolic' is from the Kido diary transcript in the Fellers Papers, MacArthur Library.

266   That Hirohito 'would have stopped the attack' is in correspondence between Fellers and Terasaki at the MacArthur Library. See also *Bridge to the Sun*.

267   'Within the hour' is Churchill in Dower, *Empire and Aftermath*, p. 223.

267   'Prepared to do almost anything' is in Dower, *Empire and Aftermath*, p. 223.

267   Churchill had full advance notice of Pearl Harbor. See Elphrick, p. 182.

267   The exchange between Tedder and Fellers about the impending attack on Pearl Harbor is reported by Elphrick, p. 435.

267   Toland first voiced the theory that Roosevelt had advance knowledge of the attack. 'I believe that FDR knew the Japanese were coming and allowed them to attack . . . I think he felt he could safely let the Japanese fire the first shot, figuring he could rile up those isolationists in the Midwest and do it at a cheap price. He never figured such a catastrophe would happen . . . It was a calculated risk taken by a ruthless man, ruthless as all presidents must be. What he did wrong came later, when he engineered the coverup.'

According to Brigadier General Carter W. Clarke, deputy chief of the Military Intelligence Service at the Pentagon, General George Marshall, army chief of staff, also knew. Clarke was closely involved with Magic. After Hull's 26 November ultimatum to Japan, coded messages from Tokyo were being 'monitored with special care'. Clarke said Japan was expected soon to attack the Dutch East Indies and – although FDR had signed a secret agreement to go to war if this happened – it would be difficult to rally support if there had been no Japanese attack on Americans.

Clarke said that on 19 November Tokyo instructed its embassies that a false weather report 'east wind and rain' would signal the go-ahead for an attack on the United States. On 4 December, Clarke said, the US Navy facility at Cheltenham, Maryland, intercepted that Japanese broadcast. When the message was deciphered, it was passed to the White House by Rear Admiral Noyes, chief of naval intelligence.

The following day, 5 December, Clarke said he was surprised that senior army and navy officers at the Pentagon appeared unconcerned. On 6 December new Magic decodes began to arrive including Tokyo's response to Hull's ultimatum. (Only at this point was FDR's personal message to the emperor sent by slow regular telegraph.) Before 8 a.m. Washington time on 7 December, Clarke said, the final bits of Japan's response were decoded, but Admiral Stark could not reach General Marshall, who (strangely under the circumstances) had decided to go horse-riding. Clarke said, 'My associates and myself on the general staff were frankly puzzled that Marshall, with war merely a few hours away, could absent himself from his office. When he returned at 11.20 a.m. he had a hurried consultation with his staff and came to the conclusion that "something is going to happen at 1 o'clock." He drafted a vague and brief instruction to General Short [in Honolulu] and then, to delay matters a bit more, phoned Admiral Stark to discuss about sending a similar instruction to Admiral Kimmel . . . Marshall had a scrambler phone on his desk by the use of which he could reach Honolulu in seven minutes.' Instead, Clarke said Marshall said the warnings to Short and Kimmel must go by RCA commercial service. Of course, they reached Hawaii too late.

Clarke: 'It was for this reason that Marshall called us together in a locked room and exacted from each of us a promise that we would never tell the truth about the details concerning Pearl Harbor. This was to go with us "to the grave".' Clarke said incriminating records were destroyed as well.

This Clarke narrative was contained in documents sent to us by Bonner Fellers's postwar secretary Bruce Merkle. These documents are also to be found in the Fellers Papers, MacArthur Library.

267   'It was . . . a blessing' is Churchill, quoted in Elphrick, p. 446.

268–9   MacArthur's fumbling, his notoriety as 'Dug-out Doug', Eisenhower's disgust with him and the gift of gold are drawn from Schaller; Spector, *Eagle against the Sun;* and Manchester, *American Caesar: Douglas MacArthur.* Urgently needing a public hero in the Pacific, Washington cynically promoted MacArthur's vainglorious image to the press.

270   For an account of how the Japanese were hamstrung and forced to cut deals with the overseas Chinese, see Seagrave, *Lords of the Rim*.

270–1   For basic information about the looting of Asia, see Seagrave, *Lords of the Rim* and *The Marcos Dynasty*, Guyot, the Cooks, McCoy, and Iris Chang.

271   Japanese who participated in Golden Lily in various capacities have given us basic details of procedure, including methods of looting, separation of gems from precious metals, the re-melting of the metal into bars by Chinese collaborators in tin-mining regions, and shipment of the bars in bronze boxes and of gemstones in oil drums. In 1988, we outlined much of this in *The Marcos Dynasty*, but we erred by attributing the looting to Japanese underworld figures working with the military. We now have cross-confirmation of the role of the princes in Golden Lily from a number of Japanese sources, and documentary evidence that will be published in a sequel to this book.

271   The Hokkien black marketeer and the smelting operation at Ipoh are described by Martin Booth in *The Dragon Syndicates*.

272   This 35-mile-long tunnel under Manila still exists and can be visited by anyone sufficiently determined. In recent years, some of its entrances have been blocked by new construction. Most Filipinos do not know it exists.

272   We have numerous eyewitness accounts of Prince Chichibu and other princes in the Philippines. Many finite details of clothing, iconography (badges, decorations), contemporary photographs, etc., have been cross-checked with experts and verified by other Japanese participants.

274   After World War II, Ferdinand Marcos learned of gold recoveries in Luzon by some of his Ilocano constituents, and made a claim on them. Thereafter he made deals with Japanese to carry out joint recoveries. In 1975 he hired Nevada mining engineer Robert Curtis to excavate a major ('777') loot burial

site at Teresa. A '777' site is one that contained 777 billion yen's worth of treasure, mostly gold and diamonds, according to the Golden Lily inventory coded on the site map drawn by Japanese engineers at the time. In 1945, the yen was pegged at between three and four to the dollar, so this site was worth around $190 billion. Curtis figured out the Japanese map codes and excavated half the site, from which Marcos removed the contents (half of the 777). Curtis built Marcos a smelting factory at Subic Bay to recast the gold and disguise its metallurgical fingerprint, so that the bullion could be moved into the world gold market without arousing suspicion about its provenance. Curtis also designed (and Marcos built) an underground vault behind the presidential retreat in Bataan; this vault was the size of a football field, and was to contain recovered war gold. See *The Marcos Dynasty*. The original Golden Lily map of this 777 site at Teresa is reproduced on page 184. Many other sites have since been recovered by Japanese and other groups. Marcos sent an intelligence officer, Colonel Vilacrusis, to Tokyo to negotiate joint venture recoveries, and documents show that Vilacrusis held talks with several imperial princes. (Prince Chichibu had died in 1953.) In these documents, Vilacrusis reported that one prince confirmed Chichibu's presence in the Philippines as head of Golden Lily, and his escape by submarine in spring 1945.

Golden Lily surveyors made several sets of coded maps of 172 'imperial' treasure sites; one set was hidden in Luzon and later confiscated by Marcos. When his life was threatened, Robert Curtis became disenchanted with President Marcos; to protect himself, Curtis photocopied the maps, burned the originals and left for America. We have copies of some of the maps.

274   For a full account of the *Nachii*, see Seagrave, *The Marcos Dynasty*.

274   The story of I-52 is in *Time*, 31 July 1995. See also Davis and Roberts, *An Occupation without Troops*,

for movements of Japanese gold offshore during the war.

274   Many court cases were provoked by the Marcoses after they fell from power. One in a Honolulu court resulted in a multi-billion-dollar judgement against the Marcos estate. One in Switzerland led to the revelation that one of the stolen gold Buddhas was in a bank vault under Zürich airport, in a Marcos account. See articles by Anderson, Bruppacher, Lucas, and McCabe, and Dingman, *Ghost of War*.

274–5   We have a videotape of the Asahi Television documentary. See also the article in the bibliography 'General Yamashita's Treasure Found,' referring to the Asahi broadcast. We were informed by Asahi staff that they wanted to launch a full investigation but were afraid of reprisals by Japanese extremists.

275   According to documents we examined, Colonel Vilacrusis said an imperial prince told him over $100 billion in treasure was hidden in the Philippines. This may only have been a figure of speech, because the 777 site that Marcos recovered half of in 1975 was worth $190 billion in all – Marcos recovering approximately $95 billion of that. There are a number of 777 sites. We have direct personal knowledge that these sites exist, and many have been recovered.

275   On the gangsters. Kodama Yoshio siphoned off great sums of loot for his private use, mostly keeping diamonds that were easy to hide and transport by plane. This was known to United States intelligence services in postwar Japan. See subsequent chapters for how Kodama cooked a deal with the USA over a portion of his loot. Kodama was not working for Golden Lily but held vice-admiral's rank in the navy under the orders of Admiral Yonai. The CIA hired Kodama and kept him on a retainer for decades, a fact that emerged during the Lockheed scandal. See Kaplan and Dubro.

275   Casualty figures are difficult to determine. In this case we relied on *The Encyclopaedia Britannica*.

275 Jewish Holocaust victims are sensitive to the fact that Japan has a long way to go in facing up to crimes in World War II. See 'Jewish Group Raps Japan over Nanjing Massacre' from *Japan Economic Newswire, Kyodo News Service*, 23 April 1998.

276 'I assume' is from Large, *Emperors,* pp. 172–3. The original information comes from the Kido diaries published in Japanese.

276 'I wanted to strike' is from The Emperor's Monologues.

276 Shortly after the Japanese defeat at Midway (in June 1942), Yoshida approached Konoe with a proposal. Konoe would be sent to Switzerland to be available as a mediator should either Britain or Germany suffer serious reverses. Dower, *Empire and Aftermath,* p. 229. See also Davis and Roberts.

277 Wealthy members of the peace group included Ikeda Seihin, a rich businessman later arrested by SCAP. He became a financier of the LDP in the 1950s. Others were Kabayama Aisuke, Amherst graduate and matchmaker; Makino Nobuaki; Imperial Way General Mazaki Jinzaburo; retired Admiral Suzuki Kantaro; and Imperial Way General Ugaki. They were 'a microcosm of the elites . . . court circles, army, navy, business and financial world, bureaucracy, police, colonial administration, diplomatic corps, and titled nobility.' Dower, *Empire and Aftermath*, p. 231.

277 Hirohito relied on Tojo. See The Emperor's Monologues.

277 'It is said that Tojo is no good' is from Large, *Emperors,* p. 175.

277 Konoe learned of secret talks between Japan's ambassador to Switzerland and Joseph Grew. What Konoe was outlining to Higashikuni was a postwar strategy in which the throne would be Japan's 'unique and final hope'. See Davis and Roberts, p. 153. A more detailed discussion is in Nakamura Masanori.

277 'Americans [have] little knowledge' is from Oka, *Konoe,* p. 197.

278   'Prince Takamatsu was drawn into [the] plan' is from *The Honjo Diary,* p. 53.

278   Mention of involving Sadako in peace moves is in *The Honjo Diary,* p. 54.

278   'If it is mishandled' is from *The Honjo Diary,* p. 54.

278   The plan to retire Hirohito is in Large, *Emperors,* p. 173.

279   '*Tennozan*' refers to the 1582 battle when a feudal leader staked his survival on the outcome of a single skirmish.

279   'If first we' is quoted from The Emperor's Monologues.

279   'If Japan wins' is from Time-Life's *Japan at War,* p. 183.

279   The admiral hid in the basement is from Time-Life's *Japan at War.*

279   That Prince Takamatsu and others thought the end would come sooner. Dower, *Empire and Aftermath,* p. 256; Large, *Emperors.*

280   Konoe's obsession with the communists is in Dower, *Empire and Aftermath.*

280   'The majority of our professional soldiers' is part of Konoe's memo to the emperor, from Oka's *Konoe,* pp. 207–8. Oka's version of the Konoe memo differs in translation from Dower's version in *Empire and Aftermath.*

280   Overthrow of the Control Group (faction) could only come from within the military itself. 'The only military faction capable of replacing the Control Faction and commanding the loyalty of the military forces was, in their view, the Imperial Way Faction . . . Their plan was to get Hirohito to replace Tojo as prime minister and war minister with General Ugaki or Mazaki, a respected military figure from the old Imperial Way . . . who would have widespread support in the army and navy. With their men in control, they would move swiftly to purge the high command of members of the Control Faction. Then they would sue for peace . . . they envisioned a revo-

lutionary upheaval if the war were not terminated quickly.' Dower, *Empire and Aftermath*, p. 236.

281   Bix argues in 'The Showa Emperor's Monologues': 'Rather than taking the initiative for peace when the war was clearly lost, Hirohito stubbornly held on. He was the chief obstacle in the moves to oust the Tojo cabinet.' Fellers noted that Hirohito's character prevented him from making the crucial decision. See 'Bonner Fellers: Japan Background' at the MacArthur Library. See also The Emperor's Monologues.

281   Konoe's confidence in the Americans and Grew is discussed in Dower, *Empire and Aftermath*, p. 270. See also Nakamura Masanori.

282   Hirohito grew silent and delayed the decision is from Oka, *Konoe*, p. 209.

282   'Running around' is Takamatsu in Dower, *Empire and Aftermath*, p. 238.

282   Fire-bombings and their effect on Tokyo are described in Time-Life's *Japan at War*, p. 164.

282   'Since the army and navy' is from The Emperor's Monologues.

282   'Having given a firm promise to Germany' is from The Emperor's Monologues.

283   The bunker is described in Time-Life's *Japan at War*, p. 168.

283   For Hirohito's relief at sharing in the experience of war, see Time-Life's *Japan at War*, p. 168.

283   'The greatest obstacle' is from Nakamura Masanori, *The Japanese Monarchy*, p. 71.

283   Dower talks of Grew's determination to reassure Japan's elite. See *Empire and Aftermath*, p. 247. See also Nakamura Masanori's study.

283   The Allied ultimatum and long discussions in Washington and Tokyo concerning wording, interpretation and acceptance are covered in Nakamura Masanori, and the unpublished papers of Grew.

285   'Ultimate form of government' is in Nakamura Masanori, pp. 78–9.

285   Kido's discovery of the leaflets is from his diary and Nakamura Masanori. Fellers was proud of his role in

psychological warfare but complained that he received no special recognition. Hirohito cultivated Fellers by conveying flattering messages through Terasaki. On 10 March 1946, Fellers wrote excitedly to his wife, 'Yesterday obtained a statement from the emperor sent to me personally . . . that [my] psychological warfare leaflets and news sheets, were very effective – maybe too effective. That . . . [my campaign] forced him to hasten the end of the war because he feared that if the soldiers got hold of those leaflets they might take drastic measures such as a coup d'etat.' Fellers Papers, MacArthur Library.

285   'I have studied the terms' is from the Pacific War Research Society. *Japan's Longest Day*, p. 81.

286   'To our good and loyal' is in Large, *Emperor Hirohito and Showa Japan,* p. 129.

286   'The nation sincerely apologizes' is in Bix, 'Showa Emperor's Monologues'.

286   'It was His Majesty himself' is quoted in Gradisher, p. 97.

CHAPTER 9: THE EXORCISTS

288   For a fine study of the way postwar Germany and postwar Japan have handled issues of war responsibility see Buruma, *Wages of Guilt*. See also Brackman, and the annotations for our prologue. As George Kennan points out in his memoirs, the fact that the occupation of Japan (and of Germany too) was run along the lines of a feudal kingdom meant that MacArthur was carrying out his own agenda, influenced by personal backers like Herbert Hoover.

289   For photos of the bunker at Matsushiro see Time-Life, *Japan at War*. For a recollection of the Korean slave labourers who built it, see the Cooks' *Japan at War*.

289   The stash of drugs is from the *New York Times*, 31 October 1945.

289–93   America's occupation. For a concise look, see Livingston *et al.*, *Postwar Japan*. Many of our discoveries came from unpublished papers of Fellers and

Hoover at the MacArthur Library and Hoover Institute. Reform versus continuity is discussed by Nakamura Masanori, Fearey, and Kennan. Unpublished papers of Grew at Harvard's East Asia Center lend insight into meddling. Those who condemned the naiveté of it all were Bisson, Gayn, Maki, and Hadley.

292   The evolution of the Central Liaison Office is from Maki. This was a purely Japanese creation, set up a week before the surrender was signed. It was under the jurisdiction of the Foreign Ministry, but not organically part of it.

292   Kase Toshikazu's career is mentioned briefly in Toland's *Rising Sun*. He was not related to Kase Shunichi, Japan's wartime ambassador to Switzerland who met secretly with Grew. This was clarified by Hamish Todd. For more, see Davis and Roberts, and Kase's own memoir. Guillain, the French journalist who stayed in Tokyo throughout the war, says Kase worked with Konoe to try to get Hirohito to surrender from 1943 onwards.

292   'Very dear friend of mine' is from the transcript of an interview by MacArthur biographer D. Clayton James with Fellers, at the MacArthur Library, Record Group 49, dated 26 June 1971.

293   For Kase's role as messenger see Grew, *Turbulent Era*, and *Silver Drum*.

293   How the CLO functioned as an intelligence organization is clear in Maki.

294   Fellers described this dinner with Kase to D. Clayton James in 1971.

294   Grew's role in reassuring Japan about the emperor's continuity is from Nakamura. Grew's own correspondence at Harvard contains many references to his ambition to protect Hirohito and the emperor system.

294   Fellers's dinner with Yoshida is in the interview by D. Clayton James. There is a long document in the Fellers Papers entitled 'Bonner Fellers: Japan Background'. On pp. 10 and 11, Fellers describes his dinner with Yoshida and says he suggested that SCAP

507

needed a Japanese liaison officer, and Crown Prince Akihito needed an American woman tutor.

294   The first interview between Terasaki and Fellers is described in the Fellers Papers and *Bridge to the Sun*. See also 'Bonner Fellers: Japan Background' at the MacArthur Library. In it, Fellers recalled: 'I was immediately impressed with Hidenari Terasaki. His face reflected enlightenment and character. His eyes were dark, deep pools of compassion and understanding . . . As the liaison between Japanese and American staffs, Terasaki, who also had access to the emperor, made a material contribution to the initial success of the occupation.' Terasaki's daughter told us he had 'no preconceived notions about the emperor's war responsibility' when given this assignment.

295   Terry's meetings with Fellers, and his work for the palace, are from Gwen Terasaki, and the letters of Fellers and Terry Terasaki at the MacArthur Library.

295   The cynicism Terasaki saw in Fellers was noted by his daughter, Mariko, in private conversations with the authors in 1998. Although Terasaki's widow Gwen and daughter Mariko were in the United States from 1950 onwards, their contact with Fellers was minimal. When Gwen's memoirs were bought by MGM, Fellers told her he was not pleased with the portrait she painted of him, protesting: 'It is utterly impossible that I could have been so rude . . . I am cast in the role of a hard-boiled, bombastic person void of understanding . . . I object to such a hide-bound reasonless portrayal.' Fellers to Gwen Terasaki, 10 September 1958, Fellers Papers, MacArthur Library.

295   Terasaki originally shared the hopes of Japan's prewar elite. Gwen's memoirs show her husband walked a tight line in Japan's foreign service in the 1930s and 1940s. The strain may have contributed to his early death from cardiac disease.

His tougher older brother Terasaki Taro, who inherited the family wealth and properties, became ambassador to Vichy France, where he was part of the peace net relaying messages to Grew. The *New York Times*, 26 June 1943, mentions his appointment. Vichy France was collaborationist.

295   Terasaki's fears about his stolen diaries were mentioned by his daughter.

296   Terasaki's uncertainty about dealing with the emperor. On 19 December 1947, after things settled down, Terry wrote to Fellers: 'I was not sure to see [the emperor] at all at the beginning of my palace days.' Fellers Papers, MacArthur Library.

296   Acts of kindness shown to Terasaki by Hirohito were recounted by his daughter Mariko to the authors.

296   Chichibu's visit to the palace on 15 September 1945 is in *Silver Drum*.

296   Discussions of Hirohito's reaction to talk of abdication are in Bix, 'Inventing the "Symbol Monarchy" in Japan'. See also Dower, *Empire and Aftermath*; Large, *Emperors*.

297   That Hirohito faced public trial with the likelihood of hanging is supported by Fellers. As we note in the prologue, 'The emperor fears you will punish him' and 'feels he is liable to lose his neck' – from a letter of Fellers to his wife, 27 September 1945.

In 'Bonner Fellers: Japan Background' he wrote: 'Among a very few influential members of General MacArthur's staff there were sinister convictions implied, but most carefully expressed, that the emperor should be tried as a war criminal. To me this was not only unjust, it was frightening. The success of the entire Occupation was dependent upon implementing the program with the emperor's endorsement.' Fellers Papers, MacArthur Library.

298   Buruma speaks of MacArthur's use of the emperor to enhance his own image. MacArthur acted in the fashion of a 'traditional Japanese strongman', using 'the imperial symbol to enhance his own power'. See *Wages of Guilt*.

298   On 2 October 1945, Fellers neatly summarized: this memo is in the Fellers Papers and a copy was provided to us by his daughter Nancy Gillespie. In a

letter to his wife, 15 July 1945, a month before the Japanese surrender, he said: 'After peace comes I don't give a hang what happens to him.' Before submitting his 2 October 1945 memo to MacArthur, 'I took a draft of my study to my life-long friend Miss Michi Kawai [they were students together at Earlham]. She was most helpful in shaping the statement accurately to reflect [what] the Japanese reaction should be [if the] emperor [were to] be indicted.' From 'Bonner Fellers: Japan Background'. According to his agenda notes for 22 September 1945, he dined with Michi Kawai and discussed the emperor. The agenda is in the Fellers Papers, MacArthur Library.

299   On Fellers and Herbert Hoover: in the Fellers Papers there is a compendium of Fellers and Hoover letters, starting in 1939 concerning MacArthur's presidential ambitions. Fellers sent Hoover a copy of his 2 October 1945 memo with a note stating, 'The Soviets want blood and revolution in Japan; hence to them all stabilizing influences are taboo.'

299   Fellers's friendship with the two Japanese co-eds at Earlham College is detailed in Liebenthal. Many letters and memos in the Fellers Papers at the MacArthur Library concern his contact with them during the occupation.

299   A copy of Fellers's treatise on the mentality of Japanese soldiers is among his papers at the MacArthur Library and Hoover Institution.

300   'I know that President Roosevelt not only respects': Fellers to Hoover, a letter at the MacArthur Library.

300   'If MacArthur should come home'. This refers to a bid for the 1944 campaign. The quote is marked, 'notes from a conversation with Mr Hoover June 26, 1943'. Fellers Papers, MacArthur Library.

300   Details about Fellers's assignments in the early 1940s are taken from his obituaries in the *New York Times* and the *Washington Post* and career summaries included in the introduction to his papers at the MacArthur Library and the Hoover Institution. On

his return from Egypt, in a breach of military protocol, he called first on Roosevelt and only later on General Marshall, chairman of the Joint Chiefs. Marshall never forgave the blunder. That he was told to report directly to Roosevelt comes from the authors' interviews with Nancy Gillespie.

300 Hoover's visit to Hitler is in the book of essays edited by Nash.

300 Hoover's views on communists were shared by Fellers who wrote to his wife on 7 March 1946: 'The things Stalin is doing are the result of and made possible by the FDR–Churchill team.' Fellers wrote to his wife on 30 January 1946 that he was going to be dealing with the Russian contingent in Tokyo and added, 'I suppose OSS experience will help me a bit.' Fellers Papers, MacArthur Library.

301 On insider knowledge Hoover acquired about secret dealings of SCAP and the Japanese government: Hoover Institution has a transcript of an interview with Fellers by Raymond Henle, for the Hoover Presidential Library. On 23 June 1967, Fellers said 'The Japanese militarists by this time in their homelands, were in thorough disrepute. They were being tried for alleged war crimes, so that Mr Hoover had no trouble in securing promises for a tremendous amount of documentation from the [Japanese] War Office on the war and how and why they went to war. Mr Hoover gave me several assignments to get this material together. He sent back an enormous number of documents from Japan.' It is not clear where these documents are.

301 'Retention of the emperor'. Grew's and Fellers's concern for postwar Japan is discussed in detail in Nakamura.

301 Our material from Grew's meeting with Truman is in Grew's unpublished papers at Harvard.

302 Truman was walking a public-relations tightrope on the issue of Hirohito's war guilt. See McCullough, *Truman*.

302 Max Bishop was a former language officer at the American Embassy in Tokyo and a personal friend of

511

General MacArthur. He then became a CIA officer. See Davis and Roberts.

302   On secret investigations conducted by Bishop and Fellers. Fellers took notes on how the surrender came about, from former prime minister Suzuki, former navy minister Yonai, Privy Seal Kido and others who were present at Supreme Council meetings where the decision to surrender was discussed. It is not clear what happened to Fellers's notes. In September 1968, a Japanese journalist wrote to Fellers: 'About your interviews with war criminals which you conducted entirely on your own almost every Sunday. You said you kept notes and such precious documents still sleep in your file boxes . . . please give me a chance to look into the historical documents which many Japanese would like to know about.' The investigations and interviews by Bishop are recorded in the Memorandum of Conversations of 6, 7 and 9 November 1945. Fellers Papers, MacArthur Library.

303   'A rat' is from the Harrieses, *Sheathing the Sword*. Although they do not name Fellers as the general who made the statement, we know that Fellers and MacArthur took a strong dislike to Konoe when they felt he was blocking their efforts to draft the constitution. The language is pure Fellers.

303   The treatment given Konoe and the unclear circumstances of his death are examined by the Harrieses in *Sheathing the Sword*.

304   The 'timely' deaths of two of Asaka's officers is noted by Iris Chang.

304   MacArthur was told in October 1945 to get on with investigating Hirohito.

304   MacArthur kept the emperor in total isolation. This is well documented by Bix. For how MacArthur ran Japan as his personal fiefdom, see Kennan, and Buruma, *Wages of Guilt*.

304   Quotes from Kennan in this chapter come from his memoirs.

305   MacArthur's statement, 'No specific and tangible evidence', is quoted from a telegram published in

Foreign Relations of the US 1946, Volume VIII The Far East, pp. 395–7. There is conflicting evidence about the impact of MacArthur's message and the timing of the decision to exonerate the emperor. Minear says the order not to prosecute Hirohito did not leave Washington until January 1946. The Harrieses in *Sheathing* say the International Prosecution Section continued investigating Hirohito's war responsibility 'at least until March 1946'.

306   While Yamashita was hanged, his superior officer was acquitted. See the Harrieses, *Sheathing*.

307   'We, who knew so well' is Princess Chichibu's tribute to Homma in *Silver Drum,* pp. 157–8.

307   There are many examples of the 1946 campaign to tidy up Hirohito's image with Americans. See the *New York Times* for examples. Mark Gayn, not a fan of the emperor or of MacArthur's policies, noted irreverently that the press corps called Hirohito 'Charlie'. He described the emperor as 'a little man, about five feet two inches in height . . . He has a pronounced facial tic, and his right shoulder twitches constantly.' Gayn, *Japan Diary*, p. 137.

307   'I am not an emperor worshiper' and other quotes from the conversation between Yonai and Fellers are from the Imperial Navy Ministry record book entitled 'General Fellers's conversation with Admiral Yonai'. These were quoted in the NHK (Japan's broadcasting corporation) broadcast of 15 June 1997. To his wife on 6 September 1945, Fellers wrote, 'Regardless it was well to use the emperor even if later he does not fit into the picture.' Fellers Papers, MacArthur Library.

308   'The best strategy' is from the NHK broadcast.

308   'I want Tojo to say' is from the Fellers–Yonai discussion quoted by NHK.

308   How Yonai avoided prosecution. Among Admiral Yonai's more sinister officers involved in looting Asia was the underworld godfather, Rear Admiral Kodama (patron/founder of the LDP). That alone should have got Yonai in trouble. But American

conservatives, and the new CIA, were cooking deals and enlisting covert assets. 'The promise of immunity – or conversely the threat of arrest – was also used to secure cooperation with SCAP.' The Harrieses, *Sheathing*, p. 100.

309   The machine-gunning incident and the fact that the issue was dropped by the British government is told in the Harrieses, *Sheathing*, p. 100. The British government remains at odds with some 20,000 former civilian and military internees who are now claiming increased compensation for their time as prisoners of the Japanese. See Chapter 13 of this book for a discussion.

309   No evidence of Unit 731 was presented to the judges. Antonio Cassese, the Dutch judge on the Tokyo tribunal, said America withheld evidence about Unit 731 'purposefully and for very sinister reasons'. Roling and Cassese, p. 49. For more on Unit 731 see Gold, Gomer *et al.*, and Sheldon Harris.

310   'As my investigation progressed' is Fellers quoted by NHK.

310   'Firstly, I asked his majesty' is Terasaki quoted by NHK.

310   About The Emperor's Monologues, we refer readers to remarks made at the start of these notes. See also Bix, 'Hirohito's War' and 'The Showa Emperor's Monologues'.

310   The men listening to Hirohito's dictation were Terasaki; Matsudaira Yoshida, the Imperial Household minister; Matsudaira Yasumasa, chief secretary to the privy seal; Kinoshita Michio, vice-grand chamberlain; and Ineda Tsuichi, a palace stenographer. There were five sessions, lasting a total of eight hours. This comes from NHK's broadcast.

310   Buruma in *Wages* is one of those who characterizes Hirohito as being well informed and belligerent.

311   'One wonders' is from the NHK broadcast.

311   Fellers was keeping Hoover informed: see Fellers Papers. He wrote to his wife on 22 April 1946 that MacArthur was 'making me Hoover's aide-de-camp

for his stay . . . and to work out this and that. Eisenhower will be here too during this period [Fellers sketched in a small frowning face]. Anyhow it will be fine to see Hoover and I hope to talk over personal matters, too.'

311   Fellers–Hoover exchanges are in Fellers Papers, MacArthur Library.

311   The copy of The Emperor's Monologues that Terasaki sent to Fellers (and Hoover) is in the section marked 'Terasaki: Terry and Gwen' in the Fellers Papers.

311   'Fellow travelers' is Hoover to Fellers, 15 October 1945. Fellers Papers.

311   'Hoover was tremendously gratified' is from the Fellers Papers.

311   'Because of American bitterness' is from a document dated 7 May 1946, in correspondence between Fellers and Hoover at the MacArthur Library.

312   Hoover told Fellers of a meeting he had with President Truman in May 1945, before Japan surrendered. 'Hoover opened the subject of peace with Japan. He explained to Truman that he believed the appointment of Suzuki as premier in April 1945 was the emperor's signal to the United States that he was seeking peace. He believed that an obstacle to peace at that time lay in the definition of unconditional surrender . . . Truman agreed, took notes as Mr Hoover talked, and said he would ask the State Department to prepare a speech along the line indicated. But this speech was never made. Mr Hoover gave the clear impression that it might easily have been Soviet influence in the State Department which insisted that the war continue until the USSR entered, and [Moscow] could have a hand in the peace and postwar settlement. In view of Mr Hoover's May conference in Washington, he feels it is most important to know exactly Japan's position toward peace, especially at the time of the Hoover–Truman meeting in May 1945.' Hoover wanted Fellers to make sure Hirohito included such statements in his dictation. See

Fellers Papers, memo of 7 May 1946, MacArthur Library.

312   Terasaki's diary for 7 May 1946, says: 'Fellers 50–50, Hoover's talk, met with majesty alone.' From NHK broadcast. In 'Bonner Fellers: Japanese Background' Fellers wrote: 'In early June 1946, . . . Hoover, with a staff of experts, flew into Japan . . . I was assigned to cut red tape.' Fellers Papers, MacArthur Library.

313   'Jealousy, intrigue': see 'Fellers, Nancy "Quaker General"'. MacArthur Library.

313   Fellers left Tokyo at the end of July 1946. He wrote to Terasaki: 'When you see your able chief – and sire – please explain that I would not leave Japan now except that I am convinced, under present circumstances, that I can contribute more towards mutual understanding between our people, in America than here.' Fellers Papers, MacArthur Library. Terasaki replied on 19 December 1947: 'The Emperor was anxious to see you and I could have arranged it, if I were not sick . . . but the Emperor . . . wants to see you here in Japan, he hopes that you will happen to come to our direction.' Fellers Papers, MacArthur Library.

314   The American panic when Tojo fluffed his lines and implicated the emperor for war responsibility is recounted in the Harrieses, *Sheathing the Sword*.

314   Kido's diary was translated as evidence for the trials. Some pages of his translation are in the Fellers Papers at the MacArthur Library. Fellers passed along copies of the Kido extracts to Hoover.

314   Many people have raised serious questions about Matsui's testimony and the way in which he was made a scapegoat for the crimes of Prince Asaka. The most recent study is by Iris Chang.

315   'The emperor asked me' is in a Terasaki letter to Fellers. Fellers Papers, MacArthur Library.

315   Fellers and Hirohito did not meet again. In 1971 Fellers received the Second Order of the Sacred Treasure, 'in recognition of your long-standing contribution in promoting friendship between Japan

and the United States'. Bruce Merkle, Fellers's secretary in Washington, said in an interview given to NHK on 26 March 1997: 'I said "was it [the medal] for your memo" [of 2 October 1945]. Fellers – "They didn't say what, they just gave it to me."' Merkle told NHK that Fellers 'was tremendously proud, pleased and honoured but he has said the ceremony was kept secret'. This was not disclosed until after Fellers's death in 1973. Merkle kindly sent the authors a transcript.

315 'There is frequent mention'. Fellers to Terasaki, 8 July 1948, Fellers Papers.

316 Hirohito's decision not to abdicate is in The Emperor's Monologues.

316 Prince Asaka's life after the war is mentioned only in a few places. One is Hane, *Eastern Phoenix*, pp. 15–16, 20. Another is in Downer.

317 Like Konoe, Kido was frank in declaring that the emperor did bear responsibility for the war. Konoe died, was probably murdered, and Kido spent time in prison as a war criminal. He was outraged by this treatment because he felt that he had cooperated with SCAP and deserved better. MacArthur wished to make it seem that everyone else was at fault, not Hirohito. Anyone reading all the Kido diaries will see that they shared complex responsibility.

317–18 MacArthur biographers noted that he was vexed at having to pass up the 7 December anniversary as the day of the executions. They fail, however, to note that the date he did choose was young Akihito's birthday.

CHAPTER 10: UNCLEAN HANDS

320 The optimistic and socially revolutionary plans for postwar Japan manifest in SCAP-1 are discussed in Pyle, *The Making of Modern Japan*, Gayn, Bisson, Bix, Hadley, and Maki.

320 'To try to graft full-fledged democracy on Japan' is in a letter from Grew to W. E. Houstoun-Boswall of 20 March 1944, in Nakamura Masanori.

320   'From what I know' is Grew in Nakamura Masanori, p. 112.

321   MacArthur's 'flealike agility' is from Kennan, p. 370.

321   Atcheson's long and short solutions are in Livingston, *et al.*

322   About investigations of Japanese wealth see Gayn, Bisson, and Hadley. Manning also talks of SCAP's financial investigations.

322   That SCAP's examination of imperial wealth turned out to be a self-audit is reported in the *New York Times,* 31 October 1945. See also Manning.

322   The great disparity in valuing Hirohito's assets is in Bix, 'Inventing the "Symbol Monarchy"', p. 326, Note 15.

323   'No representation as to accuracy' is from Manning, *Hirohito: The War Years,* p. 175. Lists of Hirohito's assets were reported in the *New York Times,* 31 October 1945.

323   On tracking Hirohito's wealth: Professor Large says that by the early 1930s Hirohito's fortune was about 30 million yen, or 15 million 1930 dollars.

323   See Gunther, *Inside Asia,* for the regular *zaibatsu* disbursements to the imperial family. This system remained in place during the war, so the emperor's bank accounts were enlarged by wartime industries.

323   At the founding of the Yokohama Specie Bank, 50 per cent of its shares were assigned to the Meiji emperor. See Sampson, *The Money Lenders*, p. 232.

323–4   'Third or fourth biggest capital enterprise' is from Gunther, *Inside Asia*, p. 15.

324   Regarding Hirohito's overseas accounts. On 30 November 1997, the *Sunday Telegraph* carried a story detailing how the Swiss government used funds sent by the Allies 'intended to relieve the plight of British and American prisoners in Japanese camps, to repatriate Swiss money from Tokyo'. Under the accord, 40 per cent of the payments for POWs and internees in Japan were used for the transfer of Swiss claims in Japan and 60 per cent were at the free disposal of the Japanese government. The article

518

referred only to a single transaction worth £3.5 million in today's money, but this was one of many such transactions. See the *Columbian,* 22 July 1997, p. A3 from www.elibrary.com.

324   It is impossible to document, but highly likely, that after Tom Lamont met privately with Hirohito in the 1920s, and Morgan became one of Japan's biggest lenders, that Morgan provided account services to the emperor over subsequent decades, as did Swiss banks. This raises interesting questions of propriety during the war and during the postwar exoneration of Hirohito.

324   Kido's 1944 conference with Japan's financial leaders and the decision to move assets to Swiss banks is from Manning, pp. 169, 175. Investment credits is from Manning, p. 175. See the *Sunday Telegraph* story cited above.

324   The role of overseas Chinese in the purchase of bullion and crediting of these sums to Swiss accounts has been witnessed personally by the authors.

324   Delay in freezing Hirohito's assets is from the *New York Times,* 21 November 1945.

325   The empty bank vaults are reported in Manning, pp. 174–5.

325   That 'MacArthur chose to ignore' Hirohito's missing gold is from Manning, p. 179. Manning could not remain in Japan without MacArthur's approval. Many journalists, including Gayn, were expelled because they did not report the story according to MacArthur's wishes. Of course, Manning's book and charges of financial deceit were only published in 1989, at Hirohito's death.

325   The princes' sale of art objects was in the *New York Times,* 15 November 1945. Hirohito's lumber donation is in the *New York Times,* 29 October 1945.

325   Princes sold palaces and properties to Tsutsumi Yasujiro. For the story of the Tsutsumis and Japan's imperial family see Downer, Havens, and news stories cited in the bibliography. In all, Tsutsumi Yasujiro purchased eleven palaces, and converted most into

hotels, the now famous Prince hotel chain. Tsutsumi Yasujiro was blacklisted by SCAP but was able to get his name removed from the list. Havens is not sure how this was achieved.

326   That the princes were 'reduced to selling empty whisky bottles' was reported in the *New York Times*, 12 July 1946.

326   For the vast profits generated by Japan's involvement in the drug trade, see the Harrieses, *Soldiers,* Jonathan Marshall, Brian Martin.

326   This subterfuge by the *zaibatsu* is in Livingston *et al.*, p. 77.

327   For Tanaka's $73 million contract and huge profit in the last days of the war, see Chapter 13. See also Hunziker and Ikuro Kamimura, *Kakuei Tanaka: A Political Biography.*

327   On Kodama Yoshio's career and the looted wealth he accumulated as a rear admiral under navy chief Admiral Yonai, see Kaplan and Dubro; Seagrave, *The Marcos Dynasty;* and Sampson, *The Arms Bazaar.*

327   Japanese whom we know have successfully recovered gold from sites in Luzon in recent decades told us that most of the gold bullion amassed in Japan itself during the war was hidden in scuttled ships offshore, in abandoned mines, or in tunnels such as the imperial bunker at Matsushiro. They said this was done by cutting side tunnels, filling them with treasure, then sealing the opening so that it was invisible. At Matsushiro the tunnels are all lined with concrete, so such side tunnels would be simple to hide. The same method was used in tunnels and catacombs under Fort Bonifacio and Fort Santiago in Manila, opened by mining engineer Robert Curtis for President Marcos.

328   The involvement of the Birch Society in gold recoveries was first reported by Jack Anderson. For a synopsis, see Seagrave, *The Marcos Dynasty*, pp. 306–8. At the time we wrote *Marcos Dynasty* we did not have information about Laurence Bunker, so we were not aware of the Birch Society connection to

SCAP in Tokyo. See Bunker's obituary in the *New York Times,* 11 October 1977, p. 123.

328   The Joint Chiefs' directive ('You will assume') is in Livingston *et al.,* p. 90.

328   On Nashimoto's arrest: see his obituary, 'Prince Nashimoto of Japan Dies', cited in the bibliography.

329   The \$2 billion stash of gold bars in Tokyo Bay and the subsequent revelation to MacArthur is from Manning, p. 193. In addition, there is a curious letter written by Fellers to his wife, 22 April 1946. In it he remarks, 'Today the Emperor asked a friend if I could be trusted – that he had something in mind and the friend said yes, go to the limit. I think it is interesting.' Fellers Papers, MacArthur Library. It is plausible that Fellers was used to convey the gold-bar information privately to MacArthur.

329   MacArthur's agreement to put the \$2 billion in gold into Japanese banks and 'Return the nation to solvency' is quoted in Manning, p. 193.

329   Manning tells us that Truman knew about the gold stash in Tokyo Bay.

329   For information about Generalissimo Chiang's deals and the release of Japanese war-criminal suspects, see Kaplan and Dubro; Seagrave, *The Marcos Dynasty* and *The Soong Dynasty*; the Harrieses, *Sheathing the Sword*. See also Kataoka on the founding of the LDP. Kodama's release and that of Kishi are in the above sources.

330   For more on the FEC-230 see Hadley and Bisson.

331   For information about the extended Morgan family and General Electric, see Davis and Roberts, Chernow, and E. Lamont.

331   The figures about American investment in Japan come from Bisson, *Zaibatsu Dissolution*.

332   'We find it difficult to understand' and 'chaos and confusion' are from the *New York Times,* 21 December 1946.

332   There are many linkages between conservative US business and the Japan Crowd. Morgan Bank was now being run by Russell Leffingwell (1948–50). The

521

Japan Crowd influenced Washington at the highest levels. Secretary of Commerce W. Averell Harriman was a principal in the investment firm of Brown Brothers, Harriman, and was part-owner of *Newsweek*. See McCullough, p. 370. Secretary of Defense James Forrestal was a key figure at the investment bank of Dillon Read. See Choate, *Agents of Influence,* pp. 65–6. Dillon Read, headed by future Treasury Secretary C. Douglas Dillon, was one of a group of investment banks called the Club of Seventeen, which handled 70 per cent of Wall Street underwriting. See Chernow, *The House of Morgan,* p. 502. Former Secretary of War Henry L. Stimson had ties to Morgan and Dillon Read through his law firm. In their thinking about Japan, all were influenced by Lamont, Hoover and Grew.

332   In public, conservative American financiers criticized Japan's monopolies, but favoured them in private. As Eleanor Hadley put it in *Antitrust in Japan*: 'American political mores require everyone to denounce monopoly and cartels, which all conservative critics were careful to observe.'

333   Information about the American Council on Japan comes from Schonberger; Davis and Roberts; the Harrieses, *Sheathing*; Livingston *et al.*

333   'Looked upon as playmates' is from the Harrieses, *Sheathing*, p. 206.

333   From Hirohito, Kern received the Order of the Sacred Treasure and Kauffman received the Order of the Rising Sun. See Davis and Roberts, p. 31. Pakenham was described as 'a friend of Hirohito and Prince Takamatsu'.

334   Castle's background is in Heinrichs, p. 104, and Davis and Roberts, p. 36.

334   Details of Eugene Dooman are from the Harrieses, *Sheathing*, Nakamura Masanori, and Heinrichs, p. 239.

334   Nakamura Masanori discusses the self-proclaimed mission of the ACJ to correct the 'excesses' of SCAP policies.

334   On the plan for Kauffman secretly to assess the break-up of the *zaibatsu*, see Davis and Roberts. Also Tamaki, *Japanese Banking: A History 1859–1959*.

334   *Newsweek*'s attack began with 'Lawyer's Report on Japan Attacks Plan to Run Occupation', 1 December 1947. See also the Harrieses, *Sheathing*, p. 206.

335   Knowland's speech attacking FEC-230 is in Livingston *et al.*, pp. 113–15. Knowland was not elected to the Senate but merely appointed to fill in for a senator who died mid-term. He habitually worked the Red-scare theme, declaring that China was 'lost' by Reds in the State Department. See McCullough, pp. 550, 774.

335   Hoover's behind-the-scenes manipulation. Hoover's own political ambitions had been disappointed. In 1945 he hoped Truman would appoint him secretary of war. Then he was passed over for the vacant Senate seat given to Knowland. He had to be content manipulating events behind the scenes, playing both kingmaker and spoiler.

336   For the Draper–Johnston mission see Livingston *et al.*, p. 106, and Hadley, *Antitrust in Japan*. More on Draper is in Schonberger, and Davis and Roberts.

336   Johnston's ties to Morgan through Chemical Bank are in Davis and Roberts.

336   Hadley describes the arguments of the Draper–Johnston mission.

337   MacArthur and Yoshida sometimes agreed, as when Yoshida denounced labour leaders as 'lawless elements'. Dower, *Empire and Aftermath*, p. 337.

337   Pyle talks about MacArthur's crackdown on Japanese labour in *The Making of Modern Japan*, p. 224.

338   MacArthur left bureaucracy intact. Japan's unreconstructed bureaucracy was a danger recognized by many; see Maki. For how this impacted on later decades, see van Wolferen; and Chalmers Johnson, *Japan: Who Governs?*

338   'If you are not prepared' is Whitney quoted by Gayn, *Japan Diary*.

339	MacArthur's biographer Manchester says the 'hand-picked Tojo Diet' approved the new constitution. *American Caesar*, p. 500.
339	'Exemplary document' is in Pyle, *The Making of Modern Japan*, p. 219.
340	Tsutsumi Yasujiro was one of the blacklisted men returned to the Diet in the 1952 elections. Tsutsumi was elected thirteen times. See Havens, *Architects of Influence*.
341	Beasley points out this tendency of many of the leaders of Japan to regard World War II as a 'minor historical aberration'.
341	For 'We had purposely relieved our erstwhile opponents' see Kennan, p. 369.
341	How Terasaki was harassed. One such event, when Terry was arrested, was recounted in a letter to Fellers from J. Woodall Greene. See Greene to Fellers, 26 March 1947, Fellers Papers, MacArthur Library.
342	Gwen Terasaki was a close friend of George Atcheson, heard of his last words from a survivor, and quoted them in *Bridge to the Sun*.
342	Terry's walk into the sea is recounted in *Bridge to the Sun,* and was also described to us by his daughter, Mariko. By the time of Atcheson's death, Terry was extremely ill. Fellers wrote to Woodall Greene in May 1947: 'I hope [Terasaki] takes care and does not overdo physically. He is one of the most valuable men in Japan and certainly the most valuable on the staff of the emperor.' Fellers Papers, MacArthur Library. Before the end of 1951, Terry was dead from cardiovascular disease and exhaustion.

CHAPTER 11: JAPANESE GOTHIC

| 343 | Much of what we know about Akihito's youth comes from three accounts written by Elizabeth Vining, his tutor after the war. She was distressed by the way he was constantly under surveillance by his staff. See *Windows*, p. 309. |
| 344 | Separation of Akihito from his parents during the |

war, and his return to Tokyo in the autumn of 1945, is from Vining, *Quiet Pilgrimage*, p. 237.

344 Hirohito's letter to his son is in Reingold, *Chrysanthemums and Thorns*, p. 29.

344 'I must study harder' is in the *New York Times*, 5 August 1989.

344 Blyth's story is in Vining, *Pilgrimage* , p. 191. Nish, Vol. 1, has an essay about Blyth.

345 Yamanashi was forced out of the Peers School under the purge orders of SCAP. Fellers disliked him, and wanted an American in charge of Akihito.

345 Other details of Blyth come from Woodward.

345 According to Fellers, he proposed that an American woman should tutor the crown prince. He said he told Yoshida this at their dinner. Fellers said he was consulted by the palace when Vining's name was put forward with another woman's. 'Being a Quaker myself and knowing Mrs Vining's superb reputation and talent, I replied: "Take Mrs Vining."' These claims are in the document, 'Bonner Fellers: Japan Background', MacArthur Library.

345 'Someone' is how Vining explained the origin of the idea to have an American to tutor Akihito. See *Pilgrimage*, p. 191.

346 Sekiya Teizaburo is in Bix, 'Inventing the "Symbol Monarchy"', p. 319.

346 'A Christian but not a fanatic' is in Vining, *Pilgrimage*, p. 192.

346 Vining learned later of the antagonism to her appointment. *Pilgrimage*, pp. 190–200. Woodward also mentions the conflict.

346 MacArthur's doubts about the sincerity of the 'emperor's request' for an American tutor are quoted by Vining, *Pilgrimage*, p. 200.

347 Other details of Vining's appointment are in the *New York Times Book Review*, 11 May 1952: 'A Quaker and the Prince of Japan' by John Gunther.

347 Gwen Terasaki's remarks about the selection of Vining are from Vining, *Pilgrimage*, p. 200.

347 'If ever' is from Gunther's book review cited above.

347   Vining's Japanese Quaker secretary and translator was Takahashi Tane. Then 29, she had attended Kawaii Michiko's Keisen School before studying in the United States. She was repatriated with the Terasakis in 1942. This and other details are from Vining's books.

348   For our Sears catalogue anecdote, see the Fellers letters exchanged with Woodall Greene. Fellers Papers, MacArthur Library.

349   Vining's recollections of Sadako appear in *Return to Japan*.

349   'Intelligent woman' is in Guillan, *I Saw Tokyo Burning*, p. 218.

350   Vining's impressions of Prince Mikasa are in *Windows*, p. 286.

350   '[She] entered' is from Gunther's book review cited above.

350   Vining (and Gunther) is frank on her difficulties with Hozumi Shigeto.

350   It was months before she was alone with the prince. *Pilgrimage*, p. 220.

350–1   Vining describes Akihito's supervisory council in *Windows*, p. 271.

351   'He seemed unable' is in *Windows*, p. 46.

351   'Chamberlains' are in *Pilgrimage*, p. 219, and *Windows*.

351   'Always on my mind'. Vining's remarks to Hirohito and Nagako are from *Pilgrimage*, pp. 242–3.

352   'He was learning' is from *Windows*, p. 121.

352   Vining talks of Matsudaira in *Windows*, pp. 26, 147; *Pilgrimage*, p. 220.

352   Tajima Michiji had been a crony of Ikeda Seihin at Mitsui Bank, a member of Yoshida's 'peace group' who was in Sugamo prison as a war-crimes suspect. See the *New York Times*, 2 June 1948.

352   When Tajima retired from the Imperial Household in 1953, he became a director of Sony. Vining, *Return*, pp. 157 and 280.

352   Tajima 'brought with him a fresh breeze' is from *Windows*, p. 147.

352   Koizumi is in *Pilgrimage,* pp. 220, 283, and *Return to Japan*, p. 115.

353   Intimacy of Akihito and Koizumi: *Saturday Evening Post*, 11 April 1959.

353   'His only defect' is in a letter to Vining by Koizumi, *Return to Japan*, p. 226.

353   'It really is very hard luck' is Ito quoted in Fujitana, p. 119.

353   In his dislike of court ladies, Koizumi resembled General Saigo.

353   'You're going to get credit' is in Fellers's interview with D. Clayton James.

354   For SCAP's 'unofficial' policy on Christianity in Japan, see Wittner.

354   'The hope and belief I entertain', 'Necessary', 'Democracy', are MacArthur quoted by Wittner.

354   Wittner remarks that Christian credentials were essential if you wanted to get into Japan as a civilian during the first two years of the occupation.

354–5   The Bible imports, brisk sales and cigarette paper are all from Wittner.

355   On rumours of the imperial family's conversion: see Woodward, pp. 272–3.

355   'How the story first got started'. The report about the empress being Christian is in a letter from Fellers to Hoover, 1 May 1946. Fellers Papers, MacArthur Library.

356   Hirohito's offer to convert and MacArthur's refusal on the grounds of 'outrageous cynicism' is from Woodward, p. 272.

356   Woodward mentions Hirohito's idea that Akihito must be exposed to Christian teachings.

356   Prince Asaka's conversion to Roman Catholicism is in the *New York Times*, 18 December 1951.

357   MacArthur's interview of Akihito is in Vining, *Windows*, pp. 218, 219.

357   Akihito was 'Arthur's only real peer': see Manchester, *Caesar*, p. 516.

358   'An ordinary boy' is in the *New York Times* magazine, 26 August 1990.

358   'I shall be emperor' is from the Gunther book review cited above.

358   'He is by no means' is in *Time*, 23 March 1959.

359   Princess Chichibu describes her husband's acute distress at the death of his mother, Dowager Empress Sadako.

359   Sadako's funeral and its political significance are discussed in Fujitana.

359   'Pathology of the ultra-right.' Criticisms of the ultra-conservatives' grip on the lives of the royals were voiced at the time of Akihito's enthronement. See the *New York Times Magazine*, 26 August 1990.

360   'How is it' is from Fujitana, p. 245.

360   Akihito's world tour is in Vining, *Pilgrimage*. By that time she was back in America.

361   Rumours of Princess Kitashirakawa Hatsuko as a bride for Akihito are mentioned in the *New York Times*, 30 July 1951. The death of her father is noted in Downer, p. 114, and in the genealogy prepared by Hamish Todd.

361   Michiko's childhood, family background and their early meetings are from Vining, the *Saturday Evening Post*, 11 April 1959, and *Time,* March 1959.

362   Akihito summered at Prince Asaka's former palace. Downer, p. 117. The palace, purchased by Tsutsumi in 1947, and renamed the Karuizawa Prince Hotel, was reserved for occupation officials till 1950. After that it was renamed Sengataki Prince Hotel, and reserved for the imperial family. See Havens. Tsutsumi was doing favours both for SCAP and for the royals.

362   Wealth of Michiko's father is in *Time*'s cover story, 23 March 1959.

362   *Saturday Evening Post,* 11 April 1959, has Koizumi saying Michiko was Akihito's choice.

362   Opposition to the match was reported in *Time*'s cover story. Hamish Todd told us of Mrs Matsudaira's opposition.

363   Diet controversy over Michiko is in Kawahara, *Hirohito and His Times*.

363   Koizumi told Vining his worries about Michiko. *Return to Japan,* p. 215.

363   How the Imperial Household fudged the choice of Michiko is in *Time,* 23 March 1959.

364   Yamanashi and Koizumi's remarks are quoted by Vining. See *Return.*

364   'Your only defect' is in *Time,* 23 March 1959.

364   The wedding of Akihito and Michiko was on 10 April 1959.

364   Using the wedding for image-building is in Irokawa, *Age of Hirohito,* p. 111.

365   Value of the gifts for the lesser royals is mentioned in Reingold.

365   'Proudly touted' is from Irokawa, *Age of Hirohito,* p. 110.

366   Akihito's promise to Michiko about their children is in the *Saturday Evening Post,* 11 April 1959.

366   Strife between Michiko and her in-laws was often in the press. See, for example, the *New York Times Magazine,* 26 August 1990. Mariko Terasaki Miller told us of a friend who turned down the post of chief lady-in-waiting to Michiko.

367   Michiko suffering 'deep sadness' is from the *New York Times Magazine,* 26 August 1990.

367   Michiko unable to speak is from the *Los Angeles Times,* 4 June 1994.

367   'If Miss Michiko thinks' was quoted in the *Sunday Times,* 17 May 1998.

368   'The emperor was so generous.' Michiko's fond remembrance of Hirohito was quoted in the *New York Times,* 5 August 1989.

368   Mikasa's first public pronouncements against the war were reported in the *New York Times,* 28 November 1951, as was his pleasure in being 'criticized'. In 1994, it was revealed that during the war he had written a stinging indictment of the conduct of the Japanese military. The document was suppressed, but one copy survived and surfaced in 1994.

370   Hirohito missed seeing Chichibu on his deathbed

because he was thwarted by the Imperial Household. *New York Times*, 13 January 1953.

370   Cremation of Chichibu. This was the first time a member of the *immediate* royal family had been cremated.

370   Princess Chichibu fondly recalled her time with Prince Charles in *Silver Drum,* and his calling her his 'Japanese grandmother'.

371   The death of Akihito's brother-in-law, Takatsukasa Toshimichi, was reported in *The Times,* 31 January 1966 and the *New York Times,* 29, 30, 31 January 1966. Further details are from Hamish Todd, memo of 30 April 1998. That Takatsukasa was depressed by the ordeal of living under the scrutiny of the Imperial Household is in the *New York Times*, 30 January 1966.

371–2   Details of Akihito's siblings come from Hamish Todd's genealogy and news articles. For stories on Atsuko and her husband see the *New York Times*, 22 May and 10, 14 October 1952.

372   Empress Nagako's public snub of Michiko, her daughter-in-law, was recounted by Kawahara in *Nagako Kotaigo*.

373   An imperial aide laid a wreath at the tomb of General MacArthur. See the *New York Times,* 7 January 1989.

373   'That unfortunate war' is in Kawahara, *Hirohito and His Times*, p. 199.

373   Both Downer and Havens give details of Asaka's business deals with Tsutsumi.

373   The Tsutsumis' acquisition of the palaces of the Higashikuni, Takeda and Kitashirakawa families is in Downer, and Havens.

374   Higashikuni's postwar life is in his obituary in the *New York Times*, 23 January 1990.

374   'I expected no victory' and Takamatsu's other revelations are in his obituary in the *New York Times*, 4 February 1987.

374   Details of Mikasa's postwar life are from Hamish Todd and Vining.

375   'I taught recruits to die' is quoted in Reingold, p. 4.

375   For the assassination attempts against the mayor of Nagasaki, see articles by Berger, Hiatt, and Sullivan.

CHAPTER 12: INVISIBLE MEN

376   Just as the oligarchs of nineteenth-century Japan hid behind the throne, so did Japan's postwar oligarchs and money politicians. See Fujitana, and Irokawa.

377   'When I speak' is Tsutsumi Yoshiaki quoted in Havens. Tsutsumi Yasujiro began the process of cultivating the LDP with generous donations. His son, Tsutsumi Yoshiaki, never ran for public office, but as Havens (pp. 91–3) puts it, he 'did not hesitate to cultivate leaders of all the major [LDP] factions as well as the opposition parties for information that might help his businesses . . . he grew to be so well connected that he could mobilize former and current prime ministers, imperial relatives, and foreign ambassadors.'

380   'I had not been in Japan 20 minutes' is from Gunther, *Inside Asia*.

381   The styling of the political parties, and their block voting, is in Kataoka, *Creating Single-Party Democracy*.

382   Rule of law, rule by law: 'Under rule *by* law there is a formal commitment to administration under the law but a lack of legal limitation on policy formation. Under rule *of* law both official discretion and policy formulation are limited by law in favor of fundamental human rights and the electoral process.' Tipton, pp. 53–4. In Japan, the bureaucracy remained *outside* the control of law, and settled disputes by informal conciliation, subject to corruption.

383   Van Wolferen talks of the 'cathartic function' of scandal in Japan.

383   There are many sources about the Recruit scandal. See Hane, *Eastern Phoenix*.

383   There is another prominent politician who deserves passing mention. Nakasone Yasuhiro was prime minister between 1982 and 1987, heading one of the

more stable postwar cabinets. He was also a leader of the LDP and held that Japan had fully recuperated from the war and had nothing to feel embarrassed about from the past. He was a powerful, manipulative politician who continues to influence power-brokering today. He was no exception when it came to dirty money, and was closely linked to the oligarchs.

383   See van Wolferen, and Johnson on structural corruption.

384–5   Hatoyama's machinations are in Dower, Kataoka, van Wolferen, and in Johnson, *Japan: Who Governs?*

385   The bureaucracy became a kingdom unto itself. Bisson warned against this in the late 1940s. Van Wolferen talks of it at length, as does Johnson in *Japan: Who Governs?*

386   'Unlike politicians' is in Miyamoto Masao, *Straitjacket Society*, p. 14.

386   Details of Kishi come from Kurzman. Kishi and Aikawa were Choshu; their families had known each other for generations. Kurzman, *Kishi and Japan,* p. 134.

387   The president of SMRC, Aikawa, was Kishi's uncle by marriage: see Montgomery, p. 381.

388   Tojo's debt to Kishi. See Montgomery, pp. 381–2.

388   'Americans aren't likely' is from Kurzman, p. 221.

388   Kodama's role in funding the LDP is documented in many sources. See van Wolferen; Johnson, *Japan: Who Governs?*; Davis and Roberts; Kaplan and Dubro; and Seagrave, *The Marcos Dynasty*. Tsutsumi Yasujiro had close ties to Kishi. His son Yoshiaki had a 'working' relationship with Tanaka, bonding with other LDP leaders like Abe Shintaro, Miyazawa Kiichi and Takeshita Noboru. See Havens, pp. 92–3.

390   Details of Tanaka are from Johnson, *Japan: Who Governs?*; van Wolferen; Hunziker; and *Kodansha Encyclopedia*.

390   Viscount Okochi's wartime businesses are in *Kodansha Encyclopedia*.

391   Tanaka's $73 million windfall is detailed in

Hunziker. While the details are skimpy on exactly how this magic was performed, keep in mind that gold bullion looted from China first came overland to Korea where it piled up awaiting shipment across the strait to Japan. It seems likely that Tanaka was permitted to go to Seoul and exchange Japanese war scrip (or a payment order) for gold bullion – before those in charge of the gold knew Japan was about to surrender, making war scrip valueless. A form of insider trading. He also did not have to do the work he was paid for. It is this kind of corruption that has crippled the Japanese banking system.

391   Tanaka's early money politics are in Johnson, *Japan: Who Governs?*; van Wolferen; and Hunziker.

392   The role of the minister of posts and the Fiscal Investment Loan Plan are explained by van Wolferen, p. 391.

392   Incest between the LDP and building contractors is detailed by Johnson, *Japan: Who Governs?*, and van Wolferen.

392–3   Rigged bidding, kickbacks and bribing opposition parties to neuter them are described by van Wolferen, p. 118.

394   Tanaka, Kodama and the Lockheed scandal are in Kaplan and Dubro; Sampson, *Arms Bazaar*; Johnson; Hunziker; and news articles.

394–7   Details about Kanemaru Shin are in Johnson, *Japan: Who Governs?*; Desmond; Parry; and many stories in the international press.

396   Sagawa's deep pockets and ties to wartime drug trading were detailed in *The Economist*, 26 September 1992.

396   Kanemaru's absurd fine is mentioned by Desmond.

397   Kanemaru's secret stash was in the *Wall Street Journal*, 11 March 1993.

398   The deep pockets of the Tsutsumis. Our information is from Downer, Havens, and numerous articles in the press cited in the bibliography.

398–9   Tsutsumi Yasujiro and Hatoyama. Neither Downer nor Havens noted the link between Tsutsumi Yasujiro and Hatoyama.

399   Asaka personally receiving $800,000: see Havens.

400   The Tsutsumi Seibu Group is mentioned in *Kodansha Encyclopedia of Japan*, but there are no details of the Tsutsumi family. Havens, while a research fellow at Waseda University, had trouble pinning down the family sources of wealth, using the words 'hidden', 'unclear' and 'murky.' Havens uses similar terms to describe how Tsutsumi Yasujiro managed to get himself de-purged at the end of the war and how he also managed to have his companies exempted from the *zaibatsu* dissolution order.

401   Unflattering appraisals of Tsutsumi Masatoshi as Princess Nori's suitor are repeated in Downer. Havens makes no mention of this connection.

401   Tsutsumi's control of the LDP is noted in Downer, p. 412, and of course by Tsutsumi's own boast quoted above by Havens.

402–3   There are many news stories about the Nagano Olympics scandal and Tsutsumi pressure and profi- teering. 'If the government' is from the *Asahi Evening News*, 12 January 1992. Tsutsumi interest in the Olympics goes back to Tsutsumi Yasujiro, who was involved in planning and backing the 1940 Tokyo Olympics, which were never held, and the 1964 Tokyo Olympics, which began shortly after his death. See Havens.

403   The Nagano expressway link: see Downer, and *The Economist*, 7 February 1998.

404   When the International Olympic Committee acknowledged in January 1999 that there was evidence of major corruption related to bidding for the Olympics, it was noted that Nagano was also being investigated. The Japanese Olympic Committee records had all been burned in 'the Japanese Way'. Kauoru Iwata, a Karuizawa resident, who is currently writing a book about Tsutsumi, says: 'He's a master at getting everything he wants through other people's

taxes. He's greedy.' This was reported in the AP on
21 February 1999.

CHAPTER 13: ECLIPSE OF THE SUN

407–8   Varied reactions of world leaders to the death of
         Hirohito were reported in *Time*, 23 January 1989.

408   'The real war criminals' is from the Cooks, p. 464.

408   'We went to war' is in Buruma, *Wages*, pp. 130–4.
         Azuma Shiro is one of a small but outspoken group
         of Japanese veterans who are determined to educate
         people about Japan's wartime atrocities. He has trav-
         elled widely and appeared at many international
         conferences on the subject. In June 1998, one of his
         colleagues was invited to give a series of lectures by
         the Global Alliance for Preserving the History of
         World War II in Asia, an organization of Chinese
         residents in the United States and Canada. He was
         refused entry to the United States. The Justice
         Department announced that 'he was on the watchlist
         as a suspected war criminal'. A few years earlier, the
         Canadian ecologist Farley Mowat, whose ideas
         clashed with those of the American government, was
         also refused entry to the United States when he wished
         to attend an ecological conference.

410   The $74 million for funeral expenses is from *Time*, 23
         January 1989.

410   Akihito's lisp and 'I find it natural' are in the *New
         York Times Magazine*, 26 August 1990.

412   For more about the comfort women, see the article
         and book by Hicks, and articles by Hoon Shim Jae,
         and Sakamachi Sachiko.

413   'You wouldn't think of inviting Hitler's son' was in
         the *Evening Standard*, 26 May 1998. Other details of
         Akihito's reception in Britain were drawn from
         British press articles during the visit.

414   Figures on compensation being demanded, and
         compensation already paid, are from *The Times*, 26
         May 1998.

414   That the compensation issue was 'settled fifty years
         ago' is in *The Times*, 27 May 1998.

414   'Bankrupt' is from Jenkins in *The Times*, 27 May
           1998.
414   Figures of £30 billion, £2 billion, are in *The Times*,
           26 May 1998.
414–15   The Swiss court ruling on comfort women was in the
           Evening Standard, 14 May 1998.
415   The number of comfort women, their ages, national-
           ities and estimated number of survivors is from Hicks,
           The Comfort Women.
415–16   Ottawa is going to compensate its citizens who were
           interned by the Japanese to the tune of $24,000 each.
           This compensation for the crimes of the Japanese will
           be paid to Canadian victims by Canadian taxpayers.
           See stories by David Lunggren and 'War Prisoners'
           New Demand'. 'Lying bastards' is from the *Daily
           Telegraph*, 26 November 1998.
417   In exchange for Japanese scrip. This story has
           appeared in many places. See *Hongkong Standard*, 25
           December 1998 and Dominic Lau writing for
           Reuters, 28 August 1996.
417   'Historical facts cannot be covered up' is Zhu Rongji
           quoted in the *New Statesman,* 13 March 1998.
417   Settlements made to the Burmese and Swiss govern-
           ments were noted in *The Times*, 26 May 1998. The
           fact that the Swiss government and banks did many
           questionable favours for Japan during the war, such
           as using money sent to feed allied POWs to repatriate
           Swiss funds from Tokyo, doubtless contributed to the
           generous postwar Swiss settlement.
417   Japan's 'perilous' economy is in London's *Evening
           Standard*, 29 April 1998.
419   Pauley's politics in the early 1940s are in
           McCullough's *Truman*, p. 300.
419   McCullough says Truman called Pauley a 'son of a
           bitch'. After Pauley returned from Tokyo, Truman
           nominated him for undersecretary of the navy, with
           an eye to promoting him to secretary of defense. But
           the nomination became a political ping-pong ball,
           and Pauley asked to be withdrawn from considera-
           tion. McCullough, pp. 483, 484.

419   Pauley's mention of hidden Japanese assets was reported in the *New York Times*, 16 November 1945. See also his official reports to the State Department cited in the bibliography.

420–1   Severino Garcia Santa Romana (born 1901, died 1974) was recruited by US military intelligence while a student in America in the 1920s. He married an American heiress, Evangeline Compton, whose subsequent death left him a wealthy man. He became one of Washington's primary agents in the Philippines and Southeast Asia during the MacArthur years, and was well known both to Bonner Fellers and Herbert Hoover. After World War II Santa Romana headed a number of front companies, which he owned under pseudonyms, and was an intimate of Lansdale, Donovan and other CIA officials and American politicians. Many of his personal bank accounts remain in place, and legal processes have been under way for many years in different countries by people who are attempting to recover the gold, or gain control of the gold.

420   An OSS agent photographed the hospital ship only after it was unloaded. See our photo where the empty ship is riding high in the water.

422   Pauley's assessment of Japan as 'a shattered empire' was in the *New York Times*, 16 November 1945.

422   The figure of $1 billion is from Hane, *Eastern Phoenix*, p. 25.

422–3   Japan's demand for reparations and the payment of same are mentioned in Livingston *et al.*, pp. 77, 96.

423   The suspension of even token reparations is noted in Davis and Roberts, p. 62.

423   'I have come to honor my signature' and the anecdotes about Japan's postwar repayment of loans to the House of Morgan come from Chernow.

426–7   Improvement of the imperial family image and the difficulties that Akihito and Michiko encountered as they tried to present a more human face are in Nakamoto Michiyo, in the *Financial Times*, 23–4 May 1998.

427–30   Details of Akihito's two sons are from many sources. Hamish Todd helped sort them out.

428   Details of Princess Kiko come from the *New York Times,* 30 June 1990.

428   Prince Akishino's alleged love affair with a catfish researcher was reported in the Kyodo News Service, 30 November 1996, and in *The Economist,* 7 December 1996.

430   The crown prince's promise to protect Owada Masako from the Imperial Household comes from the *Wall Street Journal,* 20 January 1993.

430   Backbiting and criticism of Princess Masako were reported by the Asahi News Service, 13 December 1996.

431   'Silently suffering princess' is from Kyodo News Service, 7 July 1996.

431   Princess Masako's news conference was in the Asahi News Service, 13 December 1996, entitled 'Palace Loosens the Gag'.

432   'In a recession' is from *The Economist,* 20 June 1998, p. 23.

432   Male unemployment in Japan in September 1998 was 4.2 per cent, against 4 per cent in the United States. But *The Economist* of 6 June 1998 argues that the figures are manipulated and are probably double that.

432–3   Figure of 17,500 bankruptcies is in *The Economist,* 18 April 1998, p. 59.

433   Shaky state of pension funds is in *The Economist,* 11 April 1998, p. 17.

433       $548 billion in bad loans is from *The Economist,* 27 June 1998, p. 85.

433   Amount loaned to *yakuza* is in the *San Francisco Daily Journal,* 22 June 1998.

434   Unaudited self-assessments is in *The Economist,* 27 June 1998, p. 86.

434   True value of bad loans in excess of $1 trillion is in *The Economist,* 27 June 1998, p. 85.

434   Mergers of car companies is in *The Economist,* 11 April 1998, p. 17.

434 Stories of bank insolvency and bailouts is in *The Economist*, 20, 27 June 1998.

435 The problems *yakuza* present to foreign bankers are in *The Economist*, 27 June 1998.

435 Pumping up the economy with 75 trillion yen in pointless infrastructure projects and paralysis of the bureaucracy are in *The Economist*, 21 March 1998.

435 'Goldfish shit' is from *The Economist*, 1 August 1998, pp. 52–3.

436 'The interests of the most influential clique' is from Sakaiya Taichi, *What is Japan?*, p. 140.

436 Many well-informed Japanese think it is too late. Their thoughts about the situation are in the volume edited by Ian Neary. Political scientist Kato Tetsuro, contemplating Japan's future, posits a hopeful scenario: 'There is a possibility . . . that . . . when neither politicians nor bureaucrats display a national vision, the Japanese people may be stimulated . . . to [promote] a series of (revolutionary?) changes in Japan.' He believes this may be accomplished through 'A chain of peaceful revolutions in the age of TV and rapid information spread' and 'revolutions through civic forums and round tables'. Much new thinking about the future form of government in Japan has been stimulated by great changes in Eastern Europe since the collapse of the communist bloc. Makino Noboru, president of the Mitsubishi Research Institute, told the Asahi News Service, 'We should seriously analyse the events [in Eastern Europe] and ask whether they were essentially caused by [economic collapse] or by the wearing out of the system of one-party dictatorship.'

 Inamori Kazuo, president of Kyocera Corporation, called events in Eastern Europe 'a reconfirmation of people power'. He said changes in Eastern Europe show that a government and its economic systems cannot continue if they lose 'legitimacy'. He blames Japan's bureaucracy for its over-control of the economy, and giant corporations 'which monopolize the market and conceal information'. He warned that the people of Japan may revolt against bureaucrats and big business who no longer represent their interests.

Whether Japan can change, and whether change will come from the bottom or the top, is difficult to predict. Sociologist Isono Fujiko points out deep-rooted complexities. 'For one who lived through the [occupation] period of the great expectation of a democratic Japan, I have to admit that it was partly an illusion. It is true that direct thought control by the state is no longer possible, and the principles of equality of women cannot be reversed. Nevertheless, I hesitate to boast that the democratization of Japan has been successful. The change in the occupation policy from democratization to anti-communism . . . helped the return of many former leaders, some of whom had actually been active collaborationists of the militarist regime . . . Democracy, with liberalism, [are] concepts severely attacked by the former regime as . . . forms of communism.' She is critical of postwar Japanese leadership for adopting Western technology while rejecting human rights. '[I]f you have adopted industrialization, unless you accept also the political and economic rules and ethics of an industrialized society, such as the fundamental equality of persons, the right to dissent, and democratic systems to check abuses of power, the weaker section of society will be at the mercy of the stronger.' To those who defend traditional Japanese paternalistic bureaucracy, politics and business, she points out the dangers. 'Paternalism may protect the weak, but paternalism is left to the arbitrary practice of benevolence by the superior and cannot be claimed by the inferior.' See Neary.

436 The succession: as things stand, with females being excluded, after Emperor Akihito the throne would pass to: 1) Crown Prince Naruhito, 2) Prince Akishino, 3) Prince Hitachi, 4) Prince Mikasa, 5) Prince Mikasa Tomohito (eldest son), 6) Prince Katsura (second son), 7) Prince Takamado (third

son). After that comes a problem. Of the seven princes above, 1, 3 and 6 are childless while 2, 5 and 7 have only daughters. If the law of succession is amended to include women, that would put Prince Akishino's daughters at 3 and 4, followed by Princess Nori at 6. But the Japanese could choose either the British principle whereby sons take precedence over daughters, or the Swedish principle whereby the sex is irrelevant and seniority by birth alone decides the order. Source: Hamish Todd.

BIBLIOGRAPHY

Adams, Andrew. 'When Giants Collide: Japan's Violent Ritual, Sumo'. *Geo*, July 1979.

Addis, Stephen. 'Traveling the Tokaido with Horoshige'. *Orientations*, April 1981.

Agarwal, Bina (ed.). *Structures of Patriarchy: The State, the Community and the Household*. London: Zed Books Ltd, 1988.

Aisin Gioro, Pu Yi. *From Emperor to Citizen*. Beijing: Foreign Languages Press, 1979.

Akimoto Shunkichi. *The Lure of Japan*. Tokyo: The Hukoseido Press, 1934.

Alcock, Rutherford. *The Capital of the Tycoon: A Narrative of Three Years' Residence in Japan*. New York: Greenwood Press, Publishers, 1969 reprint.

Allen, G.C. *A Short Economic History of Modern Japan: 1867–1937*. London: George Allen and Unwin Ltd, 1945.

Alletzhauser, Albert J. *The House of Nomura: The Inside Story of the Legendary Japanese Financial Dynasty*. New York: Arcade Publishing, 1990.

'Allies Sent Millions to Ease Plight of Japanese POWs. But [Swiss Banks Intervened]'. *Sunday Telegraph*, 30 November 1997.

Anderson, Jack. 'Japanese "Treasure"'. *San Francisco Chronicle*, 21 November 1986.

Ando Hiroshi-Angel. 'Japan's New "Reform" Government'. *Asian Affairs*, 1 April 1994.

Armour, Andres J.L. *Asia and Japan: The Search for Modernization and Identity.* London: The Athlone Press, 1985.

Axelbrook, Albert. *Black Star over Japan: Rising Forces of Militarism.* London: George Allen and Unwin Ltd, 1972.

Baelz, Toku (ed.). *Awakening Japan: The Diary of a German Doctor.* Bloomington: Indiana University Press, 1974.

Baerwald, Hans. H. *The Purge of Japanese Leaders under the Occupation.* Berkeley: University of California Press, 1959.

Barber, Noel. *Sinister Twilight: The Fall of Singapore.* London: Fontana, 1970.

Barclay, George W. *Colonial Development and Population in Taiwan.* Princeton: Princeton University Press, 1954.

Barthes, Roland. *Empire of Signs.* New York: Hill and Wang, 1982.

Bartu, Friedemann. *The Ugly Japanese: Nippon's Economic Empire in Asia.* Tokyo: Yenbooks, 1993.

Beasley, W.G. *The Meiji Restoration.* Stanford: Stanford University Press, 1972.

Beasley, W.G. *Japanese Imperialism 1894–1945.* Oxford: Clarendon Press, 1987.

Beasley, W.G. *The Rise of Modern Japan.* New York: St Martin's Press, 1990.

Behr, Edward. *The Last Emperor.* New York: Bantam, 1987.

Behr, Edward. *Hirohito: Behind the Myth.* New York: Villard Books, 1989.

Benda, Harry J. *et al. Japanese Military Administration in Indonesia: Selected Documents.* New Haven: Yale University Press, 1965.

Benedict, Ruth. *The Chrysanthemum and the Sword.* Tokyo: Charles E. Tuttle Company, 1954.

Benson, Stella. *The Little World.* New York: The Macmillan Company, 1925.

Bentley, Jerry H. *Old World Encounters: Cross-Cultural Contacts and Exchanges in Pre-Modern Times.* Oxford: Oxford University Press, 1993.

Bergamini, David. *Japan's Imperial Conspiracy.* London: Heinemann, 1971.

Berger, Michael. 'Outspoken Mayor of Nagasaki Shot'. *San Francisco Chronicle*, 19 January 1990.

Bernard, Condon. 'At the Crossroads: Asia'. *Forbes*, 28 July 1997.

Bingman, Charles F. *Japanese Government Leadership and Management*. London: Macmillan Press, 1989.

Bisson, T.A. *Prospects for Democracy in Japan*. New York: The Macmillan Company, 1949.

Bisson, T.A. *Zaibatsu Dissolution in Japan*. Berkeley: University of California Press, 1954.

Bix, Herbert. 'Japanese Imperialism and the Manchurian Economy 1900–1931'. *China Quarterly*, 51 (1972), pp. 425–43.

Bix, Herbert. 'Emperor Hirohito's War'. *History Today*, December 1991, pp. 12–19.

Bix, Herbert. 'The Showa Emperor's "Monologue" and the Problem of War Responsibility'. *Journal of Japanese Studies*, Vol. 18, No. 2 (1992), pp. 295–363.

Bix, Herbert. 'Inventing the "Symbol Monarchy" in Japan, 1945–1952'. *Journal of Japanese Studies*, Vol. 21, No. 2 (1995), pp. 319–63.

Blight, Richard. 'Images of Nineteenth-Century Japan'. *Orientations*, February 1981, pp. 23–33.

Booth, Martin. *Opium*. New York: Simon and Schuster, 1996.

Booth, Martin. *The Dragon Syndicates*. London: Doubleday, 1999.

Bowers, Faubion. 'The Day the General Blinked'. *New York Times*, 30 September 1988.

Brackman, Arnold. *The Other Nuremburg: The Untold Story of the Tokyo War Crimes Trials*. New York: Morrow, 1987.

Breuer, William B. *MacArthur's Undercover War*. New York: John Wiley and Sons, Inc., 1995.

Brown, Sidney DeVere. 'Kido Takayoshi (1833–1877): Meiji Japan's Cautious Revolutionary'. *Pacific Historical Review*, Vol. 25 (1958), pp. 151–62.

Brown, Sidney DeVere. 'Kido Takayoshi and the Young Emperor Meiji'. *Transactions of the Asiatic Society of Japan*, Vol. 4, No. 1 (1986), pp. 1–21.

Brunton, Richard Henry. *Building Japan: 1868–1876*. Sandgate, Folkestone, Kent: Japan Library Ltd, 1991.

Bruppacher, Balz. 'Swiss Court Gives Nod to New Claim on Marcos Fortune'. *San Francisco Examiner*, 25 March 1996.

Buckley, Roger. *Occupation Diplomacy: Britain, the United States and Japan 1945–1952*. Cambridge: Cambridge University Press, 1982.

Burgess, John. 'Emperor Hirohito as Demigod'. *Washington Post*, 27 April 1986.

Burnell, Elaine H. (ed.). *Asian Dilemma: United States, Japan and China*. Santa Barbara: Center for the Study of Democratic Institutions, 1969.

Burns, Richard D. and Edward M. Bennett (eds). *Diplomats in Crisis*. New York: ABC Clio, 1974.

Burstein, Daniel. *Turning the Tables: A Machiavellian Strategy for Dealing with Japan*. New York: Simon and Schuster, 1993.

Buruma, Ian. *Behind the Mask: On Sexual Demons, Sacred Mothers, Transvestites, Gangsters, Drifters and Other Japanese Cultural Heroes*. New York: Pantheon Books, 1984.

Buruma, Ian. 'The Redemption of Hirohito'. *Spectator*, 1 October 1988.

Buruma, Ian. *Wages of Guilt: Memories of War in Germany and Japan*. London: Vintage, 1995.

Buruma, Ian. *The Missionary and the Libertine: Love and War in East and West*. London: Faber and Faber, 1996.

Buruma, Ian. 'Why Japan's Emperor Shouldn't Apologise'. *Sunday Times*, 3 May 1998.

Calvocoressi, Peter, Guy Wint and John Pritchard. *The Causes and Course of the Second World War*. London: Penguin, 1995.

Cambridge History of Japan. Cambridge: Cambridge University Press, 1988–93.

Cameron, Rondo (ed.). *Banking and Economic Development: Some Lessons of History*. London: Oxford University Press, 1971.

Campbell, Joseph. *The Mask of God: Oriental Mythology*. Harmondsworth: Penguin, 1976.

Caruthers, Sandra T. 'Anodyne for Expansion: Meiji Japan, the Mormons, and Charles LeGendre'. *Pacific Historical Review*, Vol. 38 (1971), pp. 129–39.

Central Intelligence Agency. *Japan: Emperor Akihito's Family*. Washington, DC: CIA, 1990.

Chamberlin, William Henry. *Japan over Asia*. Boston: Little, Brown and Company, 1937.

Chang, Iris. *The Rape of Nanking: The Forgotten Holocaust of World War II*. New York: Basic Books, 1997.

Chang, Yvon. 'History of Resignations of Japanese Ministers'. Reuters, 1 January 1997.

Chapman, F. Spencer. *The Jungle is Neutral*. London: Corgi, 1957.

Chapman, William. 'Emperor Hirohito: Inheritor of Divine Power'. *Washington Post*, 7 January 1989.

Checkland, Olive. *Britain's Encounter with Meiji Japan, 1868–1912*. London: Macmillan, 1989.

Cheong Sung-hwa. *The Politics of Anti-Japanese Sentiments in Korea*. Westport, CT: Greenwood, 1991.

Chernow, Ron. *The House of Morgan*. New York: Simon and Schuster, 1990.

Chichibu Princess Setsuko. *The Silver Drum: A Japanese Imperial Memoir*. Folkestone: Global Books Ltd, 1996.

Chira, Susan. 'Hirohito, 124th Emperor of Japan, is Dead'. *New York Times*, 7 January 1989.

Chira, Susan. 'With Pomp . . . on a Global Stage'. *New York Times*, 24 February 1989.

Choate, Pat. *Agents of Influence: How Japan Manipulates America's Political and Economic System*. New York: Touchstone, 1990.

Chow Jen Hwa. *China and Japan: The History of Chinese Diplomatic Missions in Japan 1877–1911*. Singapore: Eurasia Press, 1975.

Cleary, Thomas. *The Japanese Art of War*. Boston: Shambhala, 1991.

Colegrove, Kenneth W. 'The Japanese Emperor'. *American Political Science Review*, Vol. 26, Nos 4, 5 (1932), pp. 642–59.

Comfort, William W. *Quakers in the Modern World*. New York: The Macmillan Company, 1949.

Conan, Neal. 'Empress of Japan Mum about Inability to Speak'. *National Public Radio* Morning Edition, 2 November 1993.

Congressional Record, House of Representatives, 5 November 1973. 'General Bonner Fellers in Memoriam'.

Connors, Lesley. *The Emperor's Adviser: Saionji Kinmochi and Pre-war Japanese Politics*. Kent: Croom Helm Ltd, 1987.

Cook, Haruko Taya and Theodore F. Cook. *Japan at War: An Oral History*. New York: The New Press, 1992.

Coox, Alvin D. *Nomonhan: Japan against Russia, 1939*. Stanford: Stanford University Press, 1985.

Coox, Alvin D. and Hilary Conroy (eds). *China and Japan: A Search for Balance since World War I*. Oxford: Oxford University Press, 1978.

Corbett, P. Scott. *Quiet Passages: The Exchange of Civilians between the United States and Japan during the Second World War*. Kent: Kent State University Press, 1987.

Cowley, Robert (ed.). *Experience of War*. New York: W.W. Norton and Company, Inc., 1992.

Craig, Albert M., John K. Fairbank and Edwin O. Reischauer. *East Asia: The Modern Transformation*. Boston: Houghton Mifflin, 1965.

Craig, Albert M. and Donald H. Shively. *Personality in Japanese History*. Berkeley: University of California Press, 1970.

Craig, Gordon and Felix Greene (eds). *The Diplomats, 1919–1939*. Princeton: Princeton University Press, 1953.

Crane, Burton. 'Educating a Prince'. *New York Times Magazine*, 1 December 1946.

Crump, Thomas. *The Death of an Emperor: Japan at the Crossroads*. London: Constable, 1989.

Daniels, Gordon (ed.). *Europe Interprets Japan*. Kent: Paul Norbury Publications, 1984.

Davis, Glenn and John G. Roberts. *An Occupation without Troops*. Tokyo: Yenbooks, 1996.

Daws, Gavan. *Prisoners of the Japanese: POWs of World War II in the Pacific*. New York: Morrow, 1994.

Deacon, Richard. *Kempei Tai: A History of the Japanese Secret Service*. New York: Berkeley Books, 1985.

Dear, I.C.B. (ed.). *The Oxford Companion to the Second World War*. Oxford: Oxford University Press, 1995.

Desmond, Edward W. 'Japan: Shin Kanemaru'. *Time*, 10 May 1992.

Dingman, Roger. *Ghost of War: The Sinking of the Awa Maru*. Annapolis: Naval Institute Press, 1997.

Dixon, Karl Hale. *The Extreme Right Wing in Contemporary Japan*. Dissertation, Florida State University College of Social Sciences, 1975.

Doerner, William R. 'A Delicate Burial'. *Time*, 23 January 1989.

'Dowager Empress Dies in Tokyo at 66'. *New York Times*, 18 May 1951.

Dower, John W. *Empire and Aftermath: Yoshida Shigeru and the Japanese Experience, 1878–1954*. Cambridge: Harvard University Press, 1988.

Dower, John W. *Japan in War and Peace*. London: HarperCollins, 1995.

Dower, John W. with Timothy S. George. *Japanese History and Culture from Ancient to Modern Times: Seven Basic Bibliographies*. Princeton: Markus Weiner Publishers, 1995 (2nd edn).

Downer, Lesley. *The Brothers: The Saga of the Richest Family in Japan*. London: Vintage, 1995.

Dudden, Arthur Power. *The American Pacific*. New York: Oxford University Press, 1992.

Duffy, Martha. 'The 21st Century Princess'. *Time*, 7 June 1993.

Duke, Benjamin. 'Charles Lanman and the Japanese in America (1872)'. *Japanese Quarterly*, Jan–March 1996, pp. 55–65.

Dunn, Charles. *Everyday Life in Imperial Japan*. New York: Dorset Press, 1969.

Dunn, Richard S. and Mary Maples Dunn (eds). *The World of William Penn*. Philadelphia: University of Pennsylvania Press, 1986.

Duus, Peter. *Party Rivalry and Political Chance in Taisho Japan*. Cambridge: Harvard University Press, 1968.

Duus, Peter, Ramon H. Myers and Mark R. Peattie (eds). *The Japanese Informal Empire in China, 1895–1937*. Princeton: Princeton University Press, 1989.

Editors of Institutional Investor. *The Way It Was: An Oral History of Finance*. New York: William Morrow, 1988.

Egeberg, Roger O. 'How Hirohito Kept His Throne'. *Washington Post*, 19 February 1989.

Elphrick, Peter. *Far Eastern File: The Intelligence War in the Far East, 1930–1945*. London: Hodder and Stoughton Ltd, 1997.

Emden, Paul H. *Quakers in Commerce*. London: Sampson Low, Marston and Co. Ltd, nd.

'Emperor May Sell Art Objects'. *New York Times*, 15 November 1945.

'Emperor Yoshihito Dies'. *New York Times*, 25 December 1926.

Fairbank, John K. and Edwin O. Reischauer. *East Asia: The Great Tradition*. Boston: Houghton Mifflin, 1960.

Fallows, James. *Looking at the Sun: The Rise of the New East Asian Economic and Political System*. New York: Pantheon Books, 1994.

Fearey, Robert A. *The Occupation of Japan: Second Phase 1948–1950*. New York: Macmillan, 1950.

Fellers, Bonner. *Answer to Japan*. General Headquarters South West Pacific Area, 1 July 1944.

Fellers, Bonner. 'Hirohito's Struggle to Surrender'. *Reader's Digest*, July 1947.

Fellers, Bonner. 'Our New Friends, the Japanese'. *Nation's Business*, February 1948.

Field, Norma. *In the Realm of a Dying Emperor: Japan at Century's End*. New York: Vintage Books, 1993.

Fithian, Floyd J. 'Dollars without the Flag: The Case of Sinclair and Sakhalin Oil'. *Pacific Historical Review*, Vol. 39 (1972), pp. 205–22.

'Forbes Billionaire List'. *Dow-Jones News Service*, 21 June 1998.

Foreign Relations of the United States 1946: The Far East. Vol. 8. Washington: Government Printing Office, 1971.

Frank, Richard B. *Guadalcanal*. New York: Random House, 1990.

Fraser, Mary Crawford. *A Diplomat's Wife in Japan: Sketches at the Turn of the Century (edited by Hugh Cortazzi)*. Tokyo: John Weatherhill, Inc., 1982.

Friday, Karl F. *Hired Swords: The Rise of Private Warrior Power in Early Japan*. Stanford: Stanford University Press, 1992.

Friedman, George and Meredith Lebard. *The Coming War with Japan*. New York: St Martin's Press, 1991.

Friman, H. Richard. 'Awaiting the Tsunami? Japan and the International Drug Trade'. *Pacific Review*, Vol. 6, No. 1 (1993), pp. 41–50.

Fu Poshek. *Passivity, Resistance, and Collaboration: Intellectual Choices in Occupied Shanghai, 1937–1945*. Stanford: Stanford University Press, 1993.

Fujimura Fanselow, Kumiko and Atsuko Kameda (eds). *Japanese Women: New Feminist Perspective on the Past, Present and Future*. New York: The Feminists' Press, 1995.

Fujita, Neil S. *Japan's Encounter with Christianity*. New York: Paulist Press, 1991.

Fujitana Takashi. *Splendid Monarchy: Power and Pageantry in Modern Japan*. Berkeley: University of California Press, 1996.

Fukomoto Hideko. *Femmes à l'Aube du Japon Moderne*. Paris: Des Femmes, 1997.

Fukushima Mutsuo. 'MacArthur Aide May Have Saved Emperor from Trial'. *Daily Yomiuri*, 4 January 1993.

Furiko Yoshiko. *The White Plum: A Biography of Ume Tsuda*. New York: Weatherhill, 1991.

Furiko Yoshiko *et al.* (eds). *The Attic Letters: Ume Tsuda's Correspondence to Her American Mother*. New York: Weatherhill, 1991.

Garrett, Laurie. *The Coming Plague*. New York: Penguin Books, 1994.

Gayn, Mark. *Japan Diary*. New York: William Sloane Associates, Inc., 1948.

'General Bonner Fellers Dies at 77'. *New York Times*, 10 October 1973.

551

'General Yamashita's Treasure Found'. *Weekly Post*, 1–7 April
     1996. Internet site: www.weeklypost.com

Gibney, Frank. *Japan: The Fragile Superpower*. New York:
     New American Library, 1985 (2nd edn).

Gibney, Frank. *The Pacific Century: America and Asia in a
     Changing World*. New York: Charles Scribner's Sons,
     1992.

'Girl from Outside'. *Time*, 23 March 1959.

Gluck, Carol. *Japan's Modern Myths: Ideology in the Late
     Meiji Period*. Princeton: Princeton University Press,
     1985.

Gluck, Carol and Stephen R. Graubard (eds). *Showa: The
     Japan of Hirohito*. New York: W.W. Norton, 1992.

Gold, Hal. *Unit 731 Testimony*. Tokyo: Yenbooks, 1996.

'The Golden Boat'. *Discover*, 1 January 1996.

Goldsmith, Raymond. *Financial Development of Japan,
     1868–1977*. New Haven: Yale University Press, 1983.

Gomer, Robert, John W. Powell and B.V.A. Roling. 'Japan's
     Biological Weapons 1930–1945'. *The Bulletin of the
     Atomic Scientists*, October 1981, pp. 43–53.

Gordon, Hugo. 'Hirohito's Brother Denounced War'. *Daily
     Telegraph*, 13 October 1994.

Gowens, Robert J. 'Canada and the Myth of the Japan Market,
     1896–1911'. *Pacific Historical Review*, Vol. 39 (1972),
     pp. 63–83.

Gradisher, Thomas D. *The Voice of the Crane: A Situational
     Analysis of Hirohito's August Rescript Using Mythical
     Elements*. Thesis presented to the Graduate Faculty of
     the University of Akron. May 1982.

Grew, Joseph. *Ten Years in Japan: A Contemporary Record
     Drawn from the Diaries and Private and Official
     Papers of Joseph C. Grew*. Westport, CT: Greenwood
     Press, Publishers, 1973. (First published by Simon and
     Schuster, 1944.)

Grew, Joseph. *Turbulent Era*. Boston: Houghton Mifflin,
     1952.

Griffis, William Elliot. *The Mikado: Institution and Person: A
     Study of the Internal Political Forces of Japan*.
     Princeton: Princeton University Press, 1915.

Grunebaum, Dan. 'Japan Criticizes Nanjing War Crimes Book'. *UPI*, 22 April 1998.

Guillain, Robert. *I Saw Tokyo Burning: An Eyewitness Narrative from Pearl Harbor to Hiroshima*. New York: Doubleday and Company, Inc., 1981.

Gunther, John. *Inside Asia*. New York: Harper and Brothers, 1942.

Gunther, John. 'A Quaker and the Prince of Japan'. *New York Times Book Review*, 11 May 1952.

Guyot, Dorothy. 'The Uses of Buddhism in Wartime Burma [Looting]'. *Asian Studies*, April 1969.

Haas, Margaret P. *The Emperor of Japan: A Selected Bibliography*. New York: Japan Society, Inc., 1975.

Haberman, Clyde. 'Prince Takamatsu of Japan Dies'. *New York Times*, 4 February 1987.

Hackett, Roger F. *Yamagata Aritomo in the Rise of Modern Japan, 1838–1922*. Cambridge, MA: Harvard University Press, 1971.

Hadley, Eleanor M. *Antitrust in Japan*. Princeton: Princeton University Press, 1970.

Hale, John R. *Age of Exploration*. Amsterdam: Time-Life International, 1966.

Hall, Ivan P. *Cartels of the Mind*. New York: W.W. Norton and Company, 1998.

Hall, John W. 'A Monarch for Modern Japan' in Robert E. Ward (ed.), *Political Development in Modern Japan*. Princeton: Princeton University Press, 1968.

Hall, John W. *Japan: From Prehistory to Modern Times*. Tokyo: Charles E. Tuttle Company, 1971.

Hall, John W. and Jeffrey P. Mass (eds). *Medieval Japan: Essays in Institutional History*. Stanford: Stanford University Press, 1988.

Hamada Kengi. *Prince Ito*. London: George Allen and Unwin Ltd, 1936.

Hamilton, Alan. 'Audience with the Emperor'. *The Times*, 27 May 1998.

Hamilton, Alan. 'A Day of Protest and Reconciliation'. *The Times*, 27 May 1998.

Hamm, Thomas D. *The Transformation of American*

        Quakerism: Orthodox Friends, 1800–1907. Bloomington: Indiana University Press, 1988.

Hane, Mikiso. *Eastern Phoenix: Japan since 1945*. Boulder: Westview Press, 1996.

Harries, Meirion and Susan Harries. *Sheathing the Sword: The Demilitarisation of Japan*. London: Hamish Hamilton, 1987.

Harries, Meirion and Susan Harries. *Soldiers of the Sun: The Rise and Fall of the Imperial Japanese Army*. New York: Random House, 1991.

Harris, Robert and Jeremy Paxman. *A Higher Form of Killing: The Secret Story of Chemical and Biological Warfare*. New York: Hill and Wang, 1982.

Harris, Sheldon H. *Factories of Death: Japanese Biological Warfare, 1932–45, and the American Cover-up*. London: Routledge, 1994.

Harris, Townsend. *The Complete Journal of Townsend Harris: First American Consul and Minister to Japan*. Rutland: Charles E. Tuttle Company, 1959 (2nd edn).

Harvey, Robert. *The Undefeated: The Rise, Fall and Rise of Greater Japan*. London: Macmillan, 1994.

Hasegawa Keitaro. *Japanese-Style Management: An Insider's Analysis*. Tokyo: Kodansha International Ltd, 1986.

Havens, Thomas R.H. *Architects of Affluence: The Tsutsumi Family and the Seibu-Saison Enterprises in Twentieth Century Japan*. Harvard: Harvard East Asian Monographs, 1996.

Hearn, Lafcadio, *Writings from Japan: An Anthology*. Harmondsworth: Penguin, 1984.

Heinrichs, Waldo H. Jr. *American Ambassador: Joseph C. Grew and the Development of the United States Diplomatic Tradition*. Boston: Little, Brown and Company, 1966.

Henle, Raymond. 'Oral History Interview with Bonner Fellers, 23 June 1967'. For the Herbert Hoover Presidential Library, Washington, DC.

Hersh, Philip. 'Japan Asks: What Price Olympics?' *Chicago Tribune*, 3 March 1997.

Hiatt, Fred. 'Public Debate on Japan's Emperor System'. *Washington Post*, 19 January 1989.

Hiatt, Fred. 'Mayor who Criticized Hirohito'. *Washington Post*, 19 January 1990.

Hicks, George. *The Comfort Women*. Tokyo: Yenbooks, 1995.

Hicks, George. 'Ghosts Gathering: Comfort Women Issue Haunts Tokyo'. *Far Eastern Economic Review*, 18 February 1993.

'Higashikuni, 102, Dies'. *New York Times*, 23 January 1990.

'High Tech Hunters Close in on Lost Sub'. *Baltimore Sun*, 5 October 1998.

Hillenbrand, Barry. 'Coming to Terms with History'. *Time*, 7 October 1991.

'Hirihito's Brother Hailed by Throngs'. *New York Times*, 11 April 1931.

'Hirohito's Income'. *New York Times*, 29 October 1945.

'Hirohito Outlay Curbed by Allies'. *New York Times*, 21 November 1945.

'Hirohito Son-in-law and Bar Owner Die in Her Tokyo Home'. *The Times*, 29 January 1966.

'Hirohito Thanks Hoover'. *New York Times*, 19 April 1931.

'Hirohito Will Evade Capital Levy'. *New York Times*, 7 February 1946.

'Hirohito's Worth Listed'. *New York Times*, 5 March 1946.

'History: Striking Gold at Sea. Treasure Hunters Locate a Submarine Sunk during World War II'. *Time*, 31 July 1995.

Hoehling, A.A. *December 7, 1941: The Day the Admirals Slept Late*. New York: Zebra Books, 1991.

Hoffer, Peter C. 'American Businessmen in the Japan Trade, 1931–1941: A Case Study of Attitude Formation'. *Pacific Historical Review*, Vol. 41 (1974), pp. 189–205.

Holroyd, Michael. *Augustus John: A Biography*. New York: Holt, Reinhart and Winston, 1974.

Honjo Shigeru. *Emperor Hirohito and His Chief Aide-de-Camp: The Honjo Diary, 1933–1936*. Mikiso Hane (trans.). Tokyo: University of Tokyo Press, 1967.

Hoon Shim Jae. 'Clamour for Sex-Slaves' Compensation'. *Far Eastern Economic Review*, 6 February 1993.

Hoon Shim Jae. 'Slave Wages, Government Offers Money to

Help Comfort Women'. *Far Eastern Economic Review*, 25 February 1993.

'Hoover Welcomes Royal Bridal Pair'. *New York Times*, 16 April 1931.

Hosaka Masayasu. *Chichibu no Miya to Showa Tenno*. Tokyo: Bungei Shunju, 1989.

Hosoya Chihiro *et al.* (eds). *The Tokyo War Crimes Trial*. Tokyo: Kodansha International, 1986.

Howard, Ethel. *Potsdam Princes*. London: Methuen and Co. Ltd, 1916.

Howard, Ethel. *Japanese Memories*. London: Hutchinson and Co., 1918.

Hoyt, Edwin P. *Hirohito: The Emperor and the Man*. New York: Praeger, 1991.

Hoyt, Edwin P. *Three Military Leaders: Togo, Yamamoto, Yamashita*. Tokyo: Kodansha International, 1993.

Hunt, Frazier. *The Untold Story of Douglas MacArthur*. New York: Devin-Adair Co., 1954.

Hunter, Janet E. *The Emergence of Modern Japan: An Introductory History since 1853*. London: Longman, 1989.

Hunziker, Steven and Ikuro Kamimura. *Kakuei Tanaka: A Political Biography of Modern Japan*. Singapore: Times Books International, 1996.

Idditti Smimasa. *The Life of Marquis Shigenobu Okuma: A Maker of New Japan*. Tokyo: The Hokuseido Press, 1940.

Ikegami Eiko. *The Taming of the Samurai: Honorific Individualism and the Making of Modern Japan*. Cambridge, MA: Harvard University Press, 1995.

'Imperial Japanese Diary Blasts Military'. *Boston Globe*, 6 October 1994.

Insight Guides. *Japan*. Hong Kong: APA Publications, 1995.

Irie Sukemasa. 'My 50 Years with the Emperor'. *Japan Quarterly*, Vol. 30, No. 1 (Jan–March 1983), pp. 39–43.

Iriye Akira. 'The Ideology of Japanese Imperialism: Imperial Japan and China' in Grant K. Goodman (compiler), *Imperial Japan and Asia: A Reassessment*. New York: Columbia University Press, 1967.

Iriye Akira. *Japan and China in the Global Setting.* Cambridge, MA: Harvard University Press, 1982.

Iriye Akira. *The Origins of the Second World War in Asia and the Pacific.* London: Longman, 1987.

Irokawa Daikichi. *The Culture of the Meiji Period.* Princeton: Princeton University Press, 1985.

Irokawa Daikichi. *The Age of Hirohito: In Search of Modern Japan.* New York: The Free Press, 1995.

Isaacs, Harold R. *Idols of the Tribe: Group Identity and Political Change.* New York: Harper Colophon Books, 1975.

Isaacson, Walter and Evan Thomas. *The Wise Men: Six Friends and the World They Knew.* New York: Simon and Schuster, 1986.

Ishida Takeshi. 'Pressure Groups in Japan'. *Journal of Social and Political Ideas in Japan*, December 1964, pp. 108–11.

Ishihara Shintaro. *The Japan That Can Say NO.* New York: Simon and Schuster, 1992.

Ishii, Kenneth. 'The Crown Prince Takes a Bride'. *Saturday Evening Post*, 11 April 1959.

Ishimoto Baroness Shidzue. *Facing Two Ways: The Story of My Life.* New York: Farrar and Rinehart, Inc., 1935.

Iwasaki Uichi. 'The Working Forces in Japanese Politics: A Brief Account of Political Conflicts, 1867–1920'. *Studies in History, Economics and Public Law*, Vol. 97, No. 1 (1921).

Iyer, Pico. 'The Longest Reign'. *Time*, 16 January 1989.

Jackson, Tim. *The Next Battleground: Japan, America and the New European Market.* Boston: Houghton Mifflin, 1993.

James, D. Clayton. *The Years of MacArthur. Volume II, 1941–1945.* Boston: Houghton Mifflin, 1975.

Jameson, Sam. 'Hirohito Death Reopens World War II Wounds'. *Los Angeles Times*, 18 February 1989.

Jameson, Sam. 'He Still Feels Suffering of WWII'. *Los Angeles Times*, 4 June 1994.

Jansen, Marius. *Japan and China: From War to Peace 1894–1972.* Chicago: Rand McNally, 1975.

Jansen, Marius B. (ed.). *Warrior Rule in Japan*. Cambridge: Cambridge University Press, 1995.

Japan Biographical Encyclopedia and Who's Who. Katsura Taro (ed.) Tokyo: The Rengo Press Ltd, 1958.

'Japan Court Rules in Favor of "Comfort Women"'. Reuters, 27 April 1998.

'Japan Emperor to Feel Wrath of UK POWs'. Reuters, 21 April 1998.

'Japan: Takeshita's Shadow Looms over Obuchi'. *Asahi Shimbun/Asahi Evening News*, 25 July 1998.

'Japanese'. *Fortune*, February 1942.

'Japanese Crown Prince to Have His Say on Bride'. *New York Times*, 30 July 1951.

'Japanese Emperor's Brother-in-law Killed'. *New York Times*, 2 April 1923.

'Japanese Prince's Death'. *The Times*, 3 April 1923.

'Japanese Princes Sell Belongings'. *New York Times*, 12 July 1946.

'Japanese Princess Expected to Recover'. *New York Times*, 3 April 1923.

'Japanese Resent Executive Purge'. *New York Times*, 21 December 1946.

'Japanese: Their God-Emperor Medievalism Must Be Destroyed'. *Fortune*, February 1942.

'Japan's Flourishing Empire System'. *Japan Quarterly*, Jan–March 1983.

'Japan's Policy Paralysis'. *Asian Wall Street Journal*, 2 February 1998.

'Jewish Group Raps Japan over Nanjing Massacre'. Japan Economic Newswire, Kyodo News Service, 23 April 1998.

John, Augustus. *Chiaroscuro: Fragments of Autobiography*. London: Jonathan Cape, 1954.

Johnson, Chalmers. *MITI and the Japanese Miracle*. Stanford: Stanford University Press, 1982.

Johnson, Chalmers. *Japan: Who Governs?* New York: Norton, 1995.

Jones, George E. 'Hirohito: The Man and the Emperor'. *New York Times* magazine, 23 September 1945.

Kanroji Osanaga. *Hirohito: An Intimate Portrait of the*

    Japanese Emperor. Los Angeles: Gateway Publishers, Inc., 1975.

Kaplan, David E. and Alec Dubro. *Yakuza: The Explosive Account of Japan's Criminal Underworld.* Reading, MA: Addison-Wesley Publishing Company, Inc., 1986.

Kaplan, David E. and Andrew Marshall. *The Cult at the End of the World.* London: Arrow Press, 1996.

Karlen, Arno. *Plague's Progress: A Social History of Man and Disease.* London: Victor Gollancz, 1995.

Kase Toshikazu. *Journey to the Missouri.* New Haven: Yale University Press, 1950.

Kataoka Tetsuya (ed.). *Creating Single-Party Democracy: Japan's Postwar Political System.* Stanford: Hoover Institution Press, 1992.

Kawahara Toshiaki. *Hirohito and His Times: A Japanese Perspective.* Tokyo: Kodansha International, 1990.

Kawahara Toshiaki. *Nagako Kotaigo [Dowager Empress Nagako.]* Tokyo: Bungei Shunju, 1993.

Kawai Kazuo. *Japan's American Interlude.* Chicago: The University of Chicago Press, 1960.

Kawasaki Ichiro. *Japan Unmasked.* Tokyo: Charles E. Tuttle Company, 1969.

Kearns, Robert L. *Zaibatsu America: How Japanese Firms Are Colonizing Vital US Industries.* New York: The Free Press, 1992.

Keene, Donald. *Travelers of a Hundred Ages: The Japanese as Revealed through 1,000 Years of Diaries.* New York: Henry Holt and Company, 1989.

Keene, Donald. *Living Japan: The People and Their Changing World.* New York: Doubleday and Company, Inc., nd.

Keith, Agnes. *Three Came Home: A Woman's Ordeal in a Japanese Prison Camp.* London: Eland, 1985 (reprint of 1948 edition).

Kennan, George F. *Memoirs: 1925–1950.* Boston: Little, Brown and Company, 1967.

Kennedy, Malcolm. *A History of Japan.* London: Weidenfeld and Nicolson, 1963.

Kennedy, Paul. *The Rise and Fall of the Great Powers.* New York: Random House, 1987.

Kenzo Takayanagi. 'The New Emperor System'. *Japan Quarterly*, July–September 1962, pp. 265–74.

Kerr, Alex. *Lost Japan*. Melbourne: Lonely Planet Publications, 1996.

Kester, W. Carl. *Japanese Takeovers: The Global Contest for Corporate Control*. Boston: Harvard Business School Press, 1991.

Kido Takayoshi. *The Diary of Kido Takayoshi: Volumes 1, 2, 3*. Tokyo: University of Tokyo Press, 1983.

Kitagawa, Joseph M. *Religion in Japanese History*. New York: Columbia University Press, 1990.

Kodansha Encyclopedia of Japan. Nine volumes. Tokyo: Kodansha Ltd, 1983.

Kojima Noboru. 'Militarism and the Emperor System'. *Japan Interpreter*, Spring 1973.

Koyama Itoko. *Nagako: Empress of Japan*. New York: The John Day Company, 1958.

Kuno Akiko. *Unexpected Destinations: The Poignant Story of Japan's First Vassar Graduate*. New York: Kodansha International, 1993.

Kurzman, Dan. *Kishi and Japan: The Search for the Sun*. New York: Ivan Obolensky, Inc., 1960.

Lamont, Edward M. *The Ambassador from Wall Street*. Lanham: Madison Books, 1994.

Lamont, Thomas. *Across World Frontiers*. New York: Harcourt Brace, 1951.

Lanciaux, Bernadette. 'The Influence of Economic Thought on the Political Economy of Modern Japan'. *Journal of Economic Issues*, June 1996, pp. 475–82.

Lane-Poole, Stanley. *The Life of Sir Harry Parkes*. London: Macmillan and Company, 1894.

Large, Stephen S. 'Imperial Princes and Court Politics in Early Showa Japan'. *Japan Forum*, October 1989, pp. 257–64.

Large, Stephen S. *Emperor Horohito and Showa Japan: A Political Biography*. London: Routledge, 1992.

Large, Stephen S. *Emperors of the Rising Sun: Three Biographies*. Tokyo: Kodansha Ltd, 1997.

Lasserre Philippe and Helmut Schutte. *Strategies for Asia Pacific*. London: Macmillan Press Ltd, 1995.

'Laurence Bunker, Was Aide to MacArthur and Charter Member of John Birch Society'. *New York Times*, 11 October 1977.

'Lawyer's Report on Japan Attacks Plan to Run Occupation'. *Newsweek*, 1 December 1947.

Lebra, Joyce C. *Okuma Shigenobu: Statesman of Meiji Japan*. Canberra: Australian National University Press, 1973.

Lebra, Joyce C. (ed.). *Japan's Great East Asia Co-prosperity Sphere in World War II*. Oxford: Oxford University Press, 1975.

Leonard, Jonathan N. *Early Japan*. Amsterdam: Time-Life International, 1969.

Liebenthal, Coppelia. 'A Bond War Could not Break'. *Earlhamite*, Spring 1996.

Link, Howard A. 'Neglected Masters of Rimpa'. *Orientations*, December 1980, pp. 25–34.

Livingston, Jon, Joe Moore and Felicia Oldfather (eds). *Postwar Japan: 1945 to the Present*. New York: Pantheon, 1973.

Ljunggren, David. 'Britons interned by Japan to Press UK over Money'. Reuters, 12 January 1999.

Lomax, David. *The Money Makers*. London: BBC Publications, 1986.

Lord Russell of Liverpool. *The Knights of Bushido: A Short History of Japanese War Crimes*. London: Corgi, 1958.

Lucas, Michael. 'On the Trail of a Billion-Dollar Buddha'. *Los Angeles Times*, 3 December 1996.

Lyons, Eugene. *Herbert Hoover: A Biography*. New York: Doubleday and Company, Inc., 1964.

Ma, Karen. *The Modern Madame Butterfly*. Tokyo: Charles E. Tuttle Company, 1996.

MacArthur, Douglas. *Reminiscences*. New York: McGraw Hill, 1964.

MacDougall, Terry Edward (ed.). *Political Leadership in Contemporary Japan*. Ann Arbor: Center for Japanese Studies, University of Michigan, 1982.

MacKenzie, Donald A. *China and Japan*. London: Studio Editions Limited, 1994.

Maki, John M. 'The Role of the Bureaucracy in Japan'. *Pacific Affairs*, December 1947.

561

Manchester, William. *American Caesar: Douglas MacArthur, 1880–1964*. Boston: Little, Brown and Company, 1978.

Manchester, William. *Goodbye Darkness: A Memoir of the Pacific War*. New York: Dell Publishing Co. Inc., 1979.

Manning, Paul. *Hirohito: The War Years*. New York: Bantam Books, 1989.

'Many Fetes Planned for Japanese Prince'. *New York Times*, 5 April 1931.

Maraini, Fosco. *Tokyo*. Amsterdam: Time-Life International, 1976.

March, Robert M. *The Japanese Negotiator: Subtlety and Strategy beyond Western Logic*. Tokyo: Kodansha International, 1990.

Marshall, Jonathan. 'Opium and the Politics of Gangsterism in Nationalist China, 1927–1945'. *Bulletin of Concerned Asian Scholars I*. July–September 1976, pp. 19–48.

Martin, Brian G. *The Shanghai Green Gang: Politics and Organized Crime, 1919–1937*. Berkeley: University of California Press, 1996.

Martin, John H. and Phyllis G. Martin. *Kyoto: A Cultural Guide to Japan's Ancient Imperial City*. Tokyo: Charles E. Tuttle Company, 1994.

Maruyama Masao. *Thought and Behaviour in Modern Japanese Politics*. London: Oxford University Press, 1969 (expanded edition).

Masland, John W. 'Missionary Influence upon American Far Eastern Policy'. *Pacific Historical Review*, Vol. 10, No. 3 (1944), pp. 279–96.

Masland, John W. 'Commercial Influence upon American Far Eastern Policy, 1937–1941'. *Pacific Historical Review*, Vol. 11 (1945), pp. 281–99.

Mason, Mark. *American Multinationals and Japan: The Political Economy of Japanese Capital Controls, 1899–1980*. Cambridge, MA: Harvard University Press, 1992.

Mass, Jeffrey P. (ed.). *Court and Bakufu in Japan: Essays in Kamakura History*. Stanford: Stanford University Press, 1982.

Matsubara Hisako. 'This Good World of Shinto'. *Geo*, March 1981, pp. 122–53.

Mayers, David. *The Ambassadors and America's Soviet Policy.* New York: Oxford University Press, 1995.

McCabe, Michael. 'The Hunt for Japanese Loot in the Philippines'. *San Francisco Chronicle*, 4 November 1987.

McClellan, Edwin. *Woman in the Crested Kimono.* New Haven: Yale University Press, 1985.

McCoy, Alfred W. (ed.). *Southeast Asia under Japanese Occupation.* New Haven: Yale University Press, 1985.

McCullough, David. *Truman.* New York: Simon and Schuster, 1992.

McLean, Hulda Hoover. *Genealogy of the Herbert Hoover Family.* Stanford: The Hoover Institution, 1967.

Mears, Helen. 'The Japanese Emperor'. *Yale Review*, December 1943, pp. 238–57.

Mears, Helen. *Mirror for Americans: Japan.* Boston: Houghton Mifflin, 1948.

Mee, Charles L. Jr. *Meeting at Potsdam.* New York: M. Evans and Company, Inc., 1975.

Mee, Charles L. Jr. *The End of Order: Versailles 1919.* New York: E.P. Dutton, 1980.

Menkes, Suzy. 'Kuniko Tsutsumi Tribute'. *International Herald Tribune*, 24 June 1997.

Meiji Tennoki [Annals of Emperor Meiji]. Compiled by the Imperial Household Agency. Tokyo, 1968.

Micheletti, Mary. 'Gang Land: Real Estate Investment in Japan is Tainted by Organized Crime'. *San Francisco Daily Journal*, 22 June 1998.

Miller, Merle. *Plain Speaking: An Oral Biography of Harry S Truman.* New York: Berkeley Publishing Corporation, 1973.

Miller, Roy Andrew. *Japan's Modern Myth: The Language and Beyond.* Tokyo: Weatherhill, 1982.

Minear, Richard H. *Victor's Justice: The Tokyo War Crimes Trial.* Princeton: Princeton University Press, 1971.

Mishima Akio. *Bitter Sea: The Human Cost of Minamata Disease.* Tokyo: Kosei Publishing Company, 1992.

Mitford, A.B. *Tales of Old Japan*. Rutland: Charles E. Tuttle Company, 1966.

Miyamoto Masao. *Straitjacket Society*. Tokyo: Kodansha International, 1993.

'Modern Mikado Held Prisoner by the Past: A Profile of Emperor Akihito'. *Sunday Times*, 17 May 1998.

Montgomery, Michael. *Imperialist Japan: The Yen to Dominate*. London: Christopher Helm, 1987.

Morikawa Hidemasa. *Zaibatsu: The Rise and Fall of Family Enterprise Groups in Japan*. Tokyo: University of Tokyo Press, 1992.

Morison, Samuel Eliot. *The Two-Ocean War*. Boston: Little, Brown and Company, 1963.

Morley, James (ed). *Japan's Foreign Policy 1868–1941*. New York: Columbia University Press, 1984.

Morley, John David. *Picture from the Water Trade: An Englishman in Japan*. London: Abacus, 1985.

Morris, Ivan. *The Nobility of Failure: Tragic Heroes in the History of Japan*. New York: Holt, Rinehart and Winston, 1975.

Morris, Ivan. *The World of the Shining Prince: Court Life in Ancient Japan*. Harmondsworth: Penguin, 1979.

Mosley, Leonard. *Hirohito: Emperor of Japan*. London: Weidenfeld and Nicolson, 1966.

Myers, Ramon and Mark Peattie (eds). *The Japanese Colonial Empire*. Princeton: Princeton University Press, 1984.

Nahm, Andrew C. *Korea under Japanese Colonial Rule*. Center for Korean Studies, Institute of International and Area Studies: Western Michigan University Press, 1973.

Nakamoto Michiyo. 'The God Who Fell to Earth'. *Financial Times*, 23 May 1998.

Nakamura Kaju. *Prince Ito: The Man and Statesman: A Brief History of His Life*. New York: Japanese-American Commercial Weekly, 1910.

Nakamura Masanori. *The Japanese Monarchy: Ambassador Joseph Grew and the Making of the 'Symbol Emperor System,' 1931–1991*. New York: M.E. Sharpe, Inc., 1992.

Nakane Chie. *Japanese Society*. Harmondsworth: Penguin, 1973.

Nash, George H. *The Life of Herbert Hoover: The Engineer, 1874–1914*. New York: W.W. Norton and Company, 1983.

Nash, George H. *The Life of Herbert Hoover: The Humanitarian, 1914–1917*. New York: W.W. Norton and Company, 1988.

Nash, George H. *The Life of Herbert Hoover: Master of Emergencies, 1917–1918*. New York: W.W. Norton and Company, 1996.

Nash, George H. (ed.). *Understanding Herbert Hoover: Ten Perspectives*. Stanford: Hoover Institution Press, 1987.

Neary, Ian (ed.). *War, Revolution and Japan*. Sandgate, Folkestone, Kent: Japan Library, 1993.

Neumann, William L. 'Franklin D. Roosevelt and Japan, 1913–1933'. *Pacific Historical Review*, Vol. 22 (1957), pp. 143–53.

Neumann, William L. 'Religion, Morality, and Freedom: The Ideological Background of the Perry Expedition'. *Pacific Historical Review*, Vol. 23 (1958), pp. 247–57.

Nippon Hoso Kyokai, Japan Broadcasting Corporation. 'The Showa Emperor's Two Monologues'. Broadcast in Japan, 15 June 1997.

Nish, Ian (ed.). *Britain and Japan: Biographical Portraits, Volume One*. Folkestone: Japan Library, 1994.

Nish, Ian. *Britain and Japan: Biographical Portraits, Volume Two*. Richmond, Surrey: Japan Library, 1997.

Nitobe Inazo. *Bushido: The Soul of Japan*. Tokyo: Charles E. Tuttle Company, Inc., 1991 (original edn 1905).

Nivison, David S. and Arthur F. Wright (eds). *Confucianism in Action*. Stanford: Stanford University Press, 1959.

Norman, E. Herbert. 'The Genyosha: A Study in the Origins of Japanese Imperialism'. *Pacific Affairs*, 1944, pp. 261–84.

Notehelfer, F.G. *American Samurai: Captain L.L. Janes and Japan*. Princeton: Princeton University Press, 1985.

Ogata Sadako. *Defiance in Manchuria: The Making of Japanese Foreign Policy 1931–1932*. Berkeley: University of California Press, 1964.

Ohmae Kenichi. *The Borderless World: Power and Strategy in the Global Marketplace*. London: HarperCollins, 1994.

Ohmae Kenichi. *The End of the Nation State: The Rise of Regional Economies*. London: HarperCollins, 1995.

Oka Takashi. 'The Emperor Who Meets the President Today'. *New York Times Magazine*, 26 September 1971.

Oka Yoshitake. *Five Political Leaders of Modern Japan*. Tokyo: University of Tokyo Press, 1986.

Oka Yoshitake. *Konoe Fumimaro: A Political Biography*. Lanham, MD: Madison Books, 1992.

Okazaki Hisahiko. *A Grand Strategy for Japanese Defense*. Lanham, MD: University Press of America, Inc., 1986.

Omura Bunji. *The Last Genro: Prince Saionji*. Philadelphia: J.B. Lippincott Company, 1938.

Ono Yumiko. 'Dear Empress-to-Be'. *Wall Street Journal*, 20 January 1993.

Pacific War Research Society. *Japan's Longest Day*. Tokyo: Kodansha International, 1980.

Packard, Jerrold M. *Sons of Heaven: A Portrait of Japanese Monarchy*. New York: Charles Scribner's Sons, 1987.

Papinot, E. *Historical and Geographical Dictionary of Japan*. Tokyo: Charles E. Tuttle Company, 1972.

Parillo, Mark. *The Japanese Merchant Marine in World War II*. Annapolis: Naval Institute Press, 1993.

Parrott, Lindesay. 'Hirohito is Still the Sun God'. *New York Times Magazine*, 12 May 1945.

Parrott, Lindesay. 'Hirohito Shared Zaibatsu Profits'. *New York Times*, 31 October 1945.

Parrott, Lindesay. 'Pauley Says Japan Can Pay Little in Reparations.' *New York Times*, 16 November 1945.

Parry, Richard L. 'Obituary: Shin Kanemura'. *Independent*, 29 March 1996.

Pastan, Rachel. 'Graduate Becomes Princess'. *Horizon*, 16 February 1982.

Ponsonby-Fane, Richard A.B. *The Imperial House of Japan*. Kyoto: The Ponsonby Memorial Society, 1959.

Ponsonby-Fane, Richard A.B. *The Fortunes of the Emperors: Studies in Revolution, Exile, Abdication, Usurpation* and *Deposition in Ancient Japan.* Washington, DC: University Publications of America, Inc., 1979

Powles, Cyril H. 'The Myth of the Two Emperors: A Study in Misunderstanding'. *Pacific Historical Review*, Vol. 37 (1970), pp. 35–50.

Presseisen, Ernst L. *Before Aggression: Europeans Prepare the Japanese Army.* Tucson: University of Arizona Press, 1965.

Price, Willard. *The Son of Heaven: The Problem of the Mikado.* London: William Heinemann Ltd, 1945.

'Prince Kitashirakawa Killed'. *Japan Weekly Chronicle*, 5 April 1923.

'Prince Nashimoto of Japan, 76, Dies. Only Member of the Imperial Family Arrested as a War Criminal'. *New York Times*, 2 January 1951.

'Prince and Princess Greeted by Walker'. *New York Times*, 12 April 1931.

'Prince to Remain Six Days at Capital'. *New York Times*, 11 April 1931.

'Prince Tires Aides on Capital Tour'. *New York Times*, 17 April 1931.

'Princess Chichibu: Obituary'. *Daily Telegraph*, 15 September 1995.

Pritchard, R. John and Sonia Pritchard (eds). *The Tokyo War Crimes Trial: The Complete Transcripts of the Proceedings of the International Military Tribunal for the Far East in Twenty-two Volumes.* New York: Garland, 1981.

'Problem of Comfort Women'. *The Economist*, 31 October 1992.

Pye, Lucian W. *Asian Power and Politics: The Cultural Dimensions of Authority.* Cambridge, MA: The Belknap Press, 1985.

Pyle, Kenneth B. *The New Generation in Meiji Japan: Problems in Cultural Identity, 1885–1895.* Stanford: Stanford University Press, 1969.

Pyle, Kenneth B. *The Japanese Question: Power and Purpose in a New Era.* Washington, DC: The AEI Press, 1992.

Pyle, Kenneth B. *The Making of Modern Japan.* Lexington: DC Heath and Company, 1996 (2nd edn).

'Quest Renewed for Legendary Japanese War Booty'. *Japan Economic Newswire*. Internet site: www.treasure.com.

Raistrick, Arthur. *Quakers in Science and Industry . . . during the 17th and 18th Centuries*. Whitstable: David and Charles (Holdings) Ltd, Newton Abbey, 1968.

Ramseyer, J. Mark and Frances M. Rosenbluth. *The Politics of Oligarchy: Institutional Choice in Imperial Japan*. Cambridge: Cambridge University Press, 1995.

'Ranking of the World's Richest People'. AP Online, 21 June 1998.

Record of the Proceedings of the International Military Tribunal for the Far East. Washington, DC: Library of Congress, microfilm.

Reid, T.R. 'A Damper on Japan's Royal Wedding'. *Washington Post*, 15 March 1993.

'Reign of Meiji'. *Fortune*, July 1933.

Reingold, Edwin M. *Chrysanthemums and Thorns: The Untold Story of Modern Japan*. New York: St Martin's Press, 1992.

Reischauer, Edwin O. *The Emperor of Japan: A Profile on the Occasion of the Visit by the Emperor and Empress to the United States, September 30th to October 13th, 1975*. New York: Japan Society, Inc., 1975.

Reischauer, Edwin O. *The Japanese Today: Change and Continuity*. Tokyo: Charles E. Tuttle Company, 1988.

Reischauer, Haru Matsukata. *Samurai and Silk: A Japanese and American Heritage*. Cambridge, MA: Belknap Press, 1986.

'Reluctant Prince'. *Time*, 17 October 1994.

Richie, Donald. *Geisha, Gangster, Neighbor, Nun*. New York: Kodansha International, 1987.

Richie, Donald. *The Honorable Visitors*. Rutland: Charles E. Tuttle Company, 1994.

Roberts, J.G. *Mitsui: Three Centuries of Japanese Business*. New York: Weatherhill, 1973.

Robertson, Eric. *The Japanese File: Pre-war Japanese Penetration in Southeast Asia*. Hong Kong: Heinemann Asia, 1979.

568

Robinson, Edwin A. *Selections from the Letters of Thomas Sergeant Perry*. New York: The Macmillan Company, 1929.

Robinson, Gwen. 'Hirohito's Brother Tells of War Crimes by Army'. *The Times* and *Sunday Times*, CD edn, 7 July 1994.

Roling, B.V.A. and Antonio Cassese. *The Tokyo Trial and beyond*. Cambridge: Polity Press, 1993.

Rose, Barbara. *Tsuda Umeko and Women's Education in Japan*. New Haven: Yale University Press, 1992.

Rosenfeld, Megan. 'Brig. Gen. Bonner Fellers, Ret., Dies'. *Washington Post*, 10 October 1973.

Rowland, Laura Joh. *Shinju*. New York: Random House, Inc., 1994.

'Royal Couple Due Tomorrow'. *New York Times*, 9 April 1931.

'Royal Flush'. *The Economist*, 7 December 1996.

Rusbridger, James and Eric Nave. *Betrayal at Pearl Harbor*. London: Michael O'Mara Books Ltd, 1991.

Russell, Oland D. 'Japan's War Machine'. *American Mercury*, April 1935.

Russell, Oland D. *The House of Mitsui*. Boston: Little, Brown, 1939.

Sakaiya Taichi. 'Hirohito and the Imperial Tradition'. *Php Intersect*, December 1985.

Sakaiya Taichi. *What is Japan?: Contradictions and Transformations*. Tokyo: Kodansha International, 1993.

Sakamaki Sachiko. 'Cold Comfort: Wartime Sex Slaves Offered Meagre Redress'. *Far Eastern Economic Review*, 29 June 1995.

Sampson, Anthony. *The Arms Bazaar*. London: Hodder and Stoughton, 1977.

Sampson, Anthony. *The Money Lenders: Bankers in a Dangerous World*. London: Coronet Books, 1982.

Sanford, Donald S. *Midway*. New York: Bantam, 1976.

Sanger, David E. 'She's Shy'. *New York Times*, 26 June 1990.

Sanger, David E. 'In Palace Woods, a Japanese Wedding'. *New York Times*, 30 June 1990.

Sansom, George. *A History of Japan.* Three Volumes. Tokyo: Charles E. Tuttle Company, 1974.

Sasaki Takeshi. 'Maruyama Masao and the Spirit of Politics'. *Japan Quarterly*, Jan–March 1997, pp. 59–63.

Satow, Ernest. *A Diplomat in Japan.* Tokyo: Oxford University Press, 1968.

Schaller, Michael. *Douglas MacArthur: The Far Eastern General.* Oxford: Oxford University Press, 1989.

Scherer, James A.B. *Three Meiji Leaders: Ito, Togo, Nogi.* Tokyo: The Hokuseido Press, 1936.

Schlesinger, Jacor M. 'Japan's Bid for World Leadership Haunted by War Past'. *Wall Street Journal*, 25 May 1993.

Schonberger, Howard. 'The Japan Lobby in American Diplomacy'. *Pacific Historical Review*, Vol. 44, No. 3 (August 1977), pp. 327–59.

Schreiber, Mark. *Shocking Crimes of Postwar Japan.* Tokyo: Yenbooks, 1996.

Scott-Stokes, Henry. 'A Reassessment of the Emperor: Behind Closed Doors'. *Php Intersect*, December 1985.

Seagrave, Sterling. *Soldiers of Fortune.* Alexandria: Time-Life Books, 1981.

Seagrave, Sterling. *Yellow Rain: A History of Chemical Warfare.* New York: M. Evans and Company, 1981.

Seagrave, Sterling. *The Soong Dynasty.* New York: Harper and Row, 1985.

Seagrave, Sterling. *The Marcos Dynasty.* New York: Harper and Row, 1988.

Seagrave, Sterling. *Lords of the Rim: The Invisible Empire of the Overseas Chinese.* New York: G.P. Putnam's Sons, 1995.

Seagrave, Sterling and Peggy Seagrave. *Dragon Lady: The Life and Legend of the Last Empress of China.* New York: Random House, 1990.

Seidenstucker, Edward. *Low City, High City.* New York: Knopf, 1983.

Seidenstucker, Edward. *Tokyo Rising: The City since the Great Earthquake.* Cambridge, MA: Harvard University Press, 1991.

Sewell, Brian. 'The Shaming of the Garter'. *Evening Standard*, 10 May 1998.

Shapiro, Margaret. 'Hirohito, Emperor of Japan, Dies'. *Washington Post*, 7 January 1989.

Shapiro, Margaret. 'Japan Gives Powers to Crown Prince'. *Washington Post*, 22 September 1989.

Shaplen, Robert. *A Turning Wheel: Three Decades of the Asian Revolution as Witnessed by a Correspondent of The New Yorker*. New York: Random House, 1973.

Sheldon, Charles D. 'Japanese Aggression and the Emperor, 1931–1941, from Contemporary Diaries'. *Modern Asian Studies*, Vol. 10, No. 1 (1976), pp. 1–40.

Shillony, Ben-Ami, *Revolt in Japan: The Young Officers and the February 26, 1936 Incident*. Princeton: Princeton University Press, 1973.

Shillony, Ben-Ami. *Politics and Culture in Pre-war Japan*. Oxford: Oxford University Press, 1982.

Shiroyama Saburo. *War Criminal: The Life and Death of Hirota Koki*. Tokyo: Kodansha International Ltd, 1977.

Silverman, Bernard S. and H.D. Harootunian. *Modern Japanese Leadership: Transition and Change*. Tucson: University of Arizona Press, 1963.

Sokolsky, George E. 'Again the Emperor Decides for Japan'. *New York Times* magazine, 6 December 1931.

'Son of Heaven'. *Time*, 6 September 1954.

'Sorry'. *The Economist*, 17 August 1993.

Spector, Ronald H. *Eagle against the Sun: The American War with Japan*. Harmondsworth: Penguin, 1984.

Spoto, Donald. *The Decline and the Fall of the House of Windsor*. New York: Simon and Schuster, 1995.

Statler, Oliver. *Japanese Inn: A Reconstruction of the Past*. New York: Random House, 1961.

Steinberg, Rafael. *Island Fighting*. Alexandria: Time-Life Books, 1978.

Steinberg, Rafael. *Return to the Philippines*. Alexandria: Time-Life Books, 1979.

Sterngold, James. 'South Korea Wants Japan to Return Art'. *New York Times*, 11 July 1991.

Storry, Richard. *The Double Patriots: A Study of Japanese Nationalism*. Westport, CT: Greenwood Press, Publishers, 1973 (reprint of 1957 edn).

Storry, Richard. *Japan and the Decline of the West in Asia 1894–1943*. London: Macmillan Press Ltd, 1979.

Storry, Richard. *A History of Modern Japan*. Harmondsworth: Penguin, 1990.

Sugimoto Etsu Inagaki. *A Daughter of the Samurai*. Tokyo: Charles E. Tuttle Company, 1966.

Sullivan, Kevin. 'Anti-Hirohito Mayor Shot'. *Guardian*, 19 January 1990.

Sun Fo. 'The Mikado Must Go'. *Foreign Affairs,* October 1944, pp. 17–25.

Sunderland, Riley. 'The Secret Embargo'. *Pacific Historical Review*, Vol. 29 (1962), pp. 75–80.

Supreme Commander for the Allied Powers Historical Monographs 1945–1951. Washington, DC: National Archives and Records Service, microfilm.

Swinson, Arthur. *Four Samurai: A Quartet of Japanese Army Commanders in the Second World War*. London: Hutchinson and Co. Ltd, 1968.

Taguchi Shota. 'His Majesty the Present Emperor in His Early Age'. *Cultural Nippon*, June 1940.

Takamatsu no Miya nikki [*The Diaries of Prince Takamatsu*]. Eight Volumes. Tokyo: Chuo Koronsha, 1995–7. (Special translations made from the Japanese by Hamish Todd.)

'Takeo Fukada: Obituary'. *The Economist*, 15 July 1995.

Takeskoshi Yosaburo. *Prince Saionji*. Kyoto: Ritsumeikan University, 1933.

Takeyama Michio. 'The Emperor System'. *Journal of Social and Political Ideas in Japan*, August 1964, pp. 21–6.

Takeyama Michio. *Harp of Burma*. Rutland: Charles E. Tuttle Company, 1966.

Tamaki Norio. *Japanese Banking: A History, 1859–1959*. Cambridge: Cambridge University Press, 1995.

Tanizaki Jun'ichiro. *In Praise of Shadows*. New Haven: Leete's Island Books, Inc., 1977 (written in 1933).

Tasker, Peter. *The Japanese*. New York: Meridian, 1989.

Tate, D.J.M. (compiler). *The Mikado's Japan . . . as Seen and Reported by the Illustrated London News*. Hong Kong: John Nicholson Ltd, 1990.

Taylor, Robert T. '"The Most Essential Work I Know"'. *Bible Society Record*, May 1950.

Terasaki, Gwen. *Bridge to the Sun*. Chapel Hill: University of North Carolina Press, 1957.

Terasaki, Hidenari and Mariko Terasaki Miller. *Showa Tenno Dokuhakuroku*. (The manuscript account of Terasaki's memoirs of The Emperor's Two Monologues.) Tokyo: Bungei Shunju Sha, 1991.

Teters, Barbara. 'The Genro and the National Essence Movement'. *Pacific Historical Review*, Vol. 31 (1964), pp. 359–78.

Thomas, J.E. *Modern Japan: A Social History since 1868*. London: Longman, 1996.

Thompson, Robert Smith. *A Time for War*. New York: Prentice Hall Press, 1991.

Thomson, James C., Peter Stanley and John Perry. *Sentimental Imperialists*. New York: Harper, 1982.

Thurow, Lester. *Head to Head: The Coming Economic Battle among Japan, Europe, and America*. New York: William Morrow and Company, Inc., 1992.

Time-Life Books. *Japan at War*. New York: Time Inc., 1980.

Tipton, Elise. *Japanese Police State: Tokko in Interwar Japan*. London: Athlone Press, 1991.

Titus, David A. 'Emperor and Public Consciousness in Postwar Japan'. *Japan Interpreter*, Vol. 6, No. 2 (summer 1970), pp. 182–95.

Titus, David A. *Palace and Politics in Prewar Japan*. New York: Columbia University Press, 1974.

Titus, David A. 'The Making of the "Symbol Emperor System" in Postwar Japan'. *Modern Asian Studies*, Vol. 14, No. 4 (1980), pp. 529–78.

Toland, John. *The Rising Sun: The Decline and Fall of the Japanese Empire*. New York: Bantam, 1970.

Toland, John. *Infamy: Pearl Harbor and Its Aftermath*. New York: Berkeley Books, 1983.

573

Tolischus, Otto. 'God, Emperor, High Priest'. *New York Times Magazine*, 23 November 1941.

Totman, Conrad. *Japan before Perry: A Short History*. Berkeley: University of California Press, 1981.

Trager, Frank (ed.). *Burma: Japanese Military Administration, Selected Documents, 1941–1945*. Philadelphia: University of Pennsylvania Press, 1971.

Trumbull, Robert. 'A Leader who Took Japan to War'. *New York Times*, 7 January 1989.

Trumbull, Robert. 'A New Role of the Son of Heaven'. *New York Times Magazine*, 14 September 1958.

United States Army, Office of the Chief of Military History. *War in Asia and the Pacific, 1937–1949*. New York: Garland, 1980.

United States Department of State. *Report on Japanese Assets in Manchuria to the President of the United States*. Washington, DC: Department of State, 1946.

United States Department of State. *Report on Japanese Reparations to the President of the United States, November 1945 to April 1946*. Washington, DC: Department of States Publication 3174, Far Eastern Series 25, n.d.

Van Wolferen, Karel. *The Enigma of Japanese Power: People and Politics in a Stateless Nation*. London: Macmillan, 1989.

'Veterans Turn Their Backs'. *Evening Standard*, 26 May 1998.

Vining, Elizabeth G. *Windows for the Crown Prince: Akihito of Japan*. New York: J.B. Lippincott Company, 1952.

Vining, Elizabeth G. *Return to Japan*. London: Michael Joseph, 1961.

Vining, Elizabeth G. *Quiet Pilgrimage*. Philadelphia: Lippincott, 1970.

Vogel, Ezra F. *Japan's New Middle Class*. Berkeley: University of California Press, 1963.

Volkman, Ernest. *Spies*. New York: John Wiley and Sons, Inc., 1994.

Walker, Bryce. *Earthquake*. Alexandria: Time-Life Books, Inc., 1982.

Walsh, Michael. 'The Son Also Rises'. *Time*, 16 January 1989.

Walvin, James. *The Quakers: Money and Morals*. London: John Murray, 1997.

'War Prisoners' New Demand for Compensation'. *PA Information for the Nation*, 13 January 1999.

Ward, Robert E. *Political Development in Modern Japan*. Princeton: Princeton University Press, 1968.

Ward, Robert E. and Sakamoto Yoshikazu (eds). *Democratizing Japan: The Allied Occupation*. Honolulu: University of Hawaii Press, 1987.

Watts, Anthony J. *Japanese Warships of World War II*. New York: Doubleday and Company, Inc., 1967.

Waycott, Angus. *Sado: Japan's Island in Exile*. Berkeley: Stone Bridge Press, 1996.

Weisman, Steven R. 'Japan's Imperial Present'. *New York Times Magazine*, 26 August 1990.

Wetzler, Peter. *Hirohito and War*. Honolulu: University of Hawaii Press, 1998.

Wheeler, Keith. *The Road to Tokyo*. Alexandria: Time-Life Books, 1979.

Whitney, Clara. *Clara's Diary: An American Girl in Meiji Japan*. Tokyo: Kodansha International, 1981.

Whymant, Robert. 'POWs Attack Emperor's Speech'. *The Times*, 28 May 1998.

Wildes, Harry Emerson. *Aliens in the East: A New History of Japan's Foreign Intercourse*. Philadelphia: University of Pennsylvania Press, 1937.

Wilkinson, Endymion. *Japan versus Europe: A History of Misunderstanding*. Harmondsworth: Penguin, 1983.

Willoughby, Charles A. and John Chamberlain. *MacArthur: 1941–1951*. New York: McGraw-Hill Book Company, Inc., 1954.

Wittner, Lawrence S. 'MacArthur and the Missionaries: God and Man in Occupied Japan'. *Pacific Historical Review*, Vol. 40 (1973), pp. 77–98.

'Women Had High Status in Old Japan'. *East*, Vol. 12, No. 6 (1976), pp. 11–12.

Woodward, William P. *The Allied Occupation of Japan, 1945–1952 and Japanese Religions*. Leiden: E.J. Brill, 1972.

Worswick, Clark. 'The Last Days of the Shogun'. *Geo*, March 1982, pp. 20–9.

WuDunn, Sheryl. 'Japan's King of the Mountain: The Man who Made Nagano'. *New York Times*, 6 February 1998.

Yamamura Kozo and Yasukichi Yasuba (eds). *The Political Economy of Japan: Volume 1 – The Domestic Transformation*. Stanford: Stanford University Press, 1987.

Yanaga Chitoshi. *Big Business in Japanese Politics*. New Haven: Yale University Press, 1968.

Yanaga Chitsohi. *Japan since Perry*. New York: McGraw-Hill, 1949.

Yates, Ronald. 'Horohito War Role Debated'. *Chicago Tribune*, 23 February 1989.

Yonekura Isamu. 'Kanmu . . . The Emperor Afflicted with Ghosts'. *East*, Vol. 9, No. 8 (September 1973), pp. 44–55.

Yonekura, Isamu. 'The History of the Imperial Family: Part One,' *East*, Vol. 11, No. 6 (July/August 1975), pp. 33–43.

Yonekura Isamu. 'The History of the Imperial Family: From the End of the Heian Period to the Muromachi Period: Part Two'. *East*, Vol. 11, No. 7 (September 1975), pp. 14–25.

Yonekura Isamu. 'The History of the Imperial Family: From the Muromachi Period to the Dawn of the Restoration: Part Three'. *East*, Vol. 11, No. 9 (November 1975), pp. 14–25.

Yonekura Isamu. 'The History of the Imperial Family: The Later Days of the Tokugawa Shogunate'. *East*, Vol. 11, No. 10 (December 1975), pp. 15–24.

Yonekura Isamu. 'The History of the Imperial Family: The Emperor Meiji'. *East*, Vol. 12, No. 1 (January 1976), pp. 16–28.

Yosabura Takekoshi. *Prince Saionji*. Kyoto: Ritsumeikan University, 1933.

Yoshida Shigeru. *The Yoshida Memoirs: The Story of Japan in Crisis*. Boston: Houghton Mifflin, 1962.

Yoshida Yuki. *Whispering Leaves in Grosvenor Square 1936–7*. Folkestone, Kent: Global Books Ltd, 1997 (first published 1938).

Young, A. Morgan. *Japan under Taisho Tenno: 1912–1926*. London: George Allen and Unwin Ltd, 1928.

Zich, Arthur. *The Rising Sun*. Alexandria: Time-Life Books, 1977.

INDEX

594

596

602

LORDS OF THE RIM
by Sterling Seagrave

A community of fifty-five million expatriates. Up to two trillion dollars in assets. A highly integrated network of influence and favour. A firm base on the Pacific Rim. Ambitions to influence the West. Imagine the potential power of such an organisation. You don't have to. This is the empire of the Overseas Chinese.

The Lords of the Rim uncovers a complex web of operations which already dominates the Far East and which is now making inroads into the West. Spanning thousands of years and drawing on exhaustive research, it encompasses stories of murder and betrayal, bravery and corruption, of emperors and generals, spies and pirates, and predicts just how the world will change over the coming decades.

'Highly accessible . . . A remarkable and relevant volume about a fascinating and ancient human phenomenon . . . Exceptional'
Martin Booth, *Sunday Times*

'Seagrave has uncovered a real and significant trend. There is a new economic order in the making and it is not centred on us'
Scotsman

0 552 14052 X

THE SOONG DYNASTY
by Sterling Seagrave

'A gripping book. Seagrave has tackled a mighty subject with resourcefulness and spirit'
Washington Post

The Soong Dynasty is the first full behind-the-scenes account of the extraordinary Soong family whose power and wealth dominated China and American policy towards Asia in the Twentieth century. It is an extraordinary work of historical detection which traces the family's roots from the middle of the last century and their explosive rise thereafter.

Descendants of a runaway who grew up in America under the protection of the Methodist church and who returned to their homeland to make a fortune selling Western bibles, the Soong Family became the principal rulers of China during the first half of the Twentieth century. In *The Soong Dynasty*, Sterling Seagrave describes for the first time the intricate and fascinating rise to power of Charlie Soong and his children, who he married to some of China's most powerful men to create a network of power and influence which was to last for over fifty years. It is a classic tale of power, money, corruption and greed with elements of tragedy and comedy.

'Fast paced and jammed with racy details'
New York Times Book Review

'Mr Seagrave is a fine investigative reporter – digging up information from a multitude of sources, much of it original, and piecing together a gripping account of epochal events'
Wall Street Journal

0 552 14108 9

BRIDGE ACROSS MY SORROWS
by Christina Noble with Robert Coram

'A record of grief and courage that would take a tear from a stone'
Dervla Murphy

Christina Noble's story is one of bravery and resilience in the face of deprivation and abuse on a scale most would find unimaginable. Her childhood in the Dublin slums barely merits the name: after the early death of her mother the family is split apart, their alcoholic father unable to care for them. Christina is sexually abused and later escapes from an orphanage only to become destitute on the streets of Dublin. At sixteen she is pulled into a car by four men and raped repeatedly. Later, driven to near insanity by overwork and a violent husband, she finds in a dream the will to fight back. Yet this is no vision of luxury and self-indulgence; instead Christina's hope lies in a determination to work among the *bui doi*, the street children of Vietnam.

And here the most extraordinary part of her story begins, on the streets of Ho Chi Minh City, where destitute children swarm and the rich turn a blind eye. To these needy children 'Mama Tina' became, and remains to this day, an irrepressible, unorthodox and staunch champion.

Outspoken, often angry, yet profoundly moving, *Bridge Across My Sorrows* is one of the most inspirational stories ever told.

'An extraordinarily moving story . . . Both heart-rending and inspirational' *Cameron Mackintosh*, producer of *Miss Saigon*

'We see a human spirit of shining dignity, courage and resilience – it is not a surprise when she ultimately turns her life into a magnificent act of love and generosity' *Mia Farrow*

'Christina Noble's story is heartbreaking but finally inspiring because of her own indomitable courage in the face of violence, neglect and abuse. Her spirit blazes across the page in this unforgettable book' *Sinead Cusack*

0 552 14288 3

A SELECTED LIST OF NON-FICTION TITLES AVAILABLE FROM CORGI AND BLACK SWAN

THE PRICES SHOWN BELOW WERE CORRECT AT THE TIME OF GOING TO PRESS. HOWEVER TRANSWORLD PUBLISHERS RESERVE THE RIGHT TO SHOW NEW RETAIL PRICES ON COVERS WHICH MAY DIFFER FROM THOSE PREVIOUSLY ADVERTISED IN THE TEXT OR ELSEWHERE.

13878	9	THE DEAD SEA SCROLLS DECEPTION		
			Michael Baigent & Richard Leigh	£6.99
99065	5	THE PAST IS MYSELF	Christabel Bielenberg	£7.99
14750	8	BLACK HAWK DOWN	Mark Bowden	£6.99
14493	2	THE JIGSAW MAN	Paul Britton	£6.99
14582	3	BAPTISM OF FIRE	Frank Collins	£6.99
14465	7	CLOSE QUARTER BATTLE	Mike Curtis	£5.99
13582	8	THE GOD SQUAD	Paddy Doyle	£7.99
14239	5	MY FEUDAL LORD	Tehmina Durrani	£5.99
99482	0	MILLENNIUM	Felipe Fernández-Armesto	£14.99
12833	3	THE HOUSE BY THE DVINA	Eugenie Fraser	£7.99
14489	4	THE HOLY KINGDOM	Adrian Gilbert, Alan Wilson, Baram Blackett	£6.99
99545	2	ISRAEL: A HISTORY	Martin Gilbert	£14.99
14760	5	THE CUSTOM OF THE SEA	Neil Hansen	£5.99
14694	3	VIEW FROM THE SUMMIT	Sir Edmund Hillary	£7.99
14164	X	EMPTY CRADLES	Margaret Humphreys	£6.99
14595	5	BETWEEN EXTREMES: A Journey Beyond Imagination		
			Brian Keenan & John McCarthy	£6.99
13356	6	NOT WITHOUT MY DAUGHTER		
			Betty Mahmoody	£5.99
12419	2	CHICKENHAWK	Robert C. Mason	£7.99
54536	8	SHE MUST HAVE KNOWN: THE TRIAL OF ROSEMARY WEST		
			Brian Masters	£6.99
13953	X	SOME OTHER RAINBOW	John McCarthy & Jill Morrell	£6.99
14625	0	BRAVO TWO ZERO	Andy McNab	£5.99
14288	3	BRIDGE ACROSS MY SORROWS	Christina Noble	£5.99
14607	2	THE INFORMER	Sean O'Callaghan	£6.99
14330	8	THE TEMPLAR REVELATION	Lynn Picknett & Clive Prince	£6.99
14303	0	THE HOT ZONE	Richard Preston	£5.99
14550	5	PURPLE SECRET	John Röhl, Martin Warren, David Hunt	£7.99
14052	X	LORDS OF THE RIM	Sterling Seagrave	£6.99
14108	9	THE SOONG DYNASTY	Sterling Seagrave	£8.99
99750	1	SPEAKING FOR THEMSELVES: The Personal Letters of Winston and Clementine Churchill	Mary Soames ed.	£15.00
13950	5	JESUS THE MAN	Barbara Thiering	£7.99
13288	8	IN GOD'S NAME	David Yallop	£6.99

All Transworld titles are available by post from:

Bookpost, PO Box 29, Douglas, Isle of Man, IM99 1BQ

Credit cards accepted. Please telephone 01624 836000, fax 01624 837033, Internet http://www.bookpost.co.uk or e-mail: bookshop@enterprise.net for details

Free postage and packing in the UK. Overseas customers: allow £1 per book (paperbacks) and £3 per book (hardbacks)